Baseball's Best
Short Stories

Baseball's Best
Short Stories
★ EXPANDED EDITION ★

Edited by **PAUL D. STAUDOHAR**

**CHICAGO
REVIEW
PRESS**

Copyright © 1995, 2012 by Paul D. Staudohar
All rights reserved
Illustrations © 1995 by Sean O'Neill
All rights reserved
Expanded edition
Published by Chicago Review Press, Incorporated
814 North Franklin Street
Chicago, Illinois 60610
ISBN 978-1-61374-376-8

Interior design: PerfecType, Nashville, TN

The stories in this collection originally appeared in a variety of publications. A complete list of credits and copyright notices can be found on pages 423–25.

Library of Congress Cataloging-in-Publication Data
Baseball's best short stories / edited by Paul D. Staudohar. — Expanded ed.
   p. cm.
 ISBN 978-1-61374-376-8 (pbk.)
 1. Baseball stories, American. I. Staudohar, Paul D.
 PS648.B37B4 2012
 813'.01083579—dc23

                    2011045904

Printed in the United States of America

To the memory of my father, Matt,
who taught me to love baseball

CONTENTS

PREFACE TO THE EXPANDED EDITION

*B*aseball's *Best Short Stories* was the first book on what became a series of short-fiction anthologies from the same editor and publisher. These collections are on golf, football, boxing, fishing, and hunting, and two were on a variety of sports. The most recent works were *The Best Dog Stories* (2007) and *Murder Short & Sweet* (2008).

In this expanded edition, eight new stories have been added. Three of these—by W. P. Kinsella, George Plimpton, and Richard Wilbur—predate the original collection and were somehow omitted the first time around. The other five stories were written in the 1990s and beyond by Brendan DuBois, Leslie Pietrzyk, Steven Polansky, Gary Soto, and Tobias Wolff.

PREFACE TO THE ORIGINAL EDITION

The short story has universal appeal as a staple of American fiction. Its brevity allows for consumption in a single sitting. Authors of this literary form must catch the reader's attention, hold it fast, and provide a smart conclusion. It takes a skilled writer to do this well.

Some of the best short stories are about baseball, either the game itself or morality, greed, love, envy, aging, and other literary themes that use baseball as a backdrop. Several of the best American writers have authored short stories on baseball—among the first were those in pulp magazines around the turn of the century. Shortly thereafter, writer Ring Lardner popularized the genre. The flow of good baseball stories accelerated in the 1940s and 1950s, with frequent appearances in magazines like *Collier's*, *Esquire*, and the *Saturday Evening Post*. In recent years, there has been a resurgence of interest; magazines like *The New Yorker*, *Harper's*, and *Sports Illustrated* have all published stories on the topic.

The revival of the baseball short story accompanies a wave of nostalgia for the game. Many fans deplore that the business side of baseball, its owner and player cupidity, has overshadowed the game. Yet overall fan interest remains high at the major-league level. The minor leagues have come back nicely with a surge in franchises and attendance. Hollywood's infatuation with baseball is evident from a host of recent movies. One of the top television shows in 1994 was Ken Burns' documentary *Baseball*. People are attracted, sometimes wildly, to baseball memorabilia, cards, apparel, autographs, and art.

The goal in editing this book was to collect the very best baseball short stories ever written. Excerpts from novels are not included, because they don't have compact beginnings and endings. Nonfiction was ruled out too, because it has a way of becoming dated, sooner or later. While there are some outstanding short stories from other sports, this collection is confined to baseball because of its long history and tradition and the abundance of quality material to choose from. The date of a particular story is not important. Human nature doesn't change much, and a good story can live forever.

Finding the best baseball stories is a little like playing detective. You round up the usual suspects, old tales that you've read and remembered. You talk to writers on the subject. There are some meticulously prepared bibliographies on baseball literature as well as excellent electronic databases in libraries. So, with the exception of relatively obscure sources from the distant past, it is possible to lay your hands on virtually all the significant literature. It turned out to be a far larger body of material than I imagined.

A pleasant finding from my research is that many of the truly great American authors have written short stories on baseball. Perhaps this is not surprising, since most kids grow up playing the game and it is deeply rooted in our culture. Just because a well-known writer has a baseball story, though, doesn't mean that it's one of the best. But cream has a way of rising to the top. Also, some excellent stories have been written by lesser-known authors, usually sports columnists who tried their hand at fiction.

What it came down to, once all the gathered stories were carefully considered, was making the cuts, picking the team of the very best. This process was, admittedly, a subjective one, reminiscent of Ogden Nash's limerick:

> *There once was an umpire whose vision*
> *Was cause for abuse and derision.*
> *He remarked in surprise,*
> *"Why pick on my eyes?*
> *It's my heart that dictates my decision."*

Eventually picked were twenty-eight stories, many written by authors familiar to literature buffs like Zane Grey, Robert Penn Warren, Damon Runyon, James Thurber, P. G. Wodehouse, Ring Lardner, Garrison Keillor, Frank Deford, T. Coraghessan Boyle, Stuart Dybek, and Michael Chabon. While perhaps not as famous, a number of other very successful writers grace this collection, including Eliot Asinof, W. C. Heinz, Herbert Warren Wind, J. F. Powers, Lloyd Biggle Jr., Arnold Hano, and Chet Williamson.

These stories were originally published between 1910 and 1990. Like fine wine, the older stories have aged well. Beginning with "Casey at the Bat," we find unforgettable characters, abundant humor, a touch of melancholy, and lots of great baseball talk, action, and drama. The authors aren't concerned much with transmitting facts. They try to make us think and feel, to involve the heart as well as the mind. Good thoughts, good feelings.

Batter up.

Casey at the Bat

(As it appeared in the *San Francisco Examiner* on June 3, 1888)

Ernest L. Thayer

Baseball's most famous poem is "Casey at the Bat." As much a story as a poem, it was written in 1888 by Ernest L. Thayer, a young newspaper reporter for the *San Francisco Examiner*. Whether one is reading "Casey" for the first time or the tenth, it is always fresh and loaded with imagery. Will the big slugger save the day for the Mudville team? A tasty slice of Americana served up with sparkling verse and high drama, "Casey" has spawned dozens of imitative poems and stories. For instance, sportswriter Grantland Rice's poem "Casey's Revenge" artfully changed the original outcome. Columnist Art Buchwald wrote a delightful sequel using the structure of the poem to parody baseball's allowing women reporters in the locker room. Science fiction writer Rod Serling also did a send-up on the Casey theme. But the original is still the best.

> The outlook wasn't brilliant for the Mudville nine that day;
> The score stood four to two with but one inning more to play.
> And then when Cooney died at first, and Barrows did the same,
> A sickly silence fell upon the patrons of the game.
>
> A straggling few got up to go in deep despair. The rest
> Clung to that hope which springs eternal in the human breast;

They thought if only Casey could but get a whack at that—
We'd put up even money now with Casey at the bat.

But Flynn preceded Casey, as did also Jimmy Blake,
And the former was a lulu and the latter was a cake;
So upon that stricken multitude grim melancholy sat,
For there seemed but little chance of Casey's getting to the bat.

But Flynn let drive a single, to the wonderment of all,
And Blake, the much despised, tore the cover off the ball;
And when the dust had lifted, and the men saw what had occurred,
There was Jimmy safe at second and Flynn a-hugging third.

Then from 5,000 throats and more there rose a lusty yell;
It rumbled through the valley, it rattled in the dell;
It knocked upon the mountain and recoiled upon the flat,
For Casey, mighty Casey, was advancing to the bat.

There was ease in Casey's manner as he stepped into his place;
There was pride in Casey's bearing and a smile on Casey's face.
And when, responding to the cheers, he lightly doffed his hat,
No stranger in the crowd could doubt 'twas Casey at the bat.

Ten thousand eyes were on him as he rubbed has hands with dirt;
Five thousand tongues applauded when he wiped them on his shirt.
Then while the writhing pitcher ground the ball into his hip,
Defiance gleamed in Casey's eye, a sneer curled Casey's lip.

And now the leather-covered sphere came hurtling through the air,
And Casey stood a-watching it in haughty grandeur there.
Close by the sturdy batsman the ball unheeded sped—
"That ain't my style," said Casey. "Strike one," the umpire said.

From the benches, black with people, there went up a muffled roar,
Like the beating of the storm-waves on a stern and distant shore.
"Kill him! Kill the umpire!" shouted some one on the stand;
And it's likely they'd have killed him had not Casey raised his hand.

With a smile of Christian charity great Casey's visage shone;
He stilled the rising tumult; he bade the game go on;
He signaled to the pitcher, and once more the spheroid flew;
But Casey still ignored it, and the umpire said, "Strike two."

"Fraud!" cried the maddened thousands, and echo answered fraud;
But one scornful look from Casey and the audience was awed.
They saw his face grow stern and cold, they saw his muscles strain,
And they knew that Casey wouldn't let that ball go by again.

The sneer is gone from Casey's lip, his teeth are clenched in hate;
He pounds with cruel violence his bat upon the plate.
And now the pitcher holds the ball, and now he lets it go,
And now the air is shattered by the force of Casey's blow.

Oh, somewhere in this favored land the sun is shining bright;
The band is playing somewhere, and somewhere hearts are light,
And somewhere men are laughing, and somewhere children shout;
But there is no joy in Mudville—mighty Casey has struck out.

Casey at the Bat (1988)

Frank Deford

Casey struck out. But can't there be more to the story? Frank Deford writes about the mighty swinger's colorful life before and after that fateful day at Mudville, creating a bawdy hero worthy of the "Casey at the Bat" myth. Deford's story links Casey with real-life characters like heavyweight champ John L. Sullivan and James Naismith of peach-basket fame, providing fascinating glimpses of turn-of-the-century America.

Deford, the nation's premier sportswriter during his many years with *Sports Illustrated*, also founded the critically acclaimed but ill-fated daily sports newspaper the *National*. He has written popular books with tennis personalities Arthur Ashe, Billie Jean King, Jack Kramer, and Pam Shriver and has published *The World's Tallest Midget: The Best of Frank Deford* (1978). His most-recent book is *Bliss Remembered* (2010), a novel about an elderly woman who recounts her experiences as a swimmer at the 1936 Berlin Olympics.

I f ever you loved baseball or if ever you had a hero, you surely would like to know what happened to Casey after he struck out in the bottom of the ninth on Saturday, June 2, 1888. And so . . .

The porters scrambled to grab Richard K. Fox's bag when he arrived at New York's Grand Central that bright Thursday morning, May 31, a century ago. "Boston" was all Fox said, and the lucky fellow who had ended up with Fox's valise rushed ahead to the Pullman car. Fox was not handsome, with a mustache too bushy for his little head, a nose too big by half and cold, hooded eyes. But if he lacked the sleek looks of his animal namesake, he was every bit as clever. Like so many men who have succeeded in his profession—Fox was an editor—his strength lay in the deployment of better men's talents. On his cravat he wore a horseshoe pin of gold, studded with diamonds, open side down.

Fox settled in his seat and turned to the paper he'd brought onto the train. The Democrats, party of the incumbent president, Grover Cleveland, were about to convene in St. Louis and go through the formality of renominating their man. So the press, its priorities ever straight, was much more interested in what the President's young bride, the 23-year-old beauty, Frances Folsom, had worn the day before, Memorial Day. Quickly then, Fox skimmed through the pages until he came to the sports section. He was home now.

The sports pages in the '80s—the 1880s—had become a popular force. For the cranks (as baseball fans were so aptly known), there were the major-club box scores telegraphed from all over. There were even line scores from the burgeoning minor leagues. If Fox had looked closely, for example, he would have seen the scores from the Bay State League, which included this doubleheader result: Mudville 16, 8—Lynn 5, 2. And there were stories on boxing for the fancy (as the pugilistic world was called), horse racing, crew, tennis, cricket and many other games. No one was more responsible for this boom in sports reportage—or for the profit derived from it—than Fox, who had made his magazine, the *National Police Gazette*, a successful institution largely because of sports.

An item down near the bottom of the *Tribune's* sports page caught Fox's eye: CHAMPION RETURNS FROM EUROPE. John L. Sullivan, the report said, had arrived back in Boston last month and would be engaging in some stage exhibitions. "Champion," Fox muttered, crumpling up the paper. "Fat Mick lout." Sullivan was Fox's bête noir, for he was one man in sports Fox could not control, and everything he did to thwart the Boston Strong Boy only served to enhance Sullivan's reputation. It was Fox who had put up Paddy Ryan to fight Sullivan in '82, and Sullivan's victory established him as America's first great athletic hero.

Nonetheless, Sullivan would not do Fox's bidding, would not defend his title again. Instead, he went about making a fortune fighting in exhibitions— "My name is John L. Sullivan, and I can beat any sonofabitch in the house!"

he would bellow—plus eating everything in the house, gulping bourbon from beer steins and whoring his time away. Frustrated, Fox made up a magnificent "championship" belt for the pretender, Jake Kilrain. So the whole damn city of Boston gave Sullivan an even grander bejeweled belt, and the Great John L. grew greater still.

The train pulled out of Grand Central, billowing smoke. Fox was on his way to Boston to personally goad—somehow—Sullivan into action. "The Great John L.," he muttered. "My arse."

• • •

About the time Fox's Pullman was passing through Bridgeport, Chester Drinkwater was escorting a handsome young couple into the amazing Cyclorama on Tremont Street in Boston's South End. The couple quickly became bug-eyed, for there before them—all around them, really, in a circular vista 400 feet in circumference and 50 feet high—was a painted re-creation of the Battle of Gettysburg. Timothy F. X. Casey didn't have to have it explained to him, either. He hadn't been born till '67, but his father had fought in the war, and an uncle had died at Antietam. Casey knew his America.

And America was aboomin'—the West filling, the cities bursting their seams, trolleys (some electric!) carrying the middle classes out into these new things called suburbs. Industry. Commerce. Science. Inventions. Wires were everywhere: Telegraph lines, telephone lines, electric lines. Yet America in '88 was still closer to Gettysburg than to the Ardennes, closer to Jeb Stuart than to Sergeant York, closer to Abraham Lincoln than to, uh, Babe Ruth.

Flossie Cleary had heard about Gettysburg, but because she hadn't crossed the ocean from Cork until '84, she was more impressed by the scope of the Cyclorama than by the scenes it depicted. So Casey took it upon himself to fill her in. Here's Little Round top, there Culp's Hill. . . . Pickett's Charge is over. . . . Uh, oh. His hand went out, and it grazed against Flossie. Grazed. Lingered. Then it passed on, and Casey was telling Flossie about the cavalry, but she didn't hear a word. How many times had she whispered to Father O'Reilly in the confessional that she had sinned by hoping Timothy F. X. Casey might touch her . . . and now he had . . . and now they would be alone tonight. Chaperoned, of course, by Mr. Chester Drinkwater and his sister, but alone at beautiful, alluring Nantasket Beach. Different rooms in the hotel, of course. But still. . . . There was so much about this that left Flossie uneasy.

"Ah, Timothy, but exactly who might this Mr. Drinkwater be, and why would he be doing these lovely things for you?" Flossie had asked when Casey first told her that he had this benefactor, this rich crank, who wanted to take them to Nantasket, in his own surrey, in his own sloop across Hingham Bay, put them up at the finest hotel, take them to the finest show.

"Flossie, would you be looking a gift horse in the mouth?" Casey had replied, and a bit testily. "Mr. Chester Drinkwater is not only a sporting man, but one of the most successful businessmen in Boston. He owns several trolley lines and the big amusement park in Newton."

Still, something stayed under Flossie's fair skin. On the occasion of that exchange, she and Timothy had been alone at the far end of the magnificent veranda at the house of Mr. and Mrs. Alfred L. Evans Jr., in the finest section of Mudville, where Flossie was employed as a downstairs maid. But she turned away from Casey, fretting. Things were moving too fast, and she was suspicious. Why, it had been quite enough, her falling in love with a ballist. In many quarters, ballists were dismissed as riffraff, which was fair enough, because that was what they were. Young men who played baseball, it was widely known, generally drank too much, gambled and specialized in separating young ladies from their virtue whenever the opportunity arose. Mostly, they consorted with other lowlifes, such as actors, dance hall girls, boodlers, flimflammers, second-story men, chippies, tarts and cracksmen. In fact, a great many ballists spent their off-seasons onstage or with a circus. Casey had joined the Mudville nine late in the '87 season and had met Flossie then, but he'd gone away soon enough, traveling with Barnum & Bailey. Mostly he worked as a roustabout for the sideshow, although he and another strong fellow would dress in leopard skins at showtime and go onstage to try (unsuccessfully) to hoist the fat lady.

Casey frightened Flossie some because she loved him even though he was sort of mysterious. He didn't seem to have anyone close to him. He'd grown up in Baltimore but was orphaned, and his only sibling, his left-handed twin sister, Kate, had married into a German family. He saw her only when the circus passed through Baltimore.

"It's this baseball craze, Flossie," Casey said, moving closer to her on the veranda. "People just think it's a humdinger. Not just in Mudville. Why, did you know the Beaneaters paid $10,000 to the Chicagos just to get King Kelly to come play in Boston?"

Flossie gasped. Ten thousand dollars was more money that she expected to see in her lifetime. But something was happening in the '80s. Baseball was developing as a kind of adhesive that held together the evolving city and all its diverse types. It was said that any middling city that aspired to the big time needed three things: trolley lines, an opera house and a baseball team. "What can I do, Flossie?" Casey asked. "I found out I could hit a horsehide, and now people love me for it."

Mudville had gone bonkers over its nine that spring, and it was almost entirely because of Casey. The Evanses at first didn't want Flossie to have anything to do with a ballist, but after Mr. Evans left the bank early one day and went out to the Grounds to see Mudville whip Framingham 8–1 and Casey hit two triplets and a two-bagger, he let the young fellow come call on Flossie.

Casey had kept up the tattoo all spring. Why, not a single pitcher had yet struck him out. The baseballs didn't have much bounce in them, and the wheelman delivered from only 50 feet away, but Casey had such power that soon enough the local papers were calling him Mighty Casey. He was hitting .386, too, and grumpy old Cyrus Weatherly, the town miser who owned the team and the Mudville Grounds as well, was delighted to see that the ladies and gentlemen of the town were flocking to the East Side to watch the games. Even Mrs. Evans went to a game one afternoon.

Later that same day, Casey was on the Evans's veranda with Flossie when a rather ascetic young gentleman appeared. He explained that he had been directed to this address by someone at Casey's boardinghouse, so Mr. Evans steered him out to the veranda. "Mr. Casey," the man said, "my name is Jim Naismith, and I'm a student in Canada. I'm visiting at the training school over in Springfield, considering becoming what they call a physical education instructor there."

"How do you do, sir," Casey said.

Naismith explained that word had reached Springfield that Casey had the finest natural swing in all the world. "When the season is over," Naismith said, "if they send you a rail ticket, would you come show the students your swing?"

"Gee, I don't know," Casey said, taken aback. "The past two winters I traveled with the circus."

"Oh, I see," Naismith said, clearly disappointed.

Casey glanced over at Flossie, then lowered his head. "'Course, I'm thinking maybe I won't be leaving Mudville this fall." Flossie's face turned crimson, and her heart bobbled.

"Well, now," Naismith said. "I think you'd be interested in what they do in Springfield. Besides baseball in the spring, they have gymnastics and swimming and football in the fall."

"What game do they play in the winter?" Casey asked.

"Nothing satisfactory, I'm afraid," Naismith said. "But I'm going to work on that."

Mr. Evans stepped up. "You know, Timothy, you're a bright lad and good at sport. Maybe you ought to think about *attending* that school in Springfield after the season."

Casey gulped. "But that's like a *college*, Mr. Evans."

"There's no law says a ballist can't go to college, is there, Mr. Naismith?" And then he turned to Flossie. "You wouldn't be bothered being married to a college man, would you, Flossie?"

Casey's jaw dropped. Flossie shrieked. "Faith and begorra, sir," and dashed away. Mr. Evans threw an arm about Casey's shoulders, more as he would with a son than with some roisterous ballplayer. "A real nice piece of dry goods," Mr. Evans said, winking at Casey, as they watched Flossie's trim ship sail away. "A very nice piece of calico."

Two weeks later, just before Memorial Day when Chester Drinkwater came by, Mr. Evans brought Casey right into the parlor. After Flossie had served tea, Drinkwater came to the point. "Mr. Evans, would it be possible for Flossie to come away with Mr. Casey and myself—and my sister Maud, who'll chaperon, of course—and go down to visit Nantasket Beach on Thursday?" he asked.

That week the Mudvilles would exploit Memorial Day on Wednesday by playing a doubleheader. But then they'd be off until Saturday, so Casey could get away to the beach. "I've taken a keen liking to this young man," Drinkwater said, patting Casey on the knee. "And the way baseball is taking hold, there may be a lot of cranks out there who'd love to deal with Timothy if he were a salesman for me."

"Good business," said Mr. Evans.

"It'd sure be better than trying to lift that fat lady three times a day," Casey allowed.

Mr. Evans curled his mustache, thinking. "Well, as long as she's chaperoned, and as long as she can make up the time, working her off-afternoons, I can't see why Flossie can't go to Nantasket."

"Oh, thank you, sir," Casey whooped, and he bolted into the kitchen to tell Flossie the good news.

Mr. Evans turned back to his visitor. "You know, Mr. Drinkwater, I can't tell you what a difference Casey has made to this town. Why, he's not only changed the whole spirit of Mudville, but he's got people going over to that old East Side again. We haven't had any interest out there in years, but people go out to the Grounds, see Casey wallop one, and . . . all of a sudden I've got a mortgage application on my desk for property out there. It's amazing what a team can do for a town. Something new in our modern society, I believe. Amazing. Had you ever thought about that?"

"No, I never had," Drinkwater said, lying through his teeth.

Casey's Memorial Day performance was as fine as a hitter could have: eight for twelve, two homers, eleven runs batted in. And what crowds! SRO! Waving American flags! The children hung from the trees, and all the bands from the Memorial Day parade reassembled at the Grounds, so grumpy old Cyrus Weatherly let them sit inside the center-field fence—for two bits a head—and they played music all afternoon, adding to the holiday air.

The Mudvilles had never drawn so many people, and it was only May. Word of the Mighty Casey had even reached Boston, and because the Beaneaters were away on a western swing, a few cranks took the train out from the city. Ernest Thayer, Harvard '85, a frustrated poet who was reassigned to working in one of the family's woolen mills, came in from Worcester. Flossie snuck away from the house late in the day and was at the Grounds for the eighth inning of the second game, in time to see Casey at the bat for the last time.

Hughie Barrows was on second and Johnny Flynn on first, and Casey knocked them both in with a ground-rule double that rolled into a French horn in center field. The crowd went berserk. The score didn't mean anything now. In fact, baseball didn't matter. It was mostly a matter of pride. Not only did the people of Mudville have a hero, but they also were made heroic, touched by him.

However, all Flossie could see was that glorious, innocent face on second base: Casey, standing there, his cap off, waving to the throng, beaming.

Practically all the players wore mustaches, and many of them bushy side-burns to boot. But Casey was apart. His face was as clean as it was bright, his eyes clear blue, his hair the color of a base path, his uniform happily dirty. Not poverty dirty or grubby dirty, but boyishly dirty, good dirty, thought Flossie. God, but Casey was clean. The tears poured down Flossie's cheeks. She was so in love, and maybe even better, she knew Casey loved her, too.

In the stands back of third base Thayer turned to a friend. "You know," he said, "there's that song about King Kelly."

"You mean 'Slide, Kelly, Slide'?"

"Right. And there's that barroom rhyme for John L." Thayer recited from memory:

> His colors are the Stars and Stripes.
> He also wears the green.
> And he's the greatest slugger that
> The ring has ever seen.
> No fighter in the world can beat
> Our true American:
> The champion of all champions,
> John L. Sullivan!

"Pretty good memory, Ernest."

"Yeah, well this guy Casey deserves even more. He deserves an epic poem. I think I'll come back out here Saturday."

On second base, Casey put his cap back on, and when he did, it was as if he caught a sunbeam in it and the rays wreathed his head in amber. Then he hitched up his pants and took a long lead off second.

2

Drinkwater escorted Flossie and Casey out of the Cyclorama. Her mind was still swimming at that marvel, the grandest thing she had ever seen. And now Drinkwater took her by the elbow and helped her into his rig, a magnificent surrey drawn by a pair of matching chestnuts. Why, Cinderella herself hadn't gone to the ball in anything finer, and Flossie only wished that

Mr. Drinkwater wasn't along with them so that she could snuggle up next to Timothy—and hang that anyone would see her carrying on so brazenly.

Flossie had been in the big city before, but this was different, looking from the surrey on the humanity scrambling about her. Boston had burst into a city of 400,000 people, easily double what it had been before the Civil War, and that didn't take into account the trolley suburbs. There were 231 miles of trolley lines now, carrying 85 million passengers every year—all manner of souls: Chinese men with pigtails, Jews with long beards, Poles and Gypsies, sailors, beggars and urchins. Almost three quarters of the city was immigrant or first generation. Since '85, Boston had even had an Irish mayor. What else could hold this disjointed mass together but churches, saloons and baseball?

The surrey headed south, toward Quincy and the sloop that would take them across Hingham Bay. A trolley flashed across their path, the passengers hanging on, jaunty in the warm air. Tomorrow would be June! Flossie eyed the theaters, the shops, the department stores. In one window were fancy shawls on sale for $2.25. How Flossie wanted one, but there was no time and so much to see. Druggists on every corner, curing the ails of mankind. Signs and sandwich boards boasting of nostrums to correct OBESITY! OPIUM ADDICTION! THE ILL EFFECTS OF YOUTHFUL ERRORS! SUMMER DEBILITIES! There was Lydia Pinkham's famous vegetable compound for women, and Unrivalled Eureka Pills for Weak Men who suffered from early decay and lost manhood. The way things were going, what would doctors have left to cure in the 20th Century?

When they reached Dorchester the driver pulled off the main road, and Drinkwater explained that his sister had a touch of the vapors, it seemed, and so his niece Phoebe had graciously consented to fill in as a substitute chaperon. As soon as Drinkwater got down from the rig to go in the house and fetch her, Casey turned to Flossie and, taking her by the shoulders, looked into her face.

How smooth it was. And in a world where so many people had disfiguring smallpox marks, Flossie's countenance seemed all the more polished, the rosy cheeks blushing, the green eyes enraptured, the tendrils of hair falling gently across her forehead. She knew he was going to embrace her then, kiss her right there in the surrey, in the sunlight. She also knew she wasn't going to stop him, and, indeed, when Casey didn't disappoint, when he took her in his arms and pressed his lips against hers, Flossie fell onto him and kissed him back with every bit as much fervor.

She absolutely astonished Casey, and so it was he who, finally, pulled back, wide-eyed. "You're as beautiful as Frances Folsom herself," he gasped at last, paying her the ultimate compliment.

Flossie's mother had told her about boys like him. "Am I now?"

"Oh yes, only I'm sure she doesn't kiss the President nearly so well," he smirked, making Flossie duck her head in proud embarrassment.

When she looked up, she knew Casey was going to try to kiss her again. To stop this madness, she put a finger to his lips. "Tell me now, Timothy. What *does* Mr. Drinkwater seek from you?"

Casey glared at her. "Dammit, Florence Cleary, I told you not to ask me that," he snapped. And he was so peeved at her, he sulked intermittently the rest of the trip, or at least until they put on their bathing costumes at Nantasket Beach and Casey got to see the flesh of Flossie's ankles.

Richard Fox alighted at Boston's new Park Square Terminal that afternoon. What a ride: mile-a-minute, throttle out; a sumptuous meal; exquisite comfort and service. At the Parker House his suite was ready, but before going up, Fox asked the telephone traffic operator, the hello girl, to ring up the Third Base Saloon at 940 Columbus Avenue. After a moment a voice came on. "Hello," it said.

"I'd like to talk to Mr. McGreevey," Fox said.

"This is Nuf Ced. Who's this?"

"This is Richard Fox . . . of the *Police Gazette*."

There was a pause on the other end, and Michael T. McGreevey, known by one and all as Nuf Ced, clearly let fly into a spittoon. "I don't know if I want to talk to ya."

"Is Sullivan there?"

"Maybe he is. Maybe he isn't."

"Look, Nuf Ced, I'm trying to make a lot of money for Sullivan. Tell 'im I came to Boston, and . . ."

Pit-too. "He ain't in Boston."

"So, when's he get back?"

"Maybe tomorrow." *Pit-too.*

"OK, you just tell Sullivan I'll be at your place tomorrow night."

"Aye, I'll tell 'im." *Pit-too.* "But I ain't sayin' Johnny'll like it, Fox. Nough said?" said Nuf Ced.

The reason Sullivan wasn't in Boston that Thursday was that he was the featured attraction at the Nantasket Beach show. Why should he defend his title against Jake Kilrain when he could make a king's ransom walking through exhibitions?

Drinkwater had the choicest seats for Flossie and Casey, himself and Phoebe, his niece. Truth to tell, Phoebe didn't look much like a chaperon. While she couldn't have been much older than Flossie, an aura of maturity hung on her no less than the men did. Many of those in the dining room seemed to know Drinkwater's niece as well as they knew Drinkwater. And he was a much-recognized man. The Trolley King, everyone called him.

Flossie kept her eyes on Drinkwater, though not, perhaps, quite as much as Phoebe kept hers on Casey. And how raggedy Flossie felt beside Phoebe. Flossie was in her very best Sunday gingham, but it looked absolutely shabby compared with Phoebe's magnificent brown foulard gown, with white polka dots and a parasol to match. No wonder the men stared at her so. No wonder Casey did. Flossie was relieved when they could finally get over to the pavilion to see the show.

And what a performance it was! Though Flossie had believed that nothing could possibly compare to the Gettysburg Cyclorama, this surely was entertainment unrivaled. Here was the bill:

First, Gardini and Hamlet, blackface singers. Then the solemn dramatic recitations of Amos P. Lawrence, followed by John Mahoney, who performed a "laughable trapeze," adroitly mixing humor and danger. Jessie Allyne came next, a brief novelty act. She let her magnificent hair down and down and down, until the golden tresses lay in great coiled rings at her feet. "I seen something like that in a sideshow once," Casey said, "but the lady in question wasn't nearly so grand." This was followed by the Authentic Monkey Orchestra, then Fairfax and Siegfried, human statues extraordinaire, and the ever-popular Willie Arnold, New England's favorite jig dancer.

Then it was time for the fisticuffs. First, before John L. came on, Patsey Kerrigan and George LaBlanche fought under the old ring rules, which the announcer explained meant "anything but biting." Sullivan himself would have none of that. It was odd about John L. As utterly crude as he was— almost barbaric in his personal habits—he preferred gloves and the new Marquis of Queensberry rules, with scoring by timed rounds. Still, even the fashionable Nantasket crowd showed atavistic fascination as Kerrigan and LaBlanche clawed one another.

Drinkwater leaned across to Casey. "Look about," he said. "Look at your Miss Cleary and my, uh, niece. Look all around, and you'll espy that much of the applause here comes from the dainty gloved hands." Casey nodded. "You see, Timothy, if women can favor a raw free-for-all as we've just seen, think how many of the lovelies would be attracted to a fine, clean sporting event like baseball"—Drinkwater lifted a finger—"particularly if it were played in a better part of town."

Casey started to approve this wisdom, but he was stopped cold, for at that moment the Great John L. Sullivan entered the stage, a huge green robe slung loosely over his shoulders. Casey was aghast. The Boston Strong Boy was, in fact, the Boston Fat Boy. "He's fat," Flossie said, with shock. "Disgustingly fat," said Phoebe, with disgust.

The heavyweight champion of the world, 29 years old, looked closer to 39 and packed 243 pounds on his 5'10½" frame. He was grotesquely flabby. His attendant, a spidery little sort named Smiler Pippen, laced on the champ's gloves, and that motion was enough to jiggle Sullivan's jowls and belly. John L. liked having Smiler around, for he was a self-professed druggist, who dispensed rubdowns and a favored potion, a so-called physic, which was made up of zinnia, salts and licorice. That was Sullivan's only concession to training.

He sauntered out to face one Francis Rooney, and to Casey's surprise, he had to admit that Sullivan could be remarkably nimble when he had to be—for a second or two. But he was too much the walrus to maintain any pace, and though his blows obviously devastated poor Rooney, John L. was hardly a scintillating climax to the evening. Drinkwater and his guests left a bit disappointed.

Casey had hoped then for a stroll down the boardwalk, perhaps even a little trip along the beach, but Flossie was exhausted from the long day, and he had to settle for a chaste peck on her cheek. Then Phoebe conscientiously assumed her chaperon's mantle and ushered Flossie off to her room. "A little nose paint?" Drinkwater said to Casey, beckoning to the bar, where they took a table for brandy and cigars.

"Well, Timothy, my boy, have you decided to accept my little proposition?" Drinkwater asked after they'd lit up.

"I think so, but I'm not. . . ."

"I understand. You're a prudent young man," Drinkwater said, toasting him. "So, let's run over it again. Now, you tell me you make . . ."

"Eight hundred dollars for the season. . . ."

"... playing for Mudville."

So Drinkwater took out his billfold and laid out eight $100 bills. Casey blinked.

"And if you stay with Mudville after this season, you'll be reserved," Drinkwater said. "You understand? They'll own you. 'Reserve' is just a pretty word for 'own.' Bad enough that provision was put in for the major-club players, now it's in the minors, too. What is this? This is 1888. We fought a war over this 25 years ago."

"Yes sir." The nerve of old Cyrus Weatherly and those other owners.

"Now, I'm prepared to pay you three thousand dollars"—to spell things out, Drinkwater laid down two more centuries and a pair of $1,000 bills—"to leave Mudville." Casey gasped.

"Take the summer off," Drinkwater went on. "Next season, I'll help you sign with anyone."

"The Beaneaters," said Casey.

"Why not, Timothy, my boy?"

Casey's eyes twinkled.

"And finally, and extra $500 to seal the bargain," Drinkwater said, and he laid out a $500 bill. "And I'll throw in a beautiful new gown for that young lady of yours. You get this right now"—he slid the $500 closer to Casey—"and the rest after five more games. Only you're not to get a single hit in any of those games. I don't want you just disappearing. That'd be too curious. But if all of a sudden you start striking out, it'll look like something went wrong with Mighty Casey. People will think he went lame, lost his ginger. Then you take the $3,000 and drop out of sight. Only, when you materialize next year, you're in the National League."

Casey's hand itched to reach out and take the $500, but, after hesitating, he took up the brandy glass instead. Casey was no dummy. "Mr. Drinkwater, I'm no dummy," he said. "There must be a reason you'd pay me all this."

"Of course there is, my boy. But there's an expression going around: What you don't know won't hurt you. You just have my word as a sporting man that it's not illegal. What do you say?"

Casey paused a moment. "Let me sleep on it."

"Very wise, my boy," Drinkwater said, chuckling. "Yes indeed, you sleep on it tonight. Heh, heh."

Casey entered his room. From out of the shadows Phoebe came toward him, letting her long sable hair tumble down to the brown foulard dress with the white polka dots. Only then did Casey realize that she didn't have the brown foulard dress with the white polka dots on anymore. "I thought you'd never come up, Timothy," Phoebe said with a sigh.

Later, when Phoebe had dressed, she pulled a $500 bill out of her purse and left it on the bedside table. "So, we're in business . . . with my uncle," she said. And Casey smiled and nodded.

He felt rotten, dirty and deceitful, and wondered when he could see her again.

3

Late the next afternoon, back in Boston, Casey and Flossie walked along the Charles. They'd come up from Nantasket with Phoebe and Drinkwater and had checked into the Parker House, where they planned to spent the night before heading out to Mudville the next morning for the big game. It was a glorious day—the emerald grass, the sculls and sails upon the water, the promenading swells from the Back Bay—but Casey knew that none of the ladies of Boston was as gorgeous as his Flossie.

Drinkwater had arranged for a new outfit to be waiting for Flossie at the hotel: Blue-and-white-striped silk it was, and her splendid figure filled it like one of those sails on the Charles. The dress had wide cuffs and a deep collar of white linen. And there was a leghorn straw sailor with a blue band and flowing white ribbon. Parasol to match. "You're the loveliest, Flossie," Casey said. "There's not a man on the esplanade who's not trying to catch your eye."

"Pshaw. No one would buck a gentleman so pleasing to the eye as *you*," Flossie said, giving a little flip to her parasol. She was learning quickly how much more effectively she could flirt when she was well dressed. "But, ah, I must be watching you, I must."

"Oh, how's that?"

"That Phoebe woman. I truly don't believe she's Mr. Drinkwater's niece, but I do believe she'd like to seduce you, Timothy Casey."

Casey threw his hands to his head and rolled his eyes. "Flossie, that is the most ridiculous thing I've ever heard," he said. He shook his head one more time for effect and stared out at the river.

Whew, he thought, I nipped that in the bud.

Ohhh, thought Flossie, she's seduced him already.

She turned to face him squarely. "You made your deal with Mr. Drinkwater, didn't you now?"

"Sure enough." Casey said, beaming. He pulled out the $500 bill, brandishing it and telling her all the benign details of the arrangement.

But Flossie turned away. "I love you, Timothy Casey. I surely do," she said. "But I can't be marryin' you if you're involved in . . ."

"But there's nothing illegal. I told . . ."

"Well, let me tell you," Flossie snapped, whirling around, her green eyes searing. "Mudville loves you, Mr. Casey. Why, I've heard Mr. Evans tell that you're bringin' the whole East Side back to life, you are. Can't you see what Mr. Drinkwater and that wicked lady want? They want to build a trolley line way out in the opposite direction from Mudville, practically to Devonbury, to move everything out there. Can't you understand what he'll do to Mudville?"

"Flossie, it's just good old American business know-how."

Flossie stamped her parasol on the ground as if it were a shillelagh. "Timothy Casey, would you be a dumb Mick? Can't you see? I'll bet Mr. Drinkwater's bought every bit of real estate out there. I'll wager he's going to build an amusement park, a . . . another baseball grounds. Can't you see that? You breathed life back into our little town, and now he's stealing you from us. That's worse than breakin' any law. Ah, that's breakin' th' spirit."

"But . . ." Casey began to protest, and made the mistake of holding up the $500 bill. When he did, Flossie slapped it away, and he had to scramble after it. By the time he had retrieved the money, his Flossie was weaving in and out among the strollers, disappearing.

When Casey got back to the Parker House, a package was waiting for him at the bell stand. He opened it, and there was Flossie's new dress. A note was pinned to it. It said, "Dear Timothy, I'm sorry, but I cannot accept this or what you are doing with yourself. Do not come calling on me again. Very truly yours, Florence M. Cleary."

Casey crumpled up the note in anger and rushed over to the front desk with the open package in his hands. A well-dressed man with a horseshoe pin on his cravat was standing there. He looked over Casey, looked over the dress. "Woman trouble?" he asked, but sympathetically.

Casey ignored him. To the clerk, he said, "What room is Miss Phoebe Alexander in, please?"

"Seven-eighteen."

Casey grabbed a pen, dashed off a note and called for a bellboy.

"I'm sorry," said the man with the horseshoe pin. "I didn't mean to bother you, but you look like a boxer."

"A fighter? Not me. I'm a ballist."

"Oh, well, I'm sorry. It's just that I'm a fancy man." He put out his hand. "Richard Fox, of the *Police Gazette*."

"No fooling," Casey said, licking the envelope. "Gee, I read the *Gazette* every month."

He handed the bellboy the note and a half a dime. "Seven-eighteen. And wait for the lady's reply."

Then he stuck out his hand to Fox. "I'm Timothy Casey, right fielder on the Mudville nine."

"Well, well," said Fox. "I've got a bit of business in a while, but would you join me for some nose paint while I'm waiting?"

Casey looked at Fox. The *Police Gazette*. He looked at the bellboy waiting for the elevator, and he thought of Phoebe's hair cascading over her bare shoulders. He looked back at Fox. He saw Flossie's eyes. Back to the bellboy. He was just getting on the elevator. He saw all of Flossie. He saw Flossie's love and his own shame—and in the split second it takes a horsehide to travel 50 feet to the bat, Casey dashed to the elevator and yanked the little bellboy out through the closing doors. "Keep the half a dime, but gimme the note back," he said, and then, smiling, he hustled back over to Fox.

● ● ●

Nobody had come up with the term *sports bar* in 1888, but if they had, the Third Base Saloon, Michael T. McGreevey, Prop., would surely have been recognized as the first such institution. Athletic souvenirs—especially baseball gear—cluttered the place, barely leaving room for the cranks who jammed in, particularly after Beaneater games at the South End Grounds nearby. "I call it Third Base 'cause it's the last place you stop before you steal home," McGreevey would growl. "'Nough said?"

McGreevey was stout and tiny, a terrier among men, with a handle-bar mustache, and while he had been baptized Michael Thomas, he was always called Nuf Ced. Fox explained this to Casey as they entered the Third Base Saloon and trod across the large mosaic on the floor that spelled out NUF CED. "He's here, Johnny," Nuf Ced roared from behind the bar.

"Who's here?" The great booming voice of John L. Sullivan answered from somewhere in the back. "Anybody important?"

"No, just Richard Fox, the chucklehead who gave a championship belt to Jake Kilrain." *Pit-too.*

Fox smiled facetiously, tipped his hat to Nuf Ced and bade Casey join him at a table. They ordered beers, and Fox explained they would just have to wait for Sullivan. Sure enough, it was an hour or more before Sullivan, with a big tankard of ale in one hand, appeared. He was accompanied by Smiler Pippen on the one side and by his floozy of the evening, Rosie, on the other. "All right, Fox, what is it you're wantin'?" John L. snarled, and Nuf Ced, taking his cue, came over to the table to stand between the two men.

"I just want you to fight Kilrain, Johnny."

"For you, Fox? I ain't no henhouse to let a fox into," he said, and everyone in the Third Base Saloon roared.

"Then don't do it for me," Fox went on. "Just fight him. That's what all the fancy wants. Or are you too fat, Johnny? Too old?"

"Why you goddamn—" said Sullivan, reaching down to grab Fox. John L. had taken the bait. Fox figured that Nuf Ced would jump in, and he did, but Fox didn't figure that, faster still, his new friend Casey would spring to his feet. Casey shoved Sullivan. The ale went flying, and the big fellow needed help from Smiler and Rosie before he could regain his balance. He glared at Casey, at this white-faced, clean-shaven bumpkin. "And who the hell are you, sonny?" Sullivan shouted.

Casey didn't back down. Indeed, he leaned forward a little, never taking his eyes off Sullivan. "My name is Timothy F. X. Casey, and I can beat any sonofabitch in the house."

The Third Base Saloon fell into a hush. "Is he serious?" Sullivan said at last.

"Are you serious?" Nuf Ced said. *Pit-too.*

Fox pulled at Casey's sleeve. "You're not serious, are you?" he asked.

"Sure, for a price. What are the odds on me?"

"A thousand to one," Nuf Ced said. *Pit-too.*

"I'll take anything he wants at 20 to 1," Sullivan snapped.

Immediately, Casey yanked the $500 bill out of his pocket and waved it. "You're on, John L.," he said. "For this." The crowd gasped as one.

Nuf Ced closed the bar, and the entire ensemble traipsed over to the South End Grounds, where they staked out a ring between the pitcher's box and first base. There was a good moon and enough city light.

"You sure you wanna go through with this, Casey?" Fox asked, helping him off with his coat. "I had Paddy Ryan fight him in '82, and he said it was like a telegraph pole went through him the first time Sullivan hit him."

"That was '82. I seen Sullivan last night," Casey said. "He's fat as a hog, and he's drunk a lotta ale tonight. Besides, my girl left me, and I'm mean."

"Up to scratch," Nuf Ced cried out, and the two fighters stepped forward to a line Nuf Ced had drawn in the dirt. The spectators stood about in a square, already screaming.

"Four rounds," Nuf Ced said. *Pit-too.* "No biting, scratching, gouging, tripping or wrestling."

Both men nodded. Sullivan spit on his hands. Nuf Ced raised his arm. Sullivan knew what to expect. But Casey had figured it out, too. He didn't even look at Sullivan. He kept his eyes on Nuf Ced, and the instant his arm moved, Casey ducked. Good thing. The air was shattered by the force of John L.'s blow.

Casey came up, in one motion banging his right to the big belly, and then his left. By the time Casey was standing full up, Sullivan was holding his stomach. So Casey stepped in and, with all his might, pounded his right to the champion's meaty face. And with that, barely 10 seconds into the fight, Casey had hit a home run. The Great John L. buckled and fell.

The crowd fell into utter silence, shocked. Blood trickled from the corner of Sullivan's mouth, but he wouldn't dab at it any more than Casey would grab his throbbing knuckles. Instead, the two men just glared at each other, until finally Sullivan began to rise on the count of eight. He got up like a bull elephant, slowly at first, but once he had lifted his great bulk off the ground and leaned forward, he possessed a momentum that no sleek creature could achieve. He pounded the few steps toward Casey. It would have been easy for Casey to step aside, except he was backed up against the crowd—John L.'s crowd—and the loyal spectators blocked Casey's movement. He tried to duck, but as he'd seen in Nantasket, Sullivan, for all his corpulence, still had some agility. John L. caught Casey flush with an uppercut. Casey staggered back, his face exploding, his brains rattling about.

He wanted to go down and regroup, but not only did the spectators block his fall, they also propped Casey up—and then bounced him back toward

Sullivan. Casey was a helpless target, and he could see, in his daze, John L. winding up for the knockout.

Then, inexplicably, just like that, Sullivan dropped his dukes and idly watched Casey fly past him, still propelled by the push from the crowd. Sullivan put his hands on his hips and glared at the spectators.

"John L. Sullivan doesn't need any help when he's in the ring," he bellowed. The offenders shrank back.

His rebuke complete, Sullivan turned to finish off Casey. But the moment was lost; Casey had shaken his head clear. When John L. swung, Casey hopped aside, as if he were getting away from a high inside pitch, and with everything left in him, he ducked and came up throwing, like a shortstop pegging to first. Whoosh. Into the champion's soft underbelly. Sullivan gasped. His chin was wide open, but Casey went for the tummy again. And again. The champion doubled over, and only then did Casey aim his left hand—the one that still had its knuckles intact—for Sullivan's chin. Bam! John L. crumpled to his knees and then pitched forward, spitting out blood and ale, spilling his beans.

"Start the goddam count, Nuf Ced!" Fox screamed.

Sullivan peeked up. He didn't know how Casey's hands ached. So he just waved Nuf Ced away and sank back onto the infield grass, into his own blood and guts. The Great John L. was beaten. "Congratulations, sonny," he said. "Now you can tell the whole world you was the first sonuvab. . . . You was the first man ever to beat the Great John L."

"Gimme my $10,000, and I'll never tell a soul on God's green earth," Casey said.

"Don't matter none. That viper Fox'll put it in the *Gazette*."

Fox stepped forward to Sullivan. "Not if you fight Kilrain, I won't, Johnny," he said.

"Yeah now?" said Sullivan, the possibilities dawning on him, and he looked all around at the crowd. "Any sonuvabitch here see John L. Sullivan get beat tonight?"

There was silence for another moment as the crowd looked at one another. Finally, Nuf Ced spit and spoke up: "No, indeed, not me." And then the others cried out, "Not these eyes!" "No, no, no." "I didn't see nuthin'."

Sullivan nodded. "All right, Fox. I'll fight your boy."

"Bare-knuckle."

"Yeah, bare-knuckle. One last time."

Casey started to walk away. "Get me my money, Fox," he called out, and the onlookers stepped aside for him, standing back in awe, afraid even to whisper in the presence of, let alone get in the way of, the man who beat John L.

Suddenly, Fox ran after Casey and caught him near home plate. He took his diamond-studded gold horseshoe off and pinned it on Casey's shirt. "Thanks" was all Fox said.

Casey took the pin off. "You never worked a circus, did you, Fox?" he asked.

"No."

Casey put the pin back on his shirt, but he fixed it with the open end of the horseshoe up. "You never hang a horseshoe down," said Casey. "Anybody on a circus knows that. Hang it down, all the good luck will run out."

Fox nodded and smiled.

"No wonder you never beat John L. before," Casey said.

4

Flossie was hanging the washing on the clothesline the next afternoon when Casey came tearing up to her, his face all bruised. "Timothy, what in heaven's name. . . ."

"I haven't got time," he said. "I'm already late for the game, and I gotta see Drinkwater, too."

She gritted her teeth at the mere mention of that name, but Casey only reached out and pinned the horseshoe pin above her breast. "We can pluck the diamonds out and make a proper engagement ring," he said, and with that he dashed off to the ball yard. Flossie unfastened the pin to look it over. Why, it obviously cost even more than the silk dress. How much more money was Drinkwater paying him now? And for what? Furious, Flossie pinned the horseshoe back on, and even though only half the washing had gone up on the line, she rushed off.

There had never been a larger crowd for a baseball game in Mudville. Had everybody in town skipped work? Had every kid robbed his piggy bank? Grumpy old Cyrus Weatherly had stuck the overflow behind ropes in center field. Ernest Thayer had arrived in time to get a ticket, but the crowd spilled over into the aisles, and he had a hard time seeing some of the action.

But where was Casey? Mighty Casey? Nobody knew. Only Drinkwater, sitting in his box by the Mudville bench, beamed.

Willie Flaherty, the Mudville manager, put McGillicuddy in for Casey, but the Mudvilles were at sea without their star, and the Lynns built a 4–2 lead. Then, just as Lynn made out in the seventh, here came Casey sauntering onto the diamond. The people roared and screamed his name, everyone standing and stretching for just a glance. Weatherly glowered at his tardy slugger. Drinkwater nodded his head and winked at Casey as he jogged to the bench. The kid has a real sense of theater, Drinkwater mused. To show up like this and *then* strike out—an even greater disappointment for the gullible locals. Casey went right to the manager. "I'm ready, Willie," he said.

Jimmy Blake was leading off in the seventh, so McGillicuddy was on deck—Casey's spot. But Flaherty waved the Mudville star away. "Sit down, Mr. Casey," he said. "I play the guys who are here when the game starts."

While the crowd booed, poor McGillicuddy batted—bumping a little dribbler back to the wheelman. Three up and three down. And the same in the Mudville eighth. However, when Barry O'Connor, the Mudville pitcher, retired the Lynns in order in the ninth inning, he came out of the pitcher's box and headed straight for Flaherty, to beseech him to let Casey have his licks. Flaherty spit and then said, "OK, Barry, if we get to McGillicuddy's spot, I'll give him a swing."

But the elation on the Mudville bench was short-lived because Cooney grounded out and Barrows topped a ball to first. "I've never seen such a sickly silence," Thayer said to the fellow next to him.

"Still," the other gentleman said, "I'd put up even money if Casey could get at the bat."

The pitcher for the Lynns was a wiry little guy named Kenny Landis, who was a law student pitching under the nom de baseball of Walt Mueller. In his heavy flannel, he was sweating copiously as he peered in for the final out against Johnny Flynn. Landis tried to dry his pitching hand on his trousers, but they were almost soaked through with sweat. With his wet fingers, and his being tired, too, he hung an in-shoot, and Flynn knocked it cleanly up the middle. That brought Blake to the plate, and the Mudville Grounds exploded, but even Blake knew it wasn't for him. No, the roar was for who would come after Blake: Casey, the Mighty Casey, was moving up on deck.

Casey detoured on the way, going over to speak to Drinkwater. Flossie had found her way into the Grounds by now and had worked her way to the first row in the center-field overflow. When she saw Casey consorting with

Drinkwater again—and right out in the open!—she slammed her arms folded across her chest and cursed the best way she knew how.

Blake was an old-timer, cagey when he was sober, and he decided to rip into the kid pitcher's first pitch. He rifled it down the left-field line, and when the dust was settled, he was standing on second base and Flynn on third.

Here came Casey. Poor Landis could hardly see through his sweat. But, he thought, Casey probably wants to see what kind of stuff I have, so he'll be taking. Good thinking: Casey let a waist-high fastball go by. "Strike one," said the umpire. Flossie wrung her hands and prayed that Casey would find his conscience and hit the ball.

Landis came back with an outdrop, but Casey thought it was off the plate. The umpire, standing behind the pitcher, saw it nick the corner. "Strike two," he said.

But the Mudvilles weren't worried. Casey had seen the kid's repertoire, and he was a celebrated two-strike hitter. The cranks were all on their feet, hollering, and Thayer, even on tiptoes, had to hop this way and that to follow the action. In fact, he missed it when Casey, staring out at the pitcher, spotted Flossie directly behind him, watching from straight-away center, standing out against the crowd in her maid's uniform. For just a moment Casey smiled at her, and then something came over him. Before he knew it, he had raised his bat, pointing it toward center, calling a home run right over his dear Flossie's head. The crowd roared.

"What was that? What was that?" Thayer cried.

"I couldn't see, either," the guy next to him said.

Then the crowd parted a little, and Thayer was able to watch as Casey clenched his teeth and pounded his bat. Landis sweated even more. He would have gone to the resin bag, only there weren't any resin bags yet, so he rubbed his hand on his clothes, on his cap, his socks, his hair, his mustache. Then he reared back and let the ball go. Casey saw it all the way. The pitch didn't have a thing on it. He began his swing, poised, evenly, perfectly. . . .

Casey missed it by a country mile.

Mudville blinked. Mudville couldn't believe it. Flossie could. Flossie cried. Casey had gone on the take. There was no joy in Mudville.

Only . . . wait. The pitch had darted down, and it went under the catcher's glove. It began to roll to the backstop, and here came Flynn, already bearing down on the plate. Casey began to run for first. The catcher got to the ball, picked it up, dropped it, picked it up again, and there went the throw, soaring over the first baseman's head by five feet. Flynn scored. It was 4–3. And here came old Blake right behind. Tie score. Four-up. And Casey was on his way to second. He rounded the bag, and the right fielder picked up the horse-hide down the line and threw behind Casey, to nail him as he tried to scramble back to second. Only Casey saw where the throw was going, and he put his head down and kept on for third. The second-sacker took the throw, a good one, whirled and whipped it to third. It bounced in the dirt as Casey slid, and ricocheted off the third baseman's shoulder and down the left-field line. Casey scrambled to his feet and was on his way home. The third baseman tore back, picked up the ball and fired it to the plate. Casey slid. The catcher took the ball and slapped it on him. "Safe," the umpire said.

"Curses," Chester Drinkwater muttered.

There was joy in Mudville. The crowd poured onto the field and lifted Casey to its shoulders. He had struck out, but they hoisted him up and began to parade him around.

Casey saw Flossie out in center. The rest of the crowd had run in, and she was just standing there, all alone, the tears flowing down her cheeks. "Let me down, let me down!" Casey cried, and he fought his way off the shoulders to the ground and ran to her, ran as fast as he could, ran even faster than he had when he'd circled the bases.

Only, when he grabbed her, Flossie said, "I hate you, Timothy Casey."

"Listen to me, Flossie. Dammit, listen to me! I tried. I tried! *I tried!* He just struck me out."

"I don't believe you," she said, and she twisted away from him.

"But you must," Casey screamed. "It happens. Somewhere, someday, somebody's even gonna beat John L. Sullivan. It happens."

"You cheated us all!" Flossie cried.

Before he could go on, Casey felt a tap on his shoulder. All the Lynn players were filing past, leaving the Grounds, and there was Landis, the pitcher. "Mr. Casey, no matter what happened, I just want you to know it was an honor facing you," he said. "And I want you to know that that last pitch was the best one I ever hurled in all my life. I don't even know how I did it."

"It was sure some pitch," Casey said. "If you can throw that pitch again, you can strike out King Kelly hisself."

Only Landis never did throw that pitch again. He tried. He tried holding the ball this way and that, releasing it here and there, firing it fast and slow. But all he did was give himself a sore arm and hurry himself into the judiciary. Landis didn't realize he'd mixed his sweat with his mustache wax and thrown the first spitball. Because he didn't know that, he would never do it again, and it was 14 more years before somebody invented the spitball.

Casey yanked Landis over to Flossie. "Tell her, tell her," he screamed at Landis.

"Well, ma'am," said Landis, "like I just said, that was the best pitch I ever threw."

"You hear that, Flossie?" said Casey. "He struck me out. He was just better'n me."

He chased after her some more, but she wasn't convinced. "I don't believe you," she said. "I even saw you talking to Drinkwater just before you went to the bat."

"That was because I told him I left his $500 and the silk dress with Phoebe at the Parker House, because you were right and I don't want nothing to do with his deal." He grabbed Flossie by her cheeks and held her face before his. "You hear me, Flossie? I love you! I love you!"

She appeared to be considering this, so Casey pulled out all the stops. He sank to one knee, took her hands and said, "Florence Cleary, will you do me the honor of being my wife?"

Flossie believed him. "Yes, I will," she said.

Casey jumped to his feet and kissed her, and all the cranks who were standing around watching began to cheer. Then Casey said, "It's a good thing for you that you said that, because I'm also a rich man now. I got ten $1,000 bills in my shoes."

"What?"

"I'll tell you all about it sometime, but right now. . . ." He reached over and took off the horseshoe pin, because he'd just noticed that Flossie had put it back on upside down. "Don't ever wear a horseshoe pointing down, because then all the luck will run out of it," he said, and he pinned it back on her, the right way.

Then he put his arm around her, and they walked off together, toward the sunset, as a matter of fact. "You mean if I'd worn the pin right you'd have hit a home run over my head, the way you pointed?" Flossie said.

"Nah, nobody could've hit that pitch," said Casey. "You gotta understand, darling—in baseball, even the best ballists only get a hit one out of every three times up."

Epilogue

Here is what happened to the principals after June 2, 1888.

John L. Sullivan kept his word to Richard Fox and, on July 8, 1889, fought Jake Kilrain, successfully defending his championship in 75 rounds. It was the last bare-knuckle title bout ever fought.

Richard Fox remained a pillar of popular journalism, and the *National Police Gazette* prospered until 1977. Fox's mix of sex, sport and crime serves many well even today, especially if you add weather.

Nuf Ced McGreevey continued to preside over his sports saloon until Prohibition. To this day, no Boston baseball team has won the championship of the world without Nuf Ced being present at all home games.

Jim Naismith invented basketball in 1891.

Chester Drinkwater became one of the richest men in America, gaining his fortune building ball yards and amusement parks outside the city, running streetcar lines to them and selling real estate all along the way. The only locale where this scheme did not work was Mudville, where, at considerable loss, Drinkwater let many land options lapse. Returning on the *Titanic* from his honeymoon with his fourth wife, the Countess Nina von Munschauer, 23, Drinkwater went to a watery grave.

Grumpy old Cyrus Weatherly, the town miser, refurbished Mudville Grounds after the exciting '88 season, and for decades it was know as the Jewel of the Bushes. Taking this cue, Alfred L. Evans Jr. urged his bank to support the redevelopment of the entire East Side, and the area became a national model for downtown revival. Only after World War I, when the East Side population had become largely Italian, Lithuanian and Pole, were the old Mudville Grounds razed. In 1976 a real estate developer put up middle-class housing for blacks. The area is now known as Covent Gardens Estates, and on the actual site of the diamond where Casey struck out is a 24-hour convenience store.

Timothy F. X. Casey finished the '88 season with Mudville, but though he continued to have a fine year, the events of those days in late May and early June seemed to have extracted some spirit from him that he never regained. He and Flossie became engaged, and on the day after the season ended in September, they eloped.

The Caseys spent the next couple of years traveling in America, investing their fortune in prime real estate, buying downtown tracts in such promising minor-league towns as Dallas, Seattle and Los Angeles. However, Casey had never stopped thinking about what Mr. Evans had once said to him in Mudville. So when Flossie became pregnant, he went back to school, enrolling, in the autumn of 1891, in the very first freshman class at a small new institution that was known as Leland Stanford Jr. University. He graduated with high honors in 1895.

The Caseys settled in Stockton, Calif., where he quickly made his mark in trolleys. Flossie bore him four daughters, and Casey became a pillar of the community—daily communicant, councilman and, finally, philanthropist.

Thayer's poem became more and more famous, spawning vaudeville skits, books, paintings, songs, movies, even a whole opera. The supposedly fictional Casey became something of an American Dauphin, because for years all sorts of washed-up ballplayers maintained that they had been the model for the Mighty One. But after that famous day in Mudville, the real Casey only told one person who he actually was.

That was his nephew George, son of Casey's left-handed twin sister, Kate. Once in 1909, when he had to travel East on trolley business, Casey visited Kate in Baltimore, and the young lad seemed so keen on baseball that Casey took him over to a corner table in the family saloon on Conway Street and told him the tale of '88. "But Uncle Timothy, why did Mr. Thayer end his poem the way he did?" young George asked.

"Aw, you know sportswriters. They only write what makes a good story," Casey said.

Young George especially liked the part about Casey pointing to center field, daring to foretell a home run. "Imagine a player doin' a thing like that." George said.

Over the years Casey played a lot of golf. He was long off the tee but dicey around the greens. He and Flossie traveled a lot—to Europe, to Lake Louise and to the 1932 Los Angeles Olympics. They had an even dozen grandchildren, but, of course, the name Casey had run out.

Then, in the spring of 1941, Casey's health began to fail, and he took to his bed in June. He knew by then that the jig was up. He got weaker and weaker. It was the 75th summer of his life.

Three of his daughters still lived around Stockton, but Mary Louise had moved to San Francisco, so Flossie called her on July 17 and said she had better come. She brought her youngest son, Casey's favorite grandchild, John Lawrence Sullivan Gambardella. They just made it to Stockton, to the old family house, in time and went directly to the master bedroom, where the old man lay.

"Well, Johnny, how's tricks?" Casey said, just barely getting the words out. He was going fast. Peacefully, but fast, the sands of his time, 1867–1941.

"Oh, I'm OK, Grandpop," the boy said, "but I heard on the radio the Indians got DiMaggio out tonight. So it ends at 56 in a row."

Casey shook his head a bit, and he said, "Well, if he's any good, he'll get over it."

"Yes, sir."

Mary Louise kissed her father, and then she stepped back next to her sisters so her mother could stand closest to the old man. Flossie leaned down and kissed Casey gently on the forehead and squeezed his hand. He sighed, and his eyes began to close. He could all but see the angels now. But then, somehow, Casey forced one more breath of life into his body, and he opened his eyes, even smiled a tiny little bit. Looking up at his beloved Flossie, he said. "Oh, somewhere in this favored land, the sun is shining bright."

Then Casey closed off his smile, turned down his eyes and died. Flossie kept hold of his hand and said. "The band is playing somewhere, and somewhere hearts are light."

The four daughters turned to look at one another, tears in their eyes, but wondering what in the world had come over their mother. "And somewhere men are laughing." Flossie went on. "And somewhere children shout." She smiled broadly and didn't say another word.

As for the one other principal in this story, as for baseball, it grew to become the national pastime and lived happily ever after.

The Thrill of the Grass (1984)

W. P. Kinsella

W. P. Kinsella is best known for his novel *Shoeless Joe* (1983), which was made into one of the most celebrated baseball movies of all time, *Field of Dreams*. The title of this short story is drawn from that same novel, in which Joe Jackson says, "I'd wake up in the night with the smell of the ballpark in my nose and the cool of the grass on my feet. The thrill of the grass." Kinsella's other books include *Dance Me Outside* (1977), *The Iowa Baseball Confederacy* (1986), *The Dixon Cornbelt League and Other Baseball Stories* (1995), and *Magic Time* (2001), a novel of hope, promise, and baseball. The following story depicts irate fans who take matters into their own hands during the 1981 baseball strike, which was the first lengthy and season-interrupting work stoppage in sports history.

1981: the summer the baseball players went on strike. The dull weeks drag by, the summer deepens, the strike is nearly a month old. Outside the city the corn rustles and ripens in the sun. Summer without baseball: a disruption to the psyche. An unexplainable aimlessness engulfs me. I stay later and later each evening in the small office at the rear of my shop. Now, driving home after work, the worst of the rush hour traffic over, it is the time of evening I would normally be heading for the stadium.

I enjoy arriving an hour early, parking in a far corner of the lot, walking slowly toward the stadium, rays of sun dropping softly over my shoulders like tangerine ropes, my shadow gliding with me, black as an umbrella. I like to watch young families beside their campers, the mothers in shorts, grilling hamburgers, their men drinking beer. I enjoy seeing little boys dressed in the home team uniform, barely toddling, clutching hotdogs in upraised hands.

I am a failed shortstop. As a young man, I saw myself diving to my left, graceful as a toppling tree, fielding high grounders like a cat leaping for butterflies, bracing my right foot and tossing to first, the throw true as if a steel ribbon connected my hand and the first baseman's glove. I dreamed of leading the American League in hitting—being inducted into the Hall of Fame. I batted .217 in my senior year of high school and averaged 1.3 errors per nine innings.

I know the stadium will be deserted; nevertheless I wheel my car down off the freeway, park, and walk across the silent lot, my footsteps rasping and mournful. Strangle-grass and creeping charlie are already inching up through the gravel, surreptitious, surprised at their own ease. Faded bottle caps, rusted bits of chrome, an occasional paper clip, recede into the earth. I circle a ticket booth, sun-faded, empty, the door closed by an oversized padlock. I walk beside the tall, machinery-green, board fence. A half mile away a few cars hiss along the freeway; overhead a single-engine plane fizzes lazily. The whole place is silent as an empty classroom, like a house suddenly without children.

It is then that I spot the door-shape. I have to check twice to be sure it is there: a door cut in the deep green boards of the fence, more the promise of a door than the real thing, the kind of door, as children, we cut in the sides of cardboard boxes with our mothers' paring knives. As I move closer, a golden circle of lock, like an acrimonious eye, establishes its certainty.

I stand, my nose so close to the door I can smell the faint odor of paint, the golden eye of a lock inches from my own eyes. My desire to be inside the ballpark is so great that for the first time in my life I commit a criminal act. I have been a locksmith for over forty years. I take the small tools from the pocket of my jacket, and in less time than it would take a speedy runner to circle the bases I am inside the stadium. Though the ballpark is open-air, it smells of abandonment; the walkways and seating areas are cold as basements. I breathe the odors of rancid popcorn and wilted cardboard.

The maintenance staff were laid off when the strike began. Synthetic grass does not need to be cut or watered. I stare down at the ball diamond, where just to the right of the pitcher's mound, a single weed, perhaps two inches high, stands defiant in the rain-pocked dirt.

The field sits breathless in the orangy glow of the evening sun. I stare at the potato-colored earth of the infield, that wide, dun arc, surrounded by plastic grass. As I contemplate the prickly turf, which scorches the thighs and buttocks of a sliding player as if he were being seared by hot steel, it stares back in its uniform ugliness. The seams that send routinely hit ground balls veering at tortuous angles are vivid, gray as scars.

I remember the ballfields of my childhood, the outfields full of soft hummocks and brown-eyed gopher holes.

I stride down from the stands and walk out to the middle of the field. I touch the stubble that is called grass, take off my shoes, but find it is like walking on a row of toothbrushes. It was an evil day when they stripped the sod from this ballpark, cut it into yard-wide swathes, rolled it, memories and all, into great green-and-black cinnamon-roll shapes, trucked it away. Nature temporarily defeated. But Nature is patient.

Over the next few days an idea forms within me, ripening, swelling, pushing everything else into a corner. It is like knowing a new, wonderful joke and not being able to share. I need an accomplice.

I go to see a man I don't know personally, though I have seen his face peering at me from the financial pages of the local newspaper, and the *Wall Street Journal*, and I have been watching his profile at the baseball stadium, two boxes to the right of me, for several years. He is a fan. Really a fan. When the weather is intemperate, or the game not close, the people around us disappear like flowers closing at sunset, but we are always there until the last pitch. I know he is a man who attends because of the beauty and mystery of the game, a man who can sit during the last of the ninth with the game decided innings ago, and draw joy from watching the first baseman adjust the angle of his glove as the pitcher goes into his windup.

He, like me, is a first-base-side fan. I've always watched baseball from behind first base. The positions fans choose at sporting events are like politics, religion, or philosophy: a view of the world, a way of seeing the universe. They make no sense to anyone, have no basis in anything but stubbornness.

I brought up my daughters to watch baseball from the first-base side. One lives in Japan and sends me box scores from Japanese newspapers, and Japanese baseball magazines with pictures of superstars politely bowing to one another. She has a season ticket in Yokohama; on the first-base side.

"Tell him a baseball fan is here to see him," is all I will say to his secretary. His office is in a skyscraper, from which he can look out over the city to where the prairie rolls green as mountain water to the limits of the eye. I wait all afternoon in the artificially cool, glassy reception area with its yellow and mauve chairs, chrome and glass coffee tables. Finally, in the late afternoon, my message is passed along.

"I've seen you at the baseball stadium," I say, not introducing myself.

"Yes," he says. "I recognize you. Three rows back, about eight seats to my left. You have a red scorebook and you often bring your daughter. . . ."

"Granddaughter. Yes, she goes to sleep in my lap in the late innings, but she knows how to calculate an ERA and she's only in Grade 2."

"One of my greatest regrets," says this tall man, whose mustache and carefully styled hair are polar-bear white, "is that my grandchildren all live over a thousand miles away. You're very lucky. Now, what can I do for you?"

"I have an idea," I say. "One that's been creeping toward me like a first baseman when the bunt sign is on. What do you think about artificial turf?"

"Hmmmf," he snorts, "that's what the strike should be about. Baseball is meant to be played on summer evenings and Sunday afternoons, on grass just cut by a horse-drawn mower," and we smile as our eyes meet.

"I've discovered the ballpark is open, to me anyway," I go on. "There's no one there while the strike is on. The wind blows through the high top of the grandstand, whining until the pigeons in the rafters flutter. It's lonely as a ghost town."

"And what is it you do there, alone with the pigeons?"

"I dream."

"And where do I come in?"

"You've always struck me as a man who dreams. I think we have things in common. I think you might like to come with me. I could show you what I dream, paint you pictures, suggest what might happen . . ."

He studies me carefully for a moment, like a pitcher trying to decide if he can trust the sign his catcher has just given him.

"Tonight?" he says. "Would tonight be too soon?"

"Park in the northwest corner of the lot about 1:00 AM. There is a door about fifty yards to the right of the main gate. I'll open it when I hear you."

He nods.

I turn and leave.

• • •

The night is clear and cotton warm when he arrives. "Oh, my," he says, staring at the stadium turned chrome-blue by a full moon. "Oh, my," he says again, breathing in the faint odors of baseball, the reminder of fans and players not long gone.

"Let's go down to the field," I say. I am carrying a cardboard pizza box, holding it on the upturned palms of my hands, like an offering.

When we reach the field, he first stands on the mound, makes an awkward attempt at a windup, then does a little sprint from first to about halfway to second. "I think I know what you've brought," he says, gesturing toward the box, "but let me see anyway."

I open the box in which rests a square foot of sod, the grass smooth and pure, cool as a swatch of satin, fragile as baby's hair.

"Ohhh," the man says, reaching out a finger to test the moistness of it. "Oh, I see."

We walk across the field, the harsh, prickly turf making the bottoms of my feet tingle, to the left-field corner where, in the angle formed by the foul line and the warning track, I lay down the square foot of sod. "That's beautiful," my friend says, kneeling beside me, placing his hand, fingers spread wide, on the verdant square, leaving a print faint as a veronica.

I take from my belt a sickle-shaped blade, the kind used for cutting carpet. I measure along the edge of the sod, dig the point in, and pull carefully toward me. There is a ripping sound, like tearing an old bed sheet. I hold up the square of artificial turf like something freshly killed, while all the time digging the sharp point into the packed earth I have exposed. I replace the sod lovingly, covering the newly bared surface.

"A protest," I say.

"But it could be more," the man replies.

"I hoped you'd say that. It could be. If you'd like to come back . . ."

"Tomorrow night?"

"Tomorrow night would be fine. But there will be an admission charge . . ."

"A square of sod?"

"A square of sod two inches thick . . ."

"Of the same grass?"

"Of the same grass. But there's more."

"I suspected as much."

"You must have a friend . . ."

"Who would join us?"

"Yes."

"I have two. Would that be all right?"

"I trust your judgment."

"My father. He's over eighty," my friend says. "You might have seen him with me once or twice. He lives over fifty miles from here, but if I call him he'll come. And my friend . . ."

"If they pay their admission they'll be welcome . . ."

"And they may have friends . . ."

"Indeed they may. But what will we do with this?" I say, holding up the sticky-backed square of turf, which smells of glue and fabric.

"We could mail them anonymously to baseball executives, politicians, clergymen."

"Gentle reminders not to tamper with Nature."

We dance toward the exit, rampant with excitement.

"You will come back? You'll bring others?"

"Count on it," says my friend.

They do come, those trusted friends, and friends of friends, each making a live, green deposit. At first, a tiny row of sod squares begins to inch along toward left-center field. The next night even more people arrive, the following night more again, and the night after there is positively a crowd. Those who come once seem always to return accompanied by friends, occasionally a son or young brother, but mostly men my age or older, for we are the ones who remember the grass.

Night after night the pilgrimage continues. The first night I stand inside the deep green door, listening. I hear a vehicle stop; hear a car door close with a snug thud. I open the door when the sound of soft-soled shoes on gravel tells me it is time. The door swings silent as a snake. We nod curt greetings to each other. Two men pass me, each carrying a grasshopper-legged sprinkler. Later, each sprinkler will sizzle like frying onions as it wheels, a silver sparkler in the moonlight.

During the nights that follow, I stand sentinel-like at the top of the grandstand, watching as my cohorts arrive. Old men walking across a parking lot in a row, in the dark, carrying coiled hoses, looking like the many wheels of a locomotive, old men who have slipped away from their homes, skulked down their sturdy sidewalks, breathing the cool, grassy, after-midnight air. They have left behind their sleeping, gray-haired women, their immaculate bungalows, their manicured lawns. They continue to walk across the parking lot, while occasionally a soft wheeze, a nibbling, breathy sound like an old horse might make, divulges their humanity. They move methodically toward the baseball stadium which hulks against the moon-blue sky like a small mountain. Beneath the tint of starlight, the tall light standards which rise above the fences and grandstand glow purple, necks bent forward, like sunflowers heavy with seed.

My other daughter lives in this city, is married to a fan, but one who watches baseball from behind third base. And like marrying outside the faith, she has been converted to the third-base side. They have their own season tickets, twelve rows up just to the outfield side of third base. I love her, but I don't trust her enough to let her in on my secret.

I could trust my granddaughter, but she is too young. At her age she shouldn't have to face such responsibility. I remember my own daughter, the one who lives in Japan, remember her at nine, all knees, elbows, and missing teeth—remember peering in her room, seeing her asleep, a shower of well-thumbed baseball cards scattered over her chest and pillow.

I haven't been able to tell my wife—it is like my compatriots and I are involved in a ritual for true believers only. Maggie, who knew me when I still dreamed of playing professionally myself—Maggie, after over half a lifetime together, comes and sits in my lap in the comfortable easy chair which has adjusted through the years to my thickening shape, just as she has. I love to hold the lightness of her, her tongue exploring my mouth, gently as a baby's finger.

"Where do you go?" she asks sleepily when I crawl into bed at dawn.

I mumble a reply. I know she doesn't sleep well when I'm gone. I can feel her body rhythms change as I slip out of bed after midnight.

"Aren't you too old to be having a change of life," she says, placing her toast-warm hand on my cold thigh.

I am not the only one with this problem.

"I'm developing a reputation," whispers an affable man at the ballpark. "I imagine any number of private investigators following any number of cars across the city. I imagine them creeping about the parking lot, shining penlights on license plates, trying to guess what we're up to. Think of the reports they must prepare. I wonder if our wives are disappointed that we're not out discoing with frizzy-haired teenagers?"

Night after night, virtually no words are spoken. Each man seems to know his assignment. Not all bring sod. Some carry rakes, some hoes, some hoses, which, when joined together, snake across the infield and outfield, dispensing the blessing of water. Others cradle in their arms bags of earth for building up the infield to meet the thick, living sod.

I often remain high in the stadium, looking down on the men moving over the earth, dark as ants, each sodding, cutting, watering, shaping. Occasionally the moon finds a knife blade as it trims the sod or slices away a chunk of artificial turf, and tosses the reflection skyward like a bright ball. My body tingles. There should be symphony music playing. Everyone should be humming "America the Beautiful."

Toward dawn, I watch the men walking away in groups, like small patrols of soldiers, carrying, instead of arms, the tools and utensils which breathe life back into the arid ballfield.

Row by row, night by night, we lay the little squares of sod, moist as chocolate cake with green icing. Where did all the sod come from? I picture many men, in many parts of the city, surreptitiously cutting chunks out of their own lawns in the leafy midnight darkness, listening to the uncomprehending protests of their wives the next day—pretending to know nothing of it—pretending to have called the police to investigate.

When the strike is over I know we will all be here to watch the workouts, to hear the recalcitrant joints crackling like twigs after the forced inactivity. We will sit in our regular seats, scattered like popcorn throughout the stadium, and we'll nod as we pass on the way to the exits, exchange secret smiles, proud as new fathers.

For me, the best part of all will be the surprise. I feel like a magician who has gestured hypnotically and produced an elephant from thin air. I know I am not alone in my wonder. I know that rockets shoot off in half-a-hundred chests; the excitement of birthday mornings, Christmas eves, and hometown doubleheaders boils within each of my conspirators. Our secret rites have been performed with love, like delivering a valentine to a sweetheart's door in that blue-steel span of morning just before dawn.

Players and management are meeting round the clock. A settlement is imminent. I have watched the stadium covered square foot by square foot until it looks like green graph paper. I have stood and felt the cool odors of the grass rise up and touch my face. I have studied the lines between each small square, watched those lines fade until they were visible to my eyes alone, then not even to them.

What will the players think, as they straggle into the stadium and find the miracle we have created? The old-timers will raise their heads like ponies, as far away as the parking lot, when the thrill of the grass reaches their nostrils. And, as they dress, they'll recall sprawling in the lush outfields of childhood, the grass as cool as a mother's hand on a forehead.

"Good-bye, good-bye," we say at the gate, the smell of water, of sod, of sweat, small perfumes in the air. Our secrets are safe with each other. We go our separate ways.

Alone in the stadium in the last chill darkness before dawn, I drop to my hands and knees in the center of the outfield. My palms are sodden. Water touches the skin between my spread fingers. I lower my face to the silvered grass, which, wonder of wonders, already has the ephemeral odors of baseball about it.

The Rube's Waterloo (1920)

Zane Grey

This story first appeared in Zane Grey's book *The Redheaded Outfield*, which was inspired by Grey's younger brother, Romer—or "Reddy"—who played two games for the Pittsburgh Pirates in 1903. Zane himself was quite a ballplayer. Born Pearl Zane Grey in Zanesville, Ohio, he graduated from the University of Pennsylvania, where he was the captain of the baseball team. While a student at Penn, he also played minor-league ball, under the name Pearl Zane. He continued with professional baseball after college and also tried to establish a dental practice. Grey left these pursuits to become an author, even though he was close to making the big leagues. Altogether he wrote eighty-nine books, mostly Western novels. Two special favorites are *Riders of the Purple Sage* (1912) and *The Thundering Herd* (1925).

I t was about the sixth inning that I suspected the Rube of weakening. For that matter he had not pitched anything resembling his usual brand of baseball. But the Rube had developed into such a wonder in the box that it took time for his letdown to dawn upon me. Also it took a tip from Raddy, who sat with me on the bench.

"Con, the Rube isn't himself today," said Radbourne. "His mind's not on the game. He seems hurried and flustered, too. If he doesn't explode presently, I'm a dub at callin' the turn."

Raddy was the best judge of a pitcher's condition, physical or mental, in the Eastern League. It was a Saturday and we were on the road and finishing up a series with the Rochesters. Each team had won and lost a game, and, as I was climbing close to the leaders in the pennant race, I wanted the third and deciding game of that Rochester series. The usual big Saturday crowd was in attendance, noisy, demonstrative and exacting.

In this sixth inning the first man up for Rochester had flied to McCall. Then had come the two plays significant of Rube's weakening. He had hit one batter and walked another. This was sufficient, considering the score was three to one in our favor, to bring the audience to its feet with a howling, stamping demand for runs.

"Spears is wise all right," said Raddy.

I watched the foxy old captain walk over to the Rube and talk to him while he rested, a reassuring hand on the pitcher's shoulder. The crowd yelled its disapproval and umpire Bates called out sharply, "Spears, get back to the bag!"

"Now, Mr. Umpire, ain't I hurrin' all I can?" queried Spears as he leisurely ambled back to first.

The Rube tossed a long, damp welt of hair back from his big brow and nervously toed the rubber. I noted that he seemed to forget the runners on bases and delivered the ball without glancing at either bag. Of course this resulted in a double steal. The ball went wild—almost a wild pitch.

"Steady up, old man," called Gregg between the yells of the bleachers. He held his mitt square over the plate for the Rube to pitch to. Again the long twirler took his swing, and again the ball went wild. Clancy had the Rube in the hole now and the situation began to grow serious. The Rube did not take half his usual deliberation, and of the next two pitches one of them was a ball and the other a strike by grace of the umpire's generosity. Clancy rapped the next one, an absurdly slow pitch for the Rube to use, and both runners scored to the shrill tune of the happy bleachers.

I saw Spears shake his head and look toward the bench. It was plain what that meant.

"Raddy, I ought to take the Rube out," I said, "but whom can I put in? You worked yesterday—Cairns' arm is sore. It's got to be nursed. And Henderson, that ladies' man I just signed, is not in uniform."

"I'll go in," replied Raddy, instantly.

"Not on your life." I had as hard a time keeping Radbourne from over-working as I had in getting enough work out of some other players. "I guess I'll let the Rube take his medicine. I hate to lose this game, but if we have to, we can stand it. I'm curious, anyway, to see what's the matter with the Rube. Maybe he'll settle down presently."

I made no sign that I had noticed Spears's appeal to the bench. And my aggressive players, no doubt seeing the situation as I saw it, sang out their various calls of cheer to the Rube and of defiance to their antagonists. Clancy stole off first base so far that the Rube, catching somebody's warning too late, made a balk and the umpire sent the runner on to second. The Rube now plainly showed painful evidences of being rattled.

He could not locate the plate without slowing up and when he did that a Rochester player walloped the ball. Pretty soon he pitched as if he did not care, and but for the fast fielding of the team behind him the Rochesters would have scored more than the eight runs it got. When the Rube came in to the bench I asked him if he was sick and at first he said he was and then that he was not. So I let him pitch the remaining innings, as the game was lost anyhow, and we walked off the field a badly beaten team.

That night we had to hurry from the hotel to catch a train for Worcester and we had dinner in the dining car. Several of my players' wives had come over from Worcester to meet us, and were in the dining car when I entered. I observed a pretty girl sitting at one of the tables with my new pitcher, Henderson.

"Say, Mac," I said to McCall, who was with me, "is Henderson married?"

"Naw, but he looks like he wanted to be. He was in the grandstand today with that girl."

"Who is she? Oh! a little peach!"

A second glance at Henderson's companion brought this compliment from me involuntarily.

"Con, you'll get it as bad as the rest of this mush bunch of ballplayers. We're all stuck on that kid. But since Henderson came she's been a frost to all of us. An' it's put the Rube in the dumps."

"Who's the girl?"

"That's Nan Brown. She lives in Worcester an' is the craziest girl fan I ever seen. Flirt! Well, she's got them all beat. Somebody introduced the Rube to her. He has been moony ever since."

That was enough to whet my curiosity, and I favored Miss Brown with more than one glance during dinner. When we returned to the parlor car I took advantage of the opportunity and remarked to Henderson that he might introduce his manager. He complied, but not with amiable grace.

So I chatted with Nan Brown, and studied her. She was a pretty, laughing coquettish little minx and quite baseball mad. I had met many girl fans, but none so enthusiastic as Nan. But she was wholesome and sincere, and I liked her.

Before turning in I sat down beside the Rube. He was very quiet and his face did not encourage company. But that did not stop me.

"Hello, Whit; have a smoke before you go to bed?" I asked cheerfully.

He scarcely heard me and made no move to take the proffered cigar. All at once it struck me that the rustic simplicity which had characterized him had vanished.

"Whit, old fellow, what was wrong today?" I asked, quietly, with my hand on his arm.

"Mr. Connelly, I want my release, I want to go back to Rickettsville," he replied hurriedly.

For the space of a few seconds I did some tall thinking. The situation suddenly became grave. I saw the pennant for the Worcesters fading, dimming.

"You want to go home?" I began slowly. "Why, Whit, I can't keep you. I wouldn't try if you didn't want to stay. But I'll tell you confidentially, if you leave me at this stage I'm ruined."

"How's that?" he inquired, keenly looking at me.

"Well, I can't win the pennant without you. If I do win it there's a big bonus for me. I can buy the house I want and get married this fall if I capture the flag. You've met Milly. You can imagine what your pitching means to me this year. That's all."

He averted his face and looked out of the window. His big jaw quivered.

"If it's that—why, I'll stay, I reckon," he said huskily.

That moment bound Whit Hurtle and Frank Connelly into a far closer relation than the one between player and manager. I sat silent for a while, listening to the drowsy talk of the other players and the rush and roar of the train as it sped on into the night.

"Thank you, old chap," I replied. "It wouldn't have been like you to throw me down at this stage. Whit, you're in trouble?"

"Yes."

"Can I help you—in any way?"

"I reckon not."

"Don't be too sure of that. I'm a pretty wise guy, if I do say it myself. I might be able to do as much for you as you're going to do for me."

The sight of his face convinced me that I had taken a wrong tack. It also showed me how deep Whit's trouble really was. I bade his good night and went to my berth, where sleep did not soon visit me. A saucy, sparkling-eyed woman barred Whit Hurtle's baseball career at its threshold.

Women are just as fatal to ballplayers as to men in any other walk of life. I had seen a strong athlete grow palsied just at a scornful slight. It's a great world, and the women run it. So I lay awake racking my brains to outwit a pretty disorganizer; and I plotted for her sake. Married, she would be out of mischief. For Whit's sake, for Milly's sake, for mine, all of which collectively meant for the sake of the pennant, this would be the solution of the problem.

I decided to take Milly into my confidence, and finally on the strength of that I got to sleep. In the morning I went to my hotel, had breakfast, attended to my mail, and then boarded a car to go out to Milly's house. She was waiting for me on the porch, dressed as I liked to see her, in blue and white, and she wore violets that matched the color of her eyes.

"Hello, Connie. I haven't seen a morning paper, but I know from your face that you lost the Rochester series," said Milly, with a gay laugh.

"I guess yes. The Rube blew up, and if we don't play a pretty smooth game, young lady, he'll never come down."

Then I told her.

"Why, Connie, I knew long ago. Haven't you seen the change in him before this?"

"What change?" I asked blankly.

"You are a man. Well, he was a gawky, slouchy, shy farmer boy when he came to us. Of course the city life and popularity began to influence him. Then he met Nan. She made the Rube a worshiper. I first noticed a change in his clothes. He blossomed out in a new suit, white negligee, neat tie and a stylish straw hat. Then it was evident he was making heroic struggles to overcome his awkwardness. It was plain he was studying and copying the other boys. He's wonderfully improved, but still shy. He'll always be shy. Connie, Whit's a fine fellow, too good for Nan Brown."

"But, Milly," I interrupted, "the Rube's hard hit. Why is he too good for her?"

"Nan is a natural-born flirt," Milly replied. "She can't help it. I'm afraid Whit has a slim chance. Nan may not see deep enough to learn his fine qualities. I fancy Nan tired quickly of him, though the one time I saw them together she appeared to like him very well. This new pitcher of yours, Henderson, is a handsome fellow and smooth. Whit is losing to him. Nan likes flash, flattery, excitement."

"McCall told me the Rube had been down in the mouth ever since Henderson joined the team. Milly, I don't like Henderson a whole lot. He's not in the Rube's class as pitcher. What am I going to do? Lose the pennant and a big slice of purse money just for a pretty little flirt?"

"Oh, Connie, it's not so bad as that. Whit will come around all right."

"He won't unless we can pull some wires. I've got to help him win Nan Brown. What do you think of that for a manager's job? I guess maybe winning pennants doesn't call for diplomatic genius and cunning! But I'll hand them a few tricks before I lose. My first move will be to give Henderson his release."

I left Milly, as always, once more able to make light of discouragements and difficulties.

Monday I gave Henderson his unconditional release. He celebrated the occasion by verifying certain rumors I had heard from other managers. He got drunk. But he did not leave town, and I heard that he was negotiating with Providence for a place on that team.

Radbourne pitched one of his gilt-edged games that afternoon against Hartford and we won. And Milly sat in the grandstand, having contrived by cleverness to get a seat next to Nan Brown. Milly and I were playing a vastly deeper game than baseball—a game with hearts. But we were playing it with honest motive, for the good of all concerned, we believed, and on the square. I sneaked a look now and then up into the grandstand. Milly and Nan appeared to be getting on famously. It was certain that Nan was flushed and excited, no doubt consciously proud of being seen with my affianced. After the game I chanced to meet them on their way out. Milly winked at me, which was her sign that all was working beautifully.

I hunted up the Rube and bundled him off to the hotel to take dinner with me. At first he was glum, but after a while he brightened up somewhat to my persistent cheer and friendliness. Then we went out on the hotel balcony to smoke, and there I made my play.

"Whit, I'm pulling a stroke for you. Now listen and don't be offended. I know what's put you off your feed, because I was the same way when Milly had me guessing. You've lost your head over Nan Brown. That's not so terrible, though I daresay you think it's a catastrophe. Because you've quit. You've shown a yellow streak. You've lain down.

"My boy, that isn't the way to win a girl. You've got to scrap. Milly told me yesterday how she had watched your love affair with Nan, and how she thought you had given up just when things might have come your way. Nan is a little flirt, but she's all right. What's more, she was getting fond of you. Nan is meanest to the man she likes best. The way to handle her, Whit, is to master her. Play high and mighty. Get tragical. Then grab her up in your arms. I tell you, Whit, it'll all come your way if you only keep your nerve. I'm your friend and so is Milly. We're going out to her house presently—and Nan will be there."

The Rube drew a long, deep breath and held out his hand. I sensed another stage in the evolution of Whit Hurtle.

"I reckon I've taken baseball coachin'," he said presently, "an' I don't see why I can't take some other kind. I'm only a Rube, an' things come hard for me, but I'm a-learnin'."

It was about dark when we arrived at the house.

"Hello, Connie. You're late. Good evening, Mr. Hurtle. Come right in. You've met Miss Nan Brown? Oh, of course; how stupid of me!"

It was a trying moment for Milly and me. A little pallor showed under the Rube's tan, but he was more composed than I had expected. Nan got up from the piano. She was all in white and deliciously pretty. She gave a quick, glad start of surprise. What a relief that was to my troubled mind! Everything had depended upon a real honest liking for Whit, and she had it.

More than once I had been proud of Milly's cleverness, but this night as hostess and an accomplice she won my everlasting admiration. She contrived to give the impression that Whit was a frequent visitor at her home and very welcome. She brought out his best points, and in her skillful hands he lost embarrassment and awkwardness. Before the evening was over Nan regarded Whit with different eyes, and she never dreamed that everything had not come about naturally. Then Milly somehow got me out on the porch, leaving Nan and Whit together.

"Milly, you're a marvel, the best and sweetest ever," I whispered. "We're going to win. It's a cinch."

"Well, Connie, not that—exactly," she whispered back demurely. "But it looks hopeful."

I could not help hearing what was said in the parlor.

"Now I can roast you," Nan was saying, archly. She had switched back to her favorite baseball vernacular. "You pitched a swell game last Saturday in Rochester, didn't you? Not! You had no steam, no control, and you couldn't have curved a saucer."

"Nan, what could you expect?" was the cool reply. "You sat up in the stand with your handsome friend. I reckon I couldn't pitch. I just gave the game away."

"Whit!—Whit!—"

Then I whispered to Milly that it might be discreet for us to move a little way from the vicinity.

It was on the second day afterward that I got a chance to talk to Nan. She reached the grounds early, before Milly arrived, and I found her in the grandstand. The Rube was down on the card to pitch and when he started to warm up Nan said confidently that he would shut out Hartford that afternoon.

"I'm sorry, Nan, but you're way off. We'd do well to win at all, let alone get a shutout."

"You're a fine manager!" she retorted, hotly. "Why won't we win?"

"Well, the Rube's not in good form. The Rube—"

"Stop calling him that horrid name."

"Whit's not in shape. He's not right. He's ill or something is wrong. I'm worried sick about him."

"Why—Mr. Connelly!" exclaimed Nan. She turned quickly toward me.

I crowded on full canvas of gloom to my already long face.

"I'm serious, Nan. The lad's off, somehow. He's in magnificent physical trim, but he can't keep his mind on the game. He has lost his head. I've talked with him, reasoned with him, all to no good. He only goes down deeper in the dumps. Something is terribly wrong with him, and if he doesn't brace, I'll have to release—"

Miss Nan Brown suddenly lost a little of her rich bloom. "Oh! you wouldn't—you couldn't release him!"

"I'll have to if he doesn't brace. It means a lot to me, Nan, for of course I can't win the pennant this year without Whit being in shape. But I believe I wouldn't mind the loss of that any more than to see him fall down. The boy is a magnificent pitcher. If he can only be brought around he'll go to the big league next year and develop into one of the greatest pitchers the game has ever produced. But somehow or other he has lost heart. He's quit. And I've done my best for him. He's beyond me now. What a shame it is! For he's the making of such a splendid man outside of baseball. Milly thinks the world of him. Well, well; there are disappointments—we can't help them. There goes the gong. I must leave you. Nan, I'll bet you a box of candy Whit loses today. Is it a go?"

"It is," replied Nan, with fire in her eyes. "You go to Whit Hurtle and tell him I said if he wins today's game I'll kiss him!"

I nearly broke my neck over benches and bats getting to Whit with that message. He gulped once.

Then he tightened his belt and shut out Hartford with two scratch singles. It was a great exhibition of pitching. I had no means to tell whether or not the Rube got his reward that night, but I was so happy that I hugged Milly within an inch of her life.

But it turned out that I had been a little premature in my elation. In two days the Rube went down into the depths again, this time clear to China, and Nan was sitting in the grandstand with Henderson. The Rube lost his next game, pitching like a schoolboy scared out of his wits. Henderson followed Nan like a shadow, so that I had no chance to talk to her. The Rube lost his next game and then another. We were pushed out of second place.

If we kept up that losing streak a little longer, our hopes for the pennant were gone. I had begun to despair of the Rube. For some occult reason he scarcely spoke to me. Nan flirted worse than ever. It seemed to me she flaunted her conquest of Henderson in poor Whit's face.

The Providence ball team came to town and promptly signed Henderson and announced him for Saturday's game. Cairns won the first of the series and Radbourne lost the second. It was Rube's turn to pitch the Saturday game and I resolved to make one more effort to put the lovesick swain in something like his old fettle. So I called upon Nan.

She was surprised to see me, but received me graciously. I fancied her face was not quite so glowing as usual. I came bluntly out with my mission. She tried to freeze me but I would not freeze. I was out to win or lose and not to be lightly laughed aside or coldly denied. I played to make her angry, knowing the real truth of her feelings would show under stress.

For once in my life I became a knocker and said some unpleasant things—albeit they were true—about Henderson. She championed Henderson royally, and when, as a last card, I compared Whit's fine record with Henderson's not only as a ballplayer, but as a man, particularly in his reverence for women, she flashed at me:

"What do you know about it? Mr. Henderson asked me to marry him. Can a man do more to show his respect? Your friend never so much as hinted such honorable intentions. What's more—he insulted me!" The blaze in Nan's black eyes softened with a film of tears. She looked hurt. Her pride had encountered a fall.

"Oh, no, Nan, Whit couldn't insult a lady," I protested.

"Couldn't he? That's all you know about him. You know I—I promised to kiss him if he beat Hartford that day. So when he came I—I did. Then the big savage began to rave and he grabbed me up in his arms. He smothered me; almost crushed the life out of me. He frightened me terribly. When I got away from him—the monster stood there and coolly said I belonged to him. I ran out of the room and wouldn't see him anymore. At first I might have forgiven him if he had apologized—said he was sorry, but never a word. Now I never will forgive him."

I had to make a strenuous effort to conceal my agitation. The Rube had most carefully taken my fool advice in the matter of wooing a woman.

When I had got a hold upon myself, I turned to Nan white-hot with eloquence. Now I was talking not wholly for myself or the pennant, but for this boy and girl who were at odds in the strangest game of life—love.

What I said I never knew, but Nan lost her resentment, and then her scorn and indifference. Slowly she thawed and warmed to my reason, praise, whatever it was, and when I stopped she was again the radiant bewildering Nan of old.

"Take another message to Whit for me," she said, audaciously. "Tell him I adore ballplayers, especially pitchers. Tell him I'm going to the game today to choose the best one. If he loses the game—"

She left the sentence unfinished. In my state of mind I doubted not in the least that she meant to marry the pitcher who won the game, and so I told the Rube. He made one wild upheaval of his arms and shoulders, like an erupting volcano, which proved to me that he believed it, too.

When I got to the bench that afternoon I was tired. There was a big crowd to see the game; the weather was perfect; Milly sat up in the box and waved her scorecard at me; Raddy and Spears declared we had the game; the Rube stalked to and fro like an implacable Indian chief—but I was not happy in mind. Calamity breathed in the very air.

The game began. McCall beat out a bunt; Ashwell sacrificed and Stringer laced one of his beautiful triples against the fence. Then he scored on a high fly. Two runs! Worcester trotted out into the field. The Rube was white with determination; he had the speed of a bullet and perfect control of his jump ball and drop. But Providence hit and had the luck. Ashwell fumbled, Gregg threw wild. Providence tied the score.

The game progressed, growing more and more of a nightmare to me. It was not Worcester's day. The umpire could not see straight; the boys grumbled and fought among themselves; Spears roasted the umpire and was sent to the bench; Bogart tripped, hurting his sore ankle, and had to be taken out. Henderson's slow, easy ball baffled my players, and when he used speed they lined it straight at a Providence fielder.

In the sixth, after a desperate rally, we crowded the bases with only one out. Then Mullaney's hard rap to left, seemingly good for three bases, was pulled down by Stone with one hand. It was a wonderful catch and he doubled up a runner at second. Again in the seventh we had a chance to score, only to fail on another double play, this time by the infield.

When the Providence players were at bat their luck not only held good but trebled and quadrupled. The little Texas-league hits dropped safely just out of reach of the infielders. My boys had an off day in fielding. What horror that of all days in a season this should be the one for them to make errors!

But they were game, and the Rube was the gamest of all. He did not seem to know what hard luck was, or discouragement, or poor support. He kept everlastingly hammering the ball at those lucky Providence hitters. What speed he had! The ball streaked in, and somebody would shut his eyes and make a safety. But the Rube pitched on, tireless, irresistibly, hopeful, not forgetting to call a word of cheer to his fielders.

It was one of those strange games that could not be bettered by any labor or daring or skill. I saw it was lost from the second inning, yet so deeply was I concerned, so tantalizingly did the plays reel themselves off, that I groveled there on the bench unable to abide by my baseball sense.

The ninth inning proved beyond a shadow of doubt how baseball fate, in common with other fates, loved to balance the chances, to lift up one, then the other, to lend a deceitful hope only to dash it away.

Providence had almost three times enough to win. The team let up in that inning or grew overconfident or careless, and before we knew what had happened some scratch hits, and bases on balls, and errors, gave us three runs and left two runners on bases. The disgusted bleachers came out of their gloom and began to whistle and thump. The Rube hit safely, sending another run over the plate. McCall worked his old trick, beating out a slow bunt.

Bases full, three runs to tie! With Ashwell up and one out, the noise in the bleachers mounted to a high-pitched, shrill, continuous sound. I got up and yelled with all my might and could not hear my voice. Ashwell was a dangerous man in a pinch. The game was not lost yet. A hit, anything to get Ash to first—and then Stringer!

Ash laughed at Henderson, taunted him, shook his bat at him and dared him to put one over. Henderson did not stand under fire. The ball he pitched had no steam. Ash cracked it—square on the line into the shortstop's hands. The bleachers ceased yelling.

Then Stringer strode grimly to the plate. It was a hundred to one, in that instance, that he would lose the ball. The bleachers let out one deafening roar, then hushed. I would rather have had Stringer at the bat than any other player in the world, and I thought of the Rube and Nan and Milly—and hope would not die.

Stringer swung mightily on the first pitch and struck the ball with a sharp, solid bing! It shot toward center, low, level, exceedingly swift, and like a dark streak went straight into the fielder's hands. A rod to right or left would have made it a home run. The crowd strangled a victorious yell. I came out of my trance, for the game was over and lost. It was the Rube's Waterloo.

I hurried him into the dressing room and kept close to him. He looked like a man who had lost the one thing worth while in his life. I turned a deaf ear to my players, to everybody, and hustled the Rube out and to the hotel. I wanted to be near him that night.

To my amazement we met Milly and Nan as we entered the lobby. Milly wore a sweet, sympathetic smile. Nan shone more radiant than ever. I simply stared. It was Milly who got us all through the corridor into the parlor. I heard Nan talking.

"Whit, you pitched a bad game but"—there was the old teasing, arch, coquettishness—"but you are the best pitcher!"

"Nan!"

"Yes!"

Alibi Ike (1915)

Ring Lardner

Ringold W. Lardner (1885–1933) was widely praised as one of America's best short-story writers. The great critic Edmund Wilson and others likened Lardner to Mark Twain. Britain's queen of literature, Virginia Woolf, said that "he writes the best prose to come our way." The story below, one of two by Lardner in this book, is about a ballplayer who has an excuse for everything, even what he does very well. A fine satirist, Lardner pokes fun at the delightfully goofy Alibi Ike while more broadly lampooning the apologists, complainers, and prevaricators among us.

Born in Niles, Michigan, Lardner left engineering school after two years to become a reporter for the *South Bend Tribune*. He made his early mark as a sportswriter with the *Chicago Tribune*. It was there that he wrote the first of his "You Know Me, Al" stories, which caused a national sensation when published in the *Saturday Evening Post*.

1

His right name was Frank X. Farrell, and I guess the X stood for "Excuse me." Because he never pulled a play, good or bad, on or off the field, without apologizin' for it.

"Alibi Ike" was the name Carey wished on him the first day he reported down south. O' course we all cut out the "Alibi" part of it right away for the fear he would overhear it and bust somebody. But we called him "Ike" right to his face and the rest of it was understood by everybody on the club except Ike himself.

He ast me one time, he says:

"What do you all call me Ike for? I ain't no Yid."

"Carey give you the name," I says. "It's his nickname for everybody he takes a likin' to."

"He mustn't have only a few friends then," says Ike. "I never heard him say 'Ike' to nobody else."

But I was goin' to tell you about Carey namin' him. We'd been workin' out two weeks and the pitchers was showin' somethin' when this bird joined us. His first day out he stood up there so good and took such a reef at the old pill that he had everyone lookin'. Then him and Carey was together in left field, catchin' fungoes, and it was after we was through for the day that Carey told me about him.

"What do you think of Alibi Ike?" ast Carey.

"Who's that?" I says.

"This here Farrell in the outfield," says Carey.

"He looks like he could hit," I says.

"Yes," says Carey, "but he can't hit near as good as he can apologize."

Then Carey went on to tell me what Ike had been pullin' out there. He'd dropped the first fly ball that was hit to him and told Carey his glove wasn't broke in good yet, and Carey says the glove could easy of been Kid Gleason's gran'father. He made a whale of a catch out o' the next one and Carey says "Nice work!" or somethin' like that, but Ike says he could of caught the ball with his back turned only he slipped when he started after it and, besides that, the air currents fooled him.

"I thought you done well to get to the ball," says Carey.

"I ought to been settin' under it," says Ike.

"What did you hit last year?" Carey ast him.

"I had malaria most o' the season," says Ike. "I wound up with .356."

"Where would I have to go to get malaria?" says Carey, but Ike didn't wise up.

I and Carey and him set at the same table together for supper. It took him half an hour longer'n us to eat because he had to excuse himself every time he lifted his fork.

"Doctor told me I needed starch," he'd say, and then toss a shovelful o' potatoes into him. Or, "They ain't much meat on one o' these chops," he'd tell us, and grab another one. Or he'd say: "Nothin' like onions for a cold," and then he'd dip into the perfumery.

"Better try that apple sauce," says Carey. "It'll help your malaria."

"Whose malaria?" says Ike. He'd forgot already why he didn't only hit .356 last year.

I and Carey begin to lead him on.

"Whereabouts did you say your home was?" I ast him.

"I live with my folks," he says. "We live in Kansas City—not right down in the business part—outside a ways."

"How's that come?" says Carey. "I should think you'd get rooms in the post office."

But Ike was too busy curin' his cold to get that one.

"Are you married?" I ast him.

"No," he says. "I never run round much with girls, except to shows onct in a wile and parties and dances and roller skatin'."

"Never take 'em to the prize fights, eh?" says Carey.

"We don't have no real good bouts," says Ike. "Just bush stuff. And I never figured a boxin' match was a place for the ladies."

Well, after supper he pulled a cigar out and lit it. I was just goin' to ask him what he done it for, but he beat me to it.

"Kind o' rests a man to smoke after a good work out," he says. "Kind o' settles a man's supper, too."

"Looks like a pretty good cigar," says Carey.

"Yes," says Ike. "A friend o' mine give it to me—a fella in Kansas City that runs a billiard room."

"Do you play billiards?" I ast him.

"I used to play a fair game," he says. "I'm all out o' practice now—can't hardly make a shot."

We coaxed him into a four-handed battle, him and Carey against Jack Mack and I. Say, he couldn't play billiards as good as Willie Hoppe; not quite. But to hear him tell it, he didn't make a good shot all evenin'. I'd leave him an awful-lookin' layout and he'd gather 'em up in one try and then run a couple o' hundred, and between every carom he'd say he'd put too much stuff on the ball, or the English didn't take, or the table wasn't true, or his stick was crooked, or somethin'. And all the time he had the balls actin' like they was

Dutch soldiers and him Kaiser William. We started out to play fifty points, but we had to make it a thousand so as I and Jack and Carey could try the table.

The four of us set round the lobby a wile after we was through playin', and when it got along toward bedtime Carey whispered to me and says:

"Ike'd like to go to bed, but he can't think up no excuse."

Carey hadn't hardly finished whisperin' when Ike got up and pulled it:

"Well, good night, boys," he says. "I ain't sleepy, but I got some gravel in my shoes and it's killin' my feet."

We knowed he hadn't never left the hotel since we'd came in from the grounds and changed our clo'es. So Carey says:

"I should think they'd take them gravel pits out o' the billiard room."

But Ike was already on his way to the elevator, limpin'.

"He's got the world beat," says Carey to Jack and I. "I've knew lots o' guys that had an alibi for every mistake they made; I've heard pitchers say that the ball slipped when somebody cracked one off'n 'em; I've heard infielders complain of a sore arm after heavin' one into the stand, and I've saw outfielders tooken sick with a dizzy spell when they've misjudged a fly ball. But this baby can't even go to bed without apologizin', and I bet he excuses himself to the razor when he gets ready to shave."

"And at that," says Jack, "he's goin' to make us a good man."

"Yes," says Carey, "unless rheumatism keeps his battin' average down to .400."

Well, sir, Ike kept whalin' away at the ball all through the trip till everybody knowed he'd won a job. Cap had him in there regular the last few exhibition games and told the newspaper boys a week before the season opened that he was goin' to start him in Kane's place.

"You're there, kid," says Carey to Ike, the night Cap made the 'nnouncement. "They ain't many boys that wins a big league berth their third year out."

"I'd of been up here a year ago," says Ike, "only I was bent over all season with lumbago."

2

It rained down in Cincinnati one day and somebody organized a little game o' cards. They was shy two men to make six and ast I and Carey to play.

"I'm with you if you get Ike and make it seven-handed," says Carey.

So they got a hold of Ike and we went up to Smitty's room.

"I pretty near forgot how many you deal," says Ike. "It's been a long wile since I played."

I and Carey give each other the wink, and sure enough, he was just as ig'orant about poker as billiards. About the second hand, the pot was opened two or three ahead of him, and they was three in when it come his turn. It cost a buck, and he throwed in two.

"It's raised, boys," somebody says.

"Gosh, that's right, I did raise it," says Ike.

"Take out a buck if you didn't mean to tilt her," says Carey.

"No," says Ike, "I'll leave it go."

Well, it was raised back at him and then he made another mistake and raised again. They was only three left in when the draw come. Smitty'd opened with a pair o' kings and he didn't help 'em. Ike stood pat. The guy that'd raised him back was flushin' and he didn't fill. So Smitty checked and Ike bet and didn't get no call. He tossed his hand away, but I grabbed it and give it a look. He had king, queen, jack and two tens. Alibi Ike he must have seen me peekin', for he leaned over and whispered to me.

"I overlooked my hand," he says. "I thought all the wile it was a straight."

"Yes," I says, "that's why you raised twice by mistake."

They was another pot that he come into with tens and fours. It was tilted a couple o' times and two o' the strong fellas drawed ahead of Ike. They each drawed one. So Ike throwed away his little pair and come out with four tens. And they was four treys against him. Carey'd looked at Ike's discards and then he says:

"This lucky bum busted two pair."

"No, no, I didn't," says Ike.

"Yes, yes, you did," says Carey, and showed us the two fours.

"What do you know about that?" says Ike. "I'd of swore one was a five spot."

Well, we hadn't had no pay day yet, and after a wile everybody except Ike was goin' shy. I could see him gettin' restless and I was wonderin' how he'd make the get-away. He tried two or three times. "I got to buy some collars before supper," he says.

"No hurry," says Smitty. "The stores here keeps open all night in April."

After a minute he opened up again.

"My uncle out in Nebraska ain't expected to live," he says. "I ought to send a telegram."

"Would that save him?" says Carey.

"No, it sure wouldn't," says Ike, "but I ought to leave my old man know where I'm at."

"When did you hear about your uncle?" says Carey.

"Just this mornin'," says Ike.

"Who told you?" ast Carey.

"I got a wire from my old man," says Ike.

"Well," says Carey, "your old man knows you're still here yet this afternoon if you was here this mornin'. Trains leavin' Cincinnati in the middle o' the day don't carry no ball clubs."

"Yes," says Ike, "that's true. But he don't know where I'm goin' to be next week."

"Ain't he got no schedule?" ast Carey.

"I sent him one openin' day," says Ike, "but it takes mail a long time to get to Idaho."

"I thought your old man lived in Kansas City," says Carey.

"He does when he's home," says Ike.

"But now," says Carey, "I s'pose he's went to Idaho so as he can be near your sick uncle in Nebraska."

"He's visitin' my other uncle in Idaho."

"Then how does he keep posted about your sick uncle?" ast Carey.

"He don't," says Ike. "He don't even know my other uncle's sick. That's why I ought to wire and tell him."

"Good night!" says Carey.

"What town in Idaho is your old man at?" I says. Ike thought it over.

"No town at all," he says. "But he's near a town."

"Near what town?" I says.

"Yuma," says Ike.

Well, by this time he'd lost two or three pots and he was desperate. We was playin' just as fast as we could, because we seen we couldn't hold him much longer. But he was tryin' so hard to frame an escape that he couldn't pay no attention to the cards, and it looked like we'd get his whole pile away from him if we could make him stick.

The telephone saved him. The minute it begun to ring, five of us jumped for it. But Ike was there first.

"Yes," he says, answerin' it. "This is him. I'll come right down."

And he slammed up the receiver and beat it out o' the door without even sayin' good-bye.

"Smitty'd ought to locked the door," says Carey.

"What did he win?" ast Carey.

We figured it up—sixty-odd bucks.

"And the next time we ask him to play," says Carey, "his fingers will be so stiff he can't hold the cards."

Well, we set round a wile talkin' it over, and pretty soon the telephone rung again. Smitty answered it. It was a friend of his'n from Hamilton and he wanted to know why Smitty didn't hurry down. He was the one that had called before and Ike had told him he was Smitty.

"Ike'd ought to split with Smitty's friend," says Carey.

"No," I says, "he'll need all he won. It costs money to buy collars and to send telegrams from Cincinnati to your old man in Texas and keep him posted on the health o' your uncle in Cedar Rapids, D.C."

3

And you ought to heard him out there on that field! They wasn't a day when he didn't pull six or seven, and it didn't make no difference whether he was goin' good or bad. If he popped up in the pinch he should of made a base hit and the reason he didn't was so-and-so. And if he cracked one for three bases he ought to had a home run, only the ball wasn't lively, or the wind brought it back, or he tripped on a lump o' dirt, roundin' first base.

They was one afternoon in New York when he beat all records. Big Marquard was workin' against us and he was good.

In the first innin' Ike hit one clear over that right-field stand, but it was a few feet foul. Then he got another foul and then the count come to two and two. Then Rube slipped one across on him and he was called out.

"What do you know about that!" he says afterward on the bench. "I lost count. I thought it was three and one, and I took a strike."

"You took a strike all right," says Carey. "Even the umps knowed it was a strike."

"Yes," says Ike, "but you can bet I wouldn't of took it if I'd knew it was the third one. The score board had it wrong."

"That score board ain't for you to look at," says Cap. "It's for you to hit that old pill against."

"Well," says Ike, "I could of hit that one over the score board if I'd knew it was the third."

"Was it a good ball?" I says.

"Well, no, it wasn't," says Ike. "It was inside."

"How far inside?" says Carey.

"Oh, two or three inches or half a foot," says Ike.

"I guess you wouldn't of threatened the score board with it then," says Cap.

"I'd of pulled it down the right foul line if I hadn't thought he'd call it a ball," says Ike.

Well, in New York's part o' the innin' Doyle cracked one and Ike run back a mile and a half and caught it with one hand. We was all sayin' what a whale of a play it was, but he had to apologize just the same as for gettin' struck out.

"That stand's so high," he says, "that a man don't never see a ball till it's right on top o' you."

"Didn't you see that one?" ast Cap.

"Not at first," says Ike; "not till it raised up above the roof o' the stand."

"Then why did you start back as soon as the ball was hit?" says Cap.

"I knowed by the sound that he'd got a good hold of it," says Ike.

"Yes," says Cap, "but how'd you know what direction to run in?"

"Doyle usually hits 'em that way, the way I run," says Ike.

"Why don't you play blindfolded?" says Carey.

"Might as well, with that big high stand to bother a man," says Ike. "If I could of saw the ball all the time I'd of got it in my hip pocket."

Along in the fifth we was one run to the bad and Ike got on with one out. On the first ball throwed to Smitty, Ike went down. The ball was outside and Meyers throwed Ike out by ten feet.

You could see Ike's lips movin' all the way to the bench and when he got there he had his piece learned.

"Why didn't he swing?" he says.

"Why didn't you wait for his sign?" says Cap.

"He give me his sign," says Ike.

"What is his sign with you?" says Cap.

"Pickin' up some dirt with his right hand," says Ike.

"Well, I didn't see him do it," Cap says.

"He done it all right," says Ike.

Well, Smitty went out and they wasn't no more argument till they come in for the next innin'. Then Cap opened it up.

"You fellas better get your signs straight," he says.

"Do you mean me?" says Smitty.

"Yes," Cap says. "What's your sign with Ike?"

"Slidin' my left hand up to the end o' the bat and back," says Smitty.

"Do you hear that, Ike?" ast Cap.

"What of it?" says Ike.

"You says his sign was pickin' up dirt and he says it's slidin' his hand. Which is right?"

"I'm right," says Smitty. "But if you're arguin' about him goin' last innin', I didn't give him no sign."

"You pulled your cap down with your right hand, didn't you?" ast Ike.

"Well, s'pose I did," says Smitty. "That don't mean nothin'. I never told you to take that for a sign, did I?"

"I thought maybe you meant to tell me and forgot," says Ike.

They couldn't none of us answer that and they wouldn't of been no more said if Ike had of shut up. But wile we was settin' there Carey got on with two out and stole second clean.

"There!" says Ike. "That's what I was tryin' to do and I'd of got away with it if Smitty'd swang and bothered the Indian."

"Oh!" says Smitty. "You was tryin' to steal then, was you? I thought you claimed I give you the hit and run."

"I didn't claim no such a thing," says Ike. "I thought maybe you might of gave me a sign, but I was goin' anyway because I thought I had a good start."

Cap prob'ly would of hit him with a bat, only just about that time Doyle booted one on Hayes and Carey come acrost with the run that tied.

Well, we go into the ninth finally, one and one, and Marquard walks McDonald with nobody out.

"Lay it down," says Cap to Ike.

And Ike goes up there with orders to bunt and cracks the first ball into that right-field stand! It was fair this time, and we're two ahead, but I didn't think about that at the time. I was too busy watchin' Cap's face. First he turned pale and then he got red as fire and then he got blue and purple, and finally he just laid back and busted out laughin'. So we wasn't afraid to laugh ourself when we seen him doin' it, and when Ike come in everybody on the bench was in hysterics.

But instead o' takin' advantage, Ike had to try and excuse himself. His play was to shut up and he didn't know how to make it.

"Well," he says, "if I hadn't hit quite so quick at that one I bet it'd of cleared the center-field fence."

Cap stopped laughin'.

"It'll cost you plain fifty," he says.

"What for?" says Ike.

"When I say 'bunt' I mean 'bunt,'" says Cap.

"You didn't say 'bunt,'" says Ike.

"I says 'Lay it down,'" says Cap. "If that don't mean 'bunt,' what does it mean?"

"'Lay it down' means 'bunt' all right," says Ike, "but I understood you to say 'Lay on it.'"

"All right," says Cap, "and the little misunderstandin' will cost you fifty."

Ike didn't say nothin' for a few minutes. Then he had another bright idear.

"I was just kiddin' about misunderstandin' you," he says. "I knowed you wanted me to bunt."

"Well, then, why didn't you bunt?" ast Cap.

"I was goin' to on the next ball," says Ike. "But I thought if I took a good wallop I'd have 'em all fooled. So I walloped at the first one to fool 'em, and I didn't have no intention o' hittin' it."

"You tried to miss it, did you?" says Cap.

"Yes," says Ike.

"How'd you happen to hit it?" ast Cap.

"Well," Ike says, "I was lookin' for him to throw me a fast one and I was goin' to swing under it. But he come with a hook and I met it right square where I was swingin' to go under the fast one."

"Great!" says Cap. "Boys," he says, "Ike's learned how to hit Marquard's curve. Pretend a fast one's comin' and then try to miss it. It's a good thing to know and Ike'd ought to be willin' to pay for the lesson. So I'm goin' to make it a hundred instead o' fifty."

The game wound up 3 to 1. The fine didn't go, because Ike hit like a wild man all through that trip and we made pretty near a clean-up. The night we went to Philly I got him cornered in the car and I says to him:

"Forget them alibis for a wile and tell me somethin'. What'd you do that for, swing that time against Marquard when you was told to bunt?"

"I'll tell you," he says. "That ball he throwed me looked just like the one I struck out on in the first innin' and I wanted to show Cap what I could of done to that other one if I'd knew it was the third strike."

"But," I says, "the one you struck out on in the first innin' was a fastball."

"So was the one I cracked in the ninth," says Ike.

4

You've saw Cap's wife, o' course. Well, her sister's about twict as good-lookin' as her, and that's goin' some.

Cap took his missus down to St. Louis the second trip and the other one come down from St. Joe to visit her. Her name is Dolly, and some doll is right.

Well, Cap was goin' to take the two sisters to a show and he wanted a beau for Dolly. He left it to her and she picked Ike. He'd hit three on the nose that afternoon—off'n Sallee, too.

They fell for each other that first evenin'. Cap told us how it come off. She begin flatterin' Ike for the star game he'd played and o' course he begin excusin' himself for not doin' better. So she thought he was modest and it went strong with her. And she believed everything he said and that made her solid with him—that and her make-up. They was together every mornin' and evenin' for the five days we was there. In the afternoons Ike played the grandest ball you ever see, hittin' and runnin' the bases like a fool and catchin' everything that stayed in the park.

I told Cap, I says: "You'd ought to keep the doll with us and he'd make Cobb's figures look sick."

But Dolly had to go back to St. Joe and we come home for a long serious.

Well, for the next three weeks Ike had a letter to read every day and he'd set in the clubhouse readin' it till mornin' practice was half over. Cap didn't say nothin' to him, because he was goin' so good. But I and Carey wasted a lot of our time tryin' to get him to own up who the letters was from. Fine chanct!

"What are you readin'?" Carey'd say. "A bill?"

"No," Ike'd say, "not exactly a bill. It's a letter from a fella I used to go to school with."

"High school or college?" I'd ask him.

"College," he'd say.

Then he'd stall a wile and then he'd say:

"I didn't go to the college myself, but my friend went there."

"How did it happen you didn't go?" Carey'd ask him.

"Well," he'd say, "they wasn't no colleges near where I lived."

"Didn't you live in Kansas City?" I'd say to him.

One time he'd say he did and another time he didn't. One time he says he lived in Michigan.

"Where at?" says Carey.

"Near Detroit," he says.

"Well," I says, "Detroit's near Ann Arbor and that's where they got the university."

"Yes," says Ike, "they got it there now, but they didn't have it there then."

"I come pretty near goin' to Syracuse," I says, "only they wasn't no railroads runnin' through there in them days."

"Where'd this friend o' yours go to college?" says Carey.

"I forget now," says Ike.

"Was it Carlisle?" ast Carey.

"No," says Ike, "His folks wasn't very well off."

"That's what barred me from Smith," I says.

"I was goin' to tackle Cornell's," says Carey, "but the doctor told me I'd have hay fever if I didn't stay up North."

"Your friend writes long letters," I says.

"Yes," says Ike; "he's tellin' me about a ballplayer."

"Where does he play?" ast Carey.

"Down in the Texas League—Fort Wayne," says Ike.

"It looks like a girl's writin'," Carey says.

"A girl wrote it," says Ike. "That's my friend's sister, writin' for him."

"Didn't they teach writin' at this here college where he went?" says Carey.

"Sure," Ike says, "they taught writin', but he got his hand cut off in a railroad wreck."

"How long ago?" I says.

"Right after he got out o' college," says Ike.

"Well," I says, "I should think he'd of learned to write with his left hand by this time."

"It's his left hand that was cut off," says Ike; "and he was left-handed."

"You get a letter every day," says Carey. "They're all the same writin'. Is he tellin' you about a different ball player every time he writes?"

"No," Ike says. "It's the same ball player. He just tells me what he does every day."

"From the size o' the letters, they don't play nothin' but double-headers down there," says Carey.

We figured that Ike spent most of his evenin's answerin' the letters from his "friend's sister," so we kept tryin' to date him up for shows and parties to see how he'd duck out of 'em. He was bugs over spaghetti, so we told him one day that they was goin' to be a big feed of it over to Joe's that night and he was invited.

"How long'll it last?" he says.

"Well," we says, "we're goin' right over there after the game and stay till they close up."

"I can't go," he says, "Unless they leave me come home at eight bells."

"Nothin' doin'," says Carey. "Joe'd get sore."

"I can't go then," says Ike.

"Why not?" I ast him.

"Well," he says, "my landlady locks up the house at eight and I left my key home."

"You can come and stay with me," says Carey.

"No," he says, "I can't sleep in a strange bed."

"How do you get along when we're on the road?" says I.

"I don't never sleep the first night anywheres," he says. "After that I'm all right."

"You'll have time to chase home and get your key right after the game," I told him.

"The key ain't home," says Ike. "I lent it to one o' the other fellas and he's went out o' town and took it with him."

"Couldn't you borry another key off'n the landlady?" Carey ast him.

"No," he says, "that's the only one they is."

Well, the day before we started East again, Ike come into the clubhouse all smiles.

"Your birthday?" I ast him.

"No," he says.

"What do you feel so good about?" I says.

"Got a letter from my old man," he says. "My uncle's goin' to get well."

"Is that the one in Nebraska?" says I.

"Not right in Nebraska," says Ike. "Near there."

But afterwards we got the right dope from Cap. Dolly'd blew in from Missouri and was goin' to make the trip with her sister.

5

Well, I want to alibi Carey and I for what come off in Boston. If we'd of had any idear what we was doin', we'd never did it. They wasn't nobody outside o' maybe Ike and the dame that felt worse over it than I and Carey.

The first two days we didn't see nothin' of Ike and her except out to the park. The rest o' the time they was sight-seein' over to Cambridge and down to Revere and out to Brook-a-line and all the other places where the rubes go.

But when we come into the beanery after the third game Cap's wife called us over.

"If you want to see somethin' pretty," she says, "look at the third finger on Sis's left hand."

Well, o' course we knowed before we looked that it wasn't goin' to be no hangnail. Nobody was su'prised when Dolly blew into the dinin' room with it—a rock that Ike'd bought off'n Diamond Joe the first trip to New York. Only o' course it'd been set into a lady's-size ring instead o' the automobile tire he'd been wearin'.

Cap and his missus and Ike and Dolly ett supper together, only Ike didn't eat nothin', but just set there blushin' and spillin' things on the table-cloth. I heard him excusin' himself for not havin' no appetite. He says he couldn't never eat when he was clost to the ocean. He'd forgot about them sixty-five oysters he destroyed the first night o' the trip before.

He was goin' to take her to a show, so after supper he went upstairs to change his collar. She had to doll up, too, and o' course Ike was through long before her.

If you remember the hotel in Boston, they's a little parlor where the pia-no's at and then they's another little parlor openin' off o' that. Well, when Ike come down Smitty was playin' a few chords and I and Carey was harmonizin'. We seen Ike go up to the desk to leave his key and we called him in. He tried to duck away, but we wouldn't stand for it.

We ast him what he was all duded up for and he says he was goin' to the theayter.

"Goin' alone?" says Carey.

"No," he says, "a friend o' mine's goin' with me."

"What do you say if we go along?" says Carey.

"I ain't only got two tickets," he says.

"Well," says Carey, "we can go down there with you and buy our own seats; maybe we can all go together."

"No," says Ike. "They ain't no more seats. They're all sold out."

"We can buy some off'n the scalpers," says Carey.

"I wouldn't if I was you," says Ike. "They say the show's rotten."

"What are you goin' for, then?" I ast.

"I didn't hear about it bein' rotten till I got the tickets," he says.

"Well," I says, "if you don't want to go I'll buy the tickets from you."

"No," says Ike, "I wouldn't want to cheat you. I'm stung and I'll just have to stand for it."

"What are you goin' to do with the girl, leave her here at the hotel?"

"What girl?" says Ike.

"The girl you ett supper with," I says.

"Oh," he says, "we just happened to go into the dinin' room together, that's all. Cap wanted I should set down with 'em."

"I noticed," says Carey, "that she happened to be wearin' that rock you bought off'n Diamond Joe."

"Yes," says Ike. "I lent it to her for a wile."

"Did you lend her the new ring that goes with it?" I says.

"She had that already," says Ike. "She lost the set out of it."

"I wouldn't trust no strange girl with a rock o' mine," says Carey.

"Oh, I guess she's all right," Ike says. "Besides, I was tired o' the stone. When a girl asks you for somethin', what are you goin' to do?"

He started out toward the desk, but we flagged him.

"Wait a minute!" Carey says. "I got a bet with Sam here, and it's up to you to settle it."

"Well," says Ike, "make it snappy. My friend'll be here any minute."

"I bet," says Carey, "that you and that girl was engaged to be married."

"Nothin' to it," says Ike.

"Now look here," says Carey, "this is goin' to cost me real money if I lose. Cut out the alibi stuff and give it to us straight. Cap's wife just as good as told us you was roped."

Ike blushed like a kid.

"Well, boys," he says, "I may as well own up. You win, Carey."

"Yatta boy!" says Carey. "Congratulations!"

"You got a swell girl, Ike," I says.

"She's a peach," says Smitty.

"Well, I guess she's OK," says Ike. "I don't know much about girls."

"Didn't you never run round with 'em?" I says.

"Oh, yes, plenty of 'em," says Ike. "But I never seen none I'd fall for."

"That is, till you seen this one," says Carey.

"Well," says Ike, "this one's OK, but I wasn't thinkin' about gettin' married yet a wile."

"Who done the askin'—her?" says Carey.

"Oh, no," says Ike, "but sometimes a man don't know what he's gettin' into. Take a good-lookin' girl, and a man gen'ally almost always does about what she wants him to."

"They couldn't no girl lasso me unless I wanted to be lassoed," says Smitty.

"Oh, I don't know," says Ike. "When a fella gets to feelin' sorry for one of 'em it's all off."

Well, we left him go after shakin' hands all round. But he didn't take Dolly to no show that night. Some time wile we was talkin' she'd came into that other parlor and she'd stood there and heard us. I don't know how much she heard. But it was enough. Dolly and Cap's missus took the midnight train for New York. And from there Cap's wife sent her on her way back to Missouri.

She'd left the ring and a note for Ike with the clerk. But we didn't ask Ike if the note was from his friend in Fort Wayne, Texas.

6

When we'd came to Boston Ike was hittin' plain .397. When we got back home he'd fell off to pretty near nothin'. He hadn't drove one out o' the infield in any o' them other Eastern parks, and he didn't even give no excuse for it.

To show you how bad he was, he struck out three times in Brooklyn one day and never opened his trap when Cap ast him what was the matter. Before, if he'd whiffed oncet in a game he'd of wrote a book tellin' why.

Well, we dropped from first place to fifth in four weeks and we was still goin' down. I and Carey was about the only ones in the club that spoke to each other, and all as we did was remind ourself o' what a boner we'd pulled.

"It's goin' to beat us out o' the big money," says Carey.

"Yes," I says. "I don't want to knock my own ball club, but it looks like a one-man team, and when that one man's dauber's down we couldn't trim our whiskers."

"We ought to knew better," says Carey.

"Yes," I says, "but why should a man pull an alibi for bein' engaged to such a bearcat as she was?"

"He shouldn't," says Carey. "But I and you knowed he would or we'd never started talkin' to him about it. He wasn't no more ashamed o' the girl than I am of a regular base hit. But he just can't come clean on no subjec'."

Cap had the whole story, and I and Carey was as pop'lar with him as an umpire.

"What do you want me to do, Cap?" Carey'd say to him before goin' up to hit.

"Use your own judgment," Cap'd tell him. "We want to lose another game."

But finally, one night in Pittsburgh, Cap had a letter from his missus and he come to us with it.

"You fellas," he says, "is the ones that put us on the bum, and if you're sorry I think theys a chancet for you to make good. The old lady's out to St. Joe and she's been tryin' her hardest to fix things up. She's explained that Ike don't mean nothin' with his talk; I've wrote and explained that to Dolly, too. But the old lady says that Dolly says that she can't believe it. But Dolly's still stuck on this baby, and she's pinin' away just the same as Ike. And the old lady says she thinks if you two fellas would write to the girl and explain how you was always kiddin' with Ike and leadin' him on, and how the ball club was all shot to pieces since Ike quit hittin', and how he acted like he was goin' to kill himself, and this and that, she'd fall for it and maybe soften down. Dolly, the old lady says, would believe you before she'd believe I and the old lady, because she thinks it's her we're sorry for, and not him."

Well, I and Carey was only too glad to try and see what we could do. But it wasn't no snap. We wrote about eight letters before we got one that looked good. Then we give it to the stenographer and had it wrote out on a typewriter and both of us signed it.

It was Carey's idear that made the letter good. He stuck in somethin' about the world's serious money that our wives wasn't goin' to spend unless she took pity on a "boy who was so shy and modest that he was afraid to come right out and say that he had asked such a beautiful and handsome girl to become his bride."

That's prob'ly what got her, or maybe she couldn't of held out much longer anyway. It was four days after we sent the letter that Cap heard from his missus again. We was in Cincinnati.

"We've won," he says to us. "The old lady says that Dolly says she'll give him another chance. But the old lady says it won't do no good for Ike to write a letter. He'll have to go out there."

"Send him to-night," says Carey.

"I'll pay half his fare," I says.

"I'll pay the other half," says Carey.

"No," says Cap, "the club'll pay his expenses. I'll send him scoutin'."

"Are you goin' to send him to-night?"

"Sure," says Cap. "But I'm goin' to break the news to him right now. It's time we win a ball game."

So in the clubhouse, just before the game, Cap told him. And I certainly felt sorry for Rube Benton and Red Ames that afternoon! I and Carey was standin' in front o' the hotel that night when Ike come out with his suitcase.

"Sent home?" I says to him.

"No," he says, "I'm goin' scoutin'."

"Where to?" I says. "Fort Wayne?"

"No, not exactly," he says.

"Well," says Carey, "have a good time."

"I ain't lookin' for no good time," says Ike. "I says I was goin' scoutin'."

"Well, then," says Carey, "I hope you see somebody you like."

"And you better have a drink before you go," I says.

"Well," says Ike, "they claim it helps a cold."

Three New Twins Join Club in Spring (1988)

Garrison Keillor

Garrison Keillor was born in 1942 in Anoka, Minnesota. He received his bachelor's degree in English from the University of Minnesota. Keillor is well-known for his novels, short stories, and radio program, *A Prairie Home Companion*, which features live music, humor, and variety. In 1980 this program, a staple of American Public Radio, won a George Foster Peabody Award for distinguished broadcasting. "Three New Twins Join Club in Spring," the first of two Keillor stories in the book, originally appeared in *The New Yorker*. It contains the kind of folksy Midwest humor that typifies his work.

My team won the World Series. You thought we couldn't but we knew we would and we did, and what did your team do? Not much. Now we're heading down to spring training looking even better than before, and your team that looked pitiful then looks even less hot now. Your hometown paper doesn't say so, but your lead-off guy had a bad ear infection in January and now he gets dizzy at the first sign of stress and falls down in a heap. Sad. Your cleanup guy spent the winter cleaning his plate. He had to buy new clothes in a size they don't sell at regular stores. Your great relief guy, his life has been changed by the Rama Lama Ding Dong, and he is now serenely throwing the ball from a place deep within himself, near his gall bladder.

What a shame. Your rookie outfielder set a world record for throwing a frozen chicken, at a promotional appearance for Grandma Fanny's Farm Foods. Something snapped in his armpit and now he can't even throw a pair of dice. Tough beans. Your big left-hander tried hypnosis to stop smoking and while in a trancelike state discovered he hated his mother for tying his tiny right hand behind his back and making him eat and draw and tinkle with his left. So he's right-handed now, a little awkward but gradually learning to point with it and wave good-bye. That's what your whole team'll be doing by early May.

Meanwhile, my team, the world-champion Minnesota Twins, are top dogs who look like a lead-pipe cinch to take all the marbles in a slow walk. My guys had a good winter doing youth work. Last October they pooled their Series pay to purchase a farm, Twin Acres, north of Willmar, where they could stay in shape doing chores in the off-season, and they loved it so much they stayed through Thanksgiving and Christmas (celebrating them the good old-fashioned Midwestern way), and raised a new barn, bought a powerful new seed drill to plant winter wheat with, built up the flock of pure-bred Leghorns, chopped wood, carried water, etc., along with their guests—delinquent boys and girls from St. Louis and Detroit who needed to get out of those sick and destructive environments and learn personal values such as hard work and personal cleanliness. Meanwhile, back in Minneapolis, the Twins front office wasn't asleep on its laurels but through shrewd deals made mostly before 8:15 AM added to what they had while giving up nothing in return. It seems unfair.

Other Teams Gnash Teeth or Sulk

It's considered impossible to obtain *three top premium players* without paying a red cent, but the Twins:

Traded away some useless air rights for Chuck Johnson (23, 187 lbs., 6'1", bats left, throws left), a native of Little Falls, Minnesota. Maybe that's why the scouts who work the Finger Lakes League ignored his phenomenal season with the Seneca Falls Susans. They figured, "Minnesota? Forget it!" But how can you forget thirty-eight doubles, twenty-two triples, and twenty-nine round-trippers—and in spacious Elizabeth Cady Stanton Stadium! That's a lot of power for a lifelong liberal like Chuck. And what's more, he *never struck out*. Not once. Plays all positions cheerfully.

Sent a couple in their mid-forties to the San Diego Padres in exchange for Duane (Madman) Mueller (29, 280 lbs., 6'2", right/right, a.k.a. Mule, Hired Hand, The Barber). Duane is a big secret because after he was suspended by the Texas League for throwing too hard he played Nicaraguan winter ball for three years and then spent two more doing humanitarian stuff, so scouts forgot how, back when he was with the Amarillo Compadres, nobody wanted to be behind the plate, Duane threw so hard. His own team kept yelling, "Not so *hard*, Man!" If that sounds dumb, then you never saw him throw: he threw *hard*. A devoted Lutheran, he never ever hit a batter, but in one game a pitch of his nicked the bill of a batting helmet and spun it so hard it burned off the man's eyebrows. No serious injury, but big Duane took himself out of organized ball until he could learn an offspeed pitch. He's from Brainerd, Minnesota, where he lives across the street from his folks. His mom played kittenball in the fifties and had a good arm but not like her son's. She thinks he got it from delivering papers and whipping cake mix. "I'd sure hate to have to bat against him," she says.

Gave up a dingy two-bedroom house in St. Paul (it needs more that just a paint job and a new roof, and it's near a rendering plant) to acquire and activate Bob Berg (24, 112 lbs., 5'3", right/left), the fastest man on the base paths today (we *think*), but he sat out last year and the year before last and the year before *that* because he didn't have shoes. Reason: he's so fast he runs the shoes right off his own feet. Now athletic foot specialists have studied his film clips (sad to see: three lightning strides, a look of dismay on Bob's face, and down he goes with his loose laces like a lasso round his ankles) and come up with a new pair of pigskin shoes with barbed cleats that stick in the turf and slow him down. Born and raised in Eveleth, Minnesota, he is probably the nicest fast man in baseball. Nicknamed The Hulk ("berg" means "mountain" in Norwegian). He used those three years on the bench to earn a B.A. in history, by the way.

That's Not All

Joining the team later will be Wally Gunderson (17, 191 lbs., 6'4", left/right), who dons a Twins uniform June 8th, the day after he graduates from West High in Minneapolis. The Twins have saved him a number, 18, and assigned him a locker and paid him a bonus, twelve hundred dollars, which was all he would accept. He's thrilled just to be on the team. A big lanky loose-jointed kid with long wavy blond hair and a goofy grin, he throws a screwball that comes in and up, a slider that suddenly jumps, a curve that drops off the table, and a stinkball that hangs in the air so long some batters swing twice. You don't expect so much junk from an Eagle Scout, but Wally's got one more: a fastball that decelerates rapidly halfway to the plate—a braking pitch. Some he learned from his dad and the rest he invented for a Science Fair project. "Pitching is physics, that's all," he says, looking down at his size-13 shoes, uneasy at all the acclaim.

Detroit and St. Louis offered the lad millions in cash, land, jewelry, servants, tax abatements, but he wasn't listening. "I want to play my ball where my roots are," he says quietly.

Twinsville wasn't one bit surprised. Personal character and loyalty and dedication are what got us where we are right now, and that's on top. We're No. 1. We knew it first and now you know it, too. You thought we were quiet and modest in the Midwest but that's because you're dumb, as dumb as a stump, dumber than dirt.

You're so dumb you don't know that we're on top and you're below. Our team wins and your team loses; we need your team to amuse us. Minnesota soybeans, corn, and barley; we're the best, so beat it, Charley, or we'll shell ya like a pea pod, dunk ya like a doughnut—sure be nice when the game's over, won't it—take ya to the cleaners for a brand-new hairdo. We can beat ya anytime we care to. Shave and a haircut, two bits.

A Family Game (2001)

Brendan DuBois

Parents love to watch their kids play baseball, but a father in this story displays an ugly side that spoils the fun. The author nicely paces this entertaining tale, which leads to a blockbuster finale. Brendan DuBois, a lifelong resident of New Hampshire, is the author of seven books in the Lewis Cole mystery series. Among his novels are *Resurrection Day* (1999), *Betrayed* (2003), *Primary Storm* (2006), *Twilight* (2007), *Final Winter* (2008), and *Deadly Cove* (2011). He has twice won the Shamus Award for best short story of the year. His celebrated story "The Dark Snow" appears in the anthology *Murder Short and Sweet* (2008).

The June day was surprisingly muggy and hot, especially out in the baseball field behind the Morton Regional High School, where there was no shade and the sun beat down so hard that Richard Dow could feel its strength through the baseball cap he was wearing. The cap was yellow with a blue "P" in the center, just like the caps of the dozen boys who were on the field or in the dugout this day who played for the Pine Tree Rotary youth team. He stood by first base, the team's assistant coach, and he looked over at the scoreboard, kept current by a young girl using a piece of chalk almost the size of her fist. Pine Tree Rotary, 1; Glen's Plumbing & Heating, 0. Two out, the bottom of the sixth. The game was almost over. Just one more out.

He rubbed his hands together. A boy from Glen's Plumbing & Heating was on third base. He didn't know his name. But he certainly knew the name of the boy pitching this afternoon's game: Sam Dow, age 12, who was one out away from earning Pine Tree's first victory this season. They were 1 and 5, but nobody on the team counted that solitary victory: it had been a forfeit, when the other team—Jerry's Lumberyard—didn't make it to the game because the coach's van had struck a moose on Route Four.

"C'mon, Sam!" he called out, slapping his hands together. "One more out, you can do it! Just one more out!"

Sam ignored him. Good boy. Focus on the hitter, standing there with his helmet and blue and white uniform, bat looking so large in his small hands. The attendance was good for a warm summer day in Vermont, with a smattering of parents and friends and relatives in the stands behind home plate. Someone in the stands was smoking a large cigar, and a brief breeze brought the scent over, and Richard was surprised at the hunger he felt at smelling it. God, how long had it been since he had a really good cigar . . .

Richard looked over in the stands again, saw his ten-year-old daughter, Olivia, carefully keeping score in a large looseleaf binder. He waved at her but she, too, was ignoring her father, keeping focus on the job at hand. And that's what their mother Carla was doing this early afternoon as well, working at the local travel agency.

Sam wound up and the ball flew fast for such a young boy, and the batter swung just as Richard heard the satisfying *thump!* as the ball landed in the catcher's glove. The umpire did his sideways dance and said, "Strike!" and there were a few cheers and groans, but no jeers. The umpire today was Denny Thompson, the town's fire chief, and he had a good eye and for an umpire was pretty reasonable.

"C'mon, Sam," he whispered, "one more strike. You can do it." He rubbed his hands again, looked over at the few boys of Pine Tree who weren't on the field, now leaning forward on the badly-painted green bench in the dugout. He could sense their anticipation, their youthful hunger, to feel—just once— what it would be like to win. That's all, pretty simple stuff, but for an eleven- or twelve-year-old boy, getting that first win meant everything. It had been a long time since Richard had been this young, but he remembered. He always remembered.

There. Another windup from his boy, the blur of the ball, and—*Crack!*

Richard snapped his head, tracking the flying ball, it was well-hit, pretty well-hit, but wait, it's arcing over, it's just a pop-up fly, great, a pop-up fly, that's it, it's going to happen, we're going to win, it's going to happen . . .

Then Richard noticed the slow-moving legs of the Pine Tree Rotary boy backing up in right field, one hand shading his eyes, the other hand holding up the open glove, his arm now wavering, trembling, moving back and forth like a semaphore signaler. Leo Winn. The youngest player on the team, and Richard just whispered again, "C'mon, Leo, you can do it buddy, just catch the ball, just like practice, nothing to it, nothing at all."

The ball plopped into his glove, and before the cheers could get any louder from the Pine Tree players and fans, young Leo, still moving backwards, tripped and fell on his back, the ball flying free into the freshly mown grass, the cheers and shouts now coming from the other team, as Pine Tree players and fans, including Richard, fell silent, as they lost once again.

● ● ●

After the ceremonial end-of-the-game lineup, when the players stood in line in the field and shook each other's hands, murmuring "good game, good game," Richard was in the parking lot of the school, one arm over Olivia's shoulder, the other over Sam's. Olivia was carrying the score books under her arm and said, "Sam, that was your best game ever. Three strikeouts and only one hit. And that was scored as an error."

"Yeah, I know, I know, I was there, okay?" Sam replied. "What difference does it make? We still lost."

Richard hugged his boy's shoulder. "You did well, Sam. Even Leo."

"Dad, he's no good," Sam complained.

"He's not as good as you, but he's still out there, practicing and playing," Richard said. "That counts for a lot. He could have given up a long time ago. But he didn't."

Sam didn't say a word, and Richard knew the poor guy was struggling, over showing emotion at having lost again, yet determined not to say anything that could lead to dreaded tears pouring out. For twelve-year-old boys, sometimes showing tears was worse than anything else.

Olivia spoke up. "Look, there's the other team. Going out for ice cream."

"Well, we can go, too," Richard said, seeing the smiles and happy faces of the other boys, trooping into open car and minivan doors.

"Dad . . ." Sam said. "No, let's just go home. It doesn't count. They're going for ice cream 'cause they won. Losers don't get ice cream after a game like ours."

Richard was going to say something but he noticed something going on over near the school's dumpster. He pulled out his car keys, passed them over to Sam. "Here, go in and get the car opened up. I'll be right along."

Sam said, his voice now not so despondent: "Can I start it up?"

"Yes, but move it out of park and I'll ground you till you're thirty."

His two kids ran ahead to his Lexus, and he dodged around the end of a pickup truck hauling an open trailer with a lawn mower on the back. There came a man's voice, loud and insistent, ". . . dummy, how in hell could you drop that ball? It was an easy out!"

Richard froze at what he saw. George Winn, landscaper in town—among other things, some legal, some not so legal—had his boy's T-shirt twisted up in a large fist and was shaking the poor guy back and forth. Tears were streaming down his face and his ball cap was on the ground. George was huge, with a beer gut that poked out from underneath a dark green T-shirt, and a beard that went halfway down his chest. The hand that was wrapped around the boy's T-shirt was stained with dirt and grease. Richard stepped forward. "Hey, George, lighten up, okay? It's just a game."

George turned, his face looking surprised, like he could not believe anyone would approach him for something so insignificant. "Hunh? What did you say, Dick?"

Richard hated being called Dick but let it go for now. "George, c'mon, it's just a game. Your kid did all right."

George let loose of his son's shirt, and the boy quickly went over to pick up his hat. The older man stepped closer and Richard caught a whiff of beer. "You looking for trouble, Dick?"

His hands seemed to start tingling, like they were being suddenly energized by the adrenaline. Richard recognized the sensation, tried to dampen it. "No, I'm just telling you that your kid's a good player. Hey, he's a trooper. Why don't you—"

George came over, punched a finger into Richard's chest, making him step back. "No, he ain't no trooper. He's a loser, writerman, so back off. Unless you want to settle this, right here and now."

A horn honked, and he recognized the tone. His kids were in the Lexus, urging him to hurry up so they could get home. A door slammed and he saw the small figure of Leo in the front seat of the truck. Richard stepped back, made sure his back wasn't turned to George.

"No, I don't want to settle this, right here and now."

George snorted in satisfaction. "Good. Then why don't you go home to your kiddie books and leave me and my boy the frig alone."

Richard walked over to his Lexus as the truck backed up and roared away, the front right fender brushing his pants leg as it bailed out of the parking lot. He got to his Lexus and sat still for a moment, as Sam talked more about the game and Olivia asked what he thought would be for dinner tonight, and it was like their voices were coming at him through thick cotton, for the only voice he could really make out was George's.

• • •

Dinner that night was the usual rolling chaos of dishes being prepared, voices being raised, the television set on and the phone ringing, with boys and girls calling for Sam and Olivia—and was it a genetic quirk among children everywhere, Richard thought, that they always called at dinner time?—and he managed to give Carla a quick hug and kiss as she heated up a tuna-fish casserole.

"Besides losing, how was the game?"

"Great," he said. "Sam pitched well. Got three strikeouts. Your day okay?"

"Unh-hunh," she said, handing over a head of Romaine lettuce to him. "Wash this up, will you?"

"Sure," he said, looking over at the trim figure of his blond-haired wife, her tight jeans and black flat shoes, and the light blue polo shirt that had white script on the left that said CENTRAL STREET TRAVEL. The casserole smelled all right, but he remembered a number of years ago, when Carla would prepare dishes like baked ziti and manicotti and a lobster fettucine . . . my, how good that had been. But all those food dishes had been left behind, years ago, when they had come to Vermont.

Olivia was at the kitchen counter, drawing a horse, and piped up, "I think Daddy almost got into a fight today."

That got Carla's sharp attention. "He did, did he?"

He started running the cold water, started washing the lettuce leaves. "No, he didn't. It wasn't a fight. It was just a discussion."

"That true, Olivia?" Carla asked, her voice still tense.

"Dunno, mom," she said, still working on her horse. "The car doors were closed, but the other man was pushing his finger into Daddy."

"Oh, he was, was he," she said, her brown eyes flashing at him. "I thought you said things went great."

"They did," he said, washing another leaf of lettuce.

"And who was this guy, and what was going on?" she demanded.

"Nothing much," Richard said, patting dry the leaves of lettuce on a stretch of paper towel. "We were just talking about the game and about sports dads. That sort of thing. He got a little heated up, and that was that. I just tried to remind him that it was just a family game. That's all."

"No trouble then," she asked.

He smiled at his demanding wife. "No trouble."

• • •

Some hours later he woke up in bed with Carla, staring up at the ceiling. He rolled over, checked the time on the red numerals of the nearby clock radio. It was 1 AM. Time to go. He slowly got out of bed, sitting up and letting his feet touch the floor, hoping he wouldn't disturb his wife. But Carla was too good.

She gently touched his bare back. "What's up, hon," she whispered, shifting closer to him in the darkness.

"Nothing much," he said, leaning over to a chair, picking up his pants and a pullover.

"Getting dressed?"

"Unh-hunh."

"What's going on?"

"Gotta see a guy about something."

"Something bad?"

He reached behind him, stroked her face. "No, nothing bad. Just seeing a guy about something. No big deal. I'll be back in an hour or so."

"'kay," she murmured. "You be careful, and you come back to us. *Capisce?*"

"*Capisce*," he said, leaning over to kiss her forehead.

• • •

A half hour later he was on the other side of town, at a small dirt park near the wooden covered bridge that spanned the Bellamy River. He shifted in his seat, wincing some at the uncomfortable feeling of the nine-millimeter Browning pistol stuck in his rear waistband. It was a quiet night, and he leaned his elbow outside the open window. The night sounds of crickets and frogs were pleasant enough, but he remembered other night sounds as well. Traffic, always moving, always going. Horns and sirens and brakes squeaking. Music and the rattle-roar of the subway and people talking, shouting, laughing. And behind it all, the constant hum of an island filled with millions of people, always moving, always dealing, always doing something. That sense of energy, of being plugged in, of being part of something. God, he missed it as much as the faraway scent the day before of the cigar . . .

Lights coming across the bridge. The headlights flashed twice and then the lights dimmed as the car pulled up beside him. He stepped out and kept the hood and engine block between him and the visitors.

"Richard?" came the familiar voice from the dark car. One Charlie Moore, and once again, he wished he could be in a place where he would never hear that voice again.

"The same," he said, relaxing, bringing his hand to his side from where it had been, at the rear of his shirt.

"Glad to see you," he said. "Have a visitor here. Do you mind?"

"Do you care if I mind or not?"

A laugh. "Nope, I guess not."

The footsteps came towards his Lexus, and a voice cautioned, "Watch it, light coming on." He moved his head away and a small battery-powered lamp was turned on, and was then placed on the hood of his car. In the small but bright light he made out the face of two men, one familiar, the other a stranger. The familiar one said, "Time for introductions. Bob Tuthill, Department of Justice, please meet Richard Dow. Formerly known as Ricky 'The Rifle' Dolano."

Tuthill just nodded. He had on a dark suit, white shirt, and red necktie. His companion was dressed more comfortably, in jeans and a black turtleneck shirt. Richard said, "Charlie, what's going on?"

Tuthill spoke up. "What's going on is another trial, set to start in August."

"Where?"

"California. Two days, maybe three."

"Who are you guys after?"

"Mel Flemmi," Charlie said. "Used to be in your neck of the woods, then got in trouble in San Diego. The government needs to prove a pattern of criminal conduct, which is where you come in, testifying about what he did in Jersey. That won't be a problem, will it?"

"Nope," Richard said.

Tuthill shook his head. "Sorry, Ricky, that was—"

"Richard," he interrupted. "The name is Richard Dow. Go on."

Tuthill looked over at Charlie in exasperation and said, "What I was saying is that you answered too quickly. Saying there wouldn't be a problem is a given, 'cause you know where we've got you. Set up in this little piece of paradise is part of the deal, and so is your testifying when we say so. But I don't like the way you answered Mister Moore so quickly. What I need to know is that we're going to have your full faith and cooperation in testifying against Flemmi. Understood?"

Richard folded his arms, feeling his breathing tighten, just like when he was face to face with that moron George Winn at the high school parking lot. He said, "Look, Mel Flemmi is an animal. I know enough about what he did so you guys could put him away until the next millennium, even without bringing up whatever he did in San Diego. So yeah, I don't have a problem with testifying against him. Little slug, his own teenage niece started doing drugs, started staying out late in the streets, and he whacked her, personally. So she wouldn't bring shame to his family. So that's the kind of guy he is, and so here's the story. I don't have a problem testifying against him. That good enough for you, Tuthill?"

A little smile came across the man's face. "Nice talk from someone accused of committing eleven murders in his career."

"Accused," Richard said. "Never convicted."

This time, Tuthill laughed and turned to Charlie. "What is it with these wiseguys? Man, they flip and testify at the drop of a hat. The old timers in my office, they said there used to be a time when guys like this would rather serve ten, twenty or thirty years before being accused of being a rat. They getting soft or what?"

Richard tightened his arms against his chest. "I don't know about any 'they.' All I know is that I found out my boss was cooperating with clowns like you. So I cut my own deal, to protect myself and my family. Loyalty's a two-way street, and I'm not going to Leavenworth for life for some guy who wants to get free on my back."

Tuthill laughed. "Whatever. Moore, I'm ready to go back. Oh, Richard, one more thing."

"Yes?"

Tuthill leaned over the hood of the car. "Some of your compatriots over the years, they've embarrassed the department over side deals they had going on while they were in the program. Your job, what is it? A children's book writer?"

"That's what they gave me," Richard said.

"And the publicity problem . . . ?" Tuthill asked.

"You should know," Richard said. "I write under a pseudonym. The books are for two- and three-year-olds. Not much chance of many fan letters. There's no photo on the book jackets; they say the author lives in California. The locals, they don't care. This is Vermont. You could sacrifice goats to Lucifer in your spare time, and nobody'd care, as long as you don't keep your neighbors up with the noise."

"How charming," Tuthill said. "Which brings me to my original point. Other guys like you, they've gotten bored with their agreement. They've decided to get back to their original business, like loan sharking and gambling and breaking arms and legs. Which means sleazy defense lawyers get to jump all over their character, and whether or not their testimony is truthful."

"How interesting," Richard said.

"Wait, it gets better. So what I'm telling you is that your friggin' nose better be clean. No violence, no threat of violence, not even a parking violation. This trial is important, quite important, and I'm not going to let some stoolie killer like you spoil it for me. 'Cause if you do, you and your family will be moving. How'd you like to run a pig farm in the middle of Nebraska?"

Richard said, "I like it here. You won't have a problem."

"Good," he said. "Moore, I'm ready to head back."

"Sure," Charlie said. "I'll be right there."

When the sound of a car door being slammed reached them both, Charlie sighed. "Sorry. Young guy, new in his job, wants to make his bones. Sorry about all that yapping and such."

"Not your fault," Richard said, letting his arms relax.

"Still . . ."

"Yeah?"

"Listen well to what he said, Richard. Except for one little mark against your record since you moved here, you've done okay. Keep it that way, or he will transfer you out to a pig farm. Your wife, your kids, they've adjusted over the years here, haven't they. I don't think they'd like moving again."

Richard said, "You let me worry about my family. And that so-called black mark against my record, that was bogus, and you know it. Besides, I had only been out here a month. I was still adjusting."

Charlie laughed. "You broke the headlights on some guy's car with a baseball bat and threatened to do the same to his teeth. Doesn't sound too bogus to me."

Richard smiled. "He stole a parking space from me at the shopping center. Look, I've got the message, loud and clear. I'll be a good little boy."

"Okay," Charlie said. "Here, I've got two things for you." Charlie reached into his pocket and took out a computer disk, which he tossed over to Richard. He caught it with no problem.

"Your next book," Charlie said. "*Lulu the Seasick Sea Lion.*"

"Marvelous. What's the other thing you've got for me?"

"This," Charlie said, handing over a plastic shopping bag, full and bulging. "Some souvenirs from your old haunts. Cheeses and sausages and pepperonis and spices and sauces. A little bit of everything. I figured you still missed some of that old-time food, don't you."

Richard was surprised at how much his mouth watered. "Yeah, you're right."

Charlie picked up the little lamp, switched it off. "Well, don't let it be said that the U.S. Marshall's Office doesn't have a little consideration. I'll be seeing you, Richard."

"Unfortunately, I think you're right," he said, now smelling the delicious scents coming up from the bag. His stomach began grumbling, and he hefted the bag a couple of times as he waited until the other car left the small lot. Richard waited until his eyes adjusted to the darkness, and then he walked a few yards to the beginning of the covered bridge. His feet echoed on the old wooden planks. He leaned over and heard the rushing of the Bellamy River below him, and then took the bag and threw it into the river.

He sighed, rubbed at his face. That was the only way. To follow the rules and survive, and never, absolutely never, dress or smoke or eat or do anything like you once did back home, because they were out there, still out there in the shadows, bent on revenge, and he didn't want to raise a single scent for their benefit.

He looked at the river for a couple of minutes, and then went back to his car and drove home.

• • •

At home he was in the upstairs hallway, heading to the bedroom, where he heard a murmuring noise coming from Sam's bedroom. The door was ajar and he could make out a bluish light coming from the room. Inside Sam was curled up on his side, his eyes closed, dressed in light gray pajama bottoms. On a dresser at the foot of the bed was a small color TV, and Richard made out a baseball game being played. He reached up to turn it off when a sleepy voice said, "No, Dad, don't . . . still watching it . . ."

"Sam, it's almost three in the morning."

"I know. . . . The Red Sox are in Seattle . . . it's gone extra innings . . ."

Richard looked at a little graphic in the corner of the television picture. "Sam, the score is zero to zero, and they're in the eighteenth inning."

"Mom said I could watch the game till it was over . . ."

Richard shut the little TV off. "And I'm saying it's just a game, okay? You need to get to sleep."

No answer. Just the soft noise of his boy, breathing. From the hallway light he made out posters of baseball players up on the walls, all of them Red Sox. He shrugged. He wished the boy would at least follow a winning team, like the Mets or the Yankees, but what could one expect. He bent down to kiss Sam's forehead.

"Just a game, son. Just a game."

In the morning, before she left for work and to bring the kids to a day camp, Carla brought him another cup of coffee in his small office, which was a spare bedroom when they had first moved in. He took the cup and sipped from it, and she said, "So. What went on last night?"

Other guys back then, they could spin stories to their wives about being solid waste management consultants, but not Carla. She had entered things clear-eyed and agreeable, and not once had he ever tried to pull something over her.

He put the coffee cup down on his desk. "A trip to California in a couple of months. Another testimony deal. Against Mel Flemmi."

She made a face. "Good. He sure deserves it. What else."

"What do you mean, what else?" he asked.

Carla gently whacked him on the side of his shoulder. "There's always something else with the Feds. What was it?"

He tried a casual shrug. "I've got to keep my nose clean, as always. That way, any defense lawyer won't be able to say I don't have the kind of character to testify truthfully."

"Keep your nose clean . . ." she said simply. "Does that mean not breaking some guy's headlights over a parking space?"

"It was my parking space, I'd just got there, and it won't happen again."

She leaned over, grabbed his ears and kissed him firmly on the mouth. "Good. 'Cause it ain't no game, Richard. I like it here. The kids like it here. We can continue having a good life here. Don't do anything to screw it up."

"I won't."

"Good. Because if you do, I'll kill you."

He kissed her back. "I have no doubt."

• • •

For most of the day, he stayed in his office. He played twenty-three games of computer solitaire, another computer game involving shooting and lots of fast-moving monsters—not surprisingly, he scored quite high—and spent a while on the Internet as well, seeing the combined creativity of a number of women who could just barely dress themselves, and got an idea or two for next Valentine's Day.

Then, at about 3 PM, he popped in the computer disk, called up a file called "Sea Lion," and printed out all thirty-three pages. He put the pages in an Express Mail envelope, drove to the post office, and sent the envelope to a publisher in New York City. Back home, he made another cup of coffee and waited for Carla and the kids to show up. "Man, writers have it easy," he said.

The next day was a practice one for the Pine Tree Rotary team, and he enjoyed seeing how enthusiastically all the kids took to the field—Patrick and Jeffrey and Alexander and his own Sam and even little Leo, chugging out there on his tiny legs, and all the others. They did some exercises to loosen up, and then some pitching and hitting, and some base running. He took it upon himself to spend some extra time with Leo, tossing up pop flies, and Leo managed to catch fifteen in a row.

Then he took Ron Bachman aside, the town auditor who was the team's manager. "Did you see how Leo's doing?"

"Yep," Ron said, making a note on a clipboard. "Not a single dropped ball. That's what happens when dad's not around. Plays a lot better."

"So tell me, what's the deal with his dad, George. What's his problem?"

Ron looked up from the clipboard. "What do you mean, what's his problem?"

"The way he goes after his kid, that's what."

"Oh, that," he said. "You know, George has got a lot of problems. Drinking and picking fights and being the son of the chairman of the board of selectmen, so he gets a lot of slack cut his way. He's a mean man that takes his frustrations out on his kid. Typical story. Unfortunately, it has to show itself here."

"Yeah," Richard said. "Unfortunately."

• • •

Two days later the team went on a field trip to Fenway Park in Boston, an hours-long drive that took three minivans and a number of other parents to act as chaperones. When putting kids in the vans, Richard made sure that Leo was in his van, and he glanced at the boy some while heading into Boston. He half-expected to see a haunted look in the boy's eyes, a troubled expression, but no, there was nothing like that there. Just the excitement of being in Boston and seeing the Red Sox play.

Richard took in Fenway Park as they found their seats. It was an old, tiny park, opened up in 1912, the same year the *Titanic* sunk on its maiden voyage. It had its charms, with the Green Monster out in left field and the intimacy of being close-up to the action, but Richard wasn't satisfied. It wasn't Yankee Stadium, it wasn't the House that Ruth Built, but he kept his opinions to himself.

All part of his new life.

As the game progressed, he enjoyed watching the kids almost as much as the game itself. They followed each pitch intensely and ate popcorn and hotdogs and drank sodas, and cheered when one of the Red Sox players rocketed a home run over the Green Monster, and booed when the opposing pitcher hit a Red Sox player with a fastball, causing both benches to clear. The game wasn't worth much—an early season bout with the Tigers that the Red Sox managed to lose, 4–3—but it was still fun. He was glad to be here with his boy and was glad not to be in jail, and it even looked like Leo was enjoying himself too, watching the game with wide eyes and grins, seemingly thousands of miles away from his father.

On the way back to Vermont, as Sam rode up front next to Richard, and with most of the boys in the rear seats slumbering, he said, "Dad?"

"Yeah, Sam," he said, feeling a bit juiced after driving through real city streets for a change. Here was real traffic, intersections, lights, people moving in and out. Where they now lived in Vermont, there were two traffic lights, and only a few hundred feet of sidewalk in the downtown. He liked driving in the city and rolled down his window as he drove, to hear the noises, smell the scents out there.

But now they were on a featureless stretch of asphalt, making the long drive back to Vermont.

"About the game," Sam said.

"Go on."

"When the Red Sox hitter got beaned by the pitcher, I was just surprised at how fast the other players came out of the dugout to go after the pitcher. And then, the other team . . . well, man, Dad, that fight started quick. Why do they fight like that? Couldn't it have been just an accident?"

"Maybe," he said, keeping an eye on both sides of the narrow highway as they headed home, keeping an eye open for deer or moose on the side of the road, ready to trot across and wreck several thousand dollars worth of vehicle parts. "But players like that, it's more than just that. It's a team thing. You stick up for a member of your team, no matter what. And when one of your team members gets hit, or gets in trouble, you help out. That's what happens."

"Oh," Sam said. "Like a family, right? Like you've said before, about me and Olivia helping each other out? Like a family?"

"Sure," he said. "Like a family."

He drove on a few more miles, and looked over at the drowsy face of his boy, remembered a time when he was much younger, and when they all lived in a neighborhood not unlike some of the streets they had passed through on the way to the ballpark.

"Sam?"

"Yeah, Dad."

"Besides the game, how did you like it?"

His son moved in his seat, like he was seeking a comfortable position to fall asleep in. "I dunno, what do you mean, how did I like it . . ."

"I mean the city. How did you like being in the city? You know, all those buildings, all those people. What did you think?"

Sam yawned. "It was too noisy, too dirty. I like it better back home."

"Oh."

He kept on driving, wondering if he should feel angry or glad, that his son—his own boy, raised in New York!—should now hate big cities.

• • •

A few days later, the next-to-last game of the season. Pine Tree Rotary was playing Greg's Small Engine Repair, and Richard was tired and hot and thirsty. The other team had jumped on the boys right away in the first inning, and the score was now 10 to 0. Even his boy Sam, as good as he was, grounded out twice and struck out once. About the only bright spot in the lineup was poor little Leo, who was so small that he confused the opposing team's pitcher and managed to get on base twice through walks. Even though they were walks, Leo acted like Pete "Charlie Hustle" Rose himself—of course, before getting caught up in that gambling fiasco—and raced to the first base, just so damn pleased to be there, out on the bases.

Last inning, and here was Leo. Richard checked his watch and was going to call out to the boy, when somebody with a louder voice beat him to it.

"Leo!" the man bellowed. "You better get a hit or I'll be after you! That you can bet on!"

He shaded his eyes from the glare, knew who had shown up, like a shambling bear wandering into someplace he wasn't welcome. George Winn was at the fence, his fat fingers protruding through the open metal, shouting again. "Leo! You worthless player, you! Get a hit or you'll get one from me!"

Richard yelled out, "Leo, wait for a good pitch, guy, wait for a good one!"

But Leo, his legs trembling, his face red, swung at the first three pitches that came across the plate, and promptly struck out.

• • •

He ignored Olivia. He ignored Sam. He ignored the other coaches and players and strode right out to the parking lot again, where George was hauling his kid to his truck, the clothing of the boy's shirt clenched up in his fist. Richard called out, "George, you hold on!"

George spun around, moving surprisingly fast for such a large man. He propelled Leo forward with one hand and said, "Wait in the truck! Now!"

Leo ran ahead and Richard came up to him, saying, "George, you can't yell at your boy like that. He's doing the best he can, and yelling like that—"

And George stepped forward and punched him in the chest. Richard staggered back, the force of the blow bringing back hordes of muscle memories from times past, when he had faced down and put down bigger and badder guys than this, and his fists clenched up and he was spotting his move, what he should do to put this bullying jerk down, but thinking, now, he was thinking about Carla and the kids and—

The next punch struck his jaw, and then George grabbed him and he fell to the ground, and the kicks began, one after another, and Richard curled up and protected his kidneys and groin and face as much as possible, until there were other voices, other shouts, and the kicking and punching stopped.

• • •

Later that night, in bed, Carla was next to him, gingerly wiping down his face again with a wet cloth. Her face was hard and set, and he couldn't tell from one moment to the next who she was most angry with, and he just kept his hands still and let her work and talk.

"You think I like having the children see you, their father, in a brawl right in their own school parking lot?"

It hurt to talk, so he kept his words to a minimum. "Wasn't a brawl. I didn't touch the guy."

"Well, he sure as hell touched you," she said. "Poor Olivia and Sam were crying so much, I thought they'd never stop."

"They're okay."

"Yeah, but you're not. And remember what those Feds told you, about keeping your nose clean? Is this how you're doing that?"

"Didn't file a complaint," he said. "No cops."

She wiped him down again, and he winced. Even with the painkillers, it was going to be a long night.

"Doesn't matter," she said. "Word gets out. And poor Sam . . . he thinks the whole team should get together and go on over and burn down George Winn's house. He thinks they should stick up for you. Is that right?"

"Nope."

"You're damn right," she said, getting up from the bed, walking into the bathroom, and back out again with a fresh washcloth. "But our family . . .

that's something else. I don't like what happened, not one bit. Are you going to do something about it?"

He thought for a moment. "Yeah."

She wrung out the cloth over a small metal bowl. "Are you going to tell me?"

"Not yet," he said. "Not yet."

"When?" she asked.

"Soon," he said.

• • •

The next day, in his office, playing computer solitaire and wincing in pain as he moved the fingers on his right hand, the phone rang.

"Is this Richard?" came the vaguely familiar voice.

"It is," he said. "Who's this?"

There came a slight chuckle. "Let's just say it's one of the two gentleman you spoke with the other night."

He sat up straighter in his chair. "You shouldn't be calling. It's not part of the agreement. It's not part—"

"Look, pal, here's the only agreement I care about, and that's that you testify in August, and that you stay out of trouble. Right now, you're batting five hundred, and I don't like it."

"I don't understand what you mean," Richard said.

"Wasn't there a fight yesterday? In the parking lot of a school? Right after a baseball game with your kid?"

He winced again as his hand clenched the phone tighter. "It wasn't my fault. He picked the fight, not me. There was no complaint filed with the cops."

Another chuckle. "Yeah, I heard you didn't even put up a fight. Man, you must really like that place to put up with crap like that. So here's the facts, one more time. You're right on the edge, my friend. Right on the edge. One more little problem, and I don't care whose fault it was, who threw the first punch, you're still coming out to testify. But you'll come back to that pig farm in Nebraska."

Richard didn't even bother replying, because the caller had already hung up.

He sat back in his chair, looked at the little computer mouse next to the computer, and in one flurry of motion, tore it from his desk and threw it across the room.

• • •

Two days after the phone call, he was in the kitchen when Sam came tearing through. He wanted to call out to Sam, to tell him to slow down, but instead he said, "Hey, bud. What do you have going on today?"

Sam went to the refrigerator, opened up the door, and started chugging down a couple of swallows of orange juice. His mother would never let him get away with doing anything like that, and he knew his father would. What a kid. Sam put the juice away and said, "Not much. Some fishing later with Greg over at the river."

"Want to catch a late afternoon matinee?" he asked.

Sam smiled. "Just the two of us? What would Mom and Olivia think?"

"Mom's at work," he said, "and Olivia's over with some friends, staying through till dinner. I'll leave a note for your mom. It'll be fine. Come on, you've got a big day tomorrow. Last game of the season."

Sam slammed the door of the refrigerator. "When?"

"Right now."

"Cool, Dad," he said.

• • •

The movie theater was on the outskirts of town, in a little shopping mall, and the cool interior felt comfortable. He let Sam pick the movie and it was a live-action film based on a popular comic book series Richard had never heard of. Most of the audience were kids about Sam's age, with a scattering of parents like himself, there to chaperone and make sure the little ones didn't walk out and sneak into an R-rated film. He sat in a row next to a guy he knew, some clerk at the hardware store named Paul, who was there with a boy of about eight or nine.

He checked his watch as the movie droned on with punches and gunshots and buildings blowing up. He looked at the smiling faces of the young boys, illuminated some from what was up on the screen. Smiling and young and full of energy and life. He wondered how Leo was doing, if he was dreading tomorrow's game, the last game of the year, the last chance to win one before the season was over, one more time out there in the field with his father watching and shouting at him.

One more time with his watch. Time. He leaned over to Sam and whispered, "I'm going to get some popcorn. You want another drink?"

"Unh-hunh," Sam whispered back, attention still focused on the screen.

Richard got up, stepped on Paul's foot—"Jeez, excuse me"—and walked out of the dark theater.

• • •

Later that night, he was in the living room, trying to judge which one of Olivia's drawn horses was the best one—"for a contest the library's holding, Dad, and the deadline is tomorrow!"—when the doorbell rang. Olivia looked up at him and then Carla appeared in the entranceway to the kitchen, slowly wiping a salad bowl from dinner. He looked down at Olivia and said, "Right away, squirt. Go see your mom."

"But, Dad . . ."

"Now, please," he said, and Carla added, "Olivia, listen to your father. He'll finish with your horses later."

He went to the door, wiped at his hair for a moment, remembered the many other times when he had answered evening doorbells like this one, so he wasn't surprised when he opened the door and saw the town's police chief there.

"Mister Dow?" he said quietly. "Ted Reiser. Chief of police."

The chief was about ten years older than Richard, heavyset with a black moustache and a chubby neck that spilled over the collar of his white uniform dress shirt. A gold star was in each of his collar tabs, and Richard thought the chief—who was boss of a whole six officers—looked slightly ridiculous.

"Sure," Richard said. "What can I do for you?"

The chief looked past Richard, and said, "Can I come in for a moment?"

"Absolutely, come on in," he said, and the chief came in and took a seat on the couch, balancing his gold-brimmed hat on his knees. Richard sat down and said, "If you'd like, can I get you a drink or—"

Reiser raised his hand. "Sorry, no. Look, I'm sorry, but this is an official call. I'm investigating something that occurred earlier today. Something I'm afraid that might involve you."

He made a point of folding his hands together and leaning forward in his chair. "One of my kids? Did they do something?"

The chief ignored the question, went on. "George Winn. I take it you know him."

"Sure. I coach his kid in the baseball league."

"You've also had words with him, plus one altercation. True?"

Richard nodded. "True. I try to help out his boy, and George thought the kid would work best under threats."

"But there was an altercation, nearly a week ago."

"I didn't hit him, not once. Can you tell me what's going on?"

The chief sighed. "George Winn was attacked and severely injured today. An intruder broke into his home, struck him from the rear. No description of the attacker, but I'm afraid I'll have to ask you what you were doing at about 4:45 PM today."

"Why?"

"Please, Mister Dow. You were in a fight with him last week. I need to know this."

"Should I be getting a lawyer?"

That got the chief's attention. "Do you think you need one?"

"No," Richard answered.

"Then why don't you tell me where you were this afternoon."

Richard shrugged. "All right. I was at the movies with my boy Sam, at the River Mall theater. The picture started at 3:30, got out at 5:30."

"Do you have any proof?" the chief asked.

"Sure." He dug into his pants pocket, past his handkerchief and change. "Look. Ticket stubs for the both of us."

"Anybody see you at the theater?"

"Um, a kid named Larry who took my money."

"Anybody else?"

"Let's see . . . oh, sure. Paul, who works at Twombly's Hardware. He sat next to me. In fact, I stepped on the poor guy's toes when I left to get some popcorn about halfway through the movie."

The chief moved his hat in a semicircle. "Did you know what time it was?"

"Nope."

"And what time did you get back into the theater?"

Richard looked at the chief, tried to feel what was going on behind those unblinking eyes. "I'm sorry, what did you say?"

Now it was time for the police chief to lean forward. "You said you left the theater to get some popcorn. And what I want to know is, how long were you out there?"

"Two minutes, maybe three."

"And did anybody see you come back into the theater?"

"Yeah, Paul did, I'm sure."

"Oh, you are, are you," the chief said. "And why's that?"

Richard looked at the chief calmly. "Because when I tried to get past him and sit next to my son, I accidentally poured a cold drink on his head. That's why."

• • •

Another sunny day, hot but the air was dry, with little humidity. Richard was back at his position near first base, waiting. It was the bottom of the sixth inning and the score was tied, zero to zero, but his boy Sam was on third base. He rubbed his hands together, could feel the anticipation in the air, as the next Pine Tree Rotary batter came to the plate, little Leo Winn, holding his baseball bat strong and true.

The stands were nearly full and there was Olivia, keeping score again with the large notebook on her tiny lap. Today Carla had taken the afternoon off and she was there as well, and he waved at them both, but neither waved back, as they were talking to each other. Maybe later, he thought.

He wiped his hands on his pants legs. It was a beautiful day, the best so far this summer, and there was the first pitch . . .

Thump! as the ball went into the catcher's mitt. Denny Thompson was umpiring again today, and he slowly got up. "Ball!" came the shout.

"Good eye, Leo, good eye!" Richard called out, and he looked up in the stands again, and sure enough, there was Leo's dad, George, sitting there stiffly. Richard thought about waving at George but decided that would be pushing it.

Another pitch, and this time Leo swung mightily at it, and missed. Another *thump!* of the ball into the glove.

"Strike!"

Richard clapped his hands. "That's fine, Leo, that's fine. You're doing all right," and even his teammates in the dugout joined in, calling out to Leo, encouraging him, telling him to take his time, to swing at a good pitch. It was a good sound, a wonderful sound, made even better by the fact that no one was shouting insults, no one was shouting threats. Like he had mentioned the other night in the van to his son, sometimes a team was like a family, looking out for each other. Richard looked up in the stands again, and there was George, sitting still, sitting quiet.

He clapped his hands again. "Come on, Leo, the next one's yours!"

But of course, George had no choice, for George was sitting there, jaw wired shut, after somebody broke into his house and smashed his jaw with what the police believed to be a length of lead pipe. Funny how things happen, Richard thought, and then he looked over at Carla, and waved at her.

And she raised her arm and waved back, and even at this distance, he could see the slight pain in her eyes, for she had quite the workout the previous day, and wielding a lead pipe with such a slender arm could cause some soreness. He smiled as the other team's pitcher began his windup, remembered the meeting last week with the two Feds, and how even to this day, they couldn't figure out why he had gotten away with eleven killings in his previous life. It was simple, really, if you looked at it as a game, as a family game, and he waved once more at his lovely wife.

The pitch flew by and this time, oh, this time, there was a powerful *crack!* as Leo swung his bat and the ball flew up and out, heading so far out into the sky, and the people in the stands began cheering as little Leo chugged up the baseline, his face so alive and excited, and true enough, this was just a game, but it was the best damn game in the world.

Goodwood Comes Back (1948)

Robert Penn Warren

Robert Penn Warren (1905-1989) was one of the country's most distinguished literary figures, with an unparalleled reputation as a novelist and poet. Born in Guthrie, Kentucky, he earned his bachelor's degree at Vanderbilt and his master's at Berkeley and studied at Oxford as a Rhodes scholar. Warren was a cofounder of the *Southern Review*, one of America's foremost literary and critical quarterlies. Among the best known of his many novels are *Night Rider* (1939); *At Heaven's Gate* (1943); *All the King's Men* (1946), which won the Pulitzer Prize; and *Band of Angels* (1955). Warren also authored several collections of poems, two of which won Pulitzers (*Promises: Poems 1954-1956* and *Now and Then: Poems 1976-1977*). In 1986 he was named poet laureate of the United States.

Luke Goodwood always could play baseball, but I never could, to speak of. I was little for my age then, but well along in my studies and didn't want to play with the boys my size; I wanted to play with the boys in my class, and if it hadn't been for Luke, I never would have been able to. He was a pitcher then, like he has always been, and so he would say, "Aw, let him field." When he was pitching, it didn't matter much who was fielding, anyway, because there weren't going to be any hits to amount to anything in the first place. I used to play catcher some, too, because I had the best mitt, but he pitched a mighty hard ball and it used to fool the batter all right, but it fooled me too a good part of the time so I didn't hold them so good. Also, I was a little shy about standing close up to the plate on account of the boys flinging the bat the way they did when they started off for first base. Joe Lancaster was the worst for that, and since he almost always played on the other side, being a good hitter to balance off Luke's pitching, I had to come close, nearly getting scared to death of him braining me when he did get a hit. Luke used to yell, "For Christ sake get up to that plate or let somebody else catch for Christ sake that can!"

Joe Lancaster wasn't much bigger than I was, but he was knotty and old-looking, with a white face and hair that was almost white like an old man's, but he wasn't exactly an albino. He was a silent and solemn kind of boy, but he could sure hit; I can remember how he used to give that ball a good solid crack, and start off running the bases with his short legs working fast like a fox terrier's trying to catch up with something, but his face not having any expression and looking like it was dead or was thinking about something else. I've been back home since and seen him in the restaurant where he works behind the counter. I'm bigger than he is now, for he never did grow much. He says hello exactly like a stranger that never saw you before and asks what you want. When he has his sleeves rolled up in the summertime, and puts an order on the counter for you, his arms are small like a boy's, still, with very white skin you can see the veins through.

It was Joe hit me in the head with a bat when I was catching. Luke ran up toward the plate, yelling, "You've killed him!"—for the bat knocked me clean over. It was the last time I played catcher; the next time I came out bringing my mitt, which was a good one, Luke said, "Gimme that mitt." He took it and gave it to another boy, and told me to go play field. That was the only thing I didn't like about Luke, his taking my mitt.

I stayed at the Goodwood house a lot, and liked it, even if it was so different from my own. It was like a farmhouse, outside and inside, but the town was growing out toward it, making it look peculiar set so far back off the street with barns and chicken yards behind it. There was Mr. Goodwood, who had been a sheriff once and who had a bullet in his game leg, they said, a big man one time, but now with his skin too big for him and hanging in folds. His mustache was yellow from the chewing tobacco he used and his eyes were bloodshot; some people said he was drinking himself to death, but I'll say this for him, he drank himself to death upstairs without making any fuss. He had four boys, and drink was their ruination. They say it was likker got Luke out of the big league, and none of the Goodwoods could ever leave the poison alone. Anyway, the Goodwood house was a man's house with six men sitting down to the table, counting the grandfather, and Mrs. Goodwood and her daughter going back and forth to the kitchen with sweat on their faces and their hair damp from the stove. There would be men's coats on the chairs in the living room, sometimes hunting coats with the old blood caked on the khaki, balls of twine and a revolver on the mantel-piece, and shotguns and flyrods lying around, even on the spare bed that was in the living room. And the bird dogs came in the house whenever they got good and ready. At my house everything was different, for men there always seemed to be just visiting.

Luke took me hunting with him, or sometimes one of his big brothers took us both, but my mother didn't like for me to go with the grown boys along, because she believed that their morals were not very good. I don't suppose their morals were much worse than ordinary for boys getting their sap up, but hearing them talk was certainly an education for a kid. Luke was as good a shot as you ever hope to see. He hunted a lot by himself, too, for my folks wouldn't let me go just all the time. He would get up before day and eat some cold bread and coffee in the kitchen and then be gone till after dark with his rifle or his shotgun. He never took anything to eat with him, either, for when he was hunting he was like they say the Indians were in that respect. Luke reminded you of an Indian, too, even when he was a boy and even if he was inclined to be a blond and not a brunette; he was long and rangy, had a big fine-cut nose, and looked to be setting his big feet always carefully on the ground, and came up on his toes a little, like a man testing his footing. He walked that way even on a concrete walk, probably from being in the woods so much. It was no wonder with all his hunting he never did study or make any good use and profit of his mind, which was better than most people's, however. The only good grades he made were in penmanship, copybooks still being used then in the grammar school part of school. He could make his writing look exactly like the writing at the top of the page, a Spencerian hand tilted forward, but not too much like a woman's. He could draw a bird with one line without taking the pencil off the paper once, and he'd draw them all afternoon in school sometimes. The birds all looked alike, all fine and rounded off like his Spencerian writing, their beaks always open, but not looking like any birds God ever made in this world. Sometimes he would put words coming out of a bird's bill, like "You bastard," or worse; then he would scratch it out, for he might just as well have signed his name to it, because the teachers and everybody knew how well he could draw a bird in that way he had.

Luke didn't finish high school. He didn't stop all at once, but just came less and less, coming only on bad days most of the time, for on good days he would be off hunting or fishing. It was so gradual, him not coming, that nobody, maybe not even the teachers, knew when he really stopped for good. In the summer he would lie around the house, sleeping out in the yard on the grass where it was shady, stretched out like a cat, with just a pair of old pants on. Or he would fish or play baseball. It got so he was playing baseball for little town teams around that section, and he picked up some change to buy shells and tackle.

That was the kind of life he was living when I finished school and left town. We had drifted apart, you might say, by that time, for he didn't fool around with the school kids anymore. I never found out exactly how he broke into real baseball and got out of what you call the sandlot. My sister wrote me some big man in the business saw Luke pitch some little game somewhere and Luke was gone to pitch for a team up in Indiana somewhere. Then the next year he got on the sport page in the papers. My sister, knowing I would be interested in the boy that was my friend, you might say, used to find out about the write-ups and send me clippings when the home paper would copy stories about Luke from the big papers. She said Luke was making nine thousand dollars playing for the Athletics, which was in Philadelphia. The papers called him the Boy Wizard from Alabama. He must have been making a lot of money that year to judge from the presents he sent home. He sent his mother a five-hundred-dollar radio set and a piano, and I admired him for the way he remembered his mother, who had a hard time and no doubt about it. I don't know why he sent the piano, because nobody at his house could play one. He also fixed up the house, which was in a bad shape by that time. Mr. Goodwood was still alive, but according to all reports he was spending more time upstairs than ever, and his other three boys never were worth a damn, not even for working in the garden, and didn't have enough git-up-and-git to even go fishing.

The next year Luke pitched in the World Series, for the team that bought him from the Athletics, in Philadelphia, and he got a bonus of three thousand dollars, plus his salary. But he must have hit the skids after that, drink being the reason that was reported to me. When he was home on vacation, my sister said he did some fishing and hunting, but pretty soon he was drunk all the time, and carousing around. The next year he didn't finish the season. My sister sent me a clipping about, and wrote on the margin, "I'm sure you will be sorry to know this because I know you always liked Luke. I like Luke too." For a matter of fact, I never saw a woman who didn't like Luke, he was so good-looking and he had such a mixture of wildness and a sort of embarrassment around women. You never saw a finer-looking fellow in your life than he was going down the street in summer with nothing on except old khaki pants and underwear tops and his long arms and shoulders near the color of coffee and his blondish hair streaked golden color with sunburn. But he didn't have anything to do with girls, that is, decent girls, probably because he was too impatient. I don't suppose he ever had a regular date in his life.

But the next year he was back in baseball, but not in such a good team, for he had done some training and lived clean for a while before the season opened. He came back with great success, it looked like at first. I was mighty glad when I got a clipping from my sister with the headlines, *Goodwood Comes Back*. He was shutting them out right and left. But it didn't last. The drink got him, and he was out of the big-time game for good and all, clean as a whistle. Then he came back home.

It was on a visit home I saw him after all that time. I was visiting my sister, who was married and lived there, and I had taken a lawn mower down to the blacksmith shop to get it fixed for her. I was waiting out in front of the shop, leaning against one side of the door and looking out in the gravel street, which was sending up heat-dazzles. Two or three old men were sitting there, not even talking; they were the kind of old men you find sitting around town like that, who never did amount to a damn and whose names even people in town can't remember half the time. I saw Luke coming up the road with another boy, who didn't strike me as familiar right off because he was one of those who had grown up in the meantime. I could see they were both nearly drunk, when they got under the shade of the shed; and I noticed Luke's arms had got pretty stringy. I said hello to Luke, and he said, "Well, I'll be damned, how you making it?" I said, "Fine, how's it going?" Then he said, "Fine."

After they stood there a while I could see the other boy wasn't feeling any too good with the combination of whisky and the heat of the day. But Luke kept kidding him and trying to make him go up to the Goodwood house, where he said he had some more whisky. He said he had kept it under a setting hen's nest for two weeks to age, and the other boy said Luke never kept any whisky in his life two days, let alone two weeks, without drinking it up. It was bootleg whisky they were drinking, because Alabama was a dry state then, according to the law, even after repeal; Luke must have been kidding too, because he ought to know if anybody does, whisky don't age in glass whether it's under a setting hen or not. Then he tried to make the boy go up to Tangtown, which is what they call nigger town because of the immoral goings-on up there, where they could get some more whisky, he said, and maybe something else. The other boy said it wasn't decent in the middle of the afternoon. Then he asked me to go, but I said no thanks to the invitation, not ever having approved of that, and Tangtown especially, for it looks like to me a man ought to have more self-respect. The old men sitting there were taking in every word, probably jealous because they weren't good for drinking or anything anymore.

Finally Luke and the other boy started up the road in the hot sun, going I don't know where, whether to his house or off to Tangtown in the middle of the afternoon. One of the old men said, "Now, ain't it a shame the way he's throwed away his chances." One of the others said likker always was hard on the Goodwoods. Luke, not being any piece off and having good ears even if he was drinking, must have heard them, for he stooped down and scooped up a rock from the road like a baseball player scooping up an easy grounder, and yelled, "Hey, see that telephone pole?" Then he threw the rock like a bullet and slammed the pole, which was a good way off. He turned around, grinning pretty sour, and yelled, "Still got control, boys!" Then the two of them went off.

It was more than a year before I saw him again, but he had been mentioned in letters from my sister, Mrs. Hargreave, who said that Luke was doing better and that his conduct was not so outrageous, as she put it. His mother's dying that year of cancer may have quieted him down some. And then he didn't have any money to buy whisky with. My sister said he was hunting again and in the summer pitching a little ball for the town team that played on Saturday and Sunday afternoons with the other teams from the towns around there. His pitching probably was still good enough to make the opposition look silly. But maybe not, either, as might be judged from what I heard the next time I saw him. I was sitting on the front porch of my sister's house, which is between the Goodwood house and what might be called the heart of town. It stands close up to the street without much yard like all the houses built since the street got to be a real street and not just a sort of road with a few houses scattered along it. Some men were putting in a concrete culvert just in front of the house, and since it was the middle of the day, they were sitting on the edge of the concrete walk eating their lunch and smoking. When Luke came along, he stopped to see what they were doing and got down in the ditch to inspect it. Although it was getting along in the season, there were still enough leaves on the vine on my sister's porch to hide me from the street, but I could hear every word they said. One of the workmen asked Luke when the next game would be. He said Sunday with Millville. When they asked him if he was going to win, he said he didn't know because Millville had a tough club to beat all right. I noticed on that trip home that the boys talked about their ball club, and not their ball team. It must have been Luke's influence. Then one of the men sitting on the curb said in a tone of voice that sounded righteous and false somehow in its encouragement, "We know you can beat 'em, boy!" For a minute Luke didn't say anything; then he said, "Thanks," pretty short, and turned off down the street, moving in that easy yet fast walk of his that always seemed not to be taking any effort.

It was a couple of days later when I was sitting in my sister's yard trying to cool off, that he came by and saw me there and just turned in at the gate. We said hello, just like we had been seeing each other every day for years, and he sat down in the other chair without waiting to be asked, just like an old friend, which he was. It wasn't long before he got out of the chair, though, and lay on the grass, just like he always used to do, lying relaxed all over just like an animal. I was a little bit embarrassed at first, I reckon, and maybe he was, too, for we hadn't sort of sat down together like that for near fifteen years, and he had been away and been a big league pitcher, at the top of his profession almost, and here he was back. He must have been thinking along the same lines, for after he had been there on the grass a while he gave a sort of laugh and said, "Well, we sure did have some pretty good times when we were kids going round this country with our guns, didn't we?" I said we sure did. I don't know whether Luke really liked to remember the times we had or whether he was just being polite and trying to get in touch with me again, so to speak.

Then he got to talking about the places he had been and the things he had seen. He said a man took him to a place in some city, Pittsburgh I believe it was, and showed him the biggest amount of radium there is in the world in one place. His mother having died of cancer not much more than a year before that day we were talking must have made him remember that. He told me how he shot alligators in Florida and went deep-sea fishing. That was the only good time he had away from home, he said, except the first year when the Athletics farmed him out to a smaller team. I was getting embarrassed when he started to talk about baseball, like you will when somebody who has just had a death in the family starts talking natural, like nothing had happened, about the departed one. He said his first year in Pennsylvania he got six hundred dollars a month from the club he was pitching for, plus a little extra. "Being raised in a town like this," he said, "a fellow don't know what to do with real money." So he wrote home for them to crate up his bird dogs and express them to him, which they did. He leased a farm to put his dogs on and hired somebody to take care of them for him, because he couldn't be out there all the time, having his job to attend to. Then he bought some more dogs, for he always was crazy about dogs, and bought some Chinese ring-neck pheasants to put on his farm. He said that was a good time, but it didn't last.

He told me about some other pitchers too. There was one who used to room with him when the club went on the road. Every time they got to a new city, that pitcher made the rounds of all the stores, then the boxes would begin coming to the hotel room, full of electric trains and mechanical automobiles and boats, and that grown man would sit down and play with them and after the game would hurry back so he could play some more. Luke said his friend liked trains pretty well, but boats best, and used to keep him awake half the night splashing in the bathtub. There was another pitcher up in Indiana who went to a roadhouse with Luke, where they got drunk. They got thrown out of the place because that other pitcher, who was a Polak, kept trying to dance with other people's women. The Polak landed on a rock pile and put his hand down and found all the rocks were just the size of baseballs, and him a pitcher. He started breaking windows, and stood everybody off till the cops came. But Luke was gone by that time; so the police called up the hotel to tell Luke there was a guy needed two thousand dollars to get out of jail. So he and three other players went down and put up five hundred apiece to get the fellow out, who was sobered up by that time and wanted to go to bed and get some rest. Luke didn't know that fellow very well and when the Polak went off with the team to play some little game and Luke didn't go, he figured his five hundred was gone too. The fellow didn't come back with the team, either, for he had slipped off, so he figured he had really kissed his five hundred good-bye. But the night before the trial, about three o'clock in the morning, there was a hammering on the hotel-room door and before Luke could open it, somebody stuck a fist through the panel and opened it. And there was the Polak, wearing a four-bit tuxedo and patent-leather shoes and a derby hat, and his tie under one ear, drunk. He fell flat on the floor clutching twenty-three hundred dollars' worth of bills in his hands. That Polak had gone back to the mines, having been a miner before he got in baseball, and had gambled for three days, and there he was to pay back the money as soon as he could. Luke said he wouldn't take money from a man who was drunk because the man might not remember and might want to pay him again when he got sober; so he got his the next morning. The fine and expense of fixing up the roadhouse wasn't as much as you'd expect, and the Polak had a good profit, unless a woman who got hit in the head with a rock and sued him got the rest. Luke didn't know how much she got. He said all pitchers are crazy as hell one way or another.

He told me about things that he saw or got mixed up with, but he said he never had a good time after he had to give up the farm where he had the dogs and the Chinese ring-neck pheasants. He said after that it wasn't so good anymore, except for a little time in Florida, shooting alligators and fishing. He had been raised in the country, you see, and had the habit of getting up mighty early, with all that time on his hands till the game started or practice. For a while he used to go to the gymnasium in the mornings and take a work-out, but the manager caught on and stopped that because he wouldn't be fresh for the game. There wasn't anything to do in the mornings after that, he said, except pound the pavements by himself, everybody else still being asleep, or ride the lobbies, and he didn't have a taste for reading, not ever having cultivated his mind like he should. Most of the boys could sleep late, but he couldn't, being used to getting up before sun to go fishing or hunting or something. He said he could have stood the night drinking all right, it was the morning drinking got him down. Lying there on the grass, all relaxed, it didn't look like he gave a damn either.

He had his plans all worked out. If he could get hold of a few hundred dollars he was going to buy him a little patch of ground back in the country where it was cheap, and just farm a little and hunt and fish. I thought of old Mr. Bullard, an old bachelor who lived off in a cabin on the river and didn't even bother to do any farming anymore, they said, or much fishing, either. I used to see him come in town on a Saturday afternoon, walking nine miles in just to sit around in the stores looking at people, but not talking to them, or, if the weather was good, just standing on the street. But Luke probably liked to hunt and fish better than Mr. Bullard ever did in his life, and that was something for a man to hold on to. I told Luke I hoped he got his farm, and that now was the time to buy while the depression was on and land was cheap as dirt. He laughed at that, thinking I was trying to make a joke, which I wasn't, and said, "Hell, a farm ain't nothing but dirt, anyway."

After lying there some more, having about talked himself out, he got up and remarked how he had to be shoving on. We shook hands in a formal way, this time, not like when he came in the yard. I wished him luck, and he said, "The same to you," and when he got outside the gate, he said, "So long, buddy."

About six months later he got married, much to my surprise. My sister wrote me about it and sent a clipping about it. His bride was a girl named Martha Sheppard, who is related to my family in a distant way, though Lord knows my sister wouldn't claim any kin with them. And I reckon they aren't much to brag on. The girl had a half-interest in a piece of land out in the country, in the real hoot-owl sticks, you might say, where she lived with her brother, who had the other half-share. I guessed at the time when I read the letter that Luke just married that girl because it was the only way he could see to get the little piece of ground he spoke of. I never saw the girl to my recollection, and don't know whether she was pretty or not.

I have noticed that people living way back in the country like that are apt to be different from ordinary people who see more varieties and kinds of people every day. That maybe accounts for the stories you read in papers about some farmer way back off the road getting up some morning and murdering his whole family before breakfast. They see the same faces every day till some little something gets to preying on their mind and they can't stand it. And it accounts for the way farmers get to brooding over some little falling-out with a neighbor and start bushwhacking each other with shotguns. After about a year Martha Sheppard's brother shot Luke. My sister wrote me the bad blood developed between them because Luke and his wife didn't get along so well together. I reckon she got to riding him about the way he spent his time, off hunting and all. Whatever it was, her brother shot Luke with Luke's own shotgun, in the kitchen one morning. He shot him three times. The gun was a .12-gauge pump gun, and you know what even one charge of a .12-gauge will do at close range like a kitchen.

The Rookie
(1953)

Eliot Asinof

Eliot Asinof was well-known for his screenwriting and television writing. He authored several fiction and nonfiction books—among them are *Eight Men Out: The Black Sox and the 1919 World Series* (1963), a mystery titled *The Name of the Game Is Murder* (1968), and a book about the Wilson administration and the post-World War I era called *1919: America's Loss of Innocence* (1990). Asinof passed away in 2008, and his posthumous novel, *Final Judgment*, was published later that year.

Asinof's story "The Rookie" captures the stark realism and sacrifice that many players face in struggling to make the major leagues. It's about fate and fading youth, guts and dreams, as a thirty-five-year-old rookie finally gets his big chance for glory after sixteen frustrating years in the minors.

The Rookie walked into the batter's circle behind home plate and listened to the roar of the tremendous crowd. He swung the two big bats over his head, stretching the muscles in his powerful arms, and recorded the deafening noises for his memory. Dropping to one knee, he stroked his favorite piece of shiny ash, and wiped the dirt from the tapered white barrel. He could not resist looking up toward the towering, triple-tiered stadium around him. For the fourth time today he waited there for his turn at bat; each time he would wallow in the exultation that ran through him, repeating under his breath for his senses to enjoy: "You're in the big-time, Mike. . . . At last, you're in the big-time!"

At last . . . after sixteen grueling, sweltering summers in squalid, southern towns. At last . . . after sixteen years, the whole span of a ballplayer's life. For a moment, he reveled in the thrill that beat against his insides and almost made him weep. At last . . . he was a Major Leaguer.

But now a hot wave of savage noise rose from the stands, jarring him rudely from his reverie, and brought him back to the sticky climate of this crucial September ball game. He turned to watch Red Schalk fidgeting in the batter's box, then the pitch twisting half-speed to the plate. He saw the hitter's badly timed stride and the ball curve elusively by him, the bat remaining ineptly on his shoulder. The Rookie heard the umpire's callous cry:

"Steee-rike one!"

Mike braced himself for the new roar of the crowd, multiplying the tension in this ninth-inning climax, and considered the crisis in the game. There were two men out, and the tying and winning runs danced helplessly off second and first, itching to hit pay dirt. The game was going down to the wire; it was clearly up to Red Schalk to take it there.

The Rookie added to the bellowing mob behind him, and roared aloud his desperate hopes:

"Keep alive, Red! Keep alive!"

But within him, he knew he meant something else: keep it alive for me . . . for *me*. Get on base and leave those runners sitting out there. Selfishly, Mike felt himself begging for the hero's job—to hit that long blow and bust up the game. He transferred his body into Red's, his hands on Red's bat, his power, timing, coordination, and most of all, his will into Red's. To the Rookie, this day was a personal climax, far more important to him that the goddam game. It had to be his day; for after sixteen struggling years to get here, he knew damn well he had it coming to him.

"Mike!" he heard. "The resin. Gimme the resin."

He looked up to see Red walking toward him from the plate. He picked up the resin bag and went to meet him.

"Sonovabitch!" Red muttered under his breath.

"Take it easy, Red," Mike said, trying to steady him; the "veteran" was having it rough. "Get loose."

Red rubbed the resin over his sweaty hands.

"Can't get 'em dry enough. . . ."

Scare sweat, the Rookie thought. The guy is scared up there. A chance to be a hero and the guy is scared.

"Take your time, Red. . . ."

"Sonovabitch, Mike . . . can't get loose."

"Take it easy." He noticed now the guy was shaking.

Mike went back to the batter's circle and spat his contempt. He'd give half his pay to be in this guy's spot right now, but the Redhead didn't know whether to piss or go blind. And this was a "bonus baby"—Red Schalk, the new-type ballplayer. They had handed him twenty grand for being a high school hero, for hitting .400 against the patsy pitchers, and playing with babies. Twenty Gs for merely signing his lousy name. When Mike signed to play pro ball, they gave him a nickel cigar . . . and he didn't even smoke. He thought back . . . he was just a raw kid out in a Pennsylvania mining town, hating the black mines that threatened to swallow his future. Instead, he had practically lived on the sandlots, driving his natural baseball skills to perfection, hoping to spend the rest of his life with a bat, not a pick, and wear a cap without a flashlight over the peak.

He grunted at his memories, and spat a portion of rich brown tobacco juice skillfully down the length of his extra bat.

"Com' on, Red!" he hollered, fighting back his bitterness. "Get on that sack!"

Mike watched the pitcher lean into the shadows to pick up the catcher's sign, his intense concentration hidden under the lowered peak. The pitch spun in, an exact facsimile of the previous strike . . . and it tied the Redhead in the exact same knot. Mike groaned helplessly and bit harshly at his lip as the umpire roared again:

"Steerike two!"

Fooled him twice . . . the lousy Redhead . . . fooled the big-time Major Leaguer, overanxious in the clutch like a stinking high school kid. Red had never even waved his stick. Christ . . . you'd think a guy three years in the big-time would at least know how to get set.

He shivered as an icy wind passed through him, frantic now that everything vital to him seemed so far beyond his control.

He heard Red calling him again.

"Mike. . . ." The voice was low and charged with fear. "Mike. . . ." And he spluttered his confession like a frightened, guilty child: "I . . . I don't wanna hit!"

"What!" Mike snarled, hardly believing, only conscious of something rotten happening. "What! You don't wanna hit?" Then it occurred to him that he had come across this before. The kid had found himself in a crucial spot and hated it. Some punks just weren't cut out for it; they were great only when it didn't count. The hitters with crap in their blood.

Mike looked into the quivering face, amazed at its pallor. He guessed the kid had given up on himself.

"I don't feel good, Mike," Red was saying. "I can't stand up there. . . ."

The Rookie thought of all the drunks he had sobered up; this looked like a tougher job.

"Don't tell that to the Skipper, Red," he said. "I gotta feeling he won't appreciate it."

So now the bottom was falling out; this was supposed to be the hitter who would give him a crack at the big one. Mike felt himself sinking in the field of quicksand . . . down, down he went . . . the towering steel that enclosed it seemed to loom higher, much higher. . . .

"Com' on, Red," the umpire growled at them. "Let's get the game moving."

Mike grabbed the hitter roughly by the arm. What the hell could he say? "Get back in there and hit or you'll never hit again. Not in this League, anyway." His voice was harsh with anger. "Be tough," he added. "Be tough up there!" And he turned away, spitting the taste of his words. Maybe he oughta pray, too.

Oh you crud, you mighty crud! he muttered under his breath, and he let his memory flash back four wasted years to a city in the Texas League. For there he had first come across Red Schalk, a pink-cheeked, nineteen-year-old bonus-baby out of Georgia. He remembered how they babied him, trying to justify the ridiculous twenty-grand investment. He was some big-shot scout's fair-haired boy, the big prospect. Mike had watched them coddle Red all season, letting him nurse his .302 batting average to make it look good. A year later, they moved Red Schalk up to the big-time.

Mike had burned up at the move. Hadn't he outhit Red by a dozen points, and wasn't he a dozen times the glove man? Where were the rewards for his years of consistently good ball playing? What about the promises they'd made to him . . . year after year? Why doesn't he go up? he demanded to know. Why not him?

Sure, Mike, the scout had told him; you're a fine ballplayer. But up in the Big Leagues they're after the younger kids. By all rights, you should be up there . . . and if it hadn't been for the war and those years you lost, you would be. Sorry, Mike . . . you know how it is . . . a kid of nineteen has a much longer ride ahead of him. . . .

The plain and simple truth had been made apparent to him; they just didn't want him anymore. He was over thirty by then, and they considered him a secondary piece of property.

Now he was thirty-five, an old man of thirty-five . . . a rookie of thirty-five, playing his first day in the Majors. It did not escape him that he was here by a fluke. The mother club had been riddled with injuries down the stretch, and they decided to use Mike in this crucial September series rather than some green kid. At the last minute, they called him in Texas and flew him up during the night. As he got off the plane in the morning, they hurriedly signed him to a big-league contract. He never even got a chance to get some sleep.

Sixteen years he had plugged his heart out for a crack at the big leagues; when they finally needed him, they threw it in his face.

In the locker room before the game, the Skipper came over to meet him. "You're in the lineup today, Kutner," he said tersely. "Show me something." And he walked away.

The players watched the Rookie smile sourly at this. Those who knew him saw his determination and understood it. To them, it was a matter of winning a pennant, and a few extra thousand bucks to show for it. Oh, that was something, all right. But to this man, it was much more . . . it was a test of a lifetime struggle. They all knew Mike was good, as good as almost any of them—and if the ball had bounced differently, he might have been up there all these years instead of them. But now, at thirty-five, he could be called old. Those who did not know him looked curiously across the room at the signs of his age: his partially bald head, the dark, leathery skin in back of his neck, his heavy, uneven walk . . . and they wondered how many years they had left for themselves. Respectfully, they left him alone while he dressed.

He had waited until they were all out to finish. He laced his shoes tightly and put on his new cap. His uniform was clean and he liked its fresh-sterile smell. With tremendous pride he walked over to the big mirror by the shower room and stood solidly before it. He looked at himself for a long moment, allowing the glow to penetrate his senses. A lush tingling tickled the back of his neck, bringing goose bumps to his skin. He had never felt so wonderful.

"You're here, Mike," he had said out loud. "You finally made it!" Then he clenched his fists as the tears came to his eyes. "You're here, goddamit . . . and you're not going back!"

• • •

The umpire's voice brought him out of his reverie.

"Play ball!" he hollered.

The Rookie raised his eyes to Schalk at the plate and watched him feebly wave his bat through the air like he was flagging a train. Red was now an empty shell of a man, a skeleton of bones in a big-league uniform, faking through the motions of being a hitter. Look at him, Mike thought. Look at what they picked instead of me! Suddenly, he felt the years of resentment boiling inside him, for here was the sickening symbol of his frustrations. His anger rose furiously to his throat, almost choking him, and he exploded at the Redhead with consummate violence:

"Stand up there like a pro, you goddam yellow punk!" he hollered. "Get on that goddam base!"

At once, he was conscious of what he had done. A ballplayer doesn't blow up that way. That's what you don't do. Instinctively, his mind, his bright, quick baseball mind went back to work for him. He looked out to the pitcher's mound, thinking how much he'd like to be the chucker for this one pitch. If that mug knew the insides of Schalk's guts he'd be laughing out loud. But the pitcher was fingering his own resin bag, and Mike smiled despite himself; the jerk was probably scared too. The Rookie felt like the only veteran in the ballpark.

The pitcher looked for a sign, a studied smile on his face. He'll curve him again, Mike thought. Any decent curve'll get him. Red can't even see anymore . . . just little colored spots in front of his eyes. Count him out, ump . . . Red Schalk, K.O.

The curve spun rapidly in. Red went through the motions, stepping like he knew what he was doing, as if to take his cut. The ball curved from the inside to cut the corner of the plate, but it never got there. It bounded painfully off Red's leg.

"Take yer base!" the umpire bellowed.

Red lay moaning in the dust, rubbing his thigh.

Well, kiss my butt, Mike thought as he went to him, guessing the breaking pitch might have been a good one.

"You OK, Red?" he asked. Maybe the guy did pray at that.

"Yeah, yeah. I'm OK," he said. "It's funny, Mike . . . I never saw it." And he got up, loosening his leg on the way to first.

Mike grinned. It's good you didn't, he thought . . . it's goddam good you didn't. And he turned his concentration quickly to the job before him.

Behind him, the crowd rose to a frenzy at the bases-loaded climax. The Rookie swung the two bats like a windmill and listened to the wild stampede.

It's all yours now; there's nothing left to the day but you. Go back sixteen years, Rookie, and maybe ten thousand turns at bat. None of them matter . . . none of them. Just this one, Mike; just this one, beautiful moment. . . .

He heard the Skipper's voice from the bench, and anti-climax to his mood:

"It's up to you, Kutner. Show me something!"

I'll show you something, you dumb bastard, Mike thought. He tossed away the extra stick and started to dig a foothold in the batter's box. It's all up to you . . . this game, maybe even the big pennant. This is the turn that counted. The other three meant nothing . . . the neat sacrifice bunt, the base on balls, and that long, well-hit fly ball the center fielder dragged down. They were all routine. This is the spot, Rookie. Blast one and bust up the game!

They were really down to the wire now. All around him there was a tremendous din, a wild persistent yelling that racked his ears. He looked up through the bubbling joy in his heart to face the pitcher. He saw the three runners dance anxiously off their bases. From the bench they were hollering at him: "Com' on, Mike. Clobber one!"

The pitcher was getting his sign, this time without a smile.

Here we go, Rookie. Tag one and you're a Major Leaguer for the rest of your natural-born life! To Mike, there were no doubts; as sure as he was alive he knew he was going to. He couldn't keep the smile off his face; this was the spot he had waited sixteen years for.

Mike watched the pitcher take a full, slow windup. He cocked his bat menacingly over his shoulder and waited for the throw. It came half-speed, spinning toward the outside corner. He stepped toward the pitch and lashed viciously at the ball with full power. As he finished his pivot, he knew he had gotten only a slice of it. The ball skidded off into the upper grandstand behind him.

"Steee-rike one!" he heard the umpire cry.

He leaned over to pick up dirt, muttering profanities at himself. He was set. He saw it all the way. Yet he hadn't met it squarely. Was it because he was tired? Or too eager? . . . But then he realized this had happened to him too many times over this past year. His memory flashed him pictures of powerful smashes of just such a pitch, years ago. But now he didn't always get around in time. There was something missing; the thin edge of timing and coordination that made the difference had dulled over the years. He swiped viciously at the dirt and sprayed it over the ground in anger, and remembered what the scout had told him in Texas four years ago. His age was catching up with him; he was thirty-five and past his prime.

He heard the cries from the other bench now, beamed directly to him over the stamping and screaming of the crowd.

"Hey, Pop . . . how'd you break in here?"

He took a moment to adjust his cap and looked squarely into their dugout. They were all on the front step, nervously bellowing at him.

"Hey, Baldy . . . where's your cane?"

He stepped back in the box and dug in again. He would like that pitch once more, just to prove he could clobber it. But he knew damn well he wouldn't get it now.

"Hey, Rookie. Let's see that fine head of skin again!"

Be set, Mike, and stay loose. This punk has nothing he can throw by you. The ducks are on the pond, Mike, and yours to knock in. It's a picnic, man, a picnic!

He watched the arm swing up and around, the big stride toward the plate, and the little ball spun bullet-speed toward him. It came high and tight, and Mike ducked carefully away from it.

"Steee-rike two!" the ump called.

Mike turned on him in a sudden ferocious rage that raced through him like an electric shock.

"What!" he roared. "It knocked me down! It was a waste pitch!"

"It was in there, buddy. Quit yer crying and get back in there and hit!"

The Rookie slammed the end of his bat against the ground like a sledge hammer, close to the umpire's feet. He was livid.

"No . . . goddamit . . . it knocked me down!"

In a second, the Manager and coaches were there, crowding around the ump, hammering away at him in unsuppressed rage. Not a nice word was spoken.

When the dust had cleared, Mike stood anxiously to the side, trying to collect himself. It was a terrible call, that strike, and it came at a terrible time. It put him way behind the pitcher, making it real tough for him to cut loose. He had to guard that plate now, instead of making the pitcher come in there with it. He couldn't pick out the throw he liked. Mike thought it was the kind of call an ump would never make on a star. But on a rookie. . . .

"Play ball!" the ump shouted, masking his face, trying to recover his prestige.

Mike turned, his anger still drumming in his gut.

"Take it easy, ump. I got a little something riding on this pitch . . . so take it easy."

The ump lifted his mask and leaned toward him.

"You're pretty sassy for a rookie, buddy."

Sure, Mike thought. There it was.

"Yeah . . ." he said, as sour as he could make it.

"Get up there and hit!"

Behind him he heard the Skipper again.

"To hell with him, Kutner. You got the big one left."

Sure . . . nothing to it. Sorry you had to swallow a call like that, but you still gotta produce. The sacks are loaded and only you can pull out this ball game. That's what you'll get paid for, buddy, and nothing else matters. The stinkin' ump could call another zombie against you, and you're out, just as if you whiffed one, and the game is gone. An hour later, it don't matter anymore that it wasn't your fault. You didn't produce . . . that's what mattered. It's just a big, round K.O. in the papers tomorrow. And because you're thirty-five, you're back in the bush leagues on the first train out.

Then he heard the jockeys from the other bench again.

"Grampa . . . hey, Grampa! Who does yer grandson play for?"

"Get out the rockin' chair . . . here comes Papa Kutner!"

Mike reached down again to finger some dirt at his feet. He rubbed his hands dry and gripped tightly the narrow handle of his bat. Back in the batter's box, he dug his spikes in position. He faced the pitcher and started thinking baseball again.

Get set, he told himself. Be ready for anything. It's still up to you, Mike. He can't get it by you . . . he can't get it by. . . .

"Ba-a-a-l-d-e-e-eeeeeee!"

The arm swung around again, and Mike's keen eyes followed the movement of the pitcher's hand. His sharp baseball sense picked up a tiny quirk in the pitcher's delivery that clearly indicated a curve ball. Mike set himself and moved his body toward the pitch. The ball spun down the inside and started curving late. He pivoted with all his power and met the pitch out front with the fat part of the bat. The sharp crack rang out, beautiful and clear as a bell, and everyone in the park knew that ball was really tagged.

Mike started to first, watching it sail up and up, into the sky, way above the stadium roof, soaring deep toward the left-field bleachers. He heard the tremendous, ear-splitting roar of the 50,000 who were a part of it, and the happiness beat glowingly against his ribs. It was the big one! You've done it, Mike . . . you blasted one in the clutch, with the sacks loaded! He rounded first base with tears in his eyes, for he knew, at last, that the world was all his.

As he made his turn, he looked up again to follow the end flight of the ball, wanting to feast on the sight of it disappearing into the seats out there. Suddenly his throat constricted in an agonizing gasp. The ball . . . it wasn't falling right. The wind above the roof had caught it and was pulling it toward the foul line. He followed it down now, sinking deep into the bleachers, but at an angle he could not guess. He saw the foul pole, the tall white shaft; an icy tremor ran through him as the ball fell out of sight into a scramble of spectators.

He never heard the umpire's call. Short of second base, he stopped and turned slowly back to home plate. From some place deep within him, his instincts had called the play: foul ball.

He was right.

It took him a long time to walk back to the plate. He needed all the time he could get now. A sense of doom came over him and he couldn't shake it off. For a moment he thought he'd been feeling it all day, a feeling that luck was down on him, just like always . . . the real luck, luck when you really needed it. Then he realized what he was doing to himself and he cursed his momentary weakness. Just like the Skipper said: Mike, you still got the big one left!

But the thought of trying again somehow depressed him, almost as if he were suddenly very tired. He wondered how much drive he had left in him. For sixteen years he had pushed his body and his spirit, trying with all his heart to get up this far. Now, it seemed to him, his entire effort was to be packed into one brief moment of time. One more pitch, maybe. It must be now . . . there's no more time . . . no more time.

Maybe it was too much to ask of a man.

At the plate, the batboy was holding his bat, waiting for him.

"Straighten it out, Mike," he said.

Sure, sure. . . . Stop the wind and straighten it out.

He ran his hand fondly along the end of the bat, subconsciously feeling for the dent. He wished he had more time.

"All right, Kutner," the ump called him. "Batter up!"

Mike played with his belt, trying to stall. His mind was cluttered with doubts and he wanted to shake them loose. Hitting is a state of mind, as important to coordination, timing, and power as a good pair of eyes. He was thinking of too many things now to be a hitter.

The jockeys found it timely to get back on him.

"Com' on Pop. Better get back up there before they dig you under!"

"Too bad, Baldy. . . . You shot yer wad on a foul ball!"

Somehow or other he was thinking of all the winter jobs he held over the years. He hated them all . . . gas station attendant, special delivery postman, road gangs . . . they amounted to nothing. Just wasting the winter to get to the spring. After all these years, the whole deal seemed like such a stupid waste.

"Back to the mines, Pop!" The jockeys again.

He was about to step in, and it backed him away. "Back to the mines." The words rattled around in his head like loose marbles. It made his head spin as he thought how close he was to it.

"Let's go, Kutner . . . play ball!" The ump was insistent.

Com' on, Mike. You gotta get up there. You gotta get up there and hit. Suddenly, he leaned over and picked up a tiny pebble. He told himself that unless he put it in his pocket he wouldn't hit. For a moment, he stood there, studying the pebble, debating with himself. It was a foolish superstition and he always rejected them. If you let yourself go, a million little things will deflect you, threaten you, strip you of your will to hit. He had seen guys who became slaves to their petty superstitions. Yet, something almost made him change. Compulsively, he threw the pebble away and stepped up to the plate.

They were ready for him:

"Yo, Pop. I heard you were in the war . . . which one?"

He moved his big bat around, trying to loosen the clothing on his shoulders. It didn't seem to set properly. He dug and redug his back foot in the corner of the box. He felt something about his position was different . . . some minute arrangement of his feet, or the balance of his body as he set himself. He watched the pitcher get his sign and his mind began an agonizing conjecture. Would he curve him again . . . half-speed? Would he waste one, or make him cut at something bad? Would he try to throw a hard one by him, under his chin . . . or low outside? It was hard not to guess. Don't guess, he told himself. That's suicide. You're still the hitter. Just be ready . . . be ready.

"They got a ball club back at the mines, Pop?"

He cocked his bat over his shoulder and was conscious of the wet pull of his shirt against him. He made a quick movement of his body to release it. It disturbed him, and he thought of stepping out of the box again. Then he remembered the pebble and wondered about superstitions: he regretted not saving it.

"When ya leave here, turn yer bat in for a pickax!"

Mike watched the pitcher nod and smile to the catcher. The windup was calm and kept him waiting. It seemed like an endless moment of time.

OK, Mike . . . guard that dish, he told himself. No fear . . . guard that dish. The ball spun lightly off the chucker's fingers and fluttered toward the plate. He saw it start to break, a slow curve breaking toward the outside corner. It didn't look good to him . . . but it might be. In a split second he had to decide, his own judgment shaken by his fear of the umpire. The delicate instrument of timing was shattered, and the balance of his power upset. He stepped toward the pitch and started his swing, lashing at the ball with half a will, half a prayer.

He didn't come near it . . . and the game was over.

For a moment he just stood there, wondering how sick he must have looked. He even tried to guess how far outside the plate the ball had passed.

Then the final thunderous roar of the crowd rose from the stands like a tidal wave, blasting into his ears the consequences of his failure. It was too much for him to take.

"No!" he screamed. "Goddamit . . . *no!*" And he beat the plate brutally with his bat, refusing to accept this.

He turned to face the pitcher's mound, swinging his bat like he was ready to hit again, demanding that the game go on.

"Throw the goddam ball!" he hollered savagely. "Throw the goddam ball!"

But their entire team had gathered around the pitcher, slapping his back, clutching and tearing at his triumph. They lifted him to their shoulders to cart him off the field. Mike watched them, letting their spirited laughter bite into him, as if it were aimed at him. He hated them now, the lucky sonovabitchin' pitcher, the lousy jockeys. . . . He stared at them, trying to smear them with his hatred, hoping to provoke one more derisive cat-call from them that might unleash his rage and goad him to attack them all. But they never saw him, nor even acknowledged his presence there, and he finally turned away from the plate for the long walk in.

He moved toward the bedlam of the stands now, and saw the screaming faces. A moment ago they were all yours . . . all yours, Mike. They were yelling for you. He looked into the dejection of his dugout and his naked failure came home to him. In a rage, he pulled his bat back, ready to fling it into the crowd, to scatter them and shut them up. He swallowed the top of his anger and held on.

In the stands behind the dugout, they were waiting for him, the harsh faces of the sadistic punks who wallowed in the luxury of a few last kicks at the guy who was down.

"Kutner . . . you stink!"

"You're a bum . . ."

"Oooooooohh . . . what a bum!"

He bristled at their hoots and sneering laughter and wondered how he could get through that gantlet. He gripped his bat tightly as he approached them, trying not to hurry his walk.

"Whatta star! . . . Where'd they pick you up?"

"Back to the minors, Kutner. . . ."

He felt their stale-beer spittle spray into his hot face, and he choked on his bubbling rage. A sloppy hand reached over and stole his cap from his head.

"You won't need this no more. . . ."

"Naaah . . . back to the bush leagues!"

He stopped on the bottom step and looked up at them. They taunted him, waving his cap at him, just out of reach. Inside him, suddenly the dam burst, and he flung himself toward the cap, over the dugout and into the stands. In a second he caught the terrified heckler and wrenched the cap from him. With his other hand he started smashing at him in a wild fury, bellowing hoarsely at the top of his lungs.

At once the crowd dispersed, scrambling over each other like scared chickens, and watched in their own terror. The ushers and cops came for him, four of them pulling him off, trying to hold him still, for his rage was only part spent.

They carried him down the steps again, into the dim corridors below the stands, and stood him hard against the wall, just outside the locker room.

"Take it easy, rookie . . ." a cop said, his hands tight on Mike's wrist.

Mike breathed heavily, and looked through the door at the ballplayers inside. He saw them, glum and silent on their benches, unlacing their shoes, quietly passing around smokes and cold beer. As he felt the heavy restraint of the cops, he saw Red Schalk among them, close to the door, and their eyes met. His arms were pinned to his side and he tried to wriggle loose.

"Easy, rookie . . . easy . . ." he heard again. "That ain't the way for a Major Leaguer to act. . . ."

The words knifed into him, twisting into his thoughts, and he lowered his eyes from the Redhead's. He wondered how in hell he'd ever be able to go through that door into the locker room again.

The Crab
(1920)

Gerald Beaumont

Gerald Beaumont (1886-1926) was born in California and lived in Hollywood. He was a popular writer of sports stories, which often appeared in *Redbook* magazine. Beaumont's collected stories on baseball, including "The Crab," were published in his book *Hearts and the Diamond* (1921). His popular collection of stories on horse racing is called *Riders Up!* (1922). Beaumont got many of the ideas for his stories from frequent visits to the racetracks and ballparks of southern California. He served as an official scorer for the old Pacific Coast League, which included his home team, the Hollywood Stars.

Not until the orchestra at 11:30, with a cheery flourish from the clarinets, launched into a quaint little melody, did the Crab's expression of disapproval change. Then his eyes sought a velvet curtain stretched across one end of the room. The drapery parted to admit a slip of a girl in a pink dress who came gliding down between the tables, slim white arms swaying in rhythm with her song. The Crab, obeying a sentiment he did not try to analyze, eyed her just as he had done every night for a week.

Those at the tables who had been there before nudged newcomers and whispered, "Watch her smile—it's the whole show."

It was a bright little tune—soothing as a lullaby. She sang the second chorus, looking straight at the Crab:

"Smile a-while, and I'll smile, too,
What's the good of feeling blue?
Watch my lips—I'll show you how:
That's the way—you're smiling now!"

A spotlight from the balcony darted across the room and encompassed the girl and the man to whom she was singing. Amid general laughter and applause, the Crab squirmed, reddened and achieved a sheepish grin.

The singer passed to other tables, the light playing on her yellow hair and accentuating the slimness of her figure.

"I'm the Smile Girl, so folks say—
Seems like smiles all come my way.
Want to smile? I'll show you how:
That's the way—you're smiling now."

People continued smiling and humming to the tuneful melody long after she had declined further encores. The Crab stared into the bottom of his empty glass. His face was still very red. Her fingers had brushed the Crab's sleeve as lightly as a butterfly's wing but he was exalted by the contact.

• • •

Coast League fans said of Bill Crowley that if he ever learned to moderate his crabbing, the majors would one day be bidding for the greatest third baseman in history. He was chain lightning on his feet and could hit around .290 in any company. Moreover, he had perfect baseball hands, an arm of steel, and the runner was yet to wear spikes who could scare him into exposing even a corner of the bag if the play was close.

But Bill was a crab by instinct, preference and past performances. He was hard-boiled in the dye of discontent, steeped in irritability—a consistent, chronic, quarrelsome crab, operating apparently with malice aforethought and intent to commit mischief.

Naturally the fans rode him. It is human nature to poke sticks at a crab and turn it over on its back. In time, a crustacean becomes imbued with the idea that it was born to be tormented, hence it moves around with its claws alert for pointed sticks. That was the way with Bill Crowley, third-sacker extraordinary, and kicker plenipotentiary to the court of Brick

McGovern, sorrel-topped manager of the Wolves. Looking for trouble, he found it everywhere.

At that, Bill the Crab was not without a certain justification. A third baseman has enough woes without being afflicted with boils on the back of his neck. Such ailments belong by the law of retribution to the outfield. The fact that little pink protuberances appeared every now and then due south from the Crab's collar button, where the afternoon sun could conveniently find them, was further proof that even Providence had joined in the general persecution.

No infielder or outfielder ever threw the ball right to the Crab. It was either too low, or too high, or too late, or on his "meat" hand. There wasn't a scorer on the circuit who knew the definition of a base hit. The only time the umpires were ever on top of the play was when Bill was the runner, and then they had their thumbs in the air before he even hit the dirt.

Under such circumstances there was nothing for the Crab to do but register his emphatic disapproval. This he invariably accomplished by slamming his glove on the ground and advancing on the umpire stiff-legged after the manner of a terrier approaching a strange dog. Had there been hair on the back of his neck, it would have bristled.

The arbiters of the diamond took no chances with the Crab. They waved five fingers at him when he took the first step, and held up both hands when he took the second. If that didn't hold him, they promptly bestowed the Order of the Tin Can by waving the right arm in the general direction of the shower baths. This meant in all a fine of twenty dollars and the familiar line in the sporting extras:

CROWLEY THROWN OUT FOR CRABBING

In the last game of the season, the Crab distinguished himself by clouting a home run in the first inning with the bases full, but before the contest was over he was led from the park by two policemen, having planted his cleats on the sensitive toes of Umpire Bull Feeney and thereby precipitated the worst riot of the year.

McGovern, astute pilot of a club which had won two pennants, clung to the Crab in the forlorn hope that time and patience might work one of those miracles of the diamond which are within the memory of most veteran managers.

Had anyone told the red-headed campaigner that he would yet live to see the day when the Crab would be a spineless thing of milk and water, pulling away from a runner's spikes, flinching under the taunts of the bleachers, accepting meekly the adverse decisions of the men in blue, he would have grinned tolerantly. The Crab might mellow a little with advancing years, but lose his fighting spirit? Not in this world!

• • •

It was in the spring of the following year when the team came straggling into camp for the annual conditioning process, and all but the Crab and one or two others had reported, that the Wolves were subjected to a severe jolt.

Rube Ferguson who had an eye for the dramatic waited until the gang was at morning batting practice. Then he broke the astounding news.

"The Crab's got himself a wife."

The Wolves laughed.

"*All* right," said Ferguson, "*all* right—you fellows know it all; I'm a liar. The Crab's been married three months. I stood up with him. What's more, you fellows know the girl."

He took advantage of the general paralysis that followed this announcement to sneak up to the plate out of turn. He was still in there swinging when they came to life and rushed him. News is news, but a man's turn at bat, especially after an idle winter, is an inalienable right. Rube clung to his club.

"Three more cuts at the old apple," he bargained, "and I tell you who she is."

They fell back grumbling. Ferguson's last drive screamed into left field and whacked against the fence. Grinning contentedly he surrendered his bat and took his place at the end of the waiting line.

"Not so bad—I could have gone into third on that baby standing up. Trouble with you fellows is you're growing old. Now I—"

Brick McGovern raised a club menacingly.

"Who'd the Crab marry?"

"Keep your shirt on," advised Ferguson. "I'm coming to that. It was the blonde at Steve's place."

"Not the Smile Girl?" The quick objection sprang from a dozen lips. "Not the little queen who sings—not the entertainer?"

Ferguson beamed happily. He had his sensation.

"You said it," he told them. "The Smile Girl is now Mrs. Crab. She married Bill because the whole world was picking on him and it wasn't right. Ain't that a dame for you?"

They were inexpressibly shocked. The Smile Girl—daintiest wisp of cheer in the city—married to the Crab—surliest lump of gloom in baseball. The thing seemed incredible and yet—that was just the sort of girl she was—gravitating toward anyone who was in distress. They swore in awed undertones.

"What a bonehead play," sighed Boots Purnell, "what a Joe McGee! Imagine *any*one, let alone the Smile Girl, trying to live with the Crab! Give her an error—oh, give her six!" He made his sorrowful way to the plate, moaning over the appalling blunder.

Rube Ferguson's rich tenor sounded the opening lines of the Smile Girl's own song:

"Smiling puts the blues to flight;
Smiling makes each wrong come right—"

They joined mechanically in the chorus but they did not smile.

Pee-wee Patterson, midget second baseman, expressed what was in every one's mind:

"If anyone can tame the Crab, it's Goldilocks—but I'm betting she slips him his release by June. I wonder will he bring her to camp with him?"

The Crab settled this point himself the following day by showing up—alone and unchastened. He invited no questions and they forbore to offer any. He was as truculent and peevish as ever. The food was the bunk; someone had the room that he was entitled to; the bushers were too thick for comfort; the weather was "hell," and the new trainer didn't know a "charley horse" from a last year's bunion.

"The Crab's going to have a good year," observed Pee-wee, "twenty bucks says she gives him the gate by the first of June. Who wants it?"

Rube Ferguson whistled thoughtfully.

"If Brick will advance it to me I'll see you," he hazarded. "Some Janes are bears for punishment and the Crab ain't so worse. He made her quit her job and he staked her to a set of furniture and a flat. My wife says they're stuck on one another."

Pee-wee snorted. "Flypaper wouldn't stick to Bill after the first ten minutes." He raised his voice a little in imitation of Bull Feeney addressing the grandstand: "Batt'ries for today's game," he croaked, "the Smile Girl and the Crab. Bon soir, bye-bye, good night."

The Rube grinned. "Sure is a rummy battery," he agreed ruefully, "but the bet stands." He departed in search of McGovern and a piece of the bankroll.

Those of the Wolves who had not already met the Smile Girl, and they were mostly the rookies, learned to know her in the final days of the training season when the Wolves sought their home grounds for the polishing-up process.

She was enough of a child to want to accompany the Crab to the ball park for even the morning workouts and to say pretty things to each one individually. The Crab accomplished the introductions awkwardly, but it was evident that he was very proud of her and that she was very much in love with him.

"Some guys have all the luck," lamented Boots Purnell. "If she ever benches the Crab, I'll be the first one to apply for his job."

At the opening game of the season, the Smile Girl's pink dress and picture hat were conspicuous in the front row of the grandstand just back of third base. Pink for happiness, she always said.

Rube Ferguson confided an important discovery to Brick McGovern and others between innings as they sat in the Wolf dugout.

"The Crab's keeping one eye on the batter and the other on his wife. I don't think he knows there's anybody else in the park. They've got a set of signals. Every time the Crab starts to splutter, she gives him the tip to lay off the rough stuff, and he chokes it back. Pee-wee, you lose!"

The diminutive second-sacker did not reply at once. He was searching wildly for his favorite stick. At length he found it and trotted off for his turn at the plate. He was back shortly, insisting loudly that the "last one was over his head."

"Now about the Crab," he confided to Rube, "everything's coming his way, get me? Wait until we hit the road for a while and the hot weather comes and the ace-in-the-hole boys get to working on him, then we'll see."

The Wolves, always a slow team to round to form because of the many veterans on the roster, trailed along in the second division and swung north in fifth place for their first extended road trip.

Gradually it became apparent to all that Pee-wee Patterson had called the turn on the Crab. He was plainly settling back into his old surly ways, snarling at the umpires, grumbling over the work of the pitchers, and demanding angrily that McGovern get someone behind the bat who didn't have a broken arm—this of Billy Hopper who could handcuff nine third basemen out of ten.

They were on the road four weeks and the Crab's batting average climbed steadily while his temper grew hourly worse. This was characteristic. He seemed able to vent considerable of his spite on the inoffensive leather. It was the nerves of his teammates that suffered.

"What did I tell you?" demanded Patterson, "now when we hit the home grounds next week—the Crab will get the panning of his life and the Smile Girl will break her heart over it. I tell you I'm calling the play!"

Brick McGovern and Rube Ferguson regarded their comrade-at-arms soberly. They felt that he spoke the truth.

"Well," commented Rube, "you can't bench a man that's hitting over .300 just to spare his wife's feelings." And with that understanding, the Crab was retained in the clean-up role.

• • •

Most ballplayers have a dislike for one or more cities on the circuit. The Crab's pet aversion was the St. Clair grounds. There, the huge double-decked grandstand, with its lower floor on a level with the infield itself and not forty feet from the foul lines, brought players and spectators into closer contact than was good for either. Back of the heavy screening and paralleling a well-worn path between the home plate and the dugout assigned to the home club, stretched "Sure Thing Row" where men who wagered money in downtown poolrooms before the game congregated like birds of prey to await the outcome.

"Sure Thing Row" ran to checked suits, diamonds and stacks of half dollars, the latter held lightly in one hand and riffled with the thumb and forefinger of the other. It broke no law of the land; it knew its rights and exercised every one of them.

"The Row" maintained a proprietary interest in the Crab. He was theirs by right of discovery. In him they recognized not only the strongest link in the Wolf defense but likewise the weakest. He was an unconscious instrument to be used or not as the odds might require. Now that the Crab was married, the problem was simplified.

It was in the third game of the series that Rube Ferguson, sitting beside Brick McGovern in the dugout while the Wolves were at bat, reported to his leader what was going on.

"The ace-in-the-hole boys are after the Crab. When he went up to bat just now they were whispering stuff to him about his wife—get me, Brick? They're handing him the laugh about the Smile Girl. He'll blow up before the inning's over."

McGovern nodded. His gnarled and sun-scorched hands opened and shut helplessly. "I know," he groaned, "I know—they used to hand it to me like that and if it hadn't been for my wife and kids I'd have done murder twenty times. There's no law against insulting a ballplayer. That goes with the price of admission. They'll not break the Crab's nerve but they'll get him thrown out. Ah!"

The gray-clad figures in the Wolf dugout sprang to their feet. The high-pitched yelp of the timber wolf pierced the clamor, followed by cries of "tear 'em, puppy!"

The Crab had lashed a terrific drive along the right-field foul line and was rounding first base in full stride.

McGovern tore for the coaching box with both arms raised, palms outward. Walker in right field had knocked the drive down. He had one of the best arms in the league.

"None out," yelled the Wolf leader, "two bags—play it safe! Back—go back!"

But the Crab had eyes or ears for no one. He was running wild, bent only on showing "Sure Thing Row" he was its master. Blind with rage and excitement he bore down on third base. The ball zipped into the hands of the waiting fielder in plenty of time. The Crab must have known he was out, but he arose from a cloud of dust, wildly denunciatory, and frantic under the jibs of the bleachers and the fox-faced gentry back of the screen.

In the old belligerent way, he stalked after Tim Cahill and grabbed the umpire by the arm.

"You—you—" he foamed.

McGovern dashed out on the diamond but the mischief was already done. Cahill knew his business and he stood for no breach of discipline. Freeing himself from the Crab's clutch, he jerked a thumb in the direction of the clubhouse in center field.

"You're through for the day," he snapped, "off the field or I'll nick you for a ten spot. Beat it!"

McGovern pulled his infielder away and shoved him in the direction indicated. "Don't be a fool, Dill," he advised, "you were out a mile."

The target for a storm of derisive hoots, the Crab made his way sullenly along the fence and into the clubhouse shadows. Not until he had vanished from sight did the last sibilant hiss die out.

McGovern walked back to the Wolves' pit and shot a quick glance at the Smile Girl sitting in her usual place just back of third. All around her, men were laughing at the Crab's discomfiture. She was smiling bravely but even at that distance he was certain that her chin was quivering.

"Sure Thing Row" settled back contentedly and winked. The Crab and his bludgeon had been eliminated from the crucial game of the series.

The Wolves lost by one run.

On the last day of June, just before the club left for another long swing around the circle, Rube Ferguson encountered little Patterson in front of the clubhouse. He drew the midget aside and handed him a twenty-dollar bill.

"Much obliged," acknowledged Pee-wee, "what's the idea?"

"The Crab's wife has left him."

"No!"

"Yes. She's been gone three days. She told my wife he came home and beefed because she was sewing something, and she said she could stand his crabbing about everything else but *that.*"

The second baseman looked incredulous.

"Seems like somebody's got their signals crossed, don't it?

The Rube shrugged. "What do women always sew? The money's yours."

The little infielder's eyes hardened. "I'm clean," he admitted. "I haven't got a red—but you put that twenty back in your pocket or I'll beat you to death."

Ferguson nodded his comprehension. "I feel that way about it, too. There's something likeable about the Crab but I've never found out what it is. Will he be better or worse now?"

"Does a Crab ever change?" asked Pee-wee.

During the next few weeks it seemed as though Patterson's question could admit of but one answer. The Crab drew if anything a little closer into his shell. He was more morose, more savage in the clubhouse and on the diamond. He snarled his refusals when they offered him the usual hand of poker up in Boots Parnell's hotel room. When they left the clubhouse in the afternoons, he disappeared and they did not see him until the next morning. They forbore to question him. The ballplayer's code of ethics does not include discussion of domestic averages. While he continued to hit and field as he was doing, he was entitled to behave off the diamond in any way he saw fit.

Not until August when the club was in third place and going like a whirlwind, did the Crab give any indication that he missed the slim little figure in the pink dress who used to blow him kisses from the grandstand.

Then, so gradually that they had difficulty in comprehending the process, something under the Crab's shell began to disintegrate.

It was his hitting—that infallible barometer to a ballplayer's condition, that fell off first. Not that the Crab didn't connect just as frequently as ever, but his swings lacked the old driving power. Outfielders who used to back against the fence when he came up, now moved forward and had no trouble getting under the ball. From fourth place in the batting order he was dropped to sixth and then seventh without result. His huge shoulders seemed devitalized.

Next it was his fielding. He fumbled ground balls that ordinarily would have given him no trouble. He was slow on his feet and erratic in his throwing.

Jiggs Peterson, guardian of the right-field pasture, called still another deficiency to the attention of the entire club one afternoon when, in a tight game with the Saints, a runner slid safely into third despite a perfect throw from deep right.

"I had that guy nailed by twenty feet," he complained to the Crab, "and you let him slide into the bag. What's the idea of taking the ball in back of the sack?"

The Crab's only reply was a mumbled, "You peg 'em right and I'll get 'em."

"Jiggs had called the turn," whispered Pee-wee, "the Crab is pulling away from the runner's spikes right along. I don't understand it."

"Nor I," Ferguson responded, "there was a time when he would have broken Jiggs in two for trying to call him like that."

The next day the Crab, seated beside his manager in the dugout, turned suddenly to McGovern.

"Brick—I can't find her—it's August and I can't find her."

McGovern masked his surprise. The Crab's eyes were bloodshot, the lines on his weather-beaten face sunk to unnatural depths. Several times McGovern opened his mouth but the right words did not occur to him.

"I can't find her," reiterated the Crab dully. "I lost her, and I can't find her."

McGovern scraped in the soft dirt with his cleats. He spoke as one man to another. "I'm sorry, Dill, I didn't know just how you felt about it."

The Crab contemplated the palm of a worn-out glove. The muscles of his face twitched.

"I thought it was doll clothes she was sewing, Brick—she's such a kid. Honest to God I thought it was doll's clothes. I never knew different until I read her note. Now you know why I *got* to find her."

The pilot of the four-time pennant winners was again bereft of speech. He nodded slowly.

"She left no address," continued the third baseman. "She thought I was crabbing at her because—" His voice cracked sharply.

The Wolves came trooping noisily in from across the diamond. Their sorrel-topped pilot threw an arm carelessly around the Crab's shoulders.

"The Smile Girl couldn't hold a grudge against anyone," he whispered, "you'll hear from her one of these days. Why, man, anyone could see she was nuts about you!"

The Crab's fingers closed on his leader's arm with a grip that made McGovern wince.

"You think so, Brick—on the level?"

"On the level, Bill."

That afternoon the Crab got two hits, the first he had negotiated in a week, but as the fifteenth of August approached, he slumped again, and McGovern benched him and made three unsuccessful attempts to bolster up the one weak spot in his infield. But good third basemen are not lying around loose in the middle of August. The Crab at his worst was better than the newcomers and McGovern put him back in the fray. Two of three major-league scouts who had been attracted by the Crab's hitting and who had lingered in the hope that he would emerge from his slump, packed their grips and went elsewhere. The third man was a product of the school of McGraw. He studied the Crab through half-closed eyelids and—stayed.

With seven weeks of the season still unplayed, the Wolves returned from a southern trip in second place. The fine lines of worry between McGovern's eyes deepened. He caught himself watching the apathetic figure of the Crab and praying that the third baseman would regain just a little of his old fighting spirit.

And then one afternoon just before the umpire called the Wolves and Tigers together for the opening game of the week, Rube Ferguson, idol of the right-field bleachers, tossed a number of neatly folded newspapers into the pit.

"Compliments of 'Pebble Pop,' champion groundkeeper of the world," he told them, "pipe the write-up they gave the old boy."

The Crab opened his paper listlessly, glanced over the tribute to the veteran caretaker, and permitted the pages to slip to the concrete floor of the dugout. He was in the act of thrusting the paper aside with his cleats, when his eye caught a single word in black-face type up near the top of the column on the reverse side of the sporting page. It was his own name. Hypnotically, he picked up the page and stared at it. The words that followed the black-faced capitals burned themselves into his brain.

A sharp ejaculation caused McGovern to look up. The Crab's teeth were chattering.

"What's wrong?"

"N-n-nothing," stammered the Crab. The paper rustled from his nerveless hands. He straightened up, looked around wildly and then walked up and out of the pit—straight as a chalk line to the exit back of first base. With the entire team watching him, open-mouthed, the Crab wrenched savagely at the gate. A special officer drew the bolt, and the third baseman disappeared into the crowd, uniform and all.

Pee-wee Patterson broke the silence.

"I knew it was coming. He's cuckoo. Somebody better follow him."

But Brick McGovern was scanning the paper that the third baseman had dropped.

"Cuckoo, nothing," he exclaimed, "the Crab has found his wife!"

They all saw it then—two lines of agate type that began: "CROWLEY—"

The paper was eight days old.

• • •

A sorrel-topped Irishman with a fighting face, but rather too generous about the middle for perfect condition, plodded up the steps of St. Joseph's Hospital at dusk. One hand grasped a bouquet of pink roses.

"Ah, yes," said the little woman in the office, "second floor of the Annex—Room 41."

McGovern located the room and tapped gently on the white door.

"Come in," chirped a voice.

The pilot of the Wolves turned the knob dubiously and peered into the room.

The Smile Girl was sitting up in bed. Her eyes were bright with the look that comes to a woman who has borne her mate his first man-child. She beckoned to McGovern and then held a pink finger to her lips.

"S-sh!" she whispered, "look!"

In an armchair facing the window and away from the door, McGovern made out a familiar figure, still in uniform. It was rocking gently back and forth, cleats tapping on the linoleum-covered floor, and as it rocked it sang most unmusically to a rose-colored bundle held awkwardly over one shoulder:

"Smile awhile—and I'll smile, too,
What's the good of feeling blue?
Watch my lips—I'll show you how:
That's the way—you're smiling now!"

McGovern blew his nose. The singing stopped abruptly.

"Honey," said the Smile Girl, "bring William Junior to me. You've had him for most an hour and I want to show him to Mr. McGovern."

The Crab's cleats click-clacked across the room. He held up the bundle for McGovern's inspection.

"I'd let you hold him, Brick," he confided, "but it's got to be done just a certain way. The nurse put me wise; see—you keep one hand back of the neck and shoulders, so you don't do no fumbling."

McGovern nodded. He deposited the roses on the bed and laid the tip of one pudgy finger ever so lightly on the cheek of the sleeping infant.

"Some kid," he marveled, "*some kid!*"

The Smile Girl emitted a cry of surprise. From an envelope attached to the roses she had extracted a hundred-dollar bill.

"What's that?" demanded the Crab crossly, "what you trying to put over, Brick? I haven't touched a bean of my salary for three months. I don't need—"

"Shut up!" admonished McGovern. "Can't I take an option on the little fellow's services if I want to? Look at those hands, Bill—ain't they made for an infielder—they're yours all over—he's got your eyes and your hair and—"

The baby squirmed and moved its hands restlessly. The lusty wail of a perfectly healthy and hungry man-cub brought a nurse hurrying into the room.

With obvious reluctance, Bill Crowley surrendered his possession. He brushed one hand hastily across his eyes.

"Darn little crab," he said huskily, "he *does* look like me just a little bit, *don't* he, Brick?"

• • •

Digger Grimes, base runner par excellence, flashed past first and second in an ever-widening circle and headed for third. He was well between the two bags when Pee-wee Patterson, crouched in short center, took the throw from his old and esteemed friend Rube Ferguson and with a single motion shot the ball, low and a trifle wide of the waiting figure at third.

It was the seventh inning of the last game of the season. Thirty thousand fans in bleachers and grandstand rose to their feet. The play was close, so close that men forgot to breathe. Twenty feet from the bag, the runner made his leap. Spikes flashed in the sunlight menacingly. The Digger was coming in at an angle opposite to the guardian of the bag—charging with his fangs bared!

At the same instant, a heavy-shouldered figure in the familiar uniform of the champion Wolves swept up the ball with one bare hand and flung himself headlong in the path of the plunging runner. The two figures thudded together—threshed a moment in a flurry of arms and legs and then were still.

With his cleats still six inches from the bag, Digger Grimes found himself pinned to the dirt under 180 pounds of inexorable bone and muscle.

Out from a cloud of dust, while the bleachers and grandstand rocked in a tempest of glee, came an indignant bellow:

"He's out—I tell you!—he ain't touched the bag yet—he's out!"

The Crab catapulted to his feet and advanced on Dan McLaughlin. The umpire turned mild blue eyes on the Wolf infielder.

"I called him out," he protested, "what do you want—a written notice?"

The Crab blinked a moment, and stalked back to his position. From under the visor of his cap he shot a swift glance at the crowded benches just back of third. A blur of pink and a smaller blur of blue showed up against the dark background of masculine fandom and told him all he wished to know.

The Crab's chest expanded, as is only proper when a man has got his two hits. Pounding the palm of his worn glove, he dug his cleats into the dirt and set himself for the next play.

"Come on," he called, "get the next man! Ump—it's too bad you only got one lung—can't call a play louder than a whisper, can you? Pipes all rusty, huh? Too bad!"

Over in the Wolf dugout, a red-headed manager who had seen his club climb into the lead in the closing days of the grueling struggle, smiled faintly and stared with unseeing eyes across the diamond. His fingers twisted a telegram that had come to him that morning from New York.

Ten thousand dollars cash and spring delivery is too tempting an offer for any minor-league manager to reject. But there would be a wide hole at third base next year, and Brick McGovern was already wondering how he would ever plug it.

Baseball in April (1990)

Gary Soto

This is the story of Mexican-American youngsters growing up with baseball, friendship, love, and disappointment in Fresno, California. These farmworker kids contrast culturally with more affluent Little Leaguers, but they share the same vulnerability and dreams. Author Gary Soto draws on his own experiences growing up poor and Latino in California's Central Valley. He is a prolific writer with numerous poems, novels, memoirs, and anthologies to his credit. *New and Select Poems* (1995) was a finalist for the National Book Award. A book for young readers is *Cesar Chavez: A Hero for Everyone* (2003), and a recent novel is *Accidental Love* (2006).

T he night before Michael and Jesse were to try out for the Little League team for the third year in a row, the two brothers sat in their bedroom listening to the radio, pounding their fists into their gloves, and talking about how they would bend to pick up grounders or wave off another player and make the pop-up catch. "This is the year," Michael said with the confidence of an older brother. He pretended to scoop up the ball and throw out a man racing to first. He pounded his glove, looked at Jesse, and asked, "How'd you like that?"

When they reached Romain playground the next day there were a hundred kids divided into lines by age group: nine, ten, and eleven. Michael and

Jesse stood in line, gloves hanging limp from their hands, and waited to have a large paper number pinned to their backs so that the field coaches would know who they were.

Jesse chewed his palm as he moved up the line. When his number was called he ran out onto the field to the sound of his black sneakers smacking against the clay. He looked at the kids still in line, then at Michael who yelled, "You can do it!" The first grounder, a three-bouncer, spun off his glove into center field. Another grounder cracked off the bat, and he scooped it up, but the ball rolled off his glove. Jesse stared at it before he picked it up and hurled it to first base. The next one he managed to pick up cleanly, but his throw made the first baseman leap into the air with an exaggerated grunt that made *him* look good. Three more balls were hit to Jesse, and he came up with one.

His number flapped like a broken wing as he ran off the field to sit in the bleachers and wait for Michael to trot onto the field.

Michael raced after the first grounder and threw it on the run. On the next grounder, he lowered himself to one knee and threw nonchalantly to first. As his number, a crooked seventeen, flapped on his back, he saw a coach make a mark on his clipboard.

Michael lunged at the next hit but missed, and it skidded into center field. He shaded his eyes after the next hit, a high pop-up, and when the ball came down he was there to slap it into his glove. His mouth grew fat from trying to hold back a smile. The coach made another mark on his clipboard.

When the next number was called, Michael jogged off the field with his head held high. He sat next to his brother, both dark and serious as they watched the other boys trot on and off the field.

Finally, the coaches told them to return after lunch for batting tryouts. Michael and Jesse ran home to eat a sandwich and talk about what to expect in the afternoon.

"Don't be scared," Michael said with his mouth full of ham sandwich, though he knew Jesse's batting was no good. He showed him how to stand. He spread his legs, worked his left foot into the carpet as if he were putting out a cigarette, and glared at where the ball would come from, twenty feet in front of him near the kitchen table. He swung an invisible bat, choked up on the handle, and swung again.

He turned to his younger brother. "Got it?"

Jesse said he thought he did and imitated Michael's swing until Michael said, "Yeah, you got it."

Jesse felt proud walking to the playground because the smaller kids were in awe of the paper number on his back. It was as if he were a soldier going off to war.

"Where you goin'?" asked Rosie, sister of Johnnie Serna, the playground bully. She had a large bag of sunflower seeds, and spat out a shell.

"Tryouts," Jesse said, barely looking at her as he kept stride with Michael.

At the diamond, Jesse once again grew nervous. He got into the line of nine-year-olds and waited for his turn at bat. Fathers clung to the fence, giving last-minute instructions to their kids.

By the time it was Jesse's turn, he was trembling and trying to catch Michael's eye for reassurance. He walked to the batter's box, tapped the bat on the plate—something he had seen many times on television—and waited. The first pitch was outside and over his head. The coach laughed.

He swung hard at the next pitch, spinning the ball foul. He tapped his bat again, kicked the dirt, and stepped into the batter's box. He swung at a low ball. Then he wound up and sliced the next ball foul to the edge of the infield grass, which surprised him because he didn't know he had the strength to send it that far.

Jesse was given ten pitches and got three hits, all of them grounders to the right side. One grounder kicked up in the face of a kid trying to field the ball. The kid tried to hang tough as he trotted off the field, head bowed, but Jesse knew tears were welling up in his eyes.

Jesse handed the bat to the next kid and went to sit in the bleachers to wait for the ten-year-olds to bat. He was feeling better than after that morning's fielding tryouts because he had gotten three hits. He also thought he looked strong standing at the plate, bat high over his shoulder.

Michael came up to the plate and hit the first pitch to third base. He sent the next pitch into left field. He talked to himself as he stood in the box, bouncing slightly before the next pitch, which he smacked into the outfield. The coach marked his clipboard.

After his ten hits, he jogged off the field and joined his brother in the bleaches. His mouth was fat again from holding back a smile. Jesse was jealous of his brother's athletic display. He thought to himself, Yeah, he'll make the team, and I'll just watch from the bleachers. He imagined Michael running home with a uniform under his arm while he walked home empty-handed.

They watched other kids come to the plate and whack, foul, chop, slice, dribble, and hook balls all over the field. When a foul ball bounced into the bleachers, Jesse got it. He weighed the ball in his palm, like a pound of bologna, and then hurled it back onto the field. An uninterested coach watched it roll by his feet.

After it was over, they were told to expect a phone call by the end of the week if they had made the team.

By Monday afternoon they were already anxious for the phone to ring. They slouched in the living room after school and watched "Double Dare" on TV. Every time Jesse went into the kitchen, he stole a glance at the telephone. Once, when no one was looking, he picked it up to see if it was working and heard a long buzz.

By Friday, when it was clear the call would never come, they went outside to the front yard to play catch and practice bunting.

"I should have made the team," Michael said as he made a stab at Jesse's bunt. Jesse agreed with him. If anyone should have made the team, it should have been his brother. He was the best one there.

They hit grounders to each other. A few popped off Jesse's chest, but most disappeared neatly into his glove. Why couldn't I do this last Saturday? he wondered. He grew angry at himself, then sad. They stopped playing and returned inside to watch "Double Dare."

Michael and Jesse didn't make Little League that year, but Pete, a friend from school, told them about a team of kids from their school that practiced at Hobo Park near downtown. After school Michael and Jesse raced to the park. They laid their bikes on the grass and took the field. Michael ran to the outfield, and Jesse took second base to practice grounders.

"Give me a baby roller," Danny Lopez, the third baseman, called. Jesse sidearmed a roller, which Danny picked up on the third bounce. "Good pickup," Jesse yelled. Danny looked pleased, slapping his glove against his pants as he hustled back to third.

Michael practiced catching pop-ups with Billy Reeves until Manuel, the coach, arrived in his pickup. Most of the kids ran to let him know they wanted to play first, to play second, to hit first, to hit third. Michael and Jesse were quiet and stood back from the racket.

Manuel pulled a duffel bag from the back of his pickup and walked over to the palm tree that served as a backstop. He dropped the bag with a grunt, clapped his hands, and told the kids to take the field.

The two brothers didn't move. When Pete told the coach that Michael and Jesse wanted to play, Jesse stiffened up and tried to look strong.

Because he was older, and wiser, Michael stood with his arms crossed over his chest.

"You guys are in the outfield," the coach shouted before turning to pull a bat and a ball from the bag.

Manuel was middle-aged, patient, and fatherly. He bent down on his haunches to talk to the kids, spoke softly and listened to what they had to say. He cooed "Good" when they made catches, even routine ones. The kids knew he was good to them because most of them didn't have fathers, or had fathers who were so beaten from hard work that they came home and fell asleep in front of the TV set.

The team practiced for two weeks before Manuel announced their first game.

"Who we playing?" asked Pete.

"The Red Caps," he answered. "West Fresno kids."

"What's our name?" two kids asked.

"The Hobos," the coach said, smiling.

In two weeks Jesse had gotten better. But Michael quit the team because he found a girlfriend, a slow walker who hugged her books against her chest while gazing dreamily into Michael's equally dazed face. What fools, Jesse thought as he rode off to practice.

Jesse was catcher and winced behind his mask when the batter swung, because he had no chest protector or shin guards. Balls skidded off his arms and chest, but he never let on that they hurt.

His batting, however, did not improve, and the team knew he was a sure out. Some of the older kids tried to give him tips: how to stand, follow through, and push his weight into the ball. Still, when he came up to bat, the outfielders moved in, like wolves moving in for the kill.

Before their first game, some of the team members met early at Hobo Park to talk about how they were going to whip the Red Caps and send them home crying to their mothers. Soon, others showed up to field grounders while they waited for the coach. When they spotted him, they ran to his pickup and climbed the sides. The coach stuck his head from the cab and warned them to be careful. He waited for a few minutes for the slow kids, and waved for them to get in the front with him. As the team drove slowly to the West Side, the wind running through their hair, they thought they looked pretty neat.

When they arrived, they leaped from the pickup and stood by the coach, who waved to the other coach as he hoisted his duffel bag onto his shoulder.

Jesse scanned the other team: most were Mexican like his team, but they had a few blacks.

The coach shook hands with the other coach. They talked quietly in Spanish, then roared with laughter and patted each other's shoulder. They turned around and furrowed their brows at the infield, which was muddy from a recent rain.

Jesse and Pete warmed up behind the backstop, throwing gently to each other and trying to stay calm. Jesse envied the Red Caps, who seemed bigger and scarier than his team and wore matching T-shirts and caps. His team wore jeans and mismatched T-shirts.

The Hobos batted first and scored one run on an error and a double to left field. Then the Red Caps batted and scored four runs on three errors. On the last one, Jesse stood in front of the plate, mask in hand, yelling, "I got a play! I got a play!" But the ball sailed over his head. By the time Jesse picked up the ball, the runner was already sitting on the bench, breathing hard and smiling. Jesse carried the ball to the pitcher.

He searched his face and saw that Elias was scared. "C'mon, you can do it," Jesse said, putting his arm around the pitcher's shoulder. He walked back to the plate. He was wearing a chest protector that reached almost to his knees and made him feel important.

The Red Caps failed to score any more that inning.

In their second turn at bat, the Hobos scored twice on a hit and an error that hurt the Red Caps' catcher. But by the sixth inning, the Red Caps were ahead, sixteen to nine.

The Hobos began arguing with each other. Their play was sloppy, nothing like the cool routines back at their own field. Fly balls to the outfield dropped at the feet of open-mouthed players. Grounders rolled slowly between their legs. Even the pitching stank.

"You *had* to mess up, *menso*," Danny Lopez shouted at the shortstop.

"Well, you didn't get a hit, and *I* did," the shortstop said, pointing to his chest.

From the dugout, the coach told them to be quiet when they started cussing.

Jesse came up to bat for the fourth time that afternoon with two men on and two outs. His teammates moaned because they were sure he was going to strike out or hit a pop-up. To make matters worse, the Red Caps had a new pitcher and he was throwing hard.

Jesse was almost as scared of the pitcher's fastball as he was of failing. The coach clung to the fence, cooing words of encouragement. His team yelled at Jesse to swing hard. Dig in, they shouted, and he dug in, bat held high over his shoulder. After two balls and a strike, the pitcher threw low and hard toward Jesse's thigh. Jesse stood still because he knew that was the only way he was going to get on base.

The ball hit with a thud, and he went down holding his leg and trying to hold back the tears. The coach ran from the dugout and bent over him, rubbing his leg. A few of the kids on his team came over to ask, "Does it hurt?" "Can I play catcher now?" and "Let me run for him, coach!"

Jesse rose and limped to first. The coach shooed the team back into the dugout and jogged to the coach's box at first. Although his leg hurt, Jesse was happy to be on base. He grinned, looked up, and adjusted his cap. So this is what it's like, he thought. He clapped his hands and encouraged the next batter, their lead-off man. "C'mon, baby, c'mon, you can do it!" The batter hit a high fly ball to deep center. While the outfielder backpedaled and made the catch, Jesse rounded second on his way to third, feeling wonderful to have gotten that far.

Hobo Park lost, nineteen to eleven, and went on to lose against the Red Caps four more times that season. The Hobos were stuck in a two-team league.

Jesse played until the league ended. Fewer and fewer of the players came to practice and the team began using girls to fill in the gaps. One day Manuel didn't show up with his duffel bag. On that day, it was clear to the four boys who remained that the baseball season was over. They threw the ball around, then got on their bikes and rode home. Jesse didn't show up the next day for practice. Instead he sat in front of the TV watching Superman bend iron bars.

He felt guilty though. He thought that one of the guys might have gone to practice and discovered no one there. If he had, he might have waited on the bench or, restless for something to do, he might have practiced pop-ups by throwing the ball into the air, calling, "I got it! I got it!" all by himself.

You Could Look It Up (1941)

James G. Thurber

James G. Thurber (1894-1961) was famous for his stories about people and dogs. Many of his stories appeared in *The New Yorker*, and his major literary works include *My Life and Hard Times* (1933), *The Middle-Aged Man on the Flying Trapeze* (1935), and *My World—and Welcome to It* (1942). The following story is a fine example of Thurber's talent for satirical humor and fantasy. His character Pearl du Monville is a midget who plays baseball. The story is particularly interesting because, ten years after it was written, fact followed fiction. On August 19, 1951, Bill Veeck, showman owner of the St. Louis Browns, sent Eddie Gaedel, standing forty-three inches tall and weighing sixty-five pounds, to bat in a game against the Detroit Tigers. Gaedel strode to the plate wearing number $1/8$. He walked on four straight pitches and was taken out for a pinch runner. Where do you suppose Veeck got the idea to use Eddie Gaedel? You could look it up.

I t all begun when we dropped down to C'lumbus, Ohio, from Pittsburgh to play an exhibition game on our way out to St. Louis. It was gettin' on into September, and though we'd been leadin' the league by six, seven games most of the season, we was now in first place by a margin you could a got it into the eye of a thimble, bein' only a half a game ahead of St. Louis. Our slump had given the boys the leapin' jumps, and they was like a bunch a old ladies at a lawn fete with a thunderstorm comin' up, runnin' around snarlin' at each other, eatin' bad and sleepin' worse, and battin' for a team average of maybe .186. Half the time nobody'd speak to nobody else, without it was to bawl 'em out.

Squawks Magrew was managin' the boys at the time, and he was darn near crazy. They called him "Squawks" 'cause when things was goin' bad he lost his voice, or perty near lost it, and squealed at you like a little girl you stepped on her doll or somethin'. He yelled at everybody and wouldn't listen to nobody, without maybe it was me. I'd been trainin' the boys for ten year, and he'd take more lip from me than from anybody else. He knowed I was smarter'n him, anyways, like you're goin' to hear.

This was thirty, thirty-one year ago; you could look it up, 'cause it was the same year C'lumbus decided to call itself the Arch City, on account of a lot of iron arches with electric-light bulbs into 'em which stretched across High Street. Thomas Albert Edison sent 'em a telegram, and they was speeches and maybe even President Taft opened the celebration by pushin' a button. It was a great week for the Buckeye capital, which was why they got us out there for this exhibition game.

Well, we just lose a double-header to Pittsburgh, 11 to 5 and 7 to 3, so we snarled all the way to C'lumbus, where we put up at the Chittaden Hotel, still snarlin'. Everybody was tetchy, and when Billy Klinger took a sock at Whitey Cott at breakfast, Whitey threw marmalade all over his face.

"Blind each other, whatta I care?" says Magrew. "You can't see nothin' anyways."

C'lumbus win the exhibition game, 3 to 2, whilst Magrew set in the dug-out, mutterin' and cursin' like a fourteen-year-old Scotty. He bad-mouthed everybody on the ball club and he bad-mouthed everybody offa the ball club, includin' the Wright brothers, who, he claimed, had yet to build a airship big enough for any of our boys to hit it with a ball bat.

"I wisht I was dead," he says to me. "I wisht I was in heaven with the angels."

I told him to pull hisself together, 'cause he was drivin' the boys crazy, the way he was goin' on, sulkin' and bad-mouthin' and whinin'. I was older'n he was and smarther'n he was, and he knowed it. I was ten times smarter'n he was about this Pearl du Monville, first time I ever laid eyes on the little guy, which was one of the saddest days of my life.

Now, most people name of Pearl is girls, but this Pearl du Monville was a man, if you could call a fella a man who was only thirty-four, thirty-five inches high. Pearl du Monville was a midget. He was part French and part

Hungarian, and maybe even part Bulgarian or somethin'. I can see him now, a sneer on his little pushed-in pan, swingin' a bamboo cane and smokin' a big cigar. He had a gray suit with a big black check into it, and he had a gray felt hat with one of them rainbow-colored hatbands onto it, like the young fellas wore in them days. He talked like he was talkin' into a tin can, but he didn't have no foreign accent. He might a been fifteen or he might a been a hundred, you couldn't tell. Pearl du Monville.

After the game with C'lumbus, Magrew headed straight for the Chittaden bar—the train for St. Louis wasn't goin' for three, four hours—and there he set, drinkin' rye and talkin' to this bartender.

"How I pity me, brother," Magrew was tellin' this bartender. "How I pity me." That was alwuz his favorite tune. So he was settin' there, tellin' this bartender how heartbreakin' it was to be manager of a bunch of blindfolded circus clowns, when up pops this Pearl du Monville outa nowheres.

It give Magrew the leapin' jumps. He thought at first maybe the DTs had come back on him; he claimed he'd had 'em once, and little guys had popped up all around him, wearin' red, white, and blue hats.

"Go on, now!" Magrew yells. "Get away from me!"

But the midget clumb up on a chair acrost the table from Magrew and says, "I seen that game today, Junior, and you ain't got no ball club. What you got there, Junior," he says, "is a side show."

"Whatta ya mean, 'Junior'?" says Magrew, touchin' the little guy to satisfy hisself he was real.

"Don't pay him no attention, mister," says the bartender. "Pearl calls everybody 'Junior,' 'cause it alwuz turns out he's a year older'n anybody else."

"Yeh?" says Magrew. "How old is he?"

"How old are you, Junior?" says the midget.

"Who, me? I'm fifty three," says Magrew.

"Well, I'm fifty-four," says the midget.

Magrew grins and asts him what he'll have, and that was the beginnin' of their beautiful friendship, if you don't care what you say.

Pearl du Monville stood up on his chair and waved his cane around and pretended like he was ballyhooin' for a circus. "Right this way, folks!" he yells. "Come on in and see the greatest collection of freaks in the world! See the armless pitchers, see the eyeless batters, see the infielders with five thumbs!" and on and on like that, feedin' Magrew gall and handin' him a laugh at the same time, you might say.

You could hear him and Pearl du Monville hootin' and hollerin' and singin' way up to the fourth floor of the Chittaden, where the boys was packin' up. When it come time to go to the station, you can imagine how disgusted we was when we crowded into the doorway of that bar and seen them two singin' and goin' on.

"Well, well, well," says Magrew, lookin' up and spottin' us. "Look who's here. . . . Clowns, this is Pearl du Monville, a monseer of the old, old school. . . . Don't shake hands with 'em, Pearl, 'cause their fingers is made of chalk and would bust right off in your paws," he says, and he starts guffawin' and Pearl starts titterin' and we stand there givin' 'em the iron eye, it bein' the lowest ebb a ball-club manager'd got hisself down to since the national pastime was started.

Then the midget begun givin' us the ballyhoo. "Come on in!" he says, wavin' his cane. "See the legless base runners, see the outfielders with the butter fingers, see the southpaw with the arm of a little chee-ild!"

Then him and Magrew begun to hoop and holler and nudge each other till you'd of thought this little guy was the funniest guy than even Charlie Chaplin. The fellas filed outa the bar without a word and went on up to the Union Depot, leavin' me to handle Magrew and his new-found crony.

Well, I got 'em outa there finely. I had to take the little guy along, 'cause Magrew had a holt onto him like a vise and I couldn't pry him loose.

"He's comin' along as masket," says Magrew, holdin' the midget in the crouch of his arm like a football. And come along he did, hollerin' and pro-testin' and beatin' at Magrew with his little fists.

"Cut it out, will ya, Junior?" the little guy kept whinin'. "Come on, leave a man loose, will ya, Junior?"

But Junior kept a holt onto him and begun yellin', "See the guys with the glass arm, see the guys with the cast-iron brains, see the fielders with the feet on their wrists!"

So it goes, right through the whole Union Depot, with people starin' and catcallin', and he don't put the midget down till he gets him through the gates.

"How'm I goin' to go along without no toothbrush?" the midget asts. "What'm I goin' to do without no other suit?" he says.

"Doc here," says Magrew, meanin' me—"doc here will look after you like you was his own son, won't you, doc?"

I give him the iron eye, and he finely got on the train and prob'ly went to sleep with his clothes on.

This left me alone with the midget. "Lookit," I says to him. "Why don't you go on home now? Come mornin', Magrew'll forget all about you. He'll prob'ly think you was somethin' he seen in a nightmare maybe. And he ain't goin' to laugh so easy in the mornin', neither," I says. "So why don't you go on home?"

"Nix," he says to me. "Skiddoo," he says, "twenty-three for you," and he tosses his cane up into the vestibule of the coach and clam'ers on up after it like a cat. So that's the way Pearl du Monville come to go to St. Louis with the ball club.

I seen 'em first at breakfast the next day, settin' opposite each other; the midget playin' "Turkey in the Straw" on the harmonium and Magrew starin' at his eggs and bacon like they was a uncooked bird with its feathers still on.

"Remember where you found this?" I says, jerkin' my thumb at the midget. "Or maybe you think they come with breakfast on these trains," I says, bein' a good hand at turnin' a sharp remark in them days.

The midget puts down the harmonium and turns on me. "Sneeze," he says; "your brains is dusty." Then he snaps a couple drops of water at me from a tumbler. "Drown," he says, tryin' to make his voice deep.

Now, both them cracks is Civil War cracks, but you'd of thought they was brand new and the funniest than any crack Magrew'd ever heard in his whole life. He started hoopin' and hollerin', and the midget started hoopin' and hollerin', so I walked on away and set down with Bugs Courtney and Hank Metters, payin' no attention to this weak-minded Damon and Phidias acrost the aisle.

Well, sir, the first game with St. Louis was rained out, and there we was facin' a double-header next day. Like maybe I told you, we lose the last three double-headers we play, makin' maybe twenty-five errors in the six games, which is all right for the intimates of a school for the blind, but is disgraceful for the world's champions. It was too wet to go to the zoo, and Magrew wouldn't let us go to the movies, 'cause they flickered so bad in them days. So we just set around, stewin' and frettin'.

One of the newspaper boys come over to take a pitture of Billy Klinger and Whitey Cott shakin' hands—this reporter'd heard about the fight—and whilst they was standin' there, toe to toe, shakin' hands, Billy give a back lunge and a jerk, and throwed Whitey over his shoulder into a corner of the room, like a sack a salt. Whitey come back at him with a chair, and Bethlehem broke loose in that there room. The camera was tromped to pieces like

a berry basket. When we finely got 'em pulled apart, I heard a laugh, and
there was Magrew and the midget standin' in the door and givin' us the
iron eye.

"Wrasslers," says Magrew, cold-like, "that's what I got for a ball club, Mr.
du Monville, wrasslers—and not very good wrasslers at that, you ast me."

"A man can't be good at everythin'," says Pearl, "but he oughta be good
at somethin'."

This sets Magrew guffawin' again, and away they go, the midget taggin'
along by his side like a hound dog and handin' him a fast line of so-called
comic cracks.

When we went out to face that battlin' St. Louis club in a double-header
the next afternoon, the boys was jumpy as tin toys with keys in their back. We
lose the first game, 7 to 2, and are trailin', 4 to 0, when the second game ain't
but ten minutes old. Magrew set there like a stone statue, speakin' to nobody.
Then, in their half a the fourth, somebody singled to center and knocked in
two more runs for St. Louis.

That made Magrew squawk. "I wisht one thing," he says. "I wisht I was
manager of a old ladies' sewin' circus 'stead of a ball club."

"You are, Junior, you are," says a familyer and disagreeable voice.

It was that Pearl du Monville again, poppin' up outa nowheres, swingin'
his bamboo cane and smokin' a cigar that's three sizes too big for his face. By
this time we'd finely got the other side out, and Hank Metters slithered a bat
acrost the ground, and the midget had to jump to keep both his ankles from
bein' broke.

I thought Magrew'd bust a blood vessel. "You hurt Pearl and I'll break
your neck!" he yelled.

Hank muttered somethin' and went on up to the plate and struck out.

We managed to get a couple runs acrost in our half a the sixth, but they
come back with three more in their half a the seventh, and this was too much
for Magrew.

"Come on, Pearl," he says. "We're gettin' outa here."

"Where you think you're goin'?" I ast him.

"To the lawyer's again," he says cryptly.

"I didn't know you'd been to the lawyer's once, yet," I says.

"Which that goes to show how much you don't know," he says.

With that, they was gone, and I didn't see 'em the rest of the day, nor
know what they was up to, which was a God's blessin'. We lose the nightcap,

9 to 3, and that puts us into second place plenty, and as low in our mind as a ball club can get.

The next day was a horrible day, like anybody that lived through it can tell you. Practice was just over and the St. Louis club was takin' the field, when I hears this strange sound from the stands. It sounds like the nervous whickerin' a horse gives when he smells somethin' funny on the wind. It was the fans ketchin' sight of Pearl du Monville, like you have prob'ly guessed. The midget had popped up onto the field all dressed up in a minacher club uniform, sox, cap, little letters sewed onto his chest, and all. He was swingin' a kid's bat and the only thing kept him from lookin' like a real ballplayer seen through the wrong end of a microscope was this cigar he was smokin'.

Bugs Courtney reached over and jerked it outa his mouth and throwed it away. "You're wearin' that suit on the playin' field," he says to him, severe as a judge. "You go insultin' it and I'll take you out to the zoo and feed you to the bears."

Pearl just blowed some smoke at him which he still has in his mouth.

Whilst Whitey was foulin' off four or five prior to strikin' out, I went on over to Magrew. "If I was as comic as you," I says, "I'd laugh myself to death," I says. "Is that any way to treat the uniform, makin' a mockery out of it?"

"It might surprise you to know I ain't makin' no mockery outa the uniform," says Magrew. "Pearl du Monville here has been made a bone-of-fida member of this so-called ball club. I fixed it up with the front office by long-distance phone."

"Yeh?" I says. "I can just hear Mr. Dillworth or Bart Jenkins agreein' to hire a midget for the ball club. I can just hear 'em." Mr. Dillworth was the owner of the club and Bart Jenkins was the secretary, and they never stood for no monkey business. "May I be so bold as to inquire," I says, "just what you told 'em?"

"I told 'em," he says, "I wanted to sign up a guy they ain't no pitcher in the league can strike him out."

"Uh-huh," I says, "and did you tell 'em what size of a man he is?"

"Never mind about that," he says. "I got papers on me, made out legal and proper, constitutin' one Pearl du Monville a bone-of-fida member of this former ball club. Maybe that'll shame them big babies into gettin' in there and swingin', knowin' I can replace any one of 'em with a midget, if I have a mind to. A St. Louis lawyer I seen twice tells me it's all legal and proper."

"A St. Louis lawyer would," I says, "seein' nothin' could make him happier that havin' you makin' a mockery outa this one-time baseball outfit," I says.

Well, sir, it'll all be there in the papers of thirty, thirty-one year ago, and you could look it up. The game went along without no scorin' for seven innings, and since they ain't nothin' much to watch but guys poppin' up or strikin' out, the fans pay most of their attention to the goin's-on of Pearl du Monville. He's out there in front a the dugout, turnin' handsprings, balancin' his bat on his chin, walkin' a imaginary line, and so on. The fans clapped and laughed at him, and he ate it up.

So it went up to the last a the eighth, nothin' to nothin', not more'n seven, eight hits all told, and no errors on neither side. Our pitcher gets the first two men out easy in the eighth. Then up come a fella name of Porter or Billings, or some such name, and he lammed one up against the tobacco sign for three bases. The next guy up slapped the first ball out into left for a base hit, and in come the fella from third for the only run of the ball game so far. The crowd yelled, the look a death come onto Magrew's face again, and even the midget quit his tomfoolin'. Their next man fouled out back a third, and we come up for our last bats like a bunch a schoolgirls steppin' into a pool of cold water. I was lower in my mind than I'd been since the day in nineteen-four when Chesbro throwed the wild pitch in the ninth inning with a man on third and lost the pennant for the Highlanders. I knowed something just as bad was goin' to happen, which shows I'm a clairvoyun, or was then.

When Gordy Mills hit out to second, I just closed my eyes. I opened 'em up again to see Dutch Muller standin' on second, dustin' off his pants, him havin' got his first hit in maybe twenty times to the plate. Next up was Harry Loesing, battin' for our pitcher, and he got a base on balls, walkin' on a fourth one you could a combed your hair with.

Then up come Whitey Cott, our lead-off man. He crotches down in what was prob'ly the most fearsome stanch in organized ball, but all he can do is pop out to short. That brung up Billy Klinger, with two down and a man on first and second. Billy took a cut at one you could a knocked a plug hat offa this here Carnera with it, but then he gets sense enough to wait 'em out, and finely he walks, too, fillin' the bases.

Yes, sir, there you are; the tyin' run on third and the winnin' run on second, first a the ninth, two men down, and Hank Metters comin' to the bat. Hank was built like a Pope-Hartford and he couldn't run no faster'n

President Taft, but he had five home runs to his credit for the season, and that wasn't bad in them days. Hank was still hittin' better'n anybody else on the ball club, and it was mighty heartenin', seein' him stridin' up toward the plate. But he never got there.

"Wait a minute!" yells Magrew, jumpin' to his feet. "I'm sendin' in a pinch hitter!" he yells.

You could a heard a bomb drop. When a ball-club manager says he's sendin' in a pinch hitter for the best batter on the club, you know and I know and everybody knows he's lost his holt.

"They're goin' to be sendin' the funny wagon for you, if you don't watch out," I says, grabbin' a holt of his arm.

But he pulled away and ran out toward the plate, yellin', "Du Monville battin' for Metters!"

All the fellas begun squawlin' at once, except Hank, and he just stood there starin' at Magrew like he'd gone crazy and was claimin' to be Ty Cobb's grandma or somethin'. Their pitcher stood out there with his hands on his hips and a disagreeable look on his face, and the plate umpire told Magrew to go on and get a batter up. Magrew told him again du Monville was battin' for Metters, and the St. Louis manager finely got the idea. It brung him outa his dugout, howlin' and bawlin' like he'd lost a female dog and her seven pups.

Magrew pushed the midget toward the plate and he says to him, he says, "Just stand up there and hold that bat on your shoulder. They ain't a man in the world can throw three strikes in there 'fore he throws four balls!" he says.

"I get it, Junior!" says the midget. "He'll walk me and force in the tyin' run!" And he starts on up to the plate as cocky as if he was Willie Keeler.

I don't need to tell you Bethlehem broke loose on that there ball field. The fans got onto their hind legs, yellin' and whistlin', and everybody on the field begun wavin' their arms and hollerin' and shovin'. The plate umpire stalked over to Magrew like a traffic cop, waggin' his jaw and pointin' his finger, and the St. Louis manager kept yellin' like his house was on fire. When Pearl got up to the plate and stood there, the pitcher slammed his glove down onto the ground and started stompin' on it, and they ain't nobody can blame him. He's just walked two normal-sized human bein's, and now here's a guy up to the plate they ain't more'n twenty inches between his knees and his shoulders.

The plate umpire called in the field umpire, and they talked a while, like a couple doctors seein' the bucolic plague or somethin' for the first time. Then the plate umpire come over to Magrew with his arms folded acrost his chest, and he told him to go on and get a batter up, or he'd forfeit the game to St. Louis. He pulled out his watch, but somebody batted it outa his hand in the scufflin', and I thought there'd be a free-for-all, with everybody yellin' and shovin' except Pearl du Monville, who stood up at the plate with his little bat on his shoulder, not movin' a muscle.

Then Magrew played his ace. I seen him pull some papers outa his pocket and show 'em to the plate umpire. The umpire begun lookin' at 'em like they was bills for somethin' he not only never bought it, he never even heard of it. The other umpire studied 'em like they was a death warren, and all this time the St. Louis manager and the fans and the players is yellin' and hollerin'.

Well, sir, they fought about him bein' a midget, and they fought about him usin' a kid's bat, and they fought about where'd he been all season. They was eight or nine rule books brung out and everybody was thumbin' through 'em, tryin' to find out what it says about midgets, but it don't say nothin' about midgets, 'cause this was somethin' never'd come up in the history of the game before, and nobody'd ever dreamed about it, even when they has nightmares. Maybe you can't send no midgets in to bat nowadays, 'cause the old game's changed a lot, mostly for the worst, but you could then, it turned out.

The plate umpire finely decided the contrack papers was all legal and proper, like Magrew said, so he waved the St. Louis players back to their places and he pointed his finger at their manager and told him to quit hollerin' and get on back in the dugout. The manager says the game is percedin' under protest, and the umpire bawls, "Play ball!" over 'n' above the yellin' and booin', him havin' a voice like a hog-caller.

The St. Louis pitcher picked up his glove and beat at it with his fist six or eight times, and then got set on the mound and studied the situation. The fans realized he was really goin' to pitch to the midget, and they went crazy, hoopin' and hollerin' louder'n ever, and throwin' pop bottles and hats and cushions down onto the field. It took five, ten minutes to get the fans quieted down again, whilst our fellas that was on base set down on the bags and waited. And Pearl du Monville kept standin' up there with the bat on his shoulder, like he'd been told to.

So the pitcher starts studyin' the setup again, and you got to admit it was the strangest setup in a ball game since the players cut off their beards and begun wearin' gloves. I wisht I could call the pitcher's name—it wasn't old Barney Pelty nor Nig Jack Powell nor Harry Howell. He was a big right-hander, but I can't call his name. You could look it up. Even in a crotchin' position, the ketcher towers over the midget like the Washington Monument.

The plate umpire tries standin' on his tiptoes, then he tries crotchin' down, and he finely gets hisself into a stanch nobody'd ever seen on a ball field before, kinda squattin' down on his hanches.

Well, the pitcher is sore as a old buggy horse in fly time. He slams in the first pitch, hard and wild, and maybe two foot higher'n the midget's head.

"Ball one!" hollers the umpire over 'n' above the racket, 'cause everybody is yellin' worsten ever.

The ketcher goes on out toward the mound and talks to the pitcher and hands him the ball. This time the big right-hander tries a undershoot, and it comes in a little closer, maybe no higher'n a foot, foot and a half above Pearl's head. It would a been a strike with a human bein' in there, but the umpire's got to call it, and he does.

"Ball two!" he bellers.

The ketcher walks on out to the mound again, and the whole infield comes over and gives advice to the pitcher about what they'd do in a case like this, with two balls and no strikes on a batter that oughta be in a bottle of alcohol 'stead of up there at the plate in a big-league game between the teams that is fightin' for first place.

For the third pitch, the pitcher stands there flat-footed and tosses up the ball like he's playin' ketch with a little girl.

Pearl stands there motionless as a hitchin' post, and the ball comes in big and slow and high—high for Pearl, that is, it bein' about on a level with his eyes, or a little higher'n a grown man's knees.

They ain't nothin' else for the umpire to do, so he calls, "Ball three!"

Everybody is onto their feet, hoopin' and hollerin', as the pitcher sets to throw ball four. The St. Louis manager is makin' signs and faces like he was a contorturer, and the infield is givin' the pitcher some more advice about what to do this time. Our boys who was on base stick right onto the bag, runnin' no risk of bein' nipped for the last out.

Well, the pitcher decides to give him a toss again, seein' he come closer with that than with a fast ball. They ain't nobody ever seen a slower ball throwed. It come in big as a balloon and slower'n any ball ever throwed before in the major leagues. It come right in over the plate in front of Pearl's chest, lookin' prob'ly big as a full moon to Pearl. They ain't never been a minute like the minute that followed since the United States was founded by the Pilgrim grandfathers.

Pearl du Monville took a cut at that ball, and he hit it! Magrew give a groan like a poleaxed steer as the ball rolls out in front a the plate into fair territory.

"Fair ball!" yells the umpire, and the midget starts runnin' for first, still carryin' that little bat, and makin' maybe ninety foot an hour. Bethlehem breaks loose on that ball field and in them stands. They ain't never been nothin' like it since creation was begun.

The ball's rollin' slow, on down toward third, goin' maybe eight, ten foot. The infield comes in fast and our boys break from their bases like hares in a brush fire. Everybody is standin' up, yellin' and hollerin', and Magrew is tearin' his hair outa his head, and the midget is scamperin' for first with all the speed of one of them little dashhounds carryin' a satchel in his mouth.

The ketcher gets to the ball first, but he boots it on out past he pitcher's box, the pitcher fallin' on his face tryin' to stop it, the shortstop sprawlin' after it full length and zaggin' it on over toward the second baseman, whilst Muller is scorin' with the tyin' run and Loesing is roundin' third with the winnin' run. Ty Cobb could a made a three-bagger outa that bunt, with everybody fallin' over theirself tryin' to pick the ball up. But Pearl is still maybe fifteen, twenty feet from the bag, toddlin' like a baby and yeepin' like a trapped rabbit, when the second baseman finely gets a holt of that ball and slams it over to first. The first baseman ketches it and stomps on the bag, the base umpire waves Pearl out, and there goes your old ball game, the craziest ball game ever played in the history of the organized world.

Their players start runnin' in, and then I see Magrew. He starts after Pearl, runnin' faster'n any man ever run before. Pearl sees him comin' and runs behind the base umpire's legs and gets a holt onto 'em. Magrew comes up, pantin' and roarin', and him and the midget plays ring-around-a-rosy with the umpire, who keeps shovin' at Magrew with one hand and tryin' to slap the midget loose from his legs with the other.

Finely Magrew ketches the midget, who is still yeepin' like a stuck sheep. He gets holt of that little guy by both his ankles and starts whirlin' him round and round his head like Magrew was a hammer thrower and Pearl was the hammer. Nobody can stop him without gettin' their head knocked off, so everybody just stands there and yells. Then Magrew lets the midget fly. He flies on out toward second, high and fast, like a human home run, headed for the soap sign in center field.

Their shortstop tries to get to him, but he can't make it, and I knowed the little fella was goin' to bust to pieces like a dollar watch on a asphalt street when he hit the ground. But it so happens their center fielder is just crossin' second, and he starts runnin' back, tryin' to get under the midget, who had took to spiralin' like a football 'stead of turnin' head over foot, which give him more speed and more distance.

I know you never seen a midget ketched, and you prob'ly never even seen one throwed. To ketch a midget that's been throwed by a heavy-muscled man and is flyin' through the air, you got to run under him and with him and pull your hands and arms back and down when you ketch him, to break the compact of his body, or you'll bust him in two like a matchstick. I seen Bill Lange and Willie Keeler and Tris Speaker make some wonderful ketches in my day, but I never seen nothin' like that center fielder. He goes back and back and still further back and he pulls that midget down outa the air like he was liftin' a sleepin' baby from a cradle. They wasn't a bruise onto him, only his face was the color of cat's meat and he ain't got no air in his chest. In his excitement, the base umpire, who was runnin' back with the center fielder when he ketched Pearl, yells, "Out!" and that give hysteries to the Bethlehem which was ragin' like Niagry on that ball field.

Everybody was hoopin' and hollerin' and yellin' and runnin', with the fans swarmin' onto the field, and the cops tryin' to keep order, and some guys laughin' and some of the women fans cryin', and six or eight of us holdin' onto Magrew to keep him from gettin' at that midget and finishin' him off. Some of the fans picks up the St. Louis pitcher and the center fielder, and starts carryin' 'em around on their shoulders, and they was the craziest goin's-on knowed to the history of organized ball on this side of the 'Lantic Ocean.

I seen Pearl du Monville strugglin' in the arms of a lady fan with a ample bosom, who was laughin' and cryin' at the same time, and him beatin' at her with his little fists and bawlin' and yellin'. He clawed his way loose finely and disappeared in the forest of legs which made that ball field look like it was Coney Island on a hot summer's day.

That was the last I ever seen of Pearl du Monville. I never seen hide nor hair of him from that day to this, and neither did nobody else. He just vanished into the thin of the air, as the fella says. He was ketched for the final out of the ball game and that was the end of him, just like it was the end of the ball game, you might say, and also the end of our losin' streak, like I'm goin' to tell you.

That night we piled onto a train for Chicago, but we wasn't snarlin' and snappin' any more. No, sir, the ice was finely broke and a new spirit come into that ball club. The old zip come back with the disappearance of Pearl du Monville out back a second base. We got to laughin' and talkin' and kiddin' together, and 'fore long Magrew was laughin' with us. He got a human look onto his pan again, and he quit whinin' and complainin' and wishtin' he was in heaven with the angels.

Well, sir, we wiped up that Chicago series, winnin' all four games, and makin' seventeen hits in one of 'em. Funny thing was, St. Louis was so shook up by that last game with us, they never did hit their stride again. Their center fielder took to misjudgin' everything that come his way, and the rest a the fellas followed suit, the way a club'll do when one guy blows up.

'Fore we left Chicago, I and some of the fellas went out and bought a pair of them little baby shoes, which we had 'em golded over and give 'em to Magrew for a souvenir, and he took it all in good spirit. Whitey Cott and Billy Klinger made up and was fast friends again, and we hit our home lot like a ton of dynamite and they was nothin' could stop us from then on.

I don't recollect things as clear as I did thirty, forty year ago. I can't read no fine print no more, and the only person I got to check with on the golden days of the national pastime, as the fella says, is my friend, old Milt Kline, over in Springfield, and his mind ain't as strong as it once was.

He gets Rube Waddell mixed up with Rube Marquard, for one thing, and anybody does that oughta be put away where he won't bother nobody. So I can't tell you the exact margin we win the pennant by. Maybe it was two and a half games, or maybe it was three and a half. But it'll all be there in the newspapers and record books of thirty, thirty-one year ago and, like I was sayin', you could look it up.

Smoke (1990)

Michael Chabon

Michael Chabon was born in 1963 in New York City and now lives in Berkeley, California. Chabon's gifts as a writer first came to light in *The Mysteries of Pittsburgh* (1988), a novel about a summer in the life of a gangster's son who is coming to grips with his identity. In 2001, Chabon won the Pulitzer Prize for *The Amazing Adventures of Kavalier and Clay* (2000); he recently published the nonfiction book *Manhood for Amateurs: The Pleasures and Regrets of a Husband, Father, and Son* (2009). His second book, *A Model World and Other Stories* (1991), includes the baseball story "Smoke," which was originally published in *The New Yorker*. "Smoke" is about a pitcher of diminishing skills who attends the funeral of his catcher.

I t was a frigid May morning at the end of a freak cold snap that killed all the daffodils on the lawns of the churches of Pittsburgh. Matt Magee sat in the front seat of his old red Metropolitan, struggling with the French cuffs of his best shirt. This was a deliberate and calm struggle. He did not relish the prospect of Drinkwater's funeral, and he was in no hurry to go in. He had already sat and fiddled and listened to the radio and rubbed lovingly at his left shoulder for ten minutes in the parking lot of St. Stephen's, watching the other mourners and the media arrive. Magee was not all that young anymore, and it seemed to him that he had been to a lot of funerals.

On the evening that Eli Drinkwater wrecked his Fleetwood out on Mt. Nebo Road, Magee had been sent down to Buffalo after losing his third consecutive start, in the second inning, when he got a fastball up to a good right-handed hitter with the bases loaded and nobody out. He'd walked two batters and hit a third on the elbow, and then he had thrown the bad pitch after shaking off Drinkwater's sign for a slider, because he was so nervous about walking in a run.

Eli Drinkwater had been a scholarly catcher, a redoubtable batsman, and a kind, affectionate person, but as Magee lost his stuff their friendship had deteriorated into the occasional beer at the Post Tavern and terse expressions of pity and shame. Little Coleman Drinkwater was Magee's godson, but he hadn't seen the boy in nearly four years. It was the necessity of encountering Drinkwater's widow and son at the funeral, along with his erstwhile teammates, that kept Magee hunched over behind the wheel of his car in an empty corner of the church parking lot, rolling his cuffs and unrolling them, as the car filled with the varied exhalations of his body. For eleven and a half hours now, he'd been working on a quart of Teacher's. He was not attempting to get roaring drunk, or to assuage his professional disgrace and the sorrow of Drinkwater's death, but with care and a method to poison himself. It was not only from Drinkwater that he had drifted apart in recent years; he seemed to have simply drifted apart, like a puff of breath. He was five years past his best season, and his light was on the verge of winking out.

At last Magee started to shiver in the cold. He fastened his pink tourmaline cufflinks, turned off the radio, and climbed out of the car. He was nearly six feet five, and it always gave other people a good deal of pleasure to watch him unfold himself out of the tiny Metropolitan. According to the settlement of his divorce from his wife, Elaine, he had ended up with it, even though it had been hers before. Elaine had ended up with everything else. Thanks to a bad investment Magee had made in an ill-fated chain of baseball-themed, combination laundromat-and-crabhouses, this consisted of less than seventy-one thousand dollars, a king-size mobile home in Monroeville with a dish and a Jacuzzi bathtub, and a five-year-old Shar-Pei with colitis. Magee retrieved his sober charcoal suit jacket and navy tie from the minute rear bench of the Metropolitan and slowly knotted the necktie. The tie had white clocks on it, and the suit was flecked with a paler gray. He had lost his overcoat—a Hart Schaffner & Marx—on the flight down to Florida that spring, and had hoped he wouldn't be needing one again. Just before Magee slammed the car door, he paused a moment to study his two small suitcases, side by side on the passenger seat, and allowed himself to imagine carrying them to any one of a thousand destinations other than Buffalo, New York. Then he checked his hair in the window, patted it in two places, and headed across the parking lot toward the handsome stone church.

It was warm inside St. Stephen's, and there was a wan smell of woollens and paperwhites and old furniture polish. Magee took up a place behind the last row of pews, over by the far wall, among some reporters he knew well enough to hope that they would not be embarrassed to see him. The arrangements for the funeral had been made without fanfare, and although the church was filled from front to back, there were still not as many people as Magee had expected. The minister, a handsome old man in a gilded chasuble, murmured out over the scattered heads of Drinkwater's family and teammates. There was to be a memorial ceremony later in the week which ought to pack them in. By then the newspaper eulogies would have worked their way past shock and fond anecdote and begun to put the numbers together, and people would see what they had lost. Drinkwater had led the league in home runs the past two years, and his on-base average over that period was 415. He had walked three times as often as he struck out, and had last year broken the season record for bases stolen by a catcher—not that this had been all that difficult. The lifetime won-lost percentage for games he had caught, which to Magee's mind was the most important statistic of all, was close to .600; had he not been required to catch most of the fifty-odd games Magee had lost during that period, it would have been even better. Drinkwater had been cut down in his prime, all right. And that was what the numbers would show.

"Too bad it couldn't have been you instead of him," said a gravelly female voice at his ear. He turned, startled at hearing his own thought echoed aloud. It was Beryl Zmuda, in a fur coat, and she was only kidding, in her gravelly way. Beryl was a sports columnist for the Erie morning paper, and she had known Magee ever since Magee had come up in that city, with the Cardinals organization. A laudatory article by Beryl, written after Magee's first professional shutout, had gotten things rolling for him eleven years before. In that game Magee had struck out nine batters in a row and made the last out himself by bare-handing a line drive. No one was more disappointed by what had become of Magee's career than Beryl Zmuda.

"Hey, Ber," said Magee in a whisper. "When do I get to go to your funeral?"

"It was last year. You missed it." She did not trouble to whisper. She wore a myrtle-green hat with a heron feather which he had seen many times before. "You look terrible. But as usual that's a lovely suit."

"Thanks."

They shook hands, and then Magee bent down to kiss her. She sniffled and leaned forward to accept his kiss. Her pointed nose was still red from the cold, and he found her cheeks a little wet. The sable coat felt delightful and smelled both of warm fur and of Quelques Fleurs, and he had to force himself to let go of her. They had slept together for two months during the minor-league season of 1979, and Magee still held a fond regard for her. Her uncle had been a wartime pitcher for the St. Louis Browns; she knew baseball, especially pitchers, and she could write a nice line. Because of her name, she favored the color green, and under the coat her funeral suit was a worn gabardine the somber hue of winter seawater.

"What a shame it is," he said, wiping at his own eyes. Magee was a sucker for weeping women, and lachrymose when he had been drinking.

"He had a great April," said Beryl. Her Pittsburgh accent was flat and angular. She had fifteen years on Magee, and it was starting to tell. Her hair, blond as an ashwood bat, was entirely the product of technology now, and her face was looking papery and translucent and pinched at the corners. But she still had nice legs, with the pomaceous calves of a Pittsburgh girl. She had been raised on the steep staircases of Mt. Washington.

"He did," said Magee. "Three-thirty-one with seven home runs and eighteen ribbies."

"Hey, how about you?" She looked him up and down as though he had just gotten out of the hospital. "How's the arm?"

He shrugged; the arm was fine. Magee had a problem with his mechanics. He had become balky and as wild as a loose fire hose. Although on the hill he felt the same as he had since the age of fourteen, jangling and irritable and clearheaded, some invisible element of his delivery had changed. The coaches felt that it was the fault of his right foot, which seemed to have grown half a shoe size in recent years. Whatever the cause, he could no longer find what Eli Drinkwater had called the wormhole. Drinkwater had picked up this term from Dr. Carl Sagan's television program. A pitched ball passing through the wormhole disappeared for an instant and then reappeared somewhere else entirely, at once right on target and nowhere near where it ought to be, halfway across the galaxy, right on the edge of the black. Magee's repeated, multiseasonal failure to find the wormhole had bred fear, and fear caution; he had undergone some horrendous shellings.

"It's fine," said Magee, rubbing his left shoulder. "I'm going up to Buffalo this afternoon. Right after this." He nodded in the general direction of the altar, before which sat the closed casket that held the body of Eli Drinkwater. It was a fancy black casket, whose size and finish and trim recalled those of the massive American automobiles its occupant had preferred.

The pastor finished his bit, and Gamble Wicklow, the Pittsburgh manager, rose to his feet and approached the pulpit. He was an eloquent speaker with a degree in law from Fordham—his sending down of Magee had been a masterpiece of regret and paternal solicitude—but he looked tired and elderly today. Magee could not make out what he was saying. Gamble had been sitting beside Roxille Drinkwater, in the foremost pew, and now there was a gap between Roxille and little Coleman. The sight of this gap was poignant, and Magee looked away.

"Will you look at that," said Beryl. She went up on tiptoe to get a clearer view.

"I can't," said Magee.

"Look how Roxille's looking at that casket."

The reporters on either side of them, saddened, serious as the occasion required, were still rapacious and insatiable. They turned toward the grieving widow with the simultaneity of starlings taking wing. There was indeed something odd in the face and the posture of Roxille Drinkwater. Roxille was a pretty woman, a little heavy. Her russet hair was pulled tightly against her head and tied at the back. She wore no veil, and the look in her eyes was angry and complicated, but Magee thought he recognized it. Her husband had blown away, out of her life, like an empty wrapper, like a cloud of smoke. She was wondering how she could ever have thought he was real. As Magee watched she began to rock a little in the pew, back and forth. It was hardly noticeable at first, but as Wicklow's voice rose to praise her dead husband for his constancy and steadiness, and to foretell the endurance of his presence in the game, Roxille's rocking gathered force, and Magee knew he would have to do something.

Once, on an airplane, Magee had seen Roxille lose it. It had been during a night flight from New York, where Drinkwater had gone to collect an award, to Pittsburgh, aboard a careering, rattling, moaning little two-propeller plane. Roxille had begun by rocking in her seat, rocking and staring into the darkness outside the window of the plane. She had finished by shrieking and praying aloud, and then slapping a stewardess who attempted to calm her down. Now the people sitting in the pews around Roxille exchanged worried looks. Joey Puppo, the GM, was frowning, and glancing frequently toward the reporters, who had begun to mutter and click their tongues. Magee saw that she intended, whether she knew it or not, to hurl herself across the gleaming black lid of the coffin.

"She won't do it," said Beryl, in a voice that just qualified as a whisper. She had little esteem for other women, in particular for baseball wives.

"This is a funeral," said a television sports reporter, a former outfielder named Leon Lamartine who once at Wrigley had knocked one of Magee's sliders—a high, hard one that was not quite hard enough—out onto Waveland Avenue, under a rosebush and into pictures that were shown on national TV. His tone seemed to imply not that decorum would prevent Roxille from doing something outrageous but that anything was possible at funerals.

"Hey, c'mon, you guys," said Magee. "Keep it down." But he cracked his knuckles and worked his shoulder blades a couple of times, just in case.

Gamble Wicklow was winding down now. His chin had settled into his chest, and he was commending the departed soul of Eli Drinkwater to the Man in charge of putting together the Great Roster in the Sky. Roxille licked her lips. Her eyelids fluttered. She reached out tentatively toward the stylish coffin. Three dozen cameras and recording devices turned upon her. Magee moved.

"Where you going, Matty?" said Beryl, whirling. "Oh, my. Oh, my."

". . . now that Eli Drinkwater has forever become, as I think we may truly say, All-Star," said Gamble Wicklow, putting a period to his elegy with a sad smile.

"I told you," Leon Lamartine said, pointing.

Magee had delayed too long—his timing was irrevocably off—and his initial smooth glide down the aisle toward the first pew became a two-way foot race as Gamble stepped down from the pulpit. Magee was forced to run while pretending that he was still walking, all the time trying to keep his head down and remain inconspicuous. The result was an unintentional but skilled approximation of the gait of Groucho Marx. Only the fact that Gamble and the next eulogist collided by the entrance to the chancel allowed Magee to occupy Gamble's place in the pew. Magee put his left arm around Roxille, as though to comfort her, and wrestled her back into her coat.

"Take it easy," said Magee in his softest voice.

When Gamble Wicklow saw that Magee had usurped his seat, he frowned, gave an odd little wave, then turned and trudged managerially up the aisle. His suit was of old tweed and fit him ill. The nave of St. Stephen's filled with rumor and alarm and a faint, funereal laughter.

"Magee. Oh, Magee. What in the hell am I going to do?" Roxille said quietly. Her voice was almost inaudible when she said the word "hell." Her eyes were bloodshot and lively. She was not really looking at Magee but around him, at her son, who had turned and clambered to his knees in the pew to see what was going on back there among the cameras. Coleman had grown to be a good-looking little boy, long-limbed and as dark as his father. His hair had been cut very short, and, according to the fashion, a design had been carved into the stubble at the side of his head; it looked like a couple of eyeballs.

Magee put his hand on Roxille's forearm. She had on an expensive-looking black knit dress with a black lace collar and noticeable gores. She smelled of Castile soap.

"I don't know, Roxie," he said. He blushed. He felt very out of place, here in the front row, and he was ashamed to have gone so long without visiting or speaking to her, but he was glad that he had kept her off national TV. "You'll get along."

Roxille shuddered and took a deep breath. She closed her wild eyes and then opened them carefully. The minister had regained the pulpit and managed, by dint of looking pale and disappointed, to quiet the murmuring. He then introduced the next eulogist, a writer from *Sports Illustrated*. This man had started out working at the same Erie newspaper as Beryl, and not all that long ago. He was talented and he had done well for himself. Beryl hated him, in a good-humored way, and this led Magee to wonder why he had not hated Eli Drinkwater, whose fortunes had begun to rise so soon after Magee lost sight of the wormhole. He looked at Drinkwater's coffin, now no more than a few feet away from him. The Teacher's had worn off, and all at once he felt incurably tired. It occurred to him that you could probably tell a joke whose punch line involved a choice between being dead and being outrighted to Buffalo. It didn't seem like much of a choice, but he supposed that Buffalo held a slight edge. On the other hand, at least Drinkwater didn't have to know that he had died.

He had the vague impression that something was disturbing his exhaustion and then realized that it was Coleman Drinkwater, pulling on his sleeve.

The little boy pointed at the coffin. He was watching it as though he had been told that it was going to perform a trick.

"Is my daddy in there?" he said, in a clear, thin, terribly normal voice.

Magee and Coleman looked at each other for what became several seconds. Magee, who had no children, searched for the correct answer. He wanted to say something that would be fair to Coleman and yet would not make him afraid. He wished that his head were clearer and that he were not so damn tired. He felt as though everyone in the church were waiting on his reply. His forehead grew damp and he opened his mouth, but he said nothing. Finally, helpless, he put an arm around Coleman's small shoulders, and turned back to the speaker in the pulpit. The little boy suffered his godfather's arm upon him, and as the funeral dragged on he even rested his head against Magee's rib cage. Presently he fell asleep.

After a while, Magee himself, who had been awake for some thirty-two hours, drifted into an easy sleep. He dreamed his usual dream, the one in which he had found his stuff again and was on the mound at Three Rivers throwing seven different kinds of smoke. The sunshine was fragrant and the grass brilliant. When he awoke, feeling refreshed, the funeral was over and the coffin had already been wheeled out. Beryl was standing in front of him, her arms folded, looking as she had once looked on bailing him out of the Erie County Prison. Magee smiled, rubbed his eyes, and then realized that Coleman and Roxille had gone. He spun around in time to see the little boy being towed by his mother out the front door of the church. Coleman smiled across the empty pews at Magee, who saw from this distance that the design shaved into the side of the little boy's head was not two eyeballs. It was Eli Drinkwater's uniform number, the double zero.

"Poor kid," said Beryl. "I heard what he asked you. God. I almost lost it."

"I know," said Magee, scratching his chin. He could not seem to remember what his reply had been, or if he had said anything at all.

"So," said Beryl, sitting down beside him and taking hold of his throwing hand. She began, with a firm, nursely touch, to massage it. The backs of her hands hadn't aged very much at all, and Magee, feeling nostalgic, watched them for a while as they worked him over. A soft lock of her platinum hair brushed against his cheek. "So. What are you going to do? Buffalo? You're really going to let them do that to you?"

"I want to pitch, Ber. I have to get my mechanics back. I think it'll be a little easier in Triple A."

Beryl tightened her grasp on his hand and looked at him. Her face was neither incredulous nor mocking; she only bit her lip and wrinkled the bridge of her nose. Beryl's nose, though small, could be expressive of great sadness.

"Magee," she said. "Matty. Maybe I'm wrong to even put this thought in your head. I know how hard you're trying, Matty, but—what if they're just gone, baby?" Her voice cracked sweetly as she said this. "Have you ever thought of that?"

Magee withdrew his pitching hand and flexed it a couple of times. He watched it with a puzzled expression, as though it were a new model, of uncertain capacity. Then he looked away from it, up toward the ceiling of the church, and tried, for the last time, to remember if he had answered Coleman Drinkwater, and what he had told him.

"Yes," he said to the empty choir.

One Throw
(1950)

W. C. Heinz

Originally published in *Collier's* magazine, W. C. Heinz's story "One Throw" is a wonderful morality play on the diamond. It's about a highly talented young shortstop who is stuck in the low minors playing for an unfeeling manager. What if he makes a bad throw to goad the manager into shoving him up to a higher league? Heinz (1915–2008) was the author of the highly acclaimed boxing novel, *The Professional* (1958), and published *What a Time It Was: The Best of W. C. Heinz on Sports* (2001).

I checked into a hotel called the Olympia, which is right on the main street and the only hotel in the town. After lunch I was hanging around the lobby, and I got to talking to the guy at the desk. I asked him if this wasn't the town where that kid named Maneri played ball.

"That's right," the guy said. "He's a pretty good ballplayer."

"He should be," I said. "I read that he was the new Phil Rizzuto."

"That's what they said," the guy said.

"What's the matter with him?" I said. "I mean if he's such a good ballplayer what's he doing in this league?"

"I don't know," the guy said. "I guess the Yankees know what they're doing."

"He's a nice kid," the guy said. "He plays good ball, but I feel sorry for him. He thought he'd be playing for the Yankees soon, and here he is in this town. You can see it's got him down."

"He lives here in this hotel?"

"That's right," the guy said. "Most of the older ballplayers stay in rooming houses, but Pete and a couple other kids live here."

He was leaning on the desk, talking to me and looking across the hotel lobby. He nodded his head. "This is a funny thing," he said. "Here he comes now."

The kid had come through the door from the street. He had on a light gray sport shirt and a pair of gray flannel slacks.

I could see why, when he showed up with the Yankees in spring training, he made them all think of Rizzuto. He isn't any bigger than Rizzuto, and he looks just like him.

"Hello, Nick," he said to the guy at the desk.

"Hello, Pete," the guy at the desk said. "How goes it today?"

"All right," the kid said, but you could see he was exaggerating.

"I'm sorry, Pete," the guy at the desk said, "but no mail today."

"That's all right," the kid said, turning and looking at me.

"Excuse me," the guy at the desk said, introducing us. "Pete, this is Mr. Franklin."

"Harry Franklin," I said.

"I'm glad to know you," the kid said, shaking my hand.

"I recognize you from your pictures," I said.

"Pete's a good ballplayer," the guy at the desk said.

"Not very," the kid said.

"Don't take his word for it, Mr. Franklin," the guy said.

"I'm a great ball fan," I said to the kid. "Do you people play tonight?"

"We play two games," the kid said.

"The first game's at six o'clock," the guy at the desk said. "They play pretty good ball."

"I'll be there," I said. "I used to play a little ball myself."

"You did?" the kid said.

"With Columbus," I said. "That's twenty years ago."

"Is that right?" the kid said. . . .

That's the way I got to talking with the kid. They had one of those pine-paneled taprooms in the basement of the hotel, and we went down there.

I had a couple and the kid had a Coke, and I told him a few stories and he turned out to be a real good listener.

"But what do you do now, Mr. Franklin?" he said after a while.

"I sell hardware," I said. "I can think of some things I'd like better, but I was going to ask you how you like playing in this league."

"Well," the kid said, "I suppose it's all right. I guess I've got no kick coming."

"Oh, I don't know," I said. "I understand you're too good for this league. What are they trying to do to you?"

"I don't know," the kid said. "I can't understand it."

"What's the trouble?"

"Well," the kid said, "I don't get along very well here. I mean there's nothing wrong with my playing. I'm hitting .365 right now. I lead the league in stolen bases. There's nobody can field with me, but who cares?"

"Who manages this ball club?"

"Al Dall," the kid said. "You remember, he played in the outfield for the Yankees for about four years."

"I remember."

"Maybe he is all right," the kid said, "but I don't get along with him. He's on my neck all the time."

"Well," I said, "that's the way they are in the minors sometimes. You have to remember the guy is looking out for himself and his ball club first. He's not worried about you."

"I know that," the kid said. "If I get the big hit or make the play he never says anything. The other night I tried to take second on a loose ball and I got caught in the run-down. He bawls me out in front of everybody. There's nothing I can do."

"Oh, I don't know," I said. "This is probably a guy who knows he's got a good thing in you, and he's looking to keep you around. You people lead the league, and that makes him look good. He doesn't want to lose you to Kansas City or the Yankees."

"That's what I mean," the kid said. "When the Yankees sent me down here they said, 'Don't worry. We'll keep an eye on you.' So Dall never sends a good report on me. Nobody ever comes down to look me over. What chance is there for a guy like Eddie Brown or somebody like that coming down to see me in this town?"

"You have to remember that Eddie Brown's the big shot," I said, "the great Yankee scout."

"Sure," the kid said. "I never even saw him, and I'll never see him in this place. I have an idea that if they ever ask Dall about me he keeps knocking me down."

"Why don't you go after Dall?" I said. "I had trouble like that once myself, but I figured out a way to get attention."

"You did?" the kid said.

"I threw a couple of balls over the first baseman's head," I said. "I threw a couple of games away, and that really got the manager sore. I was lousing up his ball club and his record. So what does he do? He blows the whistle on me, and what happens? That gets the brass curious, and they send down to see what's wrong."

"Is that so?" the kid said. "What happened?"

"Two weeks later," I said, "I was up with Columbus."

"Is that right?" the kid said.

"Sure," I said, egging him on. "What have you got to lose?"

"Nothing," the kid said. "I haven't got anything to lose."

"I'd try it," I said.

"I might try it," the kid said. "I might try it tonight if the spot comes up."

I could see from the way he said it that he was madder than he'd said. Maybe you think this is mean to steam a kid up like this, but I do some strange things.

"Take over," I said. "Don't let this guy ruin your career."

"I'll try it," the kid said. "Are you coming out to the park tonight?"

"I wouldn't miss it," I said. "This will be better than making out route sheets and sales orders."

It's not much ballpark in this town—old wooden bleachers and an old wooden fence and about four hundred people in the stands. The first game wasn't much either, with the home club winning something like 8 to 1.

The kid didn't have any hard chances, but I could see he was a ballplayer, with a double and a couple of walks and a lot of speed.

The second game was different, though. The other club got a couple of runs and then the home club picked up three runs in one, and they were in the top of the ninth with a 3–2 lead and two outs when the pitching began to fall apart and they loaded the bases.

I was trying to wish the ball down to the kid, just to see what he'd do with it, when the batter drives one on one big bounce to the kid's right.

The kid was off for it when the ball started. He made a backhand stab and grabbed it. He was deep now, and he turned in the air and fired. If it goes over the first baseman's head, it's two runs in and a panic—but it's the prettiest throw you'd want to see. It's right on a line, and the runner is out by a step, and it's the ball game.

• • •

I walked back to the hotel, thinking about the kid. I sat around the lobby until I saw him come in, and then I walked toward the elevator like I was going to my room, but so I'd meet him. And I could see he didn't want to talk.

"How about a Coke?" I said.

"No," he said. "Thanks, but I'm going to bed."

"Look," I said. "Forget it. You did the right thing. Have a Coke."

We were sitting in the taproom again. The kid wasn't saying anything.

"Why didn't you throw that ball away?" I said.

"I don't know," the kid said. "I had it in my mind before he hit it, but I couldn't."

"Why?"

"I don't know why."

"I know why," I said.

The kid didn't say anything. He just sat looking down.

"Do you know why you couldn't throw that ball away?" I said.

"No," the kid said.

"You couldn't throw that ball away," I said, "because you're going to be a major-league ballplayer someday."

The kid just looked at me. He had that same sore expression.

"Do you know why you're going to be a major-league ballplayer?" I said.

The kid was just looking down again, shaking his head. I never got more of a kick out of anything in my life.

"You're going to be a major-league ballplayer," I said, "because you couldn't throw that ball away, and because I'm not a hardware salesman and my name's not Harry Franklin."

"What do you mean?" the kid said.

"I mean," I explained to him, "that I tried to needle you into throwing that ball away because I'm Eddie Brown."

A Game of Catch (1953)

Richard Wilbur

This little jewel of a story is about three kids fooling around with baseball and poking fun at each other. Author Richard Wilbur taught at Harvard, Wellesley, and Wesleyan. When he turned ninety in 2011, the *Wall Street Journal* referred to him as "our finest living poet." Among his collections of poetry are *Things of the World* (1957), *Advice of a Prophet* (1961), and *The Catbird's Song* (1997). Wilbur has won many honors, including two Pulitzer Prizes and the National Book Award. He was poet laureate of the United States in 1987–1988.

Monk and Glennie were playing catch on the side lawn of the firehouse when Scho caught sight of them. They were good at it, for seventh-graders, as anyone could see right away. Monk, wearing a catcher's mitt, would lean easily sidewise and back, with one leg lifted and his throwing hand almost down to the grass, and then lob the white ball straight up into the sunlight. Glennie would shield his eyes with his left hand and, just as the ball fell past him, snag it with a little dart of his glove. Then he would burn the ball straight toward Monk, and it would spank into the round mitt and sit, like a still-life apple on a plate, until Monk flipped it over into his right hand and, with a negligent flick of his hanging arm, gave Glennie a fast grounder.

They were going on and on like that, in a kind of slow, mannered, luxurious dance in the sun, their faces perfectly blank and entranced, when Glennie noticed Scho dawdling along the other side of the street and called hello to him. Scho crossed over and stood at the front edge of the lawn, near an apple tree, watching.

"Got your glove?" asked Glennie after a time. Scho obviously hadn't.

"You could give me some easy grounders," said Scho. "But don't burn 'em."

"All right," Glennie said. He moved off a little, so the three of them formed a triangle, and they passed the ball around for about five minutes, Monk tossing easy grounders to Scho, Scho throwing to Glennie, and Glennie burning them in to Monk. After a while, Monk began to throw them back to Glennie once or twice before he let Scho have his grounder, and finally Monk gave Scho a fast, bumpy grounder that hopped over his shoulder and went into the brake on the other side of the street.

"Not so hard," called Scho as he ran across to get it.

"You should've had it," Monk shouted.

It took Scho a little while to find the ball among the ferns and dead leaves, and when he saw it, he grabbed it up and threw it toward Glennie. It struck the trunk of the apple tree, bounced back at the angle, and rolled steadily and stupidly onto the cement apron in front of the firehouse, where one of the trucks was parked. Scho ran hard and stopped it just before it rolled under the truck, and this time he carried it back to his former position on the lawn and threw it carefully to Glennie.

"I got an idea," said Glennie. "Why don't Monk and I catch for five minutes more, and then you can borrow one of our gloves?"

"That's all right with me," said Monk. He socked his fist into his mitt, and Glennie burned one in.

"All right," Scho said, and went over and sat under the tree. There in the shade he watched them resume their skillful play. They threw lazily fast or lazily slow—high, low, or wide—and always handsomely, their expression serene, changeless, and forgetful. When Monk missed a low backhand catch, he walked indolently after the ball and, hardly even looking, flung it sidearm for an imaginary put-out. After a good while of this, Scho said, "Isn't it five minutes yet?"

"One minute to go," said Monk, with a fraction of a grin.

Scho stood up and watched the ball slap back and forth for several minutes more, and then he turned and pulled himself up into the crotch of the tree.

"Where you going?" Monk asked.

"Just up the tree," Scho said.

"I guess he doesn't want to catch," said Monk.

Scho went up and up through the fat light-gray branches until they grew slender and bright and gave under him. He found a place where several supple branches were knit to make a dangerous chair, and sat there with his head coming out of the leaves into the sunlight. He could see the two other boys down below, the ball going back and forth between them as if they were bowling on the grass, and Glennie's crew-cut head looking like a sea urchin.

"I found a wonderful seat up here," Scho said loudly. "If I don't fall out." Monk and Glennie didn't look up or comment and so he began jouncing gently in his chair of branches and singing "Yo-ho, heave ho" in an exaggerated way.

"Do you know what, Monk?" he announced in a few moments. "I can make you two guys do anything I want. Catch that ball, Monk! Now you catch it, Glennie!"

"I was going to catch it anyway," Monk suddenly said. "You're not making anybody do anything when they're already going to do it anyway."

"I made you say what you just said," Scho replied joyfully.

"No, you didn't," said Monk, still throwing and catching but now less serenely absorbed in the game.

"That's what I wanted you to say," Scho said.

The ball bounded off the rim of Monk's mitt and plowed into a gladiolus bed beside the firehouse, and Monk ran to get it while Scho jounced in his treetop and sang, "I wanted you to miss that. Anything you do is what I wanted you to do."

"Let's quit for a minute," Glennie suggested.

"We might as well, until the peanut gallery shuts up," Monk said.

● ● ●

They went over and sat crosslegged in the shade of the tree. Scho looked down between his legs and saw them on the dim, spotty ground, saying nothing to one another. Glennie soon began abstractedly spinning his glove between his palms; Monk pulled his nose and stared out across the lawn.

"I want you to mess around with your nose, Monk," said Scho, giggling. Monk withdrew his hand from his face.

"Do that with your glove, Glennie," Scho persisted. "Monk, I want you to pull up hunks of grass and chew on it."

Glennie looked up and saw a self-delighted, intense face staring down at him through the leaves. "Stop being a dope and come down and we'll catch for a few minutes," he said.

Scho hesitated, and then said, in a tentatively mocking voice, "That's what I wanted you to say."

"All right, then, nuts to you," said Glennie.

"Why don't you keep quiet and stop bothering people?" Monk asked.

"I made you say that," Scho replied, softly.

"Shut up," Monk said.

"I made you say that, and I want you to be standing there looking sore. And I want you to climb up the tree. I'm making you do it!"

Monk was scrambling up through the branches, awkward in his haste, and getting snagged on twigs. His face was furious and foolish, and he kept telling Scho to shut up, shut up, shut up, while the other's exuberant and panicky voiced poured down upon his head.

"Now you shut up or you'll be sorry," Monk said, breathing hard as he reached up and threatened to shake the cradle of slight branches in which Scho was sitting.

"I *want*—" Scho screamed as he fell. Two lower branches broke his rustling, crackling fall, but he landed on his back with a deep thud and lay still, with a strangled look on his face and his eyes clenched. Glennie knelt down and asked breathlessly, "Are you O.K., Scho? Are you O.K.?" while Monk swung down through the leaves crying that honestly he hadn't even touched him, the crazy guy just let go. Scho doubled up and turned over on his right side, and now both the other boys knelt beside him, pawing at his shoulder and begging to know how he was.

Then Scho rolled away from them and sat partly up, still struggling to get his wind but forcing a species of smile on his face.

"I'm sorry, Scho," Monk said. "I didn't mean to make you fall."

Scho's voice came out weak and gravelly, in gasps. "I meant—you to do it. You   had to. You can't do—anything—unless I want—you to."

Glennie and Monk looked helplessly at him as he sat there, breathing a bit more easily and smiling fixedly, with tears in his eyes. Then they picked up their gloves and the ball, walked over to the street, and went slowly away down the sidewalk, Monk punching his fist into the mitt, Glennie juggling the ball between glove and hand.

From under the apple tree, Scho, still bent over a little for lack of breath, croaked after them in triumph and misery, "I want you to do whatever you're going to do for the whole rest of your life!"

A Pitcher Grows
Tired (1946)

Ashley Buck

Ashley Buck's poignant story "A Pitcher Grows Tired" was originally published in *Esquire* magazine. It's about an aging pitcher, still sharp but realizing his baseball mortality and hanging on to a fleeting career. This is a real nostalgia piece.

Rodkin walked across the field to the clubhouse. Burke and Peck were beside him. The crowd gathered close around and it was difficult to move. They pulled at Rodkin's uniform and slapped his back. Once he had liked that in a crowd. His heart liked it now, but their friendly grasping wore his body to exhaustion. They came to the edge of the field and walked under the bleachers and into the clubhouse. Inside there was an odor of sweat, dust, liniments and steam from the hot showers. Rodkin liked the smell: strong, human, earthly. It was a smell you never forgot and during the long winters when there was no baseball you got lonely for the smell and wanted to bring it back.

The players laughed and hurried to get dressed. They spoke of the splendid game Rodkin had pitched. He wondered if they knew how fortunate he had been. If Blake had known how tired he was he would not have been overanxious. He would have waited. Blake and others would not always be young and inexperienced.

Rodkin did not hurry. He sat down and slowly unlaced his shoes. His hands shook. All the strength was gone from them. Peck spoke to him, low, not wanting anyone else to hear: "You still got plenty of guts. You've always had the heart."

Rodkin kept his eyes on his shoes: "And I have plenty on the ball too."

"Yes," said Peck.

"I can put it anywhere Burke says."

"I know that."

There was a silence. Rodkin slipped off his shirt. The muscles in his shoulders throbbed like hearts. His eyes never met Peck's.

"You got the guts," said Peck. "I never knew you had so much. You looked like a million dollars in there."

"Yeah," said Rodkin.

"And you felt like two cents."

"I was all right."

"You were fine."

Peck moved away. There was a gnawing feeling in Rodkin's chest, a dull pressure at the back of his head.

The players left the building and only the trainer, Rodkin and Joie remained. Rodkin lay upon the table. He closed his eyes and let his body relax. It was a pleasant feeling that brought a soft ache to his stomach. He seemed to sink into nothingness.

"Take it easy," he told the trainer.

"I've taken it easy for years," said Hank.

Hank took more time to rub down Rodkin than he did anyone else. Rodkin knew this. The massaging hurt. Not a painful hurt; only the hurt of wanting to be hurt, wanting the body gently tortured for the relief that came afterward; for the fine feeling after the fingers left the sore spots.

"You and Burke won today's game with your heads," said Hank.

"Yes," said Rodkin.

"Your arm had nothing to do with it," said Hank.

"Burke's smart."

"You're smart too," said Hank. "You've always been smart."

"No one is smarter than Mr. Rodkin," said Joie.

Rodkin opened his eyes. He had forgotten Joie was there. "Forget the Mister, Joie. I'm only one of the players."

"No, you're not."

"You're anything but that," said Hank.

"Why do you call me Mister, Joie?"

"It's like I told you. There are ballplayers you call by their first names, ball players you call by nicknames and then there are the ones you call Mister. You couldn't call them anything else."

"And I'm a Mister?"

"Yes."

"If you had known Ty Cobb, what would he have been?"

"Mister Cobb."

"He was the very best, Joie. There's never been a player as great."

"You're as great a pitcher as he was an outfielder."

A strange look passed between Rodkin and Hank. Rodkin closed his eyes and turned his head away from Joie. He spoke softly: "Thanks, Joie. That's the nicest thing ever said to me. As great as Cobb."

A calmness settled over the clubhouse. The only sound was Hank's hands rubbing Rodkin's body.

Joie sat thinking. He spoke: "Cobb could hit even when he quit baseball, couldn't he, Mr. Rodkins?"

"He was always dangerous. Even at the end his eyes were sharp and few players hit better."

"It was his legs, wasn't it? He wasn't fast anymore?"

"That's right. He wasn't fast. He played his last two years in the outfield on a dime."

"But he could still hit?"

"Always."

"Damn the legs," said Joie. "Damn them!"

"Even at the finish he was beautiful to watch. He had a sixth sense. Speaker had it too. They knew where to play a ball. I've seen them not have to move two feet to take a line drive. Their legs lasted longer than most legs do."

"They were the last word," said Hank. "They had everything."

"Everything," said Rodkin.

"I never saw either of them," said Joie.

"Then you've never seen the outfield played," said Hank. "And if you never saw Sisler, you've never seen first base played either."

"That's right," said Rodkin.

"I've missed those things," said Joie, "but I've seen Mr. Rodkin pitch and that makes up for them."

A silence. Joie walked over to the table and put his hand on Rodkin's back: "How do you feel?"

"Fine."

"You're not tired?"

"No. I'm not tired."

"You pitched a swell game today."

"Thanks, Joie."

"I have to run along. I'll see you tomorrow."

"Yes."

"Good-bye."

"Good-bye."

Hank's hands never left Rodkin's body. His fingers worked in and out between the muscles. Rodkin's tiredness went away.

"OK," said Hank.

"OK," said Rodkin. He got off the table and began to dress.

"You should have married," said Hank. "A ballplayer needs a wife."

"I've never been able to find a girl who sees baseball as I do."

"It's not too late."

"Yes it is."

"More women come to the games every day."

"It's a fad," said Rodkin. "Few really like it."

"My wife likes it."

"She's different."

"When you stop winning games Joie's heart will break."

"We all stop sometime," said Rodkin.

Hank spoke, casually, quietly: "Some pitchers pitch years with their heads."

"Yes."

"I've known pitchers who stayed around two and three years that didn't have a thing on the ball—just brains."

"Johnson pitched a long time like that."

"Yeah, and Alexander too," said Hank. "If a pitcher keeps getting smarter and doesn't bear down too hard—except in the pinches—he could stay around as long as Quinn did. He was near fifty before he left the majors."

"He was a spitball pitcher."

"That makes no difference. He had nerve and a head. You have them too."

They looked at each other. Rodkin lowered his eyes. He slipped on his coat. "So long," he said.

"So long," said Hank.

Rodkin walked out of the clubhouse. He wanted to see the park again. He wanted to go back a long way. He stood in deep right field and looked across the diamond to home plate. A great stillness lay over the field and stands. There is no lonelier place in the world than a ball park when the crowd has gone and it is cleaned out and in the west the day swiftly dying and nothing remains but a quietness that seems to speak. Inside Rodkin was filled with an emptiness. An aching loneliness started at the pit of his stomach and crept slowly upward past his chest, lingering in his throat. Whenever he spoke of those men a dullness came to him. Once there had been something and now that thing was gone. Once, long ago, he had pitched to those men and now they were no more. He remembered Cobb standing at the plate, kidding him, calling him a dumb rookie. Cobb was nearing the tiring age then. Who was it that said Cobb's only weakness was a walk? It was true anyway.

His eyes went to the green of the outfield. Speaker, Hooper and Cobb were ghosts running swiftly to catch long low drives. Their figures were silhouetted against the blue horizon: satyrs racing gracefully over the fresh spring earth to catch a white ball no larger than their closed hand. They had been great men and great players. Rodkin wanted to pitch to them again, but they had gotten tired and gone away. Their hearts had remained enthusiastic but not their bodies. He too was tired and like them would some day go away. He felt fine after the rubdown, but knew he would not be able to pitch any real ball for four days. Peck would not ask him to pitch until then. Peck was saving him. Rodkin wanted to be saved. Baseball was a part of him and he could not imagine what he would do without it. There is a difference in liking to see it played and in liking to play it. He wanted to play it forever— to pitch big league ball until he died. The great players he loved were gone, but every spring would bring new players and like young Blake some would stay and grow older and become smart, that is, if they had the courage and were thoughtful and listened to what was told them and did not dissipate too much. They would stand before Rodkin with confidence, the crowd roaring or sitting in hushed stillness, and it would be their thinking against his. There would always be young players staring into the sun, dreaming of being as great as Cobb or Sisler, and maybe, one or two would reach that goal and he would then be too old to pitch to them.

And Burke? Burke must be tired. But he wasn't. Not until he straightened up a trifle to throw to second base. He would then be tired and the afternoons seem long and endless. And shortly after that time he would find there was to be no more afternoons. Rodkin never wanted to see that day. . . . To wipe the vision away he sank the palms of his hands against his eyelids.

He moved slowly away. All days wouldn't be like today. He could stay a long time if he pitched with his head. He could stay for another three years—maybe four. He would have to be careful. He would have to be smart.

Baseball Hattie
(1954)

Damon Runyon

Damon Runyon (1880-1946) was widely recognized as the greatest newspaper reporter in the country. He was born in Manhattan, Kansas, and his formal education extended only through the sixth grade. Runyon initially found fame as a columnist for the old *New York American* and a nationally syndicated writer for the Hearst newspaper chain. He became a man about town in New York, playing the horses and chumming with the likes of boxer Jack Dempsey and Giants manager John McGraw. Both a humorist and a dramatic writer, Runyon is considered one of the best short-story writers ever. Many of his fictional creations are New York-talking guys of shady character with rough grammar, a genre that is called "Runyonesque." Among his best-known works are the trilogy of collected stories: *Guys and Dolls* (1929), *Money from Home* (1931), and *Blue Plate Special* (1931).

I t comes on springtime, and the little birdies are singing in the trees in Central Park, and the grass is green all around and about, and I am at the Polo Grounds on the opening day of the baseball season, when who do I behold but Baseball Hattie. I am somewhat surprised at this spectacle, as it is years since I see Baseball Hattie, and for all I know she long ago passes to a better and happier world. But there she is, as large as life, and in fact twenty pounds larger, and when I call the attention of Armand Fibleman, the gambler, to her he gets up and tears right out of the joint as if he sees a ghost, for if there is one thing Armand Fibleman loathes and despises, it is a ghost. I can see that Baseball Hattie is greatly changed, and to tell the truth, I can see that she is getting to be nothing but an old bag. Her hair that is once as black as a yard up a stovepipe is gray, and she is wearing gold-rimmed cheaters, although she seems to be pretty well dressed and looks as if she may be in the money a little bit, at that.

But the greatest change in her is the way she sits there very quiet all afternoon, never once opening her yap, even when many of the customers around her are claiming that Umpire William Klem is Public Enemy No. 1 to 16 inclusive, because they think he calls a close one against the Giants. I am wondering if maybe Baseball Hattie is stricken dumb somewhere back down the years, because I can remember when she is usually making speeches in the grandstand in favor of hanging such characters as Umpire William Klem when they call close ones against the Giants. But Hattie just sits there as if she is in a church while the public clamor goes on about her, and she does not as much as cry out robber, or even you big bum at Umpire William Klem. I see many a baseball bug in my time, male and female, but without doubt the worst bug of them all is Baseball Hattie, and you can say it again. She is most particularly a bug about the Giants, and she never misses a game they play at the Polo Grounds, and in fact she sometimes bobs up watching them play in other cities, which is always very embarrassing to the Giants, as they fear the customers in these cities may get the wrong impression of New York womanhood after listening to Baseball Hattie awhile.

The first time I ever see Baseball Hattie to pay any attention to her is in Philadelphia, a matter of twenty-odd years back, when the Giants are playing a series there, and many citizens of New York, including Armand Fibleman and myself, are present, because the Philadelphia customers are great hands for betting on baseball games in those days, and Armand Fibleman figures he may knock a few of them in the creek. Armand Fibleman is a character who will bet on baseball games from who-laid-the-chunk, and in fact he will bet on anything whatever, because Armand Fibleman is a gambler by trade and has been such since infancy. Personally, I will not bet you four dollars on a baseball game, because in the first place I am not apt to have four dollars, and in the second place I consider horse races a much sounder investment, but I often go around and about with Armand Fibleman, as he is a friend of mine, and sometimes he gives me a little piece of one of his bets for nothing.

Well, what happens in Philadelphia but the umpire forfeits the game in the seventh inning to the Giants by a score of nine to nothing when the Phillies are really leading by five runs, and the reason the umpire takes this action is because he orders several of the Philadelphia players to leave the field for calling him a scoundrel and a rat and a snake in the grass, and also a baboon, and they refuse to take their departure, as they still have more names to call him. Right away the Philadelphia customers become infuriated in a manner you will scarcely believe, for ordinarily a Philadelphia baseball customer is as quiet as a lamb, no matter what you do to him, and in fact in those days a Philadelphia baseball customer is only considered as somebody to do something to.

But these Philadelphia customers are so infuriated that they not only chase the umpire under the stand, but they wait in the street outside the baseball orchard until the Giants change into their street clothes and come out of the clubhouse. Then the Philadelphia customers begin pegging rocks, and one thing and another, at the Giants, and it is a most exciting and disgraceful scene that is spoken of for years afterwards. Well, the Giants march along toward the North Philly station to catch a train for home, dodging the rocks and one thing and another the best they can, and wondering why the Philadelphia gendarmes do not come to the rescue, until somebody notices several gendarmes among the customers doing some of the throwing themselves, so the Giants realize that this is a most inhospitable community, to be sure.

Finally all of them get inside the North Philly station and are safe, except a big, tall, left-handed pitcher by the name of Haystack Duggeler, who just reports to the club the day before and who finds himself surrounded by quite a posse of these infuriated Philadelphia customers, and who is unable to make them understand that he is nothing but a rookie, because he has a Missouri accent, and besides, he is half paralyzed with fear. One of the infuriated Philadelphia customers is armed with a brickbat and is just moving forward to maim Haystack Duggeler with this instrument, when who steps into the situation but Baseball Hattie, who is also on her way to the station to catch a train, and who is greatly horrified by the assault on the Giants.

She seizes the brickbat from the infuriated Philadelphia customer's grasp, and then tags the customer smack-dab between the eyes with his own weapon, knocking him so unconscious that I afterwards hear he does not recover for two weeks, and that he remains practically an imbecile the rest of his days. Then Baseball Hattie cuts loose on the other infuriated Philadelphia customers with language that they never before hear in those parts, causing them to disperse without further ado, and after the last customer is beyond the sound of her voice, she takes Haystack Duggeler by the pitching arm and personally escorts him to the station.

Now out of this incident is born a wonderful romance between Baseball Hattie and Haystack Duggeler, and in fact it is no doubt love at first sight, and about this period Haystack Duggeler begins burning up the league with his pitching, and at the same time giving Manager Mac plenty of headaches, including the romance with Baseball Hattie, because anybody will tell you that a left-hander is tough enough on a manager without a romance, and especially a romance with Baseball Hattie. It seems that the trouble with Hattie is she is in business up in Harlem, and this business consists of a boarding and rooming house where ladies and gentlemen board and room, and personally I never see anything out of line in the matter, but the rumor somehow gets around, as rumors will do, that in the first place, it is not a boarding and rooming house, and in the second place that the ladies and gentlemen who room and board there are by no means ladies and gentlemen, and especially ladies.

Well, this rumor becomes a terrible knock to Baseball Hattie's social reputation. Furthermore, I hear Manager Mac sends for her and requests her to kindly lay off his ballplayers, and especially off a character who can make a baseball sing high C like Haystack Duggeler. In fact, I hear Manager Mac gives her such a lecture on her civic duty to New York and to the Giants that Baseball Hattie sheds tears, and promises she will never give Haystack another tumble the rest of the season. "You know me, Mac," Baseball Hattie says. "You know I will cut off my nose rather than do anything to hurt your club. I sometimes figure I am in love with this big bloke, but," she says, "maybe it is only gas pushing up around my heart. I will take something for it. To hell with him, Mac!" she says.

So she does not see Haystack Duggeler again, except at a distance, for a long time, and he goes on to win fourteen games in a row, pitching a no-hitter and four two-hitters among them, and hanging up a reputation as a great pitcher, and also as a hundred-percent heel.

Haystack Duggeler is maybe twenty-five at this time, and he comes to the big league with more bad habits than anybody in the history of the world is able to acquire in such a short time. He is especially a great rumpot, and after he gets going good in the league, he is just as apt to appear for a game all mulled up as not. He is fond of all forms of gambling, such as playing cards and shooting craps, but after they catch him with a deck of readers in a poker game and a pair of tops in a crap game, none of the Giants will play with him anymore, except of course when there is nobody else to play with. He is ignorant about many little things, such as reading and writing and geography and mathematics, as Haystack Duggeler himself admits he never goes to school anymore than he can help, but he is so wise when it comes to larceny that I always figure they must have great tutors back in Haystack's old home town of Booneville, Mo.

And no smarter jobbie ever breathes than Haystack when he is out there pitching. He has so much speed that he just naturally throws the ball past a batter before he can get the old musket off his shoulder, and along with his hard one, Haystack has a curve like the letter q. With two ounces of brains, Haystack Duggeler will be the greatest pitcher that ever lives. Well, as far as Baseball Hattie is concerned, she keeps her word about not seeing Haystack, although sometimes when he is mulled up he goes around to her boarding and rooming house, and tries to break down the door.

On days when Haystack Duggeler is pitching, she is always in her favorite seat back of third, and while she roots hard for the Giants no matter who is pitching, she puts on extra steam when Haystack is bending them over, and it is quite an experience to hear her crying lay them in there, Haystack, old boy, and strike this big tramp out, Haystack, and other exclamations of a similar nature, which please Haystack quite some, but annoy Baseball Hattie's neighbors back of third base, such as Armand Fibleman, if he happens to be betting on the other club.

A month before the close of his first season in the big league, Haystack Duggeler gets so ornery that Manager Mac suspends him, hoping maybe it will cause Haystack to do a little thinking, but naturally Haystack is unable to do this, because he has nothing to think with. About a week later, Manager Mac gets to noticing how he can use a few ball games, so he starts looking for Haystack Duggeler, and he finds him tending bar on Eighth Avenue with his uniform hung up back of the bar as an advertisement. The baseball writers speak of Haystack as eccentric, which is a polite way of saying he is a screwball, but they consider him a most unique character and are always writing humorous stories about him, though any one of them will lay you plenty of nine to five that Haystack winds up an umbay. The chances are they will raise their price a little, as the season closes and Haystack is again under suspension with cold weather coming on and not a dime in his pants pockets.

It is sometime along in the winter that Baseball Hattie hauls off and marries Haystack Duggeler, which is a great surprise to one and all, but not nearly as much of a surprise as when Hattie closes her boarding and rooming house and goes to live in a little apartment with Haystack Duggeler up on Washington Heights.

It seems that she finds Haystack one frosty night sleeping in a hallway, after being around slightly mulled up for several weeks, and she takes him to her home and gets him a bath and a shave and a clean shirt and two boiled eggs and some toast and coffee and a shot or two of rye whiskey, all of which is greatly appreciated by Haystack, especially the rye whiskey. Then Haystack proposes marriage to her and takes a paralyzed oath that if she becomes his wife he will reform, so what with loving Haystack anyway, and with the fix commencing to request more dough off the boarding-and-rooming-house business than the business will stand, Hattie takes him at his word, and there you are. The baseball writers are wondering what Manager Mac will say when he hears these tidings, but all Mac says is that Haystack cannot possibly be any worse married than he is single-o, and then Mac has the club office send the happy couple a little paper money to carry them over the winter. Well, what happens but a great change comes over Haystack Duggeler. He stops bending his elbow and helps Hattie cook and wash the dishes, and holds her hand when they are in the movies, and speaks of his love for her several times a week, and Hattie is as happy as nine dollars' worth of lettuce. Manager Mac is so delighted at the change in Haystack that he has the club office send over more paper money, because Mac knows that with Haystack in shape he is sure of twenty-five games, and maybe the pennant.

In late February, Haystack reports to the training camp down South still as sober as some judges, and the other ballplayers are so impressed by the change in him that they admit him to their poker game again. But of course it is too much to expect a man to alter his entire course of living all at once, and it is not long before Haystack discovers four nines in his hand on his own deal and breaks up the game.

He brings Baseball Hattie with him to the camp, and this is undoubtedly a slight mistake, as it seems the old rumor about her boarding-and-rooming-house business gets around among the ever-loving wives of the other players, and they put on a large chill for her. In fact, you will think Hattie has the smallpox. Naturally, Baseball Hattie feels the frost, but she never lets on, as it seems she runs into many bigger and better frosts than this in her time. Then

Haystack Duggeler notices it, and it seems that it makes him a little peevish toward Baseball Hattie, and in fact it is said that he gives her a slight pasting one night in their room, partly because she has no better social standing and partly because he is commencing to cop a few sneaks on the local corn now and then, and Hattie chides him for same.

Well, about this time it appears that Baseball Hattie discovers that she is going to have a baby, and as soon as she recovers from her astonishment, she decides that it is to be a boy who will be a great baseball player, maybe a pitcher, although Hattie admits she is willing to compromise on a good second basemen. She also decides that his name is to be Derrill Duggeler, after his paw, as it seems Derrill is Haystack's real name, and he is only called Haystack because he claims he once makes a living stacking hay, although the general opinion is that all he ever stacks is cards. It is really quite remarkable what a belt Hattie gets out of the idea of having this baby, though Haystack is not excited about the matter. He is not paying much attention to Baseball Hattie by now, except to give her a slight pasting now and then, but Hattie is so happy about the baby that she does not mind these pastings.

Haystack Duggeler meets up with Armand Fibleman along in midsummer. By this time, Haystack discovers horse racing and is always making bets on the horses, and naturally he is generally broke, and then I commence running into him in different spots with Armand Fibleman, who is now betting higher than a cat's back on baseball games.

It is late August, and the Giants are fighting for the front end of the league, and an important series with Brooklyn is coming up, and everybody knows that Haystack Duggeler will work in anyway two games of the series, as Haystack can generally beat Brooklyn just by throwing his glove on the mound. There is no doubt but what he has the old Indian sign on Brooklyn, and the night before the first game, which he is sure to work, the gamblers along Broadway are making the Giants two-to-one favorites to win the game.

This same night before the game, Baseball Hattie is home in her little apartment on Washington Heights waiting for Haystack to come in and eat a delicious dinner of pigs' knuckles and sauerkraut, which she personally prepares for him. In fact, she hurries home right after the ball game to get this delicacy ready, because Haystack tells her he will surely come home this particular night, although Hattie knows he is never better than even money to keep his word about anything. But sure enough, in he comes while the pigs' knuckles and sauerkraut are still piping hot, and Baseball Hattie is surprised to see Armand Fibleman with him, as she knows Armand backwards and forwards and does not care much for him, at that. However, she can say the same thing about four million other characters in this town, so she makes Armand welcome, and they sit down and put on the pigs' knuckles and sauerkraut together, and a pleasant time is enjoyed by one and all. In fact, Baseball Hattie puts herself out to entertain Armand Fibleman, because he is the first guest Haystack ever brings home.

Well, Armand Fibleman can be very pleasant when he wishes, and he speaks very nicely to Hattie. Naturally, he sees that Hattie is expecting, and in fact he will have to be blind not to see it, and he seems greatly interested in this matter and asks Hattie many questions, and Hattie is delighted to find somebody to talk to about what is coming off with her, as Haystack will never listen to any of her remarks on the subject. So Armand Fibleman gets to hear all about Baseball Hattie's son, and how he is to be a great baseball player, and Armand says is that so, and how nice, and all this and that, until Haystack Duggeler speaks up as follows, and to wit:

"Oh, dag-gone her son!" Haystack says. "It is going to be a girl, anyway, so let us dismiss this topic and get down to business. Hat," he says, "you fan yourself into the kitchen and wash the dishes, while Armand and me talk."

So Hattie goes into the kitchen, leaving Haystack and Armand sitting there talking, and what are they talking about but a proposition for Haystack to let the Brooklyn club beat him the next day so Armand Fibleman can take the odds and clean up a nice little gob of money, which he is to split with Haystack. Hattie can hear every word they say, as the kitchen is next door to the dining room where they are sitting, and at first she thinks they are joking, because at this time nobody ever even as much as thinks of skulduggery in baseball, or anyway, not much. It seems that at first Haystack is not in favor of the idea, but Armand Fibleman keeps mentioning money that Haystack owes him for bets on the horse races, and he asks Haystack how he expects to continue betting on the races without fresh money, and Armand also speaks of the great injustice that is being done Haystack by the Giants in not paying him twice the salary he is getting, and how the loss of one or two games is by no means such a great calamity.

Well, finally Baseball Hattie hears Haystack say all right, but he wishes a thousand dollars then and there as a guarantee, and Armand Fibleman says this is fine, and they will go downtown and he will get the money at once, and now Hattie realizes that maybe they are in earnest, and she pops out of the kitchen and speaks as follows:

"Gentlemen," Hattie says, "you seem to be sober, but I guess you are drunk. If you are not drunk, you must both be daffy to think of such a thing as phenagling around with a baseball game."

"Hattie," Haystack says, "kindly close your trap and go back in the kitchen, or I will give you a bust in the nose."

And with this he gets up and reaches for his hat, and Armand Fibleman gets up, too, and Hattie says like this:

"Why, Haystack," she says, "you are not really serious in this matter, are you?"

"Of course I am serious," Haystack says. "I am sick and tired of pitching for starvation wages, and besides, I will win a lot of games later on to make up for the one I lose tomorrow. Say," he says, "these Brooklyn bums may get lucky tomorrow and knock me loose from my pants, anyway, no matter what I do, so what difference does it make?"

"Haystack," Baseball Hattie says, "I know you are a liar and a drunkard and a cheat and no account generally, but nobody can tell me you will sink so low as to purposely toss off a ball game. Why, Haystack, baseball is always on the level. It is the most honest game in all this world. I guess you are just ribbing me, because you know how much I love it."

"Dry up!" Haystack says to Hattie. "Furthermore, do not expect me home again tonight. But anyway, dry up."

"Look, Haystack," Hattie says, "I am going to have a son. He is your son and my son, and he is going to be a great ballplayer when he grows up, maybe a greater pitcher than you are, though I hope and trust he is not left-handed. He will have your name. If they find out you toss off a game for money, they will throw you out of baseball and you will be disgraced. My son will be known as the son of a crook, and what chance will he have in baseball? Do you think I am going to allow you to do this to him, and to the game that keeps me from going nutty for marrying you?"

Naturally, Haystack Duggeler is greatly offended by Hattie's crack about her son being maybe a greater pitcher than he is, and he is about to take steps, when Armand Fibleman stops him. Armand Fibleman is commencing to be somewhat alarmed at Baseball Hattie's attitude, and he gets to thinking that he hears that people in her delicate condition are often irresponsible, and he fears that she may blow a whistle on this enterprise without realizing what she is doing. So he undertakes a few soothing remarks to her. "Why, Hattie," Armand Fibleman says, "nobody can possibly find out about this little matter, and Haystack will have enough money to send your son to college, if his markers at the race track do not take it all. Maybe you better lie down and rest awhile," Armand says.

But Baseball Hattie does not as much as look at Armand, though she goes on talking to Haystack. "They always find out thievery, Haystack," she says, "especially when you are dealing with a fink like Fibleman. If you deal with him once, you will have to deal with him again and again, and he will be the first to holler copper on you, because he is a stool pigeon in his heart."

"Haystack," Armand Fibleman says, "I think we better be going."

"Haystack," Hattie says, "you can go out of here and stick up somebody or commit a robbery or a murder, and I will still welcome you back and stand by you. But if you are going out to steal my son's future, I advise you not to go."

"Dry up!" Haystack says. "I am going."

"All right, Haystack," Hattie says, very calm. "But just step into the kitchen with me and let me say one little word to you by yourself, and then I will say no more." Well, Haystack Duggeler does not care for even just one little word more, but Armand Fibleman wishes to get this disagreeable scene over with, so he tells Haystack to let her have her word, and Haystack goes into the kitchen with Hattie, and Armand cannot hear what is said, as she speaks very low, but he hears Haystack laugh heartily and then Haystack comes out of the kitchen, still laughing, and tells Armand he is ready to go.

As they start for the door, Baseball Hattie outs with a long-nosed .38-caliber Colt's revolver, and goes root-a-toot-toot with it, and the next thing anybody knows, Haystack is on the floor yelling bloody murder, and Armand Fibleman is leaving the premises without bothering to open the door. In fact, the landlord afterwards talks some of suing Haystack Duggeler because of the damage Armand Fibleman does to the door. Armand himself afterwards admits that when he slows down for a breather a couple of miles down Broadway he finds splinters stuck all over him.

Well, the doctors come, and the gendarmes come, and there is great confusion, especially as Baseball Hattie is sobbing so she can scarcely make a statement, and Haystack Duggeler is so sure he is going to die that he cannot think of anything to say except oh-oh-oh, but finally the landlord remembers seeing Armand leave with his door, and everybody starts questioning Hattie about this until she confesses that Armand is there all right, and that he tries to bribe Haystack to toss off a ball game, and that she then suddenly finds herself with a revolver in her hand, and everything goes black before her eyes, and she can remember no more until somebody is sticking a bottle of smelling salts under her nose. Naturally, the newspaper reporters put two and two together, and what they make of it is that Hattie tries to plug Armand Fibleman for his rascally offer, and that she misses Armand and gets Haystack, and right away Baseball Hattie is a great heroine, and Haystack is a great hero, though nobody thinks to ask Haystack how he stands on the bribe proposition, and he never brings it up himself.

And nobody will ever offer Haystack any more bribes, for after the doctors get through with him he is shy a left arm from the shoulder down, and he will never pitch a baseball again, unless he learns to pitch right-handed. The newspapers make quite a lot of Baseball Hattie protecting the fair name of baseball. The National League plays a benefit game for Haystack Duggeler and presents him with a watch and a purse of twenty-five thousand dollars, which Baseball Hattie grabs away from him, saying it is for her son, while Armand Fibleman is in bad with one and all.

Baseball Hattie and Haystack Duggeler move to the Pacific Coast, and this is all there is to the story, except that one day some years ago, and not long before he passes away in Los Angeles, a respectable grocer, I run into Haystack when he is in New York on a business trip, and I say to him like this:

"Haystack," I say, "it is certainly a sin and a shame that Hattie misses Armand Fibleman that night and puts you on the shelf. The chances are that but for this little accident you will hang up one of the greatest pitching records in the history of baseball. Personally," I say, "I never see a better left-handed pitcher."

"Look," Haystack says. "Hattie does not miss Fibleman. It is a great newspaper story and saves my name, but the truth is she hits just where she aims. When she calls me into the kitchen before I start out with Fibleman, she shows me a revolver I never before know she has, and says to me, 'Haystack,' she says, 'if you leave with this weasel on the errand you mention, I am going to fix you so you will never make another wrong move with your pitching arm. I am going to shoot it off for you.'

"I laugh heartily," Haystack says. "I think she is kidding me, but I find out different. By the way," Haystack says, "I afterwards learn that long before I meet her, Hattie works for three years in a shooting gallery at Coney Island. She is really a remarkable broad," Haystack says.

I guess I forget to state that the day Baseball Hattie is at the Polo Grounds she is watching the new kid sensation of the big leagues, Derrill Duggeler, shut out Brooklyn with three hits.

He is a wonderful young left-hander.

Bullet in the Brain (1996)

Tobias Wolff

It's not a good idea to taunt an armed bank robber. But what does this have to do with baseball? Read this gem of a story, originally from *The New Yorker*, and find out. Distinguished contemporary author Tobias Wolff teaches in the English department at Stanford University. Among his books are *Back in the World: Stories* (1996), *The Night in Question: Stories* (1997), and *Old School: A Novel* (2003). Wolff was the editor of *The Best American Short Stories*, 1994.

Anders couldn't get to the bank until just before it closed, so of course the line was endless and he got stuck behind two women whose loud, stupid conversation put him in a murderous temper. He was never in the best of tempers anyway, Anders—a book critic known for the weary, elegant savagery with which he dispatched almost everything he reviewed.

With the line still doubled around the rope, one of the tellers stuck a POSITION CLOSED sign in her window and walked to the back of the bank, where she leaned against a desk and began to pass the time with a man shuffling papers. The women in front of Anders broke off their conversation and watched the teller with hatred. "Oh, that's nice," one of them said. She turned to Anders and added, confident of his accord, "One of those little human touches that keep us coming back for more."

Anders had conceived his own towering hatred of the teller, but he immediately turned it on the presumptuous crybaby in front of him. "Damned unfair," he said. "Tragic, really. If they're not chopping off the wrong leg or bombing your ancestral village, they're closing their positions."

She stood her ground. "I didn't say it was tragic," she said. "I just think it's a pretty lousy way to treat your customers."

"Unforgivable," Anders said. "Heaven will take note."

She sucked in her cheeks but stared past him and said nothing. Anders saw that the other woman, her friend, was looking in the same direction. And then the tellers stopped what they were doing, and the customers slowly turned, and silence came over the bank. Two men wearing black ski masks and blue business suits were standing to the side of the door. One of them had a pistol pressed against the guard's neck. The guard's eyes were closed, and his lips were moving. The other man had a sawed-off shotgun. "Keep your big mouth shut!" the man with the pistol said, though no one had spoken a word. "One of you tellers hits the alarm, you're all dead meat. Got it?"

The tellers nodded.

"Oh, bravo," Anders said. "*Dead meat.*" He turned to the woman in front of him. "Great script, eh? The stern, brass-knuckled poetry of the dangerous classes."

She looked at him with drowning eyes.

The man with the shotgun pushed the guard to his knees. He handed the shotgun to his partner and yanked the guard's wrists up behind his back and locked them together with a pair of handcuffs. He toppled him onto the floor with a kick between the shoulder blades. Then he took his shotgun back and went over to the security gate at the end of the counter. He was short and heavy and moved with peculiar slowness, even torpor. "Buzz him in," his partner said. The man with the shotgun opened the gate and sauntered along the line of tellers, handing each of them a Hefty bag. When he came to the empty position he looked over at the man with the pistol, who said, "Whose slot is that?"

Anders watched the teller. She put her hand to her throat and turned to the man she's been talking to. He nodded. "Mine," she said.

"Then get your ugly ass in gear and fill that bag."

"There you go," Anders said to the woman in front of him. "Justice is done."

"Hey! Bright boy! Did I tell you to talk?"

"No," Anders said.

"Then shut your trap."

"Did you hear that?" Anders said. "'Bright boy.' Right out of 'The Killers.'"

"Please, be quiet," the woman said.

"Hey, you deaf or what?" The man with the pistol walked over to Anders. He poked the weapon into Anders' gut. "You think I'm playing games?"

"No," Anders said, but the barrel tickled like a stiff finger and he had to fight back the titters. He did this by making himself stare into the man's eyes, which were clearly visible behind the holes in the mask: pale blue and rawly red-rimmed. The man's left eyelid kept twitching. He breathed out a piercing, ammoniac smell that shocked Anders more than anything that had happened, and he was beginning to develop a sense of unease when the man prodded him again with the pistol.

"You like me, bright boy?" he said. "You want to suck my dick?"

"No," Anders said.

"Then stop looking at me."

Anders fixed his gaze on the man's shiny wing-tip shoes.

"Not down there. Up there." He stuck the pistol under Anders' chin and pushed it upward until Anders was looking at the ceiling.

Anders had never paid much attention to that part of the bank, a pompous old building with marble floors and counters and pillars, and gilt scrollwork over the tellers' cages. The domed ceiling had been decorated with mythological figures whose fleshy, toga-draped ugliness Anders had taken in at a glance many years earlier and afterward declined to notice. Now he had no choice but to scrutinize the painter's work. It was even worse than he remembered, and all of it executed with the utmost gravity. The artist had a few tricks up his sleeve and used them again and again—a certain rosy blush on the underside of the clouds, a coy backward glance on the faces of the cupids and fauns. The ceiling was crowded with various drama, but the one that caught Anders' eye was Zeus and Europa—portrayed, in this rendition, as a bull ogling a cow from behind a haystack. To make the cow sexy, the painter had canted her hips suggestively and given her long, droopy eyelashes through which she gazed back at the bull with sultry welcome. The bull wore a smirk and his eyebrows were arched. If there'd been a bubble coming out of his mouth, it would have said, "Hubba hubba."

"What's so funny, bright boy?"

"Nothing."

"You think I'm comical? You think I'm some kind of clown?"

"No."

"You think you can fuck with me?"

"No."

"Fuck with me again, you're history. *Capiche*?"

Anders burst out laughing. He covered his mouth with both hands and said, "I'm sorry, I'm sorry," then snorted helplessly through his fingers and said, "*Capiche*—oh, God, *capiche*," and at that the man with the pistol raised the pistol and shot Anders right in the head.

The bullet smashed Anders' skull and ploughed through his brain and exited behind his right ear, scattering shards of bone into the cerebral cortex, the corpus callosum, back toward the basal ganglia, and down into the thalamus. But before all this occurred, the first appearance of the bullet in the cerebrum set off a crackling chain of ion transports and neurotransmissions. Because of their peculiar origin these traced a peculiar pattern, flukishly calling to life a summer afternoon some forty years past, and long since lost to memory. After striking the cranium the bullet was moving at 900 feet per second, a pathetically sluggish, glacial pace compared to the synaptic lightning that flashed around it. Once in the brain, that is, the bullet came under the mediation of brain time, which gave Anders plenty of leisure to contemplate the scene that, in a phrase he would have abhorred, "passed before his eyes."

It is worth noting what Anders did not remember, given what he did remember. He did not remember his first lover, Sherry, or what he had most madly loved about her, before it came to irritate him—her unembarrassed carnality, and especially the cordial way she had with his unit, which she called Mr. Mole, as in, "Uh-oh, looks like Mr. Mole wants to play," and, "Let's hide Mr. Mole!" Anders did not remember his wife, whom he had also loved before she exhausted him with her predictability, or his daughter, now a sullen professor of economics at Dartmouth. He did not remember standing just outside his daughter's door as she lectured her bear about his naughtiness and described the truly appalling punishments Paws would receive unless he changed his ways. He did not remember a single line of the hundreds of poems he had committed to memory in his youth so that he could give himself the shivers at will—not "Silent, upon a peak in Darien," or "My God, I heard this all day," or "All my pretty ones? Did you say all? O hell-kite! All?" None of these did he remember; not one. Anders did not remember his dying mother saying of his father, "I should have stabbed him in his sleep."

He did not remember Professor Josephs telling his class how Athenian prisoners in Sicily had been released if they could recite Aeschylus, and then reciting Aeschylus himself, right there, in the Greek. Anders did not remember how his eyes had burned at those sounds. He did not remember the surprise of seeing a college classmate's name on the jacket of a novel not long after they graduated, or the respect he had felt after reading the book. He did not remember the pleasure of giving respect.

Nor did Anders remember seeing a woman leap to her death from the building opposite his own just days after his daughter was born. He did not remember deliberately crashing his father's car into a tree, or having his ribs kicked in by three policemen at an antiwar rally, or waking himself up with laughter. He did not remember when he began to regard the heap of books on his desk with boredom and dread, or when he grew angry at writers for writing them. He did not remember when everything began to remind him of something else.

This is what he remembered. Heat. A baseball field. Yellow grass, the whirr of insects, himself leaning against a tree as the boys of the neighborhood gather for a pickup game. He looks on as the others argue the relative genius of Mantle and Mays. They have been worrying this subject all summer, and it has become tedious to Anders: an oppression, like the heat.

Then the last two boys arrive, Coyle and a cousin of his from Mississippi. Anders has never met Coyle's cousin before and will never see him again. He says hi with the rest but takes no further notice of him until they've chosen sides and someone asks the cousin what position he wants to play. "Shortstop," the boy says. "Short's the best position they is." Anders turns and looks at him. He wants to hear Coyle's cousin repeat what he's just said, but he knows better than to ask. The others will think he's being a jerk, ragging the kid for his grammar. But that isn't it, not at all—it's that Anders is strangely roused, elated, by those final two words, their pure unexpectedness and their music. He takes the field in a trance, repeating them to himself.

The bullet is already in the brain; it won't be outrun forever, or charmed to a halt. In the end it will do its work and leave the troubled skull behind, dragging its comet's tail of memory and hope and talent and love into the marble hall of commerce. That can't be helped. But for now Anders can still make time. Time for the shadows to lengthen on the grass, time for the tethered dog to bark at the flying ball, time for the boy in right field to smack his sweat-blackened mitt and softly chant, *They is, they is, they is.*

The Master's Touch (1951)

Herbert Warren Wind

Herbert Warren Wind (1918–2005) was a preeminent authority on golf and tennis. Primarily a nonfiction writer, his well-known books include *The Complete Golfer* (1954), *The Gilded Age of Sport* (1961), and *Game, Set, and Match* (1979). Wind wrote an outstanding baseball yarn in "The Master's Touch." The "master" in the story is a wily general manager, Calvin Shepard, who keeps a keen eye on his minor-league prospects. Trouble is, one of his finest talents is head over heels in love with a beautiful movie star of dubious reputation. As love blooms, the player's batting average plummets. Can Shepard save the day?

C alvin Cowley Shepard was methodically going through the mail stacked on his desk. He owned the largest desk in organized baseball—a foot longer and nine inches wider than Branch Rickey's by actual measurement. It was a fine July morning, the air exceptionally cool and dry for the Atlantic seaboard in summer, Shepard was thinking as he savored a testimonial from the local Elks Club to the effect that C. C. Shepard was the smartest man in the major leagues.

Reluctantly, he went on to the next letter, a routine report from the secretary of the Redlands farm team. The weather suddenly changed. The severe

207

granite contours of his face became sharper and deeper as Shepard impatiently jabbed at a buzzer on his desk.

By the time his secretary, Ray Bell, came hurrying in, Shepard looked like the Old Man of the Mountain after a rough storm.

"You're not ready to see the press yet, are you?" Ray asked. He was a slim young man in his early thirties, who spoke, as did Shepard, with slight traces of a Vermont twang.

"No, my boy, I'm not ready to see the press," Shepard said with what was supposed to be elegant sarcasm. "I see them at ten o'clock. I know that. I don't need any coaching." He paused for a moment. "I've just been reading the report from Redlands. Do you know what Walter Eamons is batting?"

"It was .274 on last month's report," Ray answered. "Probably up around .280, .285 by now. I wouldn't worry about Eamons."

"Well, for your information," Shepard said slowly, "our Mr. Eamons is now pounding the ball at a robust .221. That boy ever hit below .340 for us?"

Ray fingered his brow. "No. He was over .370 those two years in the Kitty League. Last year at Redlands, let's see—" He broke off. "Think it was .362."

Shepard leaned over and pushed one button in a battery of sixteen attached to his desk. A glass panel at the far end of the office was jerkily lighted by fluorescent tubing. At the top of the panel, *Redlands* was printed in red; beneath the name of the club, in black, the roster of players. Fifteen similar panels, each devoted to a different farm team, formed unbroken murals along the two windowless walls of the office. The installation of this equipment had been one of Shepard's first moves after he'd bought his major-league franchise, and he derived a sense of power from pressing his buttons and watching the panels light up like a pinball machine in the hands of a true artist.

"I've won three pennants in the five years I've been in baseball," Shepard resumed, slightly appeased by the panel's obedience to his wishes. "How did I do it? By building up the best organization in the game. Not a single personal relation of mine is on the payroll. How come, then, I'm only now getting word that the best prospect we own is miles off the beam?"

"You saw that note about Eamons, didn't you—the one in last month's report from Redlands?" Ray asked him. "That line about possible woman trouble."

"Woman trouble!" Shepard cut in scornfully. "How can you live and not have woman trouble! That doesn't tell me a thing. It seems that any time I want the dope on anything, I've got to get it myself. Add Redlands to the itinerary on tomorrow's trip. Tell McCrillis to get packed. I'll want both of you. And *now* you may show the gentlemen of the press in."

• • •

Late Friday afternoon, Shepard and his aides deplaned at San Bernardino and proceeded directly to the Arrowhead Springs Hotel, a plush oasis perched on the foothills of the mountains above the arid valley. Shepard had been pushing himself hard for three days but his labors had paid off in results. In Topeka, Shepard and McCrillis, his chief scout, had watched Whitey Kravchek pitch a four-hit shutout. Sid Sandler, the young left-hander with Portland, had also impressed them as having the stuff to make the big jump to the majors.

As McCrillis put it, both youngsters had a little more to learn before they were finished pitchers, but just as they were, they would probably help the club a lot more than those two base-on-balls philanthropists, Al Marineau and Blitz Baker.

With his pitching problem nicely under control, Shepard took things easy during dinner and limited himself to two long-distance calls. In addition, he made one local call, instructing Emil Hochstetter, the old Cincinnati outfielder who managed Redlands, to meet him at nine o'clock sharp on the hotel's outdoor terrace. After lighting his old cherrywood pipe, Shepard felt so pleasantly in tune with his private universe that the thought of calling a conference of the local sports writers never entered his mind.

Somewhat under the spell of the palms and a few planter's punches, Shepard and his entourage, supplemented by Hochstetter, relaxed contentedly on the terrace. They did not stop talking baseball, however, until their attention was arrested by the entrance of a tall, handsome girl whom the headwaiter guided to a table directly across the dance floor from theirs. She wore a white dress over her tan, and had whatever it is that makes people rest their drinks on the table and stare. The four baseball men looked her over as closely as they would a promising left-hander.

"Now there's the sort of girl I like!" Shepard exclaimed.

"That's very big of you," Ray said. "I thought you were an antiglamour man, boss. That girl's loaded with it."

"*Honest* glamour," Shepard said, correcting him. "That tan, for example. That isn't one of those beauty-parlor jobs. None of that grapefruit-colored hair, either. There're a lot of other tips if you know what to look for. I can tell you all about that girl."

"Like what?"

"Well, first, she's in the movies."

"That's like saying that a guy who's just fanned Kiner, Musial and Robinson is in baseball."

Shepard refused to be thrown off stride. "She's obviously an outdoor girl," he continued calmly. "Plays good tennis, rides horseback well. She's an intelligent girl, levelheaded. Probably from a solid middle-class family. I'd guess that she comes of good old New England stock."

Ray whipped out a notebook and pretended to take notes.

"I don't see what's so amusing," Shepard said to him. "I happen to be able to judge women as accurately as I can judge ballplayers. I can sense these things, just the way I knew that Eamons belonged in center field, not at shortstop."

At almost the exact moment his name was mentioned, Walter Eamons was making his way through the tables at the far end of the terrace. The four baseball men, spotting the rangy towhead immediately, watched him pick a zigzag path to the table where the levelheaded girl from the solid New England family was sitting. She and the outfielder greeted each other with the sort of kiss that can be seen nowadays only in foreign movies.

"I can see it all now," Shepard said, beaming benevolently. "It's as simple as two and two. The boy's in love. No wonder he's not hitting."

"With a dish like that around, he's lucky to be able to find his way to the ballpark," Ray said.

"Don't be cynical," Shepard said. "I wish all my players picked girls like that! Say, Emil," he said, turning to Hochstetter, "the next time you people refer to 'woman trouble' in a report, you've got to be more specific—much more specific."

"Would you like to meet her, Shep?" Hochstetter asked.

When Shepard said he would, Hochstetter padded slowly across the dance floor and returned shortly with the model young couple, smiling, in tow.

"I recognized you, all right, Mr. Shepard," Walter Eamons said as Shepard and his aides stood up to welcome him. "I didn't think you'd remember me. That's why I didn't come over."

"Of course I do," Shepard assured him. He grasped the outfielder's hand. "It's nice seeing you, Walter. Who's the lovely young lady?"

"Mr. Shepard, I'd like you to meet my fiancée, Priscilla Summers," Eamons said awkwardly, as if he had memorized the line. "We're engaged," he explained.

Miss Summers, who had been restricting herself to a smile of general cordiality, turned on the full wattage as she received the congratulations of the three baseball men. "My, you have a strong grip!" she purred to Jim McCrillis.

"Used to catch," McCrillis replied shyly.

"I've heard a lot about *you*, Mr. Shepard," Priscilla Summers continued. "You look much younger than your pictures."

Shepard took the compliment gracefully. "You're an extremely fortunate young man, Walter," he said, dropping his voice to a judicial pitch. "When's the big day?"

Eamons looked at his fiancée for guidance. "Sometime after the end of the season," she answered for them.

Shepard thought that was fine, just fine. "You kids run along now," he said. "No sense spending your time with a bunch of old fogies when you've got better things to do. I'll see you at the ballpark, Walter."

"Peach of a girl," Shepard said approvingly to Hochstetter, when the young couple had gone off to dance. "Real New England type. It's a pity, though, they couldn't have fallen in love during the off season. That's a small matter, really. Next spring the boy will be himself again."

"I don't think so," Hochstetter said shortly.

Shepard stiffened. "You don't think what?"

Hochstetter looked at his boss as if Shepard were a pitcher to whom he was going to have to break the bad news that he was yanking him. "I don't think Eamons will be any good next year, or the year after, or any year, if he marries that girl."

"Emil"—Shepard's smile was patronizing—"I don't think you know women."

"I don't claim to, Shep. But I know a hell of a lot more about this customer than you do. I wanted to tell you about her, but you didn't give me a chance. Get the picture now. She comes down to this hotel from Hollywood for the weekend. This is five, six weeks ago. She's with another actress friend. They decide they'll kill the afternoon by watching a ball game. They get themselves a couple of box seats, in the section where the players' wives sit. I got this from Lefty Blake's wife. She was sitting in the row behind them. To make a long story short, this Summers babe spots Eamons and she goes for him—"

"But he wasn't hitting," Shepard objected.

"From a woman's point of view, Eamons ain't a good outfielder or a lousy outfielder or any other kind of an outfielder," Hochstetter said. "He's a big, good-looking kid with a build. Well, round about the fourth, when he's leaning against the bat rack, she stands up and looks him over like he was a bull at a country fair. Then she announces to her friend, just as cool as you like, 'I think I want that boy.' Blake's wife told me all about it."

Shepard stared for a long minute at his pipe. "What do you know about this girl's background?" he finally asked.

"Nothing much," Hochstetter replied. "All I know, Shep, is the kid's been no good to the team since she got hold of him. She's down here every weekend, so he can't keep his mind on his work Friday, Saturday, or Sunday. Tuesday and Wednesday he's still in a fog, dreaming about the weekend. Thursday he's off on a new fog, counting the hours till she shows up on Friday."

Shepard sat silent for several minutes. Then he turned, as he did whenever his intuitive powers had let him down, to the extreme opposite pole of operation: the meticulous collecting of facts and figures with which his problem could be worked out as unemotionally as an algebraic equation. "Ray," Shepard snapped in a weak imitation of his best bark, "I want you to get up to Hollywood immediately and dig up a full dossier on Priscilla Summers. I want you back by nine tomorrow night."

"You mean you want me to leave right now?"

"That's exactly what I mean. Now get moving."

On Saturday, Shepard pushed himself through, what was, for him, an unsatisfyingly slow morning. He leafed through the special reports his office had airmailed: the team was just barely holding on to third place—something he didn't need to be told. He conferred with McCrillis on minor problems that had arisen at Topeka and Portland, and, after a short call at Lefty Blake's house on the way to the ballpark, lunched with the club secretary and was interviewed by the local reporters. After lunch he tried to rouse himself from his lethargy by okaying plans for a new scoreboard and taking batting practice with the team, but his mind was not on his work. Just before game time he motioned Walter Eamons over to his box.

"You weren't getting much of that ball during batting practice," Shepard said, in a more severe tone than he had meant to use.

"Yeah, I was kinda poppin' 'em up," Eamons said. His face took on a look of concern. "You feeling all right, Mr. Shepard?"

Shepard stared at him.

"You don't look so good as last night," Eamons went on. "You eat something that didn't agree with you?"

"I'll worry about my own digestion," Shepard sputtered. He tried to calm himself. "I'm certain I'd feel a hundred percent better, Walter, if you started to play the ball we know you're capable of. Do you know you're batting .221?"

"I just can't seem to get a good piece of the ball," Eamons answered. He broke out in a grin, as if a very funny thought had just struck him. "That ball keeps getting smaller and smaller, Mr. Shepard. Right now it looks about as tiny as . . ."

Eamons's voice trailed off as his eyes focused on something over Shepard's left shoulder. He blew a kiss in that direction. Shepard turned. Priscilla Summers, her fingers pressed against her lips, was undulating down the aisle. Shepard scrutinized the faraway look in Eamons's eyes as Priscilla walked toward them. The boy was a goner, Shepard realized, scarcely recognizable as the same lean athlete who had shown such spirit at the training camp that Shepard had soberly appraised him to a newspaperman as "one of those aggressive, old-time ballplayers who can hit, field, throw and run those bases, a true competitor, possibly another Cobb." In the shape he was in, Eamons wasn't fit to carry Cobb's Coca Cola stock, let alone his glove.

Shepard held his guard high. He just grunted when Priscilla greeted him with a warm smile and repeated her observation that photographs failed to do justice to his youthful appearance. "Walter," Shepard said curtly, as Eamons rested his elbows on the railing before the box, "I think you'd better get out in center field. The game's ready to begin."

"Now, darling," Priscilla cautioned the outfielder, patting him on the hand, "It's a terribly hot day, so don't play too hard. I've got a wonderful evening planned for us, and I don't want you to be all worn out. We're—"

"Walter, you're holding up the game," Shepard interrupted. "Miss Summers," he continued firmly, as Eamons trotted out to center field, "I don't know if you realize this or not, but all this high living and late hours—well, it's hurting the boy. I don't think you have Walter's best interests at heart."

"I think I'm a better judge of what's good for Walter than you are," Priscilla answered. "Anyhow, I don't see how what happens between Walter and me is any business of yours."

"It most certainly *is* my business," Shepard said. "Women like you don't care who you fool around with. It doesn't mean a thing to you that you're ruining the career of one of the best young ballplayers in the country. No, I can see it doesn't."

Priscilla measured Shepard coolly. "Get this through that great brain of yours, Grandpa," she said. "I don't give a damn about you and your precious baseball. If I want to marry that outfielder of yours or whatever he is, I'm going to, and there's nothing you or anybody else can do about it. Do I make myself clear?"

"You won't talk so bold tomorrow," Shepard fumed. "I've got a man in Hollywood getting the dope on you right now. You won't marry Walter Eamons. I'll see to it you won't."

"Like to bet on that?"

Shepard, barely in control of himself, pushed by Priscilla and marched out of the box.

• • •

Ray Bell knocked on the door of Shepard's suite and walked in.

"You're back earlier than I expected," Shepard said. "Let's have it."

"She was easier to check on than I thought she'd be. Everyone in Hollywood seems to know Priscilla Summers," Ray explained as he riffled through his notebook. "You were right on some things and wrong on others. Her real name is Priscilla Summers. She does come from New England. Worcester, Mass. After that, your diagnosis isn't so hot."

"I'm not paying you to tell me how stupid I am," Shepard growled. "Cut the baloney and get on with it."

"Okay, I'll give it to you quick. She's been in Hollywood not quite two years. Been in two movies. They haven't been released yet, but everybody who's seen the previews says she's going to get somewhere. Clean-cut sex appeal. Okay, going back to the beginning. Born Worcester, 1927. Father managed a movie house. Nothing but the usual studio fiction on her till 1946, year she hit New York. Made a big splash as a model. She was a blonde then. That's not important, but I thought you'd like to know. The tan is real, though. She's been on location the last six weeks, making a Western."

"*Private* life," Shepard said.

"Just coming to that. She's been married twice. First time to a lightheavyweight fighter I never heard of. Lasted less than a year. Second time to a pro football player. She's known about town as a pretty predatory gal.

Specializes in athletes, the way other women do in artists or millionaires. Just now getting around to baseball, I guess. Let's see, what else? Well, she's five-six and weighs one-nineteen and—"

"Bats right-handed and throws with both hands," Shepard broke in. "That's enough, Ray." He made an effort to smile that didn't quite come off. "I don't want any cracks out of you about how I ought to stick to judging ball-players," he muttered. "I can handle this baby. Watch me."

Shepard paced the floor for a minute or two, and then directed Ray to summon Jim McCrillis to the room.

"All right. I've got it all figured out," Shepard announced when McCrillis arrived. "We're going to call up Kravchek and Sandler. We'll send Marineau down to Topeka. They need a pitcher. I was going to give Portland Blitz Baker in exchange for Sandler, but I'm going to bring Blitz to Redlands instead. In a hot, dry climate, Blitz has a better chance of getting his arm back. Get the paperwork started on this, Ray. One other thing: We're going to bring up Eamons."

Ray jerked his head up from his note-taking.

"I don't see what else we can do," Shepard said defensively. "I suppose we could transfer Eamons to one of the other farms, but I'd feel safer having him where I can keep an eye on him myself. We're dealing with a pretty unscrupulous woman." A new thread of anxiety crept into his voice: "Jim, you go out and round up Eamons right this minute. Get a double room in the hotel for tonight and stay with him. We're starting home first thing tomorrow, and I want that boy on the plane."

• • •

On Labor Day, C. C. Shepard's team propelled itself into a tie for first place by taking both ends of a double-header. Sandler and Kravchek were the winning pitchers. They had led the team's drive to the top, and the pro-Shepard press cited their arrival in the nick of time as one further evidence of C.C.'s peerless masterminding. As was to be expected, the reporters who didn't like Shepard glossed over the remarkable showings of Sandler and Kravchek—they had won eight games between them—and lambasted Shepard for bringing up Walter "Cantaloupe" Eamons, who had succeeded in losing two games all by himself and could easily have lost more if he'd been given the opportunity.

In an important game against Boston, for example, Eamons had been inserted in the lineup in the seventh inning for defensive purposes. In the ninth, although the sun had been down for twenty minutes, for some reason he was still wearing his sunglasses. This may have accounted in part for the improbable demonstration he had put on in attempting to field a hard-hit drive that the average big-league outfielder could have handled with little or no trouble. Eamons had misjudged the sinking liner, and the ball had skidded between his legs on its first low bounce, hit the fence behind him, and rebounded right through his legs a second time.

Eamons had previously been relieved from his pinch-hitting duties after popping up three times and fanning twice. He reminded very few people of Cobb.

Off the field, Eamons dwelt in a similar fog. During his first weeks in the East, it was simply the usual haziness that enshrouds the lovesick. Then it thickened into a depression. During the last two weeks in August, Eamons, who had been hearing from Priscilla at least once a day, received no word whatever from her. His increasingly desperate phone calls to the West Coast had also gone unanswered. Jim McCrillis did everything he could to cheer up the forlorn outfielder. Assigned by Shepard to stay on as Eamons's twenty-four-hour companion, McCrillis took him to a Western movie each night and dined him at the best rathskellers. In their hotel room, he listened patiently to the boy's lamentations.

On Labor Day evening, McCrillis reported to Shepard that the situation had become impossible. "And damn unpleasant, too," he added. "I can't tell the boy why he hasn't heard from that girl. I think he knows she's dropped him. He just can't bring himself to face it."

"He'll have to eventually. Then he'll start to mend," Shepard told him. "Stick with it, Jim."

The Saturday after Labor Day, Eamons pulled another "Eamons," as his boners were now being called. In the fourth inning, he was sent in as a pinch runner, a seemingly foolproof assignment. Eamons found a way, though. No one told him to steal second, but on the third pitch he was off like a hare.

He flashed down the base line with a terrific burst of speed, and had the base stole before the catcher went through the motions of making his throw. The only trouble was that second base was already occupied by a teammate. This teammate, of course, was not prepared to jump for third, and Eamons was tagged for the rally-killing out. If there was a bright side to the incident, it was that Eamons didn't have to be used again in the game.

Shepard witnessed this "Eamons" from the center-field bleachers. He made it a practice to mingle with the fans in the bleachers from time to time in order to get, as he phrased it, "a true and undistorted picture of the real fan's attitude toward the team and the administration." On these expeditions, Shepard diguised himself in a baggy suit and dark glasses, and pulled the brim of an old hat down low over his forehead. Now and then a fan penetrated Shepard's disguise, but for the most part his identity went unsuspected. It was a bittersweet triumph. It pleased him to be a successful masquerader, but at the same time he was always hoping that, in spite of his efforts to conceal his face and figure, he would be so well known to an adoring public that they could spot him in a suit of armor with the visor shut.

"Mr. Shepard," he heard a voice saying in hushed tones as he sat in the bleachers, wondering when the fans would quiet down about Eamons's latest blunder and stop accusing C. C. Shepard of throwing away a pennant. He turned his head cautiously. It was Ray.

"Priscilla Summers wants to see you," Ray whispered excitedly in his ear. "She's up at the top of the bleachers."

Shepard's jaw sagged.

"She showed up at your box," Ray went on. "I would have brushed her off but I was afraid she'd get to Eamons."

Shepard tugged the brim of his hat down and followed Ray up the aisle of concrete steps. His mind worked furiously to bring this unsettling turn of events into some sort of focus.

Priscilla Summers sat, with her legs casually crossed, in the last row of the bleachers. She was wearing dark glasses, too. They hid the expression in her eyes, but the line of her mouth showed she was in an aggressive mood.

Shepard removed his hat in an elaborate gesture of mock courtesy. "I hope you didn't come all this distance," he said, "just to tell me I'm looking much more handsome than my recent photographs."

"Is that a nice way to speak to one of your greatest admirers?" she cooed. They faced each other like ancient foes. "I just happened to be in town," she went on coolly. "Publicity. One of my pictures opens here next week. We're greasing the wheels."

"And you came all the way out to the ballpark to give me a pair of free tickets."

"Ah, you're a cute boy," she laughed. "No, I've got news for you. Personal news. I wanted to tell you I'm going to marry one of your players next Wednesday."

Shepard tried to steady himself by clutching wildly for Ray's arm.

"I knew you'd be delighted to hear that," Priscilla smiled.

"How'd you ever work that, young lady?" Shepard sputtered feebly. "You haven't seen Eamons for a month. You haven't written him in over two weeks. You—"

"Oh, I'm not marrying Walter," she interrupted. "I'm going to marry Blitz Baker."

Shepard's instinct told him to cover up, fast. The important thing was for Priscilla to believe she had triumphed gloriously and completely. He made a titanic effort not to register the feeling of relief that surged through every fiber of his body. It was only Blitz Baker. A washed-up pitcher. Won four, lost nine. Whew! A cheap price to pay when it could have been Eamons.

"I've got to hand it to you," he said, as if he were standing gallant in defeat. "You're a faster worker than I bargained for."

"Just call me Shep," Priscilla said with frosty sarcasm. She stood up to leave. "How do you like finishing second, Grandpa?"

Shepard watched her as she disappeared down the runway exit. He shocked Ray by leading him back to the office for a good stiff drink. When his nerves had slowed down to a bumpy trot after he'd had three fingers of Scotch, Shepard peeled off his disguise and climbed back into his regular clothes. The telephone rang just as he was leaving for home. It was McCrillis, calling from the players' dressing room. He wanted to know if Shepard had seen the story in the afternoon papers about Blitz Baker and Priscilla Summers.

Shepard described the meeting in the bleachers. "I was going to call you, Jim," he said, his voice still husky with tension. "Do you think we should tell Eamons or try to keep it from him?"

"He knows about it," McCrillis said. "Somebody showed him the paper."

"How'd he take it?"

"Hard, Shep, awful hard. He's been in the shower for over a half hour. I think he's waiting till everybody goes."

"Watch him close," Shepard said to McCrillis. "Don't let him out of your sight."

• • •

Refreshed by a good night's sleep and some glowing write-ups in the morning papers, Shepard arrived at the ballpark shortly after nine on Sunday morning. His footsteps, the only sound in the vast hush of the stadium, echoed strangely as he strode through the rotunda where, three hours later, thousands would be clamoring around the ticket booths. He unlocked a gate next to the turnstiles, and was striding down the passageway under the stands when he was startled by what seemed to be the sound of bat meeting ball. He heard it again as he hurried up the nearest ramp. Probably some kids who'd stowed away over Saturday night.

He stopped short when he came to the head of the ramp, behind first base, and tried to make some sense out of the baffling scene on the diamond below him. Jim McCrillis stood on the pitcher's mound, with thirty or so practice balls scattered around him. He was pitching to Eamons. *Whack!* Shepard watched a long belt sail all the way to the wall in right center. That's the way he used to cut, thought Shepard. McCrillis picked up another ball. Into the motion. *Whack!* Shepard lowered himself into a chair and gazed at the ghostly batting practice.

Eamons slammed the last pitch against the scoreboard in dead-center field and hustled down the first-base line and on into the outfield. He picked up a ball near the wall, wheeled, and fired it in to home plate, where McCrillis stood. Eamons picked up another ball, wheeled and fired again.

McCrillis had just handled the fourth throw from the outfield when, out of the corner of his eye, he caught sight of Shepard making his way through the boxes. McCrillis cupped his glove and bare hand to his mouth and hollered to Eamons to hold it up.

Shepard clambered awkwardly over the railing and on to the field. "What goes on here, anyway?" he shouted as he walked toward the plate.

"He wanted some practice," McCrillis said, panting a little. He looked as if he had just caught both games of a double-header. "Got me out of bed at—"

"Watch your head!" Eamons's voice carried pugnaciously from the far reaches of the outfield. A rifle-shot throw kicked off the turf near the pitcher's mound. McCrillis and Shepard hit the dirt just in time, and the ball banged against the backstop. The two men dusted themselves off and moved a safe distance down the first-base line.

"He's been like that all morning. You can't do anything with him," McCrillis grumbled as the bombardment of baseballs continued. "One extreme to the other. Last night, he was like a wounded deer. Pitiful. Fell asleep right after supper. He couldn't eat any. Fell asleep with all his clothes on, in a chair. This morning—whango! I'm living with a madman. He pulls me out of bed at six o'clock. Yanks the blankets off and tells me to shut up when I ask him what's the matter. He needs some practice, he tells me; we're going to the ballpark. We've been out here three hours. He wouldn't even let me get some breakfast."

A bounding ball zipped by McCrillis's knee. He started to yell something to Eamons and then decided it was a waste of time. "When he comes in now," McCrillis complained, "I'll have to pitch that whole batch to him again or hit him fungoes. I don't mind that. But he's got no right to be sore at me. I'm not Priscilla Summers."

"I think you hit it there," Shepard said absently. He had been listening with one ear, trying to put the parts together. "He's going to take it out on everyone for a while, Jim. He's going to show the world."

Shepard and McCrillis were collecting the balls in front of the backstop and rolling them toward the pitcher's mound when Eamons came jogging in from the outfield. Shepard greeted him warmly: "Good morning, Walter."

Eamons glowered at Shepard for a moment. He spat a slug of tobacco juice an inch over Shepard's shoe and walked on to pick up a bat.

Shepard dug an elbow into McCrillis's ribs. "We've got a ballplayer again," he said.

During the week that followed, Eamons treated opposing pitchers with no more respect than he had Shepard. He delivered twice as a pinch hitter, and was given a crack at the starting lineup. In the final six games of the team's home stand, he collected twelve hits in twenty-six times at bat, stole three bases, and was impeccable in the field. His one-man rampage was the spearhead of the drive that sent the team four full games in front as it headed west to play the last twelve games on the schedule.

• • •

"And that, gentlemen," C. C. Shepard announced with a crackle of self-congratulation, "is how it worked out—precisely as we planned it." He watched the faces of the reporters whom he had summoned when the news had come through from Chicago that his team had clinched the pennant. Even his severest critics, Shepard could see, had been impressed by his account of how he had coped with his difficult midsummer problems.

Shepard basked for a moment in the admiration of his audience. "I just happen to have the ability to size up women," he went on. "Five minutes after I met this actress, I had her number. I knew Blitz Baker was exactly the type she'd go for. That's why I sent Blitz to Redlands. In two weeks she had forgotten all about Eamons. You know the rest, gentlemen. Last week she and Blitz were married. I'm afraid this will mean the finish of Blitz's baseball career. My guess, gentlemen, is that he'll be lucky to be pitching Class-D ball next year."

Ray, standing beside his boss, studied Shepard's face as he warmed up to the subject of Walter Eamons's great future. It struck Ray that he had never seen Shepard's craggy features composed in an expression of such radiant bliss.

The telephone rang, and Shepard motioned for Ray to take it.

"Who was it?" Shepard asked as Ray hung up.

"Nothing important, Mr. Shepard," Ray answered casually.

"Well, who was it?" Shepard asked again.

"Just Hochstetter," Ray said. "Nothing urgent."

"He wouldn't call me up just to congratulate me on the pennant," Shepard persisted. "What was on his mind, Ray?"

"Just some news about Blitz Baker."

"What did he do? Quit the team?" Shepard asked with a wise twinkle.

"Well, if you must know," Ray said, as if he were being pushed into something against his better judgment, "Hochstetter wanted to tell you that Blitz just pitched a no-hitter and struck out eleven men."

"As I was saying, gentlemen," Shepard resumed quickly, "this Eamons will be even better next year. With proper handling, I predict he'll develop into another Cobb. You can quote me on that."

What Did We Do Wrong? (1985)

Garrison Keillor

Garrison Keillor's tales of small-town America include runaway bestsellers like *Lake Wobegone Days* (1985) and *Leaving Home* (1987). He has written many popular short stories for *The New Yorker* and the *Atlantic Monthly*, which have been collected into *Happy to Be Here* (1982), *We Are Still Married* (1990), and *The Book of Guys: Stories* (1993). Recent books include *77 Love Sonnets* (2009) and *Cat, You Better Come Home* (2010). "What Did We Do Wrong?" originally appeared in *The New Yorker*. It gives us Annie Szemanski, the first woman to play in the major leagues.

The first woman to reach the big leagues said she wanted to be treated like any other rookie, but she didn't have to worry about that. The Sparrows nicknamed her Chesty and then Big Numbers the first week of spring training, and loaded her bed at the Ramada with butterscotch pudding. Only the writers made a big thing about her being the First Woman. The Sparrows treated her like dirt.

Annie Szemanski arrived in camp fresh from the Federales League of Bolivia, the fourth second baseman on the Sparrows roster, and when Drayton stepped in a hole and broke his ankle Hemmie put her in the lineup, hoping she would break hers. "This was the front office's bright idea," he told the writers. "Off the record, I think it stinks." But when she got in she looked so good that by the third week of March she was a foregone conclusion. Even Hemmie had to admit it. A .346 average tells no lies. He disliked her purely because she was a woman—there was nothing personal about it. Because she was a woman, she was given the manager's dressing room, and Hemmie had to dress with the team. He was sixty-one, a heavyweight, and he had a possum tattooed on his belly alongside the name "Georgene," so he was shy about taking his shirt off in front of people. He hated her for making it necessary. Other than that, he thought she was a tremendous addition to the team.

Asked how she felt being the first woman to make a major-league team, she said, "Like a pig in mud," or words to that effect, and then turned and released a squirt of tobacco juice from the wad of rum-soaked plug in her right cheek. She chewed a rare brand of plug called Stuff It, which she learned to chew when she was playing Nicaraguan summer ball. She told the writers, "They were so mean to me down there you couldn't write it in your newspaper. I took a gun everywhere I went, even to bed. *Especially* to bed. Guys were after me like you can't believe. That's when I started chewing tobacco—because no matter how bad anybody treats you, it's not as bad as this. This is the worst chew in the world. After this, everything else is peaches and cream." The writers elected Gentleman Jim, the Sparrow's PR guy, to bite off a chunk and tell them how it tasted, and as he sat and chewed it tears ran down his old sunburnt cheeks and he couldn't talk for a while. Then he whispered, "You've been chewing this for two years? Boy, I had no idea it was so hard to be a woman."

When thirty-two thousand fans came to Cold Spring Stadium on April 4th for Opening Day and saw the scrappy little freckle-faced woman with tousled black hair who they'd been reading about for almost two months, they were dizzy with devotion. They chanted her name and waved Annie flags and Annie caps ($8.95 and $4.95) and held up hand-painted bedsheets (EVERY DAY IS LADIES' DAY, A WOMAN'S PLACE—AT SECOND BASE, E.R.A. & R.B.I., THE GAME AIN'T OVER TILL THE BIG LADY BATS), but when they saw No. 18 trot out to second with a load of chew as big as if she had the mumps it was a surprise. Then, bottom of the second, when she leaned over in the on-deck circle and dropped a stream of brown juice in the sod, the stadium experienced a moment of thoughtful silence.

One man in Section 31 said, "Hey, what's the beef? She can chew if she wants to. This is 1987. Grow up."

"I guess you're right," his next-seat neighbor said. "My first reaction was nausea, but I think you're right."

"Absolutely. She's a woman, but, more than that, she's a *person*."

Other folks said, "I'm with you on that. A woman can carry a quarter pound of chew in her cheek and spit in public, same as any man—why should there be any difference?"

And yet. Nobody wanted to say this, but the plain truth was that No. 18 was not handling her chew well at all. Juice ran down her chin and dripped onto her shirt. She's bit off more than she can chew, some people thought to themselves, but they didn't want to say that.

Arnie (the Old Gardener) Brixius mentioned it ever so gently in his "Hot Box" column the next day:

> It's only this scribe's opinion, but isn't it about time baseball cleaned up its act and left the tobacco in the locker? Surely big leaguers can go two hours without nicotine. Many a fan has turned away in disgust at the sight of grown men (and now a member of the fair sex) with a faceful, spitting gobs of the stuff in full view of paying customers. Would Frank Sinatra do this onstage? Or Anne Murray? Nuff said.

• • •

End of April, Annie was batting .278, with twelve R.B.I.s, which for the miserable Sparrows was stupendous, and at second base she was surprising a number of people, including base runners who thought she'd be a pushover on the double play. A runner heading for second quickly found out that Annie had knees like ball-peen hammers and if he tried to eliminate her from the play she might eliminate him from the rest of the week. One night, up at bat against the Orioles, she took a step toward the mound after an inside pitch and yelled some things, and when the dugouts emptied she was in the thick of it with men who had never been walloped by a woman before. The home-plate ump hauled her off a guy she was pounding the cookies out of, and a moment later he threw her out of the game for saying things to him, he said, that he had never heard in his nineteen years of umpiring. ("Like what, for example?" writers asked. "Just tell us one thing." But he couldn't; he was too upset.)

The next week, the United Baseball Office Workers local passed a resolution in support of Annie, as did the League of Women Voters and the Women's Softball Caucus, which stated, "Szemanski is a model for all women who are made to suffer guilt for their aggressiveness, and we declare our solidarity with her heads-up approach to the game. While we feel she is holding the bat too high and should bring her hips into her swing more, we're behind her one hundred per cent."

Then, May 4th, at home against Oakland—seventh inning, two outs, bases loaded—she dropped an easy pop-up and three runs came across home plate. The fans sent a few light boos her way to let her know they were paying attention, nothing serious or overtly political, just some folks grumbling, but she took a few steps toward the box seats and yelled something at them that sounded like—well, like something she shouldn't have said, and after the game she said some more things to the writers that Gentleman Jim pleaded with them not to print. One of them was Monica Lamarr, of the *Press*, who just laughed. She said, "Look. I spent two years in the Lifestyles section writing about motherhood vs. career and the biological clock. Sports is my way out of the gynecology ghetto, so don't ask me to eat this story. It's a hanging curve and I'm going for it. I'm never going to write about day care again." And she wrote it:

SZEMANSKI RAPS FANS AS "SMALL PEOPLE" AFTER DUMB ERROR
GIVES GAME TO A'S
FIRST WOMAN ATTRIBUTES BOOS TO SEXUAL INADEQUACY IN STANDS

Jim made some phone calls and the story was yanked and only one truckload of papers went out with it, but word got around, and the next night, though Annie went three for four, the crowd was depressed, and even when she did great the rest of the home stand, and became the first woman to hit a major-league triple, the atmosphere at the ballpark was one of moodiness and deep hurt. Jim went to the men's room one night and found guys standing in line there, looking thoughtful and sad. One of them said, "She's a helluva ballplayer," and other guys murmured that yes, she was, and they wouldn't take anything away from her, she was great and it was wonderful that she had opened up baseball to women, and then they changed the subject to gardening, books, music, aesthetics, anything but baseball. They looked like men who had been stood up.

Gentleman Jim knocked on her door that night. She wore a blue chenille bathrobe flecked with brown tobacco-juice stains, and her black hair hung down in wet strands over her face. She spat into a Dixie cup she was carrying. "Hey! How the Fritos are you? I haven't seen your Big Mac for a while," she said, sort of. He told her she was a great person and a great ballplayer and that he loved her and wanted only the best for her, and he begged her to apologize to the fans. "Make a gesture—*anything*. They *want* to like you. Give them a chance to like you."

She blew her nose into a towel. She said that she wasn't there to be liked, she was there to play ball.

• • •

It was a good road trip. The Sparrows won five out of ten, lifting their heads off the canvas, and Annie raised her average to .291 and hit the first major-league home run ever by a woman, up into the left-field screen at Fenway. Sox fans stood and cheered for fifteen minutes. They whistled, they stamped, they pleaded, the Sparrows pleaded, umpires pleaded, but she refused to come out and tip her hat until the public-address announcer said, "No. 18, please come out of the dugout and take a bow. No. 18, the applause is for you and is not intended as patronizing in any way," and then she stuck her head out for 1.5 seconds and did not tip but only touched the brim. Later, she told the writers that just because people had expectations didn't mean she had to fulfill them—she used other words to explain this, but her general drift was that she didn't care very much about living up to anyone else's image of her, and if anyone thought she should, they could go watch wrist wrestling.

The forty thousand who packed Cold Spring Stadium June 6th to see the Sparrows play the Yankees didn't come for a look at Ron Guidry. Banners hung from the second deck: WHAT DID WE DO WRONG? and ANNIE COME HOME and WE LOVE YOU, WHY DO YOU TREAT US THIS WAY? and IF YOU WOULD LIKE TO DISCUSS THIS IN A NONCONFRONTATIONAL, MUTUALLY RESPECTFUL WAY, MEET US AFTER THE GAME AT GATE C. It was Snapshot Day, and all the Sparrows appeared on the field for photos with the fans except you know who. Hemmie begged her to go. "You owe it to them," he said.

"Owe?" she said. "*Owe?*"

"Sorry, wrong word," he said. "What if I put it this way: it's a sort of tradition."

"*Tradition*?" she said. "I'm supposed to worry about *tradition*?"

That day, she became the first woman to hit .300. A double in the fifth inning. The scoreboard flashed the message, and the crowd gave her a nice hand. A few people stood and cheered, but the fans around them told them to sit down. "She's not that kind of person," they said. "Cool it. Back off." The fans were trying to give her plenty of space. After the game, Guidry said, "I really have to respect her. She's got that small strike zone and she protects it well, so she makes you pitch to her." She said, "Guidry? Was that his name? I didn't know. Anyway, he didn't show me much. He throws funny, don't you think? He reminded me a little bit of a southpaw I saw down in Nicaragua, except she threw inside more."

All the writers were there, kneeling around her. One of them asked if Guidry had thrown her a lot of sliders.

She gave him a long, baleful look. "Jeez, you guys are out of shape," she said. "You're wheezing and panting and sucking air, and you just took the elevator down from the press box. You guys want to write about sports you ought to go into training. And then you ought to learn how to recognize a slider. Jeez, if you were writing about agriculture, would you have to ask someone if those were Holsteins?"

Tears came to the writer's eyes. "I'm trying to help," he said. "Can't you see that? Don't you know how much we care about you? Sometimes I think you put up this tough exterior to hide your own insecurity."

She laughed and brushed the wet hair back from her forehead. "It's no exterior," she said as she unbuttoned her jersey. "It's who I am." She peeled off her socks and stepped out to her cubicle a moment later, sweaty and stark naked. The towel hung from her hand. She walked slowly around them. "You guys learned all you know about women thirty years ago. That wasn't me back then, that was my mother." The writers bent over their notepads, writing down every word she said and punctuating carefully. Gentleman Jim took off his glasses. "My mother was a nice lady, but she couldn't hit the curve to save her Creamettes," she went on. "And now, gentlemen, if you'll excuse me, I'm going to take a shower." They pored over their notes until she was gone, and then they piled out into the hallway and hurried back to the press elevator.

Arnie stopped at the Shortstop for a load of Martinis before he went to the office to write the "Hot Box," which turned out to be about love:

Baseball is a game but it's more than a game, baseball is people, dammit, and if you are around people you can't help but get involved in their lives and care about them and then you don't know how to talk to them or tell them how much you care and how come we know so much about pitching and we don't know squat about how to communicate? I guess that is the question.

• • •

The next afternoon, Arnie leaned against the batting cage before the game, hung over, and watched her hit line drives, fifteen straight, and each one made his head hurt. As she left the cage, he called over to her. "Later," she said. She also declined a pregame interview with Joe Garagiola, who had just told his NBC "Game of the Week" television audience, "This is a city in love with a little girl named Annie Szemanski," when he saw her in the dugout doing deep knee bends. "Annie! Annie!" he yelled over the air. "Let's see if we can't get her up here," he told the home audience. "Annie! Joe Garagiola!" She turned her back to him and went down into the dugout.

That afternoon, she became the first woman to steal two bases in one inning. She reached first on a base on balls, stole second, went to third on a sacrifice fly, and headed for home on the next pitch. The catcher came out to make the tag, she caught him with her elbow under the chin, and when the dust cleared she was grinning at the ump, the catcher was sprawled in the grass trying to inhale, and the ball was halfway to the backstop.

The TV camera zoomed in on her, head down, trotting toward the dugout steps, when suddenly she looked up. Some out-of-town fan had yelled at her from the box seats. ("A profanity which also refers to a female dog," the *News* said.) She smiled and, just before she stepped out of view beneath the dugout roof, millions observed her right hand uplifted in a familiar gesture. In bars around the country, men looked at each other and said, "Did she do what I think I saw her do? She didn't do that, did she?" In the booth, Joe Garagiola was observing that it was a clean play, that the runner has a right to the base path, but when her hand appeared on the screen he stopped. At home, it sounded as if he had been hit in the chest by a rock. The screen went blank, then went to a beer commercial. When the show resumed, it was the middle of the next inning.

On Monday, for "actions detrimental to the best interests of baseball," Annie was fined a thousand dollars by the Commissioner and suspended for two games. He deeply regretted the decision, etc. "I count myself among her most ardent fans. She is good for baseball, good for the cause of equal rights, good for America." He said he would be happy to suspend the suspension if she would make a public apology, which would make him the happiest man in America.

Gentleman Jim went to the bank Monday afternoon and got the money, a thousand dollars, in a cashier's check. All afternoon, he called Annie's number over and over, waiting thirty and forty rings, then trying again. He called from a pay phone at the Stop 'N' Shop, next door to the Cityview Apartments, where she lived, and between calls he sat in his car and watched the entrance, waiting for her to come out. Other men were parked there, too, in front, and some in back—men with Sparrows bumper stickers. After midnight, about eleven of them were left. "Care to share some onion chips and clam dip?" one guy said to another guy. Pretty soon all of them were standing around the trunk of the clam-dip guy's car, where he also had a case of beer.

"Here, let me pay you something for this beer," said a guy who had brought a giant box of pretzels.

"Hey, no. Really. It's just good to have other guys to talk to tonight," said the clam-dip owner.

"She changed a lot of very basic things about the whole way that I look at myself as a man," the pretzel guy said quietly.

"I'm in public relations," said Jim, "but even I don't understand all that she has meant to people."

"How can she do this to us?" said a potato-chip man. "All the love of the fans, how can she throw it away? Why can't she just play ball?"

Annie didn't look at it that way. "Pall Mall! I'm not going to crawl just because some Tootsie Roll says crawl, and if they don't like it, then Ritz, they can go Pepsi their Hostess Twinkies," she told the writers as she cleaned out her locker on Tuesday morning. They had never seen the inside of her locker before. It was stuffed with dirty socks, half-unwrapped gifts from admiring fans, a set of ankle weights, and a small silver-plated pistol. "No way I'm going to pay a thousand dollars, and if they expect an apology—well, they better send out for lunch, because it's going to be a long wait. Gentlemen, good-bye and hang on to your valuable coupons." And she smiled her most winning smile and sprinted up the stairs to collect her paycheck. They waited for her outside the Sparrows office, twenty-six men, and then followed her down the ramp and out of Gate C. She broke into a run and disappeared into the lunch-time crowd on West Providence Avenue, and that was the last they saw of her—the woman of their dreams, the love of their lives, carrying a red gym bag, running easily away from them.

Horseshoes (1914)

Ring Lardner

Although Ring Lardner was personally articulate, modest, and somewhat prudish, his fictional baseball players are usually just the opposite. In his later short stories, Lardner branched out to other sports and aspects of the American scene and character. This widened his popularity and burnished his image as one of the great American writers. His books, many of which are collections of his short stories, include *You Know Me, Al* (1916), *Round Up* (1929), *The Big Town* (1925), and *Collected Stories of Ring Lardner* (1941).

The series ended Tuesday, but I had stayed in Philadelphia an extra day on the chance of there being some follow-up stuff worth sending. Nothing had broken loose; so I filed some stuff about what the Athletics and Giants were going to do with their dough, and then caught the eight o'clock train for Chicago.

Having passed up supper in order to get my story away and grab the train, I went to the buffet car right after I'd planted my grips. I sat down at one of the tables and ordered a sandwich. Four salesmen were playing rum at the other table and all the chairs in the car were occupied; so it didn't surprise me when somebody flopped down in the seat opposite me.

I looked up from my paper and with a little thrill recognized my companion. Now I've been experting round the country with ballplayers so much that it doesn't usually excite me to meet one face to face, even if he's a star. I can talk with Tyrus without getting all fussed up. But this particular player had jumped from obscurity to fame so suddenly and had played such an important though brief part in the recent argument between the Macks and McGraws that I couldn't help being a little awed by his proximity.

It was none other than Grimes, the utility outfielder Connie had been forced to use in the last game because of the injury to Joyce—Grimes, whose miraculous catch in the eleventh inning had robbed Parker of a home run and the Giants of victory, and whose own homer—a fluky one—had given the Athletics another World's Championship.

I had met Grimes one day during the spring he was with the Cubs, but I knew he wouldn't remember me. A ballplayer never recalls a reporter's face on less than six introductions or his name on less than twenty. However, I resolved to speak to him, and had just mustered sufficient courage to open a conversation when he saved me the trouble.

"Whose picture have they got there?" he asked, pointing to my paper.

"Speed Parker's," I replied.

"What do they say about him?" asked Grimes.

"I'll read it to you," I said:

"'Speed Parker, McGraw's great third baseman, is ill in a local hospital with nervous prostration, the result of the strain of the World's Series, in which he played such a stellar role. Parker is in such a dangerous condition that no one is allowed to see him. Members of the New York team and fans from Gotham called at the hospital to-day, but were unable to gain admittance to his ward. Philadelphians hope he will recover speedily and will suffer no permanent ill effects from his sickness, for he won their admiration by his work in the series, though he was on a rival team. A lucky catch by Grimes, the Athletics' substitute outfielder, was all that prevented Parker from winning the title for New York. According to Manager Mack, of the champions, the series would have been over in four games but for Parker's wonderful exhibition of nerve and—'"

"That'll be a plenty," Grimes interrupted. "And that's just what you might expect from one o' them doughheaded reporters. If all the baseball writers was where they belonged they'd have to build a annex to Matteawan."

I kept my temper with very little effort—it takes more than a peevish ballplayer's remarks to insult one of our fraternity; but I didn't exactly understand his peeve.

"Doesn't Parker deserve the bouquet?" I asked.

"Oh, they can boost him all they want to," said Grimes; "but when they call that catch lucky and don't mention the fact that Parker is the luckiest guy in the world, somethin' must be wrong with 'em. Did you see the serious?"

"No," I lied glibly, hoping to draw from him the cause of his grouch.

"Well," he said, "you sure missed somethin'. They never was a serious like it before and they won't never be one again. It went the full seven games and every game was a bear. They was one big innin' every day and Parker was the big cheese in it. Just as Connie says, the Ath-a-letics would of cleaned 'em in four games but for Parker; but it wasn't because he's a great ballplayer—it was because he was born with a knife, fork and spoon in his mouth, and a rabbit's foot hung round his neck.

"You may not know it, but I'm Grimes, the guy that made the lucky catch. I'm the guy that won the serious with a hit—a home-run hit; and I'm here to tell you that if I'd had one-tenth o' Parker's luck they'd of heard about me long before yesterday. They say my homer was lucky. Maybe it was; but, believe me, it was time things broke for me. They been breakin' for him all his life."

"Well," I said, "his luck must have gone back on him if he's in a hospital with nervous prostration."

"Nervous prostration nothin'," said Grimes. "He's in a hospital because his face is all out o' shape and he's ashamed to appear on the street. I don't usually do so much talkin' and I'm ravin' a little to-night because I've had a couple o' drinks; but—"

"Have another," said I, ringing for the waiter, "and talk some more."

"I made two hits yesterday," Grimes went on, "but the crowd only seen one. I busted up the game and the serious with the one they seen. The one they didn't see was the one I busted up a guy's map with—and Speed Parker was the guy. That's why he's in a hospital. He may be able to play ball next year; but I'll bet my share o' the dough that McGraw won't reco'nize him when he shows up at Marlin in the spring."

"When did this come off?" I asked. "And why?"

"It come off outside the clubhouse after yesterday's battle," he said; "and I hit him because he called me a name—a name I won't stand for from him."

"What did he call you?" I queried, expecting to hear one of the delicate epithets usually applied by conquered to conqueror on the diamond.

"'Horseshoes!'" was Grimes' amazing reply.

"But, good Lord!" I remonstrated, "I've heard of ballplayers calling each other that, and Lucky Stiff, and Fourleaf Clover, ever since I was a foot high, and I never knew them to start fights about it."

"Well," said Grimes, "I might as well give you all the dope; and then if you don't think I was justified I'll pay your fare from here to wherever you're goin'. I don't want you to think I'm kickin' about trifles—or that I'm kickin' at all, for that matter. I just want to prove to you that he didn't have no license to pull that Horseshoes stuff on me and that I only give him what was comin' to him."

"Go ahead and shoot," said I.

"Give us some more o' the same," said Grimes to the passing waiter. And then he told me about it.

• • •

Maybe you've heard that me and Speed Parker was raised in the same town—Ishpeming, Michigan. We was kids together, and though he done all the devilment I got all the lickin's. When we was about twelve years old Speed throwed a rotten egg at the teacher and I got expelled. That made me sick o' schools and I wouldn't never go to one again, though my ol' man beat me up and the truant officers threatened to have me hung.

Well, while Speed was learnin' what was the principal products o' New Hampshire and Texas I was workin' round the freight-house and drivin' a dray.

We'd both been playin' ball all our lives; and when the town organized a semipro club we got jobs with it. We was to draw two bucks apiece for each game and they played every Sunday. We played four games before we got our first pay. They was a hole in my pants pocket as big as the home plate, but I forgot about it and put the dough in there. It wasn't there when I got home. Speed didn't have no hole in his pocket—you can bet on that! Afterward the club hired a good outfielder and I was canned. They was huntin' for another third baseman too; but, o' course, they didn't find none and Speed held his job.

The next year they started the Northern Peninsula League. We landed with the home team. The league opened in May and blowed up the third week in June. They paid off all the outsiders first and then had just money enough left to settle with one of us two Ishpeming guys. The night they done the payin' I was out to my uncle's farm, so they settled with Speed and told me I'd have to wait for mine. I'm still waitin'!

Gene Higgins, who was manager o' the Battle Creek Club, lived in Houghton, and that winter we goes over and strikes him for a job. He give it to us and we busted in together two years ago last spring.

I had a good year down there. I hit over .300 and stole all the bases in sight. Speed got along good too, and they was several big-league scouts lookin' us over. The Chicago Cubs bought Speed outright and four clubs put in a draft for me. Three of 'em—Cleveland and the New York Giants and the Boston Nationals—needed outfielders bad, and it would of been a pipe for me to of made good with any of 'em. But who do you think got me? The same Chicago Cubs; and the only outfielders they had at that time was Schulte and Leach and Good and Williams and Stewart, and one or two others.

Well, I didn't figure I was any worse off than Speed. The Cubs had Zimmerman at third base and it didn't look like they was any danger of a busher beatin' him out; but Zimmerman goes and breaks his leg the second day o' the season—that's a year ago last April—and Speed jumps right in as a regular. Do you think anything like that could happen to Schulte or Leach, or any o' them outfielders? No, sir! I wore out my uniform slidin' up and down the bench and wonderin' whether they'd ship me to Fort Worth or Siberia.

Now I want to tell you about the miserable luck Speed had right off the reel. We was playin' at St. Louis. They had a one-run lead in the eighth, when their pitcher walked Speed with one out. Saier hits a high fly to center and Parker starts with the crack o' the bat. Both coachers was yellin' at him to go back, but he thought they was two out and he was clear round to third base when the ball come down. And Oakes muffs it! O' course he scored and the game was tied up.

Parker come in to the bench like he'd did something wonderful.

"Did you think they was two out?" ast Hank.

"No," says Speed, blushin'.

"Then what did you run for?" says Hank.

"I had a hunch he was goin' to drop the ball," says Speed; and Hank pretty near falls off the bench.

The next day he come up with one out and the sacks full, and the score tied in the sixth. He smashes one on the ground straight at Hauser and it looked like a cinch double play; but just as Hauser was goin' to grab it the ball hit a rough spot and hopped a mile over his head. It got between Oakes and

Magee and went clear to the fence. Three guys scored and Speed pulled up at third. The papers come out and said the game was won by a three-bagger from the bat o' Parker, the Cubs' sensational kid third baseman. Gosh!

We go home to Chi and are havin' a hot battle with Pittsburgh. This time Speed's turn come when they was two on and two out, and Pittsburgh a run to the good—I think it was the eighth innin'. Cooper gives him a fast one and he hits it straight up in the air. O' course the runners started goin', but it looked hopeless because they wasn't no wind or high sky to bother anybody. Mowrey and Gibson both goes after the ball; and just as Mowrey was set for the catch Gibson bumps into him and they both fall down. Two runs scored and Speed got to second. Then what does he do but try to steal third—with two out too! And Gibson's peg pretty near hits the left-field seats on the fly.

When Speed comes to the bench Hank says:

"If I was you I'd quit playin' ball and go to Monte Carlo."

"What for?" says Speed.

"You're so dam' lucky!" says Hank.

"So is Ty Cobb," says Speed. That's how he hated himself!

First trip to Cincy we run into a couple of old Ishpeming boys. They took us out one night, and about twelve o'clock I said we'd have to go back to the hotel or we'd get fined. Speed said I had cold feet and he stuck with the boys. I went back alone and Hank caught me comin' in and put a fifty-dollar plaster on me. Speed stayed out all night long and Hank never knowed it. I says to myself: "Wait till he gets out there and tries to play ball without no sleep!" But the game that day was called off on account o' rain. Can you beat it?

I remember what he got away with the next afternoon the same as though it happened yesterday. In the second innin' they walked him with nobody down, and he took a big lead off first base like he always does. Benton throwed over there three or four times to scare him back, and the last time he throwed, Hobby hid the ball. The coacher seen it and told Speed to hold the bag; but he didn't pay no attention. He started leadin' right off again and Hobby tried to tag him, but the ball slipped out of his hand and rolled about a yard away. Parker had plenty o' time to get back; but, instead o' that, he starts for second. Hobby picked up the ball and shot it down to Groh—and Groh made a square muff.

Parker slides into the bag safe and then gets up and throws out his chest like he'd made the greatest play ever. When the ball's throwed back to Benton, Speed leads off about thirty foot and stands there in a trance. Clarke signs for a pitch-out and pegs down to second to nip him. He was caught flat-footed—that is, he would of been with a decent throw; but Clarke's peg went pretty near to Latonia. Speed scored and strutted over to receive our hearty congratulations. Some o' the boys was laughin' and he thought they was laughin' with him instead of at him.

It was in the ninth, though, that he got by with one o' the worst I ever seen. The Reds was a run behind and Marsans was on third base with two out. Hobby, I think it was, hit one on the ground right at Speed and he picked it up clean. The crowd all got up and started for the exits. Marsans run toward the plate in the faint hope that the peg to first would be wild. All of a sudden the boys on the Cincy bench begun yellin' at him to slide, and he done so. He was way past the plate when Speed's throw got to Archer. The bonehead had shot the ball home instead o' to first base, thinkin' they was only one down. We was all crazy, believin' his nut play had let 'em tie it up; but he comes tearin' in, tellin' Archer to tag Marsans. So Jim walks over and tags the Cuban, who was brushin' off his uniform.

"You're out!" says Klem. "You never touched the plate."

I guess Marsans knowed the umps was right because he didn't make much of a holler. But Speed sure got a pannin' in the clubhouse.

"I suppose you knowed he was goin' to miss the plate!" says Hank sarcastic as he could.

Everybody on the club roasted him, but it didn't do no good.

Well, you know what happened to me. I only got into one game with the Cubs—one afternoon when Leach was sick. We was playin' the Boston bunch and Tyler was workin' against us. I always had trouble with left-handers and this was one of his good days. I couldn't see what he throwed up there. I got one foul durin' the afternoon's entertainment; and the wind was blowin' a hundred-mile gale, so that the best outfielder in the world couldn't judge a fly ball. That Boston bunch must of hit fifty of 'em and they all come to my field.

If I caught any I've forgot about it. Couple o' days after that I got notice o' my release to Indianapolis.

Parker kept right on all season doin' the blamedest things you ever heard of and gettin' by with 'em. One o' the boys told me about it later. If they was playin' a double-header in St. Louis, with the thermometer at 130 degrees, he'd get put out by the umps in the first innin' o' the first game. If he started to steal the catcher'd drop the pitch or somebody'd muff the throw. If he hit a pop fly the sun'd get in somebody's eyes. If he took a swell third strike with

the bases full the umps would call it a ball. If he cut first base by twenty feet
the umps would be readin' the mornin' paper.

Zimmerman's leg mended, so that he was all right by June; and then Saier
got sick and they tried Speed at first base. He'd never saw the bag before; but
things kept on breakin' for him and he played it like a house afire. The Cubs
copped the pennant and Speed got in on the big dough, besides playin' a
whale of a game through the whole serious.

Speed and me both went back to Ishpeming to spend the winter—though
the Lord knows it ain't no winter resort. Our homes was there; and besides,
in my case, they was a certain girl livin' in the old burg.

Parker, o' course, was the hero and the swell guy when we got home. He'd
been in the World's Serious and had plenty o' dough in his kick. I come home
with nothin' but my suitcase and a hard-luck story, which I kept to myself. I
hadn't even went good enough in Indianapolis to be sure of a job there again.

That fall—last fall—an uncle o' Speed's died over in the Soo and left him
ten thousand bucks. I had an uncle down in the Lower Peninsula who was
worth five times that much—but he had good health!

This girl I spoke about was the prettiest thing I ever seen. I'd went with
her in the old days, and when I blew back I found she was still strong for me.
They wasn't a great deal o' variety in Ishpeming for a girl to pick from. Her
and I went to the dance every Saturday night and to church Sunday nights.
I called on her Wednesday evenin's, besides takin' her to all the shows that
come along—rotten as the most o' them was.

I never knowed Speed was makin' a play for this doll till along last
Feb'uary. The minute I seen what was up I got busy. I took her out sleigh-
ridin' and kept her out in the cold till she'd promised to marry me. We set the
date for this fall—I figured I'd know better where I was at by that time.

Well, we didn't make no secret o' bein' engaged; down in the poolroom
one night Speed come up and congratulated me. He says:

"You got a swell girl, Dick! I wouldn't mind bein' in your place. You're
mighty lucky to cop her out—you old Horseshoes, you!"

"Horseshoes!" I says. "You got a fine license to call anybody Horseshoes!
I suppose you ain't never had no luck?"

"Not like you," he says.

I was feelin' too good about grabbin' the girl to get sore at the time; but
when I got to thinkin' about it a few minutes afterward it made me mad clear
through. What right did that bird have to talk about me bein' lucky?

Speed was playin' freeze-out at a table near the door, and when I started home some o' the boys with him says:

"Good night, Dick."

I said good night and then Speed looked up.

"Good night, Horseshoes!" he says.

That got my nanny this time.

"Shut up, you lucky stiff!" I says. "If you wasn't so dam' lucky you'd be sweepin' the streets." Then I walks on out.

I was too busy with the girl to see much o' Speed after that. He left home about the middle o' the month to go to Tampa with the Cubs. I got notice from Indianapolis that I was sold to Baltimore. I didn't care much about goin' there and I wasn't anxious to leave home under the circumstances, so I didn't report till late.

When I read in the papers along in April that Speed had been traded to Boston for a couple o' pitchers I thought: "Gee! He must of lost his rabbit's foot!" Because, even if the Cubs didn't cop again, they'd have a city serious with the White Sox and get a bunch o' dough that way. And they wasn't no chance in the world for the Boston Club to get nothin' but their salaries.

It wasn't another month, though, till Shafer, o' the Giants, quit baseball and McGraw was up against it for a third baseman. Next thing I knowed Speed was traded to New York and was with another winner—for they never was out o' first place all season.

I was gettin' along all right at Baltimore and Dunnie liked me; so I felt like I had somethin' more than just a one-year job—somethin' I could get married on. It was all framed that the weddin' was comin' off as soon as this season was over; so you can believe I was pullin' for October to hurry up and come.

One day in August, two months ago, Dunnie come in the clubhouse and handed me the news.

"Rube Oldring's busted his leg," he says, "and he's out for the rest o' the season. Connie's got a youngster named Joyce that he can stick in there, but he's got to have an extra outfielder. He's made me a good proposition for you and I'm goin' to let you go. It'll be pretty soft for you, because they got the pennant cinched and they'll cut you in on the big money."

"Yes," I says; "and when they're through with me they'll ship me Hellan-gone, and I'll be raggin' down about seventy-five bucks a month next year."

"Nothin' like that," says Dunnie. "If he don't want you next season he's go to ask for waivers; and if you get out o' the big league you come right back here. That's all framed."

So that's how I come to get with the Ath-a-letics. Connie give me a nice, comf'table seat in one corner o' the bench and I had the pleasure o' watchin' a real ball club perform once every afternoon and sometimes twice.

Connie told me that as soon as they had the flag cinched he was goin' to lay off some o' his regulars and I'd get a chance to play.

Well, they cinched it the fourth day o' September and our next engagement was with Washin'ton on Labor Day. We had two games and I was in both of 'em. And I broke in with my usual lovely luck, because the pitchers I was ast to face was Bochling, a nasty left-hander, and this guy Johnson.

The mornin' game was Bochling's and he wasn't no worse than some o' the rest of his kind. I only whiffed once and would of had a triple if Milan hadn't run from here to New Orleans and stole one off me.

I'm not boastin' about my first experience with Johnson though. They can't never tell me he throws them balls with his arm. He's got a gun concealed about his person and he shoots 'em up there. I was leadin' off in Murphy's place and the game was a little delayed in startin', because I'd watched the big guy warm up and wasn't in no hurry to get to that plate. Before I left the bench Connie says:

"Don't try to take no healthy swing. Just meet 'em and you'll get along better."

So I tried to just meet the first one he throwed; but when I stuck out my bat Henry was throwin' the pill back to Johnson. Then I thought: Maybe if I start swingin' now at the second one I'll hit the third one. So I let the second one come over and the umps guessed it was another strike, though I'll bet a thousand bucks he couldn't see it no more'n I could.

While Johnson was still windin' up to pitch again I started to swing—and the big cuss crosses me with a slow one. I lunged at it twice and missed it both times, and the force o' my wallop throwed me clean back to the bench. The Ath-a-letics was all laughin' at me and I laughed too, because I was glad that much of it was over.

McInnes gets a base hit off him in the second innin' and I ast him how he done it.

"He's a friend o' mine," says Jack, "and he lets up when he pitches to me."

I made up my mind right there that if I was goin' to be in the league next year I'd go out and visit Johnson this winter and get acquainted.

I wished before the day was over that I was hittin' in the catcher's place, because the fellers down near the tail-end of the battin' order only had to face him three times. He fanned me on three pitched balls again in the third, and when I come up in the sixth he scared me to death by pretty near beanin' me with the first one.

"Be careful!" says Henry. "He's gettin' pretty wild and he's liable to knock you away from your uniform."

"Don't he never curve one?" I ast.

"Sure!" says Henry. "Do you want to see his curve?"

"Yes," I says, knowin' the hook couldn't be no worse'n the fast one.

So he give me three hooks in succession and I missed 'em all; but I felt more comf'table than when I was duckin' his fastball. In the ninth he hit my bat with a curve and the ball went on the ground to McBride. He booted it, but throwed me out easy—because I was so surprised at not havin' whiffed that I forgot to run!

Well, I went along like that for the rest o' the season, runnin' up against the best pitchers in the league and not exactly murderin' 'em. Everything I tried went wrong, and I was smart enough to know that if anything had depended on the games I wouldn't of been in there for two minutes. Joyce and Strunk and Murphy wasn't jealous o' me a bit; but they was glad to take turns restin', and I didn't care much how I went so long as I was sure of a job next year.

I'd wrote to the girl a couple o' times askin' her to set the exact date for our weddin'; but she hadn't paid no attention. She said she was glad I was with the Ath-a-letics, but she thought the Giants was goin' to beat us. I might of suspected from that somethin' was wrong, because not even a girl would pick the Giants to trim that bunch of ourn. Finally, the day before the serious started, I sent her a kind o' sassy letter sayin' I guessed it was up to me to name the day, and askin' whether October twentieth was all right. I told her to wire me yes or no.

I'd been readin' the dope about Speed all season, and I knowed he'd had a whale of a year and that his luck was right with him; but I never dreamed a man could have the Lord on his side as strong as Speed did in that World's Serious! I might as well tell you all the dope, so long as you wasn't there.

The first game was on our grounds and Connie give us a talkin' to in the clubhouse beforehand.

"The shorter this serious is," he says, "the better for us. If it's a long serious we're goin' to have trouble, because McGraw's got five pitchers he can work and we've got about three; so I want you boys to go at 'em for the jump and play 'em off their feet. Don't take things easy, because it ain't goin' to be no snap. Just because we've licked 'em before ain't no sign we'll do it this time."

Then he calls me to one side and ast me what I knowed about Parker.

"You was with the Cubs when he was, wasn't you?" he says.

"Yes," I says; "and he's the luckiest stiff you ever seen! If he got stewed and fell in the gutter he'd catch a fish."

"I don't like to hear a good ballplayer called lucky," says Connie. "He must have a lot of ability or McGraw wouldn't use him regular. And he's been hittin' about .340 and played a bang-up game at third base. That can't be all luck."

"Wait till you see him," I says; "and if you don't say he's the luckiest guy in the world you can sell me to the Boston Bloomer Girls. He's so lucky," I says, "that if they traded him to the St. Louis Browns they'd have the pennant cinched by the Fourth o' July."

And I'll bet Connie was willin' to agree with me before it was over.

Well, the Chief worked against the Big Rube in that game. We beat 'em, but they give us a battle and it was Parker that made it close. We'd gone along nothin' and nothin' till the seventh, and then Rube walks Collins and Baker lifts one over that little old wall. You'd think by this time them New York pitchers would know better than to give the guy anything he can hit.

In their part o' the ninth the Chief still had 'em shut out and two down, and the crowd was goin' home; but Doyle gets hit in the sleeve with a pitched ball and it's Speed's turn. He hits a foul pretty near straight up, but Schang misjudges it. Then he lifts another one and this time McInnes drops it. He'd ought to of been out twice. The Chief tries to make him hit at a bad one then, because he'd got him two strikes and nothin'. He hit at it all right—kissed it for three bases between Strunk and Joyce! And it was a wild pitch that he hit. Doyle scores, o' course, and the bugs suddenly decide not to go home just yet. I fully expected to see him steal home and get away with it, but Murray cut into the first ball and lined out to Barry.

Plank beat Matty two to one the next day in New York, and again Speed and his rabbit's foot give us an awful argument. Matty wasn't so good as usual and we really ought to of beat him bad. Two different times Strunk was on second waitin' for any kind o' wallop, and both times Barry cracked 'em down the third-base line like a shot. Speed stopped the first one with his stomach and extricated the pill just in time to nail Barry at first base and retire the side. The next time he threw his glove in front of his face in self-defense and the ball stuck in it.

In the sixth innin' Schang was on third base and Plank on first, and two down, and Murphy combed an awful one to Speed's left. He didn't have time to stoop over and he just stuck out his foot. The ball hit it and caromed in two hops right into Doyle's hands on second base before Plank got there. Then in the seventh Speed bunts one and Baker trips and falls goin' after it or he'd of threw him out a mile. They was two gone; so Speed steals second, and, o' course, Schang has to make a bad peg right at that time and lets him go to third. Then Collins boots one on Murray and they've got a run. But it didn't do 'em no good, because Collins and Baker and McInnes come up in the ninth and walloped 'em where Parker couldn't reach 'em.

Comin' back to Philly on the train that night, I says to Connic:

"What do you think o' that Parker bird now?"

"He's lucky, all right," says Connie smilin'; "but we won't hold it against him if he don't beat us with it."

"It ain't too late," I says. "He ain't pulled his real stuff yet."

The whole bunch was talkin' about him and his luck, and sayin' it was about time for things to break against him. I warned 'em that they wasn't no chance—that it was permanent with him.

Bush and Tesreau hooked up next day and neither o' them had much stuff. Everybody was hittin' and it looked like anybody's game right up to the ninth. Speed had got on every time he come up—the wind blowin' his fly balls away from the outfielders and the infielders bootin' when he hit 'em on the ground.

When the ninth started the score was seven apiece. Connie and McGraw both had their whole pitchin' staffs warmin' up. The crowd was wild, because they'd been all kinds of action. They wasn't no danger of anybody's leavin' their seats before this game was over.

Well, Bescher is walked to start with and Connie's about ready to give Bush the hook; but Doyle pops out tryin' to bunt. Then Speed gets two strikes and two balls, and it looked to me like the next one was right over the heart; but Connolly calls it a ball and gives him another chance. He whales the groove ball to the fence in left center and gets round to third on it, while Bescher scores. Right then Bush comes out and the Chief goes in. He whiffs Murray and has two strikes on Merkle when Speed makes a break for home—and o' course, that was the one ball Schang dropped in the whole serious!

They had a two-run lead on us then and it looked like a cinch for them to hold it, because the minute Tesreau showed a sign o' weakenin' McGraw was sure to holler for Matty or the Rube. But you know how quick that bunch of ourn can make a two-run lead look sick. Before McGraw could get Jeff out o' there we had two on the bases.

Then Rube comes in and fills 'em up by walkin' Joyce. It was Eddie's turn to wallop and if he didn't do nothin' we had Baker comin' up next. This time Collins saved Baker the trouble and whanged one clear to the woods. Everybody scored but him—and he could of, too, if it'd been necessary.

In the clubhouse the boys naturally felt pretty good. We'd copped three in a row and it looked like we'd make it four straight, because we had the Chief to send back at 'em the followin' day.

"Your friend Parker is lucky," the boys says to me, "but it don't look like he could stop us now."

I felt the same way and was consultin' the time-tables to see whether I could get a train out o' New York for the West next evenin'. But do you think Speed's luck was ready to quit? Not yet! And it's a wonder we didn't all go nuts durin' the next few days. If words could kill, Speed would of died a thousand times. And I wish he had!

They wasn't no record-breakin' crowd out when we got to the Polo Grounds. I guess the New York bugs was pretty well discouraged and the bettin' was eight to five that we'd cop that battle and finish it. The Chief was the only guy that warmed up for us and McGraw didn't have no choice but to use Matty, with the whole thing dependin' on this game.

They went along like the two swell pitchers they was till Speed's innin', which in this battle was the eighth. Nobody scored, and it didn't look like they was ever goin' to till Murphy starts off that round with a perfect bunt and Joyce sacrifices him to second. All Matty had to do then was to get rid o' Collins and Baker—and that's about as easy as sellin' silk socks to an Eskimo.

He didn't give Eddie nothin' he wanted to hit, though; and finally he slaps one on the ground to Doyle. Larry made the play to first base and Murphy moved to third. We all figured Matty'd walk Baker then, and he done it. Connie sends Baker down to second on the first pitch to McInnes, but Meyers don't pay no attention to him—they was playin' for McInnes and wasn't takin' no chances o' throwin' the ball away.

Well, the count goes to three and two on McInnes and Matty comes with a curve—he's got some curve too; but Jack happened to meet it and—Blooie! Down the left foul line where he always hits! I never seen a ball hit so hard in my life. No infielder in the world could of stopped it. But I'll give you a thousand bucks if that ball didn't go kerplunk right into the third bag and stop as dead as George Washington! It was child's play for Speed to pick it up and heave it over to Merkle before Jack got there. If anybody else had been playin' third base the bag would of ducked out o' the way o' that wallop; but even the bases themselves was helpin' him out.

The two runs we ought to of had on Jack's smash would of been just enough to beat 'em, because they got the only run o' the game in their half— or, I should say, the Lord give it to 'em.

Doyle'd been throwed out and up come Parker, smilin'. The minute I seen him smile I felt like somethin' was comin' off and I made the remark on the bench.

Well, the Chief pitched one right at him and he tried to duck. The ball hit his bat and went on a line between Jack and Eddie. Speed didn't know he'd hit it till the guys on the bench wised him up. Then he just had time to get to first base. They tried the hit-and-run on the second ball and Murray lifts a high fly that Murphy didn't have to move for. Collins pulled the old bluff about the ball bein' on the ground and Barry yells, "Go on! Go on!" like he was the coacher. Speed fell for it and didn't know where the ball was no more'n a rabbit; he just run his fool head off and we was gettin' all ready to laugh when the ball come down and Murphy dropped it!

If Parker had stuck near first base, like he ought to of done, he couldn't of got no farther'n second; but with the start he got he was pretty near third when Murphy made the muff, and it was a cinch for him to score. The next two guys was easy outs; so they wouldn't of had a run except for Speed's boner. We couldn't do nothin' in the ninth and we was licked.

Well, that was a tough one to lose; but we figured that Matty was through and we'd wind it up the next day, as we had Plank ready to send back at 'em. We wasn't afraid o' the Rube, because he hadn't never bothered Collins and Baker much.

The two left-handers come together just like everybody'd doped it and it was about even up to the eighth. Plank had been goin' great and, though the score was two and two, they'd got their two on boots and we'd hit ourn in. We went after Rube in our part o' the eighth and knocked him out. Demaree stopped us after we'd scored two more.

"It's all over but the shoutin'!" says Davis on the bench.

"Yes," I says, "unless that seventh son of a seventh son gets up there again."

He did, and he come up after they'd filled the bases with a boot, a base hit and a walk with two out. I says to Davis:

"If I was Plank I'd pass him and give 'em one run."

"That wouldn't be no baseball," says Davis—"not with Murray comin' up."

Well, it mayn't of been no baseball, but it couldn't of turned out worse if they'd did it that way. Speed took a healthy at the first ball; but it was a hook and he caught it on the handle, right up near his hands. It started outside the first-base line like a foul and then changed its mind and rolled in. Schang run away from the plate, because it looked like it was up to him to make the play. He picked the ball up and had to make the peg in a hurry.

His throw hit Speed right on top o' the head and bounded off like it had struck a cement sidewalk. It went clear over to the seats and before McInnes could get it three guys had scored and Speed was on third base. He was left there, but that didn't make no difference. We was licked again and for the first time the gang really begun to get scared.

We went over to New York Sunday afternoon and we didn't do no singin' on the way. Some o' the fellers tried to laugh, but it hurt 'em. Connie sent us to bed early, but I don't believe none o' the bunch got much sleep—I know I didn't; I was worryin' too much about the serious and also about the girl, who hadn't sent me no telegram like I'd ast her to. Monday mornin' I wired her askin' what was the matter and tellin' her I was gettin' tired of her foolishness. O' course I didn't make it so strong as that—but the telegram cost me a dollar and forty cents.

Connie had the choice o' two pitchers for the sixth game. He could use Bush, who'd been slammed round pretty hard last time out, or the Chief, who'd only had two days' rest. The rest of 'em—outside o' Plank—had a epidemic o' sore arms. Connie finally picked Bush, so's he could have the Chief in reserve in case we had to play a seventh game. McGraw started Big Jeff and we went at it.

It wasn't like the last time these two guys had hooked up. This time they both had somethin', and for eight innin's runs was as scarce as Chinese policemen. They'd been chances to score on both sides, but the big guy and Bush was both tight in the pinches. The crowd was plumb nuts and yelled like Indians every time a fly ball was caught or a strike called. They'd of got their money's worth if they hadn't been no ninth; but, believe me, that was some round!

They was one out when Barry hit one through the box for a base. Schang walked, and it was Bush's turn. Connie told him to bunt, but he whiffed in the attempt. Then Murphy comes up and walks—and the bases are choked. Young Joyce had been pie for Tesreau all day or else McGraw might of changed pitchers right there. Anyway he left Big Jeff in and he beaned Joyce with a fast one. It sounded like a tire blowin' out. Joyce falls over in a heap and we chase out there, thinkin' he's dead; but he ain't, and pretty soon he gets up and walks down to first base. Tesreau had forced in a run and again we begun to count the winner's end. Matty comes in to prevent further damage and Collins flies the side out.

"Hold 'em now! Work hard!" we says to young Bush, and he walks out there just as cool as though he was goin' to hit fungoes.

McGraw sends up a pinch hitter for Matty and Bush whiffed him. Then Bescher flied out. I was prayin' that Doyle would end it, because Speed's turn come after his'n; so I pretty near fell dead when Larry hit safe.

Speed had his old smile and even more chest than usual when come up there, swingin' five or six bats. He didn't wait for Doyle to try and steal, or nothin'. He lit into the first ball, though Bush was tryin' to waste it. I seen the ball go high in the air toward left field, and then I picked up my glove and got ready to beat it for the gate. But when I looked out to see if Joyce was set, what do you think I seen? He was lyin' flat on the ground! That blow on the head had got him just as Bush was pitchin' to Speed. He'd flopped over and didn't no more know what was goin' on than if he'd croaked.

Well, everybody else seen it at the same time; but it was too late. Strunk made a run for the ball, but they wasn't no chance for him to get near it. It hit the ground about ten feet back o' where Joyce was lyin' and bounded way over to the end o' the foul line. You don't have to be told that Doyle and Parker both scored and the serious was tied up.

We carried Joyce to the clubhouse and after a while he come to. He cried when he found out what had happened. We cheered him up all we could, but he was a pretty sick guy. The trainer said he'd be all right, though, for the final game.

They tossed up a coin to see where they'd play the seventh battle and our club won the toss; so we went back to Philly that night and cussed Parker clear across New Jersey. I was so sore I kicked the stuffin' out o' my seat.

You probably heard about the excitement in the burg yesterday mornin'. The demand for tickets was somethin' fierce and some of 'em sold for as high as twenty-five bucks apiece. Our club hadn't been lookin' for no seventh game and they was some tall hustlin' done round that old ballpark.

I started out to the grounds early and bought some New York papers to read on the car. They was a big story that Speed Parker, the Giants' hero, was goin' to be married a week after the end o' the serious. It didn't give the name o' the girl, sayin' Speed had refused to tell it. I figured she must be some dame he'd met round the circuit somewhere.

They was another story by one o' them smart baseball reporters sayin' that Parker, on his way up to the plate, had saw that Joyce was about ready to faint and had hit the fly ball to left field on purpose. Can you beat it?

I was goin' to show that to the boys in the clubhouse, but the minute I blowed in there I got some news that made me forget about everything else. Joyce was very sick and they'd took him to a hospital. It was up to me to play!

Connie come over and ast me whether I'd ever hit against Matty. I told him I hadn't, but I'd saw enough of him to know he wasn't no worse'n Johnson. He told me he was goin' to let me hit second—in Joyce's place—because he didn't want to bust up the rest of his combination. He also told me to take my orders from Strunk about where to play for the batters.

"Where shall I play for Parker?" I says, tryin' to joke and pretend I wasn't scared to death.

"I wisht I could tell you," says Connie. "I guess the only thing to do when he comes up is to get down on your knees and pray."

The rest o' the bunch slapped me on the back and give me all the encouragement they could. The place was jammed when we went out on the field. They may of been bigger crowds before, but they never was packed together so tight. I doubt whether they was even room enough left for Falkenberg to sit down.

The afternoon papers had printed the stuff about Joyce bein' out of it, so the bugs was wise that I was goin' to play. They watched me pretty close in battin' practice and give me a hand whenever I managed to hit one hard. When I was out catchin' fungoes the guys in the bleachers cheered me and told me they was with me; but I don't mind tellin' you that I was as nervous as a bride.

They wasn't no need for the announcers to tip the crowd off to the pitchers. Everybody in the United States and Cuba knowed that the Chief'd work for us and Matty for them. The Chief didn't have no trouble with 'em in the first innin'. Even from where I stood I could see that he had a lot o' stuff. Bescher and Doyle popped out and Speed whiffed.

Well, I started out makin' good, with reverse English, in our part. Fletcher booted Murphy's ground ball and I was sent up to sacrifice. I done a complete job of it—sacrificin' not only myself but Murphy with a pop fly that Matty didn't have to move for. That spoiled whatever chance we had o' gettin' the jump on 'em; but the boys didn't bawl me for it.

"That's all right, old boy. You're all right!" they said on the bench—if they'd had a gun they'd of shot me.

I didn't drop no fly balls in the first six innin's—because none was hit out my way. The Chief was so good that they wasn't hittin' nothin' out o' the infield. And we wasn't doin' nothin' with Matty, either. I led off in the fourth and fouled the first one. I didn't molest the other two. But if Connie and the gang talked about me they done it internally. I come up again—with Murphy on third base and two gone in the sixth, and done my little whiffin' specialty. And still the only people that panned me was the thirty thousand that had paid for the privilege!

My first fieldin' chance come in the seventh. You'd of thought that I'd of had my nerve back by that time; but I was just as scared as though I'd never saw a crowd before. It was just as well that they was two out when Merkle hit one to me. I staggered under it and finally it hit me on the shoulder. Merkle got to second, but the Chief whiffed the next guy. I was gave some cross looks on the bench and I shouldn't of blamed the fellers if they'd cut loose with some language; but they didn't.

They's no use in me tellin' you about none o' the rest of it—except what happened just before the start o' the eleventh and durin' that innin', which was sure the big one o' yesterday's pastime—both for Speed and yours sincerely.

The scoreboard was still a row o' ciphers and Speed'd had only a fair amount o' luck. He'd made a scratch base hit and robbed our bunch of a couple o' real ones with impossible stops.

When Schang flied out and wound up our tenth I was leanin' against the end of our bench. I heard my name spoke, and I turned round and seen a boy at the door.

"Right here!" I says; and he give me a telegram.

"Better not open it till after the game," says Connie.

"Oh, no; it ain't no bad news," I said, for I figured it was an answer from the girl. So I opened it up and read it on the way to my position. It said:

"Forgive me, Dick—and forgive Speed too. Letter follows."

Well, sir, I ain't no baby, but for a minute I just wanted to sit down and bawl. And then, all of a sudden, I got so mad I couldn't see. I run right into Baker as he was pickin' up his glove. Then I give him a shove and called him some name, and him and Barry both looked at me like I was crazy—and I was. When I got out in left field I stepped on my own foot and spiked it. I just had to hurt somebody.

As I remember it the Chief fanned the first two of 'em. Then Doyle catches one just right and lams it up against the fence back o' Murphy. The ball caromed round some and Doyle got all the way to third base. Next thing I seen was Speed struttin' up to the plate. I run clear in from my position.

"Kill him!" I says to the Chief. "Hit him in the head and kill him, and I'll go to jail for it!"

"Are you off your nut?" says the Chief. "Go out there and play ball—and quit ravin'."

Barry and Baker led me away and give me a shove out toward left. Then I heard the crack o' the bat and I seen the ball comin' a mile a minute. It was headed between Strunk and I and looked like it would go out o' the park. I don't remember runnin' or nothin' about it till I run into the concrete wall head first. They told me afterward and all the papers said that it was the greatest catch ever seen. And I never knowed I'd caught the ball!

Some o' the managers have said my head was pretty hard, but it wasn't as hard as that concrete. I was pretty near out, but they tell me I walked to the bench like I wasn't hurt at all. They also tell me that the crowd was a bunch o' ravin' maniacs and was throwin' money at me. I guess the ground-keeper'll get it.

The boys on the bench was all talkin' at once and slappin' me on the back, but I didn't know what it was about. Somebody told me pretty soon that it was my turn to hit and I picked up the first bat I come to and starts for the plate. McInnes come runnin' after 'em and ast me whether I didn't want my own bat. I cussed him and told him to mind his own business.

I didn't know it at the time, but I found out afterward that they was two out. The bases was empty. I'll tell you just what I had in my mind: I wasn't thinkin' about the ball game; I was determined that I was goin' to get to third base and give that guy my spikes. If I didn't hit one worth three bases, or if I didn't hit one at all, I was goin' to run till I got round to where Speed was, and then slide into him and cut him to pieces!

Right now I can't tell you whether I hit a fastball, or a slow ball, or a hook, or a fader—but I hit somethin'. It went over Bescher's head like a shot and then took a crazy bound. It must of struck a rock or a pop bottle, because it hopped clear over the fence and landed in the bleachers.

Mind you, I learned this afterward. At the time I just knowed I'd hit one somewheres and I starts round the bases. I speeded up when I got near third and took a runnin' jump at a guy I thought was Parker. I missed him and sprawled all over the bag. Then, all of a sudden I come to my senses. All the Ath-a-letics was out there to run home with me and it was one o' them I'd tried to cut. Speed had left the field. The boys picked me up and seen to it that I went on and touched the plate. Then I was carried into the clubhouse by the crazy bugs.

Well, they had a celebration in there and it was a long time before I got a chance to change my clothes. The boys made a big fuss over me. They told me they'd intended to give me five hundred bucks for my divvy, but now I was goin' to get a full share.

"Parker ain't the only lucky guy!" says one of 'em. "But even if that ball hadn't of took that crazy hop you'd of had a triple."

A triple! That's just what I'd wanted; and he called me lucky for not gettin' it!

The Giants was dressin' in the other part o' the clubhouse; and when I finally come out there was Speed, standin' waitin' for some o' the others. He seen me comin' and he smiled. "Hello, Horseshoes!" he says.

He won't smile no more for a while—it'll hurt too much. And if any girl wants him when she sees him now—with his nose over shakin' hands with his ear, and his jaw a couple o' feet foul—she's welcome to him. They won't be no contest!

∙ ∙ ∙

Grimes leaned over to ring for the waiter.

"Well," he said, "what about it?"

"You won't have to pay my fare," I told him.

"I'll buy a drink anyway," said he. "You've been a good listener—and I had to get it off my chest."

"Maybe they'll have to postpone the wedding," I said.

"No," said Grimes. "The weddin' will take place the day after tomorrow—and I'll bat for Mr. Parker. Did you think I was goin' to let him get away with it?"

"What about next year?" I asked.

"I'm goin' back to the Ath-a-letics," he said. "And I'm goin' to hire somebody to call me 'Horseshoes!' before every game—because I can sure play that old baseball when I'm mad."

Fielder's Choice (1946)

Edward L. McKenna

Edward L. McKenna's story "Fielder's Choice" originally appeared in *Esquire* magazine. A period piece (thirty-five cents for a magazine, a baseball game for a buck), it features a player's heroism in a dangerous situation. The baseball fiction writers of the 1940s and 1950s, of whom McKenna is typical, reveled in characters who had courage, grace, and personal modesty along with talent. This is also a reflection of the actual ballplayers of that era, more of whom seem to have been authentic heroes. "Where have you gone, Joe DiMaggio?"

It was seldom enough that Charles J. Horton went to see a ball game. He worked for the Third National, and from the beginning he had taught himself to remember that although a bank closes at three o'clock it doesn't pay to rush right off as soon as your books for the day are finished. No; you stay right on, making yourself useful and noticeable to your superiors. You're painfully careful about everything, and you never make an error. You take the extension courses at the University, even though you already have a Phi Beta Kappa key from the little school up-state. You attend the lectures given by the Institute of Banking. You carry the *Wall Street Journal,* or the *Commercial and Financial Chronicle,* and you read magazines that cost at least thirty-five cents. You pay some attention to your appearance, shaving each morning after your cold shower and your setting-up exercises, and your habit is costly as your purse can buy. You economize on beggars and waiters, and live at your college club, where the food is so bad it reminds you of the old fraternity house. Still, you get the stationery for nothing, and it gives you a certain cachet, or so you imagine. Your favorite book is your own bankbook, and you put by a little every month. You don't get married, and you're other-wise thrifty, neither drinking nor smoking nor going on parties, because if you really feel the need of recreation, can't you go to the movies or a theatre or a good restaurant all by yourself? You're really much better than most other people, and you've determined to get on, and so, perhaps, you will.

The program was working well enough for Charlie Horton. At twenty-eight, he was out of a teller's cage, and back of a desk and on the slow road to fortune. He had subordinates to whom he could be distant and severe, and two thousand dollars in his savings account, and a few good bonds, though he carried no life insurance whatsoever.

So, on this bright Saturday afternoon he was sitting behind first base, among people he rather disliked, and watching the acrobatics of eighteen ath-letes for whom, as individuals, he felt a faint contempt. One of them he knew, though he hadn't spoken to him for years. They'd gone to school together. Joe Marchand had been a popular hero, and Charlie Horton had been almost nobody.

Joe Marchand was more or less a popular hero still, though most experts agreed that he was slipping a little. He played right field for the Eagles, and had batted .342 last season. His arm was still all right, but he wasn't so fast in the field or on the bases. That was to be expected. He was almost thirty.

Joe had never finished high school. When he was seventeen, he was pick-ing up a few dollars playing semiprofessional ball, and then he played two seasons for Scranton and one in the Southern League. Somebody saw him down there, and picked up his contract, and ever since then he'd been in the big money. There'd been seasons when he'd made eight and ten thousand. It was generally understood that he wasn't getting anything like that any-more, but Joe never said so. Whatever it was, he never saved a cent more than enough to take him and his wife and his three kids through the winter.

Outside of his family, the things Joe liked best were baseball, close har-mony, and twenty-five-cent-limit draw. He had always been crazy about playing ball, crazy about every sort of sport, every sort of game. Boxing, horse-racing, ice-hockey, hunting, fishing, cards, dice, billiards, and even golf fascinated him always. He wasn't a drinking man, and he didn't chase around, but he did like to gamble, and to watch games, and to play them.

He weighed a hundred and ninety pounds, and his face and neck and hands looked as if they'd been dipped in some brown stain. After a game they'd won, or on the Pullman, or back at the hotel, he and Art Herman and Petey Grant would start harmonizing. Joe had a barytone voice, not nearly so good as he imagined, but he knew a thousand songs all full of barber-shop and pleasing sentiment, and he never forgot a new wow, a new combination of confluent chords. Songs in which there were two separate and distinct first-tenor parts were his delight.

The only people he disliked in all the world were fresh fans and fresh bushers, and even the bushers soon got used to Joe, and the fans didn't ride him, as a rule. Anyhow, he played in right field. Nobody took him too seriously, except left-handers; he could murder them. His one great weakness was this: he was a bad waiter. When the count was two and two, unless he had a signal, he'd be apt to take a crack at the next one, whatever it was, for to be called out on strikes without swinging just ruined his afternoon. Also, it did not give him much pleasure to knock one into the infield, even though he scratched a hit out of it. Joe liked to sock them. From his first days in the league it was his great delight to watch the fielders playing deep for him, dropping back toward the fence and the bleachers when he walked out toward the plate. He wasn't a scientific hitter, but he certainly could lean on them.

He'd helped to win two pennants; this year, the Eagles weren't even in the first division. That didn't worry him or any of them. They were playing away, in a big town they liked, against the leaders of the league, and the Eagles didn't think so much of them, outside of their pitchers. It was a doubleheader, and the games made a difference in the league's standing, though not to them. Everybody felt pretty good. Contenders who amount to anything always like a crack at the champion, whether they beat him or not. Forty thousand people were out there to watch them, to jeer them in a pleasant enough sort of way, with the good-natured contempt of victors, even vicarious ones. It was August, the sun was nice, and not too bright, and the dry, scorched grass was good to feel beneath their feet. Some of them were kids, with years before them, some of them were on their way out, like Joe. Anyhow, they had this fine long summer afternoon.

The thing happened, in the beginning of the fourth.

Joe was coaching a runner on first, so he was nearest to it. He heard all the noise, the screaming, and turned around, and peered up at the stands behind him.

Just back of first base, the crowds were giving way to right and left, pushing and leaping. A sea of people was surging in each direction, and seats were breaking beneath them as they went, but there was almost nowhere for them to go. Out into the aisles they came, and fell upon those seated in the next section, and that in turn went rolling onward till the next aisle was reached. There was the crashing and creaking of rotted timber, the snap of arms of broken chairs, the thin sharp yelp of men in fear.

The first-base stand was collapsing.

"Hi!" shouted Joe. "Hi! Come on, you guys." With that, he went into the falling stand.

He didn't know quite what he was going to do. All he knew was that he was going where the trouble was, to do his best. There weren't many who followed him. A few policemen charged into that stand, too. Cops haven't much sense either.

There was a pretty bad fifteen minutes or so in there. Maybe it was only ten, maybe it was only five. It didn't turn out to be so serious. Only a little part of the stands had actually fallen. Twenty-two people were killed, and about a hundred injured, not counting scratches, and black eyes, and torn clothing, and nervous systems somewhat impaired, or strengthened. Some five thousand men had looked suddenly upon the face of death. It leered at them, and as quickly turned away, and it only cost them a dollar apiece, and a bruise or two.

Joe came out of it all right, except that his right arm felt sort of funny. He hunched his shoulder up and around; it still felt funny. "Wonder how I got that?" he said to himself. He wouldn't have known. He'd made three or four trips into the middle of it, yelling and cursing, and pushing and pulling, and trying to do whatever he could. He remembered getting one man out from underfoot; the *Record* said he got three.

The shoulder was dislocated, he found that out at the clubhouse. "Tough luck, Joe," they said. "Ah, a coupla weeks," he said, to them, but to himself he said, "That's curtains. That's curtains."

It wasn't curtains. He played ball again, plenty of it. What was more, the owner of the club came to the hotel, the next day, with a copy of the *Record* in his hand.

"This true?" he said.

"No. It's my press-agent," said Joe.

"My daughter was in that stand," said the owner.

Joe looked at him.

"You go in there, you have no call to go in. You cripple yourself, for the sake of other people. All right. You got a job with this club, as long as I'm in baseball. Bum wing, or no bum wing. You hear me?"

"Yeah," said Joe. "Your—your daughter OK?"

"Yes. She's OK," said the owner. His name was, and is, Ben Siegal, and he is known to all the world as a soft-hearted, hot-headed sentimental slob who'd rather lose money in baseball than make it brewing beer.

There's a line in that *Record* story that Joe has never noticed. Under "Dead" there is this: Horton, Charles J. 28. Bank clerk, employed by Third National Bank.

Brooklyns Lose (1954)

William Heuman

"Brooklyns Lose" was written by William Heuman for *Sports Illustrated* in 1954, the first year of the magazine's existence and a few short years before the Dodgers headed west. The sting of a loss to the Reds is revealed in the soul of a diehard Bums fan who, with his son, is plodding home after a long day at the ballpark. And who should be at the house to greet them but Uncle Nathan, a gloating Giants fan? This scenario is richly served up by Heuman in dialectal "Brooklynese," a literary treat.

I t's one of those long, drawn-out games at Ebbets Field, and it's not over till nearly six o'clock. We come out hot and tired, and with a little headache— you know how it is after a game—and the kid says he wants a hot dog.

"I like the long ones, Pop," he says.

You know the kind they sell outside the park at those little hot-dog stands, long and skinny and rubbery.

"Never mind," I tell him.

We're hurrying for the trolley car, and the big crowd is pouring out of the exit gates. It's almost six o'clock and Madge has the supper on the table, and I can see her fuming, and the kid's talking about hot dogs.

"Forget it," I tell him.

Who thinks about food when the Dodgers lose? You sit there for nearly three and a half hours and you try to root them home. You're with them every minute, every play, and you have it in the bag, and then it's gone over the wall.

"That was some home run," the kid says.

"Shut up," I tell him. "Keep quiet."

"Well, it was good, Pop. Way out toward center field."

A home run in the last inning which wins the ball game and sends the Brooklyns down to defeat is never a *good* home run. What the kid means is that it was well hit. I admit that. I'm a Brooklyn fan, but I admit that. The ball travels maybe four hundred feet before it clears the fence in right center, so it's a good hit. All right, but don't rub it in. Three and a half hours I sit there in the bleachers on a hot day and we lose anyway. So what's good about it?

A guy on the trolley says to me, "They shoulda passed him, that Kluszewski."

"Alston didn't wanna put the winning run on base," I tell him. "That's baseball. You play the averages."

"He didn't put Kluszewski on, neither," this guy says, grinning. "Klu hit it an' kept goin'."

This guy jokes, yet. This is a time for jokes when you have a ball game sewed up eight-to-seven in the ninth, and you lose it with a home-run ball.

I look out the window, and the guy says, "So tomorrow's another day."

I don't even look at him. That kind of guy I don't look at.

You don't mind losing a ball game now and then, but when you lose to Cincinnati it hurts, especially when you got it sewed up, and especially in September and you're way out of first place and that old lost column can murder you.

The kid's getting wise here. He's eleven now, and I've had him down to a lot of ball games, and he argues baseball with the other kids on the block.

He says now, "They shoulda took Oiskin out."

"Never mind," I tell him. "Forget about it."

Why can't they let it drop? It's over and we lose it, so it goes down in the records, and you never change the records, not even if the Russians come over and take this country. It's down in the books.

So maybe Alston should have taken Erskine out, and maybe put in Johnny Podres, and Podres walks three-four guys and it's over anyway, and Alston's a dope again. He should have left Erskine in.

I don't like to second-guess the manager. The guy is out there with his job to do, and he knows more about it than anybody else. Just like me in the shop. In the shop I know my job and I do it. I don't like a guy coming around and telling me it might work out better some other way.

I'm just saying, though, that if it was me in Alston's shoes I'd have had Shuba pinch-hit for Erskine the end of the eighth, and maybe bring us in another run or two, so when this big clown belts one over the wall in the ninth we still got the lead. With Erskine out for a pinch hitter I'd have stuck Roe in there for one inning with that slow stuff. It might have been a different ball game.

Like I say, though, you can't second-guess, and it's silly to work yourself up into a stew because we dropped one. Just forget about it; let it drop.

I hear a guy in the seat behind me say, "They shoulda pulled a squeeze in the seventh with Reese on third. When Dressen was runnin' this club we worked a lot of squeeze plays. We'd of had that extra run, and when Kluszewski hits that homer it's only tied up, an'—"

You see how they try to dope it out? It's dead; it's in the record books. So who's up when Reese is on third and one away? Gil Hodges is up, and Gil is a long-ball hitter. Since when do you ask your long-ball hitter to bunt? That guy behind me is crazy. Any kind of fly ball would have brought Reese in. So Hodges struck out; so Alston knew he was gonna strike out?

If it was me I'd have had Reese try to steal home when it was two out. This Cincinnati guy was taking a long windup. I'm not telling Alston how to run his ball club, but you can see how it goes around and around inside your head. I've heard of guys going off their trolley arguing points like this.

Madge says when we come into the house at about six-thirty:

"What were you doing—standing outside the field asking for their autographs?"

She has that look on her face. The pots are still on the stove, all covered up, and they've been there for some time, I can see.

"It was a long game," I tell her.

"It's always a long game down there," she says, and the way she says "there" you'd think she was talking of some gin mill somewhere.

She should be married to a heavy drinker or a guy who plays the horses like some of them in the shop. I don't have any bad habits; I have a glass of beer now and then; I go to Ebbets Field. That's wrong?

"Sit down and eat your supper," Madge says.

"Pop wouldn't buy me a hot dog," the kid tells her.

"I'm not surprised," Madge says. "He probably didn't even know you were with him."

"I bought him two in the park," I snap. "He wants another one on the way home. What am I—Rockefeller?"

"He'd have had a better time at Brighton Beach," Madge says as she's banging the pots around on the stove.

"My vacation," I tell her. "Monday we go to the beach. Wednesday we go to the beach. What am I—a seal?"

"Sit down," she says.

I notice that there are four plates set out and I know who the other plate is for. He comes in from the parlor, snapping at his suspenders—the last guy I want to see tonight.

Uncle Nathan is my brother-in-law, a bachelor, and he lives in a rooming house around the corner from us. Every once in a while—and even once is too often—Madge invites him around for supper. I'm practically supporting this guy, and I think that, secretly, he likes the Giants.

"Lost again," Uncle Nathan grins as he sits down opposite me. "Heard it on the radio."

"Again," I tell him acidly. "Don't I know it's again?"

"The Reds," Uncle Nathan says. "The Cincinnati Reds from Cincinnati."

He's a guy who never goes to a ball game, but he can make remarks like that. He don't know first base from second.

"Kluszewski hit a home run and won the game in the ninth inning," the kid says, and I have to hear that over again.

"They should have a man like Kluszewski on first base for Brooklyn," Uncle Nathan says.

"What's wrong with Hodges?" I ask him. "What's wrong with a guy who hits over three hundred and drives in all them runs?"

"Eat your supper," Madge says.

Who feels like eating, especially with Uncle Nathan sitting across from you, smirking? Uncle Nathan is a small, pot-bellied guy with a circle of fuzzy hair around his bald head. All his life he's lived in Brooklyn, twenty minutes from the field, and never saw a game. That's a citizen!

"Who was it beat them this afternoon?" Uncle Nathan says. "I never heard of the guy."

"How many guys you ever heard of in baseball?" I ask him.

"Eat your supper, Joe," Madge says. "You'd all be a lot better off if you spent your time on something more educational."

I could make some remarks about that, too, but I don't. I got arguments up to the neck, already. Education. What's education but knowing something, and what's better to know than Brooklyn wins?

"Hear the Giants won this afternoon," Uncle Nathan says, without looking up from his plate. "Three-to-one over the Cardinals. They got it made."

"They'll fade in the stretch," I say. "They'll drop a few, and we'll catch them in the last week. We got a three-game series here, remember."

Imagine a guy talking about the Giants down here in Flatbush. A guy like that is crazy. He should be arrested.

I don't eat much tonight because I'm not hungry, and I guess I don't say much, either, because Madge says, as she's bringing out the dessert:

"All afternoon you yell your head off at the game. When you come home, you shut up like a clam."

"What's to say?" I ask her. "I gotta talk every minute?"

"He'd be talkin' plenty," Uncle Nathan says, "if the Dodgers had won."

I don't even bother to answer.

The kid, sitting next to me at the table, says, "That Kluszewski sure can hit."

We have pork chops for supper, but they don't taste good; the peas don't taste good either. Imagine a guy with a name you can't even pronounce licking the Dodgers? Down at the field I hear this Kluszewski's name pronounced about nine different ways. Any way you say it, though, it goes down in the books as a Brooklyn loss.

My wife says, "I spend the afternoon making a supper and he eats it like he was a bird."

"So I have to stuff myself every meal?" I say. "That's smart?"

I'm glad when I can get outside. I go down to the basement and get out the plastic hose. We live in a nice section in Flatbush here—two-family houses, with a little plat of ground out front. It's not much as far as ground goes, maybe six feet from the house to the sidewalk. Most everybody has a little shrubbery.

I get out the hose and I water the shrubbery because we haven't had any rain in a week. Next to me lives Saul Ruskin, who is my neighbor. Saul is sitting in one of those aluminum-and-plastic chairs that folds up, and you wonder how it holds his weight.

The plat out in front of Saul's house he's filled in with cement, so he has sidewalk from the house all the way to the curb, and no shrubbery, no grass or weeds to worry about.

"I should be a farmer?" Saul says. "I wanna raise crops, I move out to the suburbs."

Saul watches me as I hook up the hose. He has a stub of cigar in his mouth, and he says around the cigar, "A tough one to lose, Joe. Them Reds allus get hot against us."

"They have to win once in awhile," I tell him.

Saul is a dyed-in-the-wool Brooklyn rooter. I see he don't feel too good about this one, either, and it makes me feel a little better.

"These clubs come in here loaded," Saul says. "They save their best pitchers for Brooklyn. They do all their hittin' at Ebbets Field. It ain't right."

"That's baseball," I tell him as I start to squirt the shrubbery.

"Couple of Sundays back I see Pittsburgh," Saul says. "They score eighteen runs in two games. They don't score eighteen runs in a whole season. That's the way it goes."

"I know," I tell him sympathetically.

"That home run Klusoositz hits," Saul says. "It was a fluke, Joe?"

"He tagged it, Saul," I tell him. "He hits that long ball."

"Allus against us," Saul scowls. He pauses and then adds, "Alston maybe shoulda passed him, a guy hits like that."

"Man on second an' one out," I tell him. "Kluszewski ain't made a hit all day."

"Then he was due," Saul says. "You can't shut out a guy like that four-five times in one game. He was due."

"They took a chance. Erskine got him before."

The guy lives upstairs from me is just coming back from Sam Klein's candy store, where he has bought some cigarets, and he stops to talk. He says: "A good game, Joe?"

"Brooklyns lose, Lennie," Saul says. "That's a good game?"

"You know what I mean," Lennie says. "That lucky Klookitz."

"Kluszewski," I tell him.

"How the hell you say it," Lennie says, "It's still a home run. That right, Joe?"

We stand there for a while, chewing the rag while I squirt the shrubbery. Saul puffs on the cigar and sits there with his arms folded across his chest. Lennie Brannick sits on the stoop and lights up a cigaret.

"You give Dressen a club hitting like this," Lennie says, "an' he'd never lose a ball game. You know what I mean? Allus liked Dressen—a noisy guy, but a great manager."

"Alston's all right," I tell him.

"That club we got this year," Saul puts in, "a two-headed zebra could manage. They oughtta win for anybody; they oughtta even win for your brother-in-law Nathan, Joe."

"Leave us not get on that subject," I tell him.

My wife calls through the screen door, "If you're going down to Klein's, stop at the delicatessen and pick up a few bottles of beer, Joe. The empties are on the back step."

I turn off the water because them shrubs have enough now. I say to Saul Ruskin under my breath, "I have to feed him beer now. It's not enough he eats my food. Luxuries he gets."

"That's relatives for you," Saul nods. "I got a cousin like that."

I get the empty bottles from the back doorstep and I head down the street toward Klein's. This is my neighborhood; this is where I was born, not on this block, but a few blocks away. This is a nice block, nice people, all good Brooklyn rooters. You feel bad, and everybody feels bad with you. That's neighbors.

Outside Klein's is the usual bunch of kids, seventeen and eighteen years old, and it's all baseball with them, too. It's arguments about baseball, and what these kids don't know about the game you can stick in your hat and forget about.

One kid who knows me says, "Hello, Mr. Armbruster."

"How's it," I say.

"You up the game?" he asks. "You see that Klusookitz?"

"He kills that ball," I tell him.

"I see Roe strike that bum out three times," another boy says. "You give him that fastball an' he moiders."

Inside, I talk to Sam Klein about the game.

"A hard one to lose," Sam says, "but you can't win 'em all, Joe."

"I know," I say.

"If he'd passed this Klusowsky," Sam says, "somebody else would have homered. That's fate, Joe."

"Maybe we can still afford to lose one," I tell him.

"Sure," Sam says. "Look how it used to be years ago. You win two out of five an' you think you done somethin'."

"It's still a great club," I tell him. "The best ever."

I come out of Klein's and stop by the delicatessen for some beer. I'm feeling pretty good now, the best since Kluszewski hit that home run and robbed us of a game. You know how it is when you have good neighbors? Everybody's on your side; everybody's rooting for you and with you. You can even stand a guy like Uncle Nathan. Where do you find neighbors like this?

I come down the walk toward my house, and Saul Ruskin hasn't moved from his chair on the sidewalk. I go past Saul, and he lifts two fingers in the for-victory sign.

"Tomorrow," says Saul.

How can you beat neighbors like that? How can you beat Brooklyn?

Uncle Nathan is standing by the screen door when I come in, and he says, "You gonna slit your throat tonight, Joe, because the Dodgers lost?"

"Jump in the lake," I tell him. "Take a long run an' jump in the lake."

Tomorrow we'll get 'em.

The Pitcher and the Plutocrat (1910)

P. G. Wodehouse

It is said that baseball has its origins in the British game of rounders. How fitting, therefore, that one of baseball's best stories is from the pen of one of Britain's most celebrated writers, Pelham Grenville Wodehouse (1881–1975). A master of English style, imagery, and wit, P. G. Wodehouse was one of the most prolific writers of all time. Besides ninety-two books, he wrote stories, plays, and lyrics for Broadway musicals. Called the "funniest writer in the world," Wodehouse was educated at Dulwich College, honored by a doctor of letters from Oxford, and knighted by the Queen. In 1956 he obtained citizenship in the United States. Among his books are *My Man Jeeves* (1919), *Ukridge* (1924), *The Butler Did It* (1957), and *The Golf Omnibus* (1973). Written in 1910, "The Pitcher and the Plutocrat" is the oldest story in this collection.

T he main difficulty in writing a story is to convey to the reader clearly yet tersely the natures and dispositions of one's leading characters. Brevity, brevity—that is the cry. Perhaps, after all, the play-bill style is the best. In this drama of love, baseball, frenzied finance, and tainted millions, then, the principals are as follows, in their order of entry:

Isabel Rackstraw (a peach)
Clarence Van Puyster (a Greek god)
Old Man Van Puyster (a proud old aristocrat)
Old Man Rackstraw (a tainted millionaire)

More about Clarence later. For the moment let him go as a Greek god. There were other sides, too, to Old Man Rackstraw's character; but for the moment let him go as a Tainted Millionaire. Not that it is satisfactory. It is too mild. He was *the* Tainted Millionaire. The Tainted Millions of other Tainted Millionaires were as attar of roses compared with the Tainted Millions of Tainted Millionaire Rackstraw. He preferred his millions tainted. His attitude toward an untainted million was that of the sportsman toward the sitting bird. These things are purely a matter of taste. Some people like Limburger cheese.

It was at a charity bazaar that Isabel and Clarence first met. Isabel was presiding over the Billiken, Teddy Bear, and Fancy Goods stall. There she stood, that slim, radiant girl, buncoing the Younger Set out of its father's hard-earned with a smile that alone was nearly worth the money, when she observed, approaching, the handsomest man she had ever seen. It was—this is not one of those mystery stories—it was Clarence Van Puyster. Over the heads of the bevy of gilded youths who clustered round the stall their eyes met. A thrill ran through Isabel. She dropped her eyes. The next moment Clarence had bucked center; the Younger Set had shredded away like a mist; and he was leaning toward her, opening negotiations for the purchase of a yellow Teddy Bear at sixteen times its face value.

He returned at intervals during the afternoon. Over the second Teddy Bear they became friendly; over the third, intimate. He proposed as she was wrapping up the fourth Golliwog, and she gave him her heart and the parcel simultaneously. At six o'clock, carrying four Teddy Bears, seven photograph frames, five Golliwogs, and a Billiken, Clarence went home to tell the news to his father.

Clarence, when not at college, lived with his only surviving parent in an old red-brick house at the north end of Washington Square. The original Van Puyster had come over in Governor Stuyvesant's time in one of the then fashionable ninety-four-day boats. Those were the stirring days when they were giving away chunks of Manhattan Island in exchange for trading-stamps; for the bright brain which conceived the idea that the city might possibly at some remote date extend above Liberty Street had not come into existence. The original Van Puyster had acquired a square mile or so in the heart of things for ten dollars cash and a quarter interest in a pedler's outfit. "The Columbus Echo and Vespucci Intelligencer" gave him a column and a half under the heading: "Reckless Speculator. Prominent Citizen's Gamble in Land." On the proceeds of that deal his descendants had led quiet, peaceful lives ever since. If any of them ever did a day's work, the family records are silent on the point. Blood was their long suit, not Energy. They were plain, homely folk, with a refined distaste for wealth and vulgar hustle. They lived simply, without envy of their richer fellow citizens, on their three hundred thousand dollars a year. They asked no more. It enabled them to entertain on a modest scale; the boys could go to college, the girls buy an occasional new frock. They were satisfied.

Having dressed for dinner, Clarence proceeded to the library, where he found his father slowly pacing the room. Silver-haired old Vansuyther Van Puyster seemed wrapped in thought. And this was unusual, for he was not given to thinking. To be absolutely frank, the old man had just about enough brain to make a jay-bird fly crooked, and no more.

"Ah, my boy," he said, looking up as Clarence entered. "Let us go in to dinner. I have been awaiting you for some little time now. I was about to inquire as to your whereabouts. Let us be going."

Mr. Van Puyster always spoke like that. This was due to Blood.

Until the servants had left them to their coffee and cigarettes, the conversation was desultory and commonplace. But when the door had closed, Mr. Van Puyster leaned forward.

"My boy," he said quietly, "we are ruined."

Clarence looked at him inquiringly.

"Ruined much?" he asked.

"Paupers," said his father. "I doubt if when all is over, I shall have much more than a bare fifty or sixty thousand dollars a year."

A lesser man would have betrayed agitation, but Clarence was a Van Puyster. He lit a cigarette.

"Ah," he said calmly. "How's that?"

Mr. Van Puyster toyed with his coffee-spoon.

"I was induced to speculate—rashly, I fear—on the advice of a man I chanced to meet at a public dinner, in the shares of a certain mine. I did not thoroughly understand the matter, but my acquaintance appeared to be well versed in such operations, so I allowed him to—and, well, in fact, to cut a long story short, I am ruined."

"Who was the fellow?"

"A man of the name of Rackstraw. Daniel Rackstraw."

"Daniel Rackstraw!"

Not even Clarence's training and traditions could prevent a slight start as he heard the name.

"Daniel Rackstraw," repeated his father. "A man, I fear, not entirely honest. In fact, it seems that he has made a very large fortune by similar transactions. Friends of mine, acquainted with these matters, tell me his behavior toward me amounted practically to theft. However, for myself I care little. We can rough it, we of the old Van Puyster stock. If there is but fifty thousand a year left, well—I must make it serve. It is for your sake that I am troubled, my poor boy. I shall be compelled to stop your allowance. I fear you will be obliged to adopt some profession." He hesitated for a moment. "In fact, work," he added.

Clarence drew at his cigarette.

"Work?" he echoed thoughtfully. "Well, of course, mind you, fellows do work. I met a man at the club only yesterday who knew a fellow who had met a man whose cousin worked."

He reflected for a while.

"I shall pitch," he said suddenly.

"Pitch, my boy?"

"Sign on as a professional ballplayer."

His father's fine old eyebrows rose a little.

"But, my boy, er—the—ah—family name. Our—shall I say *noblesse oblige*? Can a Van Puyster pitch and not be defiled?"

"I shall take a new name," said Clarence. "I will call myself Brown." He lit another cigarette. "I can get signed on in a minute. McGraw will jump at me."

This was no idle boast. Clarence had had a good college education, and was now an exceedingly fine pitcher. It was a pleasing sight to see him, poised on one foot in the attitude of a Salome dancer, with one eye on the batter, the other gazing coldly at the man who was trying to steal third, uncurl abruptly like the main spring of a watch and sneak over a swift one. Under Clarence's guidance a ball could do practically everything except talk. It could fly like a shot from a gun, hesitate, take the first turning to the left, go up two blocks, take the second to the right, bound in mid-air like a jack rabbit, and end by dropping as the gentle dew from heaven upon the plate beneath. Briefly, there was class to Clarence. He was the goods.

Scarcely had he uttered these momentous words when the butler entered with the announcement that he was wanted by a lady at the telephone.

It was Isabel.

Isabel was disturbed.

"Oh, Clarence," she cried, "my precious angel wonder-child, I don't know how to begin."

"Begin just like that," said Clarence approvingly. "It's fine. You can't beat it."

"Clarence, a terrible thing has happened. I told papa of our engagement, and he wouldn't hear of it. He was furious. He c-called you a b-b-b—

"A p-p-p—"

"That's a new one on me," said Clarence, wondering.

"A b-beggarly p-pauper. I knew you weren't well off, but I thought you had two or three millions. I told him so. But he said no, your father had lost all his money."

"It is too true, dearest," said Clarence. "I am a pauper. But I'm going to work. Something tells me I shall be rather good at work. I am going to work with all the accumulated energy of generations of ancestors who have never done a hand's turn. And some day when I—"

"Good-by," said Isabel hastily, "I hear papa coming."

The season during which Clarence Van Puyster pitched for the Giants is destined to live long in the memory of followers of baseball. Probably never in the history of the game has there been such persistent and widespread mortality among the more distant relatives of office-boys and junior clerks. Statisticians have estimated that if all the grandmothers alone who perished between the months of April and October that year could have been placed end to end they would have reached considerably further than Minneapolis. And it was Clarence who was responsible for this holocaust. Previous to the opening of the season skeptics had shaken their heads over the Giants' chances for the pennant. It had been assumed that as little new blood would be forthcoming as in other years, and that the fate of Our City would rest, as usual, on the shoulders of the white-haired veterans who were boys with Lafayette.

And then, like a meteor, Clarence Van Puyster had flashed upon the world of fans, bugs, chewing-gum, and nuts (pea and human). In the opening game he had done horrid things to nine men from Boston; and from then onward, except for an occasional check, the Giants had never looked back.

Among the spectators who thronged the bleachers to watch Clarence perform there appeared week after week a little, gray, dried-up man, insignificant except for a certain happy choice of language in moments of emotion and an enthusiasm far surpassing that of the ordinary spectator. To the trained eye there is a subtle but well-marked difference between the fan, the bug, and—the last phase—the nut of the baseball world. This man was an undoubted nut. It was writ clear across his brow.

Fate had made Daniel Rackstraw—for it was he—a tainted millionaire, but at heart he was a baseball spectator. He never missed a game. His library of baseball literature was the finest in the country. His baseball museum had but one equal, that of Mr. Jacob Dodson of Detroit. Between them the two had cornered, at enormous expense, the curio market of the game. It was Rackstraw who had secured the glove worn by Neal Ball, the Cleveland shortstop, when he made the only unassisted triple play in the history of the game; but it was Dodson who possessed the bat which Hans Wagner used as a boy. The two men were friends, as far as rival connoisseurs can be friends; and Mr. Dodson, when at leisure, would frequently pay a visit to Mr. Rackstraw's country home, where he would spend hours gazing wistfully at the Neal Ball glove buoyed up only by the thought of the Wagner bat at home.

Isabel saw little of Clarence during the summer months, except from a distance. She contented herself with clipping photographs of him from the evening papers. Each was a little more unlike him than the last, and this lent variety to the collection. Her father marked her new-born enthusiasm for the national game with approval. It had been secretly a great grief to the old buccaneer that his only child did not know the difference between a bunt and a swat, and more, did not seem to care to know. He felt himself drawn closer to her. An understanding, as pleasant as it was new and strange, began to spring up between parent and child.

As for Clarence, how easy it would be to cut loose to practically an unlimited extent on the subject of his emotions at this time. One can figure him, after the game is over and the gay throng has dispersed, creeping moodily—but what's the use? Brevity. That is the cry. Brevity. Let us on.

The months sped by. August came and went, and September; and soon it was plain to even the casual follower of the game that, unless something untoward should happen, the Giants must secure the National League pennant. Those were delirious days for Daniel Rackstraw. Long before the beginning of October his voice had dwindled to a husky whisper. Deep lines appeared on his forehead; for it is an awful thing for a baseball nut to be compelled to root, in the very crisis of the season, purely by means of facial expression. In this time of affliction he found Isabel an ever-increasing comfort to him. Side by side they would sit at the Polo Grounds, and the old man's face would lose its drawn look, and light up, as her clear young soprano pealed out above the din, urging this player to slide for second, that to knock the stitching off the ball; or describing the umpire in no uncertain voice as a reincarnation of the late Mr. Jesse James.

Meanwhile, in the American League, Detroit had been heading the list with equal pertinacity; and in far-off Michigan Mr. Jacob Dodson's enthusiasm had been every whit as great as Mr. Rackstraw's in New York. It was universally admitted that when the championship series came to be played, there would certainly be something doing.

But, alas! How truly does Epictetus observe: "We know not what awaiteth us around the corner, and the hand that counteth its chickens ere they be hatched ofttimes graspeth but a lemon." The prophets who anticipated a struggle closer than any on record were destined to be proved false.

It was not that their judgment of form was at fault. By every law of averages the Giants and the Tigers should have been the two most evenly matched nines in the history of the game. In fielding there was nothing to choose between them. At hitting the Tigers held a slight superiority; but this was balanced by the inspired pitching of Clarence Van Puyster. Even the keenest supporters of either side were not confident. They argued at length, figuring out the odds with the aid of stubs of pencils and the backs of envelopes, but they were not confident. Out of all those frenzied millions two men alone had no doubts. Mr. Daniel Rackshaw said that he did not desire to be unfair to Detroit. He wished it to be clearly understood that in their own class the Tigers might quite possibly show to considerable advantage. In some rural league down South, for instance, he did not deny that they might sweep all before them. But when it came to competing with the Giants—Here words failed Mr. Rackstraw, and he had to rush to Wall Street and collect several tainted millions before he could recover his composure.

Mr. Jacob Dodson, interviewed by the Detroit "Weekly Rooter," stated that his decision, arrived at after a close and careful study of the work of both teams, was that the Giants had rather less chance in the forthcoming tourney than a lone gumdrop at an Eskimo teaparty. It was his carefully considered opinion that in a contest with the Avenue B Juniors the Giants might, with an effort, scrape home. But when it was a question of meeting a live team like Detroit—Here Mr. Dodson, shrugging his shoulders despairingly, sank back in his chair, and watchful secretaries brought him round with oxygen.

Throughout the whole country nothing but the approaching series was discussed. Wherever civilization reigned, and in Jersey City, one question alone was on every lip: Who would win? Octogenarians mumbled it. Infants lisped it. Tired business men, trampled under foot in the rush for the West Farms express, asked it of the ambulance attendants who carried them to hospital.

And then, one bright, clear morning, when all Nature seemed to smile, Clarence Van Puyster developed mumps.

New York was in a ferment. I could have wished to go into details to describe in crisp, burning sentences the panic that swept like a tornado through a million homes. A little encouragement, the slightest softening of the editorial austerity, and the thing would have been done. But no. Brevity. That was the cry. Brevity. Let us on.

The Tigers met the Giants at the Polo Grounds, and for five days the sweat of agony trickled unceasingly down the corrugated foreheads of the patriots who sat on the bleachers. The men from Detroit, freed from the fear of Clarence, smiled grim smiles and proceeded to knock holes through the fence. It was in vain that the home fielders skimmed like swallows around the diamond. They could not keep the score down. From start to finish the Giants were a beaten side.

Broadway during that black week was a desert. Gloom gripped Lobster Square. In distant Harlem red-eyed wives faced silently scowling husbands at the evening meal, and the children were sent early to bed. Newsboys called the extras in a whisper.

Few took the tragedy more nearly to heart than Daniel Rackstraw. Each afternoon found him more deeply plunged in sorrow. On the last day, leaving the ground with the air of a father mourning over some prodigal son, he encountered Mr. Jacob Dodson of Detroit.

Now, Mr. Dodson was perhaps the slightest bit shy on the finer feelings. He should have respected the grief of a fallen foe. He should have abstained from exulting. But he was in too exhilarated a condition to be magnanimous. Sighting Mr. Rackstraw, he addressed himself joyously to the task of rubbing the thing in. Mr. Rackstraw listened in silent anguish.

"If we had had Brown—" he said at length.

"That's what they all say," whooped Mr. Dodson. "Brown! Who's Brown?"

"If we had had Brown, we should have—" He paused. An idea had flashed upon his overwrought mind. "Dodson," he said, "listen here. Wait till Brown is well again, and let us play this thing off again for anything you like a side in my private park."

Mr. Dodson reflected.

"You're on," he said. "What side bet? A million? Two million? Three?"

Mr. Rackstraw shook his head scornfully.

"A million? Who wants a million? I'll put on my Neal Ball glove against your Hans Wagner bat. The best of three games. Does that go?"

"I should say it did," said Mr. Dodson joyfully. "I've been wanting that glove for years. It's like finding it in one's Christmas stocking."

"Very well," said Mr. Rackstraw. "Then let's get it fixed up."

Honestly, it is but a dog's life, that of the short-story writer. I particularly wished at this point to introduce a description of Mr. Rackstraw's country home and estate, featuring the private ballpark with its fringe of noble trees. It would have served a double purpose, not only charming the lover of nature, but acting as a fine stimulus to the youth of the country, showing them the sort of home they would be able to buy some day if they worked hard and saved their money. But no. You shall have three guesses as to what was the cry. You give it up? It was "Brevity! Brevity!" Let us on.

The two teams arrived at the Rackstraw house in time for lunch. Clarence, his features once more reduced to their customary finely chiseled proportions, alighted from the automobile with a swelling heart. He could see nothing of Isabel, but that did not disturb him. Letters had passed between the two. Clarence had warned her not to embrace him in public, as McGraw would not like it; and Isabel accordingly had arranged a tryst among the noble trees which fringed the ballpark.

I will pass lightly over the meeting of the two lovers. I will not describe the dewy softness of their eyes, the catching of their breath, their murmered endearments. I could, mind you. It is at just such descriptions that I am particularly happy. But I have grown discouraged. My spirit is broken. It is enough to say that Clarence had reached a level of emotional eloquence rarely met with among pitchers of the National League, when Isabel broke from him with a startled exclamation, and vanished behind a tree; and, looking over his shoulder, Clarence observed Mr. Daniel Rackstraw moving toward him.

It was evident from the millionaire's demeanor that he had seen nothing. The look on his face was anxious, but not wrathful. He sighted Clarence, and hurried up to him.

"Say, Brown," he said, "I've been looking for you. I want a word with you."

"A thousand, if you wish it," said Clarence courteously.

"Now, see here," said Mr. Rackstraw. "I want to explain to you just what this ball game means to me. Don't run away with the idea I've had you fellows down to play an exhibition game just to keep me merry and bright. If the Giants win today, it means that I shall be able to hold up my head again and look my fellow man in the face, instead of crawling around on my stomach and feeling like thirty cents. Do you get that?"

"I am hep," replied Clarence with simple dignity.

"And not only that," went on the millionaire. "There's more to it. I have put up my Neal Ball glove against Mr. Dodson's Wagner bat as a side bet. You understand what that means? It means that either you win or my life is soured for keeps. See?"

"I have got you," said Clarence.

"Good. Then what I wanted to say was this. Today is your day for pitching as you've never pitched before. Everything depends on whether you make good or not. With you pitching like mother used to make it, the Giants are some nine. Otherwise they are Nature's citrons. It's one thing or the other. It's all up to you. Win, and there's twenty thousand dollars waiting for you above what you share with the others."

Clarence waved his hand deprecatingly.

"Mr. Rackstraw," he said, "keep your dough. I care nothing for money."

"You don't?" cried the millionaire. "Then you ought to exhibit yourself in a dime museum."

"All I ask of you," proceeded Clarence, "is your consent to my engagement to your daughter."

Mr. Rackstraw looked sharply at him.

"Repeat that," he said. "I don't think I quite got it."

"All I ask is your consent to my engagement to your daughter."

"Young man," said Mr. Rackstraw, not without a touch of admiration, "you have gall."

"My friends have sometimes said so," said Clarence.

"And I admire gall. But there is a limit. That limit you have passed so far that you'd need to look for it with a telescope."

"You refuse your consent."

"I never said you weren't a clever guesser."

"Why?"

Mr. Rackstraw laughed. One of those nasty, sharp, metallic laughs that hit you like a bullet.

"How would you support my daughter?"

"I was thinking that you would help to some extent."

"You were, were you?"

"I was."

"Oh?"

Mr. Rackstraw emitted another of those laughs.

"Well," he said, "it's off. You can take that as coming from an authoritative source. No wedding-bells for you."

Clarence drew himself up, fire flashing from his eyes and a bitter smile curving his expressive lips.

"And no Wagner bat for you!" he cried.

Mr. Rackstraw started as if some strong hand had plunged an auger into him.

"What!" he shouted.

Clarence shrugged his superbly modeled shoulders in silence.

"Say," said Mr. Rackstraw, "you wouldn't let a little private difference like that influence you any in a really important thing like this ball game, would you?"

"I would."

"You would hold up the father of the girl you love?"

"Every time."

"Her white-haired old father?"

"The color of his hair would not affect me."

"Nothing would move you?"

"Nothing."

"Then, by George, you're just the son-in-law I want. You shall marry Isabel; and I'll take you into partnership this very day. I've been looking for a good, husky bandit like you for years. You make Dick Turpin look like a preliminary three-round bout. My boy, we'll be the greatest team, you and I, that ever hit Wall Street."

"Papa!" cried Isabel, bounding happily from behind her tree.

Mr. Rackstraw joined their hands, deeply moved, and spoke in low, vibrant tones:

"Play ball!"

Little remains to be said, but I am going to say it, if it snows. I am at my best in these tender scenes of idyllic domesticity.

Four years have passed. Once more we are in the Rackstraw home. A lady is coming down the stairs, leading by the hand her little son. It is Isabel. The years have dealt lightly with her. She is still the same stately, beautiful creature whom I would have described in detail long ago if I had been given half a chance. At the foot of the stairs the child stops and points at a small, wooden object in a glass case.

"Wah?" he says.

"That?" says Isabel. "That is the bat Mr. Wagner used to use when he was a little boy."

She looks at a door on the left of the hall, and puts a finger to her lip.

"Hush!" she says. "We must be quiet. Daddy and grandpa are busy in there cornering wheat."

And softly mother and child go out into the sunlit garden.

Gandhi at the Bat (1983)

Chet Williamson

Chet Williamson's short fiction has appeared in many popular magazines, including *The New Yorker*, *Playboy*, and *Esquire*. He is also a well-known novelist, with several books to his credit. Among his books are *Second Chance* (1995), *The Searchers* (1998), *100 Ghastly Little Ghost Stories* (2003), and *Zombies! Zombies! Zombies!* (2011). "Gandhi at the Bat" is a truly original baseball yarn about the Indian statesman. It originally appeared in *The New Yorker*.

History books and available newspaper files hold no record of the visit to America in 1933 made by Mohandas K. Gandhi. For reasons of a sensitive political nature that have not yet come to light, all contemporary accounts of the visit were suppressed at the request of President Roosevelt. Although Gandhi repeatedly appeared in public during his three-month stay, the cloak of journalistic silence was seamless, and all that remains of the great man's celebrated tour is this long-secreted glimpse of one of the Mahatma's unexpected nonpolitical appearances, written by an anonymous press-box denizen of the day.

Yankee Stadium is used to roaring crowds. But never did a crowd roar louder than on yesterday afternoon, when a little brown man in a loincloth and wire-rimmed specs put some wood on a lefty Grove fastball and completely bamboozled Connie Mack's A's.

It all started when Mayor John J. O'Brien invited M. K. ("Mahatma") Gandhi to see the Yanks play Philadelphia up at "The House That Ruth Built." Gandhi, whose ballplaying experience was limited to a few wallops with a cricket bat, jumped at the chance, and 12 noon saw the Mayor's party in the Yankee locker room, where the Mahatma met the Bronx Bombers. A zippy exchange occurred when the Mayor introduced the Lord of the Loincloth to the Bambino. "Mr. Gandhi," Hizzoner said, "I want you to meet Babe Ruth, the Sultan of Swat."

Gandhi's eyes sparkled behind his Moxie-bottle lenses, and he chuckled. "Swat," quoth he, "is a sultanate of which I am not aware. Is it by any chance near Maharashtra?"

"Say," laughed the Babe, laying a meaty hand on the frail brown shoulder, "you're all right, kiddo. I'll hit one out of the park for you today."

"No hitting, please," the Mahatma quipped.

In the Mayor's front-row private box, the little Indian turned down the offer of a hot dog and requested a box of Cracker Jack instead. The prize inside was a tin whistle, which he blew gleefully whenever the Bambino waddled up to bat.

The grinning guru enjoyed the game immensely—far more than the A's, who were down 3–1 by the fifth. Ruth, as promised, did smash a homer in the seventh, to Gandhi's delight. "Hey, Gunga Din!" Ruth cried jovially on his way to the Yankee dugout. "Know why my battin' reminds folks of India? 'Cause I can really Bangalore!"

"That is a very good one, Mr. Ruth!" cried the economy-size Asian.

By the top of the ninth, the Yanks had scored two more runs. After Mickey Cochrane whiffed on a Red Ruffing fastball, Gandhi remarked how difficult it must be to hit such a swiftly thrown missile and said, "I should like to try it very much."

"Are you serious?" Mayor O'Brien asked.

"If it would not be too much trouble. Perhaps after the exhibition is over," his visitor suggested.

There was no time to lose. O'Brien, displaying a panache that would have done credit to his predecessor, Jimmy Walker, leaped up and shouted to the umpire, who called a time-out. Managers McCarthy and Mack were beckoned to the Mayor's side, along with Bill Dinneen, the home-plate umpire, and soon all of Yankee stadium heard an unprecedented announcement:

"Ladies and gentlemen, regardless of the score, the Yankees will come to bat to finish the ninth inning."

The excited crowd soon learned that the reason for such a breach of tradition was a little brown pinch-hitter shorter than his bat. When the pinstriped Bronx Bombers returned to their dugout after the last Philadelphia batter had been retired in the ninth, the Nabob of Nonviolence received a hasty batting lesson from Babe Ruth under the stands.

Lazzeri led off the bottom of the stanza, hitting a short chop to Bishop, who rifled to Foxx for the out. Then, after Crosetti fouled out to Cochrane, the stadium became hushed as the announcer intoned, "Pinch-hitting for Ruffing, Mohandas K. Gandhi."

The crowd erupted as the white-robed holy man, a fungo bat propped jauntily on his shoulder, strode to the plate, where he remarked to the crouching Mickey Cochrane, "It is a very big field, and a very small ball."

"C'mon, Moe!" Ruth called loudly to the dead-game bantam batter. "Show 'em the old pepper!"

"I will try, Mr. Baby!" Gandhi called back, and went into a batting stance unique in the annals of the great game—his sheet-draped posterior facing the catcher, and his bat held high over his head, as if to clobber the ball into submission. While Joe McCarthy called time, the Babe trotted out and politely corrected the little Indian's position in the box.

The time-out over, Grove threw a creaming fastball right over the plate. The bat stayed on Gandhi's shoulder. "Oh, my," he said as he turned and observed the ball firmly ensconced in Cochrane's glove. "That *was* speedy."

The second pitch was another dead-center fastball. The Mahatma swung, but found that the ball had been in the Mick's glove for a good three seconds before his swipe was completed. "Steerike two!" Dinneen barked.

The next pitch was high and outside, and the ump called it a ball before the petite pundit made a tentative swing at it. "Must I sit down now?" He asked.

"Nah, it's a ball," Dinneen replied. "I called it before you took your cut."

"Yes. I *know* that is a ball, and I did swing at it and did miss."

"No, no, a ball. Like a free pitch."

"Oh, I see."

"Wasn't in the strike zone."

"Yes, I see."

"So you get another swing."

"Yes."

"And if you miss you sit down."

"I just *did* miss."

"Play ball, Mister."

The next pitch was in the dirt. Gandhi did not swing. "Ball," Dinneen called.

"Yes, it is," the Mahatma agreed.

"Two and two."

"That is four."

"Two balls, two strikes."

"Is there not but one ball?"

"Two balls."

"Yes, I see."

"And two strikes."

"And if I miss I sit down."

Ruth's voice came booming from the Yankee dugout: "Swing early, Gandy baby!"

"When is early?"

"When I tell ya! I'll shout 'Now!'"

Grove started his windup. Just as his leg kicked up, the Bambino's cry of "*Now!*" filled the park.

The timing was perfect. Gandhi's molasses-in-January swing met the Grove fastball right over the plate. The ball shot downward, hit the turf, and arced gracefully into the air toward Grove. "*Run*, Peewee, *run!*" yelled Ruth, as the crowd went wild.

"Yes, yes!" cried Gandhi, who started down the first-base line in what can only be described as a dancing skip, using his bat as a walking stick. An astonished Grove booted the high bouncer, then scooped up the ball and flung it to Jimmie Foxx at first.

But Foxx, mesmerized by the sight of a sixty-three-year-old Indian in white robes advancing merrily before him and blowing mightily on a tin whistle, failed to descry the stitched orb, which struck the bill of his cap, knocking it off his head, and, slowed by its deed of dishabille, rolled to a stop by the fence.

Gandhi paused only long enough to touch first and to pick up Jimmie's cap and return it to him. By the time the still gawking Foxx had perched it once more on his head, the vital vegetarian was halfway to second.

Right fielder Coleman retrieved Foxx's missed ball and now relayed it to Max Bishop at second, but too late. The instant Bishop tossed the ball back to the embarrassed Grove, Gandhi was off again. Grove, panicking, overthrew third base, and by the time left fielder Bob Johnson picked up the ball, deep in foul territory, the Tiny Terror of Tealand had rounded the hot corner and was scooting for home. Johnson hurled the ball on a true course to a stunned Cochrane. The ball hit the pocket of Cochrane's mitt and popped out like a muffin from a toaster.

Gandhi jumped on home plate with both sandalled feet, and the crowd exploded as Joe McCarthy, the entire Yankee squad, and even a beaming Connie Mack surged onto the field.

"I ran home," giggled Gandhi. "Does that mean that I hit a run home?'

"A home run, Gandy," said Ruth. "Ya sure did."

"Well, technically," said Umpire Dinneen, "it was a single and an over-throw and then—"

"Shaddup," growled a dozen voices at once.

"Looked like a homer to me, too," the ump corrected, but few heard him, for by that time the crowd was on the field, lifting to their shoulders a joyous Gandhi, whose tin whistle provided a thrilling trilling over the mob's acclaim.

Inside the locker room, Manager McCarthy offered Gandhi a permanent position on the team, but the Mahatma graciously refused, stating that he could only consider a diamond career with a different junior-circuit club.

"Which club would that be, kid?" said the puzzled Bambino.

"The Cleveland Indians, of course," twinkled the Mahatma.

An offer from the Cleveland front office arrived the next day, but India's top pinch-hitter was already on a train headed for points west—and the history books.

The Curious Case of Sidd Finch (1985)

George Plimpton

George Plimpton (1927–2003) was a cofounder of *The Paris Review* and served as its editor during his lifetime. He is best known as a journalist who participated in big-league sports. His initial venture was memorialized in *Out of My League* (1961), when he pitched against major-league hitters like Willie Mays and Ernie Banks. He went to training camp as a quarterback for the Detroit Lions, which became a book and a movie called *Paper Lion*, and played goalie for the Boston Bruins, which he chronicled in *Open Net* (1968).

The following story appeared in *Sports Illustrated* on April 1, 1985. Plimpton concocted the Buddhist pitcher, Sidd Finch, who had a 168-mile-an-hour fastball and was supposedly under wraps at the New York Mets training camp. A lot of readers were taken in by this April Fool's Day spoof.

He's a pitcher, part yogi and part recluse. Impressively liberated from our opulent life-style, Sidd's deciding about yoga—and his future in baseball.

The secret cannot be kept much longer. Questions are being asked, and sooner rather than later the New York Mets management will have to produce a statement. It may have started unraveling in St. Petersburg, Fla., two weeks ago, on March 14, to be exact, when Mel Stottlemyre, the Met pitching coach, walked over to the 40-odd Met players doing their morning calisthenics at the Payson Field Complex not far from the Gulf of Mexico, a solitary figure among the pulsation of jumping jacks, and motioned three Mets to step out of the exercise. The three, all good prospects, were John Christensen, a 24-year-old outfielder; Dave Cochrane, a spare but muscular switch-hitting third baseman; and Lenny Dykstra, a swift center fielder who may be the Mets' lead-off man of the future.

Ordering the three to collect their bats and batting helmets, Stottlemyre led the players to the north end of the complex where a large canvas enclosure had been constructed two weeks before. The rumor was that some irrigation machinery was being installed in an underground pit.

Standing outside the enclosure, Stottlemyre explained what he wanted. "First of all," the coach said, "the club's got kind of a delicate situation here, and it would help if you kept reasonably quiet about it. O.K.?" The three nodded. Stottlemyre said, "We've got a young pitcher we're looking at. We want to see what he'll do with a batter standing in the box. We'll do this alphabetically. John, go on in there, stand at the plate and give the pitcher a target. That's all you have to do."

"Do you want me to take a cut?" Christensen asked.

Stottlemyre produced a dry chuckle. "You can do anything you want."

Christensen pulled aside a canvas flap and found himself inside a rectangular area about 90 feet long and 30 feet wide, open to the sky, with a home plate set in the ground just in front of him, and down at the far end a pitcher's mound, with a small group of Met front-office personnel standing behind it, facing home plate. Christensen recognized Nelson Doubleday, the owner of the Mets, and Frank Cashen, wearing a long-billed fishing cap. He had never seen Doubleday at the training facility before.

Christensen bats right-handed. As he stepped around the plate he nodded to Ronn Reynolds, the stocky reserve catcher who has been with the Met organization since 1980. Reynolds whispered up to him from his crouch, "Kid, you won't believe what you're about to see."

A second flap down by the pitcher's end was drawn open, and a tall, gawky player walked in and stepped up onto the pitcher's mound. He was wearing a small, black fielder's glove on his left hand and was holding a baseball in his right. Christensen had never seen him before. He had blue eyes, Christensen remembers, and a pale, youthful face, with facial muscles that were motionless, like a mask. "You notice it," Christensen explained later, "when a pitcher's jaw isn't working on a chaw or a piece of gum." Then to Christensen's astonishment he saw that the pitcher, pawing at the dirt of the mound to get it smoothed out properly and to his liking, was wearing a heavy hiking boot on his right foot.

Christensen has since been persuaded to describe that first confrontation.

"I'm standing in there to give this guy a target, just waving the bat once or twice over the plate. He starts his windup. He sways way back, like Juan Marichal, this hiking boot comes clomping over—I thought maybe he was wearing it for balance or something—and he suddenly rears upright like a catapult. The ball is launched from an arm completely straight up and *stiff*. Before you can blink, the ball is in the catcher's mitt. You hear it *crack*, and then there's this little bleat from Reynolds."

Christensen said the motion reminded him of the extraordinary contortions that he remembered of Goofy's pitching in one of Walt Disney's cartoon classics.

"I never dreamed a baseball could be thrown that fast. The wrist must have a lot to do with it, and all that leverage. You can hardly see the blur of it as it goes by. As for hitting the thing, frankly, I just don't think it's humanly possible. You could send a blind man up there, and maybe he'd do better hitting at the *sound* of the thing."

Christensen's opinion was echoed by both Cochrane and Dykstra, who followed him into the enclosure. When each had done his stint, he emerged startled and awestruck.

Especially Dykstra. Offering a comparison for SI, he reported that out of curiosity he had once turned up the dials that control the motors of the pitching machine to maximum velocity, thus producing a pitch that went approximately 106 miles per hour. "What I looked at in there," he said, motioning toward the enclosure, "was whistling by another third as fast, I swear."

The phenomenon the three young batters faced, and about whom only Reynolds, Stottlemyre and a few members of the Mets' front office know, is a 28-year-old, somewhat eccentric mystic named Hayden (Sidd) Finch. He may well change the course of baseball history. On St. Patrick's Day, to make sure they were not all victims of a crazy hallucination, the Mets brought in a radar gun to measure the speed of Finch's fastball. The model used was a JUGS Supergun II. It looks like a black space gun with a big snout, weighs about five pounds and is usually pointed at the pitcher from behind the catcher. A glass plate in the back of the gun shows the pitch's velocity—accurate, so the manufacturer claims, to within plus or minus 1 mph. The figure at the top of the gauge is 200 mph. The fastest projectile ever measured by the JUGS (which is named after the oldtimer's descriptive—the "jug-handled" curve-ball) was a Roscoe Tanner serve that registered 153 mph. The highest number that the JUGS had ever turned for a baseball was 103 mph, which it did, curi-ously, twice on one day, July 11, at the 1978 All-Star game when both Goose Gossage and Nolan Ryan threw the ball at that speed. On March 17, the gun was handled by Stottlemyre. He heard the pop of the ball in Reynolds's mitt and the little squeak of pain from the catcher. Then the astonishing figure 168 appeared on the glass plate. Stottlemyre remembers whistling in amazement, and then he heard Reynolds say, "Don't tell me, Mel, I don't want to know. . . ."

The Met front office is reluctant to talk about Finch. The fact is, they know very little about him. He has had no baseball career. Most of his life has been spent abroad, except for a short period at Harvard University.

The registrar's office at Harvard will release no information about Finch except that in the spring of 1976 he withdrew from the college in midterm. The alumni records in Harvard's Holyoke Center indicate slightly more. Finch spent his early childhood in an orphanage in Leicester, England, and was adopted by a foster parent, the eminent archaeologist Francis Whyte-Finch, who was killed in an airplane crash while on an expedition in the Dhaulagiri mountain area of Nepal. At the time of the tragedy, Finch was in his last year at the Stowe School in Buckingham, England, from which he had been accepted into Harvard. Apparently, though, the boy decided to spend a year in the general area of the plane crash in the Himalayas (the plane was never actually found) before he returned to the West and entered Harvard in 1975, dropping for unknown reasons the "Whyte" from his name. Hayden Finch's picture is not in the freshman yearbook. Nor, of course, did he play baseball at Harvard, having departed before the start of the spring season.

His assigned roommate was Henry W. Peterson, class of 1979, now a stockbroker in New York with Dean Witter, who saw very little of Finch. "He was almost never there," Peterson told SI. "I'd wake up morning after morn-ing and look across at his bed, which had a woven native carpet of some sort on it—I have an idea he told me it was made of yak fur—and never had the sense it had been slept in. Maybe he slept on the floor. Actually, my assump-tion was that he had a girl in Somerville or something, and stayed out there. He had almost no belongings. A knapsack. A bowl he kept in the corner on the floor. A couple of wool shirts, always very clean, and maybe a pair or so of blue jeans. One pair of hiking boots. I always had the feeling that he was very bright. He had a French horn in an old case. I don't know much about French-horn music but he played beautifully. Sometimes he'd play it in the bath. He knew any number of languages. He was so adept at them that he'd be talking in English, which he spoke in this distinctive singsong way, quite Oriental, and he'd use a phrase like 'pied-à-terre' and without knowing it he'd sail along in French for a while until he'd drop in a German word like 'angst' and he'd shift to that language. For any kind of sustained conversation you had to hope he wasn't going to use a foreign buzz word—especially out of the Eastern languages he knew, like Sanskrit—because that was the end of it as far as I was concerned."

When Peterson was asked why he felt Finch had left Harvard, he shrugged his shoulders. "I came back one afternoon, and everything was gone—the little rug, the horn, the staff. . . . Did I tell you that he had this long kind of shepherd's crook standing in the corner? Actually, there was so little stuff to begin with that it was hard to tell he wasn't there anymore. He left a curious note on the floor. It turned out to be a Zen koan, which is one of those puzzles which cannot be solved by the intellect. It's the famous one about the live goose in the bottle. How do you get the goose out of the bottle without hurting it or breaking the glass? The answer is, "There, it's out!" I heard from him once, from Egypt. He sent pictures. He was on his way to Tibet to study."

Finch's entry into the world of baseball occurred last July in Old Orchard Beach, Maine, where the Mets' AAA farm club, the Tidewater Tides, was in town playing the Guides. After the first game of the series, Bob Schaefer, the Tides' manager, was strolling back to the hotel. He has very distinct memories of his first meeting with Finch: "I was walking by a park when suddenly this guy—nice-looking kid, clean-shaven, blue jeans, big boots—appears alongside. At first, I think maybe he wants an autograph or to chat about the game, but no, he scrabbles around in a kind of knapsack, gets out a scuffed-up baseball and a small, black leather fielder's mitt that looks like it came out of the back of some Little League kid's closet. This guy says to me, 'I have learned the art of the pitch. . . .' Some odd phrase like that, delivered in a singsong voice, like a chant, kind of what you hear in a Chinese restaurant if there are some Chinese in there.

"I am about to hurry on to the hotel when this kid points out a soda bottle on top of a fence post about the same distance home plate is from the pitcher's rubber. He rears way back, comes around and pops the ball at it. Out there on that fence post the soda bottle *explodes*. It disintegrates like a rifle bullet hit it—just little specks of vaporized glass in a *puff*. Beyond the post I could see the ball bouncing across the grass of the park until it stopped about as far away as I can hit a three-wood on a good day.

"I said, very calm, 'Son, would you mind showing me that again?'

"And he did. He disappeared across the park to find the ball—it had gone so far, he was after it for what seemed 15 minutes. In the meantime I found a tin can from a trash container and set it up for him. He did it again—just kicked that can off the fence like it was hit with a baseball bat. It wasn't the accuracy of the pitch so much that got to me but the *speed*. It was like the tin can got belted as soon as the ball left the guy's fingertips. Instantaneous. I thought to myself, 'My god, that kid's thrown the ball about 150 mph. Nolan Ryan's fastball is a change-up compared to what this kid just threw.'

"Well, what happens next is that we sit and talk, this kid and I, out there on the grass of the park. He sits with the big boots tucked under his legs, like one of those yoga guys, and he tells me he's not sure he wants to play big-league baseball, but he'd like to give it a try. He's never played before, but he knows the rules, even the infield-fly rule, he tells me with a smile, and he knows he can throw a ball with complete accuracy and enormous velocity. He won't tell me how he's done this except that he 'learned it in the mountains, in a place called Po, in Tibet.' That is where he said he had learned to pitch . . . up in the mountains, flinging rocks and meditating. He told me his name was Hayden Finch, but he wanted to be called Sidd Finch. I said that most of the Sids we had in baseball came from Brooklyn. Or the Bronx. He said his Sidd came from 'Siddhartha,' which means 'Aim Attained' or 'The Perfect Pitch.' That's what he had learned, how to throw the perfect pitch. O.K. by me, I told him, and that's what I put on the scouting report, 'Sidd Finch.' And I mailed it in to the front office."

The reaction in New York once the report arrived was one of complete disbelief. The assumption was that Schaefer was either playing a joke on his superiors or was sending in the figment of a very powerful wish-fulfillment dream. But Schaefer is one of the most respected men in the Met organization. Over the past seven years, the clubs he has managed have won six championships. Dave Johnson, the Met manager, phoned him. Schaefer verified what he had seen in Old Orchard Beach. He told Johnson that sometimes he, too, thought he'd had a dream, but he hoped the Mets would send Finch an invitation so that, at the very least, his own mind would be put at rest.

When a rookie is invited to training camp, he gets a packet of instructions in late January. The Mets sent off the usual literature to Finch at the address Schaefer had supplied them. To their surprise, Finch wrote back with a number of stipulations. He insisted he would report to the Mets camp in St. Petersburg only with the understanding that: 1) there were no contractual commitments; 2) during off-hours he be allowed to keep completely to himself; 3) he did not wish to be involved in any of the team drills or activities; 4) he would show the Mets his pitching prowess in privacy; 5) the whole operation in St. Petersburg was to be kept as secret as possible, with no press or photographs.

The reason for these requirements—he stated in a letter written (according to a source in the Met front office) in slightly stilted, formal and very polite terminology—was that he had not decided whether he actually wanted to play baseball. He wrote apologetically that there were mental adjustments to be made. He did not want to raise the Mets' expectations, much less those of the fans, and then dash them. Therefore it was best if everything were carried on in secret or, as he put it in his letter, "in camera."

At first, the inclination of the Met front office was to disregard this nonsense out of hand and tell Finch either to apply, himself, through normal procedures or forget it. But the extraordinary statistics in the scouting report and Schaefer's verification of them were too intriguing to ignore. On Feb. 2, Finch's terms were agreed to by letter. Mick McFadyen, the Mets' groundskeeper in St. Petersburg, was ordered to build the canvas enclosure in a far corner of the Payson complex, complete with a pitcher's mound and plate. Reynolds's ordeal was about to start.

Reynolds is a sturdy, hardworking catcher (he has been described as looking like a high school football tackle). He has tried to be close-lipped about Finch, but his experiences inside the canvas enclosure have made it difficult for him to resist answering a few questions. He first heard about Finch from the Mets' general manager. "Mr. Cashen called me into his office one day in early March," Reynolds disclosed. "I was nervous because I thought I'd been traded. He was wearing a blue bow tie. He leaned across the desk and whispered to me that it was very likely I was going to be a part of baseball history. Big doings! The Mets had this rookie coming to camp and I was going to be his special catcher. All very hush-hush.

"Well, I hope nothing like that guy ever comes down the pike again. The first time I see him is inside the canvas coop, out there on the pitcher's mound, a thin kid getting ready to throw, and I'm thinking he'll want to toss a couple of warmup pitches. So I'm standing behind the plate without a mask, chest protector, pads or anything, holding my glove up, sort of half-assed, to give him a target to throw at . . . and suddenly I see this windup like a pretzel gone loony, and the next thing, I've been blown two or three feet back, and I'm sitting on the ground with the ball in my glove. My catching hand feels like it's been hit with a sledgehammer."

He was asked: "Does he throw a curveball? A slider? Or a sinker?"

Reynolds grinned and shook his head. "Good questions! Don't ask me."

"Does it make a sound?"

"Yeah, a little *pft, pft-boom!*"

Stottlemyre has been in direct charge of Finch's pitching regimen. His own playing career ended in the spring of 1975 with a rotator-cuff injury, which makes him especially sensitive to the strain that a pitching motion can put on the arm. Although as close-lipped as the rest of the staff, Stottlemyre does admit that Finch has developed a completely revolutionary pitching style. He told SI: "I don't understand the mechanics of it. Anyone who tries to throw the ball that way should fall flat on his back. But I've seen it. I've seen it a hundred times. It's the most awesome thing that has ever happened in baseball."

Asked what influences might have contributed to Finch's style and speed, Stottlemyre said, "Well, *cricket* may have something to do with it. Finch has taken the power and speed of the running throw of the cricket bowler and has somehow harnessed all that energy to the pitching rubber. The wrist snap off that stiff arm is incredible. I haven't talked to him but once or twice. I asked him if he ever thought of snapping the *arm*, like baseball pitchers, rather than the wrist: It would increase the velocity.

"He replied, very polite, you know, with a little bob of the head: 'I undertake as a rule of training to refrain from injury to living things.'

"He's right, of course. It's Ronn Reynolds I feel sorry for. Every time that ball comes in, first you hear this *smack* sound of the ball driving into the pocket of the mitt, and then you hear this little gasp, this *ai yee!*—the catcher, poor guy, his whole body shakin' like an angina's hit it. It's the most piteous thing I've ever heard, short of a trapped rabbit."

Hayden (Sidd) Finch arrived in St. Petersburg on Feb. 7. Most of the rookies and minor-leaguers stay at the Edgewater Beach Inn. Assuming that Finch would check in with the rest of the early arrivals, the Mets were surprised when he telephoned and announced that he had leased a room in a small boardinghouse just off Florida Avenue near a body of water on the bay side called Big Bayou. Because his private pitching compound had been constructed across the city and Finch does not drive, the Mets assigned him a driver, a young Tampa Bay resident, Eliot Posner, who picks him up in the morning and returns him to Florida Avenue or, more often, to a beach on the Gulf where, Posner reports, Finch, still in his baseball outfit and carrying his decrepit glove, walks down to the water's edge and, motionless, stares out at the windsurfers. Inevitably, he dismisses Posner and gets back to his boardinghouse on his own.

The Met management has found out very little about his life in St. Petersburg. Mrs. Roy Butterfield, his landlady, reports (as one might expect) that "he lives very simply. Sometimes he comes in the front door, sometimes the back. Sometimes I'm not even sure he spends the night. I think he sleeps on the floor—his bed is always neat as a pin. He has his own rug, a small little thing. I never have had a boarder who brought his own rug. He has a soup bowl. Not *much*, is what I say. Of course, he plays the French horn. He plays it very beautifully and, thank goodness, softly. The notes fill the house. Sometimes I think the notes are coming out of my television set."

Probably the member of the Met staff who has gotten the closest to Finch is Posner. When Posner returns to the Payson complex, inevitably someone rushes out from the Mets' offices asking, "Did he say anything? What did he say?"

Posner takes out a notebook.

"Today he said, 'When your mind is empty like a canyon you will know the power of the Way.'"

"Anything else?"

"No."

While somewhat taxed by Finch's obvious eccentricities, and with the exception of the obvious burden on the catchers, the Mets, it seems, have an extraordinary property in their camp. But the problem is that no one is sure if Finch really wants to play. He has yet to make up his mind; his only appearances are in the canvas enclosure. Reynolds moans in despair when he is told Finch has arrived. Sometimes his ordeal is short-lived. After Finch nods politely at Reynolds and calls down "*Namas-te!*" (which means "greetings" in Sanskrit), he throws only four or five of the terrifying pitches before, with a gentle smile, he announces "*Namas-te!*" (it also means "farewell") and gets into the car to be driven away.

One curious manifestation of Finch's reluctance to commit himself entirely to baseball has been his refusal to wear a complete baseball uniform. Because he changes in his rooming house, no one is quite sure what he will be wearing when he steps through the canvas flap into the enclosure. One afternoon he turned up sporting a tie hanging down over the logo on his jersey, and occasionally—as Christensen noticed—he wears a hiking boot on his right foot. Always, he wears his baseball cap back to front—the conjecture among the Met officials is that this sartorial behavior is an indication of his ambivalence about baseball.

In hopes of understanding more about him, in early March the Mets called in a specialist in Eastern religions, Dr. Timothy Burns, the author of, among other treatises, *Satori, or Four Years in a Tibetan Lamasery.* Not allowed to speak personally with Finch for fear of "spooking him," Burns was able only to speculate about the Mets' newest player.

According to sources from within the Met organization, Burns told a meeting of the club's top brass that the strange ballplayer in their midst was very likely a *trapas,* or aspirant monk.

A groan is said to have gone up from Nelson Doubleday. Burns said that Finch was almost surely a disciple of Tibet's great poet-saint Lama Milaraspa, who was born in the 11th century and died in the shadow of Mount Everest. Burns told them that Milaraspa was a great yogi who could manifest an astonishing phenomenon: He could produce "internal heat," which allowed him to survive snowstorms and intense cold, wearing only a thin robe of white cotton. Finch does something similar—an apparent deflection of the huge forces of the universe into throwing a baseball with bewildering accuracy and speed through the process of *siddhi,* namely the yogic mastery of mind-body. He mentioned that *The Book of Changes, the I Ching,* suggests that all acts (even throwing a baseball) are connected with the highest spiritual yearnings. Utilizing the Tantric principle of body and mind, Finch has decided to pitch baseballs—at least for a while.

The Mets pressed Burns. Was there any chance that Finch would come to his senses and *commit* himself to baseball?

"There's a chance," Burns told them. "You will remember that the Buddha himself, after what is called the Great Renunciation, finally realized that even in the most severe austerities—though he conquered lust and fear and acquired a great deal of self-knowledge—truth itself could not necessarily be found. So after fasting for six years he decided to eat again."

Reached by SI at the University of Maryland, where he was lecturing last week, Burns was less sanguine. "The biggest problem Finch has with baseball," he said over the phone, "is that *nirvana*, which is the state all Buddhists wish to reach, means literally 'the blowing out'—specifically the purifying of oneself of greed, hatred and delusion. Baseball," Burns went on, "is symbolized to a remarkable degree by those very three aspects: *greed* (huge money contracts, stealing second base, robbing a guy of a base hit, charging for a seat behind an iron pillar, etc.), *hatred* (players despising management, pitchers hating hitters, the Cubs detesting the Mets, etc.) and *delusion* (the slider, the pitchout, the hidden-ball trick and so forth). So you can see why it is not easy for Finch to give himself up to a way of life so opposite to what he has been led to cherish."

Burns is more puzzled by Finch's absorption with the French horn. He suspects that in Tibet Finch may have learned to play the *rkang-gling*, a Tibetan horn made of human thighbones, or perhaps even the Tibetan long trumpet, the *dung-chen*, whose sonorous bellowing in those vast Himalayan defiles is somewhat echoed in the lower registers of the French horn.

The Met inner circle believes that Finch's problem may be that he cannot decide between baseball and a career as a horn player. In early March the club contacted Bob Johnson, who plays the horn and is the artistic director of the distinguished New York Philomusica ensemble, and asked him to come to St. Petersburg. Johnson was asked to make a clandestine assessment of Finch's ability as a horn player and, even more important, to make contact with him. The idea was that, while praising him for the quality of his horn playing, Johnson should try to persuade him that the lot of a French-horn player (even a very fine one) was not an especially gainful one. Perhaps *that* would tip the scales in favor of baseball.

Johnson came down to St. Petersburg and hung around Florida Avenue for a week. He reported later to SI: "I was being paid for it, so it wasn't bad. I spent a lot of time looking up, so I'd get a nice suntan. Every once in a while I saw Finch coming in and out of the rooming house, dressed to play baseball and carrying a funny-looking black glove. Then one night I heard the French horn. He was playing it in his room. I have heard many great horn players in my career—Bruno Jaenicke, who played for Toscanini; Dennis Brain, the great British virtuoso; Anton Horner of the Philadelphia Orchestra—and I would say Finch was on a par with them. He was playing Benjamin Britten's *Serenade*, for tenor horn and strings—a haunting, tender piece that provides great space for the player—when suddenly he produced a big, evocative *bwong* sound that seemed to shiver the leaves of the trees. Then he shifted to the rondo theme from the trio for violin, piano and horn by Brahms—just sensational. It may have had something to do with the Florida evening and a mild wind coming in over Big Bayou, and the sound of the tree-frog chorus in the background; it was *remarkable*. I told this to the Mets, and they immediately sent me home—presuming, I guess, that I was going to hire the guy. That's not so far-fetched. He can play for the Philomusica anytime."

Meanwhile, the Mets are trying other ways to get Finch into a more positive frame of mind about baseball. Inquiries among American lamaseries (there are more than 100 Buddhist societies in the U.S.) have been quietly initiated in the hope of finding monks or priests who are serious baseball fans and who might persuade Finch that the two religions (Buddhism and baseball) are compatible. One plan is to get him into a movie theater to see *The Natural*, the mystical film about baseball, starring Robert Redford. Another film suggested is the baseball classic *It Happens Every Spring*, starring Ray Milland as a chemist who, by chance, discovers a compound that avoids wood; when applied to a baseball in the film, it makes Milland as effective a pitcher as Finch is in real life.

Conversations with Finch himself have apparently been exercises in futility. All conventional inducements—huge contracts, advertising tie-ins, the banquet circuit, ticker-tape parades, having his picture on a Topps bubble-gum card, chatting on *Kiner's Korner* (the Mets' postgame TV show) and so forth—mean little to him. As do the perks ("You are very kind to offer me a Suzuki motorcycle, but I cannot drive"). He has very politely declined whatever overtures the Mets have offered. The struggle is an absolutely internal one. He will resolve it. Last week he announced that he would let the management know what he was going to do on or around April 1.

Met manager Davey Johnson has seen Finch throw about half a dozen pitches. He was impressed ("If he didn't have this great control, he'd be like the Terminator out there. Hell, that fastball, if off-target on the inside, would carry a batter's kneecap back into the catcher's mitt"), but he is leaving the situation to the front office. "I can handle the pitching rotation; let them handle the monk." He has had one meeting with Finch. "I was going to ask him if we could at least give him a decent fielder's mitt. I asked him why he was so attached to the piece of rag he was using. 'It is,' the guy told me, 'the only one I have.' Actually, I don't see why he needs a better one. All he will ever need it for is to catch the ball for the next pitch. So then I said to him, 'There's only one thing I can offer you, Finch, and that's a fair shake.'"

According to Jay Horwitz, the Mets' public-relations man, Finch smiled at the offer of the fair shake and nodded his head politely—perhaps because it was the only nonmaterial offer made. It did not encroach on Finch's ideas about the renunciation of worldly goods. It was an ingenious, if perhaps unintentional, move on the manager's part.

Nelson Doubleday is especially hopeful about Finch's ultimate decision. "I think we'll bring him around," he said a few days ago. "After all, the guy's not a nut, he's a Harvard man."

In the meantime, the Mets can only wait. Finch periodically turns up at the enclosure. Reynolds is summoned. There are no drills. Sometimes Finch throws for five minutes, instantly at top speed, often for half an hour. Then he leaves. Security around the enclosure has been tight. Since Finch has not signed with the Mets, he is technically a free agent and a potential find for another club. The curious, even Met players, are politely shooed away from the Payson Field enclosure. So far Finch's only association with Met players (other than Reynolds) has been the brief confrontation with Christensen, Cochrane and Dykstra when the front office nervously decided to test his control with a batter standing in the box. If he decides to play baseball, he will leave his private world of the canvas enclosure and join manager Johnson and the rest of the squad. For the first time Gary Carter, the Mets' regular catcher, will face the smoke of the Finch pitch, and the other pitchers will stand around and gawk. The press will have a field day ("How do you spell Siddhartha? How do you grip the ball? How do you keep your balance on the mound?"). The Mets will try to protect him from the glare and help him through the most traumatic of culture shocks, praying that in the process he will not revert and one day disappear.

Actually, the presence of Hayden (Sidd) Finch in the Mets' training camp raises a number of interesting questions. Suppose the Mets (and Finch himself) can assuage and resolve his mental reservations about playing baseball; suppose he is signed to a contract (one wonders what an ascetic whose major possessions are a bowl, a small rug, a long stick and a French horn might demand); and suppose he comes to New York's Shea Stadium to open the season against the St. Louis Cardinals on April 9. It does not matter that he has never taken a fielding drill with his teammates. Presumably he will mow down the opposition in a perfect game. Perhaps Willie McGee will get a foul tip. Suppose Johnson discovers that the extraordinary symbiotic relationship of mind and matter is indefatigable—that Finch can pitch day after day at this blinding, unhittable speed. What will happen to Dwight Gooden? Will Carter and the backup catchers last the season? What will it do to major-league baseball as it is known today?

Peter Ueberroth, baseball's new commissioner, was contacted by SI in his New York office. He was asked if he had heard anything about the Mets' new phenomenon.

No, he had not. He had heard some *rumors* about the Mets' camp this spring, but nothing specific.

Did the name Hayden (Sidd) Finch mean anything to him?

Nope.

The commissioner was told that the Mets had a kid who could throw the ball over 150 mph. Unhittable.

Ueberroth took a minute before he asked, "Roll that by me again?"

He was told in as much detail as could be provided about what was going on within the canvas enclosure of the Payson compound. It was possible that an absolute superpitcher was coming into baseball—so remarkable that the delicate balance between pitcher and batter could be turned into disarray. What was baseball going to do about it?

"Well, before any decisions, I'll tell you something," the commissioner finally said, echoing what may very well be a nationwide sentiment this coming season. "I'll have to see it to believe it!"

Jamesie (1947)

J. F. Powers

James Farl Powers was born in 1917 in Jacksonville, Illinois. He was widely respected as a brilliant satirist and meticulous craftsman. Much of his fiction is deeply rooted in Catholic values and religious themes. Powers's best-known book is *Morte D'Urban* (1962), which won the National Book Award and is now included in the Modern Library's collection of great books of the world. His other books include *The Presence of Grace* (1956), *Look How the Fish Live* (1975), and *Wheat That Springeth Green* (1988). "Jamesie" is based on Powers's own childhood in Illinois, where he played baseball, basketball, and football. The story originally appeared in a collection of his stories called *Prince of Darkness and Other Stories* (1947).

There it was, all about Lefty, in Ding Bell's Dope Box.

"We don't want to add coals to the fire, but it's common knowledge that the Local Pitcher Most Likely to Succeed is fed up with the home town. Well, well, the boy's good, which nobody can deny, and the scouts are on his trail, but it doesn't say a lot for his team spirit, not to mention his civic spirit, this high-hat attitude of his. And that fine record of his—has it been all a case of him and him alone? How about the team? The boys have backed him up, they've given him the runs, and that's what wins ball games. They don't pay off on strikeouts. There's one kind of player every scribe knows—and wishes he didn't—the lad who gets four for four with the willow, and yet, somehow, his team goes down to defeat—but does that worry this gent? Not a bit of it. He's too busy celebrating his own personal success, figuring his batting average, or, if he's a pitcher, his earned-run average and strikeouts. The percentage player. We hope we aren't talking about Lefty. If we are, it's too bad, it is, and no matter where he goes from here, especially if it's up to the majors, it won't remain a secret very long, nor will he. . . . See you at the game Sunday. Ding Bell."

"Here's a new one, Jamesie," his father said across the porch, holding up the rotogravure section.

With his father on Sunday it could be one of three things—a visit to the office, fixing up his mother's grave in Calvary, or just sitting on the porch with all the Chicago papers, as today.

Jamesie put down the *Courier* and went over to his father without curiosity. It was always Lindy or the *Spirit of St. Louis*, and now without understanding how this could so suddenly be, he was tired of them. His father, who seemed to feel that a growing boy could take an endless interest in these things, appeared to know the truth at last. He gave a page to the floor—that way he knew what he'd read and how far he had to go—and pulled the newspaper around his ears again. Before he went to dinner he would put the paper in order and wish out loud that other people would have the decency to do the same.

Jamesie, back in his chair, granted himself one more chapter of *Baseball Bill in the World Series*. The chapters were running out again, as they had so many times before, and he knew, with the despair of a narcotic, that his need had no end.

Baseball Bill, at fifty cents a volume and unavailable at the library, kept him nearly broke, and Francis Murgatroyd, his best friend . . . too stingy to go halves, confident he'd get to read them all as Jamesie bought them, and each time offering to exchange the old Tom Swifts and Don Sturdys he had got for Christmas—as though that were the same thing!

Jamesie owned all the Baseball Bills to be had for love or money in the world, and there was nothing in the back of this one about new titles being in preparation. Had the author died, as some of them did, and left his readers in the lurch? Or had the series been discontinued—for where, after *Fighting for the Pennant* and *In the World Series*, could Baseball Bill go? *Baseball Bill, Manager*, perhaps. But then what?

"A plot to *fix* the World Series! So that was it! Bill began to see it all. . . . The mysterious call in the night! The diamond necklace in the dressing room! The scribbled note under the door! With slow fury Bill realized that the peculiar odor on the note paper was the odor in his room now! It was the odor of strong drink and cigar smoke! And it came from his midnight visitor! The same! Did he represent the powerful gambling syndicate? Was *he* Blackie Humphrey himself? Bill held his towering rage in check and smiled at his visitor in his friendly, boyish fashion. His visitor must get no inkling of his true thoughts. Bill must play the game—play the very fool they took him for! Soon enough they would discover for themselves, but to their everlasting sorrow, the courage and daring of Baseball Bill. . . ."

Jamesie put the book aside, consulted the batting averages in the *Courier*, and reread Ding Bell. Then, not waiting for dinner and certain to hear about it at supper, he ate a peanut butter sandwich with catsup on it, and left by the back door. He went down the alley calling for Francis Murgatroyd. He got up on the Murgatroyd gate and swung—the death-defying trapeze act at the circus—until Francis came down the walk.

"Hello, Blackie Humphrey," Jamesie said tantalizingly.

"Who's Blackie Humphrey?"

"You know who Blackie Humphrey is all right."

"Aw, Jamesie, cut it out."

"And you want me to throw the World Series!"

"Baseball Bill!"

"In the World Series. It came yesterday."

"Can I read it?"

Jamesie spoke in a hushed voice. "So you're Blackie Humphrey?"

"All right. But I get to read it next."

"So you want me to throw the World Series, Blackie. Is that it? Say you do."

"Yes, I do."

"Ask me again. Call me Bill."

"Bill, I want you to throw the World Series. Will you, Bill?"

"I might." But that was just to fool Blackie. Bill tried to keep his towering rage in check while feigning an interest in the nefarious plot. "Why do you want me to throw it, Blackie?"

"I don't know."

"Sure you know. You're a dirty crook and you've got a lot of dough bet on the other team."

"Uh, huh."

"Go ahead. Tell me that."

While Blackie unfolded the criminal plan Bill smiled at him in his friendly, boyish fashion.

"And who's behind this, Blackie?"

"I don't know."

"Say it's the powerful gambling syndicate."

"It's them."

"Ah, ha! Knock the ash off your cigar."

"Have I got one?"

"Yes, and you've got strong drink on your breath, too."

"Whew!"

Blackie should have fixed him with his small, piglike eyes.

"Fix me with your small, piglike eyes."

"Wait a minute, Jamesie!"

"Bill. Go ahead. Fix me."

"OK. But you don't get to be Bill all the time."

"Now blow your foul breath in my face."

"There!"

"Now ask me to have a cigar. Go ahead."

Blackie was offering Bill a cigar, but Bill knew it was to get him to break training and refused it.

"I see through you, Blackie." No, that was wrong. He had to conceal his true thoughts and let Blackie play him for a fool. Soon enough his time would come and . . . "Thanks for the cigar, Blackie," he said. "I thought it was a cheap one. Thanks, I'll smoke it later."

"I paid a quarter for it."

"Hey, that's too much, Francis!"

"Well, if I'm the head of the powerful—"

Mr. Murgatroyd came to the back door and told Francis to get ready.

"I can't go to the game, Jamesie," Francis said. "I have to caddy for him."

• • •

Jamesie got a ride with the calliope when it had to stop at the corner for the light. The calliope was not playing now, but yesterday it had roamed the streets, all red and gold and glittering like a hussy among the pious, black Fords parked on the Square, blaring and showing off, with a sign, Jayville vs. Beardstown.

The ballpark fence was painted a swampy green except for an occasional new board. Over the single ticket window cut in the fence hung a sign done in the severe black and white railroad manner. "Home of the Jayville Independents," but everybody called them the "Indees."

Jamesie bought a bottle of Green River out of his savings and made the most of it, swallowing it in sips, calling upon his will power under the sun. He returned the bottle and stood for a while by the ticket window making designs in the dust with the corrugated soles of his new tennis shoes. Ding Bell, with a pretty lady on his arm and carrying the black official scorebook, passed inside without paying, and joked about it.

The Beardstown players arrived from sixty miles away with threatening cheers. Their chartered bus stood steaming and dusty from the trip. The players wore gray suits with "Barons" written across their chests and had the names of sponsors on their backs—Palms Café, Rusty's Wrecking, Coca-Cola.

Jamesie recognized some of the Barons but put down a desire to speak to them.

The last man to leave the bus, Jamesie thought, must be Guez, the new pitcher imported from East St. Louis for the game. Ding Bell had it in the Dope Box that "Saliva Joe" was one of the few spitters left in the business, had been up in the Three Eye a few years, was a full-blooded Cuban, and ate a bottle of aspirins a game, just like candy.

The dark pitcher's fame was too much for Jamesie. He walked alongside Guez. He smelled the salt and pepper of the gray uniform, saw the scarred plate on the right toe, saw the tears in the striped stockings—the marks of bravery or moths—heard the distant chomp of tobacco being chewed, felt—almost—the iron drape of the flannel, and was reduced to friendliness with the pitcher, the enemy.

"Are you a real Cuban?"

Guez looked down, rebuking Jamesie with a brief stare, and growled. "Go away."

Jamesie gazed after the pitcher. He told himself that he hated Guez—that's what he did, hated him! But it didn't do much good. He looked around to see if anybody had been watching, but nobody had, and he wanted some-body his size to vanquish—somebody who might think Guez was as good as Lefty. He wanted to bet a million dollars on Lefty against Guez, but there was nobody to take him up on it.

The Indees began to arrive in ones and twos, already in uniform but car-rying their spikes in their hands. Jamesie spoke to all of them except J. G. Nickerson, the manager. J.G. always glared at kids. He thought they were stealing his baseballs and laughing about it behind his back. He was a great one for signaling with a scorecard from the bench, like Connie Mack, and Ding Bell had ventured to say that managers didn't come any brainier than Jayville's own J. G. Nickerson, even in the big time. But if there should be a foul ball, no matter how tight the game or crucial the situation, J.G. would leap up, straining like a bird dog, and try to place it, waving the batboy on without taking his eyes off the spot where it disappeared over the fence or in the weeds. That was why they called him the Foul Ball.

The Petersons—the old man at the wheel, a red handkerchief tied tight enough around his neck to keep his head on, and the sons, all players, Big Pete, Little Pete, Middle Pete, and Extra Pete—roared up with their legs hanging out of the doorless Model T and the brass radiator boiling over.

The old man ran the Model T around in circles, damning it for a runaway horse, and finally got it parked by the gate.

"Hold'er, Knute!" he cackled.

The boys dug him in the ribs, tickling him, and were like puppies that had been born bigger than their father, jollying him through the gate, calling him Barney Oldfield.

Lefty came.

"Hi, Lefty," Jamesie said.

"Hi, kid," Lefty said. He put his arm around Jamesie and took him past the ticket taker.

"It's all right, Mac," he said.

"Today's the day, Lefty," Mac said. "You can do it, Lefty."

Jamesie and Lefty passed behind the grandstand. Jamesie saw Lefty's father, a skinny, brown-faced man in a yellow straw katy.

"There's your dad, Lefty."

Lefty said, "Where?" but looked the wrong way and walked a little faster.

At the end of the grandstand Lefty stopped Jamesie. "My old man is out of town, kid. Got that?"

Jamesie did not see how this could be. He knew Lefty's father. Lefty's father had a brown face and orange gums. But Lefty ought to know his own father. "I guess it just looked like him, Lefty," Jamesie said.

Lefty took his hand off Jamesie's arm and smiled. "Yeah, that's right, kid. It just looked like him on account of he's out of town—in Peoria."

Jamesie could still feel the pressure of Lefty's fingers on his arm. They came out on the diamond at the Indees bench near first base. The talk quieted down when Lefty appeared. Everybody thought he had a big head, but nobody could say a thing against his pitching record, it was that good. The scout for the New York Yankees had invited him only last Sunday to train with them next spring. The idea haunted the others. J.G. had shut up about the beauties of teamwork.

J.G. was counting the balls when Jamesie went to the suitcase to get one for Lefty. J.G. snapped the lid down.

"It's for Lefty!"

"Huh!"

"He wants it for warm up."

"Did you tell this kid to get you a ball, Left?"

"Should I bring my own?" Lefty said.

J.G. dug into the suitcase for a ball, grunting. "I only asked him." He looked to Jamesie for sympathy. He considered the collection of balls and finally picked out a fairly new one.

"Lefty, he likes 'em brand new," Jamesie said.

"Who's running this club?" J.G. bawled. But he threw the ball back and broke a brand new one out of its box and tissue paper. He ignored Jamesie's ready hand and yelled to Lefty going out to the bull pen, "Coming at you, Left," and threw it wild.

Lefty let the ball bounce through his legs, not trying for it. "Nice throw," he said.

Jamesie retrieved the ball for Lefty. They tossed it back and forth, limbering up, and Jamesie aped Lefty's professional indolence.

When Bugs Bidwell, Lefty's battery mate, appeared with his big mitt, Jamesie stood aside and buttoned his glove back on his belt. Lefty shed his red blanket coat with the leather sleeves and gave it to Jamesie for safekeeping. Jamesie folded it gently over his arm, with the white chenille "J" showing out. He took his stand behind Bugs to get a good look at Lefty's stuff.

Lefty had all his usual stuff—the fast one with the two little hops in it, no bigger than a pea; his slow knuckler that looked like a basketball, all the stitches standing still and staring you in the face; his sinker that started out high like a wild pitch, then dipped a good eight inches and straightened out for a called strike. But something was wrong—Lefty with nothing to say, no jokes, no sudden whoops, was not himself. Only once did he smile at a girl in the bleachers and say she was plenty . . . and sent a fast one smacking into Bug's mitt for what he meant.

That, for a moment, was the Lefty that Jamesie's older cousins knew about. They said a nice kid like Jamesie ought to be kept away from him, even at the ballpark. Jamesie was always afraid it would get back to Lefty that the cousins thought he was poor white trash, or that he would know it in some other way, as when the cousins passed him on the street and looked the other way. He was worried, too, about what Lefty might think of his Sunday clothes, the snow-white blouse, the floppy sailor tie, the soft linen pants, the sissy clothes. His tennis shoes—sneakers, he ought to say—were all right, but not the golf stockings that left his knees bare, like a rich kid's. The tough guys, because they were tough or poor—he didn't know which—wore socks, not stockings, and they wore them rolled down slick to their ankles.

Bugs stuck his mitt with the ball in it under his arm and got out his Beechnut. He winked at Jamesie and said, "Chew?"

Jamesie giggled. He liked Bugs. Bugs, on loan from the crack State Hospital team, was all right—nothing crazy about him; he just liked it at the asylum, he said, the big grounds and lots of cool shade, and he was not required to work or take walks like the regular patients. He was the only Indee on speaking terms with Lefty.

Turning to Lefty, Bugs said, "Ever seen this Cuban work?"

"Naw."

"I guess he's got it when he's right."

"That so?" Lefty caught the ball with his bare hand and spun it back to Bugs. "Well, all I can promise you is a no-hit game. It's up to you clowns to get the runs."

"And me hitting a lousy .211."

"All you got to do is hold me. Anyhow what's the Foul Ball want for his five bucks—Mickey Cochrane?"

"Yeah, Left."

"I ought to quit him."

"Ain't you getting your regular fifteen?"

"Yeah, but I ought to quit. The Yankees want me. Is my curve breaking too soon?"

"It's right in there, Left."

●　●　●

It was a pitcher's battle until the seventh inning. Then the Indees pushed a run across.

The Barons got to Lefty for their first hit in the seventh, and when the next man bunted, Lefty tried to field it instead of letting Middle Pete at third have it, which put two on with none out. Little Pete threw the next man out at first, the only play possible, and the runners advanced to second and third. The next hitter hammered a line drive to Big Pete at first, and Big Pete tried to make it two by throwing to second, where the runner was off, but it was too late and the runner on third scored on the play. J.G. from the bench condemned Big Pete for a dumb Swede. The next man popped to short center.

Jamesie ran out with Lefty's jacket. "Don't let your arm get cold, Lefty."

"Some support I got," Lefty said.

"Whyn't you leave me have that bunt, Lefty?" Middle Pete said, and everybody knew he was right.

"Two of them pitches was hit solid," Big Pete said. "Good anywhere."

"Now, boys," J.G. said.

"Aw dry up," Lefty said, grabbing a blade of chew. "I ought to quit you bums."

Pid Kirby struck out for the Indees, but Little Pete walked, and Middle Pete advanced him to second on a long fly to left. Then Big Pete tripled to the weed patch in center, clear up against the Chevrolet sign, driving in Little Pete. Guez whiffed Kelly Larkin, retiring the side, and the Indees were leading the Barons 2 to 1.

The first Baron to bat in the eighth had J.G. frantic with fouls. The umpire was down to his last ball and calling for more. With trembling fingers J.G. unwrapped new balls. He had the batboy and the batboy's assistant hunting for them behind the grandstand. When one fell among the automobiles parked near first, he started to go and look for himself, but thought of Jamesie and sent him instead. "If anybody tries to hold out on you, come and tell me."

After Jamesie found the ball he crept up behind a familiar blue Hupmobile, dropping to his knees when he was right under Uncle Pat's elbow, and then popping up to scare him.

"Look who's here," his cousin said. It had not been Uncle Pat's elbow at all, but Gabriel's. Uncle Pat, who had never learned to drive, sat on the other side to be two feet closer to the game.

Jamesie stepped up on the running board, and Gabriel offered him some popcorn.

"So you're at the game, Jamesie," Uncle Pat said, grinning as though it were funny. "Gabriel said he thought that was you out there."

"Where'd you get the cap, Jamesie?" Gabriel said.

"Lefty. The whole team got new ones. And if they win today J.G. says they're getting whole new uniforms."

"Not from me," Uncle Pat said, looking out on the field. "Who the thunder's wearing my suit today?"

"Lee Coles, see?" Gabriel said, pointing to the player. Lee's back— Mallon's Grocery—was to them.

Uncle Pat, satisfied, slipped a bottle of near beer up from the floor to his lips and tipped it up straight, which explained to Jamesie the foam on his mustache.

"You went and missed me again this week," Uncle Pat said broodingly. "You know what I'm going to do, Jamesie?"

"What?"

"I'm going to stop taking your old *Liberty* magazine if you don't bring me one first thing tomorrow morning."

"I will." He would have to bring Uncle Pat his own free copy and erase the crossword puzzle. He never should have sold out on the street. That was how you lost your regular customers.

Uncle Pat said, "This makes the second time I started in to read a serial and had this happen to me."

"Is it all right if the one I bring you tomorrow has got 'Sample Copy' stamped on it?"

"That's all right with me, Jamesie, but I ought to get it for nothing." Uncle Pat swirled the last inch of beer in the bottle until it was all suds.

"I like the *Post*," Gabriel said. "Why don't you handle the *Post*?"

"They don't need anybody now."

"What he ought to handle," Uncle Pat said, "is the *Country Gentleman*."

"How's the Rosebud coming, Jamesie?" Gabriel asked. "But I don't want to buy any."

Uncle Pat and Gabriel laughed at him.

Why was that funny? He'd had to return eighteen boxes and tell them he guessed he was all through being the local representative. But why was that so funny?

"Did you sell enough to get the bicycle, Jamesie?"

"No." He had sold all the Rosebud salve he could, but not nearly enough to get the Ranger bicycle. He had to be satisfied with the Eveready flashlight.

"Well, I got enough of that Rosebud salve now to grease the Hup," Gabriel said. "Or to smear all over me the next time I swim the English Channel— with Gertrude Ederle. It ought to keep the fishes away."

"It smells nice," Uncle Pat said. "But I got plenty."

Jamesie felt that they were protecting themselves against him.

"I sent it all back anyway," he said, but that was not true; there were six boxes at home in his room that he had to keep in order to get the flashlight. Why was that the way it always worked out? Same way with the flower seeds. Why was it that whenever he got a new suit at Meyer Brothers they weren't giving out ball bats or compasses? Why was it he only won a half pound of bacon at the carnival, never a Kewpie doll or an electric fan? Why did he always get tin whistles and crickets in the Cracker Jack, never a puzzle, a ring, or a badge? And one time he had got nothing! Why was it that the five-dollar bill he found on South Diamond Street belonged to Mrs. Hutchinson? But he *had* found a quarter in the dust at the circus that nobody claimed.

"Get your aunt Kate to take that cap up in the back," Uncle Pat said, smiling.

Vaguely embarrassed, Jamesie said, "Well, I got to get back."

"If that's Lefty's cap," Gabriel called after him, "you'd better send it to the cleaners."

When he got back to the bench and handed the ball over, J.G. seemed to forget all about the bases being crowded.

"Thank God," he said. "I thought you went home with it."

The Barons were all on Lefty now. Shorty Parker, their manager, coaching at third, chanted, "Take him out. . . . Take him out. . . . Take him out."

The Barons had started off the ninth with two clean blows. Then Bugs took a foul ball off the chicken wire in front of the grandstand for one out,

and Big Pete speared a drive on the rise for another. Two down and runners on first and third. Lefty wound up—bad baseball—and the man on first
started for second, the batter stepping into the pitch, not to hit it but to spoil
the peg to second. The runner was safe; the man on third, threatening to
come home after a false start, slid yelling back into the sack. It was close and
J.G. flew off the bench to protest a little.

After getting two strikes on the next batter, Lefty threw four balls, so
wide it looked like a deliberate pitchout, and that loaded the bases.

J.G. called time. He went out to the mound to talk it over with Lefty, but
Lefty waved him away. So J.G. consulted Bugs behind the plate. Jamesie, lying
on the grass a few feet away, could hear them.

"That's the first windup I ever seen a pitcher take with a runner on first."

"It was pretty bad," Bugs said.

"And then walking that last one. He don't look wild to me, neither."

"He ain't wild, J.G.; I'll tell you that."

"I want your honest opinion, Bugs."

"I don't know what to say, J.G."

"Think I better jerk him?"

Bugs was silent, chewing it over.

"Guess I better leave him in, huh?"

"You're the boss, J.G. I don't know nothing for sure."

"I only got Extra Pete to put in. They'd murder him. I guess I got to leave
Lefty in and take a chance."

"I guess so."

When J.G. had gone Bugs walked halfway out to the mound and spoke to
Lefty. "You all right?"

"I had a little twinge before."

"A little what?"

Lefty touched his left shoulder.

"You mean your arm's gone sore?"

"Naw. I guess it's nothing."

Bugs took his place behind the plate again. He crouched, and Jamesie,
from where he was lying, saw two fingers appear below the mitt—the signal. Lefty nodded, wound up, and tried to slip a medium-fast one down the
middle. Guez, the batter, poled a long ball into left—foul by a few feet. Bugs
shook his head in the mask, took a new ball from the umpire, and slammed
it hard at Lefty.

Jamesie saw two fingers below the mitt again. What was Bugs doing? It wasn't smart baseball to give Guez another like the last one!

Guez swung and the ball fell against the left-field fence—fair. Lee Coles, the left fielder, was having trouble locating it in the weeds. Kelly Larkin came over from center to help him hunt. When they found the ball, Guez had completed the circuit and the score was 5 to 2 in favor of the Barons.

Big Pete came running over to Lefty from first base, Little Pete from second, Pid Kirby from short, Middle Pete from third. J.G., calling time again, walked out to them.

"C'mere, Bugs," he said.

Bugs came slowly.

"What'd you call for on that last pitch?"

"Curve ball."

"And the one before that?"

"Same."

"And what's Lefty give you?"

"It wasn't no curve. It wasn't much of anything."

"No," J.G. said. "It sure wasn't no curve ball. It was right in there, not too fast, not too slow, just right—for batting practice."

"It slipped," Lefty said.

"Slipped, huh!" Big Pete said. "How about the other one?"

"They both slipped. Ain't that never happened before?"

"Well, it ain't never going to happen again—not to me, it ain't," J.G. said. "I'm taking you out!"

He shouted to Extra Pete on the bench, "Warm up! You're going in!" He turned to Lefty.

"And I'm firing you. I just found out your old man was making bets under the grandstand—and they wasn't on us! I can put you in jail for this!"

"Try it," Lefty said, starting to walk away.

"If you knew it, J.G.," Big Pete said, "whyn't you let us know?"

"I just now found it out, is why."

"Then I'm going to make up for lost time," Big Pete said, following Lefty, "and punch this guy's nose."

Old man Peterson appeared among them—somebody must have told him what it was all about. "Give it to him, son!" he cackled.

Jamesie missed the fight. He was not tall enough to see over all the heads, and Gabriel, sent by Uncle Pat, was dragging him away from it all.

"I always knew that Lefty was a bad one," Gabriel said on the way home. "I knew it from the time he used to hunch in marbles."

"It reminds me of the Black Sox scandal of 1919," Uncle Pat said. "I wonder if they'll hold the old man, too."

Jamesie, in tears, said, "Lefty hurt his arm and you don't like him just because he don't work, and his father owes you at the store! Let me out! I'd rather walk by myself than ride in the Hupmobile—with you!"

• • •

He stayed up in his room, feigning a combination stomachache and headache, and would not come down for supper. Uncle Pat and Gabriel were down there eating. His room was over the dining room, and the windows were open upstairs and down, but he could not quite hear what they said. Uncle Pat was laughing a lot—that was all for sure—but then he always did that. Pretty soon he heard no more from the dining room and he knew they had gone to sit on the front porch.

Somebody was coming up the stairs. Aunt Kate. He knew the wavering step at the top of the stairs to be hers, and the long pause she used to catch her breath—something wrong with her lungs? Now, as she began to move, he heard ice tinkling in a glass. Lemonade. She was bringing him some supper. She knocked. He lay heavier on the bed and with his head at a painful angle to make her think he was suffering. She knocked again. If he pinched his forehead it would look red and feverish. He did. Now.

"Come in," he said weakly.

She came in, gliding across the room in the twilight, tall and white as a sail in her organdy, serene before her patient. Not quite opening his eyes, he saw her through the lashes. She thought he was sick all right, but even if she didn't, she would never take advantage of him to make a joke, like Uncle Pat, prescribing, "A good dose of salts! That's the ticket!" Or Gabriel, who was even meaner, "An enema!"

He had Aunt Kate fooled completely. He could fool her every time. On Halloween she was the kind of person who went to the door every time the bell rang. She was the only grownup he knew with whom it was not always the teeter-totter game. She did not raise herself by lowering him. She did not say back to him the things he said, slightly changed, accented with a grin, so that they were funny. Uncle Pat did. Gabriel did. Sometimes, if there was company, his father did.

"Don't you want the shades up, Jamesie?"

She raised the shades, catching the last of that day's sun, bringing the ballplayers on the wall out of the shadows and into action. She put the tray on the table by his bed.

Jamesie sat up and began to eat. Aunt Kate was the best one. Even if she noticed it, she would say nothing about his sudden turn for the better.

She sat across from him in the rocker, the little red one he had been given three years ago, when he was just a kid in the first grade, but she did not look too big for it. She ran her hand over the front of his books, frowning at Baseball Bill, Don Sturdy, Tom Swift, Horatio Alger, Jr., and the Sporting News. They had come between him and her.

"Where are the books we used to read, Jamesie?"

"On the bottom shelf."

She bent to see them. There they were, his old friends and hers—hers still. Perseus. Theseus. All those old Greeks. Sir Lancelot. Merlin. Sir Tristram. King Arthur. Oliver Twist. Pinocchio. Gulliver. He wondered how he could have liked them, and why Aunt Kate still did. Perhaps he still did, a little. But they turned out wrong, most of them, with all the good guys dying or turning into fairies and the bad guys becoming dwarfs. The books he read now turned out right, if not until the very last page, and the bad guys died or got what was coming to them.

"Were they talking about the game, Aunt Kate?"

"Your uncle was, and Gabriel."

Jamesie waited a moment. "Did they say anything about Lefty?"

"I don't know. Is he the one who lost the game on purpose?"

"That's a lie, Aunt Kate! That's just what Uncle Pat and Gabriel say!"

"Well, I'm sure I don't know—"

"You *are* on their side!"

Aunt Kate reached for his hand, but he drew it back. "Jamesie, I'm sure I'm not on anyone's side. How can I be? I don't know about baseball—and I don't care about it!"

"Well, I do! And I'm not one bit sick—and you thought I was!"

Jamesie rolled out of bed, ran to the door, turned, and said, "Why don't you get out of my room and go and be with them! You're on their side! And Uncle Pat drinks *near beer*!"

He could not be sure, but he thought he had her crying, and if he did it served her right. He went softly down the stairs, past the living room, out the back door, and crept along the house until he reached the front porch. He huddled under the spiraea bushes and listened to them talk. But it was not about the game. It was about President Coolidge. His father was for him. Uncle Pat was against him.

Jamesie crept back along the house until it was safe to stand up and walk. He went down the alley. He called for Francis.

But Francis was not home—still with his father, Mrs. Murgatroyd said.

Jamesie went downtown, taking his own special way, through alleys, across lots, so that he arrived on the Square without using a single street or walking on a single sidewalk. He weighed himself on the scales in front of Kresge's. He weighed eighty-four pounds, and the card said, "Cultivate your good tastes and make the most of your business connections."

He bought a ball of gum from the machine in front of the Owl Drugstore. It looked like it was time for a black one to come out, and black was his favorite flavor, but it was a green one. Anyway he was glad it had not been white.

He coveted the Louisville Sluggers in the window of the D. & M. Hardware. He knew how much they cost. They were autographed by Paul Waner, Ty Cobb, Rogers Hornsby, all the big league stars, and if Lefty ever cracked his, a Paul Waner, he was going to give it to Jamesie, he said.

When Lefty was up with the Yankees—though they had not talked about it yet—he would send for Jamesie. He would make Jamesie the bat boy for the Yankees. He would say to Jake Ruppert, the owner of the Yankees, "Either you hire my friend, Jamesie, as bat boy or I quit." Jake Ruppert would want his own nephew or somebody to have the job, but what could he do? Jamesie would have a uniform like the regular players, and get to travel around the country with them, living in hotels, eating in restaurants, taking taxicabs, and would be known to everybody as Lefty's best friend, and they would both be Babe Ruth's best friends, the three of them going everywhere together. He would get all the Yankees to write their names on an Official American League ball and then send it home to Francis Murgatroyd, who would still be going to school back in Jayville—poor old Francis; and he would write to him on hotel stationery with his own fourteen-dollar fountain pen.

And then he was standing across the street from the jail. He wondered if they had Lefty locked up over there, if Uncle Pat and Gabriel had been right—not about Lefty throwing a game—that was a lie!—but about him being locked up. A policeman came out of the jail. Jamesie waited for him to cross the street. He was Officer Burkey. He was Phil Burkey's father, and Phil had shown Jamesie his father's gun and holster one time when he was sleeping. Around the house Mr. Burkey looked like everybody else, not a policeman.

"Mr. Burkey, is Lefty in there?"

Mr. Burkey, through for the day, did not stop to talk, only saying, "Ah, that he is, boy, and there's where he deserves to be."

Jamesie said "Oh yeah!" to himself and went around to the back side of the jail. It was a brick building, painted gray, and the windows were open, but not so you could see inside, and they had bars over them.

Jamesie decided he could do nothing if Mr. Burkey was off duty. The street lights came on; it was night. He began to wonder, too, if his father would miss him. Aunt Kate would not tell. But he would have to come in the back way and sneak up to his room. If it rained tomorrow he would stay in and make up with Aunt Kate. He hurried home, and did not remember that he had meant to stay out all night, maybe even run away forever.

* * *

The next morning Jamesie came to the jail early. Mr. Burkey, on duty, said he might see Lefty for three minutes, but it was a mystery to him why anyone, especially a nice boy like Jamesie, should want to see the bum. "And don't tell your father you was here."

Jamesie found Lefty lying on a narrow iron bed that was all springs and no covers or pillow.

"Lefty," he said, "I came to see you."

Lefty sat up. He blinked at Jamesie and had trouble getting his eyes to see.

Jamesie went closer. Lefty stood up. They faced each other. Jamesie could have put his hand through the bars and touched Lefty.

"Glad to see you, kid."

"Lefty," Jamesie said, "I brought you some reading." He handed Lefty Uncle Pat's copy of *Liberty* magazine.

"Thanks, kid."

He got the box of Rosebud salve out of his pocket for Lefty.

"Well, thanks, kid. But what do I do with it?"

"For your arm, Lefty. It says 'recommended for aches and pains.'"

"I'll try it."

"Do you like oranges, Lefty?"

"I can eat 'em."

He gave Lefty his breakfast orange.

A funny, sweet smell came off Lefty's breath, like perfume, only sour. Burnt matches and cigar butts lay on the cell floor. Did Lefty smoke? Did he? Didn't he realize what it would do to him?

"Lefty, how do you throw your sinker?"

Lefty held the orange and showed Jamesie how he gripped the ball along the seams, how he snapped his wrist before he let it fly.

"But be sure you don't telegraph it, kid. Throw 'em all the same—your fast one, your floater, your curve. Then they don't know where they're at."

Lefty tossed the orange through the bars to Jamesie.

"Try it."

Jamesie tried it, but he had it wrong at first, and Lefty had to reach through the bars and show him again. After that they were silent, and Jamesie thought Lefty did not seem very glad to see him after all, and remembered the last gift.

"And I brought you this, Lefty."

It was *Baseball Bill in the World Series*.

"Yeah?" Lefty said, momentarily angry, as though he thought Jamesie was trying to kid him. He accepted the book reluctantly.

"He's a pitcher, Lefty," Jamesie said, "Like you, only he's a right-hander."

The sour perfume on Lefty's breath came through the bars again, a little stronger on a sigh.

Wasn't that the odor of strong drink and cigar smoke—the odor of Blackie Humphrey? Jamesie talked fast to keep himself from thinking. "This book's all about Baseball Bill and the World Series," he gulped, "and Blackie Humphrey and some dirty crooks that try to get Bill to throw it, but . . ." He gave up; he knew now. And Lefty had turned his back.

After a moment, during which nothing happened inside him to explain what he knew now, Jamesie got his legs to take him away, out of the jail, around the corner, down the street—away. He did not go through alleys, across lots, between buildings, over fences. No. He used the streets and sidewalks, like anyone else, to get where he was going—away—and was not quite himself.

Leg (1995)

Steven Polansky

In this story, a father carelessly injures his leg in a church-league softball game. His thirteen-year-old son has been treating him contemptuously for no legitimate reason. Perhaps the leg wound will move their relationship toward greater respect. Author Steven Polansky was a professor for many years at St. Olaf College and Macalester College, both in Minnesota. "Leg," originally published in *The New Yorker*, also appeared in *The Best American Short Stories* in 1995. Polansky has published stories in *Harper's* and *New England Review*, and his collected stories appear in *Dating Miss Universe* (1999). He has also written a novel, called *The Bradbury Report* (2009).

W hen Dave Long tagged up and tried for third, everyone had to laugh. A bone-head move, and, for Dave—typically a prudent guy—uncharacteristic. As he took off, Dave laughed, too, at his own folly. Church-league softball, one gone in the last inning, not a blessed thing on the line—the game was without meaning and out of reach—and he went on a shallow fly to left.

"Good Lord," his wife, Susan, said to the woman next to her. She was sitting in the aluminum bleachers with the rest of the Bethany Baptist bunch. She had arrived late—barely in time to see Dave reach second on an overthrow. He was surprised to see her. Susan Long was a busy, charitable woman. She worked half the time keeping the books for Nuñez Chiropractic and gave her afternoons and evenings to business of the church, the school, the community. Before the game, Dave and his son, Randy, grabbed some food downtown—as they did two or three times a week. Given her responsibilities at the church, which included a leadership role in Christian education, her several Bible studies and support groups, her involvement in such service arms as Member Care and Prayer Chain and Meals on Wheels, Susan had little time to prepare supper, or eat it. "What the heck is he doing?" she said.

Dave was trying for third. There was no question: he knew he should stay at second, he should not go, and he went. The left fielder, Pastor Jeff, of the Alliance Church, had a cannon. He looked at Dave as if Dave were pursued by demons. Pastor Jeff spoke to him. In shallow left field he was close enough to speak to Dave as he headed for third.

"Where are you going, Dave?" Pastor Jeff said. "You're dead, man."

Dave smiled. He liked Pastor Jeff. On the street. He hadn't cared for his manner in the pulpit, the few times he'd heard him preach. Pastor Jeff was too tall—he was six feet nine—and his preaching posture was stooped and condescending. He was also too familiar and digressive for Dave, who had been raised in the cooler, straighter logic of the Episcopalians. But Pastor Jeff had the straight truth there: Dave *was* dead. To rights. Dave had been fast, but he was forty-four now, and he was too slow to pull this sort of stunt.

Dave's son, his only child, Randy, stood a way off, down the third-base line, behind the Cyclone fence. He was hanging from the fence as if tethered there, his arms stretched out above his head, his fingers laced through the wire, the toes of his sneakers wedged in the bottommost holes. He shook his head back and forth, almost violently. Randy was thirteen. He had not wanted to come watch his father play.

"God," he said when Dave tagged up. "Stupid. You're stupid."

Randy was a big, strong kid. He was, almost all the time now, angry at his father. He could tolerate his mother, but everything about Dave, who you would have thought the more approachable parent, enraged him.

Randy hated the way Dave dressed. He hated his whole wardrobe, in particular a blue down jacket Dave had had for years and wore when he drove Randy to school on winter mornings.

"You garbageman," Randy would say to him. "You look like a garbageman. You grunge monkey."

Dave liked this latter expression; he tried not to smile.

"Laugh," Randy said. "Laugh. The garbagemen dress better than you do."

Dave's beard, which he kept respectably trimmed, made Randy angry.

"No kisses, wolfman," Randy said, if Dave bent over his bed to kiss him good night. "You werewolf. You're scaring me, wolfman."

Randy spoke with stage disdain of Dave's friends. Dave's car, a Taurus wagon, was boring and dumb—for Randy, an emblem of all that was insufferable and pedestrian about his father. But the thing that really drove Randy wild was that Dave liked to read. Dave rose every morning at five so he could spend a quiet hour reading and thinking and praying. Which left him irredeemable in Randy's eyes. If Dave sent Randy to his room or otherwise disciplined him—this happened more often than Dave wanted—Randy would say, in his cruelest, most hateful voice, "Who don't you just go read a book, Mr. Reading Man. Mr. Vocabulary. Go pray, you praying mantis."

Watching Randy in his father's presence—the way his face went tight, the way his back stiffened—listening to the explosive, primitive noises he made in place of speech, you could see the boy's anger was beyond his control and understanding. It had sandbagged the kid, hit him blind side. It made Dave very sad. He missed the easy love of his son. He missed talking to Randy, he missed his companionship, and he felt sorry for him, because in the periodic rests between peals of rage, when he took breath, Randy was clearly dazed and spent and, himself, sad.

Sometimes it was hard for Dave to remember that this abrasive scowling thing, always coming at him, was his own son. Randy would bump him or leer or growl, make some foul and belligerent gesture, and before he'd had time to set or check himself, Dave would have responded in kind. "You shut your mouth, punk, or I'll shut it for you," Dave might say. He would grab Randy's arm above the elbow and squeeze it hard, trying to hurt him, and he would fill with regret and shame.

Randy said, "Stupid. You're stupid," and Dave, slow but hellbent for third, heard him.

Shoot, Dave thought. Poor kid. What am I doing?

Pastor Jeff threw a rope to the third baseman, also named Jeff, who worked in an auto-salvage yard. This layman Jeff caught the ball and straddled the bag, waiting for Dave, who was still only halfway there.

"Dumb," Randy said. "You are stupid." He untangled himself from the fence and turned his back to the field.

The third-base coach, Pastor Rick, senior pastor at Bethany Baptist, was at a loss. When the ball left the bat, a weak fly, he had raised his hands, palms out, signaling Dave to stay put. "Hold up, Gomer," he shouted, but it was too late—Dave had committed himself.

Pastor Rick was Dave's age. They met downtown once a week for lunch to discuss Scripture and Dave's personal journey in faith. They had that day, over turkey melts and iced tea, considered Matthew 7:13–14, a familiar passage Dave had lately found compelling and vexing: "Enter through the narrow gate. For wide is the gate and broad is the road that leads to destruction, and many enter through it. But small is the gate and narrow the road that leads to life, and only a few find it." After a space of silent meditation, Pastor Rick asked Dave what he thought the Gospel writer might have meant by the word "narrow." They had their Bibles on the table before them.

"Apart from the obvious?" Dave said.

"Yes," said Pastor Rick.

"Are you asking because you know, or because you want to know?"

"The second," Pastor Rick said. "I don't know. How would I know?"

"You're Baptist."

"No shit," Pastor Rick said.

"If we knew what the Hebrew was," Dave said. "Or the Greek."

"Good question. I don't. So?"

Dave thought a moment.

"Maybe as in severe," he said. "I don't know. Narrow. As in pinched. It pinches you as you go through. What's the word? Straits. Straitened. Maybe exclusive. Most people are excluded. They are left out. Unpopular. Maybe narrow as in simple. Sheer. Simple. Severe. Did I already say that?"

"Yes, you did."

"Yeah, well that's what I come up with."

"Good stuff," Pastor Rick said.

"What have you got?" Dave said.

"Half my sermon. Thanks."

A female fan on the Bethany side was yelling, "Slide, Dave, slide!" This was a joke, because no one slid in church league—the guys were too old, too sedate—and, besides, Dave was wearing shorts. Everyone laughed. Dave heard the call for him to slide, and he, too, found the proposition laughable.

Then he slid. He raised his right hand in a first. He yelled, "Oh, mama!" And from six feet away, and at what was for him top speed, he slid into third. Under the tag. Around the tag, really. No one who watched could believe it. It was the best, the only hook slide anyone had even seen in that church league.

The base paths were a hard, dry, gravelly dirt, and Dave tore up his leg. He stood up, called time, and limped off the bag. He looked down at his leg, the left, which was badly abraded from ankle to knee. Beneath a thin film of dirt, which Dave tried to wipe off with his hand, the leg was livid, strawberry, a crosshatch of cuts and gashes, bits of sand and gravel in the wounds.

Pastor Rick was beside him. He put his arm around Dave.

"Wild man. You O.K.?" Pastor Rick said. "Nice slide."

"Thanks. I'm O.K. I think."

"Can you walk? You want a runner?"

"Nah," Dave said. "I'm fine."

"You sure?"

"Yeah," Dave said.

Pastor Rick patted Dave on the rump. "All right, then. Go get 'em."

Dave turned to the crowd. He smiled sheepishly and waved.

Susan stood up in the stands.

"I'm O.K.," he said.

"Big jerk," she said to herself as she sat down. Then, to the woman next to her, "I don't believe it." She took a magazine out of her purse and looked at the cover. She stood up. She shook the magazine at Dave. He pretended to cower, and the crowd laughed.

Randy, who had wheeled to watch the play from the left-field foul line, was embarrassed: that his father slid; that his father slid in shorts and hurt himself sliding; that the slide, in this context—a game for coots and feebs and wacko fundamentalists—was inordinately, ridiculously good; and, on top of it all, that his mother had got into this bad circus act. Randy began to drift in his father's direction, up the line. Dave watched his unwitting tack with gratitude and wonder. He looked at Randy, shrugged his shoulders, and smiled, a bit goofily.

It was only when Dave smiled at him that Randy realized he was moving toward his father. He wrenched himself away. Randy turned and headed for the parking lot.

Dave's leg looked bad, painful, but it didn't really begin to hurt until after the next batter, Lloyd Weeks, who worked for Dave at the cereal plant, tapped a ground ball to the pitcher, stranding Dave at third and rendering perfectly gratuitous his miracle slide.

• • •

Randy caught a ride with his mother, who left as soon as the game ended, taking time only to tell Dave to get home and clean up his leg. To give Randy some time for his anger, Dave stayed to help gather the equipment, then wound up going for a beer with Pastor Rick and a few of the men. His leg was stinging. He doused it with cold water from a spigot by the backstop. At Tiny's, he ordered a beer and a Scotch. He poured out the Scotch on his napkin and swabbed at his leg.

"Shoot," Dave said. "That stings."

"That is one ugly leg," said Pastor Rick.

Pastor Jeff of the Alliance Church held up his diet Coke and waggled it. "Just for the record," he said. "And if anyone asks, I wasn't here."

"Who was?" said Pastor Rick.

"Great slide," said Pastor Jeff to Dave. "I had you nailed."

"Never in doubt," Dave said.

Dave nursed his beer, listening to Pastor Rick and Pastor Jeff disagree about glossolalia and about the dangers (Pastor Jeff) and the appeals (Pastor Rick) of ecumenism, and then commiserate about the unremitting demands of the lectionary.

"I'll do it for nothing," said Pastor Jeff. "You preach what I write."

"Sure, sure," said Pastor Rick. He looked over at Dave. "My guys couldn't handle it."

"Talk about speaking in tongues," Dave said.

Pastor Jeff laughed, then sat up very straight.

"I cast thee out, little feller," he said to Dave.

"I was just leaving," Dave said.

When Dave got home it was half past nine, and Susan was already asleep. Randy was closed up in his room listening to his music. Dave stood outside the door. Randy had the volume down, but Dave could still feel in his feet the pulse of the bass and the drum. It was a song he knew.

They
They betray
I'm your only
true friend now
They
They'll betray
I'm forever there

He knew the song, he knew the CD. Metallica. Randy played it often and loud, and Dave had listened to it several times, on his own, when Randy wasn't around.

Hate
I'm your hate
I'm your hate
When you want love

The boy had taste. This music was virtuoso stuff, and Dave thought it might lead him to other forms. But the lyrics, which seemed to speak to Randy so nearly—the spirit, pitch-dark and bereft, to which Randy vibrated with such sympathy—made Dave unhappy and fearful. He'd told Randy, once, that he liked the music.

Randy needed no time to work into his rage. "You don't like it. You don't know anything about it. You've never even heard it."

"I've heard it," Dave said, backing off. "I think it's good. Forget it."

"You don't know anything," Randy said. "Keep out of my room. Don't touch my stuff."

Dave showered, and dabbed his leg with a soapy washcloth. The injury was worse than he'd thought. There was almost no skin left on the wound, which covered a sizable portion of the leg, from the ankle to the knee. It looked as if someone had gone at his leg with a cheese grater. The tissue around the lesions was pink and swollen. When they were clean, they would not stop bleeding. The blood didn't flow so much as pool up, and he used a roll of toilet paper trying to staunch it. When it still would not stop, he wrapped his lower leg tightly in some gauze bandage he dug out of the vanity drawer and fastened with that adhesive tape. Almost at once, his leg began to throb. It felt hot. It was already infected, he figured. He lay down on the living-room couch and elevated his leg with a cushion. After a few minutes the blood had seeped through the gauze, and Dave gingerly removed it. There would be no way to stitch the thing—the surface area was far too large and irregular. He thought about going over to the emergency room. Instead, he boiled some water in a pot. He soaked a fresh dish towel in the water, lifted it out with salad tongs, and, thinking to cauterize the wound, applied it to his leg. It scalded him. He cried out but held the towel to his leg as long as he could bear to.

Then he sat down on the kitchen floor, his left leg stretched out before him, and prayed.

His praying was rarely premeditated or formal. More often it was a phototropic sort of turn, a moment in which he gave thanks or stilled himself to listen for guidance. He shied from petitionary prayer. With all he had, it felt scurvy—scriptural commendation notwithstanding—to ask for more. This night, his leg hurting to the bone, he permitted himself a request.

"Father," he said quietly, "please help me to see what I can do for Randy. He is in great pain. I love him. If it is your will, show me what I might do to bring him peace."

Dave looked up. Randy was watching him from the bottom of the stairs.

"Amen," Dave said. He smiled. "Hey bud."

Randy said nothing. He stood looking at Dave.

Dave got to his feet.

"Man, this sucker hurts," he said. "What are you up to?"

"You screamed," Randy said. He did not move from his spot on the stairs.

"I burned myself," Dave said.

"I came down."

"Thanks," Dave said. "I'm O.K."

Randy snorted. He shook his head and went back upstairs.

● ● ●

The doctors used the word "suppuration." Despite Dave's homespun palliatives, the wound had begun to form and discharge pus. So much that by the end of the next day, when Dave came home from work and called the doctor, the pants he'd worn to the plant were sodden and glued to his leg.

"You'd better come in and let me look at it," the doctor said. "Can you come in sometime tomorrow?"

"I can't," Dave said. "I can't get away. What do I do for it on my own?"

"You keep it clean," the doctor said. "You use a topical dressing. Bacitracin. Neosporin. I'll tell you this: if it's as infected as it sounds, you'll need a course of oral antibiotics. Perhaps even intramuscular."

"Or what?" Dave said.

"What are you asking?"

"I'm asking what might happen."

"That's not a question," the doctor said. "All sorts of things *might* happen. Which is why we don't fool around. Staph. Strep. Massive swelling. You want more? Gangrene. Sepsis. Work at it, you could lose your leg. Does that scare you?"

"Yes," Dave said.

"Good," the doctor said. "Because we're not negotiating. You come in. Day after tomorrow."

"If I can," Dave said.

"No, no. Not if you can. You come in."

• • •

The leg continued to weep. After several days, the pain was so bad, so deep, he could not put any weight on it. Though he tried keeping it clean, it had begun to smell. At night he removed the dressing and left the wound open to the air.

"Randy gone?" Susan said. She was on her way to Nuñez Chiropractic and stopped in the kitchen to sit with Dave for a minute while he ate breakfast.

"He's gone," Dave said.

"How did he go?"

"He was peaceful," Dave said. "I don't know—light. He seemed lighter. I said good-bye. Then he said good-bye. No agony. No outburst. We had ourselves a regular morning."

"What's your day like?" Susan said.

"Good," he said. "The same. The usual. What about yours? You busy?"

"The usual," she said. "Listen a minute. I'm concerned about you. About your leg."

"Don't be," he said.

"It's bad."

"Not too bad," he said. "It's better today."

"I've thrown away two pairs of your pants," she said. "And I can see. You can't walk. How can you say it's better?"

"It is. I'll be fine."

"Why don't you go to the doctor? Did you call him?"

"I did call," Dave said. "He told me what to do for it. I've got an ointment. What about dinner? We out or in?"

"I'll make something," Susan said. "Dinner. You tell me now. What's going on?"

"What?" he said.

"Tell me what you're doing. Because I'm concerned. I'm worried. And I've got to go. Please. What are you doing?"

"Nothing."

"Nothing," she said.

"Hacking around. Whatever. You know me."

"I know you," she said. "We're talking about your leg."

"It will be fine," he said.

• • •

Dave did not go to work. Without crutches or a cane he could not make it to the car. He phoned his secretary and told her he'd be out of town for several days, maybe a week. He devised, halfheartedly, a story about his mother, who suddenly needed tending to. His secretary was confused by the story, but she did not question him. He would call her again, that afternoon, he said, to fill her in. Could she handle things for a while in his absence?

He spent the morning stretched out on the couch, the living-room curtains drawn, in prayer. At one point he woke from a near trance to find his heart wildly beating, as if he'd just run a set of wind sprints. He was not flushed or dizzy or short of breath. He felt calm and relaxed, except for the steady thrum of pain in his leg and his heart thumping away. The strangeness of it made him laugh. He took a few deep breaths and closed his eyes.

In the afternoon, just before Randy got home from school, the doctor called.

"I called your office," the doctor said. "You weren't there."

"I'm here," Dave said. He was, by then, on the cool kitchen floor, supine, three crocheted hot pads beneath his head, his left leg raised slightly, the foot resting on a cookie tin.

"Your secretary said you were out of town."

"I haven't left yet," Dave said.

"I want to know how your leg is, David, and why you didn't come in as I asked."

"The leg is fine," Dave said. "I put that ointment on it. It's looking good."

"No more discharge?"

"None."

"It's healing?" the doctor said. "The pain is subsiding?"

"Seems to be," Dave said.

"So. Good. That's good. You're lucky. These things can turn nasty if they're not attended to. You got lucky. The next time I tell you to come in I want you to come in."

"I will," Dave said. "Thanks for calling."

Dave was on the kitchen floor when Randy came home from school. He thought about getting to his feet, but he had found a comfortable, if somewhat ludicrous, position and was unwilling, even for Randy, to suffer the pain that would attend trying to stand up. Randy came into the kitchen for his snack. He looked at Dave lying on the floor and stepped over him on his way to the refrigerator.

"Thanks for not stomping on me," Dave said.

Randy got out the milk and poured himself a glass. "What are you doing?" he said.

"It's cool down here. I'm having a little trouble standing."

"What is it?" Randy said, without looking at him. "Your leg again?"

This was the first mention Randy had made of Dave's leg, though Dave could see, in the way Randy had behaved the past few days—restrained, even equable—that he'd been aware of it.

"How was school?"

"O.K.," Randy said.

"Any trouble?"

"No."

"Have you got homework?"

"No. A little."

"Get yourself something to eat," Dave said.

"I am," Randy said, and he began probing the refrigerator. He took out packages of Muenster cheese and sliced ham and a jar of mayonnaise. "Where's Mom?"

"Out," Dave said. "What do you need?"

"Nothing. Where are we going for dinner?"

"Here," Dave said.

Randy made himself a sandwich.

"You hungry?" Dave said. A question he regretted as soon as he had asked it. It was the sort of question—nervous and dumb and self-evidently poised to fill the uneasy space between him and his son—that invariably caused in Randy a detonation.

"Starving," Randy said.

"Well, leave some room for dinner."

"I am," Randy said.

• • •

Sunday afternoon was hot, and Pastor Rick came by the house, in cutoff jeans, tank top, baseball cap, and flip-flops, to see Dave. Susan had put him up to it. She'd lingered in the narthex after the service to talk to him. Pastor Rick had begun to worry about Dave on his own. He hadn't heard from him in nearly a week, and seeing Susan at church alone that morning, he thought something might be wrong. Dave was as steadfast a parishioner as Pastor Rick had. Susan was undisguisedly afraid. She said the whole thing was inexplicable. Dave could no longer walk at all. No matter how tenderly she urged, no matter how forcefully she insisted, he would not go to the doctor. He claimed it was simply a matter of keeping off the leg for a few more days. But, so far as she could see, it was worse. She admitted that he seemed calm and reasonable and in amazingly good spirits, but he could not get off the couch, and spent his time now in the living room.

"Where is that gimp?" Pastor Rick said, loudly enough for Dave to hear. Susan had gone to the door to let him in. "Why is this room so dark? What is this thing on the couch? Can't we open the curtains?"

"It's cooler like this," Dave said. He was glad to see Pastor Rick. "Sit down. Relax. You're not in charge here. This is my house, bud."

"Tough guy," Pastor Rick said as he sat in a cane rocker opposite Dave, who, to receive his friend, had worked himself up to a sitting position.

"What's with you?" Pastor Rick said.

"Not much."

"Where you been?"

"Here and there. Mostly here."

"You missed a game. Susan, you got anything to drink?"

"What would you like?" She was standing at the entrance to the living room.

"You got a beer?"

"We do," she said.

"Cold?"

She nodded.

"Bring it on," he said. "You want one, Dave?"

"I'm fine," Dave said.

The two men talked for about an hour in the darkened room. Susan delivered the beer, then left them alone. They talked, first, about baseball. At one point Pastor Rick turned on the TV, and they watched the last two innings of a game. They talked about their children, their faith. Pastor Rick had been chafing under denominational expectations, these having especially to do, as he described it to Dave, with his maverick preference for the indicative Gospel over the imperative, for the good news over the dos and don'ts. There were, likewise, the expectations of the particular body of believers at Bethany Baptist, which he divided roughly into two camps. Those with what he called a "mature" faith were at ease with a theology and homiletics less than prescriptive. The others, new to the faith, or unable to push beyond a relatively simplistic version of it, were skittish without a neatly packaged set of rules and admonishments.

"I think you got in backward," Dave said.

"Oh, yeah? How's that?"

"It's we mature ones who need the hard line. We don't know what to do with grace once we've got it. It's too much for us. It's too much. We don't know how to behave. And so we behave as we always did, grace or no. I've been thinking about this."

"I see that," said Pastor Rick.

"I have. We're sloppy. We're slack. We're smug. We're just flat-out disappointing. You got to whip us into shape, or we embarrass ourselves. And each other."

"Be careful what you ask for," Pastor Rick said.

Just before he left, he turned the conversation directly to the question of Dave's leg.

"You don't need to do this," he said. "It isn't called for."

"I know," Dave said.

"It's crazy."

"What do I say?"

"You don't say anything," Pastor Rick said. "You go to the doctor, is what you do."

"Maybe I will."

"Don't, and I'll be back to take you myself."

• • •

The family had supper that night in the living room—Dave ate on the couch, Susan on the cane rocker from a tray, and Randy on the floor in front of the television. Susan fixed a light salad and made fresh lemonade; it was too hot to eat much else, though Randy asked for a grilled-cheese sandwich. It was a quiet meal. Dave and Susan hardly spoke. Randy watched a sports-magazine show; he was subdued, well-mannered. Dave, who was light-headed and running a low-grade fever, was happy. After supper he fell asleep on the couch. He was not aware of Susan and Randy going up to bed.

At two in the morning, he woke when Randy came down the stairs. Dave turned on the table lamp behind his head, and when his eyes got used to the light, he could see that Randy was crying. He was standing at the foot of the couch, a plaid cotton blanket draped shawl-like over his shoulders. He was wearing boxer shorts and nothing else, and he was weeping. Dave looked at him for a moment, certifying that he was neither dream nor delirium.

"Randy," Dave said. "You O.K.? What time is it?"

"I don't know," the boy said. "Two. I'm O.K."

"What's wrong?"

"I came down."

"Have you been asleep?"

"No."

"I was out cold," Dave said. "What's going on?"

"Nothing," Randy said.

"You're crying."

"I'm not crying," Randy said. "I came down because I want to say something. Go to the doctor. That's all I came down for."

"Hold a minute," Dave said. "Let me get up here."

Without thinking, Dave swung his feet off the couch and tried to stand up. He wanted to touch Randy. To make some sort of physical contact with his son. To comfort him, put his arm around his shoulder, hold him. Dave's left foot touched the floor, and the pain in his leg was astonishing. It knocked him flat on the couch.

"Whoa," Dave said. "Hold the doors. Good Christ."

"Do you see?" Randy said. "For shit's sake, Dad. Do you see? Are you nuts? What are you doing?"

"I'm not sure," Dave said. "I'm really not sure."

"Oh, man. Oh, man. What are you doing? Go to the doctor."

It was, by then, too late. He would lose the leg.

"That's not a bad idea," Dave said. "I will."

The Crambury Tiger (1942)

Arthur "Bugs" Baer

Arthur "Bugs" Baer's story "The Crambury Tiger" was originally published in *Collier's*. The story is partially based on some actual events in the life of the legendary Ty Cobb. In May 1912 Cobb responded to a heckler during a game by jumping into the stands and beating him up with flying fists. The fan was handicapped, and when Cobb was given a ten-day suspension without pay by American League president Ban Johnson, Cobb's Detroit Tigers teammates refused to play in a game against the Philadelphia Athletics. This one-day "strike" is believed to be the first in the history of major-league baseball. (Alas, if it were only the last.) But the game was played anyway, as the Tigers owner rounded up a team of semipro players to take the field. The real outcome of the game is told in Baer's story, albeit with colorful exaggeration. Parts of the story were depicted by Hollywood in the 1994 movie *Cobb*.

Sure, the trouble was over a girl. What isn't?

Tink was too good-looking for his own good before there were movies. He had the tickets to make the big leagues but he was as lazy as a fed cat. Tink could pitch at times.

Nippers had the general appearance of an accident looking for a lawyer and he had a profile you could saw lumber with. He couldn't field good enough to stop a water wheel in a dry spell. But he sure shook that pepper-box around the infield.

Playing semipro baseball in the summer was a softer touch than face powder. We got around like ringworms and if we weren't bums we would certainly do until bums came along.

I called myself a semipro although it might have been closer to three-eighths. Too much beer in Bustleton is what stopped me in addition to other habits that would have tightened the hide on a bloodhound's jowls. John McGraw once sent a scout to look me over but he decided I was too much of a grandstand player when I wasn't throwing them into the bleachers.

At the bat I couldn't hit all the leather in the world if I owned all the lumber. But both Tink and Nippers could throw their weight around at the plate. I was so round-shouldered I had to have my coats made twice as long in the back as in the front. I guess I played in more places than sunbeams in a forest. I wound up as the only left-handed shortstop in semipro baseball, but I finished better than Tink.

Fast as Nippers got a girl in the small towns Tink would take her away from him. But once he gave Nippers a girl, and it was just too bad.

It was all the fault of Ty Cobb. And a bit over like a baker's dozen.

Now, I know that Ty never heard of us cow-pasture punks who used a fence post for a bat and slid into a lot of things that weren't second base. But when he came up from Georgia to the Detroits he was gamer than a dentist pulling his own teeth and could take it like a carpet on the line. But he was as touchy as fingerprint powder and would climb a mountain to take a punch at an echo.

Ty fought everybody on the Detroits until the other Tigers realize that all he wants to do is win baseball games. Then they get in back of him as solid as wet sand and Detroit cops the berries in 1907, '08 and '09—and almost repeats in '10 and '11. But they go very bad in the spring of '12 and Cobb is sorer than ingrown hairs on a porcupine.

There's no living with Ty when he's in that mood, so when a grandstand manager in New York named Lucas or Lookis or something like that gives him the Bronx roll call from the dollar seats, Ty climbs into the stands and hands him a dry shave with his knuckles. The other Yankee fans choose up sides and Cobb is elected Queen of the May on the sixteenth of that month as I remember. The Yanks fans were sure going to town on Ty's transportation system when the entire Detroits barge into the stands and rescue him with their baseball bats. When the cops pull everybody loose from their pet holds it turns out that the fellow Cobb popped has no fingers on his right hand.

Well, Ty didn't know that and Lucas or Lookis has certainly used some pretty rough talk. That doesn't stop Ban Johnson from giving Cobb the indefinite works with the option of making it permanent.

The entire Detroits club their mad money in a lump and send Ban a testimonial telegram: "Feeling that Mr. Cobb is being done an injustice by your action in suspending him, we the undersigned refuse to play in another game until such action is adjusted to our satisfaction. We want him reinstated or there will be no game. If players cannot have protection we must protect ourselves." (Signed) Sam Crawford, Jim Delahanty, Davey Jones, Oscar Stanage, Oscar Vitt, George Moriarity, Jack Onslow, Ed Willett, Bill Burns, Covington, Paddy Bauman, Louden, George Mullen and all the others.

That makes it serious for the Detroit owners if they don't put a team in the field on Saturday, May 18, 1912, in Philly where their next game is. Owner Navin can lose his franchise and can be plastered with a five-grand fine.

Manager Hughey Jennings comes to Philly at the Aldine Hotel and gives out word that he is in the market for a brand-new Detroit team and no reasonable offer will be refused. Any ballplayer who can stop a grapefruit from rolling uphill or hit a bull in the pants with a bass fiddle has got a chance of going direct from the semipros to the Detroits and no questions asked.

Tink, Nippers and me are booked to play for Millville in southern Jersey the next day but we light out for the Aldine Hotel in time to run into a parade of seven hundred semipros all anxious to fill Ty Cobb's shoes. A baseball writer named Isaminger on the *North American* said that seven hundred was about the right number. The seven hundred of us semipros walk single file past Jennings and he taps the ones he wants on the shoulder with a pool cue like we were buttons on a wire over a billiard table. He runs us fifty or no count and that's his team for tomorrow.

Out of that fifty he will pick nine players who will get fifty smackers each. Then he will pick a couple more for emergency who will get twenty-five just for sitting on the bench. That was almost a full season's salary for a semipro in Philly. Tink and me are among the fifty but Nippers can't score with the pool cue even though he has a piece of chalk in his vest pocket.

That all gets into the papers and the Georgia folks get behind Cobb. A congressman named William Schley Howard made a speech about it in Washington and sent Ty a wire as follows: "As Georgians we commend your action in resenting uncalled-for insult in New York. We hope for your complete exoneration and reinstatement in clean sport of baseball. Congratulations to you as a leader and fighter of your profession."

Howard signed the telegram and it was seconded by a famous senator from Georgia named Hoke Smith. Howard also tagged Senator Bacon's name to it. One more signature and Gordon McKay of the *Inquirer* said it would have been an amendment to the Constitution. Cobb got thousands of wires and letters and the Wall Street brokers got up a petition for him that I guess they could use themselves now.

Cobb spent that Friday night in conference with his fellow Detroits and they sent a telegram or two. The White Sox were playing the Red Sox in Boston, so Ty wired Harry Lord of the Chicagos and Smokey Joe Wood of the Bostons asking if they would join a protective association of players with short tempers. That was thirty years ago and Lord and Wood are still giving the matter their serious consideration. Us ballplayers stick together like a wishbone in a pulling contest.

Philly is giving the strike of the Detroits a lot of publicity because their Athletics look like sure pennant winners even though the Red Sox finally cop and Washington winds up second. So, even if Nippers doesn't make the grade he decides to cut Millville and watch us play for the Detroits. When you're a semipro, your schedule is as loose as a skeleton on roller skates. The three of us light out for the A's park Saturday morning at eight o'clock. We swiped a bottle of milk and a loaf of bread off a porch and ate it under a bridge.

At ten, Jennings drives up with his trunks and bats. He has picked fifty ballplayers on suspicion and he wants to see if we are guilty or not. He also has two faithful Detroits with him named Sugden and McGuire and I'll tell you about them. They are so old they can sleep in a swamp without mosquito netting. At the present time Jennings was using them for coaches and scouts but he announces McGuire will catch anything that comes near him, and Sugden will play first base for everything except fast grounders and overthrows. Jennings elects himself captain, manager, coach and utility. I know my baseball and I remember Sugden was with Baltimore in 1889 and here it is 1912. He was a fatigued old gent who should have spent his summers pointing out sea shells for his grandkids to pick up.

There was a McGuire with Washington in 1892 when Washington was in the National League. I think he bobbed around a lot and finally tried umpiring, but he has spots before his eyes and gives a batter his base on four of them.

That leaves seven positions for Jennings to fill and Tink and me are out. But we make the bench for twenty-five smackers and that suits us. He picks a semipro named Travers to pitch and a good lightweight fighter Billy McHarg for third. There are also a couple of old-timers from Georgetown University and a few more sandlotters who can field all right but can't hit their weight on a diet.

The fellow who got the toughest break was the semipro picked to play Ty Cobb's spot in center. His monicker was too wide for the printers and it came out in the Sunday papers this way, "L'n'h's'r." Today nobody knows whether his name was Loopenhouser or Lagenhassigner and I bet his wife still calls him a liar when he says he once played on the Detroits.

Anyway, the fans didn't ask for their money back when they saw a lot of bums in Tigers' clothing. Here's the way the game came out in the box scores:

DETROIT					
	A	BH	O	A	E
McGarr, 2b	4	0	3	0	1
McHarg, 3b	1	0	2	0	0
Irwin, 3b, c	3	2	1	2	1
Travers, p	3	1	7	0	1
McGarvey, lf	3	0	1	0	3
L'n'h's'r, cf	4	0	1	0	0
Sugden, 1b	3	1	2	1	1
McGuire, c	2	1	3	1	2
Smith, 3b	1	0	1	0	0
Meaney, ss	2	0	3	0	1
Ward, rf	2	0	0	0	0
x Jennings	1	0	0	0	0
Totals	29	4	24	4	9
x Batted for exercise					

ATHLETICS					
	A	BH	O	A	E
Maggert, lf	4	3	0	0	0
Strunk, cf	6	4	0	0	0
Collins, 2b	6	5	0	1	0
Baker, 3b	5	2	0	0	0
Murphy, rf	3	2	1	0	0
McInnis, 1b	6	3	7	0	0
Barry, ss	4	2	3	1	1
Lapp, c	4	1	16	1	0
Coombs, p	1	0	0	1	0
Brown, p	3	2	0	2	0
Pennock, p	1	1	0	1	0
Totals	43	25	27	7	1

		Runs	Hits	Errors
DETROIT	0 0 0 0 2 0 0 0 0	2	4	9
ATHLETICS	3 0 3 0 8 4 4 2 x	24	25	1

SUMMARY OF THE GAME

RUNS, Sugden, McGuire, Maggert 2, Strunk 2, Collins 4, Baker 3, Murphy 4, McInnis 2, Barry 2, Lapp, Brown 2, Pennock.

TWO-BASE HITS, Maggert, Strunk, Barry, Pennock.

THREE-BASE HITS, Strunk, Baker, Murphy, Irwin 2, Brown, Maggert.

SACRIFICE HIT, Lapp.

SACRIFICE FLY, Barry.

STOLEN BASES, Collins 4, Baker, Murphy, McInnis 2, McGarvey.

STRUCK OUT, By Coombs 3, by Brown 5, by Pennock 7, by Travers 1.

DOUBLE PLAY, McGarvey and Smith.

LEFT ON BASES, Detroit 4, Athletics 4.

FIRST BASE ON ERRORS, Athletics 2.

BASES ON BALLS, Coombs 1, Pennock 1, Travers 7.

TIME OF GAME, One hour and forty minutes.

UMPIRES, Dineen and Perrine.

Outside of shooing Sugden and McGuire around the bases for old times' sake the A's bore down all the way like guards putting a straitjacket on the star pupil in a laughing academy. Eddie Collins did more yelling than Solomon's thousand wives catching him out with another dame. Eddie hustled all the way like a long-haired rabbit in a prairie fire. This was a regular baseball contest and it held the Detroit franchise. I still feel sorry for L'n'h's'r, who blew his big chance like a pyromaniac sneezing on his last match. It was just as well that I never got into the game because I raised a pompadour of goose pimples on the bench.

Jennings saved the bacon for Navin but when Ban Johnson got the result of the game between the A's and the Pick-ups and heard that four apostrophes were playing center field for Cobb he called himself out on that one strike.

For the first time in his life Ban copped a plea and let Cobb off with a ten-day suspension. The regular Detroits played again and got their uniforms back from the semipros. All except the one shirt that Tink wore home under his coat. It belonged to Ty.

Tink wore the Detroit shirt next Monday morning out on the sandlots in the park and word went around that he was one of the striking Detroits who refused to go back. There's a Glassboro scout there and when he hears that, he gets hotter than a one-cycle engine. He offers Tink fifteen dollars a game but Tink is stringing a couple of towns along and finally nails twenty bobbins for himself for Crambury on Decoration Day. I went with the deal and got eight dollars for playing shortstop.

Tink won for Crambury by his pitching and batting and actually lived up the Detroit "D" on his shirt. The visiting team couldn't holler about it because they were padded like an idiot's cell themselves. The Crambury fans and the local girls thought he was the top berries and there was one pretty little girl who went for him big.

Going home on the train that night Tink told me her name was Jennie and her father was a motorman. Well, that's society for Tink. He pitches four Saturdays straight for Crambury and wins against Big Timber, Tacony, Southwark and Upper Darby. But for some reason he switches to Pennsylvania towns in August even though Crambury is offering him up to thirty-five dollars a game. I'm still playing short for short dough and I see Jennie each Saturday afternoon looking for Tink. She asked me about him and I said he had sprained his arm and gone back home to Philly. She doesn't even know his last name.

Well, the biggest day in semipro baseball in Jersey and Pennsylvania is Labor Day. Crambury is going to play its big rival North Chester for the weedbending championship and it wants Tink. But Tink is going to Bound Brook for less money and I know why. I tell the Crambury manager I can get a pretty good man named Nippers but he says the local folks want a big leaguer and I tell him that maybe I can get one. He says he will pay forty for a leaguer and raise me from eight to ten. I tell Nippers about it and he tells Tink he will split the forty with him if he will lend Nippers his Cobb shirt for Labor Day.

That's twenty more in the bag for Tink and he grabs it. When I tell the Crambury manager that I have another Detroit pitcher who walked out with Cobb and didn't go back he snaps it up.

Nippers touched up the big D on his chest with black ink until it stood out like a frog's eyes. On Labor Day he looked like a leaguer and pitched all the way like one coming down to the ninth. North Chester is leading one to nothing mostly because they have a ringer from the Tri-State who can pitch and bat. He smacks a homer in the first half of the ninth and is a little winded, so he hits a Crambury in the ribs, passes one, and they move up on an infield out. The next bird is a soft touch and it brings Nippers up with two on, two out and a single needed to cop.

It gets down to three and two on Nippers and it's closer than beds in a charity ward. Nippers is waving his bat at the big Tri-Stater, who winds up and is about to let it go when he sees he is pitching to two men at the plate. The other fellow is a middle-aged gent and he is packing a shotgun, which is aimed at Nippers. The Crambury manager claims a balk but the umpire disallows because nobody can out-pitch a shotgun. The fellow with the gun then explains himself.

"I've lived in this town for sixty years," he said, "and the population has been exactly six hundred and thirty-two from 1852 to 1912. The reason for that is every time somebody is born somebody leaves town."

Well, Nippers wants to know what that has to do with him. The old boy said, "My daughter told me to look for a fellow with a Detroit D on his shirt," so I know now it's the motorman speaking, "and you're going to marry her."

Well, we plead with the old man to let the game go on and settle the matter in a legal way. But he swings the gun around to the umpire and says, "Pridemore, you're the Justice of the Peace and you're going to marry my daughter with this Detroit fellow." He calls out, "Jennie," and Jennie walks out of the crowd with her head down and a handkerchief stuffed in her mouth to hold her sobs back. She never once looks up during the ceremony, not even when the Crambury runner on third tries to steal home when Pridemore is asking, "Do you take this man for your lawful wedded husband?"

He goes back when the shotgun swings his way for Jennie's daddy knows his baseball. Then the ceremony is over and Jennie looks up and sees it isn't Tink and she faints. She's married to Ty Cobb's shirt all because Lucas or Lookis or something had to shoot his face off. Pridemore makes a wave of his hand that declares the couple married and starts the game again.

The fans go back to their places, everybody on the field gets set, the runners take a big lead and the Tri-Stater winds up and lets her go.

Nippers takes a toehold on some loose dust and swings. Well, the happy bridegroom misses it farther than a dunce getting Constantinople in a spelling bee.

Nippers is now in a fine spot. He is struck-out and married on a wide outshoot.

Jennie's daddy has brought her around OK and he also collects Nippers and they go down the road looking like Daniel Boone moving his family farther west. I get myself invited to the wedding supper and the motorman isn't a bad sort of apple-knocker if you let him have his way. I tell Nippers that I will take the Detroit shirt back to Tink, but I advise him to keep the whole forty buttons for himself for he has earned it. Nippers keeps the shirt.

Let me tell you something about Ty's shirt. It must be magic because the bird who wears it acts like a leaguer. It is better for nailing a job in a small town than an average of 99.9 in a civil service quiz for letter carriers. Nippers has a couple more pitching jobs that fall and wins both. He gets sixty-five dollars for the last game of the season. Along about February at the end of winter I hear the population of Crambury has finally hopped to six-hundred and thirty-three. Also that Nippers is offered a trial with a Hoss and Buggy League in Carolina.

Down there he meets Tink, fights him for the shirt and hammers him to a blister. They meet a second time that season and Nippers breaks the blister. The man wearing Cobb's shirt gets to think he is Ty and when the war busts loose in 1917 Nippers enlists and wins a whole flock of decorations.

He goes over the top in his Detroit shirt and eighty-seven Germans surrender to him because they think a new nation has declared war on the Kaiser.

When he got home to Crambury, Jennie and number six hundred and thirty-three are waiting for him. He starts in pitching again and he gets offers from the Three-Eye, the International and the South Atlantic leagues. But he refuses to play in any town that doesn't fit his shirt.

And, Believe It or the Marching Chinese, before the 1919 season is half over, the population of Crambury is one less than its average for sixty years, for Jennie and six hundred and thirty-three have packed up and gone west with Nippers, who is a fine husband and loving father, but once he gets out there on that baseball field, is meaner than the man who invented uphill.

And he gives Ty Cobb his shirt back. For Nippers now has a Detroit shirt of his own.

What We All Want (2003)

Leslie Pietrzyk

A thirty-year-old pitcher who reached as high as Triple-A is now toiling in the Mexican league, his career gradually slipping away. But he's having a pretty good year, and his wife, standing by her man, will do anything to help him realize his dream of reaching the majors. Leslie Pietrzyk's short stories have appeared in outlets such as *TriQuarterly, Iowa Review*, and *Columbia: A Journal of Literature and Art*. She has also written two novels: *Pears in a Willow Tree* (1998) and *A Year and a Day* (2004).

We came here because of Fernando. Everyone knew what had happened to Fernando Valenzuela, how he'd pitched for the L.A. Dodgers in the 1980s until his wondrous arm collapsed. Then he disappeared. Several years later a scout from the Baltimore Orioles found him pitching here in Mexico, striking out batters like it was as easy as drinking water. Want to try it again? the scout asked him. He did. The arm was back. In '93 he was a starting pitcher for the Orioles.

If it could happen to Fernando . . . I sat in the stands and watched them each think it. Luis Torres, Manuel Ramirez, all the rest, and especially my husband, Lee. During batting practice, during warm-ups, during a game, the words rose from the dusty field: Then it could happen to me.

Why not? In baseball it's a way of life, not a question.

• • •

It was Lee's birthday. What do you do in Oaxaca, Mexico, when your husband turns thirty? I bought a baseball piñata and filled it with foil-wrapped chocolates that looked like baseballs that my sister Fed-Exed from Dallas. I woke up early and hung the piñata where it would sway in the breeze coming through the balcony. While I waited for Lee I watched the women in the plaza below pull the coverings off the booths where all day they sold brightly colored weavings or plastic bags of fruit slices while their children splashed in the fountain. At night the men came by to collect the money and escort their families back to the villages in the mountains.

Lee came in after he finished shaving; there was a tissue dot on his cheek, and he still looked sleepy. His neck popped when he stretched.

"Happy birthday," I said, pointing to the piñata.

He didn't even look. "Jenny, I'm not doing this," he said.

"All you do is hit it with the bat," I said.

He shook his head. "It's not my birthday," and he walked out. I heard his feet thump down the stairs of our rooming house, I heard Señora Martinez call out good morning, I heard Señora Martinez's daughter ask in awkward English if he wanted juice for breakfast. He didn't answer, just more footsteps until I looked out the balcony and saw him walking across the plaza, not slowing as the women called after him to buy their weavings, their embroidered blouses, their flowers, their fruit, and finally he broke into a jog and turned the corner out of my sight.

I picked up the bat, gave the piñata one good whack, and candy showered down, rolled across the wooden floor. So now it was just a mess to sweep up.

Lee pitched that night, and his slider was sending down batters. I sat where I always sat, with the wives. Only two others made every game the way I did: Ruth from South Carolina and Tanya from Phoenix. We were the only American wives. *Las gringas*, we called ourselves, but we only saw each other at games. We'd never think to meet for coffee or shopping or anything like that. They were younger than I was, just as their husbands were younger than mine. Mexican League baseball was a matter of filling out the year for these husbands, getting in some practice before heading to the States for single-A ball in the spring, and on to double-A, triple-A, the majors. It was simple as climbing stairs. To hear Ruth and Tanya talk, their husbands had contracts that promised "1-2-3." Phil had been on the "Hot Prospect" list, and Randall's batting average in the last year's College World Series was .402.

But when Ruth and Tanya started going on about "just a matter of time" and "when he gets to the majors" and comparing how many Corvettes they'd buy or on which beach they'd build their vacation houses, I wanted to jump in with, "Don't count your chickens." But saying anything that sounded like good advice got me one of those looks: "There she goes again, talking like an old lady." So I let them go on about the leather coats and diamond earrings and all the rest.

Ruth said, "Lee's looking good tonight. Isn't he?" We were sitting only two rows off the field, but Ruth was watching home plate through binoculars. She'd asked me to teach her how to call pitches. "Wasn't that a ball?" she asked, as the umpire gestured a strike.

I said, "Caught the corner."

"You always say that," she said.

"Because that's what always happens," I said. "Because Lee's some kind of pitcher."

I took the binoculars so I wouldn't see Tanya and Ruth give each other that look they had, "If he's so good, why's he down here at thirty years old?"

I studied my husband's face through the binoculars. He used to practice glaring in the mirror until his face ached because someone once told him he looked too nice to be a pitcher. Lee and I met at our fathers' company picnic, and after the softball game was over, he took me aside to teach me how to throw. "You throw like a girl," he said. I said, "Because I *am* a girl," and he leaned over and kissed me with lips that tastes like mustard. We were fifteen. He said, "Someday I'm going to pitch in the World Series." He said it just like that, like someone had shown him it would be that way, and later, when the local sports reporters talked about Lee's authority on the mound, I knew what they meant.

"I miss hot dogs," Tanya said. "Sitting in a bleacher makes me want to eat hot dogs."

I said, "When Lee was pitching for the Prince William Cannons, they sold grilled hot dogs over by right field. They'd bring them to the guys in the dugout."

"The Cannons? That's single-A?" Ruth asked.

"You're getting to be a real baseball wife," I said.

"What charity are you going to work for when Randall gets to the majors?" Ruth asked Tanya. "I'm doing March of Dimes."

"It's better to do something local," Tanya said. "You know, set up a foundation. Then you can actually be in charge of instead of just showing up at luncheons and celebrity auctions."

Ruth nodded. "Suppose so." She took the binoculars from me.

Tanya said, "Anti-drug stuff is usually a good bet. Or some kind of stay in school program."

Ruth said, "Can I do stay in school when Phil didn't really graduate? Does GED count as graduating?"

Tanya said, "Sure."

Ruth said, "Was that a slider?"

"Fastball," I said.

Tanya said, "Wasn't it Lee's birthday coming up?"

"No," I said.

"Thought you went and got some special piñata or something?"

"Wedding anniversary," I said.

"How many years?" Ruth said. "Pitch was outside."

She was about to repeat her question, so I said, "You're right about the pitch."

She wasn't, but she smiled and high-fived Tanya. "I'm getting there," Ruth said. "Just a matter of time."

● ● ●

That night in bed, Lee said, "The piñata was great. Sorry I was a jerk."

"Thirty's tough," I said.

He said, "Never thought I'd spend my thirtieth birthday in fucking Mexico."

"Fernando did," and I didn't know when the hell Fernando's birthday was, but couldn't it have been during the Mexican League season? Why not? "He turned thirty when he was down here pitching. There was a big party for him at the hotel, and everyone was drinking tequila and making toasts and all the pretty girls lined up to kiss him, and the next day he went out and pitched a ten-inning no-hitter."

There was a pause. I thought there was a chance I convinced him. Then he said, "God, I love you for saying that."

I leaned over and kissed him, kissed his ear, his neck, but he rolled away from me, sat up and looked towards the open window, tapped his bare feet on the floor. In the dark like this he didn't look any age at all.

"I was good today," he said. "The plate was all mine."

I agreed, sat up and kissed his hard, bare shoulder.

"Fuck," he said. "Thirty years old, and I've never paid a mortgage. Got no kids. What do I have? Nothing."

I said, "It's going to work out this time; it really is."

"I'm the oldest guy on the team," he said. "I never told you. Everywhere I go now, I'm the oldest. Know what that's like? Pitchers like me are even old in the majors. And here I am playing down in bumfuck Mexico, no contract."

"Age is in your head. Everyone was saying you looked great tonight. I know it will be your year."

"What makes you so sure?"

"Nothing makes me sure," I said. "Just being sure makes me sure."

"That doesn't make any sense."

"Why should it?" I asked. "Why should any of it?" and I was thinking of Fernando, discovered, discarded, discovered again, the way his eyes rolled up to the heavens with every pitch he threw as if to say, Why not? I said, "You tell me what makes sense about baseball."

Outside I heard a group of drunk men singing badly, the chatter of women packing up their goods for the night. It could have been what I heard outside our windows all the other nights that were like this one: trucks criss-crossing the interstate, neighbors squabbling over the last beer, someone's bug zapper.

Because you know it happens this way doesn't make it easy. Because you know that your fastball will drop from 92 mph to 89 and then down to 85, 84, even 80, even lower, doesn't make you any less afraid. I wanted Lee to think I understood that.

"What makes sense about baseball?" he repeated. I watched the glow of the clock while I rubbed my palm in tight circles along his back. Finally he laughed. "Designated hitter rule, for one thing," and I laughed, too. So it would be all right. So he was thirty, and we were in Mexico, and it would be his year. It just had to be.

• • •

The next morning I was hurrying through the plaza on my morning walk, trying to ignore the calls of the women urging me to buy their things. I looked down at the sidewalk as I passed, shaking my head, but one woman jogged alongside me, tugging my arm harder and harder until I stopped. I smiled, shook my head. "No, thank you," I said. "*No gracias*. No."

She didn't smile back, instead reeled off a string of words. The only ones I recognized were "*su marido*" and "*mi marido*," which meant "your husband" and "my husband."

"*No comprendo*," I said.

She extended her hand as if for a handshake, but then she curled in her lower fingers, leaving only the index finger pointing at me. She triggered downwards with her thumb and said, "Bang-bang." Her son toddled up and clutched at her skirt, poked his thumb in his mouth.

I pulled some pesos out of my pocket, handed her the bills. Sometimes that was just quickest.

She tucked them in a pouch tied to her waist but said very slowly, "*Su marido* buy bang-bang. Buy." There was more then, in Spanish, that I didn't understand but she watched me as if I should. Then there was silence.

I shook my head. "My husband wouldn't buy a gun. Why would he need a gun?"

But she didn't follow the words in English, and she pointed her finger at me and twitched her thumb. "Bang-bang," she said. Her son thought it was funny and screamed, "Bang-bang-bang!" pointing his finger first at me, then at his own face. She slapped his hand away and glared at me before picking up her son and lugging him back to her booth of embroidered blouses.

When I asked Lee that night, he said, "I felt sorry for the guy. He needed the money." Maybe there was something about my face because he added, "Of course I threw away the gun, Jenny. Why would I want a gun?"

But afterwards, I couldn't sleep; there was too much moonlight sneaking through the curtains or the blankets were too hot or something, and I got out of bed and went into the bathroom where we kept our suitcases shoved behind the door, and there was a hard small lump in the zippered side pocket of Lee's duffel bag—a gun. It fit easily into my hand, and I knelt on the cool tile floor tilting it to catch the light from the bare bulb hanging off the ceiling. I thought about wanting something so much, this much. Then I slipped the gun back in the duffel bag, zipped it shut.

I heard a rustling behind me, but I didn't turn around or move my head. Looking up, I saw Lee's hand wrapped around the door jamb.

"I want it to happen for us so bad, baby," he whispered. "Is that crazy?"

"Not when you want it," I said.

Even though I threw away the gun the next morning, it wasn't really gone.

• • •

When Lee's record got to 5–1, they started calling him *Señor Poncho*—Mr. Strikeout. "This is where it starts," Tanya told me. "He gets a nickname, people talk so there's a buzz, and next thing is he's got himself a contract."

Ruth said, "Lee made it up to Triple-A once or twice already, didn't he?"

I nodded. Three times, actually.

"And then what happened?" she asked. "How'd he end up all the way back down here?"

Tanya said, "What matters now is he's got a nickname, right, Jenny? Right *Señora Poncho*?" and she smiled the kind of smile you save for someone you don't care much about.

I said to Ruth, "Same old story. Injuries, bad luck, bad manager. It could happen to anyone."

"Oh sure, I know," but Ruth was twisting in her seat to wave at someone a couple rows behind us, had forgotten we were having this conversation.

"Lee was on the 'Hot Prospect' list," I said. "Same as Phil."

"Don't worry, Jenny," Tanya said. "Next time we all meet, it'll be at the World Series."

"Or the All-Star Game," Ruth said. "Isn't that better?"

"No," Tanya and I said together.

Ruth said, "Hey, I'm new to all this. Cut me a break."

Tanya pointed to the opposition pitcher taking his warm-up pitches on the field. "See how he flips his glove like that? That tells the catcher he's throwing a curve ball next. Right, Jenny?"

"Right." Lee told me that when I was fifteen. These girls would have been, what, three and seven, something like that?

"Gees, I'll never learn it all," Ruth said.

"Sure you will," Tanya said. "Before long you'll know as much about baseball as Jenny does."

"Like knowing baseball does us any good," I said, and something must have been wrong with the way I said it, or the way they thought I meant it, because they looked away quick. The pitcher flipped his glove again. Once you knew to watch for that, you couldn't not notice.

Ruth said, "What's that supposed to mean?"

I shrugged. "Doesn't really matter what we know or don't know. We're just the wives. All we're supposed to do is believe them every time they tell us this is their year."

Ruth said to Tanya, "What's with her lately?" and she pressed the binoculars to her face.

Tanya said, "Come on, guys, we've only got two more weeks to go," and she bought us *paletas*—popsicles—from the boy tramping up and down the aisles.

After a short pause, Tanya said, "It's no hot dog."

"Phil wants nine children," Ruth said. The *paleta* had stained her tongue red. "He comes from a big family."

"Nine!" Tanya said. "Get busy, girl!"

"As soon as we get back home," Ruth said. "Then I start popping them out. That's the plan."

Tanya shook her head. "Two's as many as I plan to handle, and Randall knows it. You're brave."

"Or stupid. Phil's already got the names lined up," Ruth said. "He wants six boys and three girls. He says that—"

I interrupted: "What about you? What do you want?"

Ruth set the binoculars in her lap. "Why, Jenny," she said. "Same as what we all want." She pulled off her cap and shook her hair. She was pretty enough that a man could forget she was smart. That was maybe the smartest thing about her.

The bat cracked, rousing the crowd. Our first baseman Luis Torres has sent another one sailing straight out over center field, way over the fence. A swarm of kids raced to find the ball. The outfielders didn't bother to move; they'd recognized the sound, what it meant. So did I. An entire stadium collectively looking at their scorecards and thinking, I'll have to remember this guy. That's how it happens. It's not your first home run or tenth or even thirtieth. It's simply that one hit on that one day or that one pitch on that one day. I'd seen it happen to other guys on other teams—guys whose names everyone knows now. It's better than a nickname. Better than a buzz. It's what you wait for all your life, that pitch, that hit. That moment.

The manager stalked to the mound, and the pitcher handed him the ball and slunk into the dugout. A new pitcher trotted out, but it was too late. Luis Torres had been marked for the future.

"He's good," Ruth said, picking up the binoculars to follow Luis's path around the bases. "Right?"

Tanya nodded. "This is his first year."

"He's only seventeen," I said.

"Think the scout came to check him out?" Ruth asked.

I pretended to watch the new pitcher throw his warm-up pitches. He wasn't like Lee; he had no tricks, just the fastball making a lot of noise in the catcher's mitt. I guessed 93, 94 maybe. What you throw when you can muscle your way through an inning rather than having to rely on finesse.

Tanya collected our *paleta* sticks and wrappers and went to find a trash can, to go to the bathroom.

Ruth repeated, "Think the scout came to check him out?" A ball game is never really quiet, but that's how it felt just then, all quiet with only the sound of the ball smacking the catcher's mitt too hard, too fast.

Finally I said, "There are no scouts here, Ruth."

She looked at me, and with Tanya gone, it was clear that Ruth didn't much like me, that she called me "stuck-up" or something like that. She handed me the binoculars, pointed towards the third-base line.

Through the binoculars I saw a man trying to control his three sons while flirting with two pretty girls sitting behind him. The kids were swatting each other with their baseball caps. I saw the boy selling two *paletas* to a fat man wearing a Chicago Bulls T-shirt that had faded to pink in the armpits. I was about to challenge Ruth when I looked again and saw an American man sitting next to the father. There was no reason to think he was a scout. There was no reason to think he wasn't. He didn't fit into the usual Oaxaca categories: tourist, burned-out hippie, Peace Corps dropout, stray journalist. And there was something so unobtrusive about him. Yet when he glanced at the game in progress, his eyes narrow to a tight squint that pulled in each detail, if a batting stance should be opened up or which corner of the bag was stepped on rounding second.

Ruth nudged me. "That was a fastball, and it was inside."

I watched the scout light up a cigarette, smile as the littlest boy whacked him with a baseball cap. The father apologized, and the two girls giggled behind their hands, tossed back their hair. The scout smiled at them, too, said something that made them laugh and clutch at each other's arms.

Ruth murmured, "Fastball. Too low."

One girl whispered in the other's ear, and the scout made a goofy face that got the little boys laughing. He waved over the *paleta* boy, and the boy pulled popsicles out of his box one after the other as the scout pointed first to the little boys, then to the girls, next to the father, and finally to himself. Hurry up, I wanted to scream, there isn't all the time in the world, but the scout counted out his money slowly, fumbling some coins, and the boy couldn't fund the proper change, so the scout took one more *paleta* which he handed to the fat man in the Chicago Bulls shirt.

"Do you mind?" Ruth said, and I returned the binoculars because the batter had been hit by a pitch and now Phil was up and I knew because she'd told us plenty of times that she liked to watch his butt when he batted.

• • •

I didn't want it to be like I was just someone else coming up to him after the game. That wasn't the way to get these guys to listen. So I waited, and then I went to the hotel where I figured he'd be staying, the fanciest hotel in Oaxaca, the famous one where Pancho Villa once slept. I didn't have to ask around or even look hard; he was in the bar, sitting along at a table that looked onto the courtyard garden. A half-finished margarita was on the table, an overflowing ashtray, a section of an English-language newspaper that hadn't been opened, an unlit candle. Two waiters were in the back, whispered to the bartender, but otherwise we were alone.

I stepped in front of his view, smiled. "Mind if I join you?" It was a line I'd heard plenty of people say in the movies, usually those heart-of-gold hookers you know will be redeemed before the final credits.

He didn't say yes right away, just picked up his drink and tinkled the ice in the glass. He said, "The ice is okay in the hotel, right? Or am I going to spend all day tomorrow regretting this margarita?"

"The hotel purifies its water," I said.

"So regretting the margaritas depends on how many I have." He smiled at me, then held out his hand. "Chuck Dunbar."

I shook his hand, sat down. "My name's Jenny."

"There's a name I haven't heard for a while," he said. "Seems like most Jennys turned into Jennifers somewhere along the line." He gestured a "two more" flip of his wrist to the waiter without asking what I wanted.

"Thank you," I said. My lipstick felt too thick, and I tried to lick some of it off.

"Expense account," he said. "Thank my company," and to make sure there was no mistake, I asked who he worked for, and he said, "No business talk, okay? Meetings are for business. Bars are for booze and broads and old baseball stories." It was the kind of line he liked to say, to throw around a word like "broads."

The waiter brought two margaritas and a small bowl of shelled peanuts. Chuck popped a handful of peanuts into his mouth. "Peanuts are my weakness," he said. "I'll put these away in ten minutes. My ex-wife was a peanut farmer's daughter and that kept us together longer than anything else. Nothing beats good Georgia peanuts."

So I took a few from the bowl. They tasted stale. I said, "How do you like Oaxaca?"

"Thing about this hotel is I could be anywhere," he said. "Know what I mean?"

I nodded.

"Course who says that's all bad?" he said. "Knowing what to expect."

"Do you travel a lot?" I asked.

"Some," he said.

There was a silence. I watched him look me over the way he'd look at any prospect, trying to whittle all of me down to three or four quick, perfect words. Good hitter, weak on defense. Throws heat, no endurance. It was what he did, what he was paid for.

I licked the salt from the rim of my glass. I wanted to explain to him, to the waiters, to the bartender that I'd never done anything like this before.

I cleared my throat, looked away, said, "Have you eaten any *molé* yet? Oaxaca is famous for it."

He kept watching me, and I went on: "They call Oaxaca the land of seven *molés*, and each tastes different. There's a restaurant where you can get—"

He interrupted: "Honey, I know you're married, so why don't you tell me straight up what this is about."

"Is being married a problem?" I asked, looking down at my left hand. The rings were in my pocket.

"Depends on what exactly we're talking about," he said, putting more peanuts in his mouth, chewing quickly. "What are *you* talking about?"

"I don't know what you mean," I said.

"This about baseball?" he asked. "Or something else."

"Why would I want to talk about baseball?" and I leaned forward, smiled, set my hand on top of his. The skin felt hard, thick.

"I didn't get to where I got by not being able to see what's going on between each and every line," he said, slipping his hand out from under mine. "Show me an eighteen-year-old kid, and I gotta know exactly how long that hot arm of his'll stay hot. I gotta know his knee's not giving out anytime soon. Gotta figure out what's lucky streak and what's long-haul talent the club can use. Above all, I gotta know all this within five minutes of watching the kid on the field. So don't insult me. Which one of those guys out there're you married to?"

"Lee Dupree," I said.

"Well, Mrs. Dupree, now we're getting somewhere." He took all that remained of the peanuts and shoved them in his mouth, crunched noisily. "Lee Dupree. I remember seeing him go up against Rickey Dawson in the Carolina League finals couple years back. Hell of a game. But I thought by now he'd— how old is he? Thirty-one? Thirty-two? I'd've guessed he'd've settled down by now, started selling insurance, coaching his son's Little League team."

I shook my head.

"They can't all make it, Mrs. Dupree. Least he got close. Got some stories to tell his kids. Any kids, Mrs. Dupree?"

"Not yet."

He finished his drink in two swallows, swiped his mouth with the back of his hand, traced his finger around the rim of his glass to knock all the salt onto the table. I knew exactly what sex with him would be like.

"How long are you going to be down here?" I asked.

"I'm leaving after tomorrow's game," he said. "It's my granddaughter's first Christmas."

"Stay one more day to see Lee pitch."

"I saw what I came to see," he said.

"He's 5 and 1," I said.

He shook his head. "Didn't come here looking for a pitcher."

"Don't insult me," I said. "Everyone's always looking for a pitcher."

He waved for the bill, and the waiter trotted over. "Can you read this?" he asked, handing it to me. "Too damn dark in here." The waiter quickly bent and lit the candle on the table.

"It's right," I said.

He signed the check and pulled some pesos from his pocket, threw them on the table for the waiter. It was way too many.

"Nice meeting you, Mrs. Dupree," he said.

"They call him *Señor Poncho*," I said. "Mister Strikeout. He's good."

"You're a nice lady," he said, patting my shoulder. "But I've got to shove off now," and he picked up his unread newspaper, turned to walk away.

I quickly looked around. No one else had entered the bar. I stood up and pulled my shirt off over the top of my head. "Mr. Dunbar," I called, and he turned. "One more day."

The waiters in the back were suddenly silent. I tossed my shirt at him; he caught it underhanded, held it away from his body.

"Why not?" I said, and I unhooked my bra. I'd changed into the blue one that fastened in the front, the one Lee liked best.

He looked at my shirt in his hand, then shook it out and sort of folded it, the awkward way a man folds clothes, and he draped it over the chair back nearest to where he stood. He looked at my breasts, and I could feel him wanting to reach out and grab them the way he'd done with the peanuts, and he stepped closer. In a low voice he said, "Don't embarrass yourself like this, Mrs. Dupree."

"Who's embarrassed?"

"I know you've never done anything like this before," he said. "You'll wake up tomorrow and be sorry."

"Not if the day after you're watching Lee pitch a game," I said. I cupped my hands around my breast, brushed my fingers against the nipples so they stiffened. Maybe I threw like a girl. Maybe it didn't matter how much I knew about baseball because the fact was I'd never be out there on the field. But this I could do.

I watched his eyes watch my hands. It was too easy. I said, "Should we go to your room?"

He said, "Lord knows I'm no saint, but this isn't right."

I stepped closer and picked up one of his hands, placed it between my breasts. His fingers were cold. I felt callouses in different places than the callouses on Lee's hands, and I almost backed away. Instead I leaned in to kiss him; he ducked aside so all I got was air.

He said, "Don't take this the wrong way."

I looked down at his hand between my breasts, at the uneven, broken nails; the knuckles thickened from years of getting cracked; the way the veins protruded.

"This isn't what you really want," he said.

"You don't know what I want," I said. "I want Lee to have a chance."

He spoke quietly, as if explaining something to a child. "He already had his chance. Now don't do this to yourself. Please."

Something behind me caught his attention. Reflected in the mirror behind the bar I saw the other side of the courtyard where the two Mexican girls from the afternoon's game leaned up against a stone pillar. Short skirts, high heels, bright red lipstick, flowers in their hair. What you wear on a date. What you wear when you're young and beautiful and you think maybe you're in love. What I wore when Lee took me to the movies the first time.

"You're too smart for this kind of thing, Mrs. Dupree." His voice was almost too scratchy, like he tried to talk a certain way he thought he should talk.

"What do you mean, too smart?" I said. "How do you know how smart I am?"

"You're a classy, intelligent lady," he said. "Something like this is beneath you." He slid his hand up to my shoulder, patted it, thought I didn't see him wave to the girls. They smiled and waved back before they stepped out of my view. Then he smoothed his hair, shoved his hands into his pockets.

"I'm too old," I said. "That's what you mean."

"Now, Mrs. Dupree," and I could see he was afraid I was going to cry. "Now, now," he said. "You're a beautiful woman, I know your husband loves you." He picked up my shirt, held it to me. "Go ahead and put this back on."

I slapped him as hard as I could. His cheek was spongy and I would've liked to hit him again, it felt that good.

He nodded. "No one has to know about this," he said. "You just want to help your husband. I respect that," and he made nudging motions with my shirt, trying to get me to take it from his hand.

"How old are you?" I asked.

He looked embarrassed, dropped my shirt on the table in front of me. "I'm meeting Luis Torres for dinner," he said. "And I'm already late."

"How old?"

He sighed. "Forty-five, fifty, give or take. More like give."

I nodded.

He said, "I get offers all the time. I'd have to be Superman to keep up."

"Or an eighteen-year-old," I said.

"Bingo," he said. The silence that followed was finally broken by the sound of the two girls giggling. He shook my hand hard as if I were any prospect, said, "Good-bye, Mrs. Dupree. And good luck."

I hate when people say that. There's no way to feel after hearing it but pathetic.

As if he could read my mind, he turned at the archway out to the lobby and called, "Don't you know luck is what you want most in baseball?" The two girls stepped out of the shadows. He draped his arms around their shoulders as the three of them left.

• • •

I waited for Lee at the café where we were meeting for a late dinner. The plaza was busy; people were crowding in from the villages for market day tomorrow where they'd sell and buy special items for Christmas, visit family members, light a candle at the church, leave a request for St. Jude. I sipped my hot chocolate, tried to look a certain way so people wouldn't stare, wouldn't think they could approach to sell me cheap souvenirs. I'd never been in a place long enough to fit in. That came from following Lee around. I could have been like some of the wives—just stopping somewhere and saying, "This is it," and buying a house there. Someone like Tanya I imagined picking a place on the map, saying to Randall, "Here." Someone like Tanya wouldn't go long without her house, her children, her career, the things she wanted. Unlike me, she always knew what to say, when to say it.

Lee slid into the seat next to me, put his hand on mine on the table, said, "Chuck Dunbar's here from the Angels." He pushed his other hand through his hair, squinted as if he were looking into the sun. A waiter brought us two menus that we didn't open.

"He was at the game," I said.

Lee shook his head. "Remember when it was me they'd come out to see?"

"Maybe it was you," I said. "Maybe it was the famous *Señor Poncho* who brought the scout down to Mexico."

"Don't."

There was a long silence. The waiter started to walk over, but something in our faces made him back off. Lee folded his arms tightly together as if he were holding all the pieces of himself.

There should have been something better to say. I said, "Why not? It could be you."

The church bell rang, and I glanced at my watch. Nine o'clock.

"What do you want for Christmas?" he asked.

"What?"

"Isn't it almost Christmas?"

"Three days," I said.

"So what do you want?"

What do we all want for Christmas? Peace? Love? Hope? Understanding? Enough faith to get through another year? What do we get? Sweaters and jewelry. I looked at Lee's face, at the squint lines burrowed deep, at where the freckles used to be before they faded, at the lips he licked every time he threw a slider. It's not that he looked tired, but he definitely looked scuffed, like your first glove, the one you learned to play catch with. The lucky one you can't bear to throw away.

"So, Jenny, what do you want?" he asked again.

I was ready to say it. Give it up, let's go home, get a job selling insurance— we'll buy a house and have a baby. We're not getting any younger. Life's too short. Blah, blah, blah. They were words I'd been practicing since I left the hotel.

Lee sat back in his chair as if he knew what I was about to say. His face closed up. He could've been thinking anything.

The moment stretched longer and longer. I thought about that gun in my hand, thought about what had made Lee buy it. Thought about what if Chuck Dunbar had said yes. Was there really a time when I wouldn't have believed these kinds of things could happen? When a place like Mexico was only a haze in the distance?

The words were right there: Let's give up. But I said, "What I want for Christmas is . . . a moose head."

"A moose head? That's the craziest damn thing I ever heard."

"That's exactly why I want it," I said. "A big one."

"But why a moose head?"

I shook my head, smiled, giggled. "Why not?"

"Why not?" he repeated. "What's that supposed to mean?"

"I don't know." I was laughing now. "But you better find one. It's all I want." I didn't know what I was going to do if he didn't laugh soon. It was all so ridiculous, just a game you played with bats and balls, a game for children.

He smiled. "Okay, Jenny. I'll get you a moose head."

"The biggest one you can find."

"I'll do it," he said, starting to laugh. "I swear I will."

"Remember—it has to be really, really big."

"It'll be the biggest damn moose head you ever saw."

We were both laughing hard now, and I accidentally knocked my hot chocolate onto the ground. That made us grab each other and laugh even harder, so hard the tears finally came, and the waiter hurried to sweep away the broken pieces of the mug, rolling his eyes as he moved his broom across the mess, looking for all the world like Fernando on the mound, about to put one right over the plate.

Who's on First?
(1960)

Lloyd Biggle Jr.

Lloyd Biggle Jr. (1923-2002) was born in Waterloo, Iowa, and earned his PhD from the University of Michigan. He authored more than twenty books, mostly in the areas of science fiction and mystery. Two of his science-fiction novels, *The World Menders* (1971) and *Monument* (1976), are especially well-known. Biggle's "Who's on First?" is from his collection titled *A Galaxy of Strangers* (1976). The story was written in 1960, and the events are set in 1998.

> *Priority Rating: Routine*
> *From: Jard Killil, Minister of Juvenile Affairs*
> *To: All Planetary Police Organizations*
> *All Interplanetary Patrol Units*
> *Subject: Juvenile Detention Escapee Muko Zilo*
> *Enclosures: Character analysis, film strips, retinal patterns*
>
> *All law enforcement agencies are hereby informed of the escape of Muko Zilo from the Juvenile Rehabilitation Center on Philoy, Raff III, Sector 1311. Escapee is presumed to have fled the planet in a stolen space yacht, Stellar Class II, range unlimited. His probable destination is unknown.*

*Escapee is not considered dangerous. He possesses low-grade intelligence
and has no psi ability higher than Class F.*

Kindly notify Philoy JRC immediately upon detention.

The major-league baseball season of 1998 was only two weeks old, and
Manager Pops Poppinger wished it was over and done with. Since opening
day his Pirates had managed to lose fourteen games while winning none, and
Pops had only the Baseball Managers' Tenure Act of 1993 to thank for the fact
that he was still gainfully employed. He'd had that same act to thank for his
regular paychecks during the 1996 and 1997 seasons.

"But it can't last," he muttered. "Congress will repeal the thing and cite
me as the reason."

He strode through the locker room without a glance at his lounging ballplayers, entered his private office, and slammed the door. He did not want to
talk to anyone, especially if that anyone happened to be wearing a Pirate's
uniform. He dropped an armful of newspapers onto his desk, tilted back in
his chair until he could plant his size-thirteen feet in a comfortable position,
and opened the top paper to the sports pages. The headline made him wince.
"WHEN IS A PIRATE?" it demanded. Pops stuck a cigar in his mouth as he read
and forgot to light it.

"In the venerable days of yore," the article said, "when professional athletic organizations found it necessary to attach themselves to some unfortu-
nate city in the mistaken belief that civic loyalty would induce the population
to attend games in person and pay for the privilege, the fair city of Pittsburgh
spawned two notable gangs of thieves, the baseball Pirates and the football
Steelers. Both organizations had their days of glory. Within the memories
of men now living, if you care to believe it, the Pirates won five consecutive
world championships and the Steelers four.

"Those days of myth and fable are far behind us. If the Steelers stole anything worth mentioning during the football season just concluded, it escaped
this writer's attention. The 1998 Pirates are so far removed from thievery that
they will not take a game as a gift. They emphatically demonstrated their
moral uprightness yesterday, when their opposition was stricken with that
most tragic of baseball diseases, paralytic generosity. The Dodgers committed
six errors and presented the Pirates with nine unearned runs. The Dodgers
won, 27 to 9."

Pops crumpled the paper and tossed it over his shoulder. "Bah! Let 'em rave. It's for sure I ain't got any ballplayers but I got lots of tenure."

The telephone rang, and he picked it up and growled a response.

"Who's pitching today, Pops?" a cheerful voice asked.

"I dunno," Pops said. "If you reporters find some guy in the press box that ain't got a sore arm, send him down."

He slammed down the phone and reached for another paper. "PIRATES STILL IN REVERSE," the headline said. Pops tossed that one aside without reading it.

A knock rattled the door. Pops ignored it. The knock sounded again, and the door opened wide enough to admit the large, grinning face of Dipsey Marlow, the Pirates' third-base coach.

"Scram!" Pops snapped

"Some kid here to see you, Pops."

"Tell him I got a bat boy. I got a whole team of bat boys."

"He's older that that—I think. He says he's got a letter for you."

Pops straightened up and grinned. "From Congress?"

"He says it's from Pete Holloway."

"Send him in."

The kid shuffled in awkwardly. His dimensions looked to be about five feet five inches—in both directions. Oddly enough, he was not fat. There was an unhealthy thinness about his freckled face, and his overly large ears gave his features a whimsical grotesqueness, but he was shaped like a box and he moved like one. He dragged to a stop in front of Pops's desk, fumbled through four pockets, and came up with a letter.

"Mr. Poppinger?"

The high, squeaky voice made Pops's ears ring. "I'm ashamed to admit it." Pops said, "but that's my name."

"Mr. Holloway told me to give this to you."

"The last I heard of Pete Holloway, he was lost in the woods up in Maine."

"He still is, sir. I mean, he's still in Maine."

"You came clear out here to California just to give me this?"

"Yes, sir."

Pops took the envelope and ripped it open.

"Dear Pops," he read. "This here kid Zilo is the most gawdawful ballplayer I ever see on two legs. He is also the luckiest man south of the North Pole. Put him in center with a rocking chair and a bottle of beer and every ball hit to the outfield will drop in his lap. He'll even catch some of them. Sign him and you'll win the pennant. Yours, Pete. P.S. He also is lucky with the bat."

Pops scratched his head and squinted disbelievingly at Zilo. "What d'ya play?"

"Outfield," Zilo said. He quickly corrected himself. "Outfield, sir."

"Where in the outfield?"

"Anywhere, sir. Just so it's the outfield, sir."

Pops wasn't certain whether he should throw him out or go along with the gag. "I got three outfielders that get by. How about second or short? Between first and third I got nothing but grass."

"Oh, no, sir. Mr. Holloway had me play short, and I made nine errors in one inning. Then he moved me to the outfield."

"I'm surprised he didn't kill you," Pops said. He continued to eye Zilo disbelievingly. "You actually played baseball for Pete?"

"Yes, sir. Last summer, sir. I went to see him a week ago to find out when I could start playing again, and he said he thought you could use me because your season started before his does."

"What'd you bat?"

"Six forty, sir."

Pops winced. "What'd you field?"

"A thousand, sir. In the outfield. In the infield it was zero."

Pops got up slowly. "Son, Pete Holloway is an old friend of mine, and he never gave me a bad tip yet. I'll give you a tryout."

"That's very kind of you, sir."

"The name is Pops. And it ain't kind of me after what happened yesterday."

• • •

Pops was standing in the corner of dugout with Ed Schwartz, the club secretary, when the new Pirate walked out onto the field. Pops took one look, clapped his hand to his forehead, and gasped, "My God!"

"I told you I'd find him a uniform," Ed said. "I didn't guarantee to find him one that fit. He just isn't made the way our uniforms are made, and if I were you I'd make sure I wanted to keep him before I called the tailor. Otherwise, if you release him we'll have a set of uniforms on our hands that won't fit anyone or anything except maybe that oversized water cooler in the league offices."

Pops walked over to the third-base coaching box, where Dipsey Marlow was standing to watch batting practice. The Dodger dugout had just got its first incredulous look at Zilo, and Pops waited until the uproar subsided somewhat before he spoke.

"Think Pete is pulling my leg?" he asked.

"It wouldn't be like Pete, but it's possible."

"The way things is going, he ought to know better. I'll look him up when the season is over and shoot him."

Dipsey grinned happily. He was rather pleased with himself in spite of yesterday's loss. As third-base coach he'd been the loneliest man in the Western Hemisphere for seven straight days while the Pirates were being shut out without a man reaching third. Even if his team was losing, he liked to have some traffic to direct.

"You got nothing to lose but ball games," he said.

Zilo had taken his place in the batter's box. He cut on the first pitch, and the ball dribbled weakly out toward the pitcher's mound.

"He's a fly swatter," Dipsey said disgustedly.

Zilo poked two more lazy ground balls and lifted a pop fly to the third baseman. Apparently satisfied, he borrowed a glove and wandered out to left field. He dropped a couple of balls that were hit right at him and stumbled over his own feet when he tried to go a few steps to his left.

"It's a joke," Pops said. "Pete must have seen him catch one. That's what he meant by him being lucky."

Dipsey walked out to left field to talk with Zilo. He came back looking foolish. "The kid says it's all right—he's just testing the atmosphere. It'll be different when the game starts."

"He says he hit six forty," Pops said dreamily.

"You going to use him?"

"Sure I'll use him. If I'm gonna shoot Pete, I gotta have a reason that'll stand up in court. As soon as we get ten runs behind, in he goes."

Pops headed back toward the dugout, and some tourists in box seats raised a lusty chorus of boos as he passed. Pops scowled and quickened his pace. The dratted tourists were ruining the game. There had been a time when a manager could concentrate on what he was doing, but now he had to operate with a mob of howling spectators literally hanging over his shoulder and shouting advice and criticism into his ears. It got on the players' nerves, too. There was the Giants' Red Cowan, who'd been a good pitcher until they opened the games to tourists. The noise so rattled him that he had to retire.

"Why can't they stay home and see it on TV, like everybody else?" Pops growled.

"Because they pay money, that's why," Ed Schwartz said. "There's a novelty or something in seeing a ball game in the flesh, and it's getting so some of these tourists are planning their vacations so they can take in a few games. Bill Willard—the *L.A. Times* man—was saying that the National League now is California's number-one tourist attraction. The American League is doing the same thing for Arizona."

The boos sounded again, and Pops ducked into the dugout out of sight. "I don't mind their watching," he said, "if only they'd keep their mouths shut. When I started managing there wasn't anyone around during a game except the TV men, and they were too busy to be giving me advice. Even the sportswriters watched on TV. Now they camp here the whole season, and you can't go out after the morning paper without finding one waiting for an interview."

"The tourists are here to stay, so you might as well get used to them," Ed said. "There's even some talk about putting up hotels for them, so they won't have to commute from Fresno to see the games."

Pops sat down and borrowed Ed's pen to make out his lineup. Ed looked over his shoulder and asked, "How come you're not using that new guy?"

"I'm saving him until we get far enough behind."

"You mean until the second inning?" Ed said, and ducked as Pops fired a catcher's mask.

"That's the trouble with those tenure laws," Pops said. "They had to go and include the club secretaries."

The game started off in a way sadly familiar to Pops. The Dodgers scored three runs in the first inning and threatened to blast the Pirates right out of the league. Then, with the bases loaded and one out, the Pirate's third baseman managed to hang on to a sizzling line drive and turn it into a double play. Pops's breathing spell lasted only until the next inning. Lefty Effinger, the Pirates' pitcher, spent a long afternoon falling out of one hole and into another. In nine innings he gave up a total of seventeen hits, but a miraculous succession of picked-off runners, overrun bases, and double plays kept the Dodgers shut out after those first three runs.

In the meantime, Dodger pitcher Rip Ruster was having one of his great days. He gave up a scratch single in the second and a walk in the fourth, and by the ninth inning he had fanned twelve, to the gratification of the hooting, jeering tourists.

The last of the ninth opened with Ruster striking out the first two Pirates on six pitches, and the Pirates in the dugout started sneaking off to the dressing room. Then first baseman Sam Lyle ducked away from an inside pitch that hit his bat and blooped over the infield for a single. Pops called for the hit and run, and the next batter bounced the ball at the Dodger shortstop. The shortstop threw it into right field, and the runners reached second and third. Ruster, pacing angrily about the mound, walked the next batter on four pitches.

Pops jumped from the dugout and called time. "Hit six forty, did he?" Pops muttered and yelled, "Zilo!"

The beaming Zilo jumped up from the far end of the bench. "Yes, sir?"

"Get out there and hit!"

"Yes, sir!"

He shuffled toward the plate, and the uproar sent up by the tourists rocked the grandstand. Dipsey Marlow called time again and hurried over to the dugout.

"You off you rocker? We got a chance to win this one. Get that thing out of there and use a left-hander."

"Look," Pops said, "You know derned well the way Ruster is pitching we're lucky to get a loud foul off of him. That hit was luck, and the error was luck, and the base on balls happened only because Ruster got mad. Now he'll cool off, and the only thing that keeps this going is more luck. Pete says the kid's lucky, and I want some of it."

Marlow turned on his heel and stalked back to the coaching box.

Ruster coiled up and shot a bullet at home plate. Zilo swatted at it awkwardly—and popped it up.

The second baseman backed up three steps, waved the rest of the infield away, and got ready to end the game. The base runners, running furiously with two out, came down the stretch from third in a mournful procession. Zilo loped along the base path watching the Dodger second baseman and the ball.

The ball reached the top of its arc and suddenly seemed to carry. The second baseman backed confidently into position, changed his mind, and backed up again. The ball continued to float toward the outfield. The second baseman turned and raced toward center field with his eyes on the misbehaving ball.

The center fielder had been jogging toward the infield. Now he broke into a run. The second baseman leaped for the ball. The center fielder dove for it. Neither man touched it, and they went down in a heap as the ball bounced and frolicked away.

The lumbering Zilo crossed home plate before the startled right fielder could retrieve the ball. The Pirates had won, 4 to 3, and they hoisted Zilo to their shoulders and bore him off to the dressing room. The Dodgers quitted the field to an enthusiastic chorus of boos.

Pops went out to the third-base coaching box, where Dipsey Marlow still stood gazing vacantly toward the outfield.

"Luck," Pops said and gently led him away.

• • •

Rodney Wilks, the Pirates' brisk little president, flew over from L.A. that evening and threw a victory celebration in the ultramodern building that housed the National League offices. All of the players were there, and those who had families brought them. Women and children congregated in one room and the men in another. Champagne and milk shakes flowed freely in both rooms.

National League President Edgar Rysdale looked in on the party briefly but approvingly. A team in a slump was bad for all the teams—bad for the league. When the race was a good one, fans frequently paid a double TV fee, watching two games at once or, if they had only one set, switching back and forth. If one team was floundering, National League fans would watch only one game. They might even patronize the American League. So the victory pleased the league president and also the other owners, who stopped by to sample the champagne and talk shop with Wilks.

Fred Carter, the Dodger manager, also looked in on the party. Zilo's freak pop fly had ruined a nine-game winning streak for him, but he seemed more puzzled than mournful. He backed Pops into a corner and said with a grin, "I been watching pop flies for thirty-five years, and I never saw one act like that. Did the kid magnetize his bat, or something?"

Pops shrugged. "I been watching baseball forty-five years, and I see something new seven times a week."

"Just the same, the next time that kid comes up I'm passing out the butterfly nets. He don't look like much of a hitter. Where'd you get him?"

"Pete Holloway sent him out."

Carter arched his eyebrows. "He must have something, then."

"Pete says he ain't got a thing except luck."

"Isn't that enough? I'm going over to watch the Reds and Giants. Want to come?"

"Nope. Now that I finally won one, I'm gonna get some sleep tonight."

Pops saw Ed Schwartz talking with Zilo, and he went over to see what line the club secretary might be handing out. Ed was talking about the old days, and Zilo was listening intently, his dark eyes sparkling.

"Each team had its own city," Ed said, "and its own ballpark. Think of the waste involved. Eventually there were twenty-four teams in each league, which meant forty-eight ballparks, and even during the playing season they were in use only half the time, when the teams were playing at home. And the season only lasted six months. And there was all that traveling. We froze one day in Montreal and baked the next in New Orleans. Our hotel bill for the season used to look like the national debt, not to mention the plane fares. It was rough on the players in other ways. They only saw their families when they were playing at home, and just as they got settled somewhere they'd be traded and maybe have to move clear across the country—only to be traded again the next season or even the next week. Putting the entire league in one place solved everything. The climate is wonderful, and we almost never have a game postponed because of bad weather. We're down to eight teams in a league, which anyway is as many as the fans can keep track of. We have two fields, and they're used twice a day, for two afternoon and two night games. Each team has its own little community. Baseball, Cal is growing, boy, and lots of players are settling here permanently and buying their own homes. You'll want to, too. It's a wonderful place."

"It's a soft place for club secretaries," Pops growled. "Ed used to have to worry about baggage, plane schedules, hotel reservations, and a million and one other things. Now all he has to do is get the equipment moved a couple of hundred yards from one park to the other, now and then, and he gripes about it. Has he stopped talking long enough to get you settled?"

"Oh, yes, sir," Zilo said. "I'm rooming with Jerry Fargo."

"All right. Come out early tomorrow. You gotta learn to catch a fly ball without getting hit on the head."

Dipsey Marlow nudged Pops's arm and pulled him aside. "Going to play him tomorrow?"

"Might. We could use a little luck every day."

"I been listening to the big boys. Know what they're going to do? Put up a flock of temporary stands at World Series time. They think they might get fifteen thousand people out here for every game."

"That's their business," Pops said.

"Just tell me why anyone wants to take a trip and pay a stiff price to see a ball game when he can sit at home and see it for fifty cents?"

"People are funny," Pops said. "Sometimes they're almost as funny as ballplayers."

President Wilks came over and placed a full glass in Pops's hand. Pops sipped the champagne and grimaced. "It's all right, I guess, but it'll never take the place of beer."

"Finish in first division," Wilks said, "and I'll buy you enough beer to take you through the off season."

Pops grinned. "How about putting that in my contract?"

"I will," Wilks promised. "Do you want it in bottles or kegs?"

"Both."

"I'll take care of it first thing in the morning." He grinned and prodded Pops in the ribs, but behind the grin his expression was anxious. "Do you think we have a chance?"

"Too early to say. Sure, we only won one out of fifteen, but we're only ten games out of first. We been looking like a bunch of schoolkids, and if we keep that up we finish last. If we snap out of it—well, the season's got a long way to go."

"I hope you snap out of it," Wilks said. "Managers have tenure, but club presidents haven't."

Pops found a bottle of beer to kill the taste of the champagne, and he made a quiet exit after instructing Marlow to get the players home to bed at a reasonable hour. The National League's two playing fields were a blaze of light, and the shouts of the two crowds intermingled. There seemed to be a lot of tourists in attendance—and tourists at night games made even less sense than tourists at afternoon games. It'd be midnight before some of them got back to their hotels. Pops walked slowly back to Pirateville, grumbling to himself. The large mansion intended for the manager Pops had turned over to Dipsey Marlow, who needed the room for his eight kids. Pops lived in a small house a short distance down the street. His middle-aged daughter Marge kept house for him, and she was already in bed. She didn't like baseball.

Priority Rating: Routine
From: Jard Killil, Minister of Juvenile Affairs
To: All Planetary Police Organizations, Sectors 1247; 2162; 889; 1719
All Interplanetary Patrol Units, Sectors 1247; 2162; 889; 1719
Subject: Juvenile Detention Escapee Muko Zilo
Reference: Previous memorandum of 13B927D8 and enclosures

Information from several sources indicates that an unidentified ship, possibly that of Escapee Zilo, traveled on a course roughly parallel to Trade Route 79B, which would take it into or through your sectors. Because of the time elapsed since his escape, it is assumed that Zilo has found an effective planetary hiding place. Immediate investigation requested. Escapee is not—repeat—not dangerous.

Kindly notify Philoy JRC immediately upon detention.

Pops opened a three-game series against the Cubs with Zilo in left field. He figured the youngster would do the least damage there, since he was pitching Simp Simpson, his best right-hander, and the Cubs had seven left-handed batters in their lineup. At least that much of his strategy worked. In the first six innings only two balls were hit to left. One was a line drive single that Zilo bobbled for an error as the runner reached second. The other was a foul fly on which Zilo seemed about to make a miraculous catch until his feet got tangled and spilled him. At the plate he waved his bat futilely and struck out twice while the Cubs were taking a five-run lead.

In the last of the sixth the Pirates got men on first and second. It was Zilo's turn to bat. Dipsey Marlow called time, and as the tourists hooted impatiently he strode to the dugout. "Take him out," he said.

"Why?" Pops asked. "He's still batting .333. That's better than the rest of these dopes."

"You gotta understand this luck thing. Yesterday it was luck to put him in. Today it's luck to take him out. I found a spider in my locker today, and that means—"

"Hit and run on the first pitch," Pops said.

Zilo fanned the air lustily and dribbled a grounder toward the first baseman. Suddenly it took an unaccountable eight-foot bounce over his head and rolled into the outfield, picking up speed. Zilo pulled up at first, breathing heavily, and the two runners scored.

Sam Lyle followed with a lazy fly ball to right. Zilo moved off first base and halted to watch the progress of the ball. The right fielder seemed to be having difficulties. He wandered about shading his eyes, backed up, and finally lost the ball in the sun. The center fielder had come over fast, and he shouted the right fielder away, backed up slowly, and finally turned in disgust to watch the ball drop over the fence. Lyle trailed the floundering Zilo around the bases, and the Pirates trailed by a run, 5 to 4.

Three fast outs later, Dipsey Marlow returned to the dugout and squeezed in beside Pops. "I take it all back," he said. "I won't argue with you again the rest of the season. But this spider of mine—"

Pops cupped his hands and shouted. "Let's HOLD 'em now. Let's WIN this one!"

"—this spider of mine was in my sweatshirt, and my old mother always used to say spider in your clothes means money. Will the players get a cut of what those fifteen thousand tourists pay to watch a Series game?"

"The World Series is still a couple of hundred games away," Pops said. "Let's worry about it later. Get to work and pick us off a sign or two."

In the eighth inning, Zilo got a rally started with a pop fly that three infielders chased futilely. He moved to second on a ground ball that took a bad hop and he scored on a soft line drive that curved sharply and landed between the outfielders. The Pirates pushed over two more runs on hits that were equally implausible and took a two-run lead into the ninth.

The Cubs came back with a vengeance. The first two batters lashed out sizzling singles. Pops prodded his bullpen into action and went out to talk with Simpson. They stood looking down at the next Cub batter, the burly catcher Bugs Rice.

"Don't let him pull one," Pops said.

"He won't pull one," Simp said determinedly through clenched teeth.

Rice did not pull one. He didn't have to. He unloaded on the first pitch and drove it far, far away into left field, the opposite field. Pops sat down with the crack of the bat and covered his face with his hands.

"Now we gotta come from behind again," he moaned. "And we won't. I know we ain't *that* lucky."

Suddenly the men on the bench broke into excited cheers, and a scattering of applause came from the tourists. Pops looked up, saw runners on second and third, saw the scoreboard registering one out.

"What happened?" he yelped.

"Zilo caught it," Dipsey Marlow said. "Didn't think he had it in him, but he backed up to the fence and made a clean catch. Took so much time getting the ball back to the infield that the runners had time to touch up and advance, but he caught it."

"He didn't. I heard it hit the bat, and I saw it go. It should have cleared the fence by twenty feet."

"Your eyes and ears aren't as young as they used to be. Zilo caught it against the fence."

Pops shook his head. He huddled down in a corner of the dugout while Simpson fanned one batter and got another on a tap to the infield, and the Pirates had won two in a row.

• • •

That was the beginning. The Pirates pushed their winning streak to twelve, lost one, won eight more. They were twenty and fifteen and in fourth place. Zilo became a national sensation. Lucky Zilo Fan Clubs sprang up across the country, and he kept his batting average around the .450 mark and even got another home run when a solid fly ball to the outfield took crazy bounces in nineteen directions while Zilo lumbered around the bases. The rest of the team took courage and started playing baseball.

But not even a lucky Zilo could lift the Pirates above fourth place. Pops's pitching staff was a haphazard assortment of aching, overage veterans and unpredictable, inexperienced youths. One day they would be unhittable; the next day they'd be massacred, and Pops found to his sorrow that luck was no answer to a nineteen-run deficit. Still, the season drifted along with the Pirates holding desperately to fourth, and Pops began to think they might even stay there.

Then Zilo sprained his ankle. The trainer outfitted him with crutches and applied every known remedy and a few unknown ones that Zilo suggested, but the ankle failed to respond.

"It beats me," the trainer said to Pops. "Things that should make it better seem to make it worse."

"How long will he be out?" Pops asked gloomily.

"I won't even guess. The way it's reacting, it could last him a lifetime."

Pops breathed a profane farewell to first division.

Zilo hobbled to every game on his crutches and watched with silent concentration from a box behind the dugout. Oddly enough, for a time the team's luck continued. Ground balls took freakish bounces, fly balls responded to unlikely air currents, and on some days opposition pitchers suffered such a loss of control that they would occasionally wander in and stare at home plate, as though to assure themselves that it was still there. Ollie Richards, the Reds' ace and one of the best control pitchers in either league, walked seventeen batters in three innings and left the game on the short end of a 6 to 3 score without having given up a hit.

Zilo's good-natured, freckled face took on an unhealthy pallor. Wrinkles furrowed his brow and his eyes held a tense, haunted look. As the team's luck began to fade, he grew increasingly irritable and despondent. On the day they slipped to fifth place, he met Pops after the game and asked, "Could I speak with you, sir?"

"Sure," Pops said. "Come along."

Pops held the door as Zilo swung through on his crutches. He got the youngster seated and then he settled back with his own feet propped up on his desk. "Ankle any better?"

"I'm afraid not, sir."

"Takes time, sometimes."

"Sir," Zilo said, "I know I'm not a good ballplayer. Like they say, I'm just lucky. Maybe this will be the last season I'll play."

"I wouldn't say that," Pops said. "You're young, and luck has took a lot of men a long way in baseball."

"Anyway, sir, I like to play, even if I'm not good. And I'd like to have us win the pennant and play in the World Series."

"Wouldn't mind having another winner myself before I retire."

"What I'd like to do, sir, is go home for a while. I think I could get my ankle fixed up there, and I'd like to bring back some friends who could help us."

Pops was amused. "Ballplayers?"

"I think they'd be better than I am, sir. Or luckier, maybe. Do you—would you give them a trial?"

"I'd give anybody a tryout," Pops said seriously. "Especially shortstops and second basemen and pitchers, but I'd have a look at anybody."

Zilo pushed himself erect on his crutches. "I'll get back as soon as I can."

"All right. But leave a little of that luck here, will you?"

Zilo turned and looked at Pops strangely. "I wish I could, sir. I really wish I could."

Ed Schwartz took Zilo to L.A. and put him on a plane for the East. For Maine. And at Baseball, Cal, the Pirates won two more games and went into a cataclysmic slump. They lost ten straight and slipped to sixth place. Pops put through a phone call to the Maine address Zilo had given him and was informed that there was no such place. Then he called Pete Holloway.

"I wondered what was happening to you," Pete said. "I haven't seen the kid. He dropped out of nowhere last summer and played a little sandlot ball for me. He never told me where he came from, but I don't think it was Maine. If he shows up again, I'll get in touch with you."

"Thanks," Pops said. He hung up slowly.

Ed Schwartz said thoughtfully, "I suppose I better get a detective on it."

"Detectives," Pops said and wearily headed for the field and another shellacking.

Two more weeks went by. The detectives traced Zilo to Maine, where he seemed to have vanished from the ken of mortal man. The Pirates were tottering on the brink of last place.

Then Pops received an airmail letter from Zilo from Brazil.

"I got lost," he wrote plaintively. "We crashed in the jungle and they won't let us leave the country."

Pops called President Wilks into conference, and Wilks got on the phone to Washington. He knew enough of the right people to make the necessary arrangements and keep the matter out of the papers. Zilo was flown back on a chartered plane, and he brought four friends with him.

Ed Schwartz met them in L.A. and rushed them out to Baseball, Cal, in President Wilks's own plane. They arrived during the fourth inning of another Pirate beating.

"How's the ankle?" Pops demanded.

Zilo beamed. "Just fine, sir."

"Get in there, then."

Zilo got his friends seated in the president's box and then he went out to loft a long fly ball over the fence for a home run. The Pirates came to life. Everyone hit, and a 10 to 0 drubbing was transformed like magic into a 25 to 12 victory.

After the game Zilo introduced his friends. They were John Smith, Sam Jones, Robert White, and William Anderson. Smith and Jones, Zilo said, were infielders. White and Anderson were pitchers.

Ed Schwartz took in their proportions with a groan and went to work on the uniform problem. They were built like Zilo but on a much more lavish scale. They towered over Pops, answered his questions politely, and showed a childlike interest in all that went on about them.

Pops called one of his catchers over and introduced him to White and Anderson. "See what they got," he said. The catcher led them away, and Pops took Smith and Jones out for infield practice. He watched goggle-eyed as they covered ground like jet-propelled gazelles and made breathtaking leaps to pull down line drives.

The catcher returned, drew Pops aside, and said awesomely, "They got curves that break three feet. They got sliders that do a little loop-the-loop and cross the plate twice. They got fastballs that I'm scared to catch. They got pitches that change speed four times between the mound and the plate. If you're figuring on pitching those guys, you can get yourself another catcher."

Pops turned the ceremony of signing them over to Ed Schwartz, handed releases to four players who weren't worth the space they were taking up on the bench, and went home to his first good night's sleep in more than a month.

Priority Rating: Urgent
From: Jard Killil, Minister of Juvenile Affairs
To: All Planetary Police Orzanizations
All Interplanetary Patrol Units
Subject: Juvenile Detention Escapees
Enclosures: Character analyses, film strips, retinal patterns

All law enforcement agencies are hereby informed of the escape of four inmates of the Juvenile Rehabilitation Center on Philoy, Raff III, Sector 1311. Escapees have high psi ratings and may use them dangerously. Kindly give this matter top priority attention and notify Philoy JRC immediately upon detention.

The next day Pops started Anderson against the Braves. The Pirates bounced forty hits over and through and around the infield and scored thirty-five runs. Anderson pitched a no-hit game and struck out twenty-seven. White duplicated the performance the following day. Thereafter Pops pitched them in his regular rotation. He wasn't sure whether they hypnotized everyone in the park or just the ball, but as Dipsey Marlow put it, they made the ball do everything but stop and back up.

Pops's other pitchers suddenly looked like champions with Smith and Jones playing behind them. In spite of their boxlike builds, they ranged about the infield with the agility of jack rabbits. No one ever measured exactly how high they went up after line drives, but one sportswriter claimed they were a hazard to air traffic and should be licensed as aircraft. They sped far into the outfield after fly balls. Jones made more catches in right field than the right fielder, and it was not an unusual sight to see Jones and Smith far out in center contesting the right to a descending ball while the center fielder beat a hasty retreat. And both men swung murderous bats.

The Pirates had won fifty-seven games in a row and rewritten the record book when Zilo timidly knocked on the door of Pops's office. He was carrying a newspaper, and he looked disturbed.

"Sir," he said anxiously, "it says here that we're ruining baseball."

Pops chuckled. "They always say that when one team starts to pull away."

"But—is it true?"

"Well, now. If we kept on winning the way we are now, that won't do the game any good. People like to see a close race, and if one team wins too much, or loses too much, a lot of people stop watching the games. But don't let it worry you. We'll do our best to go on winning, but we'll drop a few, one of these days, and things will be back to normal. Your friends been playing over their heads and we've been luckier than usual."

"I see," Zilo said thoughtfully.

That evening Pops ruefully wished he'd kept his big mouth shut. Talk about jinxing a winning streak!

Anderson got knocked out in the first inning and lost his first game. White failed the next day, and the Pirates dropped five straight. Then they got off on another winning streak, but the talk about their ruining the game had quieted down. Pops never bothered to remind Zilo about how right he'd been. He wasn't going to jinx the team again.

• • •

"Those baseball players of yours," his daughter said to him one evening. "You know—the funny-looking ones."

"Sure, I know," Pops dead-panned. "What about 'em?"

"They're supposed to be pretty good, aren't they?"

Pops grinned wickedly. "Pretty fair." It would have been a waste of time referring Marge to what was left of the record book.

"I was over at the bowling alley with Ruth Wavel, and they were there bowling. They had everybody excited."

"How'd they do?"

"I guess they must be pretty good at that, too. They knocked all the pins over."

Pops grinned again. Marge's idea of a sport was crossword puzzles, and she could go through an entire season without seeing a single game. "Nothing unusual about that," he said. "Happens all the time."

She seemed surprised. "Does it? The people there thought it was something special."

"Someone was pulling your leg. How many strikes did they get?"

"How many what?"

"How many times did they knock all the pins down?"

"They knocked all of them down every time. All evening. It was the first time they'd ever bowled, too."

"Natural athletic ability," Pops muttered. They'd never played baseball before, either, except that Zilo had coached them a little. The more he thought about it, the odder it seemed, but he wasn't one to argue with no-hit games and home runs and sensational fielding plays.

"What'd you say?" Marge asked.

"Never look a gift ballplayer in the mouth," Pops said and went to bed.

To all ships of the Space Navy Sectors 2161, 2162, 2163. General Alert. Five escapees Juvenile Rehabilitation Center Philoy Raff III piloting stolen space yacht Stellar Class II range unlimited have been traced through Sector 2162. Destination unsurveyed quadrant C97. Contact base headquarters Sector 2162 for patrol assignments. Acknowledge. Zan First Admiral.

The pennant race leveled into a five-team contest for first place. The Pirates stayed in first or second, playing sometimes with unbelievable brilliance and sometimes with incredible ineptitude. Pops took the race stoically and tried to ignore the tourist hysteria that enveloped Baseball, Cal. He was doing so much better than anyone expected—so much better than he had thought possible even in his wildest moments of pre-season optimism—that it really didn't matter where he finished. He was a cinch to be Manager of the Year. He might add a pennant and a World Series, or he might not. It didn't matter.

Another season might see him in last place again, and a smart manager went out as a winner—especially a smart manager who was well along in his sixties. Pops called a news conference and announced his retirement at the end of the season.

"Before or after the World Series?" a reporter asked.

"No comment," Pops said.

The club owners erected their World Series stands early, and the tourists jammed them—fifteen thousand for every game. Pops wondered where they came from. National League President Rysdale wandered about smiling fondly over the daily television receipts, and President Wilks sent Pops a load of beer that filled his basement.

Over in Baseball, Arizona, the American League officials were glum. The Yankees, who were mainly distinguished for having finished last more frequently than any other team in major-league history, had suddenly and inexplicably opened up a twenty-game lead, and nobody cared any longer what happened in the American League.

"Three weeks to go," Pops told his team. "What d'ya say we wrap this thing up?"

"Right!" Zilo said happily.

"Right!" Smith, Jones, Anderson, and White chorused.

The Pirates started another winning streak.

To all ships of the Space Navy patroling unsurveyed quadrant C97. Prepare landing parties for planetary search. This message your authorization to investigate any planet with civilization at level 10 or below. Contact with civilizations higher than level 10 forbidden. Space intelligence agents will be furnished each ship to handle high-civilization planets. Acknowledge. Zan First Admiral.

The last week of the season opened with the Pirates in first place, two games ahead of the Dodgers. A provident schedule put the Dodgers and Pirates in a three-game series. The league hastily erected more stands, and with twenty-two thousand howling tourists in attendance and half of Earth's population watching on TV, White and Anderson put together no-hit games and the Pirate batters demolished the Dodger pitching staff. The Pirates took all three games.

Pops felt enormously tired and relieved that it was finished. He had won his pennant and he didn't see how he could lose the World Series. But he had never felt so old.

President Wilks threw another champagne party, and the sportswriters backed Pops into a corner and fired questions.

"How about that retirement, Pops? Still going through with it?"

"I've gone through with it."

"Is it true that Dipsey Marlow will take your place?"

"That's up to the front office. They ain't asked my opinion."

"What if they did ask your opinion?"

"I'd faint."

"Who'll start the series? Anderson or White?"

"I'll flip a coin," Pops said. "It don't matter. Either of them could pitch all thirteen games and not feel it."

"Does that mean you'll go all the way with just Anderson and White?"

"I'll use four starters, like I have most of the season."

"Going to give the Yankees a sporting chance, eh?"

"No comment," Pops said.

President Wilks and League President Rysdale rescued him from the reporters and took him to Rysdale's private office.

"We have a proposal from the American League," Rysdale said. "We'd like to know what you think of it and what you think the players would think of it. They want to split up the Series and play part of the games here and part of them in Arizona. They think it would stir up more local interest."

"I wouldn't like it," Pops said. "What's wrong with the way it is now? Here one year, there the next year, it's fair to both sides. What do they want to do—travel back and forth between games?"

"We'd start out with four games here, and then play five in Arizona and the last four back here. Next year we'd start out with four in Arizona. It used to be done that way years ago."

"One ballpark is just like another," Pops said. "Why travel back and forth?"

"They think we would draw more tourists that way. As far as we're concerned, we're drawing capacity crowds now. It might make a difference in Arizona, because there are fewer population centers there."

"They suggested it because it's in California this year," Pops said. "Next year they'd want to change back."

"That's a thought," Rysdale said. "I'll tell them it's too late to make the change this year, but we might consider it for next year. That'll give us time to figure all the angles."

"For all I care, you can play in Brazil next year," Pops told him.

In the hallway, Pops encountered half a dozen of his players crowding around infielder Jones. "What's up?" he asked Dipsey Marlow.

"Just some horsing around. They were practicing high jumps, and Jones cleared three meters."

"So?"

"That's a world record by almost half a meter. I looked it up."

To Jard Killil, Minister of Juvenile Affairs. Space ship presumed that of JRC escapees found in jungle unsurveyed. Quadrant C97 planet has type 17D civilization. Intelligence agents call situation critical. Am taking no action pending receipt further instructions. Requesting Ministry take charge and assume responsibility. Zan First Admiral.

Pops retired early the night before the Series opened. He ordered his players to do the same. Marge was out somewhere. Pops hadn't gone to sleep, but he was relaxing comfortably when she came in an hour later.

She marched straight through the house and into his bedroom. "Those ballplayers of yours—the funny-looking ones—they were at the bowling alley."

Pops took a deep breath. "They were?"

"They'd been drinking!"

Pops sat up and reached for his shoes. "You don't say."

"And they were bowling, only—they weren't bowling. They'd pretend to throw the ball but they wouldn't throw it, and the pins would fall down any way. The manager was mad."

"No doubt," Pops said, pulling on his trousers.

"They wouldn't tell anyone how they did it, but every time they waved the ball all the pins would fall down. They'd been drinking."

"Maybe that's how they did it," Pops said, slipping into his shirt.

"How?"

"By drinking."

He headed for the bowling alley at a dead run. The place was crowded with players from other teams, American and National League, and quite a few sportswriters were around. The writers headed for Pops, and he shoved them aside and found the manager. "Who was it?" he demanded.

"Those four squares of yours. Jones, Smith, Anderson, White."

"Zilo?"

"No. Zilo wasn't here."

"Did they make trouble?"

"Not the way you mean. They didn't get rough, though I had a time getting them away from the alleys. They left maybe ten minutes ago."

"Thanks," Pops said.

"When you find them, ask them how they pulled that gag with the pins. They were too drunk to tell me."

"I got some other things to ask them," Pops said.

He pushed his way through the crowd to a phone booth and called Ed Schwartz.

"I'll take care of it," Ed said. "Don't you worry about a thing."

"Sure. I won't worry about a thing."

"They may be back at their rooms by now, but we won't take any chances. I'll handle it."

"I'll meet you there," Pops said.

He slipped out a side door and headed for Bachelor's Paradise, the house where the unmarried Pirates lived with a couple of solicitous houseboys to look after them. All the players were in bed—except Smith, Jones, Anderson, White, and Zilo. The others knew nothing about them except that Zilo had been concerned about his friends and gone looking for them.

"You go home," Ed said. "I'll find them."

Pops paced grimly back and forth, taking an occasional kick at the furniture. "You find them," he said, "and I'll fine them."

He went home to bed, but he did not sleep. Twice during the night he called Ed Schwartz, and Ed was out. Pops finally reached him at breakfasttime, and Ed said, trying to be cheerful, "No news is supposed to be good news, and that's what I have. No news. I couldn't find a trace of them."

The reporters had picked up the story, and their headlines mocked Pops over his coffee. PIRATE STARS MISSING!

Ed Schwartz had notified both President Wilks and President Rysdale, and the league president had called in the FBI. By ten o'clock, police in every city in the country and a number of cities in other countries were looking for the missing Pirates, but they remained missing.

When Pops reached the field for a late-morning workout, there still was no word. He banned newsmen from the field and dressing room, told Lefty

Effinger he might have to start, and went around trying to cheer up his play-ers. The players remembered only too vividly their fourteen-game losing streak at the beginning of the season and the collapse that followed Zilo's departure. Gloom hung so thickly in the dugout that Pops wished he could think of a market for it. He could have bottled and sold it.

An hour before game time, Pops was called to the telephone. It was Ed Schwartz, calling from L.A. "I found them," he said. "They're on their way back. They'll be there in plenty of time."

"Good," Pops said.

"Bad. They're still pretty high—all except Zilo. I don't know if you can use them, but that's your problem."

Pops slammed down the phone.

"Did they find 'em?" Dipsey Marlow asked.

"Found 'em dead drunk."

Marlow rubbed his hands together. "Just let me at 'em. Ten minutes, that's all I ask. I'll have 'em dead sober."

"I dunno," Pops said. "These guys may not react the way you'd expect."

The delinquent players were delivered with time to spare, and Marlow went to work enthusiastically. He started by shoving them into a cold shower, fully dressed. Zilo stood looking on anxiously

"I'm sorry," he said to Pops. "I'd have stopped them, but they went off without me. And they never had any of that alcohol before and they didn't know what it would do to them."

"That's all right," Pops said. "It wasn't your fault."

Zilo had tears in his eyes. "Do you think they can play?"

"Leave 'em to me," Marlow said. "I'm just getting started." But when he emerged later, he looked both confused and frustrated. "I just don't know," he said. "They tell me they're all right, and they look all right, but I think they're still drunk."

"Can they play?" Pops demanded.

"They can walk a straight line. I won't say how long a straight line. I sup-pose you got nothing to lose by playing them."

"There ain't much else I can do," Pops said. "I could start Effinger, but what would I use for infielders?"

• • •

Even Pops, who had seen every World Series for forty-five years as player, manager, or spectator, had to admit that the winter classic had its own unique flavor of excitement. He felt a thrill and a clutching emptiness in his stomach as he moved to the top step of the dugout and looked out across the sunlit field. Along both foul lines, the temporary stands were jammed with tourists. Beyond them, areas were roped off for standees, and the last tickets for standing room had been sold hours before. There was no space left of any kind.

Ed Schwartz stood at Pops's elbow looking at the crowd. "What is it that's different about a submarine sandwich when you buy it at the ballpark?" he asked.

"Ptomaine," Pops growled.

Clutching his lineup card, he strode toward home plate to meet the umpires and Yankee manager Bert Basom.

Basom grinned maliciously. "Your men well rested? I hear they keep late hours."

"They're rested well enough," Pops said.

A few minutes later, with the National Anthem played and the flag raised, Pops watched critically as Anderson took his last warmup pitches. He threw lazily, as he always did, and if he was feeling any aftereffects it wasn't evident to Pops.

But Anderson got off to a shaky start. The Yankees' leadoff man clouted a tremendous drive to left, but Zilo made one of his sensational, lumbering catches. The second batter drove one through the box. Jones started after it, got his feet tangled, and fell headlong. Smith flashed over with unbelievable speed, gloved the ball, and threw to first—too late. Anderson settled down, then, and struck out the next two batters.

Zilo opened the Pirates' half of the first with one of his lucky hits, and Smith followed him with a lazy fly ball that cleared the fence. The Pirates led, 2 to 0.

The first pitch to Jones was a called strike. Jones whirled on the umpire, his large face livid with rage. His voice carried over the noise of the crowd. "You wouldn't know a strike zone if I measured it out for you!"

Pops started for home plate, and Jones saw him coming and meekly took his place in the box. Pops called time and went over to talk to Dipsey Marlow.

"Darned if I don't think he's still tight. Maybe I should lift him."

"Let him bat," Dipsey said. "Maybe he'll connect."

The pitcher wasted one and followed it with a curve that cut the outside corner. "Strike two!" the umpire called.

Jones's outraged bellow rattled the center-field fence. "What?" he shrieked. He stepped around the catcher and stood towering over the umpire. "Where's the strike zone? Where was the pitch?"

The umpire gestured impatiently to show where the ball had crossed the plate. Pops started out of the dugout again. The umpire said brusquely, "Play ball!"

Still fuming, Jones moved back to the batter's box. His high-pitched voice carried clearly. "You don't even know where the strike zone is!"

The pitcher wound up again, and as the ball sped plateward Jones suddenly leaped into the air—and stayed there. He hovered six feet above the ground. The ball crossed the plate far below his dangling legs, was missed completely by the startled catcher, and bounced to the screen.

The umpire did not call the pitch. He took two steps forward and stood looking up at Jones. The crowd came to its feet, and players from both teams edged from their dugouts. A sudden, paralyzed hush gripped the field.

"Come down here!" the umpire called angrily.

"What'd you call that pitch? Strike, I suppose. Over the plate between my knees and armpits, I suppose."

"Come down here!"

"You can't make me."

"Come down here!"

"You show me where it says in the rules that I have to bat with both feet on the ground!"

The umpire moved down the third-base line and summoned his colleagues for a conference. Pops walked out to home plate, and Zilo followed him.

"Jones," Zilo said pleadingly.

"Go to hell," Jones snarled. "I know I'm right. I'm still in the batter's box."

"Please," Zilo pleaded. "You'll spoil everything. You've already spoiled everything."

"So what? It's time we showed them how this game should be played."

"I'm taking you out, Jones," Pops said. "I'm putting in a pinch-hitter. Get back to the dugout."

Jones shot up another four feet. "You can't make me."

The umpire returned. "I'm putting you out of the game," he said. "Leave the field immediately."

"I've already left the field."

Pops, Zilo, and the umpire stood glaring up at Jones, who glared down at them. Into that impasse came Smith, who walked slowly to home plate, soared over the heads of those on the ground, and clouted Jones on the jaw. Jones descended heavily. Smith landed nearby, calmly drying his hands on his trousers.

Effective as his performance was, nobody noticed it. All eyes were on the sky, where a glistening tower of metal was dropping slowly toward the outfield. It came ponderously to rest on the outfield grass while the outfielders fled in panic. The crowd remained silent.

A port opened in the tower's side, and a landing ramp came down. The solitary figure that emerged did not use it. He stepped out into midair and drifted slowly toward the congregation at home plate. There he landed, a tremendous figure, square like Zilo and his friends but a startling nine feet tall and trimly uniformed in a lustrous brown with ribbons and braid in abundance.

Zilo, Jones, and Smith stood with downcast eyes while the others stared. Anderson and White moved from the dugout and walked forward haltingly. The stranger spoke one crisp sentence that no one understood—except Zilo, Jones, Smith, Anderson, and White.

Smith and Jones lifted slowly and floated out to the ship, where they disappeared through the port. Anderson and White turned obediently and trudged to the outfield to mount the ramp. Only Zilo lingered.

A few policemen moved nervously from the stands and surrounded the ship. The hush continued as the tourists stared and half of Earth's population watched on TV.

Zilo turned to face Pops. Tears streaked his face. "I'm sorry, Pops," he said. "I hoped we could finish it off for you. I really wanted to win this World Series. But I'm afraid we've got to go."

"Go where?" Pops asked.

"Where we came from. It's another world."

"I see. Then—then that's how come you guys played so well."

Zilo blubbered miserably, trying to wipe his eyes. His good-natured, freckled face looked tormented. "The others did," he sobbed. "I'm only a Class F telekinetic myself, and that isn't much where I come from. I did the best I could, but it was a terrible strain keeping the balls I hit away from the fielders and stopping balls from going over the fence and holding balls up until I could catch them. When I hurt my ankle I tried to help out from the bench, and it worked for a while. Sometimes I could even control the ball enough to spoil a pitcher's control, but usually when the ball was thrown fast or hit hard I couldn't do anything with it unless I was in the outfield and it had a long way to go. So I went home where I could get my ankle fixed, and when I came back I brought the others. They're really good—all of them Class A. Anderson and White—those are just names I had them use—they could control the ball so well they made it look like they were pitching. And no matter how hard the ball was hit, they could control it, even when they were sitting on the bench."

Pops scratched his head and said dazedly, "Made it look like they were pitching?"

"They just pretended to throw, and then they controlled the ball—well, with their minds. Any good telekinetic could do it. They could have pitched just as well sitting on the bench as they did on the pitcher's mound, and they could help out when one of our other pitchers was pitching. And Smith and Jones are levitators. They could cover the ground real fast and go up as high as they wanted to. I had a terrible time keeping them from going too high and spoiling everything. I was going to bring a telepath, too, to steal signs and things, but those four were the only ones who'd come. But we did pretty good anyway. When we hit the ball, Anderson and White could make it go anywhere they wanted, and they could control the balls the other team hit, and nothing could get past Smith and Jones unless we wanted it to. We could have won every game, but the papers said we were spoiling baseball, so we talked it over and decided to lose part of the time. We did the best we could. We won the pennant, and I hoped we could win this World Series, but they had to go and drink some of that alcohol, and I guess Jones would have spoiled every thing even if we hadn't been caught."

The stranger spoke another crisp sentence, and Zilo wiped the tears from his face and shook Pops's hand. "Good-bye, Pops," he said. "Thanks for everything. It was lots of fun. I really like this baseball."

He walked slowly out to the ship, passing the police without a glance, and climbed the ramp.

Reporters were edging out onto the field, and the stranger waved them back and spoke English in a booming voice. "You shall have a complete explanation at the proper time. It is now my most unpleasant duty to call upon your nation's President to deliver the apologies of my government. Muko Zilo says he did the best he could. He did entirely too much."

He floated back to the ship. The ramp lifted, and the police scattered as the ship swished upward. The umpire-in-chief shrugged his shoulders and gestured with his mask. "Play ball!"

Pops beckoned to a pinch hitter, got a pitcher warming up to replace Anderson, and strode back to the dugout. "They been calling me a genius," he muttered to himself. "Manager of the year, they been calling me. And how could I lose?"

A sportswriter leaned down from the stands. "How about a statement, Pops?"

Pops spoke firmly. "You can say that the best decision I made this year was to resign."

An official statement was handed out in Washington before the game was over. That the Yankees won the game, 23 to 2, was irrelevant. By that time, even the players had lost interest.

Priority Rating: Routine
From: Jard Killil, Minister of Juvenile Affairs
To: Milz Woon, Minister of Justice
Subject: Escapees from the Juvenile Rehabilitation Center, Philoy, Raff III, Sector 1311.

A full report on the activity of these escapees no doubt has reached your desk. The consequences of their offense are so serious they have not yet been fully evaluated. Not only have these escapees forced us into premature contact with a Type 17D civilization for which neither we nor they were prepared, but our best estimate is that the escapees have destroyed a notable cultural institution of that civilization. I believe that their ages should not be used to mitigate their punishment. They are juveniles, but they nevertheless are old enough to know right from wrong, and their only motive seems to be that they were enjoying themselves. I favor a maximum penalty.

Baseball, as students of the game never tired of pointing out, was essentially a game of records and statistics. The records were there for all to see—incredible records, with Jones and Smith tied with 272 home runs and batting above .500, with Anderson and White each hurling two dozen no-hit games, and with the strikeouts, and the extra base hits, and the double plays, and the games won, and the total bases, and the runs batted in, and the multitudinous individual and team records that the Pirates had marked up during the season. The record book was permanently maimed.

Who had done this? Four kids, four rather naughty kids, who—according to the strange man from outer space—were not especially bright. And these four kids had entered into a game requiring the ultimate in skill and intelligence and training and practice, entered into it without ever playing it before, and made the best adult ballplayers the planet Earth could produce look like a bunch of inept Little Leaguers.

The records could be thrown out, but they could not be forgotten. And it could not be forgotten that the four kids had made those records when they weren't half trying—because they didn't want to make Earth's ballplayers look too bad. No one cared to consider what would have happened had the people from outer space sent a team made up of intelligent adults.

The Yankees took the World Series in seven straight games, and few people cared. The stands were empty, and so sparse was the TV audience that the Series ended as a financial catastrophe. A committee met to decide what to do about the aliens' records and reached no decision. Again, no one cared.

The baseball establishment, fussing futilely with long-range plans to correct the damage, suddenly realized that the awards for the Most Valuable Players and Managers of the Year and the various individual championships had not been made. The oversight was not protested. People had other things on their minds.

And when a dozen TV comedy teams simultaneously resurrected an ancient, half-legendary, half-forgotten comedy sketch, they got no laughs whatsoever. The sketch was called "Who's on First?"

Death of a
Right Fielder
(1990)

Stuart Dybek

Stuart Dybek grew up in Chicago and teaches at Western Michigan University. He is the author of two books of poetry, *Brass Knuckles* (1979) and *Streets in Their Own Ink* (2004), and three short-story collections: *Childhood and Other Neighborhoods* (1980), *The Coast of Chicago* (1990), and *I Sailed with Magellan* (2003). "Death of a Right Fielder" was published in *Harper's* magazine and is included in *The Coast of Chicago*. His story is reminiscent of A. E. Houseman's poem "To an Athlete Dying Young."

After too many balls went out and never came back, we went out to check. It was a long walk—he always played deep. Finally we saw him; from a distance he resembled the towel we sometimes threw down for second base.

It was hard to tell how long he'd been lying there, sprawled on his face. Had he been playing infield, his presence, or lack of it, would of course have been noticed immediately. The infield demands communication—the constant, reassuring chatter of team play. But he was remote, clearly an outfielder. The infield is for wisecrackers, pepper pots, gum-poppers; the outfield is for loners, onlookers, brooders who would rather study clover and swat gnats than holler. People could pretty much be divided between infielders and outfielders. Not that one always has a choice. He didn't necessarily choose right field so much as accept it.

There were several theories as to what killed him. From the start, the most popular was that he'd been shot. Perhaps from a passing car, possibly by that gang calling themselves the Jokers, who played sixteen-inch softball in the center of the housing project on the concrete diamond with painted bases, or by the Latin Lords, who didn't play sports, period. Or maybe some pervert with a telescopic sight, shooting from a bedroom window, or a mad sniper from a water tower, or a terrorist with a silencer from the expressway overpass, or maybe it was an accident, a stray slug from a robbery, or shoot-out, or assassination attempt miles away.

No matter who pulled the trigger, it seemed more plausible to ascribe his death to a bullet than to natural causes like, say, a heart attack. Young deaths are never natural; they're all violent. Not that kids don't die of heart attacks. But he never seemed the type. Sure, he was quiet, but not the quiet of someone always listening for the heart murmur his parents repeatedly warned him about since he was old enough to play. Nor could it have been leukemia. He wasn't a talented enough athlete to die of that. He'd have been playing center, not right, if leukemia was going to get him.

The shooting theory was better, even though there wasn't a mark on him. Couldn't it have been, as some argued, a high-powered bullet traveling with such velocity that its hole fused behind it? Still, not everyone was satisfied. Other theories were formulated, rumors became legends over the years: He'd had an allergic reaction to a bee sting; been struck by a single bolt of lightning from a freak, instantaneous electrical storm; ingested too strong a dose of insecticide from the grass blades he chewed; or sonic waves, radiation, pollution, etc. And a few of us like to think it was simply that, chasing a sinking liner, diving to make a shoestring catch, he broke his neck.

There was a ball in the webbing of his mitt when we turned him over. His mitt had been pinned under his body and was coated with an almost luminescent gray film. The same gray was on his black high-top gym shoes, as if he'd been running through lime, and it was on the bill of his baseball cap—the blue felt one with the red C that he always denied stood for the Chicago Cubs. He may have been a loner, but he didn't want to be identified with a loser. He lacked the sense of humor for that, lacked the perverse pride that sticking with a loser season after season breeds, and the love. He was just an ordinary guy, .250 at the plate, and we stood above him not knowing what to do next. By then the guys from the other outfield positions had trotted over. Someone, the shortstop probably, suggested team prayer. So we all just stood there, silently bowing our heads, pretending to pray while the shadows moved darkly across the outfield grass. After a while the entire diamond was swallowed and the field lights came on.

In the bluish squint of those lights, he didn't look like someone we'd once known—nothing looked quite right—and we hurriedly scratched a shallow grave, covered him over, and stamped it down as much as possible so that the next right fielder, whoever he'd be, wouldn't trip. It could be just such a seemingly trivial stumble that would ruin a great career before it had begun, or hamper it years later the way Mantle's was hampered by bum knees. One can never be sure the kid beside you isn't another Roberto Clemente; and who can ever know how many potential Great Ones have gone down in the obscurity of their neighborhoods? And so, in the catcher's phrase, we "buried the grave" rather than contribute to any further tragedy. In all likelihood, the next right fielder, whoever he'd be, would be clumsy too, and if there was a mound to trip over he'd find it and break his neck, and soon right field would get the reputation as haunted, a kind of sandlot Bermuda Triangle, inhabited by phantoms calling for ghostly fly balls, where no one but the most desperate outcasts, already on the verge of suicide, would be willing to play.

Still, despite our efforts, we couldn't totally disguise it. A fresh grave is stubborn. Its outline remained visible—a scuffed bald spot that might have been mistaken for an aberrant pitcher's mound except for the bat jammed in the earth with the mitt and blue cap hooked over the handle. Perhaps we didn't want to make it disappear completely—a part of us was resting there. Perhaps we wanted the new right fielder, whoever he'd be, to notice and wonder about who played there before him, realizing he was not the only link between past and future that mattered.

As for us, we walked back, but by then it was too late—getting on to supper, getting on to the end of summer vacation, time for other things, college, careers, settling down and raising a family. Past thirty-five the talk starts about being over the hill, about a graying Phil Niekro in his forties still fanning them with the knuckler as if it's some kind of miracle, beating the odds. And maybe the talk is right. One remembers Willie Mays, forty-two years old and a Met, dropping that can-of-corn fly in the '73 Series, all that grace stripped away and with it the conviction, leaving a man confused and apologetic about the boy in him. It's sad to admit it ends so soon, but everyone knows those are the lucky ones. Most guys are washed up by seventeen.

The Umpire Was a Rookie (1956)

Arnold Hano

Arnold Hano's "The Umpire Was a Rookie" comes from the *Saturday Evening Post*. Besides his short stories, Hano is well-known for his sports biographies, including *Roberto Clemente: Batting King* (1973), *Kareem! Basketball Great* (1975), and *Muhammad Ali: The Champion* (1977). This story is about an umpire's first game in the big leagues, and what a hectic day it is.

His name was Bill Needy, a man of up-and-down lines and high shoulders, not broad and tapering like the ballplayers who had trudged up the same iron stairway. So the fans clustered below did not ask him for autographs, even though he carried the same sort of black bag in his right hand.

He heard a hoarse voice say, "Must be a new trainer or somethin'," and then he was out of the chilly mid-April sunshine, moving quickly through the white-tile corridor to the door marked UMPIRE'S DRESSING ROOM.

The three other men were already in their dark uniforms, and their eyes swung to him as he threw his bag onto a long wooden bench and began swiftly to undress.

The biggest of the three, a red-faced, white-haired man with a jaw that unhinged like a swinging lantern, put down the ball-and-strike indicator he was playing with, and walked over.

Needy knew him, of course. He was McQuinn, the senior umpire in the league. McQuinn, whom he had watched on his living-room screen during last year's World Series, a man with a bellowing voice and a quietly domineering manner.

"You Needy?" McQuinn said, and Needy was amused at how soft-spoken McQuinn really was, off the diamond.

Needy stood up. He was shirtless now, white-skinned compared with the others, thin and bony-chested. He sensed the difference between himself and them, and he hoped that it went no further than the tans they had acquired during spring training down South.

"Yes," he said, "I'm Needy." He was annoyed at the squeak in his voice. "You're Mr. McQuinn."

McQuinn laughed, and Needy heard the bellow. "You hear that? Mr. McQuinn. I hope you two bums learn something from that."

The tallest one, a turkey-necked, red-headed man, walked over, and even in those three steps, Needy saw the boy from the plow who had become one of the finest pitchers the league had seen in the last quarter century. He drawled, "I'm Carlson," and Needy wanted to say, "Yes, I've seen you pitch." Carlson had been with the Cubs for fourteen years until his fastball deserted him. Five years ago he had returned to the major leagues as an umpire.

But Needy couldn't say that, because he had never seen Carlson pitch. He had never, in fact, been inside a major-league park before this day.

He nodded and took the tall man's hand and felt all the pressure that was at the same time warm and crushing.

The third man, short and thick through the waist, bowlegged and bald, waddled over to Needy. "If you mister me," he said, "I'll fall down dead. All I ever hear is insults. I'm Jankowicz."

"Needy," he said again, clearing his throat, and he stood there, wondering whether he would ever match up to them or even come close.

They eyed him with frank curiosity. He was the new man in the league, called up just yesterday to replace Jake Mandell, the umpire who had broken his leg getting off a plane at Idlewild, flying in from an exhibition in Cleveland. The doctors said Mandell would be staring up at the ceiling for nearly two months.

Wiley, the league president, had wired the three top minor-league heads for their recommendations. They all had different choices, but Needy's league president had called the commissioner of all baseball on his private phone and talked for a half hour. The commissioner spoke to Wiley. Wiley picked Needy.

So the three other umpires stood a few yards off and watched Needy. And Needy felt the perspiration trickle down his ribs.

McQuinn broke the silence finally. He said, "I suppose you've boned up on the ground rules?"

Needy nodded. "Your league has pretty much the same rules we had back in the Association. That makes it easier."

McQuinn nodded his great head. "It does," he said, "but this is a tough park."

Needy frowned. He had shown his new league badge to the park attendant earlier that day and walked all over Robin Field, studying the angles and the shadows, the high fence in right field where balls sometimes stuck in the chicken wire, the sharp corner in left where the play got out of sight unless the third-base umpire was swift in getting back. Needy was not to umpire at third, and he guessed that was why. He was to be at second base, where the plays were often tough and dusty and bruising, but where they fell into a pattern: double play, hit-and-run, steal, force-out, pick-off.

In a way, Needy was glad he was going to be at second. It might force a quick showdown. Tad Roush was the Robin manager. He also was the Robin shortstop. Needy knew Roush firsthand. The two had tangled in the Association five years ago.

Then Carlson broke in. "Not the playing field, son," he said, and Needy smiled thinly. They must have been within five years of the same age. "He means the park. The fans."

And Needy understood. The fans were different here, so Needy had heard, men and women who had become a legend, just as their borough on the wrong side of the muddy river had become a legend. They were fans who came early and started howling long before the first pitch—and Needy could hear them even now through the thick white-tile walls—fifty-two thousand of them, the most vociferous, partisan fans in the world.

Jankowicz said, "They're tough out here, all right." He shook his head and grinned. "I've had my share of beer in my day, but I hate to have it thrown at me."

"With soft tomatoes as a side dish," McQuinn added.

"I've been through it," Needy said quietly.

"Good," McQuinn said. "When you've been through it, you either go one way or the other. You must have gone the right way, boy, or you wouldn't be here today. They don't take chickens or lilies in this league. Now, the other league—" He snorted in contempt.

The other two laughed. Needy knew how each big league thought it was the only league. But Needy wasn't laughing. McQuinn didn't know the real trouble. Needy had seen fans litter the field with vile epithets and pulpy fruit. It had never bothered him much. The real trouble was himself and Roush. McQuinn didn't know about that. Needy doubted that anybody knew about it or remembered. Maybe Roush hadn't remembered. After all, it was an unimportant game, five years back, and Roush had gone a long way since then.

A bell rang softly in the dressing room and the three other men seemed to stiffen a bit, their smiles fading. "Come on," McQuinn said, taking Needy's arm; "let's go meet them." And the four umpires moved swiftly through the door and onto the gravel path, through the exit door next to the Robins' dugout.

They stepped to the plate while the fans called down their stereotyped insults, and Needy grinned. They weren't so tough. And then a raucous voice from the stands yelled, "All right, McQuinn, don't call 'em like you did when the Phils were in last time, you blind bum!" And a snicker filtered from the stands.

Needy stiffened. Lord, he thought, they remembered from one season to the next. They were riding McQuinn for a call he'd made no more recently than last September, at least seven months ago.

Needy stood at the plate, watching the opposing pitchers wheel in their last practice throws, while the ground crew motored its rollers over the moist, sweet-smelling infield dirt, and from the stands came a rising murmur as the new season rushed up.

And Roush came out of the Robin dugout, a prancing man with toed-in steps, head down, a sheet of paper in his hand. The fans saw him and began to roar, and Roush waved his free hand without looking up. From the Titan dugout came Chub Fowler, the lineup in his hand, too, and Needy heard Roush shoot a word at Fowler. The Titan manager's face flushed hot and angry. Roush, Needy knew then, hadn't changed.

Needy moved away from the cluster at the plate so that Roush would have to see him. He wanted that part over quickly. But Roush, head down, pushed by as though he knew he had the center of the stage. He was a show-boat, Needy knew, and then, in his grudging heart, he added, *but a hell of a ballplayer.*

Roush stopped and nodded curtly to McQuinn and Carlson and Jankow-icz. "Good afternoon, you blind bats," he said softly. Then he turned to Needy. He put his hands on his hips and said, "Hello, choke-up."

Needy felt his throat tighten, and he knew the flush was rising to his temples.

McQuinn pushed past Jankowicz, coming chest to chest with Roush. "Cut it," he said quietly, but there was a bristling quality to his voice. "Cut it, I say. I won't stand for your language."

Roush didn't budge a half inch. His voice was as low as McQuinn's, but rasping and hard. "Listen," he said, "when you bums yell play ball, I'll watch my tongue. But right now you're just guests in this house, and my boss owns this house. Until that first pitch comes in, this game is in the hands of the club owners. Not you." He whirled on Needy again, and the venom lay in his throat. "Choke-up Needy, the yellowest umpire ever to call 'em wrong. Too chicken to call 'em as he sees 'em." Then he spun away and stalked off.

McQuinn roared this time. "Roush! Come here." And Roush turned, wide-eyed. "The ground rules," McQuinn said.

Roush waved his hands. "Whatever you say, Mac. We won't need any rules today." And he minced to the dugout.

McQuinn turned to Chub Fowler. He said, "I'm sorry, Chub. The smiling little skipper is off to his usual start."

Fowler growled and handed McQuinn his lineup. "Maybe we'll run some of it off," he said, and he ambled to the visiting dugout.

Needy watched Fowler, and then he looked at McQuinn, and he froze. The big umpire was staring at him with icy blue eyes. "You're a major-league umpire, Needy," he said. "Act like one."

Needy nodded and tried to say something, but his voice failed him, and then McQuinn waved the three of them to their bases before he bent to the plate, whisk broom in his gnarled hand.

The field was empty except for the four umpires, and then the Robins poured from the dugout, Roush leading them, and the fifty-two thousand fans got up and roared. They stayed standing as the PA system crackled and the announcer said, "Ladies and gentlemen, our national anthem."

But Needy barely heard it. He turned to center field to watch the flag go up into the blue sky, and he remembered. . . .

It hadn't been an important game, though Needy knew now how impor-tant it really was. And, more than that, how important they all are, the 10–2 games between a first-place team and a cellar team, and a 2–1 affair between two clubs battling for the lead. To an umpire, they're all the same. Needy knew it now.

It was the end of September, and Roush's club had already clinched the Association flag. They were playing at home, three days before the season would end, most of the regulars resting, but Roush still in there. Roush's team was losing 6–1, though Roush had started one double play and pivoted like a flying ghost on two others, and now, in the bottom of the ninth, with two out, he had hit the ball to the center-field wall for a triple.

It was a hot day, Needy remembered, fearfully hot, and it had been a hot month, a hot summer. Needy was behind the plate, weighted down with mask and protector. Somebody had once said an umpire takes hell, but that the hours couldn't be beat. That was before night ball, Needy thought, and hot days like this.

So he leaned in behind the catcher, the ball-and-strike indicator telling him it was two out, one out away from the dressing room and a quick beer, and the pitcher missed twice with curve balls, as Roush pranced down the line from third base.

Nobody was watching very closely, most of the fans having gone home in the seventh inning when Roush's pitcher was hammered for four runs. Not that there had been many to begin with. Maybe twelve hundred, Needy thought. No more than five hundred still remained.

So, when Roush started down the line and seemed to stumble, Needy hoped he'd come in all the way, for he'd surely be out, and the game would be over. The pitcher hadn't started his motion, but Roush had had a bad start. Then the batter suddenly put his hand to his eyes and stepped out of the box. Four or five times that day, swirling spirals of dust had attacked home plate, and Needy had been forced to call "Time," each time a batter stepped out.

But somehow, as his hand went up and he started to say "Time," he saw Roush continue down the line, and he saw the pitcher quickly throw to the plate. The catcher took the toss, blocked off Roush and put the tag on the runner.

There was a feeble cheer from the stands, and five hundred people slowly began to walk across the field to the exit gates. Roush got up and looked at Needy. He jabbed the edge of his hand against his own throat. "You choke-up rat," he said, "why didn't you call time?"

Needy hadn't said anything, but he knew Roush was right. He had quit on his assignment. It wasn't important whether Roush stole home or not; it was only important that Needy call it as he saw it. And he had seen the batter step out before the pitcher went into action toward the plate. He knew it and Roush knew it, and maybe the batter knew it, but he hadn't seemed to care.

Roush cared. It was baseball, and baseball was life and blood to him. Needy knew he, too, should have cared. He should have called time even then, with the five hundred fans scattered all over the diamond, paper falling to the grass, the bags being ripped up by the ground-keepers. He should have waved his hands and roared until he had controlled them, and then resumed play.

But he hadn't. He had just walked past Roush, trying to reason that it hadn't mattered, that the ball game wouldn't have changed, that the team standings wouldn't have changed. He tried to forget. . . .

And standing here at second base in Robin Field, the flag flapping against the blue sky, he knew he had never forgotten it.

Nor had Roush. The ball came spinning out from behind the plate, and Roush had it, tossing it to his second baseman, and then turning to Needy.

"Choke-up," he whispered to the umpire. "Chicken minor-leaguer."

Needy knew he didn't have to take it. The game was still not in the umpires' hands, but he was a human being being abused. There wasn't much he could do. But he could answer Roush, fire a hot word at the shortstop to let him know he was alive and fighting back.

Instead he moved behind the bag and slightly to the left of second base, as the first Titan moved in and McQuinn bellowed, "Play ball!" And just as quickly, Roush seemed to forget all about Needy, close to the bag. He bent slightly, his body swaying, his arms hanging, knees slightly hinged, and Needy watched his mouth move and a flow of words waft to the pitcher's mound. The game began.

Needy had heard it said that a major-league baseball game is unlike any minor-league game, no matter the quality of play. Now he believed it. A cloak hung over the field, a shimmering wave of electricity that coursed through the action, crackled in the air with every pitch, rose and fell with hits and outs. And behind the cloak was the booming that whooshed from the stands, like a heavy hand or the ocean rolling in. It was lightning and thunder, Needy thought, the sizzling atmosphere on the diamond and the roaring from the stands.

The Titans scored first. In the fourth inning, the Titan batter, a man named Jewell who batted left-handed and choked up on his stick three inches, pulled a line drive down the first-base line past Rogers, the Robin first baseman, and into the corner where the Robin bull-pen crew sat beneath a sun canopy.

The Robin right fielder raced to the line and into foul territory, took the rolling ball with his gloved hand, whirled and threw into second base. It was a fine throw, but Jewell hooked to the center of the diamond and grabbed off the inside edge of the bag. Needy bent to the play, head through the low cloud of dust, and he spread-eagled his hands.

Instantly Roush was at him, feet stamping, voice raised in indignant clamor, but Needy stood firm and when Roush wouldn't quit, he turned his back and walked away. It was not a serious beef, Needy knew, because Roush knew as well as he that Jewell had beaten the throw. So Roush growled and kicked dirt and went back to his position, and Needy grinned. Roush had played it four-square, fighting a close call against his team, but watching his tongue. Maybe, Needy thought, the Robin manager was going to let bygones be bygones.

The next hitter was Thomas, another left-hander, and though the Robin pitcher threw on the outside, Thomas still dragged his bunt down the first-base line, moving Jewell to third.

And Mayo, the Titans' No. 4 hitter, the league's home-run king and stolen-base leader, hit to the edge of the center-field wall, where Earl Rider had just enough room to make the catch. Jewel sauntered home and the Titans led 1–0.

It stayed that way into the seventh, a 1–0 game that was taking longer to play than any 1–0 game Needy had ever seen. The pitchers violated the twenty-second rule on nearly every pitch, and Needy knew how foolish the rule was.

When Mayo came up, there was always a short conference, and even after it ended, the Robin pitcher would lean in for a full thirty seconds, his eyes boring a path to the plate, trying to find the groove past Mayo's lunging bat. And Earl Rider had the Titan pitcher in the same grip, the long look, the signals shaken off again and again, catcher Festrun calling time and insisting on a pitch while the fans muttered and buzzed and called down their timeless hue.

In the seventh, Roush came up with one out. He slashed two bats at the grass, talking as he minced forward, and then he threw one behind him, and dug himself in.

The Titan pitcher threw, a quick white blur, and Roush was flat on his back. The mutter from the stands grew thick and ugly. But Roush was up, wiping himself off, snarling an obscenity that McQuinn behind the plate pretended he didn't hear. And Roush drilled the next pitch past the Titan pitcher's left ear and into center field.

At first base, Roush pointed his finger at the pitcher, and the Titan came down from the mound two steps to hurl a word at the Robin manager. McQuinn then hustled forward, waving his arms. And time dragged, while the sun faded, dipping to the lip of the stands over first base, lengthening the shadows.

Roush led off from first and taunted the pitcher with three quick steps down the line, drew a throw, and then started his lead again. On the second pitch, he went.

Festrun came out of his crouch with the ball in his clenched fist and he threw, true and swiftly, to the second baseman covering the bag. Needy drifted over, eyes searching, and Roush came in, one leg high. The tag was made and Needy started to go up with his right hand, but then the ball came squirting out of the glove, rolling toward the shortstop. Needy broke off his call and dropped his hands down low, yelling, "Safe, safe!"

The second baseman rolled to his feet and called "Time!" and held up his dripping red wrist.

The Titan doctor came out and cleaned the dirt from the spike wound, and then started to lead the infielder away. But the Titan insisted he could play, and the doctor shrugged, slapped on a piece of plaster and walked away, shaking his head.

Then the second baseman turned to Needy and said, "He kicked me, you know."

Needy nodded. "I guess he did, son. Nothing I can do about it. Kick him back next time," and Roush laughed out loud.

It was part of the game Needy didn't like, but there was nothing anybody ever did to remedy it. It was the way the game was played. There were rules about interference and roughness, but the line could seldom be drawn. So the umpire ignored the contact and watched the bases.

Now Roush led away, and the Titan pitcher threw four times to big Rogers, wasting one, and Rogers swung and missed three times.

The Titan pitcher then took off his glove and wiped his hand with a towel that he directed from the dugout, when Earl Rider took his bent-over stance, waving a big brown bat. And on the first pitch, Needy heard the pitcher groan with the delivery. It was what Casey Stengel liked to call a dead fish, a fastball, down the pipe, waist high, thrown to Rider's strength.

The ball disappeared over the right-field wall, clearing it by about forty feet, and the Robins led, 2–1.

They stayed that way through the eighth, and Needy looked at his watch and saw that two and a half hours had gone by as they came into the ninth. The public-address announcer made his usual statement about fans not being allowed on the playing field until all players had reached the dugouts, and the fans made a derisive sound.

It was then Needy realized that the game was nearly over, that Roush was not riding him any more than he was the other umpires. Needy felt suddenly that the problem had somehow resolved itself. He gave a short little laugh, and Roush, twelve feet away, looked at him cold-eyed, his mouth mocking and twisted. Needy felt the afternoon chill, and he knew he was wrong. It wasn't resolved. It wouldn't be until he and Roush had tangled again.

The first man in the ninth was a pinch hitter for the Titan pitcher, a red-faced man with a plug of tobacco in his cheek and the grinning self-confidence of a man who believed no pitcher on earth could get him out. He was Joads, who couldn't catch fly balls and couldn't throw, so he didn't play regularly, but who hit close to .350 in his two hundred at bats each season.

The Robin pitcher tried to curve Joads, but the ball hung on the inside corner, and Joads stroked it off the wall, where the right fielder made a swift recovery, and Joads lumbered into first, the grin still splitting his wide red face. Then he lumbered off again, for a pinch runner, and Roush spoke sharply with his pitcher.

Finally Roush called his catcher, a man named Camps, to the hill and they talked until McQuinn pushed his way to the mound.

Needy heard the big umpire say, "What's it to be, Roush? You sticking with him or you calling in the reliefer?"

Roush said, "I dunno. That's a real tough one."

McQuinn flushed and towered over Roush. "Don't con me," he said. "Make up your mind. I won't stand for any stalling."

Roush said, "Who's stalling? I'm trying to think. Get your beef off me, and I'll be able to figure it out."

McQuinn said quietly, "I'll give you fifteen seconds, Roush."

Roush stared at the sky and squinted, and Needy could see the Robin's manager's lips moving. Needy tried to hide his grin. Roush was actually counting off the seconds.

Then he stopped and said, "I got it. It's the reliefer." He waved to the bull pen with his right hand, and the right-handed knuckle-ball thrower strolled in, carrying his jacket, and began to warm up.

Needy watched from behind second, marveling that Camps could catch such a thing as the reliefer threw. Every one was a knuckler, writhing in mid-air like a drunken butterfly. Then McQuinn held up his hand for the game to pick up where it had stopped, a Titan on first, nobody out, the ninth inning, and the Robins leading, 2–1.

The knuckler got Lark, the Titan lead-off hitter, to go for a chest-high floater, and the Titan hit it straight up in the air. The ball disappeared in Camps' mitt, and there was one out.

But Jewell, who hadn't been stopped all afternoon, singled to right field and the Titan runner fled past Needy into third.

The thunder was two-edged now, the Titan fans who had braved the river and crossed into enemy territory, and the Robins, upset and grumbling as the lead teetered.

Roush raised his hand and yelled "Time!" and turned to the bull pen. He wanted a left hander to pitch to Thomas.

The sun fell over the edge of the stands, and the field lay in shadow, but lightning still hovered over the players' heads. Needy felt himself waiting with the fans now, impartial as ever concerning the game's outcome, yet intensely interested.

He watched the left-hander, a stocky hurky-jerky man named Lombardo, pitch curve balls to Thomas, but they were breaking too much and too soon, and on six pitches the bases were loaded.

Again Roush stopped the game, and a third time he signaled to the bull pen. The hitter was Mayo, the big, fleet Titan who could do everything so well. And when time was in again, Needy saw that Roush had his team playing halfway. Roush wanted to cut off the tying run at the plate, but he wasn't all the way in. The double play could still be made, though Needy knew that Mayo was as fast a man getting down the line as anybody in baseball.

The new pitcher eyed the bases, Thomas coming off first. The other Titan runners drifted away, and Roush kept darting toward second, feinting Jewell back to the bag. Roush's mouth was still moving, the words flowing to the mound, and Needy felt them hang like drones in the air.

"Come on, boy," Roush was saying. "Come on, boy; nobody hits." Then the reliefer took a deep breath and threw hard to Mayo.

It was a fastball, Needy thought, on the inside, and Mayo started to lunge. The pitch broke. It had not been a fastball at all, but a curve, thrown hard and loose, fooling the big Titan.

But Mayo somehow got a piece of it, hitting it on a high bounce past the mound, headed for the hole between second base and Roush. Needy moved in toward the bag from behind, seeing Thomas hurtling down the line, Mayo bulleting his way toward first and Roush gliding over, surefooted, a swift ghost on the brown dirt.

The thought crossed Needy's mind that Thomas would be an easy force, once Roush came up with the ball, but the winging Mayo would be a different story. Then Needy banished the thought; his problem lay at second, not first.

Roush reached to his left with his gloved hand while on the dead run eight feet from second base, and then he plucked the ball out with his right hand, leveled his arm back and threw like a rifle to first, a split second before his foot hit second base, kicking dust high into the air.

It was then that Needy's ankle buckled under him and he fell, sprawling heavily while the picture of Roush making his throw before he touched second became frozen-fixed in his mind. Needy never knew that big Rogers, at first, stretched into the diamond while Mayo leaped for the bag. Nor did Needy hear the ball spank into the first baseman's glove, umpire Carlson booming, "He's out!" All Needy heard was the thunder pounding out from the stands as he rolled to his feet to make his call.

But nobody was watching him, the players fleeing to the dugouts, and fifty-two thousand people starting to pour onto the field. Even Roush was gone. Only Thomas was near, sitting on second base, staring up at Needy, openmouthed.

For Needy stood stock-still, arms spread-eagled, yelling, "Safe, safe, safe!" He knew why Thomas couldn't believe the call. Roush had him beaten by five full steps. But Roush had taken the chance that Needy wouldn't have the guts to make the insane call he was now making. Roush had thrown the ball before his foot touched second, and the force play had never been made.

Needy knew it, and he knew why it had happened. He'd have bet his life on it. Roush had seen what he had seen. The shortstop knew that Mayo, moving like a whippet down the first-base line, would beat the throw unless he got rid of the ball right away. The tying run was thundering homeward.

It was McQuinn who finally noticed Needy, still standing at second, arms held out and low, the time-honored sign of a man being called safe.

The big ump charged to second base and said, "What's the matter, man? Are you crazy?"

Needy looked at his chief. The park cops were in a tight cordon at the foul lines, keeping the fans from trampling the young infield grass, but they couldn't keep them from roaming all over the outfield. It was a swirling, still roaring throng, most of them happy, all of them knowing they had seen a fine game, and glad to be on their way home.

"I'm sorry, Mac, but the man is safe."

McQuinn looked at him peculiarly and said, "Roush touched the bag. I saw the dust rise up."

Needy shook his head stubbornly. He thought, *What am I getting into?* The field was strewn with debris. It was like that day five years ago, except a thousand times worse. He said, "He touched the bag after he got rid of the ball. Thomas is safe."

McQuinn started to rub his jaw and then he began to grin, and finally he started to laugh out loud, a bellowing laugh that brought tears to his eyes. "I swear," he said, "if you weren't standing here, I wouldn't believe it. Now what do we do?"

Needy said, "We get the game going again."

McQuinn turned and yelled, "Carl, Janko, come here! This crazy pup's starting a rhubarb and we'll have to back him up!" The two umpires raced to second and scratched their heads as McQuinn filled them in.

Thomas suddenly got up from his perch on second base and said, "Excuse me, but if I'm safe, is time still in?" He was ready to keep running.

McQuinn roared. "Hell no! I call time right now!"

Thomas began to yell to the near-empty Titan dugout. "Hey, I'm safe, I'm safe!"

Needy said, "And your club is leading three–two."

McQuinn howled, "Now, what the devil does that mean?"

Carlson grinned. "I get him, chief. He means the men on second and third. They both scored. As a matter of fact," he said, winking at McQuinn, "I noticed Jewell touch home plate in case you didn't. The lad's right. The Titans are ahead, three–two."

"And probably piling out of their uniforms this minute," Jankowicz said. "What happens now?"

Needy said, "You boys wouldn't want me to change my decision, would you? Because," he said, "I won't, you know."

A handful of Titans began to drift onto the field. The word began to spread through the filing throng and Needy heard the first ominous mutter.

Somebody said. "Whaddya mean, the game's not over? Sure it is."

"No," somebody else said, fifteen feet from second. "That new jerk of an umpire says Thomas ain't out. They ought to mobilize the bum."

McQuinn turned to Needy. "All right, bum, take it from here."

Needy said, "It's very simple. The rules don't cover it, but you're in charge. Make an announcement over the PA that the game isn't over, that you'll give everybody—fans and players—a half hour to get back in their seats and to their positions, and that the game will continue."

Carlson said, "We could have 'em play it off some other time."

Jankowicz grinned. "No," he said. "That's too easy. I like the lad's idea. . . . Go on, Mac, make the announcement."

"Not me," McQuinn said. "Don't pass the buck to me. Let the lad do it."

Jankowicz said, "Go to it, boy. I must say you've got guts. Are they going to love you here!"

Needy shook his head. He knew it didn't matter. Love him or hate him, it didn't matter. Respect him. That was all. He started to walk to the Robin dugout to ask where the PA mike was. It would have been very easy to make the out call, he knew. But he had never even thought of it.

And thirty minutes later, before a crowd gone blood-mad as it heaped abuse on Needy, Tad Roush led his ball club back onto the field.

The shortstop took his post, raised two fingers in the air and called, "Two out, men, two out! We'll get it back!"

Then Roush turned, before his pitcher threw, and said to Needy, "Welcome to the big league, you blind bat." He was grinning. Needy ignored him, to watch the ball game.

The Hector Quesadilla Story (1986)

T. Coraghessan Boyle

T. Coraghessan Boyle was born in 1948 in New York's Hudson Valley and now resides outside Santa Barbara, California. He is the founder and director of the University of Southern California's creative writing program. Boyle's fiction has appeared in *The New Yorker*, *Harper's*, the *Atlantic Monthly*, and *Playboy*. He has written thirteen novels, most recently *When the Killing's Done* (2011). "The Hector Quesadilla Story" appears in his book *Greasy Lake and Other Stories* (1986).

He was no Joltin' Joe, no sultan of Swat, no Iron Man. For one thing, his feet hurt. And God knows no legendary immortal ever suffered so prosaic a complaint. He had shinsplints too, and corns and ingrown toenails and hemorrhoids. Demons drove burning spikes into his tailbone each time he bent to loosen his shoelaces, his limbs were skewed so awkwardly his elbows and knees might have been transposed, and the once-proud knot of his *frijole*-fed belly had fallen like an avalanche. Worse: he was old. Old, old, old, the graybeard hobbling down the rough-hewn steps of the Senate building, the ancient mariner chewing on his whiskers and stumbling in his socks. Though they listed his birth date as 1942 in the program, there were those who knew better: it was way back in '54, during his rookie year for San Buitre, that he had taken Asunción to the altar, and even in those distant days, even in Mexico, twelve-year-olds didn't marry.

When he was younger—really young, nineteen, twenty, tearing up the Mexican League like a saint of the stick—his ears were so sensitive he could hear the soft rasping friction of the pitcher's fingers as he massaged the ball and dug in for a slider, fastball, or change-up. Now he could barely hear the umpire bawling the count in his ear. And his legs. How they ached, how they groaned and creaked and chattered, how they'd gone to fat! He ate too much, that was the problem. Ate prodigiously, ate mightily, ate as if there were a hidden thing inside him, a creature all of jaws with an infinite trailing ribbon of gut. *Huevos con chorizo* with beans, tortillas, *camarones* in red sauce, and a twelve-ounce steak for breakfast, the chicken in *mole* to steady him before afternoon games, a sea of beer to wash away the tension of the game and prepare his digestive machinery for the flaming *machaca*-and-pepper salad Asunción prepared for him in the blessed evenings of the home stand.

Five foot seven, one hundred eighty-nine and three-quarters pounds. Hector Hernán Jesus y María Quesadilla. Little Cheese, they called him. Cheese, Cheese, Cheesus, went up the cry as he stepped in to pinch-hit in some late inning crisis, Cheese, Cheese, Cheesus, building to a roar until Chavez Ravine resounded as if with the holy name of the Saviour Himself when he stroked one of the clean line-drive singles that were his signature or laid down a bunt that stuck like a finger in jelly. When he fanned, when the bat went loose in the fat brown hands and he went down on one knee for support, they hissed and called him *Viejo*.

One more season, he tells himself, though he hasn't played regularly for nearly ten years and can barely trot to first after drawing a walk. One more. He tells Ascunción too—One more, one more—as they sit in the gleaming kitchen of their house in Boyle Heights, he with his Carta Blanca, she with her mortar and pestle for grinding the golden petrified kernels of maize into flour for the tortillas he eats like peanuts. *Una más*, she mocks. What do you want, the Hall of Fame? Hang up your spikes, Hector.

He stares off into space, his mother's Indian features flattening his own as if the legend were true, as if she really had taken a spatula to him in the cradle, and then, dropping his thick lids as he takes a long slow swallow from the neck of the bottle, he says: Just the other day driving home from the park I saw a car on the freeway, a Mercedes with only two seats, a girl in it, her hair out back like a cloud, and you know what the license plate said? His eyes are open now, black as pitted olives. Do you? She doesn't. Cheese, he says. It said Cheese.

Then she reminds him that Hector Jr. will be twenty-nine next month and that Reina has four children of her own and another on the way. You're a grandfather, Hector—almost a great-grandfather if your son ever settled down. A moment slides by, filled with the light of the sad waning sun and the harsh Yucatano dialect of the radio announcer. *Hombres* on first and third, one down. *Abuelo*, she hisses, grinding stone against stone until it makes his teeth ache. Hang up your spikes, *abuelo*.

● ● ●

But he doesn't. He can't. He won't. He's no grandpa with hair the color of cigarette stains and a blanket over his knees, he's no toothless old gasser sunning himself in the park—he's a big leaguer, proud wearer of the Dodger blue, wielder of stick and glove. How can he get old? The grass is always green, the lights always shining, no clocks or periods or halves or quarters, no punch-in and punch-out: this is the game that never ends. When the heavy hitters have fanned and the pitchers' arms gone sore, when there's no joy in Mudville, taxes are killing everybody, and the Russians are raising hell in Guatemala, when the manager paces the dugout like an attack dog, mind racing, searching high and low for the canny veteran to go in and do single combat, there he'll be—always, always, eternal as a monument—Hector Quesadilla, utility infielder, with the .296 lifetime batting average and service with the Reds, Phils, Cubs, Royals, and L.A. Dodgers.

So he waits. Hangs on. Trots his aching legs round the outfield grass before the game, touches his toes ten agonizing times each morning, takes extra batting practice with the rookies and slumping millionaires. Sits. Watches. Massages his feet. Waits through the scourging road trips in the Midwest and along the East Coast, down to muggy Atlanta, across to stormy Wrigley and up to frigid Candlestick, his gut clenched round an indigestible cud of meatloaf and instant potatoes and wax beans, through the terrible night games with the alien lights in his eyes, waits at the end of the bench for a word from the manager, for a pat on the ass, a roar, a hiss, a chorus of cheers and catcalls, the marimba pulse of bat striking and the sweet looping arc of the clean base hit.

And then comes a day, late in the season, the homeboys battling for the pennant with the big-stick Braves and the sneaking Jints, when he wakes from honeyed dreams in his own bed that's like an old friend with the sheets that smell of starch and soap and flowers, and feels the pain stripped from his body as if at the touch of a healer's fingertips. Usually he dreams nothing, the night a blank, an erasure, and opens his eyes on the agonies of the martyr strapped to a bed of nails. Then he limps to the toilet, makes a poor discolored water, rinses the dead taste from his mouth, and staggers to the kitchen table where food, only food, can revive in him the interest in drawing another breath. He butters tortillas and folds them into his mouth, spoons up egg and melted jack cheese and *frijoles refritos* with the green *salsa*, lashes into his steak as if it were cut from the thigh of Kerensky, the Atlanta relief ace who'd twice that season caught him looking at a full-count fastball with men in scoring position. But not today. Today is different, a sainted day, a day on which sunshine sits in the windows like a gift of the Magi and the chatter of the starlings in the crapped-over palms across the street is a thing that approaches the divine music of the spheres. What can it be?

In the kitchen it hits him: *pozole* in a pot on the stove, *carnitas* in the saucepan, the table spread with sweetcakes, *buñuelos*, and the little marzipan *dulces* he could kill for. *Feliz cumpleaños*, Asunción pipes as he steps through the doorway. Her face is lit with the smile of her mother, her mother's mother, the line of gift givers descendant to the happy conquistadors and joyous Aztecs. A kiss, a *dulce*, and then a knock at the door and Reina, fat with life, throwing her arms around him while her children gobble up the table, the room, their grandfather, with eyes that swallow their faces. Happy birthday, Daddy, Reina says, and Franklin, her youngest, is handing him the gift.

And Hector Jr.?

But he doesn't have to fret about Hector Jr., his firstborn, the boy with these same great sad eyes who'd sat in the dugout in his Reds uniform when they lived in Cincy and worshipped the pudgy icon of his father until the parish priest had to straighten him out on his hagiography; Hector Jr., who studies English at USC and day and night writes his thesis on a poet his father has never heard of, because here he is, walking in the front door with his mother's smile and a store-wrapped gift—a book, of course. Then Reina's children line up to kiss the *abuelo*—they'll be sitting in the box seats this afternoon—and suddenly he knows so much: he will play today, he will hit, oh yes, can there be a doubt? He sees it already. Kerensky, the son of a whore. Extra innings.

Koerner or Manfredonia or Brooksie on third. The ball like an orange, a mango, a muskmelon, the clean swipe of the bat, the delirium of the crowd, and the gimpy *abuelo*, a big leaguer still, doffing his cap and taking a tour of the bases in a stately trot, Sultan for a day.

● ● ●

Could things ever be so simple?

In the bottom of the ninth, with the score tied at five and Reina's kids full of Coke, hotdogs, peanuts, and ice cream and getting restless, with Asunción clutching her rosary as if she were drowning and Hector Jr.'s nose stuck in some book, Dupuy taps him to hit for the pitcher with two down and Fast Freddie Phelan on second. The eighth man in the lineup, Spider Martinez from Muchas Vacas, D.R., has just whiffed on three straight pitches, and Corcoran, the Braves' left-handed relief man, is all of a sudden pouring it on. Throughout the stadium a hush has fallen over the crowd, the torpor of sup-pertime, the game poised at apogee. Shadows are lengthening in the outfield, swallows flitting across the face of the scoreboard; here a fan drops into his beer, there a big mama gathers up her purse, her knitting, her shopping bags and parasol and thinks of dinner. Hector sees it all. This is the moment of catharsis, the moment to take it out.

As Martinez slumps toward the dugout, Dupuy, a laconic, embittered man who keeps his suffering inside and drinks Gelusil like water, takes hold of Hector's arm. His eyes are red-rimmed and paunchy, doleful as a basset hound's. Bring the runner in, Champ, he rasps. First pitch fake a bunt, then hit away. Watch Booger at third. Uh-huh, Hector mumbles, snapping his gum. Then he slides his bat from the rack—white ash, tape-wrapped grip, personally blessed by the Archbishop of Guadalajara and his twenty-seven acolytes—and starts for the dugout steps, knowing the course of the next three minutes as surely as his blood knows the course of his veins. The famil-iar cry will go up—Cheese, Cheese, Cheesus—and he'll amble up to the bat-ter's box, knocking imaginary dirt from his spikes, adjusting the straps of his golf gloves, tugging at his underwear and fiddling with his batting helmet. His face will be impenetrable. Corcoran will work the ball in his glove, maybe tip back his cap for a little hair grease and then give him a look of psychopathic hatred. Hector has seen it before. Me against you. My record, my career, my house, my family, my life, my mutual funds and beer distributorship against yours. He's been hit in the elbow, the knee, the groin, the head. Nothing fazes him. Nothing. Murmuring a prayer to Santa Griselda, patroness of the sun-blasted Sonoran village where he was born like a heat blister on his mother's womb, Hector Hernán Jesus y María Quesadilla will step into the batter's box, ready for anything.

But it's a game of infinite surprises.

Before Hector can set foot on the playing field, Corcoran suddenly doubles up in pain, Phelan goes slack at second, and the catcher and shortstop are hustling out to the mound, tailed an instant later by trainer and pitching coach. First thing Hector thinks is a groin pull, then appendicitis, and finally, as Corcoran goes down on one knee, poison. He'd once seen a man shot in the gut at Obregón City, but the report had been loud as a thunderclap, and he hears nothing now but the enveloping hum of the crowd. Corcoran is rising shakily, the trainer and pitching coach supporting him while the catcher kicks meditatively in the dirt, and now Mueller, the Atlanta *cabeza*, is striding big-bellied out of the dugout, head down as if to be sure his feet are following orders. Halfway to the mound, Mueller flicks his right hand across his ear quick as a horse flicking its tail, and it's all she wrote for Corcoran.

Poised on the dugout steps like a bird dog, Hector waits, his eyes riveted on the bullpen. Please, he whispers, praying for the intercession of the Niño and pledging a hundred votary candles—at least, at least. Can it be? Yes, milk of my Mother, yes—Kerensky himself strutting out onto the field like a fighting cock. Kerensky!

Come to the birthday boy, Kerensky, he murmurs, so certain he's going to put it in the stands he could point like the immeasurable Bambino. His tired old legs shuffle with impatience as Kerensky stalks across the field, and then he's turning to pick Asunción out of the crowd. She's on her feet now, Reina too, the kids come alive beside her. And Hector Jr., the book forgotten, his face transfigured with the look of rapture he used to get when he was a boy sitting on the steps of the dugout. Hector can't help himself: he grins and gives them the thumbs-up sign.

Then as Kerensky fires his warm-up smoke, the loudspeaker crackles and Hector emerges from the shadow of the dugout into the tapering golden shafts of the late-afternoon sun. That pitch, I want that one, he mutters, carrying his bat like a javelin and shooting a glare at Kerensky, but something's wrong here, the announcer's got it screwed up: BATTING FOR RARITAN, NUMBER THIRTY-NINE, DAVE TOOL. What the—? And now somebody's tugging at his sleeve and he's turning to gape with incomprehension at the freckle-faced batboy, Dave Tool striding out of the dugout with his big forty-two-ounce stick, Dupuy's face locked up like a vault, and the crowd, on its feet, chanting Tool, Tool, Tool! For a moment he just stands there, frozen with disbelief. Then Tool is brushing by him and the idiot of a batboy is leading him toward the dugout as if he were an old blind fisherman poised on the edge of the dock.

He feels as if his legs have been cut from under him. Tool! Dupuy is yanking him for Tool? For what? So he can play the lefty-righty percentages like some chess head or something? Tool, of all people. Tool, with his thirty-five home runs a season and lifetime B.A. of .234, Tool who's worn so many uniforms they had to expand the league to make room for him, what's he going to do? Raging, Hector flings down his bat and comes at Dupuy like a cat tossed in a bag. You crazy, you jerk, he sputters. I woulda hit him, I woulda won the game. I dreamed it. And then, his voice breaking: It's my birthday for Christ's sake!

But Dupuy can't answer him, because on the first pitch Tool slams a real worm burner to short and the game is going into extra innings.

• • •

By seven o'clock, half the fans have given up and gone home. In the top of the fourteenth, when the visitors came up with a pair of runs on a two-out pinch-hit home run, there was a real exodus, but then the Dodgers struck back for two to knot it up again. Then it was three up and three down, regular as clockwork. Now, at the end of the nineteenth, with the score deadlocked at seven all and the players dragging themselves around the field like guts-hot horses, Hector is beginning to think he may get a second chance after all. Especially the way Dupuy's been using up players like some crazy general on the western front, yanking pitchers, juggling his defense, throwing in pinch runners and pinch hitters until he's just about gone through the entire roster. Asunción is still there among the faithful, the foolish, and the self-deluded, fumbling with her rosary and mouthing prayers for Jesus Christ Our Lord, the Madonna, Hector, the home team, and her departed mother, in that order. Reina too, looking like the survivor of some disaster, Franklin and Alfredo asleep in their seats, the *niñitas* gone off somewhere—for Coke and dogs, maybe. And Hector Jr. looks like he's going to stick it out too, though he should be back in his closet writing about the mystical so-and-so and the way he illustrates his poems with gods and men and serpents. Watching him, Hector can feel his heart turn over.

In the bottom of the twentieth, with one down and Gilley on first—he's a starting pitcher but Dupuy sent him in to run for Manfredonia after Manfredonia jammed his ankle like a turkey and had to be helped off the field—Hector pushes himself up from the bench and ambles down to where Dupuy sits in the corner, contemplatively spitting a gout of tobacco juice and saliva into the drain at his feet. Let me hit, Bernard, come on, Hector says, easing down beside him.

Can't, comes the reply, and Dupuy never even raises his head. Can't risk it, Champ. Look around you—and here the manager's voice quavers with uncertainty, with fear and despair and the dull edge of hopelessness—I got nobody left. I hit you, I got to play you.

No, no, you don't understand—I'm going to win it, I swear.

And then the two of them, like old bankrupts on a bench in Miami Beach, look up to watch Phelan hit into a double play.

• • •

A buzz runs through the crowd when the Dodgers take the field for the top of the twenty-second. Though Phelan is limping, Thorkelsson's asleep on his feet, and Dorfman, fresh on the mound, is the only pitcher left on the roster, the moment is electric. One more inning and they tie the record set by the Mets and Giants back in '64, and then they're making history. Drunk, sober, and then drunk again, saturated with fats and nitrates and sugar, the crowd begins to come to life. Go Dodgers! Eat shit! Yo Mama! Phelan's a bum!

Hector can feel it too. The rage and frustration that had consumed him back in the ninth are gone, replaced by a dawning sense of wonder—he could have won it then, yes, and against his nemesis Kerensky too—but the Niño and Santa Griselda have been saving him for something greater. He sees it now, knows it in his bones: he's going to be the hero of the longest game in history.

As if to bear him out, Dorfman, the kid from Albuquerque, puts in a good inning, cutting the bushed Braves down in order. In the dugout, Doc Pusser, the team physician, is handing out the little green pills that keep your eyes open and Dupuy is blowing into a cup of coffee and staring morosely out at the playing field. Hector watches as Tool, who'd stayed in the game at first base, fans on three straight pitches, then he shoves in beside Dorfman and tells the kid he's looking good out there. With his big cornhusker's ears and nose like a tweezer, Dorfman could be a caricature of the green rookie. He says nothing. Hey, don't let it get to you, kid—I'm going to win this one for you. Next inning or maybe the inning after. Then he tells him how he saw it in a vision and how it's his birthday and the kid's going to get the victory, one of the biggest of all time. Twenty-four, twenty-five maybe.

Hector had heard of a game once in the Mexican League that took three days to play and went seventy-three innings, did Dorfman know that? It was down in Culiacán. Chito Mariti, the converted bullfighter, had finally ended it by dropping down dead of exhaustion in center field, allowing Sexto Silvestro, who'd broken his leg rounding third, to crawl home with the winning run. But Hector doesn't think this game will go that long. Dorfman sighs and extracts a bit of wax from his ear as Pantaleo, the third-string catcher, hits back to the pitcher to end the inning. I hope not, he says, uncoiling himself from the bench, my arm'd fall off.

Ten o'clock comes and goes. Dorfman's still in there, throwing breaking stuff and a little smoke at the Braves, who look as if they just stepped out of *Night of the Living Dead*. The home team isn't doing much better. Dupuy's run through the whole team but for Hector, and three or four of the guys have been in there since two in the afternoon; the rest are a bunch of ginks and gimps who can barely stand up. Out in the stands, the fans look grim. The vendors ran out of beer an hour back, and they haven't had dogs or kraut or Coke or anything since eight-thirty.

In the bottom of the twenty-seventh Phelan goes berserk in the dugout and Dupuy has to pin him to the floor while Doc Pusser shoves something up his nose to calm him. Next inning the balls-and-strikes ump passes out cold, and Dorfman, who's beginning to look a little fagged, walks the first two batters but manages to weasel his way out of the inning without giving up the go-ahead run. Meanwhile, Thorkelsson has been dropping ice cubes down his trousers to keep awake, Martinez is smoking something suspicious in the can, and Ferenc Fortnoi, the third baseman, has begun talking to himself in a tortured Slovene dialect. For his part, Hector feels stronger and more alert as the game goes on. Though he hasn't had a bite since breakfast he feels impervious to the pangs of hunger, as if he were preparing himself, mortifying his flesh like a saint in the desert.

And then, in the top of the thirty-first, with half the fans asleep and the other half staring into nothingness like the inmates of the asylum of Our Lady of Guadalupe where Hector had once visited his half-wit uncle when he was a boy, Pluto Morales cracks one down the first-base line and Tool flubs it. Right away it looks like trouble, because Chester Bubo is running around right field looking up at the sky like a bird-watcher while the ball snakes through the grass, caroms off his left foot, and coasts like silk to the edge of the warning track. Morales meanwhile is rounding second and coming on for third, running in slow motion, flat-footed and hump-backed, his face drained of color, arms flapping like the undersized wings of some big flightless bird. It's not even close. By the time Bubo can locate the ball, Morales is ten feet from the plate, pitching into a face-first slide that's at least three parts collapse and that's it, the Braves are up by one. It looks black for the home team. But Dorfman, though his arm has begun to swell like a sausage, shows some grit, bears down and retires the side to end the historic top of the unprecedented thirty-first inning.

Now, at long last, the hour has come. It'll be Bubo, Dorfman, and Tool for the Dodgers in their half of the inning, which means that Hector will hit for Dorfman. I been saving you, Champ, Dupuy rasps, the empty Gelusil bottle clenched in his fist like a hand grenade. Go on in there, he murmurs, and his voice fades away to nothing as Bubo pops the first pitch up in back of the plate. Go on in there and do your stuff.

Sucking in his gut, Hector strides out onto the brightly lit field like a nineteen-year-old, the familiar cry in his ears, the haggard fans on their feet, a sickle moon sketched in overhead as if in some cartoon strip featuring drunken husbands and the milkman. Asunción looks as if she's been nailed to the cross, Reina wakes with a start and shakes the little ones into consciousness, and Hector Jr. staggers to his feet like a battered middleweight coming out for the fifteenth round. They're all watching him. The fans whose lives are like empty sacks, the wife who wants him home in front of the TV, his divorced daughter with the four kids and another on the way, his son, pride of his life, who reads for the doctor of philosophy while his crazy *padrecito* puts on a pair of long stockings and chases around after a little white ball like a case of arrested development. He'll show them. He'll show them some *cojones*, some true grit and desire: the game's not over yet.

On the mound for the Braves is Bo Brannerman, a big mustachioed machine of a man, normally a starter but pressed into desperate relief service tonight. A fine pitcher—Hector would be the first to admit it—but he just pitched two nights ago and he's worn thin as wire. Hector steps up to the plate, feeling legendary. He glances over at Tool in the on-deck circle, and then down at Booger, the third-base coach. All systems go. He cuts at the air twice and then watches Brannerman rear back and release the ball: Strike one. Hector smiles. Why rush things? Give them a thrill. He watches a low outside slider that just about bounces to even the count, and then stands there like a statue as Brannerman slices the corner of the plate for strike two. From the stands, a chant of *Viejo, Viejo*, and Asunción's piercing soprano, Hit him, Hector!

Hector has no worries, the moment eternal, replayed through games uncountable, with pitchers who were over the hill when he was a rookie with San Buitre, with pups like Brannerman, with big leaguers and Hall of Famers. Here it comes, Hector, 92 mph, the big *gringo* trying to throw it by you, the matchless wrists, the flawless swing, one terrific moment of suspended animation—and all of a sudden you're starring in your own movie.

How does it go? The ball cutting through the night sky like a comet, arching high over the center fielder's hapless scrambling form to slam off the wall while your legs churn up the base paths, rounding first in a gallop, taking second, and heading for third . . . but wait, you spill hot coffee on your hand and you can't feel it, the demons apply the live wire to your tailbone, the legs give out and they cut you down at third while the stadium erupts in howls of execration and abuse and the *niñitos* break down, faces flooded with tears of humiliation, Hector Jr. turning his back in disgust, and Asunción raging like a harpie, *Abuelo! Abuelo! Abuelo!*

Stunned, shrunken, humiliated, you stagger back to the dugout in a maelstrom of abuse, paper cups, flying spittle, your life a waste, the game a cheat, and then, crowning irony, that bum Tool, worthless all the way back to his washerwoman grandmother and the drunken muttering whey-faced tribe that gave him suck, stands tall like a giant and sends the first pitch out of the park to tie it. Oh, the pain. Flat feet, fire in you legs, your poor tired old heart skipping a beat in mortification. And now Dupuy, red in the face, shouting: The game could be over but for you, you crazy gimpy old beaner washout! You want to hide in your locker, bury yourself under the shower-room floor, but you have to watch as the next two men reach base and you pray with fervor that they'll score and put an end to your debasement. But no, Thorkelsson whiffs and the new inning dawns as inevitable as the new minute, the new hour, the new day, endless, implacable, world without end.

But wait, wait: who's going to pitch? Dorfman's out, there's nobody left, the astonishing thirty-second inning is marching across the scoreboard like an invading army and suddenly Dupuy is standing over you—no, no, he's down on one knee, begging. Hector, he's saying, didn't you use to pitch down in Mexico when you were a kid, didn't I hear that someplace? Yes, you're saying, yes, but that was—

And then you're out on the mound, in command once again, elevated like some half-mad old king in a play, and throwing smoke. The first two batters go down on strikes and the fans are rabid with excitement, Asunción will raise a shrine, Hector Jr. worships you more than all the poets that ever lived, but can it be? You walk the next three and then give up the grand slam to little Tommy Oshimisi! Mother of God, will it never cease? But wait, wait, wait: here comes the bottom of the thirty-second and Brannerman's wild. He walks a couple, gets a couple out, somebody reaches on an infield single, and the bases are loaded for you, Hector Quesadilla, stepping up to the plate now like the Iron Man himself. The wind up, the delivery, the ball hanging there like a *piñata*, like a birthday gift, and then the stick flashes in your hands like an archangel's sword, and the game goes on forever.

ACKNOWLEDGMENTS

Several people deserve acknowledgment in putting together the expanded edition. Publisher Cynthia Sherry made valuable suggestions, as she has with other books in the series, and project editor Kelly Wilson did an outstanding job. Professor Tim Morris from the University of Texas at Arlington was helpful in gathering recent stories. Denise Crozier from California State University, East Bay, did fine administrative work. Thanks also to Sarah Dudley Plimpton and the librarians at Cal State East Bay: Todd H. Charles, Dana S. Edwards, Doug Highsmith, Paula Kapteyn, and Paul Maclennan.

Many people gave generously of their time and expertise to make the original edition possible. Research help was provided by Roger Siebert of the library at California State University, Hayward. Florence Bongard of Cal State served as secretary for the project. Thanks also to the Paul Ziffren Sports Resource Center in Los Angeles, especially librarian Shirley Ito. Leonard Koppett, former sportswriter for the *New York Times*, gave early direction and inspiration. So did baseball fiction writers Mark Harris and Ron Carlson from Arizona State University. Peter C. Bjarkman, author and editor of baseball books, was a valuable consultant. Also deserving of credit for their input on the literature were Stephen Jay Gould of Harvard University, Frederick T. Courtright of Macmillan Publishing Company, Richard L. Wentworth of the University of Illinois, Daniel J. J. Ross of the University of Nebraska, Lawrence J. Malley of Duke University, and Frank Koughan of *Harper's*. Kudos to my baseball pals, who offered useful thoughts at games of the Oakland Athletics and San Francisco Giants: E. D. Conklin, Ron Friis, Harry Koplan, Nick McIntosh, and fellow professors Robert E. Kelly, Donald Wort, and Richard Zock. And, most of all, special appreciation to Amy Teschner, editorial director of Chicago Review Press, who held everything together with such style, enthusiasm, and intelligence.

CREDITS

Grateful acknowledgment is extended to the following authors and publications:

Ernest L. Thayer, "Casey at the Bat," originally published in the *San Francisco Examiner*, June 3, 1888.

Frank Deford, "Casey at the Bat," from *Sports Illustrated*, July 18, 1988, pp. 52–75. Reprinted by permission of the publisher.

W. P. Kinsella, "The Thrill of the Grass," from *The Thrill of the Grass* by W. P. Kinsella, copyright © 1984 by W. P. Kinsella. Used by permission of Viking Penguin, a division of Penguin Group (USA) Inc.

Zane Grey, "The Rube's Waterloo," from *The Redheaded Outfield and Other Stories*, (New York: Grosset and Dunlap Publishers, 1920). Copyright © 1921 by Zane Grey, renewed 1949 by Lina Elise Grey.

Ring Lardner, "Alibi Ike," originally published in the *Saturday Evening Post*, 1915.

Garrison Keillor, "Three New Twins Join Club in Spring." Copyright © 1988 by Garrison Keillor. First published in *The New Yorker*, from *We Are Still Married: Stories and Letters* by Garrison Keillor. Used by permission of Viking Penguin, a division of Penguin Books USA Inc.

Brendan DuBois, "A Family Game," from *Murderers' Row: Baseball Mysteries*, edited by Otto Penzler, 2001. Reprinted by permission of the author.

"Goodwood Comes Back," from *The Circus in the Attic and Other Stories*, copyright © 1941, renewed 1969 by Robert Penn Warren, reprinted by permission of Harcourt Brace and Company.

William Heuman, "Brooklyns Lose," originally published in *Sports Illustrated*, 1954.

P. G. Wodehouse, "The Pitcher and the Plutocrat," originally published in *Collier's*, 1910.

Chet Williamson, "Gandhi at the Bat," from *The New Yorker*, June 20, 1983. Courtesy of Chet Williamson.

George Plimpton, "The Curious Case of Sidd Finch," originally published in *Sports Illustrated*, April 1, 1985. Reprinted by permission from Sarah Dudley Plimpton.

J. F. Powers, "Jamesie," originally published in *Prince of Darkness and Other Stories*. Courtesy of J. F. Powers.

Steven Polansky, "Leg," originally published in *The New Yorker* in 1995. Reprinted by permission of the author.

Arthur "Bugs" Baer, "The Crambury Tiger," originally published in *Collier's*, 1942.

Leslie Pietrzyk, "What We All Want," from *Bottom of the Ninth: Great Contemporary Baseball Short Stories*, edited by John McNally, 2003. Reprinted by permission of the author.

Lloyd Biggle Jr., "Who's on First?," from *A Galaxy of Strangers*, Copyright © renewed by the author, 1986. Courtesy of Lloyd Biggle Jr.

"Death of a Right Fielder," from *The Coast of Chicago* by Stuart Dybek. Copyright © 1990 by Stuart Dybek. Reprinted by permission of Alfred A. Knopf Inc.

Arnold Hano, "The Umpire Was a Rookie," originally published in the *Saturday Evening Post*, 1956.

"The Hector Quesadilla Story," from *Greasy Lake and Other Stories* by T. Coraghessan Boyle. Copyright © 1979, 1981, 1982, 1983, 1984, 1985 by T. Coraghessan Boyle. Used by permission of Viking Penguin, a division of Penguin Books USA Inc.

Rising from the
Dark Side of Life

Books of Joseph C. Plourde

Rising from the Dark Side of Life

Both Feet on the Spiritual Path

Rising from the Dark Side of Life

One Man's Spiritual Journey from Fear to Enlightenment

By the Grace of God I was Rescued

Joseph C. Plourde

iUniverse, Inc.
Bloomington

Rising from the Dark Side of Life
One Man's Spiritual Journey from Fear to Enlightenment

iUniverse books may be ordered through booksellers or by contacting:

iUniverse
1663 Liberty Drive
Bloomington, IN 47403
www.iuniverse.com
1-800-Authors (1-800-288-4677)

Because of the dynamic nature of the Internet, any Web addresses or links contained in this book may have changed since publication and may no longer be valid. The views expressed in this work are solely those of the author and do not necessarily reflect the views of the publisher, and the publisher hereby disclaims any responsibility for them.

Any people depicted in stock imagery provided by Thinkstock are models, and such images are being used for illustrative purposes only.

Certain stock imagery © Thinkstock.

ISBN: 978-1-4502-1039-3 (sc)
ISBN: 978-1-4502-1038-6 (ebook)
ISBN: 978-1-4502-1037-9 (dj)

Printed in the United States of America

iUniverse rev. date: 1/29/2011

Contents

Preface

I have written *Rising from the Dark Side of Life* in hopes that the reader will visualize my own life and realize how fortunate one can be, to not have to go through life as my family and I did. I hope my readers will also understand how wonderful it can be to be rescued by the wonderful Grace of God, our Heavenly Father.

This is the story of my childhood, and how I lived through very harsh poverty. It is a story about how I experienced some very troublesome difficulties fighting with a demon for some time. And, it is a story about how I was finally rescued by the wonderful grace of God and live to tell about it—and go on to live a happy, productive, and successful life.

The story in this book is the real truth about me and my family. I spent a great deal of time researching to gather all of the real true information that I needed. I wrote *Rising from the Dark Side of Life* with love, and with the intention of helping anyone who may have experienced living with the kinds of difficulties I lived with, so that they can understand the real problems that they once had or are still having. I hope this book helps people learn how to deal with these problems and finally get rid of them completely, so that they can also live a happy life with peace of mind. Everyone deserves to live a happy life, in harmony and with success and prosperity, for we all know that is God's will for everyone, and there is no exception because everyone is equal in the eyes of the Lord.

Amen.

Introduction

It is my true and sincere pleasure to introduce *Rising from the Dark Side of Life* to you, and to be able to talk to you as a concerned friend and brother in Christ, someone who is always ready and willing to do whatever it takes to help anyone in any way I can.

I welcome you to go through this life journey with me. I am certain that it will open your eyes, and I am certain that you will be happy and you will appreciate what you learn from the words in this book.

I have written *Rising from the Dark Side of Life* in hopes that it will be easy for anyone to read and understand. I want my readers to grasp the realization of how fortunate so many people are, not having to live through a devastating and troubled life such as the one I lived as a child with my family.

The content of this book has been sitting on the back burner, as we say, for quite a long time, and, after gathering enough truthful information, I found it was time to reveal the truth about myself and the very poor family I grew up with.

Our family lived in a very poor southeastern part of Canada during the first half of the twentieth century. Some passages of this text will probably touch some readers emotionally because of the hard times and struggle that I experienced through my life's journey, especially because I ended up with more problems than the others in my family had.

You will realize how powerful prayers can be when we are at the bottom of the barrel, as we say, and call upon the Lord to help and rescue us from the enemy— the devil—and how wonderful it is to be rescued by the grace of God, especially when you need him the most.

I am very happy to have the opportunity to introduce to you *Rising from the Dark Side of Life* because I know that it will be a great help to anyone who reads it carefully, and pays close attention to what it's revealing. It is my hope that readers will realize for themselves how fortunate they are that they don't have to go through life as I did in my early years. But, I did come out of it with the glorious help of God, and readers will probably find more appreciation for their own lives, and will certainly realize how much they really take for granted. I hope this book will also give them the opportunity to see life itself in a different perspective, which will make them feel happier with themselves and with the life all around.

I am certain that, by the time readers have finished the book, they will come to understand the purpose of life and its reality for everyone. They should also come to know how to deal with personal problems, and how to get rid of those problems—even problems that may have kept them in a certain bondage for so long in their lives. Readers may be able to find the answers to problems that they couldn't find before, and grow through life to become happy and successful as I did.

The main reason that I wrote *Rising from the Dark Side of Life* is that I know there are many people in this world who are having difficulties coping with life, and don't seem to be able to know and see the real joy of living. Sometimes it seems as if there is no one that they can find to help them; however, many times reading a book such as this one can give them the information and hope they need to overcome their problems. Some people are too shy to talk to someone else about their problems; they may be afraid that others might just think there is something wrong with them. We all deserve to turn ourselves around and start living more promising and glorious lives. I really feel for people who don't know who they can entrust their problems to ... who they can talk to and get help from with respect and dignity and confidentiality. Many people don't realize that God is always there ready and willing to help anyone as soon as he is called upon for help.

Therefore, I wrote *Rising from the Dark Side of Life* with the understanding that it will be a great help to anyone, and it is certainly my aim to reach out and help anyone I can help in any way I can. I believe that this is the best way that I can reach out to so many wonderful people. That is my goal—to reach those who need help. And, with the help of God, I am now on my way to reaching the goal that I set for myself so long ago. This book wouldn't have been written without the help of God.

I have also reached another one of my goals, one that I set previously to this one. In the fulfillment of that goal I also reached out to help people from all over the world by writing a book called *Both Feet on the Spiritual Path*. It has been a true joy and happiness for me to be able to reach out and help so many wonderful people. I have been a Christian since the early part of 1980s, and God has called upon me to spread his holy word to anyone who is willing to listen and learn from it. God has guided me to write books that will help anyone physically, emotionally, and spiritually.

I now live a happy life in the village of Lac Du Bonnet in Manitoba, Canada. I enjoy my work as a carpenter, plumber, preacher, and writer.

I have been called by God to preach the gospel and to reach out to any of God's people and help in any way I can. God has been guiding me through my life for quite some time, and I enjoy every minute of the journey.

I also play music and sing to congregations in and for the glory of God.

My heart is with you, and I wish you all the best in your future.

I pray for God to help you with your understanding and bring you peace of mind and happiness in all the years to come.

I love you and I will keep you in my prayers.

May God bless you with special blessings of happiness, joy, success, and prosperity.

Amen.

Joseph Claude Plourde

Chapter 1
The Beginning of a Troubled Family

This story may be disturbing to some readers, but it has been a very true reality for a very poor and troubled family, especially for one of the children—myself—who had a very difficult problem to conquer. Our family lived in a very poor area of southeastern Canada in the early part of the 1900s when it was very difficult for many families to make a decent living. In fact, because of the two world wars in the first half of the 1900s, it was very difficult for some families to make a decent living anywhere in the world.

This true story is about a man who has experienced life at the bottom of the barrel, as we say, as a young child, and grew to become successful with the help of the Lord Jesus Christ. I hope you will realize how truthful this text is, and how powerful Jesus Christ really is when you call upon him for help, especially when you really mean it with all your heart.

My parents, Camil and Ida, were both from eastern Canada. Camil was from the small town of Blue River in the province of Quebec, and Ida was from the city of Edmundston in the province of New Brunswick. They met while Camil was working in Edmundston; they were married in 1926. Eventually, they raised a family of twelve children. I was born in December of 1946 during very difficult times just after the Second World War had ended. Therefore, we might say that I was born during the hardest times of all, and struggled to survive just like the others.

When I was born, my parents were still living in the province of Quebec, but when I was only three years of age, they decided to move back to where it had all started—Edmundston, New Brunswick, where the eleventh child was born three and a half years after I was born.

I must say that, during those years, it seemed that no one was interested in going to church, as if no one believed in it, but still my father always made sure that all the children said the rosaries every night before going to bed.

Mother never said very much about religion or going to church on Sundays; it seemed as if she didn't have the smallest interest in religion; therefore, she never tried to influence our religious beliefs. As children, we didn't know anything about religion until we grew a little older and Father wanted us to go to church every Sunday.

I suppose Father must have understood about God and his son Jesus, and how important it is to know about them. He probably sent us to church because he knew that we would be learning something good from the experience.

Now I really thank my father and appreciate his teachings. Even though we thought at the time that he was just being hard on us, and making us do things that we didn't like to do, I for one am very happy now that I had a father who cared enough to make us learn about some spirituality, even though he didn't understand much of it himself. At least he knew that there was something good in it for us, and, even though we were very poor, he cared enough to try to prepare us for our future the best way he knew how. For that

I respect him very much. He may have been hard on us at times, but now I realize that he was trying to use tough love on us, so that we wouldn't forget what he was teaching us. I thank him and love him for all that he has done, and for all that he taught us.

Chapter 2
Trout River

While we lived in the city, I remember very well when the eleventh child was born into our family—a boy my parents named Jacque. I was, at the age of three and a half, somewhat disturbed by this newborn baby, because I wasn't the baby anymore—Jacque was taking over all the attention. Because of this, I had the opportunity to grow up quickly, and develop some better understanding about what life is all about. Even though I was still very young, it was a start for me.

After living in the city for a while, my parents decided to try the farming again, but this time in New Brunswick. My father looked around and found a very small country farm about ten miles from the city in an area called Trout River. It seemed that no one else wanted to live there, or just didn't want to have anything to do with the place, but nevertheless we moved there. There was nothing to start a farm with, but my parents were willing to work hard, and the three oldest boys, Roland, Emil, and Armand, were old enough to do their share of the work.

Well, because there were some big enough trees on that property, Father planned to also put the boys to work cutting and selling logs. He probably thought that things were going to be good there for a change, and, after we had been living there for just a short time, another baby arrived—a girl my parents named Lilianne. That brought the total count of our family to fourteen. For a short time, Father and the three oldest boys cut and sold logs to a saw mill operation in the city, and there was actually more food to feed fourteen people every day than there had been before with eight or ten children.

Roland, Emil, and Armand were helping Father with the log cutting, and the two oldest girls, Jeannette and Yolande, were helping Mother with the work in and around the house. Things seemed to be going well enough for some time.

But something else came in the way again to prevent my parents from succeeding at this place, but no one really knew what this problem was, or that it even existed; therefore, no one was prepared for it. Until one night, shortly after we moved onto this little farm where no one else wanted to live, when I had a terrible encounter with a devastating problem. This was a problem that was much different from any of the other problems that the rest of the family had, or was experiencing at the time. This problem was with the house.

I was a boy of six by this time, and I was also the tenth child in the family. One night I went upstairs to go to bed all alone ahead of everyone else. That was the custom during those days—the youngest would go to bed first, to be followed by the others afterwards. When I went to bed, it was already dark and there weren't any lights upstairs. It was such an old house, there wasn't any electricity, and we had to use kerosene or coal oil lamps for light. I was the youngest to sleep upstairs; the two babies slept downstairs with my parents.

Just a few minutes after I went upstairs and into bed, I started feeling something strange, as if there was a presence near me ... someone or something that I couldn't see. There was a small amount of light coming from the lamp downstairs through the opening of the trap door at the top of the stairway, and I should have been able to see something—someone or some kind of image—but there wasn't anything to be seen. I got a bit scared and got quickly under the blankets, and put them over my head. Then I said a prayer. I never told anyone about this experience at first, but the same thing went on each time I went upstairs to bed alone after it was dark. And it got worse.

That was a very scary, fearful thing for a young boy to experience. Sometimes there were sounds from up in the attic, as if someone was walking, but, at the same time, as if the person was dragging one foot while walking. Sometimes while I was trying to say my prayers while kneeling by the bedside, this presence would make a sound like, shishhhhhhhhhhh. It seemed then that the presence was only about five to six feet from me, and I would jump into bed and under the blankets. I would quickly pull the blankets over my head, and I would pray while shaking in fear. The presence seemed to be just standing by the bedside. I wondered if it was watching for me to stick my head out from under the blankets to talk to it. But I was far too scared to just take that chance, because I knew that this presence was there ... I could feel it. Sometimes it even felt as if someone was breathing heavily on top of the blankets, but there was nothing that could make me move from my position, for I thought I was safe as long as I stayed under the blankets and prayed. As soon as the others came upstairs to bed, then this presence would go away.

Sometimes I would talk to my older brother Ronald about this. Ronald was almost two years older then I, and we were very close in relationship. But Ronald would say, "Yeah, yeah, I've experienced things upstairs before too, but that don't scare me a bit." I thought that Ronald was just trying to laugh at me, and that he was just acting tough.

There were even sounds, at times, that came from up in the attic that sounded as if a chain was being pulled and dragged along the floor of the attic and as if it was dragging against the wall and coming down the stairs. One would think that the chain would just simply fall down, but instead it sounded as if it were dragging against the wall as it was coming down, and coming around the corner and toward my bed.

Sometimes I actually thought that I was finished—that this thing would kill me or take me away somewhere and make me suffer. I really thought that this was the end of the road for me, and the only thing that I could do was to get under the blankets and curl up and pray as hard as I could, really asking Jesus to come and help me. And somehow I was never touched by this evil thing, and, without realizing it, I was saved by Jesus Christ, the one to whom I had called for help in the beginning.

At one time, I decided to make myself a bed in a large clothes closet that was in a different part of the upstairs from my bedroom, closer to the stairway. This closet was open, with no doors, as if the work was never completed, and served as separator between two parts of the upstairs. I went inside the closet and tried to make myself a bed with lots of coats and cloaks, thinking that I would be really comfortable there, but, from where I was standing in the closet, I could see part of the floor around the staircase. There was a certain amount of light that was coming from the kerosene lamp that burned downstairs. I suddenly felt that the presence was moving around upstairs. Then, at the edge of the staircase, I saw an image that looked like a small sailboat. Part of it was a faded pink, and part of it was a faded grey, and it looked as if someone was pulling it along by a string, but I couldn't see any string or anyone pulling it. The sound it made, however, was the same sound that I had heard before up in the attic; it sounded like someone dragging a foot on the floor while walking. This little sail boat that was about twelve inches high and about sixteen inches long. It stopped at the edge of the stairs and turned toward me, as if it was looking at me. I stared at it for a moment without making a move or a sound—or even blinking—and this little sailboat turned back the other way and headed downstairs. But, as it was entering into the line of the light from downstairs, it disappeared into the light until it was all gone. The spirit that was pulling the little sail boat never came back to bother me that night; in fact, it didn't come back for a few days. I never saw that little sailboat again. Later on I got to thinking that it must have been a small child pulling the little sailboat, making a noise that sounded like someone dragging a foot while walking. But I never realized that at the time because I was too scared to think anything.

Maybe this presence that was always bothering me was just a small child looking for help, or for another child to play with, but I didn't realize that at the time because I was so afraid. It seemed to be so frightening and such an evil presence. But then I figured there had to be at least two entities—one child and one adult, and maybe the child could have been friendly. I didn't think the adult one was friendly.

If only I hadn't been so scared, I probably could have played with this child's spirit whenever it showed up. The child was probably just looking for someone to play with, or just looking for someone to rescue him or her from bondage. If only I had known...

Another night when I was going to bed, I didn't have to wait for anything because this evil presence was already there waiting for me. I turned around and ran downstairs in such fear! I finally told my parents that I couldn't sleep upstairs anymore because there was something evil there and I was too scared to go back upstairs. My parents let me sleep downstairs with my two oldest sisters, Jeannette and Yolande. Between the two of them, that night I felt safe and had the best sleep that I had had in a long time.

I was allowed to sleep downstairs with my sisters for a few days, but then my parents decided that I should go back sleeping upstairs again. They told me that everything would be all right from that time on. I was hoping that what they said was true, so I went upstairs again. But the presence was still there waiting for me, and I felt that it was upset with me for sleeping downstairs for a few days. Even though I couldn't see this evil presence, I certainly could feel it, and I knew that it was upset with me. I continued as I had before, hiding under the blankets and praying until I was tired enough to fall asleep—or until some of the others had come upstairs to bed, as it seemed that when the others were upstairs, this evil thing would go away.

Waking up in the morning in the daylight was the best thing that happened to me every day. I woke knowing that the fear was gone for another day. I tried to tell my parents and my oldest brothers about my fears, but they just joked about it, saying that I was only afraid because I had been bad, or that I'd just had nightmares because I'd eaten too much at suppertime. During this time, I, as a small child, was having a hard time coping with this thing. I was living in such fear all the time—and I was starting to get very tired of that.

One night, I asked my brother Ronald to come upstairs with me. I thought that, if we both knelt down by the bedside and said a prayer together, this thing would go away and never come back. Ronald also really knew that there was something that wasn't normal upstairs at night, but he'd never said anything to anyone about it. He did, however, immediately agree to my request. So, after it got dark, we both went upstairs and knelt down by the bedside. We started to pray together. Suddenly, this thing was about five or six feet from us. In an angry tone, it started making a terrible sound as it had before—shishhhhhhhhhhh. In no time, Ronald and I were both in the bed with the blankets over our heads. We held on to each other and prayed as hard as we could. It was very hot under those blankets. Well, we never moved from there until we fell asleep. I don't know what time that was, but probably after the others had come upstairs to bed, which was usually about two hours after my bedtime.

During those years, Father always made sure that every child knelt down by a chair at 7:00 PM to follow the rosaries as they were said over the radio. As soon as the program was finished, then the youngest child would have to go to bed. Especially in the wintertime, by that time it had been dark for a while already. The two babies slept downstairs in the same room as the parents, so I was the youngest child to sleep upstairs.

Ronald used to pretend with me that he was strong and tough because he was almost two years older than I, but that night he wasn't any braver or tougher than I was. That evil thing got the best of both of us.

Well, the next morning, Ronald and I approached our parents. Because he was older than I, he told them what had happened the night before. He told them that he, by himself, had experienced something like that upstairs before, but had never said anything to anyone. Our parents both saw that there was really something that wasn't normal in that house, and it was getting too hard for us to deal with. Whatever it was, Mother said to Father, "Camil, we have to get out of this place." And our parents began to make plans to move.

By that time, things had become harder. My father and brothers had cut and sold almost all the logs from our small piece of property. Three of the oldest children had found loved ones, and, in a short time, they had married and left home. Another child moved to the city and found work there and didn't return home. After the four oldest ones were gone from home, we were ten, including Mother and Father. By that time, it seemed that there wasn't anything left there for us anyway, on that little farm with no animals and no logs. Things were getting bad again, so Father went looking for work and found a job in the city, so we moved to a small town just outside the city.

Moving from that house to a different place—especially to a different town—was very good news to me. I was so happy just to get out of that place that it just couldn't ever be soon enough for me.

During all this time, I was too young to know much about evil spirits, and what they can do to ruin a person's life, if the person lets them have their way. I certainly didn't know that evil spirits can also secretly travel from place to place and attack a person again.

Enemies like this evil entity are very smart and very sneaky. They can be watching for someone—a target—and, when this person is not aware of this enemy, it will strike without warning. It can come into a person's life and pretend to be nice and loving, but that is just one of its tricks. So, be on your guard and don't let that happen to you. You know that God will always be by your side as long as you accept him, and let him help you every day of your life. No harm can come to you as long as you have God by your side. Don't ever let go of him because he is our refuge.

Amen.

Chapter 3
Moving to Saint Jacque

We moved to a small town called Saint Jacque, which was about eight miles from our farm. Father traveled to and from work by bus, and things went well enough while that job lasted.

But not so long after we moved there, it seemed to me that the evil presence had followed me—or found me again. I couldn't stay alone after it was dark because this evil presence was bothering me again. At least in that house, which was so small, we had to sleep three or four in the same bed, so I felt safe because there were so many there with me. I knew by that time that the entity would never bother me while I was with lots of people—or at least with more than two people. I always made sure that I wasn't alone at any time at night. Nevertheless, I always knew that this thing wouldn't leave me alone, and that it would always wait for a chance to get me by myself.

I asked my brother Ronald if he was still experiencing this evil presence, but he said that he never had felt or seen anything like it since we had left Trout River. He did know, however, that this evil spirit was still haunting me, but there was nothing we could do about it, except pray to God and ask him to take the evil thing away from me, so that I could live in peace like everyone else.

Sometimes it just seemed as if my prayers were too weak, or I didn't have enough faith in my prayers. I felt almost as if God was testing my faith. Because I would get no response at all from God, it just seemed as if he didn't hear me, or didn't want to have anything to do with me any more, or just wasn't there. That made the situation so much harder on me, because I was depending on Jesus to help me, and to rescue me from this evil thing.

I used to feel safe whenever I would pray. Occasionally I would feel some relief because I felt that Jesus had heard me and was responding. Then I felt free for a while. But, when there was no response from him, it was scary for me because I really felt alone.

At that time, I was far too young to know anything about haunted houses, or that some evil spirits could come into our lives and try to destroy our lives. During those years, we didn't even know what a television looked like, and there probably wasn't anything on the radio or the TV that would have informed us about evil entities anyway. And our parents wouldn't tell us anything about evil entities even if they knew. But, after we moved from that little farmhouse to the town about eight miles away, my father did say that there had been rumors that the house on the farm was haunted, and that was the reason that no one wanted to live there—or have anything to do with it.

My father, being a very brave man who wasn't ever scared of anything or anyone, probably thought that he would be able to take care of the haunting. But I suppose he must have realized that it wasn't that easily done, even though he wasn't afraid of that sort of thing. My guess is that he had never really had to deal with the real thing before; therefore, he didn't realize how much damage an evil entity could do to a person, or even to the whole family. I think that, when

Mother and Father saw the real fear on my face and on Ronald's face that morning, they realized that the situation was worse than they thought, and that we had no choice but to move away from that house.

Not very long after we moved from that house, someone burned the house and the barn and even cut down all the apple trees that were by the house, so there was absolutely nothing left on that property except just an empty field. I certainly know why everything was burned. I probably know things about that place that no one else could ever know.

Sometimes I used to think that this particular evil spirit was just after the young ones, because they were probably easier to get or easier to scare. Maybe the entity thought it could scare the young ones enough so that they would give in to it. I always rejected the entity, but it was very stubborn with me, and it just wouldn't quit bothering me. I never knew why it kept haunting me until later on in my life.

Nevertheless, after a while, the job that Father had in the city ended, and the money stopped coming in. It wasn't always easy to find a job during those years, especially around that area. Soon the grocery bill at the local store got bigger and bigger, and eventually the credit stopped. Father and Mother could not pay the rent. Father tried to find work to feed the family, but he was not successful. We had to move again.

During all this time, it seemed that Father was always joking around and always trying to make everyone laugh most of the time, as if everything was good. But we children just didn't realize at that time that he was just trying to bring a little joy into the family during a very difficult time for him and Mother.

Chapter 4
Little Cold House in Saint Jacque

This time, we moved to a very small house. It was very close to the railroad track in the same town, and that was probably one of the worst—if not the very worst—place that we ever lived.

After we moved into that little, cold house, things got worse ... much worse in many different ways, especially for me. Let me tell you, this was real ... very real ... and I am not exaggerating. What you read in this book is what it really was, and there is no mistaking it. I know, because I experienced it ... I lived through it. You can feel fortunate that you don't have to live through a life like I had to live through, until I got rescued by the wonderful Grace of God. Maybe you have experienced something like the evil entity that scared me, or maybe you are experiencing it now. By the time you finish reading this book, you will probably realize what or who is causing it, and how to stop it, but you certainly will know how to get rid of it.

This was a very small and very cold house. There were no woods nearby to supply wood for the stove, and there wasn't any money to buy wood, so some of us children had to go walking down by the railroad track to try to find fuel for the stove. It isn't very easy to find wood in a place like that in the wintertime. Meanwhile, Father was trying to find some work so he could get money for food and to buy wood from the neighbor. Sometimes some of us children would go down the railroad track about three-quarters of a mile or a mile away where there was some brush, and we would cut some wood with a small bucksaw, put it on our small sled, and drag it home by the way of the railroad track. Then we would be set to make a fire for another day.

By this time, there were still seven children yet at home, and in that terrible place we almost froze to death. I am not just saying this … it was real. And we almost starved to death, and this is also the real truth. I can honestly tell you that I remember very well when there was only salt and pepper in the kitchen cupboards, and absolutely nothing else at all to eat for some days. I certainly remember going to bed at night and wondering if I would wake up the next morning or if I would be dead from starvation, and it was hard to go to sleep. My stomach hurt from being hungry, and I felt weak. I did not know how long a child could live without eating; I didn't know how long I could last. I was just a small, skinny kid without much strength to fight anything.

I remember very well part of the summer that we lived there. For about a month or so, I went to school with bare feet because I simply didn't have any shoes. I certainly remember some of the other kids trying to step on my toes all the time. As children, they thought that was just a funny joke, but it sure wasn't a very funny joke for me, because they hurt me a few times, and I always had to watch for those kids.

We very well know that when children see something out of the ordinary, they get curious and they will try anything for a game, and they had their fun with it.

It wasn't easy for a child of seven or eight years of age to live that kind of life, but, nevertheless, I have forgiven whoever or whatever caused the hardship. It is easy to forgive, but not so easy to forget. Those years were the worst years of my life, but, for whatever reason, it doesn't matter to me now, because I just live on with peace of mind, in harmony with the world around me, and with the whole of society.

I use this experience as a teaching aid for myself. I have knowledge from a past that not very many people experience in their lives, and that makes me realize how fortunate I am now that I don't have to go through that kind of living anymore. I certainly hope that no one else ever has to go through what I've been through, because, even though that gave me experiences and knowledge about life and its realities, I certainly don't want anyone else to go through such suffering. For one thing, probably many wouldn't make it through. I say this because I know that the good Lord protected me from being completely destroyed.

After you read my story, I am certain that you will feel blessed that you didn't have to experience a life like mine. You will realize how fortunate you really are today. Sixty to seventy years ago, everyone had to work so very hard just to make ends meet, but our parents couldn't even make ends meet, which is why I say that our family was probably worse off than many other families. Even other poor families were making fun of us; that's just how bad it was.

But, again, after a while something came up. Father must have found a short job or something, because he brought home a box of food one day. I can remember that as if it happened only a week ago, because I knew that I wasn't going to die of starvation—at least not yet. We all ate until we were filled, and there was happiness in the house that day. I was eight years of age by this time.

But don't forget that that dark cloud—or evil spirit— was still bothering me, and it got lot worse when we were living in the little house near the railroad. I even faced the demon face to face in that terrible house. I always called it hell on earth, and I certainly have my reasons to call it that because that was the worst winter of my entire life.

As I've said earlier, that winter I almost froze to death, almost starved to death, and fought with a demon that wanted my soul so badly that it was even trying to be very nice and really loving to me, just so

I would give in to it. But no! My answer was always no, and I would always call on Jesus, and he would set me free.

One evening when I went upstairs to bed, I had just had time to lie down in my bed when I could feel the presence. But, this time, it felt as if it was very tender and loving. It grabbed me by the hand, and I let it. It lifted me up off the bed, and we both floated in the air, about six or eight inches above the bed. We went floating from the surface of the bed to the underside of the bed (those old beds were about eighteen or twenty inches from the floor). Even though it was dark, I could see the entity. I could make it out! This little demon was smaller and shorter than I. I never did have the chance to see if it was good looking or ugly, but my guess is that I am probably lucky that I didn't get to see its face properly, because it probably looked like hell. Somehow, I still knew that he or it was the wrong one and that Jesus was the right one, and, while we were still under the bed and still floating in the air just above the floor, I strongly rejected it and called on my Jesus. Suddenly, it let go of my hand and I fell to the floor, which was only about six inches away. The entity immediately disappeared as soon as it let go of my hand. My father heard the noise from downstairs and called up to ask what was going on. But I didn't answer, so he just said to get to bed and go to sleep. I suppose he probably thought that I was playing upstairs with something instead of going to bed. I didn't say anything and just went back to bed, and I remember that, after that, I felt safe and secure because of Jesus, and I wasn't afraid of anything that night and I sure slept well. I knew that Jesus was protecting me again that night.

I have to thank my father for teaching me the little that he knew about Jesus. His teaching was probably the main reason that I always rejected that evil spirit, and whenever it tried to get me by being really nice and loving to me, I would call on my Jesus, and the evil spirit would immediately go away—or at least leave me alone for a while. I remember that, whenever I called on Jesus and the demon fled, I really felt at peace, and rested and happy, with no worries whatsoever, and I slept so well. The next day, I would feel good and strong as if nothing bad had ever happened to me in my life. I know now that Jesus was the one who was giving me that strength and those good feelings. When I felt that way, I knew I wouldn't be bothered by that evil spirit again for a few days—or even four or five days sometimes.

It seemed that, whenever the evil spirit came back and bothered me again, it was trying harder, and I just had to call harder on Jesus. But the evil spirit was very stubborn. He must have said to himself, *This is really a true stubborn Frenchman*, because I never gave in to it. Every time I told it to leave me alone and it didn't go away, I would call on Jesus for help, and this stubborn Frenchman—with Jesus' help—would overcome that stubborn demon. What a fight between two stubborn beings! But, with Jesus on my side, the stubborn Frenchman prevailed. Amen.

There is one time when it is good to be stubborn— when it is to defeat a demon or any negative that may cross our path. Sometimes I prefer to say I was *persistent*; it just feels like a better word than *stubborn*.

Not very far from this house there was a river, which was called Trout River. It came down from the area where we had lived before. The railroad track crossed the river by way of a bridge, which was high above the river.

In the spring season, Trout River, as do most rivers, rose high and ran fast. One spring day, my brother Ronald and I went for a walk on the railroad track. When we came to the bridge, we decided to throw stones and sticks into the water below. When we threw a long stick into the water, it would come shooting back out of the water. While I was bending over the edge of the railing of the bridge, watching for my sticks, I lost my balance and fell into the river below.

The current was very strong, and it swept me away. Even though I didn't know how to swim, I still tried, but I kept going down and then coming back up again. After I had gone down and come back up about three times, I could see my brother running along the edge of the river. He was yelling at me to grab the board that he held in his hands and stretched out toward me. As I reached toward it, the current brought my back against a clump of bushes that grew in the water along the shore. Then, just as the current was about to take me under again, I reached out my hand and grabbed the board that Ronald was holding. He pulled me to shore.

I lay down on the ground for a bit and then we went home, but, before I went into the house, I told Ronald to go inside and get me some dry pants so I could change. I planned to dry my wet clothes by myself. I didn't want Mother to know what had happened, because I knew that she would give me the biggest torturing of my life.

Well, while I was waiting in the ditch for Ronald to bring me dry pants, all of a sudden I saw Mother coming. She was holding a peace of broom handle in her hand. Right then I said to myself, *I'm dead for sure this time.* I could see it in her face that she was really going to give it to me.

Well, I am still alive to tell you about it, but let me tell you that I got it so bad that, after a while, I couldn't even feel my but, or anything from the bottom of my back down to my knees. I couldn't walk—my brothers had to help me to the house and into bed, and I couldn't move for a while. But, after a couple of days, I couldn't believe that my bones were not all busted at the bottom of my back. Still, it took close to a week before I was back to normal again.

We have to realize that the broom handles that we had in those days were not small handles like we have nowadays; they were almost twice the size. The one Mother used on me was about two feet long—it was the same stick that she used to use for washing clothes. It was also her weapon of choice, and she used it many times on her children.

Later, when my sister Rita got a little older, she used to get upset at Mother and tell her how stupid it was to do that to her children—even that she could get in trouble with the law for doing it. Mother would tell her to just mind her own business.

I have to say that, when Mother started pounding on one of us, she didn't know when to stop, and it seemed that her anger would grow stronger and stronger until she got tired. I can honestly say that many times she got very upset with us for things that I would now just call nonsense.

As I said before, it is easy to forgive, but it isn't so easy to forget, and, because I do remember, I must reveal the truth as it was, because I promised to speak the truth in this text, and I wouldn't feel completely honest if I didn't reveal all of the truth that I know about my childhood.

I don't hold any grudges against my parents. As I've said before, I forgive them and I certainly hope that they also forgave me my trespasses, because I do understand that we have to forgive to be forgiven.

Therefore, I know that it is the right thing to do … it is the only thing to do so that we can keep on living in harmony with everyone. The past is dead, today is new, and tomorrow will take care of itself. That is what I've learned from studying the word of God.

Chapter 5
Last Place I Lived with
Mother and Father

The next summer, Father found a better job in the city. He bought an old garage outside of the town and converted it into a house. He wasn't a bad carpenter; therefore, it was a nice enough home—that wasn't the first time that he had built a house.

We couldn't wait for Father to finish building this house. We were all so anxious to move and get out of that terrible place we were in. So, we moved into our new house even before it was all completed, and we gradually completed it after a short time. Everyone was so happy with this new location, but the best part was that, this time, we really owned our home, and no one else could throw us out of our home after this.

After Father finished building this house and we moved in, it seemed as if everything was all right for a while. I remember being so happy with Jesus for getting rid of that demon for me forever—I thought. I was finally able to live as a normal child, and enjoy life the way a normal child would. Everything was good, and life was wonderful most of the time.

But one day about a year or so later, the terrible, evil thing appeared again, trying to get at me. I got so upset at it that I began calling it down. I used all kinds of evil names—anything that I could think of—without realizing that this was exactly what this demon wanted me to do … to swear and curse. I must admit that I surprised myself at the age of nine with the words I could come up with when I was really angry and had to do battle with a demon. I asked God to forgive me for using that kind of language against that evil thing, and I truly believe that he did forgive me.

To be honest, it seemed as if the evil entity had lost me for a while, and then finally found me again. It seemed very upset with me over this … as if it had really missed me while I was gone. I knew I still had a fight on my hands.

I began to get a little more mouthy with the demon by this time because I knew that, with Jesus on my side, I couldn't go wrong. I was a little older, so I was getting a little braver. I was still scared, though, and frustrated and sick and tired of the battle, so I spoke to Jesus about it, and asked him to get rid of this evil thing from me forever. But it almost seemed as if Jesus didn't hear me, or that he didn't want to have anything to do with me for a while, and that evil demon was at me every chance it got.

I very well remember one scary night. My parents had gone to a dance; my two oldest sisters who were still living at home, Rita and Simone, had also gone out with their boyfriends; the two youngest, Jacque and Lilianne, had gone to bed fairly early; and Ronald and Aline, another one of my sisters, who was about one and a half years older than Ronald, were in the dining room sitting at the table playing cards. I was supposed to go to bed at a certain time—before Ronald and Aline went to bed because I was younger than they were. So, when I went to bed, there was no one else in the bedroom that I was sleeping in, and I knew very well that this was a very good opportunity for the demon to get at me.

You can imagine that I didn't really want to go to bed all alone, but Ronald and Aline told me to go ahead and that they would also be coming to bed shortly after me. So I went to my bed in the back bedroom. As soon as I walked into the bedroom, I didn't see anything, but I sure heard something. It sounded as if someone was rushing to hide under the bed, and I heard a weird sound coming from there. It was a terrible, creepy sound that was coming out of some kind of beast. It kind of sounded like a beast that was trying to talk with its mouth full of something. But this "thing" had gone under the bed so fast, while making that awful sound, I thought, *Well, if you want to hide under the bed, you can also stay there, you evil thing.*

I knew that no one from my family could be under that bed; therefore, I knew what it was. So I ran and jumped onto the bed. Because I knew that this evil thing was *under* the bed, I stood up right in the middle of the bed so that it wouldn't—or couldn't—reach me. At the very least, I would be able to see it if it came out from under the bed because the light was shining enough into the bedroom for me to see. I thought I would be safe as long as I remained standing there.

Well, while I was standing there in the middle of the bed, the center of the mattress, right where I was standing, started moving upward, and it made a sharp hump right under my feet. The hump kept rising higher and higher until I couldn't keep my balance. I slipped and then I just jumped right off that hump and ran as fast as I could out of the bedroom and into the dining room where Ronald and Aline were. As soon as they saw the fearful expression on my face, they knew that this evil thing had been after me again in the bedroom, and they told me to stay in the dining room with them, and that the three of us would stay there until our parents came home.

I know that they were also scared to go into that bedroom, because they asked me what had made that awful sound in there just as I was running out of it. I said that I hadn't heard anything, but they insisted that they had heard an awful sound—like the hissing of a mad cat. But we didn't have any cats. I suppose I was far too preoccupied escaping to have time to hear anything. I just had no time for anything but running as fast as I could to save my life.

After our parents came home, we told them what had happened, and they told us not to go to bed alone, and to make sure that we were accompanied by someone else all the time. But, after we were all in bed, after a while, I heard Mother and Father talking in real low voices. Then their voices grew louder and louder, and they were arguing about something. I thought that something had happened while they were at the dance, because Father said to Mother, "You promised that you wouldn't do that anymore, but you broke your promise again, and look at what is happening again!" He said, "Ida, you have to stop that. That's not right and that's not fair to them." I remember Father saying, "I will throw them in the stove and burn them!" Well, I tried to figure out what in the world they were talking about, but I didn't have any idea, so I decided to just leave it alone and try to go to sleep.

The next day, I asked Mother what she and Father had been talking about the night before, but she got a bit upset with me and told me to mind my own business and go play outside.

I suppose that's what the devil likes to hear. He probably enjoyed every moment of it, and I suppose he knew that he had really scared me and Ronald and Aline while our parents were gone, and he probably thought that he had me scared enough to give in to him.

He probably figured he could just keep on bothering me more than ever before, but I kept rejecting it. I called it all kinds of evil names, and told it that I didn't want to have anything to do with it anymore—that was it, I was finished ... or I would have to call on my Jesus again, and that time would be the last time, because Jesus would really fix it. I don't recall everything I said exactly, but it must have worked, because the demon left me alone after that for a while.

I suppose that, without realizing it, I was defeating the devil with the power of the faith that I had in Jesus Christ, our Lord and Savior, and that was a power that the devil couldn't ignore; in fact he couldn't stand against it--- therefore he was defeated.

I always kept my faith and my trust in my God, no matter what happened or how bad the situation got. I never gave up on my God because I always knew that he was much stronger than anything or anyone else. I knew that he would rescue me from this evil thing, and that some day I would live a happy life as I wanted to ... a normal life like everyone else.

Chapter 6
Period of Illness

After I had my last talk with that demon and told it that it would be defeated by Jesus, something happened to me, and I'm not sure if it came from the demon, from threatening it, or if it just happened. Over the next day or two, I became very ill, and no one was able to determine what the illness was. I almost died; I was unconscious. It was as if I was dead—or almost dead—for five days. Members of my family were praying for me—especially one of my sisters, Rita, who was also always checking on me.

Well, I remember that I finally woke up on the fifth day and opened my eyes. The first person I saw was Rita. She was holding a cold cloth on my forehead, and, when she realized that I was awake, she yelled at Father to tell him. She was so happy! I remember hearing Father tell her to give me some bread with molasses on it right away. I guess that was to strengthen me quickly, and she did as he said.

I started getting better very slowly. I remember struggling just to chew and to swallow the food that Rita was giving me. She had to feed me for a while because I couldn't even lift my hands to do anything at first. I was still far too weak to get out of bed for a few more days. But I came around again, and I probably would have come around sooner, but I was just a skinny little kid, and probably not as strong as other members of the family. But, nevertheless, I got some strength back. In about one to two weeks, I was back to my normal health again, and I was able to do whatever kids usually do again.

But the best thing was that, after I got better, I knew that the demon was gone for good, and I could live at peace without having to watch for it, and having to fight with it all the time. I was finally free.

That demon never bothered me anymore after that. My fight with that evil thing was finally over and done with, but I sometimes wondered if it hadn't been that demon that had tried to kill me because I'd defeated it with the power of Jesus. Maybe it was so upset with me that it tried to kill me with some kind of evil sickness. But I was saved by Jesus because I had called upon him to save me from that evil thing forever.

Whatever it was or whatever happened, I know that I was blessed with the power of the Holy Spirit, and there is absolutely no doubt whatsoever in my mind that Jesus had something—if not everything—to do with my being rescued and saved from that terrible, evil, miserable kind of living. Everything changed for the better in my life from that time onward. It has been a slow process in getting better, but, nevertheless, it did get better and better year after year.

We very well know that any battle with a demon is never an easy battle, but, when a stubborn demon battles with a stubborn Frenchman, well, that's no easy task, let me tell you. When the stubborn Frenchman says "No!" to the stubborn demon, he means business, and there is no changing his mind. Therefore, the stubborn Frenchman wins the battle, and again the demon has to flee, and the Frenchman is set free. Amen,

Over the years, as I've gotten older and studied the Bible, I've come to realize that I went through something like Job did. In the book of Job in the Bible,

God has a discussion with Satan. He tells Satan that he can take Job's belongings and all his wealth, but that he cannot take his life. And, because Job always keeps his faith in his God, then God makes him wealthier than he had been before. So, in this story too, Satan is defeated and has to leave Job alone to serve his God.

Shortly after I started feeling better and got my strength back, there was something that happened to me—something that I certainly didn't understand or know anything about.

One day, I started speaking in an unknown tongue. I really didn't know what it was or how I was able to do it. I couldn't even understand the language I was speaking. One thing I know is that I so enjoyed speaking whatever language it was. Sometimes it seemed that I had such an urge to speak it. It was as if I just had to speak it once in a while for some unknown reason.

Once in a while, my brother Ronald would ask me to speak this language. It seemed as if he would be thrilled to listen to me. For some reason that I didn't understand at that time, I always really loved and enjoyed speaking that language. Whenever I did,

I would feel so good inside. There was some kind of happiness inside of me, but I didn't know why I felt it. I certainly can tell you now that I sure wish I had known then what that was all about, but I suppose that was the Lord's way to make me feel happy. Therefore, I am satisfied with the way that I understand it at this point and time in my life. I thank Jesus for all the great blessings that he has poured on and through me over the years.

From the time that I started speaking in an unknown tongue, I can honestly say that I always felt really bad every time I did something wrong. I have committed sins once in a while. Many times, however, I have been tempted by others, but have refused to follow their bad example for the simple fact that I knew that I just shouldn't do it … that I should just chose to walk away, even though some of my friends thought that I really should have gone with them. Now I am really happy that I have followed my heart. Don't get me wrong here, I have done lots of bad things in my life that I am certainly not proud of, but I am not worried about them anymore because I have repented, and I have learned to forgive myself. I also know that God has also forgiven me my trespasses. Therefore, I can live with peace of mind in harmony with the rest of society.

Amen.

Chapter 7
Living on the Farm

While I was still nine years of age, I went to live on a farm that belonged to my brother-in-law Maxim and my oldest sister Jeannette. I lived there for almost three years. I really loved animals, and I learned how to work with horses, and how to take care of the other animals. I even learned how to milk cows by hand. I learned about gardening and all the other work that must be done on a farm. Even though it was hard work, I enjoyed every moment of my farming experience.

I was always especially happy whenever there were newborn animals on the farm—little chicks, lambs, foals, calves, and so on. I used to say that they were beautiful creations of God, and I really took good care of them—just as if they were my own.

But, at the same time, I developed a love for working with wood … making things out of wood. I made wooden toys, wheelbarrows, and sleds. And I fixed things around the house. My brother-in-law used to call me "The Patentor" because I was always building something out of the ordinary, which was unusual and amazing for a child of my age. I always had the imagination to make something that no one had ever seen before, and I found that thrilling.

I just loved Wednesday afternoons at school because that was when we had wood class. I was always one of the best woodworkers in the class. I was good at designing new things, and I was very handy with the tools that were available to us. I believe that the woodworking class and math were probably the two things I really liked the most at school. I wasn't very much interested in anything else. If only I had known then what I know now, however, I probably would have tried to be much better than I was with my schooling because it would make my work much easier than it is now.

My father didn't have any education at all and probably wasn't aware of what he was really missing in his life; therefore, he couldn't explain to us what we would be missing if we didn't have the proper schooling. And Mother wasn't very well educated either. But my father's goal for us boys was to make good, hard-working men out of us, and with that I suppose he believed that we would make out all right in the future.

I certainly don't blame my parents for not giving us a better education. After all, it was also up to us to want to go to school and learn. Nevertheless, some of us have gone on to take some higher education programs. Our upgraded education now makes our work and our lives easier to cope with. I for one am very glad that I recognized what I was lacking and took steps to fill in the gaps. Now I do respect education for everyone; it is very much needed in everyone's life, and more now than ever before with the world changing so rapidly, and all the new technology that is continually developing.

For myself, I certainly am not a highly educated person, but I've learned lots through the years, and I never will cease my learning because I realize that the more I know, the easier my life becomes.

When I was twelve years of age, I decided to move back home with my parents and brothers and sisters for a while. By that time, there were still four children at home with Mother and Father. I had been getting lonesome for them, and they had also been getting lonesome for me. It certainly was nice to be back together again for a while.

After I moved back home, one day I went into the shed and I saw some cabinet doors that were stacked up there. I asked my mother about the doors and what they were for. She told me that Father had bought them and that he was going to build a new set of kitchen cabinets for her, but she also said that he was very slow at starting on them and that she was tired of waiting for them. So I told Mother that I would build her cabinets for her. I promised that she would be happy with them, but I begged her not to tell Father about our plan. I would get everything ready one day, and start the project the next day when he was at work. There were to be upper and lower cabinets, each eight feet long. I figured I could build them in one day.

Well, at first Mother kind of had her doubts because she thought that I would probably just ruin Father's materials. But I promised her that she would be happy with her new cabinets, and that she wouldn't be disappointed with me. At the same time, I wanted to surprise Father. I finally talked her into it, and we did has I had planed. One day I got everything ready, and then I was up and ready early the next morning. As soon as Father was gone, I got to work. I didn't even stop for lunch. I worked right through the day, and, by the time Father came home in the evening, the cabinets were built. All we had to do was paint them to have them completed. Mother was so happy with them. I still remember the moment that Father got home and saw the cabinets. He looked at Mother and said to her, "You just couldn't wait, could you? You had to go hire someone else to do that when I was going to do it as soon as I could, and you know that we can't afford to pay someone!" And mother, with a smile on her face said, "I didn't have to hire anyone. We have a carpenter in the family— right there." She pointed at me. At first, he didn't know what to say, than he looked at me and asked me if it was true that I had built the cabinets. I said, "Yes, I did. Do you like them?" He examined the cabinets for a bit and asked me where I got the design from, and who had taught me how to do such work. I told him that I had designed them in my mind and then just built them. He said, "I see that you were born a carpenter, and do you know that

Jesus Christ was also a carpenter?" I had heard that, but it made me happy to hear my father say it. After I had the chance to really think about it, I realized how fortunate I was after all that I'd been through. It certainly was then—and still is to this day—a real thrill to know that I had something in common with Jesus besides our other relationship. How fortunate I am to have Jesus on my side. He had saved me from the devil in the past, and he is still working with me. I owe him all the thanks.

We all have to realize that, when we have Jesus on our side, we don't have to worry about anything. He takes care of everything for us. As long as we recognize him and let him work with us, everything is well taking care of, so don't make the mistake of forgetting Him.

During this time, my brother Ronald was 13-14 years of age and was old enough to help and do certain jobs for the neighbors to make some spending money.

Well, unfortunately while he was working for one of our neighbors, he was sexually abused by an older man and that brought another disaster in the family, it wasn't the same after that, especially for Ronald, the abuser got charged and all of us children weren't allowed to go to that neighbor anymore. That was noticeable that Ronald wasn't the same after that, he wasn't happy, his life was damaged for ever, but at that time we didn't know how to help him with this problem, therefore unfortunately he was on his own, struggling with this problem, how I wish I would have known then what I know now and helped him.

Well, time went by and about a year after I was lonesome for life on the farm with my sister Jeannette and Maxim, the kids, and the animals, so I decided to go back to the farm. I felt so happy with them there, and I lived there for about two more years, until I moved back home with my parents, and youngest brother Jacque and youngest sister Lilianne, who were the last two children that were still living with my parents. They were in school, and it seemed so different to see the family so small.

Not so long after I moved back home, Father wasn't feeling well. He didn't know what was wrong with him, but he didn't believe in doctors. I still remember him saying—before he was ill and felt really good—that he would probably live until he was a hundred years old without ever seeing a doctor. But this changed just a few years afterwards.

I wonder sometimes how things can change so fast in a person's life. One day a person can be feeling quite good and healthy, and still that same person can be gone within five or ten years. And that loss changes the whole family—their lives, habits, and styles—so fast. Most of the time, we can't control any of that. I believe that, when God calls us, we just have to go at his will.

When I was almost sixteen, I didn't want to go to school any longer. Instead, I wanted to go to work in the forest, cutting pulp, working with a horse and a chainsaw. I already had the experience that I needed to do that kind of work, so my father said that, if I didn't want to go to school, I would have to go work. That suited me just fine because that's what I really wanted. I didn't realize at that time how important school would be for my future, and I didn't realize how much I was throwing away. My parents didn't try to force me to stay in school; they didn't even try to talk me into staying in school because they knew that, if I went to work, I could help with the expenses at home. My contribution would be welcomed because there were still two children at home, and Father wasn't very well by that time.

By any means, I don't regret for a moment what I did to help with the support at home. I believe that it was God's will for me to go to work and help at that time, and I'm glad that I did. In fact, I am very happy and satisfied with myself for giving my support while I could. That's what family members should do for each other in time of need. I wanted to go to work, and I did. I have always loved working—especially working hard. I've always been recognized for being a hard-working man, and people have always trusted me to work for them, no matter what the task. I have always tried with the best of my ability to satisfy my employers, and I have always had good results from my efforts.

Chapter 8
Supporting the Family at Fifteen

During those years, the wage in New Brunswick was 75¢ per hour. I remember when I got a raise to 95¢. There were others working from the same camp who didn't get a raise. It was a while before they found out that only some had received the raise. Ad it wasn't long before the big boss had some questions to answer. Finally, everyone got a raise and things went along much smoother.

Before I go any further, I must confess that I have always had a very bad temper. I could have gotten it from my father, but, then, I could have gotten it from my mother—they both had very bad tempers. In any case, when someone with a temper is out in the forest working with a stubborn horse, well, that person's temper grows stronger and wilder. So, one day, I had been working with a particular horse for a while. I really hate to admit it, but the truth is that there were many words that came out of my mouth that I am certainly not proud of. My relationship with Jesus at that time wasn't the same as it had been before. I know that Jesus didn't just leave me behind and forget all about me. It was I who left him behind. It seemed as if I didn't have enough time for him, and that was very sad after all that he had done for me before.

After I realized what was happening in my life, especially with my relationship with Jesus, then I decided to make some changes. I wasn't so happy with myself, and certainly not satisfied with the way my life was going. So, I waited for my brother Ronald to come for a visit while I was home for a weekend. He was, by this time, working in the province of Quebec. Not long afterwards, he came to visit, and I asked him if there might be work out there for me. He was happy that I was interested in moving to Quebec to work, so he told me that there was a possibility for me to get a job there. The wages there were $2.10 per hour to start, which was a big jump from my 75¢ per hour.

I decided to move to Quebec and work there with Ronald. My boss and my friends couldn't understand why I would leave just when I'd just gotten a raise. When I told them that I was going to work at a place called Bay Como in the province of Quebec, and that I was going to make $2.10 an hour to start, they thought I was lying. They thought that I would be sorry that I left my job, and figured that, before long, I would be back. But they were wrong. I never went back, and I earned my wages just as Ronald had told me. We worked for a paper mill company in the summer, and we went on unemployment insurance for the winter months. Then we returned to our jobs again in the following spring. So, I received a biweekly paycheck through the whole year.

For a while, until the summer of 1968, I lived at my sister Rita and brother in-law's place in a small town called Point Lebelle.

Things were going well enough living in Point Lebelle, and with my work also.

However, in the early spring of 1967 we had heard on the news that there was an 18 year of age girl that was lost and believed to be kidnapped and they were looking for her, she was lost for about 3 weeks already and they were asking for everyone's help to find her.

One day in the beginning of May I encountered something that I will never forget for as long as I live, two of my friends asked me to go for a ride with them while they were bringing a load of garbage with a trailer to the garbage dump, I accepted and went with them, after we were at the dump and ready to unload I told them that I would use the shovel and unload it for them, while they were standing about 10 feet from the trailer talking and I was unloading the trailer, I really felt that there was something that was effecting me, effecting my nerves somehow without realizing at first what it really was that was doing this to me, every time I would turn around in the trailer and turn a certain way, I would get something like an electric shock going through me, and I finally realized that every time I would turn I would get a quick glance of what I certainly didn't expect to see that day, I suddenly stopped and told my two friends while I wasn't looking but pointing with my finger in that direction, guys you know about "Giselle Guy" the girl that they lost and looking for, well there she is right there, then I turned my head to really look at it, I was about 20 feet from the body, I got down from the trailer and walked closer to have a better look, I told them that it was "Giselle Guy" because she was the only one that was lost, but I couldn't see her face, the killer had placed her face down and her arms along side her body and had covered her naked body with an old blanket and jacket from the dump, the blanket was covering her body from her feet to about half way up her back, the jacket had covered the top part of her body and her head, but the wind had blown the jacket from the top part of her body, therefore I was able to see the back of her head and the upper part of her back, I could see four cuts on her back where a knife went in, we found out later that she had been stabbed 14 times right through her body from the back, but I could only see four of the cuts.

As you can imagine, even though that didn't bother me much right away but that picture was in my head for a long time, for four days when I was trying to sleep at night, I would open my eyes and looking at the window that was in my door which I still could see the brightness of the sky through the window, all I could see was the part of her that I could see that wasn't covered, with the four cuts in her back, I didn't know how long that was going to last but I prayed to God to release me of that and let me rest properly, and talking with my sister and brother and my friends was probably a big help also, I finally got over that picture that I had stuck in my head but I will always remember that same picture for as long as I'll live, but I've learned to not let that effect my life and live in piece after that.

Not so long after, I was invited to work and live in Thompson, Manitoba, and I didn't pass up the offer; I went.

Chapter 9
Moving to Manitoba

In 1968, my brother Emil wanted me to go work in Thompson in the province of Manitoba, Canada. There was lots of work there. The town of Thompson was rapidly developing into a city because of the mining industry.

Because of the growth of the town, there was lots of carpentry work to be done. Construction companies were building houses and garages. Everyone was busy. I got a job with a construction company that was working at the mine site. We were enlarging the mine buildings. In the summer of 1969, we were asked to build a large stage on the mine property, because the queen was coming. She would give a speech, and declare Thompson a city. Everything went well. The Queen arrived and did declare Thompson a city.

I really enjoyed my work there. I started as a carpenter's helper, and then was promoted to carpenter after proving myself. The people at this company were good to me, and I tried to please them with my hard work.

About a year later, our company finished their work there, so they moved on to another location in Canada, but I decided to stay in that city at my brother Emil's place.

By that time, I was making $3.65 an hour. I thought I was going to be rich in no time, but I was wrong, because, forty-five years later, I'm still not rich.

I started working for the mining company, which was called International Nickel Company (INCO). I worked in a department called the smelter for a short time, and transferred to the Refinery, where I worked for about two years. The job was good, and I must admit that I was good at my job. I worked the night shift at INCO and then worked in the city for a construction company during the day until 3:00 or 4:00 in the afternoon, when I would go home and eat supper and go to bed until it was time to go back to work at INCO at 11:30 pm. I did this three or four days per week.

One day, I had the opportunity to work on the construction of a hydro dam in the northern part of Manitoba, near a small town by the name of Gillam. I enjoyed my work there as a carpenter and cement finisher part time. I liked the place, and I enjoyed the people that I was working with. I made lots of new friends, and things were going well for me.

After the construction was almost completed, I had to look for another job because some of the workers were laid off. As I had been one of the last ones hired, unfortunately, I was in the first or second group to be laid off.

One of my new friends, Philip, also got laid off at the same time. Fortunately, he had the opportunity to go work for the highway's department of another small community in the western part of Manitoba. He invited me to go with him.

We had to travel by train from Gillam to Thompson, but, since I had my car in Thompson, Philip asked me if I would give him a ride home, which was 210 miles from Thompson, to a small town called Cranberry Portage, Manitoba, he was going to see if he could get me on the same job and work with him, I told him I would.

When we arrived at Thompson, we stopped to visit my brother Emil and his family for a while, Emil told me that there was a big fire in Notre Dame Du Lac, PQ.

A senior home burned to the ground, our grand mother which was our father's mother was in it and she also burned, they were all burned to the point of beyond recognition, while we were still there we watched the news on television and there were people picking up body parts with shovels and putting them in bags, our grand mother was one of them but certainly couldn't tell who she was, that was a terrible thing to see.

My friend and I had to get going we had a long way to drive, we talked about this almost all the way to his place, after we arrived there, we didn't work for a couple days to rest, but Philip went to the highway's department and asked if I could work there with him, there were no problem at all, we were working together the next day.

About two weeks after, one day Philip's father and mother in-law came driving to where we were working, she had tears in her eyes, she approached me and said that she had bad news for me, there was a terrible accident and my brother Ronald was killed in the car accident, Philip and I got in the car and went to town, I went to a phone and phoned Maryanne, Emil's wife and confirmed that it was true and what had happened, well, at first it didn't seem to bother me all that much, but about ½ hour latter it suddenly hit me, I couldn't stop crying all afternoon, couldn't eat until the next day, but I finally cooled down and started getting back to normal and back to work, I was getting better every day, but the part that bothered me the most was the fact that I knew that he had taken his own life, he was still suffering from his sexual abuse and couldn't cope with it any longer, he was just waiting for the opportunity to do something about it and when the opportunity came he took it, I will never forget when I left Point Lebelle PQ to move to Thompson MB, he came to see me and was crying and practically begging me to stay at Point Lebelle with him, and he also said that it was probably the last time I would ever see him, I told him that was none sense and that maybe later he could come and work there also, I told him that I was young and I wanted to travel, but I would see him before long, he said no that will not happen, I really thought that he was just talking like that just to change my mind and stay there, instead of moving to Thompson, I had made up my mind and I wanted to go traveling and go learn something new and I did, but those words kept going through my mind so many times, but I learned to finally get that out of my mind, and went on living a normal life like everyone else.

About two weeks later, my brother Emil came to see me at Cranberry Portage, he had more bad news for me, he told me that our father had past away, well, I was getting hurt again, but this time not as much as it did for Ronald, because we already knew that he was dying from cancer, we just didn't know when, but it still added to the pain that I already had from the previous ones, that was three of them in a very short time, I didn't really have time to get over one and another thing would happen, for a while I was kind of wondering if it will ever stop, and it did, thank God.

I kept on working with Philip until winter came and we were laid off for the winter. After that, I decided to go back to Thompson because I knew that I would get work there right away.

Next, I worked for a diamond drilling company. I had been interested in this sort of work for a while, so I was pleased to take advantage of the opportunity.

I was young, and I wanted to try everything I could put my hands on. I wanted to learn everything, so I was always ready and willing to try new things.

After I worked on diamond drilling for a while, my brother Emil, who was living in Thompson, got transferred to Sudbury, Ontario, where he was going back to work for the same company he'd been working for. I had to rent a room at a family house so I could store my belongings and also my car, since I had to travel by plane to a town called Lynn Lake. We would travel the remaining of the way by truck on a winter road. I went to work for a diamond drilling company that was back in the northern part of Manitoba.

It never seemed to matter what I tried, I always returned to carpentry. It has always been my favorite, and, even though I was good at many other jobs, I was always best at carpentry. I was born a carpenter and I will always be a carpenter. I believe that was a gift from Jesus Christ.

While I was diamond drilling at a place that was called, at that time, Ruttan Lake, which has changed afterwards, I worked with a gentleman there by the name Howard Wood. We became very good friends. Shortly after the Christmas Holidays of 1970, the drilling was completed at that area; therefore, we had to go home for a while until the company called us to work again. Howard was from a small town named Manigotagan, Manitoba, which, in the English language, means "bad throat."

Chapter 10
Moving to Manigotagan

Howard and I planned to travel together. I was to let Howard off at the city of Winnipeg and keep going on my way to spend some time in Quebec on my sister Jeannette's farm. She and her husband, and all their animals, had moved from New Brunswick to Quebec.

But I decided to drive my friend home first, and then get on my way. But, after I stayed in that small town for a couple days, well, things changed. My plans vanished. I loved the people there; they took me in as if I was one of them, which made me feel good and …
I met my wife Judy there.

It wasn't too long afterwards that we were together living as a common-law couple and started a family.

We spent the remaining of the winter there, but, in the spring, I got a job working for a mining company at a place called Madsen, Ontario, Canada.

During this time, I wasn't spending much time speaking to Jesus. It seemed that I was too preoccupied with my love life with my wife, and partying with my new friends.

This was 1971. I liked this little town, but this mine was about to close down, so I applied for another job at another mine, and I was accepted immediately. This little mining town was called Warner Lake. It was still in Ontario, so Judy and I moved there and that was where our first child was born, a boy called Robert Lee. We were so happy and proud; he was born in 1971. We felt that we were really blessed by God because Judy had been told by her doctor that she probably wouldn't ever have any children because of a car accident that she had been involved in about three years before.

We met lots of people in Warner Lake, and that wasn't long before we made lots of new friends, especially a young married couple, Edward and Linda Veronneau. We are still close friends to this day. Ed and Linda were expecting their first child in the spring of 1972. Linda and Judy were both pregnant at the same time with their firstborn. Ed and Linda had a beautiful little girl, and everyone was happy and proud. They were fortunate enough to have two more children afterwards, two boys—a beautiful little family.

We always had a good time whenever we would get together. We lived a good life. We didn't make any trouble; we only wanted to be happy and have a good time together.

While I was working at the mine in the mill at Warner Lake, I was also doing carpentry work part time at other places on my days off.

In 1972, when we knew that the mine was going to shut down, my little family and I moved back to Manigotagan and rented a small house there. I began work as a full-time carpenter, building cabinets in a small garage that came with the house we were renting.

By this time, I was starting to feel that we should go to church on Sundays. Even though things were going well for us, I still felt that there was something missing in my life. Since Judy was also a Catholic believer, we began to go to the Catholic church. I could feel that God was trying to do something with me, but

I still was too preoccupied with my everyday life. I did begin to talk to God more often by this time, and it seemed that it felt good to go to church with my little family. We were happy.

From the summer of 1973 to the winter of 1974 I built houses for Manitoba Housing and Renewal Corporation (MHRC). After that, I worked as a carpenter for the Community of Manigotagan. Everything was going very well for our little family.

In 1973, we had another child, a beautiful little girl we named Pamela Lynn. Again we were so happy and proud, and we thought it was just perfect, a boy first and then a girl. We thought the boy could take care of his sister as they grew up. Unfortunately that was all the children we could have; however, Judy and I really felt blessed with two beautiful children, and we thanked God for all of his blessings. Even though we weren't Christians at the time, we still understood that we had been blessed.

When it was nearing winter, we bought one of the houses that I just finished building, and by the Christmas holidays, we were happily moved in.

I kept on working for MHRC and for the surrounding communities as a carpenter and plumber.

In the 1970s, I also had the chance to cut pulp with my friends when carpentry work slowed down for a while, and I enjoyed it. I had fun working with my friends, and I really enjoyed being in the forest. I find peace when I'm in the forest.

By this time, it seemed that I wanted to be more involved with church activities. I also became involved with a Mennonite Mission in Manigotagan. There were wonderful and really loving people who were working for this church. Judy and I started going to bible studies with them. We could feel that our lives were blooming; we were as happy as we could be, and I know that God was also happy with us.

I also did lots of work for a very good friend of mine by the name of Arthur Bostrom. I have always respected Arthur and his wife Diane for being good to me and my family. They appreciated my work, and I appreciated working for them. They owned a grocery store, garage, and restaurant. This was a very good experience for me, and I appreciated the chance that they gave me to learn more about how to deal with people and how to serve them the proper way. In the late 1970s, I built my first squared log home, and it was for Arthur's parents. It is a very nice and very comfortable home, and they were so happy with it.

In 1980, I became a town councilor, fire chief, town water system operator, and a member of the Hollow Water School building committee. I was very busy, but I enjoyed it. I always enjoy pleasing people in anyway I can, and serving in these positions was one way of helping people.

In 1981, I became the first-ever chairman of the police commission for the communities of Manigotagan, Seymourville, and Aghauming. I also worked with the Hollow Water detachment, and I got called to work as a carpenter at a mine at another small town called Bissett about thirty miles from Manigotagan. After a while, I left that job because I felt that God wanted me to devote all my time to community work. I never regretted giving up the job at the mine because I know I was needed in my other capacities.

In 1982 I was hired by Department of Natural Resources to build a round log building, which they would use as a new office building. In 1983, they hired me again to build a cut three-sided log building for what is called their technical assistance contract (TAC) crew building. I really enjoyed working for them because they treated me well, and, in return, I treated them well also. I felt blessed to have the opportunity to work for them. The pay was good, and they were happy with my work. Everything continued to go very well in my life, and I have God to thank for all the happiness that I was experiencing.

In 1983 I was also hired by the Frontier School Division to build another square log house; it was to be used as a home for some of their teachers.

I was also sent to different northern communities to do some work for Indian and *Northern Affairs Canada* (INAC) and other government departments, but most of the time I worked in the surrounding communities, and still for the same departments. It seemed that God was using me to work for so many different places, and meet so many people, and I always felt so good about this. It seemed that life was good and easy during those years. There were so many people who wanted me to work for them. It made me feel very good inside that they trusted me. I was far more blessed than I realized.

I really enjoyed working for them all as a carpenter and plumber, and I wouldn't change that for anything else. I met so many nice people all over the country and made lots of friends along the way, and I also wouldn't change that for anything. Lots of the people I've met were Christians; I always found that they were always so nice ... so loving.

During these years, I always had God by my side, and I never forgot about what Jesus had done for me in the past. Even though I still didn't know much about Christianity, and never read the Bible except for a few Bible studies that we had, I was always curious about it. I didn't know why, but I always knew that Jesus was always watching over me. Many times I actually felt his presence, but I was spiritually blind and I didn't know what to do about it. I had a hard time believing that Jesus cared enough about me to spend some of his time just to be with me. But then I knew enough to know that nothing is impossible for him to do, so sometimes I felt that he really loved me that much. After so many years, I started thinking that I was somewhat special to him, and that he had chosen me for something, even though I didn't know what it was. It made me feel very good inside to think I was special to Jesus, but I didn't want to tell anyone about it, especially the friends I used to party with, because I thought they would laugh at me. Therefore, I just kept my thoughts to myself and sometimes I didn't even tell Judy about it.

In the last few years before I became a Christian, I had several experiences that I believe were sent from God. These experiences kept getting stronger and more frequent. I did mention some of it to Judy, but she didn't understand me, or maybe she knew what was happening but didn't want to say anything at the time. In any case, I didn't say much to anyone about my experiences, but, nevertheless, I was starting to feel really good about them. They were also giving me strength, and I felt that I was going to get even stronger, and I actually felt that I was getting smarter by the month. I was enjoying all of this, and still I found that it was almost scary for a while because I didn't know what to expect next.

In the summer of 1983, after driving about seven or eight miles during a trip from Manigotagan to Bissett with my family and two of my nephews, I felt that something strange was happening to me. I felt as if I was being washed inside and out with warm water … as if the water was going right through me from my head right down to my toes. I started feeling as if there was no weight to me. I stopped the car, and one of my nephews seemed to know that there was something strange happening to me. Even before I had stopped the car, he asked me what was happening. I asked him to drive the car, and I sat on the other side of Judy on the front seat. I didn't say anything for about two minutes. They all were looking at me as if they saw something strange about me, but no one was saying anything. Finally I asked them if they could see me! Judy looked at me as if I were "losing it." I told them how I really felt—as if I didn't weigh anything and as if I was invisible. Even though I could see myself, I wasn't sure if they could see me!

I told them that I had felt warm water or a warm wind go right through me, and I didn't feel the same as I had felt before. I felt that I was pure and holy, and that I could see things that I had never seen before. I told them how good I really felt and how beautiful everything was, even the trees along the roadside and the stones on the road. Even the weeds in the ditches were beautiful. I felt as if I could just say the word and I would be able to float out of the car through the window opening, and just fly into the air ahead of them … just float in the air at my own command. Judy said, "It sounds to me like you are being touched by God in some way." I truly believe that I was shown what it is like when we become an angel.

We went to Bissett, and, on our way back, I could feel that this experience was gradually fading away. Even though I tried to stay in the experience, I just couldn't. It took three days, however, before it was totally gone.

There was something that happened to me there that I didn't talk about it for a long time, and that was because I knew that I could get anything I wanted, right then and there … anything at all. I looked around and I said, "I have everything I need; I don't need anything else at all. I am as happy as anyone could be just the way I am." And, with what I had and what I'd seen, I just had to say thank you but, I don't need any more. I saw that, as long as I was happy, I had everything I needed, and no more could be added.

In my view, if a person is happy, it's usually because he or she is satisfied. If I am satisfied, I don't need any more. If people keep wanting more than they can use, that is selfish. If people are selfish, they can't be satisfied; therefore, they cannot be truly happy.

How I wished I could have kept that feeling … that experience going forever. But, after three days, it was gone. I shed tears when it went away. I've asked God to let me experience it again, but, no matter how long I have waited, it hasn't come back for a long time after. I was really disturbed by this, and I felt that God was playing tricks on me, and was just teasing me. But, at the same time, I was so happy that I had been touched by God, and I believed that the experience would come back again some day, so I thanked God for what he had shown me.

I had other experiences after that in the same year, but not as great as that one. It seemed as if God had left me for a while. Even when I would pray, nothing would happen. I didn't feel anything or seen anything out of the ordinary, as if he didn't hear me anymore, and I was really disturbed by this. Regardless, I just kept on talking to him, hoping that I would get something from him again soon. I never gave up; I just kept on praying to God every chance I got, because I knew that, if he had been there before, he would be there again. In the meantime, it seemed that this holiness of God was getting farther and farther from me, and I was starting to feel really empty inside.

One day in the spring of 1984, I decided to go and spend some time at a cabin I had built beside the Sandy

River, about ten miles from Manigotagan. I usually did some trapping there every spring. By this time, I was getting sad and frustrated with everything and everyone around me. My nerves were getting bad, and I was even losing interest in life. It seemed as if nothing could go right for me, and I even got to the point where I was so depressed that I even thought of taking my own life so I could just get away from everything.

One afternoon, I was at my cabin all alone. I was sitting on the steps with my gun across my knees as I always did, in case I spotted a beaver or a muskrat. This afternoon, however, it crossed my mind to put the gun to my head. *How quick it would be,* I thought. Then everything would be over with—no more problems. And, the more I thought about it, the more it made sense to me. But, just as I was going to make the decision to take my life, I felt another warm wind blow right through me, even though there was absolutely no wind at all at the time. I shook my head and said to myself, *what in the hell was I thinking? What the hell was I about to do? This is stupid!* I realized what had just happened: the wind that had just blown right through me was from God. God was keeping me from doing something so stupid.

Then I realized that God wanted me alive and well, so I decided to go back home. I convinced myself that I could see something good in life at this time. But, when I was going down the highway, I came to a bridge, and then again these evil thoughts came through my mind. It almost seemed as if there was some kind of power that was doing this to me, and I couldn't do anything about it. Again, I just couldn't see anything worth living for. All of this was happening quickly, and, as I was approaching the bridge, and again was about to make a decision to end my life, I felt this warm wind blowing right through me. Instantly I was changed again, and I could again see all the beauty of the world. I felt so happy inside, and I hurried to go home, because all of a sudden I got so lonely for my wife and children. I never said anything to anyone about that for a long time.

The proper kind of understanding about life didn't come to me for a long time, but when it started coming to me—when I finally saw the real picture of it all— then I understood why I had always felt the way I had whenever I sinned. I had never shared with anyone else how I felt about it; I always kept it secret to myself. No one else ever knew who I really was—my inner self that is—or what was going on in my mind, or what I honestly felt about many things that were happening in my life. I'm sure some of my friends probably didn't agree with some of my ways sometimes, but now I am happy that I lived my life my way, and not the way someone else might have wanted me to. Now I can say that I feel better about myself because my beliefs certainly helped me cut down on my wrongdoings to a great degree.

Even before I became a Christian, when I knew only a little bit about Christianity, I always felt that Jesus was watching me all the time; however, I must admit that sometimes I would just ignore it, or at least try to ignore my sins, but that was probably the reason that I felt so bad about my behavior afterwards. I was probably ashamed of whatever I had done, even if it was just something very small that I shouldn't have been feeling so bad about. I probably felt bad because I realized that Jesus was really watching me, and sometimes just talking to him, and asking him to forgive me for what I had done, made me feel like a hypocrite. Then I would experience a bad feeling about myself, and I wouldn't know for certain if Jesus had really forgiven me or not. For that reason, I never felt free from my sins, and never had true peace of mind. All of this made my life a little harder to cope with, but it was only because of my own weakness and stubbornness.

I do realize that most of us go through these kinds of difficulties with our personal conduct sometimes in our lives, but this is certainly no excuse for failing to do the right things, especially when we already know ahead of time that we will be doing something wrong, and still go ahead and do it anyway, but thank God I learned before it was too late.

I thank and praise the Good Lord for being by my side every time I needed him to rescue me from the negative energy that came across my path so often in my life, because I know that, without him, I would have lost many battles.

Chapter 11
Becoming Christian in Hospital 1984

Shortly after I experienced these wonderful blessings from God, I was hired by the government to build a square log house for a friend of mine who was living in Manigotagan. I had some problems while I was building this house; my nerves were really bad by this time, but I always tried not to show it, and I thought that I could overcome the problem. But it was more difficult than I thought it would be. Soon this house was almost completed, and all there was to do was hang interior doors and complete little touch-ups.

One day, I went to a town called Pine Falls, which was forty-five miles away from Manigotagan, to exchange some doors. As I was nearing Pine Falls, I dropped off the doors at the lumber yard. I wasn't feeling very well—I started feeling stiff and hot at the back of my neck and my head. I kept getting hotter and hotter. I reached with my hand to the back of my neck and head and felt that it was really hot, and I felt a bit dizzy.

I got a bit scared and I drove to the local hospital. To my surprise, I didn't have to wait in the waiting room; I was sent through immediately to see the doctor. It was almost as if they already new that I was coming and as if I already had an appointment. As soon as I told the doctor what was happening, he immediately called for a nurse to come with a wheelchair. As soon as she arrived, he told her to take me up to a room. He told me that someone would see me immediately. I was so surprised to see and hear this. I told them that I could walk, and that I certainly didn't need a wheelchair.

Well, the doctor told me not to argue and just to sit in the chair, so I did. The nurse took me to a room and settled me there. In just a few minutes, another nurse came and gave me some medication. As she was about to walk away, I asked her what was wrong with me. She replied that she didn't know; all that she knew was that she had been told by the doctor to come and give me this medicine immediately. She said that the doctor would come and see me later, which turned out to be the next morning, because they'd gotten occupied in the surgery room.

About an hour after the nurse had left my room, I started getting those terrible thoughts again, just as I had had before. I started feeling as if I wasn't worth anything, and that there was nothing that I was good for. I felt so empty inside—as if I was hollow, and I remember saying to myself, *an old, rotten stump in the wilderness is worth more than I am.* I looked at myself and I didn't like what I saw. I looked at my body— my legs and arms—and there was nothing there that I felt was even worth looking at. For a moment, I felt that I was nothing … just an empty shell.

Then the glory of the Lord fell upon me, and his blessings ran right through me, and I was instantly changed forever. By his touch, I was made whole.

At this time, I was lying on the bed. I put myself completely under the sheets, and, as soon as I pulled the sheet over my head, it was just as if Jesus was unfolding under the sheet and putting himself face to face with me. I felt as if he was over me, but under the sheet. I could see his image in the sheet, and he said to me that, from that moment on, I was a new person, and that I was in perfect health, and that there would be a new job waiting for me when I got home.

Instantly, I knew everything that was in the Bible, even though I had never read the entire Bible in my life. I didn't know which passages were which, but that didn't matter; I knew the content. Then, he left. All of this, I believe, probably happened in the period of about five to ten seconds, if it was even that long. Everything came right through me instantly, just like magic.

I didn't see him physically; I just saw an image under or through the sheet—just like a painting on a cloth. And I certainly felt his presence. It was just as if he had been woven into the fabric of the sheet. I certainly heard his voice. After he left, I called for him to come back, but it didn't happen, and I kept the sheet over my head for a long time because I was hoping he would come back. After a while, I removed the sheet from myself. I felt so holy. This was just like the experience I had had before. I felt weightless and as if I was transparent—like an angel from God. I also felt that I was ready to go to Heaven, because I already knew everything there was to know. I felt so holy that I should be in Heaven already.

I knew everything that I needed to know, and I felt so good. After a while I got anxious to get home and tell Judy all that I knew about the Bible. But I waited until the next morning to see the doctor, because I knew that was what I was supposed to do. But I already knew that I was in perfect health. Nevertheless I didn't want to break their rules and regulations, and that gave me the chance to work on my patience. When the doctor came to check me out the next morning, he was accompanied by two other doctors. One of them looked at me and said, "This man is in better health then all of us put together!" He said that I should go home. My doctor asked me if I felt ready to go home. I answered, "This man is right. I am in perfect health and I am ready to go home." But my doctor looked at me and he seemed puzzled. Nevertheless, he checked me out and released me, and told me that, if I felt anything unusual, I should not hesitate to come right back and see him immediately.

I thanked my doctor and got ready and went home. All the way home, I was praying to God and thanking him for all that he had done for me again, and I asked him to just keep it coming. I just loved what was happening to me. It was so wonderful, I didn't want it to ever stop. I wanted these feelings and wonderful experiences to go on forever.

After I got home, I told Judy what had happened to me. I told her that there was supposed to be a big job waiting for me, and I asked her if she knew about it. She said yes, that the Community of Seymourville wanted me to build a new administration building for them, and they needed me to help with the plans. They wanted to start as soon as possible.

I asked her to sit for a moment, because I had something marvelous to tell her. I had never read the Bible before, but she had. I told her that I knew the whole Bible from cover to cover—that Jesus had given me that knowledge of the Bible. I started telling her about some passages from the Bible—from the Old Testament and from the New Testament.

She said she really believed what I was saying because there was no other way that I could have learned all of that in just one day. She saw and felt the happiness that I had in me. I felt so holy, and she could feel that also. She was stunned by this, but I knew that she had no choice but to believe what she was seeing and hearing. But she already had experienced things that had happened to me before, so I don't think it was much of a shock to her.

I believe that she already knew that sometime soon God was going to do something with me, especially after I told her what Jesus had done for me when I was a child, even though I didn't tell her everything about it. She felt that God was working on me, because of my actions and some of the things I said sometimes. Therefore, it didn't come as too much of a surprise to her when I proved to her that Jesus had spoken to me.

For myself, I always prayed to God to talk to me somehow, and I was just waiting for his answer. But the real problem was with me because I did not have enough patience. I would get frustrated when I had to wait for something and it seemed to take forever for it to come. Impatience can be very damaging sometimes. As I said in another book that I've written, *Both Feet on the Spiritual Path,* patience is a virtue, and, without enough patience, then faith can become very weak. And, if our faith is too weak, then we can't accomplish anything worth accomplishing.

Lack of patience had always been a problem before in my life, and, because of that, I struggled for many years in my life. The problem was made worse because I was too stubborn to admit, at least to myself, that I had this problem and that I had to do something about it. Like many other people, I didn't want to find myself being wrong, and, because of that, I almost took my own life.

When we don't have enough patience, then obviously we can get very frustrated, and that's when negative influences set in, and things keep getting worse and worse. We feel we can never seem to see the light in our lives. I believe that this is the main reason that so many people take their own lives—they get to the point where they can't handle it any more, and they just want to get out of this life. They just can't see the real joy that there is in life, and they just don't understand the real purpose of living.

Learning to be more patient was certainly a great lesson to me—and certainly a lesson that I'm not about to soon forget. Don't get me wrong, I have to admit that I am still a little stubborn from time to time, but not like before—not to the point where it could hurt me or anyone else. I would never fall into that trap again because I know how hard it is to get out of it. Take my advice: if you want faith to work in your life, you have to have patience. If you don't have patience, then you can't say that you have the proper faith that you need to make things happen, or you would be lying to yourself. Lack of patience weakens faith.

Now, after I'd spoken with Judy about what had happened to me, I got on the phone and called my friend Henry from Seymourville about the new job. He asked me if I could go to see him and look at the plans with him. I did, and I liked it, and started the project about a week later. Everything went very well on that project right until it was completed.

During this time, God was really working hard on me, and, in the late summer of 1984, I was invited by another great friend of mine, Dave, to participate in a men's retreat at a place called Portage La Prairie. This was a three-day retreat, starting Friday and ending Sunday afternoon.

I accepted the offer and went. I was surprised to see so many of my friends there. Among them was my close friend Edward, of whom I spoke earlier. I knew by this time that he was also a Christian. We shared some of our experiences that we had had with God, and we were both happy to see each other as Christians. We also shared lots of good fortune with our other friends from down home, and with the new friends that we made during this weekend. That was certainly one of the best, if not the best, reunion that I've ever experienced. Everyone was happy throughout the whole weekend. We received many blessings during the three days that we were there, and everyone went home happy, blessed, and full of Spirit. The guest speaker was Reverend David Diamond, a very loving person who reached out to help anyone who was ready and willing to learn from his messages. Everyone had fun and laughed at his stories and jokes about when he first became a Christian, and the things that he had experienced during his time as a "newcomer," as we call it.

That weekend was certainly one of the best weekends I have ever experienced, and I believe that it would be safe to say the same for many others also who were there with us; everyone felt so very much blessed that weekend.

We felt the presence of the Holy Spirit, and certainly also its power. We saw some people getting healed, and it was such marvelous thing to experience. Speaking for myself, I was a smoker before that weekend, but Reverend Diamond taught us how to get rid of some bad habits or sicknesses with the proper faith and by using the power of the Holy Spirit.

During one of our breaks, I went outside as I used to do to light up a cigarette, but this time, after Reverend Diamond had me flying so high in the Holy Spirit, I just walked up to a large garbage container that was sitting by the parking lot. I grabbed my pack of cigarettes with both hands. I cursed it and rebuked the negative influence that was in it. I broke the cigarettes all apart while I was cursing them, and threw them all into the garbage container.

Well, right from that moment, I was set free from smoking. My body was instantly healed, and I didn't have any desire to smoke after that. This was a real miracle, and, with the faith that I had in me at that time, there wasn't anything that I couldn't do. As Jesus very well said in the book of Matthew in the Bible, if we have the proper faith nothing is impossible to us.

Having faith is such wonderful and beautiful thing. It is so amazing to actually see yourself with your own eyes how it works just like magic. I have to say that it would be difficult to discover a stronger or more marvelous experience than that; sometimes you just have to shake your head and realize and accept the fact that faith is the true reality of life ... it is the true life and nothing less.

Again, by the power of the Holy Spirit, I was instantly healed and I was set free ... free from the habit of smoking. But, most importantly, I was instantly healed from it, and I was even left with absolutely no desire whatsoever to ever smoke again. It only took a few seconds and it was all done and over with.

After the weekend was over and everyone was so happy with how successful it had been, we all were anxious to share this beautiful experience with other people. For myself, I was certainly anxious to get home and share this with my family, but I was also very anxious to get back to work Monday morning and share it with the men that I was working with.

After I got home, I shared my experiences with my family, and, obviously, they could see how happy I really was, and how full of the Holy Spirit I really was. There was real happiness in the house among all of us.

After I got back to work Monday morning, I shared my experience with my friends. Some asked me when there would be another retreat like that because they were interested, but I didn't know at the time. I did find out, however, and gave them all the information they needed.

As I've said before, God was really working hard on me, or maybe I should say it like the name of a great song, written by Chris Beach "Jesus Is Working Overtime on Me," a very strong and really touching song.

During this time, God was already using me to minister to the men I was working with. I was aware of the ones who were being touched as well as the ones who were not so interested. Nevertheless, God had me working on them. I never depended on my own effort while talking to others; I left it to God to let me know when, who, how, and where. The thing that I found so amazing, was that, when he would tell me to speak to a certain person, at a certain time, it seemed that he would put it in that person's mind that I was going to talk to him or her.

I knew who the person was ahead of time, and many times this person would come to me and ask me certain questions. He or she would open up the conversation, and God always gave me the right answers to give at any time. I was never stuck for words because he always put the words into my mouth. All I had to do was speak them, which I found very easy to do—because I like to talk! But, it truly is always such joy to speak out the words that God gives me to say, and it is such blessing to know that God is working with me and that I can serve him.

God was using me to help and minister to people in places other than work—especially in the communities of Manigotagan, Seymourville, Winnipegow, Pine Falls, and anywhere I went, as well as at home with my own family. We were blessed by God many times. I've gotten so used to it that, whenever I go somewhere, I know ahead of time that there will be someone with whom I am supposed to talk about spiritual matters— someone who needs help so desperately.

Again, just like magic, people will come to me, as if they already knew that I am the one who is supposed to talk to them. Usually they ask me certain questions or ask for advice. All I have to do is answer them with words that God puts into my mouth. I just open my mouth and speak the words. At first that used to amaze me—how I could come up with the right answers so easily, and how could I say certain words that I normally couldn't even dream of saying. But, at the right time, the words are there and I just have to say them. Sometimes it feels as if I couldn't stop even if I tried.

I enjoyed that so much because, every time God speaks through me, people are touched with the power that is in those words. I want that to go on forever. I praise God and talk to him every chance I get, and he just keeps on giving me work to do for someone that needs help.

I found that God was working on more people than I thought. And, the more work he gives me to do, the more I like it, because I felt so blessed, and I am respected by everyone because they can feel the love of God flowing right through me and strait to them. Let me tell you that there is nothing better than feeling the love of God coming into you. It doesn't matter who he's using to transfer this wonderful power and blessing, it just comes to you, because God can use anyone who is willing to be his servant to help anyone.

In the early 1980s, I knew a wonderful couple in Manigotagan by the name of Dave and Edith Hiebert. They were working for the Mennonite Mission and were full of love. They certainly also liked to share it with anyone. (Dave was the friend that I spoke about earlier who invited me to the men's retreat at Portage La Prairie). In the mid 1980s, a man by the name of Neil Unrau came to replace them at the mission. But, just for a short while, another wonderful young couple came to work at the mission. They were Tom and Carrie Sprunger from Burn, Indiana. This was during the time that God was working on and with me the most. We certainly had wonderful times together at Manigotagan, especially at the Mennonite Mission. I used to love helping Tom in the little chapel on Sunday morning by giving a speech to the congregation, and also speaking at the Bible studies that we had every week. I know that they appreciated my help, and I certainly appreciated them and their help also.

I must say that the main reason that I mention these wonderful people by their names is simply because they all helped me and my family a very great deal with our spiritual walk. I want to thank them all with all my heart for their loving help, and for being such wonderful people. I will always remember them and always have them in my heart.

We all knew that the Good Lord was working with us, and he was pouring all kinds of blessings upon us.

We were just flying high in the spirit, and we were certainly living a truly happy life, I taught Tom how to play guitar, and we ended up playing guitar and singing together in the little chapel. Tom was so happy that he could sing and play guitar for the Lord.

Tom's family and mine had so many wonderful moments together. The children loved to get together. Every time we were together, I knew that God was working in our lives. I know that he was happy with both families, and he just kept on blessing us, and we very well knew it.

These people certainly helped me become a better and more loving person. I was living a happy life, and everyone felt it. I developed more respect for others, and they also had more respect for me in return. I liked to make people happy because I enjoyed seeing people happy and laughing. It is always a joyful thing to see someone else happy—at least it is for me.

During this time, I was working at Seymourville. I was treated respectfully by my employer, and also by the men I was working with at all time. After we were finished working on the administration building, they had me working on other projects throughout the community, repairing houses and other things. I really enjoyed working for these people. I treated them right, and, in return, they treated me right also—and with respect, and that made me love these people even more.

In the winter of 1985–86, I was still working for the same community.

One evening in November I really felt the presence of God around me, I felt really light as if there was no weight to me, for some reason I felt like going to bed early even though I wasn't tired at all, Judy was washing the dishes and I told her how I felt, she asked me if I was sick but I said no I feel good but for some strange reason I want to go to bed early, so I went, well as soon as I put my head on my pillow God started talking to me.

It was loud and clear in my mind and there wasn't any mistaking, no ifs or buts, I couldn't say that I didn't know or that I didn't hear anything, it was printed in my mind.

He said, *I want you to go and see your sister Yoland in New Brunswick, she will be leaving this world very soon and I want you to go and be with her and pray with her, she's waiting for you, when you're there with her I want you to put your hands on her head and I will tell you what to do and what to say, go now.*

I jumped up and went to Judy as she was washing the dishes and told her what had just happened, she looked at me and saw that I was serious about what I was telling her, I asked her what should I do about this?

She said that's for you to know not me, God spoke to you so that's for you to decide what you should do about it, I told her, how can I go anywhere, I have a job to take care of, people are working under my authority, I can't leave just like that and just put the project on hold, and I don't have enough money to go there anyway, so I was finding all kinds of excuses and I didn't know what my employer would say if I go to him and tell him that God spoke to me and what He said to me and that's why I have to go, I was a bit afraid of what he might think of me.

The next day I decided to ask God if I really have to do this, to tell me that again and tell me how I can do this, well He didn't answer.

I kept on working anyway but that was really bothering me, I was really hoping that nothing would happen to my sister, nevertheless I knew the message that I couldn't forget.

One day my employer and I went to the city on a business trip, which was 5 days after I had received that message from God, when we arrived back to my place I asked him to come in and have a cup of coffee with me before he goes home, he accepted the offer and when we walked in the house Judy came walking to me crying, I asked her what the problem was and she said to me, you know what you told me the other day about God telling you to go see your sister Yoland, well it's to late for that now she's dead, she said I just received a phone call from your other sister telling me all about it, she said that she got run over by a truck.

I felt so terrible while the thought of those words from God were going through my mind and realizing how important that message was and that I had refused to obey God that had been so good for me in the past, I felt like a real coward, but when my employer heard that and realized what had happened, he said don't worry about anything, you go to your sister's funeral, I'll take care of everything for you, he said I'll put the job on hold until you return and I'll pay you what you have coming until now and I will also give you an advance to make sure that you have enough money until you return back to work, I accepted his offer and I went, everything worked out well and I was back in about 10 day but I had to rest for a couple days before I could return to work, since I drove I was tired.

Then I was back at work and back to normal, but I will never forget this message, *never say no to God, listen and obey.*

We were just starting the construction of a new outdoor skating rink, and again I was the foreman. We had to drill six-inch-wide, three-foot-deep holes into the frozen ground around the perimeter of the rink at eight feet on center. Two men and two women had been chosen to work with me. Well, we had fun. I can tell you that many women can be better workers then many men, but this time I believe that the work was fairly even. These two men were good workers, but I think that these two women were so happy to have a job working outside, and earning their own money, they were working hard, and I certainly let them know that I was proud of them—all of them.

I really loved these people, and I treated them with love. I would never hesitate to let them know that I loved them, and that I was happy to be working with them. In return, they all thought the world of me. They thought that I couldn't do anything wrong. They told me many times that I was certainly a man of God, and that was the reason that it didn't seem that I could do anything wrong. Well, I have to admit that it was exactly the way I felt many times, but that's just the way it is when you let God control your life, instead of trying to control it yourself.

I believe that the years of 1984 through 1986 were probably the best and happiest years of my life, especially spiritually, not counting the lost of my sister. The summer of 1984 was when Jesus spoke to me in the hospital, and changed my life forever. I got filled with the Holy Spirit, and, after that, God worked in me and with me at all time. I was so happy because my life was so filled with the Holy Spirit. It seemed that I could do no wrong, and God was controlling my life to the fullest. I felt so wound up with the Holy Spirit in me that I was just flying high. With this power, God was taking me for the best ride of my life, and I wanted it to keep going forever. There certainly wasn't any turning back for anything; I had no time to look back in life, I was just doing whatever God wanted me to do.

I wouldn't hesitate to do his will whenever he called on me, except for my failure for my sister.

In the fall of 1985, I was again invited to join a men's retreat. This one was also at Portage La Prairie. This time, the guest speaker was a man who was probably in his mid sixties. He had been a reverend for about forty years, and was a very loving and powerful man in his work. He was a very strong and wise speaker ... truly a man of God.

On the second day of the retreat, some of us were called to the front of the congregation, and we were prayed on. We were supposed to receive the gift of tongue. Well, the other men started speaking in an unknown tongue, but I didn't. There was another reverend there who was probably well into his sixties. He came to me, put one of his hands on my chest, and the other on my back. He immediately asked me why I didn't want to let it out. I told him that I wasn't a hundred percent certain that they were really speaking in an unknown tongue. He said, "I know that it is. It wants to come out of you. You need to let it out." I said, "It may sound funny to you, but here it comes." And I spoke it out. He asked how long I had been speaking in an unknown tongue. I said for a long time, but I didn't tell him how long, and he didn't ask. He told me not to hold it back next time, because it is not good to hold back God's language.

Therefore I realized that, if it is God's language, then I won't be making any mistakes while I speak, because there can't be any mistakes in God's language. I got to speak this language more often then ever, and, even though I didn't understand what I was saying, it didn't matter because I knew that God knew what I was saying.

Amen.

Chapter 12
Finding Out the Cause of My Childhood Problems

Later on during the evening of the second day, I had the chance to talk one on one with the guest speaker. He seemed a little curious about me, and asked me why I hadn't wanted to speak in the unknown tongue earlier. I told him that I wasn't sure about what I felt like speaking, because I had been doing it since I was nine years old. He asked me to tell him some of my unknown tongue so I did. He looked at me and he said, "You are telling me that you've been speaking in tongues since you were nine years of age?" I said, "Yes, that is right." He looked straight into my eyes for a few seconds, and he said, "You don't know me at all from before yesterday, do you?" I said that I didn't. He said, "All right, let me tell you something. You are from a large family, are you not?" I told him I was. He said, "When you were just a young child, you experienced some very hard and difficult times, did you not?" Again, I told him he was right. He said, "I feel that there was a satanic power in the home during your childhood, is that true?" I said there had been, and I started shedding tears.

The gentleman said, "Listen to me, now is not time to cry, it is time to rejoice." He told me there had been someone in the family who was doing the devil's work, and he asked me who it was. I told him that my mother used to do witchcraft with a deck of cards, and she was very good at it. She could tell anyone that she had never met before their past and their future, and for many years she never made a mistake that I know of. He said that God is a just God, and, because Satan already had one from the household, therefore he also took one. And he said that I must have been bothered by that satanic power more then anyone else in the family. I told him he was perfectly right. He told me that, right at that moment, God was giving him all that information. "I am getting this message from God," he said, "and the reason that you were chosen by God at that time was that you were the one that the devil was trying to get for himself, and God said to him, 'No you don't, you already have one; therefore, this one is mine!' And, when you were saved by God that's when you received the gift of tongue, and that was the sign that you belonged to God, and that there was absolutely nothing that Satan could do about it."

I wasn't really surprised that God was giving all of this information to him, because I had experienced many things from God myself, but I was certainly amazed, because this man was a complete stranger to me. I had never met him before that weekend. He told me everything, just as if he had been there living with us in the same houses that we lived in for all those years.

I certainly thank God for giving me the opportunity to meet with this gentleman… for bringing us together and revealing the whole truth to me. It took only about five minutes or so for the whole picture to be revealed to me.

That meeting really opened my eyes because, after that, I understood everything about my past. I could see the whole picture of it all … the meaning of it all, and why it had been me instead of someone else in the family, and why it had lasted for so long, and why the devil had been so stubborn with me.

I believe that it was God's doing to let this man know all about it and to reveal all of that information to me. Now I could leave some things behind and not let them bother me anymore. And I could also reach out and help others who may be in need of the same kind of information. There are probably many more people than we think who really need this kind of information. My wish is to be able to help anyone in any way I can—any time, anywhere. May God bless you all with his mighty power. He has this power for everyone, and he is just waiting patiently for us to call on him for help. Amen.

God works in mysterious ways with his children—even when we don't understand what he is doing, or why he lets certain things happen that we think shouldn't happen.

In my life—especially in 1984 through 1987—I experienced miracle after miracle with the power of the Holy Spirit. I experienced all kinds of visions from God. I performed miracles to show people how powerful God really is. God spoke to me. He told me what to do, and I just did it. I've shown people how powerful prayers really are when they are put in the proper order. I've proven to people how powerful a person can be, and that nothing is impossible to a man when he has enough faith and lives by the power of the Holy Spirit, according to God's will. Nothing can go wrong; just try it and see for yourself.

God had me preach to people, spreading his word and teaching others about his powers and abilities, which we can also use if we understand them and use them properly at any time we want. Jesus said that nothing is impossible to a man who has the proper faith, and that we could perform miracles as he did— and even greater things that he did when he was here on earth in a physical form. He taught us the truth better than any one could ever teach it; this we can find in the beatitudes in the book of Matthew of the Bible.

This isn't just something that I feel like saying. This is reality—the true reality of life—and I've proven it many times to many people, individuals, and groups. I have proven how powerful anyone can be with the power of the Holy Spirit. I've had people come to me for help, and I have always had great results in my efforts to provide the help they need.

God brings them to me, and he tells me what to do and what to say. As I said before, in the beginning, that used to amaze me so much, because that was just like magic. The words that came out of my mouth didn't really come from me, they came from God through me. There were ways that I would talk and words that I would say that I couldn't even imagine myself speaking on my own.

I used to stop and think about it afterwards and realize what had happened, and that used to thrill me so much. I would thank and praise God for using me in such beautiful ways, and for bringing such happiness into my life. Even when I was doing something physical for someone—and I was happy to do these things—it was just as if God was working with my hands. I could do no wrong. Everything came out so beautiful. And these people used to be amazed with me because of the beautiful work that I was able to do. I have to admit that I always was a good carpenter, but the real truth is that, without God's guidance, I wasn't as good a carpenter. But most people just didn't realize this fact; therefore, they thought that I was naturally just that good.

Some people did tell me that I certainly was a true man of God simply because it seemed to them as if I could do no wrong or say anything wrong. These wonderful people and great friends used to respect me very well, and I respected them as well. I would sometimes tell them that God was working in and with me, but some of them, unfortunately, didn't understand what I was saying to them. But some of them knew what I was talking about.

Sometimes people have asked me why God doesn't talk to them as he does to me, and I just have to tell them that many times God speaks to them, but they don't hear him. It is because they simply don't pay enough attention to him. They just talk to him occasionally. But you have to make sure that you pay attention and listen to him very carefully. Then you will hear him, and you will know when he's talking to you, and you will know what he's saying to you. All you have to do is obey him and you will soon find that he will talk to you more often than ever before. You will realize that he is very happy talking to you. Don't worry, you'll know when he is talking to you. But don't ever try to fool him because he will rebuke you.

I could mention so many more things that I have experienced with the abilities that God had given me, and the power that he has let me use to help others. Maybe I should say that he has used me to transfer his power to other people. It certainly is always such an honor to be his servant. I always have enjoyed every moment of it, and still do whenever he calls on me to do his work. I never hesitate to do whatever he asks because it pleases me so much, and it is always so wonderful to be able to use such abilities and powers, which are way beyond my own abilities. It is a true blessing, and I absolutely love it with all my heart, mind, and soul.

I thank you, Lord, for choosing me to be your servant.

During the years of 1984 and 1985, I had experiences that were not really normal sometimes, at least not according to my understanding about the Bible. During those two years, eighteen people died in and around the Manigotagan area, in a radius of only about fifteen miles.

These experiences made me feel good for certain reasons, but bad for others. These experiences foretold the deaths of these people. I could always tell ahead of time that someone was going to die, and this went on for all eighteen people who died during that year-long stretch of time.

I used to tell Judy about it—that someone else in the area was about to die—and I could tell if it was a relative or not, and how many days it would be before the death occurred.

Well, at first Judy wouldn't believe me that I could do that, but each time, after I would come home after work, I would tell her, "Judy, I'm sorry but this one isn't the last one yet. There is another that will be going soon." And I would tell her how many days it would be. After a while, she started getting tired of me telling her all the time because I was right every time.

I remember one time when I came home after work and told her that the most recent death wouldn't be the last one. This was at the time of about the tenth or eleventh death. Judy started crying and she told me to stop it, and she looked at me and asked me if I was the one that was making that happen.

Well, I was bothered by her question and asked her if she was losing her mind … that I couldn't help it if I knew those things … that it was a voice that was telling me at the back of my head—or just some kind of knowledge that was entering my mind. I just knew about those deaths. Finally she believed that I had some kind of power or ability that we had never seen before.

But, fortunately, after the eighteenth death, I came home after work and told her the good news—that it was the last one for a long time. Well, she was so happy to hear that and she simply said, "Finally, are you sure?" I said, "Yes I am. In fact I know that's it. It's over for a while anyway." And it was the last one for a long time.

I wasn't doing any witchcraft or anything like that. I was just going to church, bible studies and worshipping God our heavenly father and his son and our brother Jesus Christ, the only one that I trusted and had faith in. I was always working for and with God and no one else.

But I remember one summer evening, I believe it was in 1985. My family and I went to spend the weekend at our friends Ed and Linda's place. We used to enjoy so much being with them. After a nice weekend, we were driving home on Sunday evening. It was about

11:00 PM, we were on the road to Manigotagan, and my wife and our two children were sleeping.

As I drove, I suddenly got a very strong feeling. I had been looking at the sky and the clouds once in a while. Off and on, the moon would hide behind the clouds. Suddenly I got this feeling that, if I wanted to, I could just look up into heaven and concentrate for a minute, and I would be able to tell the future—as if I could see the future right through the sky. I really felt that I was getting that ability.

Then I realized that this wasn't according to the bible, so why was I getting this powerful feeling? I couldn't get this part properly, so I said to myself, *If this isn't according to God's word or his will, then there is only another one who could be playing tricks on me, and I know who that would be.* While I was thinking about this, I started to be afraid, so I spoke to God and told him that, if these thoughts were from him, to let me know and let it happen. But I also told Satan that, if the thoughts were from him, well, I certainly didn't want any part of them whatsoever. I certainly didn't want to have anything to do with him!

Immediately, a hand grabbed me by the hair on the back of the head, and squeezed so hard, it was almost lifting me right off my seat. It hurt so much that tears came to my eyes, and I was about to yell when it finally let me go.

As we were approaching a bridge, I thought, *What if this evil power tries to make us go off the bridge, and fall into the river?* Well, I slowed down and prayed to God to protect us and take us home safely, and he did. After we got home, I shared this experience with Judy, so we both prayed and thanked God for keeping us safe.

I can tell you that this was an experience that I will never forget for as long as I live, especially knowing how powerful Satan can be when he wants to get someone, and especially when it is someone who really wants to follow God. Satan wants to stop that; he can get very sneaky.

Therefore, don't ever underestimate Satan because he is very real and is not to be ignored. He is the enemy, and he will try anything to stop anyone from following God. He is sneaky and sly and a liar. Don't trust him. Be on your guard at all times.

Satan is always looking for someone who is blind to him … someone who doesn't know about him, or how powerful he can be, especially with someone who isn't ready to reject him. He also tries to prevent anyone from getting to God. We always have to be on our guard. Just remember that, as long as we have God on our side, we are safe, and, as long as we keep remembering that God is always on our side, then we don't have to worry about anything—especially about Satan—because we will be protected.

I knew that God was always by my side and that he wanted me to do things to the best of my ability for others. As long as I did that, then I knew that he would always help me with anything that I did. And that is the reason that I was often so thrilled about the things I could do. I use to surprise myself sometimes, without realizing at that time that my accomplishment was probably due to the fact that God was helping me with whatever I was doing—as long as I asked him to work with me on certain projects. But sometimes we seem to forget for a moment that he is helping us.

Jesus was a carpenter, and I was born a carpenter; therefore, whenever I asked him to work with me on a project, it just couldn't go wrong. And now I realize more then ever before why, when I used to get home for supper after work, I used to be so happy with my day's work. My wife Judy and my children Robert and Pamela use to ask me why I was always so happy when I came home, and I would tell them that I had had a very good day, and that I was happy to be back home with them. I would tell them that God had made me have a nice day, and that's about all I would say about it.

After supper, whenever I had such wonderful day, I would be anxious to go back outside and do more work around the house or in the shop. I used to hate to see darkness come because that was the sign that the day was over and we had to retire for the night. I wanted to do more, and it seemed as if there was no end to me sometimes. I know that I was getting my strength and happiness from God. I know that I couldn't do all that I was doing every day without the help of God.

I thank Jesus Christ for all the blessings that I've received from Him through the years because I know that, without Him, I would simply be lost.

Chapter 13
I was Blessed Working in a Movie

This is all so wonderful, and I know that, by now, you're getting the message. We all know that sometimes in life things go so well that we really feel glorified, but then some other times things don't seem to be so glorifying. But we can't just quit having faith in ourselves and in our God; we just have to keep on searching for an answer to our problems, and be willing to do whatever it takes to fix the problem. If we are honest and strong about our situation, everything will turn out right. We have to work it out; this is the reality in our lives.

We must be willing to take the bull by the horns, as we say, face the problem, stand on the ground, and conquer it. We very well know that it takes some dedication and determination to be able to understand

and conquer any negative that may cross our path and try to destroy our happiness and our well being. But, once you've conquered that negative influence and stay or get back on the right path, then you've succeeded in your life.

To find or to have success in our lives, we have to be honest with ourselves and with the world around us. We have to be strong and be willing to make sacrifices. If we can do those things, then we can be sure to find happiness and success for as long as we want in our lives. There is nothing that any negative influence can do about it.

Now, still in 1986, The National Film Board of Canada came into the area where I was, and they were interested in producing a four-part movie named *Daughters of The Country*. I was approached by a beautiful lady who was looking for a carpenter to build things for them—a fort, a fur trading post, and so on. Everything was to look as if it existed in the late part of the 1700s. Well, with no hesitation on my part, I accepted the offer.

While I was doing this work for them, one day this same beautiful lady approached me again. She seemed to be very pleased with my work, and she asked me if I would like to participate in the movie. She didn't know that I had already asked God to give me a chance to get in that movie, but there was my answer—a perfect opportunity. Well, again with no hesitation, I accepted the offer, which was to take part in the first part of the four parts of the movie, which is called "Ikwe."

My participation in this project ended up being threefold—as carpenter, voyageur, and cast member. Again, God had answered my prayer and granted me my request. But, again, God had a plan for me. Someone needed help and support with some understanding about spirituality—how we get to live as Christians and how we can get God to talk to us when we need him. There were a few there that were interested, and they really appreciated my help. Some needed love in their lives; they needed to feel the real power of love. In fact, one of the ladies asked me to write a prayer for her so she could take it with her, and use it when she went to bed at night. After I told them about this prayer, they understood the power that was in it, and how it could help them, especially when they felt alone and lonely. Like many people, they needed a lift, and they really felt that this prayer would get them out of some bad situations. The prayer gave them some faith in themselves and also in their God. Well, they left with a happy smile, and that made me happy.

Working on this movie was another very great experience for me that I will never forget. I very much loved working for and with these people. They were so loving and helpful. I learned so much while working for this company, and I certainly appreciated all the help and understanding that I received from all of them. We had a good time, and everyone worked together so well. It seemed as if we were just one big family. Everything went very well, and "Ikwe" has been a great success all over the world. All of us who worked on the project are proud of all the hard and wonderful work that was put into it.

This four-part movie is being used in workshops all over the world as a training program, especially for people who work in jails, and those who work in self awareness training and other training. I truly believe that God had lots to do with the real success of this film.

After the film was completed and all the work of restoring and clean up was finished, all the members of the film board went back to the city of Winnipeg. I have to admit that, for a while after they were all gone, I felt lonesome for them all and I wished to get working for them again before long. Unfortunately, I haven't had the opportunity yet, but I still hope that maybe some day I will have this great opportunity again.

As I've said before, sometimes in our lives things go so well and we feel so glorified. But sometimes things do not go so well. Then we just have to keep striving for happiness and success and not lose our faith in ourselves and especially in our God. Things do turn out on the right road again, and again we find happiness, success, and prosperity.

I believe that this filming company came just at the right time for us, because, not so long after that was all finished, the economy in Canada started dropping, and times started to get a little harder.

People were afraid, but thank God a new government got elected, and things started changing for the better.

I thank my Lord for this filming company and for giving me the opportunity to work with it as I did, because it certainly was a great blessing to me and for many other people around the area.

Chapter 14
Downfall in My Christian Life

In 1987, unfortunately, things changed. Things did not go so well for a while. It seemed as if God had left me alone … as if he didn't want to do anything with me anymore. I didn't know why or what to do about it. It seemed that I was being attacked by some unknown force. Things were happening in my life that I wouldn't ever want to see happening. It almost seemed as if I was a different person all together at times. I would talk to God and ask him to tell me what was going on, but I wouldn't get any answers. And things just kept getting worse as the months went by. It seemed that I was losing control of my life, and I couldn't do anything about it. Many times I would find myself walking on the wrong path in life, and it was just as if there was some unknown or unseen force that was doing this to me. Unlike before, I just couldn't do anything about it; I couldn't stop it. It was almost as if I was living in a dream and couldn't wake up out of it. There were some unpleasant things that happened that I certainly, with all my heart, would never wish for. During the time that these things were happening, the economy was getting worse in Canada. People were starting to get on edge, and frustration was building up among the population. There wasn't much work in the area where I was; it certainly was not like it had been before. Everyone was afraid that there might be another depression like the one in the 1930s. Being a carpenter wasn't helping my own struggle. For a while, things went from bad to worse, and that lasted for about two to three years until I could finally start seeing the light again. It took me a while before I could even start feeling that I was finally getting some answers from God again, but I never gave up. I always talked to God and always praised him no matter what. Before I knew it, I was getting back to normal, and things were going the right way again.

I must admit that probably one of the reasons that God stopped working with me as he had done before, was that I disobeyed him. I have to realize that God didn't walk away from me; the truth is, I walked away from him when I refused to obey his command.

After a short time, a different government came into power and things started getting better in our country again. The economy improved, and the people's frustration started fading away. I could see happiness building up everywhere. I could see more smiling faces. It certainly was something beautiful to see. I suppose that probably helped me get some of my strength back, so that I could return to the faith that I had had before. Mostly it helped me get rid of any doubt that was haunting me, and causing me to lose some faith, or even weaken my faith and replace it with doubt rather than strengthening my faith in myself and in my God.

I was fortunate enough to go to work for a friend of mine by the name of Ray Gelean, who was also a Christian. We had lots of carpentry work, and especially lots of roofing to do. Things were going well, but in July of 1995 the gold mine at Bissett, Manitoba, reopened. Immediately they called for me, and I went to work for the mine again, because that was all-year-round work instead of just seasonal, and the pay was a little better.

Because I had worked at this place before and I knew the place very well, it was very easy for me to work there. The people knew me, and they were interested in giving me the position of surface foreman, which I accepted as soon as it was offered to me, because I knew that I would do well at that job. I enjoyed doing that kind of work, mainly because I enjoyed teaching— especially carpentry and plumbing. It would please me whenever I could help others learn something that they were interested in.

During that time, I had the urge to write a book because I believed that I possessed lots of information on the real truth about the reality of life. I truly believed that I should share this information with other people all over the world. For some time already, I had been studying and researching this matter, so I started gathering all of my notes and started putting them in proper order for when that day would come when I was ready to put it all into a book.

My interest in writing the book was growing stronger and stronger, and I was getting anxious to get working, even though I had never written a book before. I was amazed whenever I went through my notes to see how much information I had gathered throughout the years. But I knew that I wasn't ready for this book yet, and that I still didn't have all the information that I wanted and needed. Therefore, I had to be patient and work harder on studying and gathering more information. I knew that this project wasn't something that I could rush, especially because this was going to be a book designed and written to reach out and help people all over the world, and help with the proper understanding about the whole system of life and its reality physically and spiritually,

I also knew that I absolutely had to know the real truth on this matter, and that there couldn't be any mistaking at all. I was curious about the subject matter, and I wanted to know more and more. I asked the Good Lord to help me with my studies and my research.

I know that God did help me with this because I don't believe that I could have done it the way that I did without his help—having him by my side along the way while I was working. In the beginning, I still didn't know what the name of this book would be, only what it would probably be. I thought that the name wasn't so important so I left that for later on. I believed that, when I got closer to completing the book, I would find the exact or the proper name. My patience paid off in the end.

After a few years, unfortunately the mine closed down again, in December 1997, and everyone had to go searching for other employment. Well, for me, it was easy enough because I was on unemployment insurance for the winter, and, in the springtime, I just went to work for my friend again as I had before, doing carpentry work and roofing. Ray always welcomed my work, and there always was lots of work for a period of six or seven months.

One year, after I had stopped working for the winter, I contacted the Manitoba Housing Authority (MHA) and told them that I was interested in going to work for them again if they had any work for me. Immediately they told me that they had lots of work for me, and they wanted to know when I could start. Well, the next morning I was at the office getting hired, and the next day I was working—repairing units in senior homes. I worked for them from February 2001 as a carpenter, plumber, and painter. I also did minor electrical work and everything else in between. In the summer of 2002, I applied for a caretaker position for a senior home that belonged to MHA, which would add to my daily work.

I had to put in a bid for this job, and it turned out that my bid was the one that was accepted. I was certainly busy. I was taking care of a senior home and doing repairs at other senior homes and other houses that were all owned by MHA. I tell you, I wanted work—well, I got work! For about a year and a half I didn't have any days off. I worked seven days per week, and they were long days. I don't need to tell you how tired I was getting to be after a while.

I worked for MHA until 2006, when the gold mine reopened again at Bissett and I got called to work there again. I accepted. I had to present my resignation to MHA one month before I could leave my position as a caretaker. At the mine, I started as a contract worker, and about one year later I got transferred to work directly as an employee of the company

There I was again, working at this same gold mine for the third time since 1982; I believe that I will retire from this kind of work at this place.

I really enjoyed my work here, and I appreciated the opportunity to be working at this place again. But, during this time, I knew that I should get back working on my book. I really felt that God was letting me know that I was ready for it; I felt that he wanted me to get going with it. Whenever I prayed about it, I got the same answer—get to it—so I did.

Chapter 15
Writing Helpful Books

When I decided to get back to working on my book, I realized that I had enough information to start putting it together. That was lots of work, but everything went very well, and my publishing firm was a very big help to me. By the time the work was nearly finished, I had found the proper name for it: *Both Feet on the Spiritual Path*. The book has been very successful. I strongly suggest that you find a copy of this book and read it carefully, if you haven't already. I know that you will be very happy that you did.

Even before I finished working on that book, I started writing another one—this very book that you are reading right now. I have to say that I have had my share of inspiration while working on these books, especially inspiration from God, because I asked him to bless and help me work on these projects. Because I wrote these books to satisfy my desire to help others along the way, my God certainly did bless me and my work, and has made me successful. I hope I have been successful in helping my readers to develop a proper understanding about ourselves and life and its realities.

Therefore, this is how my life has been—I began as a very young child living in fear and misery, and I rose from that dark part of my life to become successful in different ways in my life—physically as well as spiritually. By now you probably can understand why the title of this book is *Rising from the Dark Side of Life*.

I thank my Lord for rescuing me from the dark part of my life and for helping me rise up and become successful after so many years.

It has been quite a journey until now, and I am happy that I am where I am now and out of that darkness. Thank you, Jesus. Amen.

I ask the good Lord to bless you through your life so that you will live a happy life in prosperity, success, and harmony with the world because I love you with the power of love that God has given me to share with you. Bless you in all your future.

Amen.

Conclusion

I certainly hope with all my heart that *Rising from the Dark Side of Life* has been a very good help to you, because by the time you finish reading and working with a text such as this one, you should be contented, and you also should be happy with yourself and with your life. If you've had problems in your life similar to mine, by now you should be able to deal with them, and put them behind you forever and never have to worry about them anymore.

My main purpose in writing *Rising from the Dark Side of Life* was to reach out and help all those who have experienced or are still experiencing these kinds of problems in their lives.

You can use this book as a tool to gain the ability to conquer your problems. We all know that we can't just walk away from our problems; we have to deal with them … find a solution and get rid of them in a way that will keep them from coming back to haunt us later on in our lives.

If you read and study this book, you certainly will be equipped with the proper tools to conquer any problem that may cross your path. If you paid good attention to what this text revealed to you, then you have the proper tools to get rid of your problems forever, and prevent them from crossing your path again in your future. No matter what, though, you always have to be on your guard; that's what a wise person usually does.

So please work with this tool and practice with it, and you will see for yourself the great results that will come from using it. Once you've read it, please don't put it away … keep it close to your favorite reading spot so that you can read it again whenever you want to; it is always good to read a helpful book more than once.

I have to admit that, when I was working on writing *Rising from the Dark Side of Life,* I had some very emotional moments, because I had to relive my life in my mind so that I could explain it properly and with the real truth. But it was all for a great cause, and I wouldn't have it any other way.

Now that all is said and done, I can say that I have reached another one of my goals, and I have done it with the help of God. Thank you, my Lord.

I want you to know that my heart is open to you, and I pray for the Good Lord to be with you for the remaining years of your life, with many of his special blessings.

I thank you for being patient with me throughout this journey, and I love you for it.

I hope with all my heart that this journey has been a great help to you.

Amen.

Joseph Claude Plourde

About The Author

I have been a Christian since the early 1980s. This is the story of my life. I have also written *Both Feet on the Spiritual Path*, a very powerful book. I enjoy my work as carpenter, plumber, preacher, and writer.

Joseph Claude Plourde